THE PLANET OF THE ELOHIM

The Planet of the Elohim

Cryton Daehraj

iUniverse, Inc.
Bloomington

The Planet of the Elohim

iUniverse books may be ordered through booksellers or by contacting:

iUniverse
1663 Liberty Drive
Bloomington, IN 47403
www.iuniverse.com
1-800-Authors (1-800-288-4677)

ISBN: 978-1-4759-4065-7 (sc)
ISBN: 978-1-4759-4067-1 (hc)
ISBN: 978-1-4759-4066-4 (e)

Library of Congress Control Number: 2012913781

Printed in the United States of America

iUniverse rev. date: 08/16/2012

Chapter One:

The Cave

"J'son, we are here what you are there. You are here what we are there. I have never met anyone quite like you."

T'mar in the cave with J'son

His first conscious thought was that he was cold and laying on something hard. He was on his stomach with his left arm providing the pillow. His floor was of packed dirt on top of rock or some other similar material, but he didn't know that yet. His thoughts swirled around him, disconnected and strange. He didn't even know his own name. The words that formed within him seem alien and not his own. A strange name surfaced within his mind, a name he didn't recognized but knew belonged to him on some level.

"J'son."

The sound of it echoed painfully around in his head. J'son? What was that? Was that his name, or someone else? And if it was his name, like he now believed it to be, then why did it sound so strange and unfamiliar? Even his thoughts, which were slowly beginning to churn under their own direction, sounded different, like pronounced in a foreign language. His head hurt; his eyes hurt, like needles had been shoved up underneath his lids: spiky, white-hot pokers jabbed deep into his forehead. Thinking hurt, and the images dancing before his eyes spoke of an exotic, unfamiliar content and texture. Where was he? And why did he hurt so much? Why did his name, J'son, sound so unfamiliar?

Slowly opening one, sleep-encrusted eye, his forehead lying on the back of his hand, J'son tried to focus on what was directly underneath him. The smell of dirt flooded his awareness and the small puff of air exiting his body as he breathed stirred up a tiny dust storm. Inhaling the fine particles irritated his nose, causing him to sneeze and then cough. Raising his head a few inches above the floor, he opened both eyes now and looked around him. Still on his stomach but arching his back to see, J'son slowly came to the realization that he wasn't in a room but lying on the floor of a cave. Peering into the back of the cave, squinting into the darkness, he could just make out the walls of uneven rock and a ceiling that disappeared into shadows. Slowly turning his throbbing head left and right, J'son was able to see that the mouth of the cave lay behind him. He could see light filtering in and the opening was outlined in a fiery red color.

Sitting up, his head swam with disconnected images, faces that he knew he should know but couldn't bring to mind their names. Or rather the words which came to mind didn't sound like any names he had ever known. The name Tammy came up but was immediately transformed into T'mii. Although the first name sounded right, it didn't feel right in his mouth, just like speaking a foreign language. He scooted over to one of the walls and leaned against it. He closed his eyes again and his swimming vision settled down. It was quiet and he could hear the sound of wind blowing outside. He opened his eyes again and looked out the mouth of the cave.

"Where the hell am I?" He asked aloud, but the words sounded foreign to his ears. He tried to form an answer for himself but the words coalescing within his mind had a strange texture and sound. The words seemed right, but the sound was peculiar. What was the last thing he had done, he wondered. Fully awake now, he blinked several times trying to take in his surroundings. Filtered daylight lit up the cave and gave it an eerie, reddish glow, reflecting off of something deep within the cave. J'son stood up slowly, placing one of his hands against the wall to steady himself. He was breathing heavily now and his vision was swaying this way and that. He reached up with his other hand and felt for the ceiling, trying to get an idea of the size of the cave. The entrance to the cave was smaller than the inside and he found that his hand disappeared into the gloomy darkness overhead.

Gaining his equilibrium, J'son shuffled over to the opening of the cave and looked out. The first thing he noticed was that he was high up the side of a mountain standing on a narrow ledge maybe a thousand feet up. Looking down he saw a craggy, rock-splintered landscape falling away for about one hundred yards and then the tops of dense, furry trees: a forest that covered the lower portion of the mountain in a velvety cloud, extending out for some miles. The leaves of these trees looked more like feathers, even from this distance. Closer to him, growing between the crags and folds, tiny shrubs swayed in the light breeze. From his vantage point he couldn't see any movement or signs of life at all. By all appearances he seemed to be alone in this strange place. The ledge he stood on extended a few feet past the mouth of the cave and the bright daylight burned away the shadows surrounding the opening. He wasn't too sure at all how he got up here or why he had fallen asleep.

The fact that he didn't know where he was, or that he couldn't remember what he had been doing before, didn't bother him too much yet. His thinking was too confused to really even consider what he had been doing. Where he was, he was sure, was somewhere in his home state of Alabama. He loved to go camping and hiking, but this place didn't look anything like home. In fact, even the sun looked funny. It didn't have that yellow color he was used to. It had more red to it and seemed to be curving into the horizon rather than climbing overhead. There was also a wavy haze to it, like seeing the sun from a few feet under water. His impression was that of a sun rising on another planet. Above the arc of the sun, twinkling in the distance, were vague points of lights that he took to be stars. J'son studied these objects for a moment then gave up trying to identify any familiar constellations. Nothing looked right.

The sun disappeared behind a large outcropping to his left in the distance and then reappeared on the other side, arcing higher into the sky but still on a course that wouldn't take it directly overhead. The sound of scattering rocks was heard in the distance and J'son thought he could hear the disturbing cackle of some kind of bird or animal. Maybe he wasn't as alone as he at first thought. A small cloud of dust rose from the floor of the canyon and he thought he could just make out what looked like a lizard of some sort sunning itself on a ledge about fifty feet below. He tried to see if there was a trail to get down but couldn't locate one. Still, he figured he had got up there somehow and after his headache went away he would remember what was going on.

He went back into the cave and the darkness felt good on his eyes. It took a minute for his eyes to readjust to the dark and he stood there, his back facing the opening, until he could see the contour of the cave. He felt a slight, cold breeze caress his face and was startled to discover it originated from somewhere deep in the cave. "Maybe that's how I got up here," he thought, gazing deeper into the cave. "But where is 'here'?"

J'son started for the rear of the cave, but then stopped, staring deep into the darkness. He thought he heard something, like the shuffling of feet. A loose rock falling, there! He did hear something. Thoughts of a hibernating bear crossed his mind, but then, perplexed, J'son wondered what time of the year it was. Bears only hibernate in the winter. Was it winter? He looked over his shoulder at the opening and saw the hazy, reddish light spilling in. It didn't look like it was winter.

"Where the hell am I?" he asked again to no one in particular. His voice echoed back into the cave and reverberated around the large, rocky room. He sat back down and leaned against one of the walls with his head between his knees. The pain in his forehead had subsided a bit and he tried to think back to what he had been doing before he woke up here. In his mind's eye, dim images of a place far away and faces of people he knew but couldn't decide his relationship to them, flashed across his awareness. A face of a boy, a young man like himself, stood out clearly in his memory. The boy's name was … T'mmy! His name is T'mmy and he is J'son's friend.

Something had happened. J'son and T'mmy had been together and something had happened. There had been a battle, a battle of the mind. There had been a force of some kind. It was powerful and destructive. He had attacked that power with his mind, hurting it and him, but it got away, whatever it was. He had followed it, and there was a woman, too! That's right, he thought. She was there, that woman from his dreams. Wait a minute. Was he dreaming now? Did this place actually exist? What was her name? Where did we go? What is this place? All these questions raced through his mind.

His head was spinning and he felt like he needed to puke. He leaned over and spit on the floor, wiping the spittle away with the back of his hand. He straightened up and closed his eyes, tilting his head back. Images danced across his awareness, jumbling his thoughts. Confusion and anxiety gripped him. Beads of sweat formed at his temples and trickled down the sides of his face. J'son felt cold and sick. He closed his eyes tight, hoping that maybe this was some kind of dream. Visuals played out tiny little dramas in his mind, but they were disjointed and choppy. "Did I drink last night?"

"J'son, are you okay?" The feminine voice sounded surprised but happy. "J'son! You're awake. How do you feel?" Standing before him, coming out of the darkness at the back of the cave, stood a beautiful woman dressed in what appeared to be some kind of organic, furry material he had never seen before. Her feet were clad in leather-like sandals that extended up to about mid calf. Her footwear didn't have any laces but stayed snug on her legs, like elastic or something. Her short skirt, tan in color, hung easily on her hips at an angle that displayed her belly button and a large amount of skin. Her breasts were covered with the same material as her skirt and appeared to be made of one piece, form fitting and supportive. Emerald green eyes looked out at him, smiling, framed in fiery red hair that fell below her shoulders. Her lips parted slightly and J'son could just make out the soft pink tip of her tongue as it brushed against her bottom teeth. Her smile faded into a question and she said, "J'son?"

J'son had been staring at her for what must have been several seconds, mouth agape. Not only did her presence surprise him, her physical appearance left him breathless. Here stood the girl from his dreams: A female Amazon who was looking at him in a very familiar way, cocking her head to the side and smiling a sweet, seductive smile J'son recognized. The way she was looking at him made him physically arouse, embarrassing him and causing him to drop his hands into his lap.

"T'mar?" he asked, looking up at her shyly.

"Yes, J'son, it's me. Whew. You were just staring at me and I was starting to get scared. I thought at first you were a residual holdover from Earth but now I see you're real. Honestly, I didn't know what to think. I'm not too sure how you got here. I'm not even sure you are supposed to be here. This shouldn't have happened. When T'mer gets here, he will know what's going on."

"What? T'mar, what's going on? Where am I? How come I can't remember what happened to me? Why does your name sound so funny? And why are you dressed like some guy's male fantasy?" J'son stood up and for the first time he noticed how he was dressed. He had on a skirt, too, with sandals that covered his feet only up to his ankle. His straight, dirty blonde hair hung around his face and rested just above his shoulders. His chest and abdomen were slightly ripped and he could see the contours of his arms and legs. He looked and felt muscular and strong. He flexed his arms several times, looking at his biceps, not recognizing his own body.

"I can explain," she said, gently reaching out with her hand to touch his cheek. She made contact with his face and J'son felt something akin to a bolt of electricity buzz his head. The sensation extended down his arms and legs. Then a bubble of static electricity erupted out of his chest, surrounded them and spread out, encompassing them in an energy field that seemed self-generated. T'mar withdrew her hand with a gasp and turned away. The field around them collapsed immediately and J'son saw that T'mar looked scared.

"I'm sorry," she said. "I just…"

As confused as he was, though, he was man enough to feel a strong, sexual attraction to her and he reached out with both hands, placing them around her bare waist, saying "That's ok. I want—"

J'son jerked away, startled, throwing his hands into the air, feeling that same electric transmission, like static electricity but more intense. In that one moment of contact he could sense what she was feeling and he liked what he felt. His attraction to her overwhelmed his hesitancy and he boldly reached out to her again, hoping to touch her once more. This time he touched her with just the tips of his fingers. She followed suite and the two of them made contact. A small, bluish sphere appeared between them just inches away from his chest. It grew larger, enveloping them and changing colors from blue to red.

The field seemed charged with electricity, growing just enough to enclose them, diffusing out at the edges. Lowering his hands, hoping not to break contact, he pulled her closer to him and embraced her, wrapping his arms tightly around her waist. Images flooded his mind, images of passion and lust. He burned for her and he knew, somehow, that she wanted him, too. He could read her thoughts, her desires. They had made contact with each other physically the way they did whenever he used to dream about her. The feeling was incredibly intimate and sexual at the same time. He had the feeling like the two of them had merged on some level, their bodies belonging to each other, one and the same. He leaned in close to kiss her, their lips almost touching and then…

"J'son, we shouldn't," she said, pulling away from him and breaking contact. The field collapsed and disappeared, leaving a slight electrical tingle in the air between them. "It's not proper. Our fields aren't the same. I could hurt you."

She knew this wasn't true and it bothered her to say it. Her energy field told her explicitly that he was a good match and even now she could feel her body wanting him. Was this the same boy from Earth? There, he was just a teenage boy with a crush, but now he looked grown up and well endowed. It appeared his human form was hiding something, she thought. She felt the passion of desire welling up within her and now it was her that had the crush. They stood together, their bodies just inches away from touching. She could feel the heat of his body radiating out to her, wanting her as much as she wanted him. She knew then that if he reached out to her again she wouldn't be able to control herself, nor did she want to. It may be wrong, she thought, but I don't care.

Just as she was hoping to touch him again, J'son broke the silence and the sexual tension between them by saying, "Can you at least tell me what is going on?" Apprehension replaced lust and he sounded to her like that scared kid back on Earth. A scared kid with tremendous power, she reminded herself. Or would he still possess those abilities? How else could he have gotten here? And he didn't look like that skinny kid anymore. He was very attractive and she smiled quietly to herself.

"J'son, I'm not too sure why you are here. You shouldn't be. Connection between your would and ours is only supposed to be one way; from here to there, not the other way around. When B'el left your reality, I pursued him, or rather his energy signature, back here. My thought was that you would wake up back on Earth, not clear across the galaxy. That shouldn't have happened. You really shouldn't be here. It doesn't make any sense."

"So where is here and why can't I remember anything?" He was still looking at her. It was hard not to.

"This is where I am from. This is my world. This reality is B'el's stronghold. Things here are very different." T'mar looked beyond J'son to the mouth of the cave. "You shouldn't have come through. You should only exist as a dream to me. But here you are. I'll have to educate you quickly. Do you remember anything?"

"Just bits and pieces. I keep flashing on faces and places that seem familiar, but they feel more like a dream. I remember you, but you don't look like you. I mean you seem different. And I remember we were following some… thing that possessed awesome power. "

"That would be B'el. What else do you remember of Earth?"

Earth? Then this isn't Earth, just like he thought. J'son stared at T'mar again, wanting to reach out and touch her soft skin. Her deep emerald eyes shined out at him, smiling slightly, playfully. He thought about the two of them being here alone together and the thought made him want to caress her body.

"J'son, we were following B'el, trying to capture him and bring him before the celestial courts so he may be judged for what he has done. We were on Earth in your hometown of Hope, Alabama. Do you remember? I found you in your dreams and we teamed up to get him. We had a battle and he slipped away from us, disappearing into the ethereal realms. When he disappeared, I thought he would materialize somewhere else on Earth. Instead, the thread of his essence, his energy signature, led us here, to our planet. I still don't know how you came through. When earthlings dream, you call out to us and we answer you. Your dreams are what pull us through to your world. We are able to materialize because we feed off of your imagination. The energy created by your thoughts allows us to manipulate matter and become solid. The image of me on Earth is just a residual hologram of what I am here. I seem different to you because I am different. On Earth, I became your fantasy. My physical appearance was a direct result of some kind of composite picture you have of the female form. In short, I was perfect according to your expectations. The sexual energy..."

T'mar trailed off at this point. Her high cheek bones took on a crimson color and she turned her head away from J'son, looking down.

"B'el! That's right. I remember him now. He came to me in my dreams. Wait a minute. Now I remember. He killed my dog. And all those people back home." J'son started to tear up. There was so much death from before. Thoughts flooded his awareness and within a moment he was staring into space, oblivious of his surroundings. J'son had entered a trance of sorts and saw things he didn't understand. Confusion gripped his mind and he wasn't sure about what was real. In his mind, he struggled to hold on to the image of his home town, hold on to the reality of Hope, Alabama. His life there seemed to be slipping away only to be replaced by images of this world. Why was it getting so hard to remember home?

From T'mar's point of view, J'son was staring off into space, but from his perspective he was deep within himself, reliving the scene from another time and place. In his mind's eye he saw someone that he recognized. Someone in authority, like a police officer, but that seemed to be in the past. The scene changed and the cop no longer had a badge but he stilled carried a gun. He's a detective now, J'son thought. The detective was sitting behind an old wooden desk. A phone rang and he picked it up. "This is Dunn," the man said.

"W-W-What?" J'son snapped back, fully here again. His eyes were wide and showed signs of panic.

"What did you see?" T'mar asked.

I think I was home, back on Earth. There was this man named D'unn. I think I know him, but not like he is now."

"Do you think it was the present or the future?"

"The future? I don't understand." J'son was really getting scared now. It seemed like whenever he closed his eyes, he was taken back to a place in his memory, a place from his past, or was it the present? Why did T'mar think he was seeing the future? And yet, as soon as she asked him if that was the case he knew that it was. "The future, I think."

"If you concentrated hard enough, do you think you could 'wake up' back there? You really need to get back to Earth while you have a chance. The only way we can enter your reality is to have someone from your world call out to us. It is only through dreams that we can materialize on your planet. I only have a short time that I can help you. You see, here we quickly forget the reality of your world. It begins to fade like a dream. Soon, I will only have a vague memory of what happened there. You being here may help me to remember, though.

"Here, we study very hard to remember and have used what you would call Occult methods to hold those memories in our mind's eye. Imagination is very important to us. In fact, it's everything. It's the essence of power that only a few can safely manipulate. We use that power to call out to ourselves from your world. It is in that manner that we can travel back and forth to your world. It is said that B'el never forgets and can travel back and forth easily. When we are called out of this world by one of you, we never know what to expect. We maintain the image of ourselves on your world through the practice of religion, in all of its forms. On your world, we are constantly reminded of who we are. The same is not true here."

"But what about your power, like back on Earth?" J'son was trying really hard to process what T'mar was saying, but at the same time he was struggling with his new-found ability to travel across time and space.

Unlike what she was saying, he was remembering more and more about his life back on Earth, not less. He had no doubt that T'mar and this world were real and he was starting to understand the complexities of his situation. But also, why did T'mar seem so anxious? Back home, she possessed incredible power. She could manipulate matter and disappear at will. She even taught him how to control and direct his power. Now, she seemed helpless and a little scared. His presence here really did cause her some concern. Was it true that he had the power to fold space and time?

"Our power is bound here," she said after a moment's pause. "It's very limited, almost non-existent. To practice that art-" She was struggling to articulate what she wanted to say. She lowered her head and put a hand on her hip, thinking. Slowly, she spoke again, "It's the only way we can protect ourselves against him. The only way we can hide."

T'mar fell quiet. Waves of confusion shadowed her face. J'son could see the conflict. But more than that, he felt her confusion. It was remote at first, just on the edge of his awareness. Then it grew to the point that he could sense it on some level. It was like he could read her aura. The images forming in his mind conveyed the impression of someone caught doing something they shouldn't be doing. There was shame there, intermingled with the confusion. And guilt, too. As attractive as she was to him, physically, what he was receiving from her repulsed him. He wasn't sure why this was so and fought against the impression, but it was too late. He had seen a side of T'mar that he didn't like, didn't respect. She's really not all that pretty anyway, he thought.

"Say, when you travelled back just now, was D'unn asleep? Did he seem like he was having a dream?"

"Uh, no. He was sitting at a desk talking on the phone. How would I know if he was dreaming? And how would I know if he was dreaming about me?"

"Did he see you? Did he interact with you? Did his movements seem programmed?" Her questions were quick and rapid-fire. She was digging for information. She was hoping, also, that maybe she could hold on to her memory of Earth.

"No. You were telling me about B'el and all of the sudden I felt carried away. The cave was here at first, but it faded into the background. Then walls of wood and plaster appeared and I found myself looking at a man seated behind a desk. I don't even know if I had a body or not."

T'mar put both hands on her hips and sighed. She was looking at J'son and the confusion that haunted her looks a moment before vanished. She was calming down and emitting an entirely different set of impressions. Dropping her hands to her sides she moved closer to J'son, stopping just inches away from him. She made a move to reach out and touch him, but stopped short. Like touching a light switch in winter, a small electric spark jumped between them, startling her. She could feel the power radiating from him. He almost seemed to be glowing.

"J'son, I want you to close your eyes and try to see if you can make contact again. This is very important. Try to clear your mind and allow thoughts of D'unn to appear. Concentrate on that image. Try to speak to him and see if he is aware of you. If he can't see you or sense you, then maybe it is just a residual image and that won't help us. If he can sense you, then we can use him as our portal. We need a door way, J'son. We need a way to get you back to Earth, a way to escape if we need one."

"I'll try, but I'm not too sure I understand." Closing his eyes, J'son took a deep breath and slowly let out it out. He breathed in again, holding it for a few seconds before letting it out. On his third breath, images flowed into his awareness and J'son felt some part of himself leaving the confines of the cave. In his mind's eye he beheld a bird's-eye view of the town square back home. He had the distinct feeling he was flying but was unsure as to how that was accomplished. Looking down, he caught a glimpse of a light post and instantly he was at that level, still floating about five feet above the pavement.

Turning his attention to the large, plate-glass window on his left, he saw that he was now in front of Sandy's bar looking at a reflection of himself in the front glass. What he saw was a small, bluish sphere the size of a softball. "What's that?" he thought.

"What did you see? Did you see yourself? Did you look like a person?" T'mar had heard him mumble something but didn't make it out. From her perspective, J'son had entered a trance, had stood perfectly still and was barely breathing. He stood that way for several minutes before he began to mumble.

"No." he said, sounding groggy even to his own ears. "I looked like a small balloon. I was blue. It reminded me of those dreams I have. "

"If you tried again, do you think you could call out to me? Try saying my name or maybe just concentrate on me. Do you think you can remember what I look like? I've never met anyone who could come and go on his own without anyone calling out to him." Well, that wasn't exactly true. T'mar had met someone before who could do that. B'el had studied the occult arts long ago and had accumulated a vast body of knowledge of the mysteries and could manipulate reality anyway he pleased. It was scary the power B'el possessed, but also exciting. That knowledge was forbidden and to practice those arts could bring damnation. At least that is what all sentient creatures knew instinctively.

Something was building up within T'mar, that old lust for power she had felt before. It was a power she had tasted a long time ago, in a different age of the universe, when she was a student of B'el. A disciple, she reminded herself. It shamed her to think about the price she had paid to study under B'el. But here was someone who could do what B'el could do. If she played her cards right, maybe she could learn from J'son now. She could pick up her studies and... Fear rose up in her thoughts. Thoughts of blasphemy and the power that came from practicing the black arts dominated her awareness. I shouldn't have followed B'el here, she thought nervously.

"I'll try," J'son said, sounding defeated and pathetic. Once again he closed his eyes and tried to clear his mind. Images of stars set in the blackness of deep space entered his awareness, tiny points of lights calling out across the universe. The scene only lasted a moment or two, and then those same stars streaked away from him leaving white linear trails tracking before his eyes. The streaks blurred and merged into a wall of white, then in a prism-like way colors fanned out from the center and were transformed into the familiar buildings and streets of his home in Hope, Alabama.

Chapter Two:

The Storm

"I am what you would call a Goddess, only I won't require your worship."

T'mar speaking to J'son in the cave

J'son found himself at street level and he felt like he had a head that he could turn and move around. Glancing down, he saw himself having the shape of a human being with legs and arms and a torso. He held out his hands and looked at his palms, flexing his fingers repeatedly, opening and closing them. Then remembering what he was supposed to do:

"Tamara, can you hear me?" The sound of his voice caught him off guard, but the echo that came back surprised him even more. The street and building that he had been standing in front of dissolved into a million points of light, the solid brick and mortar disappearing altogether only to be replaced by solid rock with T'mar standing beside him.

"I heard you say my name," she said, moving closer to him. "It was very clear, but the sound didn't come from your body here. It was like hearing someone calling out from a great distance using a bullhorn. Usually when I feel someone reach out with their mind it is while they are in the dream state. Most of the time, the dreamer doesn't even know that they are being used and a portal opens within the ethereal realm, the birthplace of dream. My entry into that realm is usually accompanied by swirling images and creations of the disembodied ego, but this time I didn't see anything. The portal didn't open."

"What happened?" J'son asked, still coping with a feeling of disorientation.

"You were standing there so still that I thought you had left your body behind and were exploring the astral realms out-of-body. This is very strange. We'll have to try again later. J'son, any chance you get to go back you must take it. See if you can solidify yourself and maintain hold of your body image before you call out again. That may give you some stability. We need access to a portal or we'll be stuck here. I don't want to confront B'el without the means of being able to escape. If he finds you here, I'm not too sure what he would do. He hates your race."

"Ok, T'mar. What's going on?" Astral realms? Trans-dimensional dreams? The need to escape? J'son still wasn't convinced that this place, this world, was real. The way T'mar talked it was this planet that had reality and the places on Earth were mere dream images coming from people who had eaten a slice of bad pizza. "Where are we and why do I feel like I am in two different worlds at the same time?"

"J'son, for lack of a better analogy you are on the planet of the gods of your forefathers. We were banished here millennia ago for crimes against the Good. We are what you would call the fallen angels of the Bible, although we don't consider ourselves as evil. That designation was given to us by inferior beings (Inferior beings?!) that have no idea what they are talking about. As for 'where' we are, I have no idea. Because we were found guilty of interfering in human development, we were sent millions of light years across the universe, away from Earth so that we wouldn't inherit… I mean take… I mean… We're being punished for something that we didn't do and wasn't even our fault. We were only trying to help."

"Help who? Us? If it were your race that got banished, why do you say you were trying to help? If we're a million light years away from Earth, how is it you remained in contact with us?"

"It was only when your race started to call out to us that we were able to find a way back to you. It was through your dreams that we gained access to your world again. Even though we lost contact with your race you still called out to us, believing that we existed. That's what I was trying to say before. We are able to attach ourselves to your dream stream and with it pull ourselves through to your side. Without someone from your world to dream us into existence, we would never be able to return. It is only through dreams that we have access to you, so we can help your race."

"Help us? You just said you were being punished for helping us. What exactly are you being punished for?" T'mar's answers were disjointed and scattered and if he understood what she was saying a little condescending. Had he been used? It sure seemed like that was what she was saying. J'son was getting impatient. He could feel his blood pressure rising and the headache he had had earlier was starting to grow again, mostly right behind his eyes.

"'When the sons of God saw the daughters of man were fair, they took to themselves wives from the race of Man.' This is something that should never have happened, J'son. Your leaders, your captains of industry, those at the top, all those that have authority over you are in reality the offspring of us. You are our children, the sons and daughters of the gods. Your world has been enslaved by those who wish to take your inheritance for their own selfish reasons. Your world is a battle ground between the forces of good and the forces of evil. B'el is the leader of the forces of evil, the power that wants your world and your reality."

J'son was pacing around the cave digesting what she was saying. He had read up on conspiracy theories that suggested what she was saying, but the reality of what she stated went against his religious upbringing. And now she was talking about a battles between Good and Evil, like something out of the Book of Revelations. This was too much. "T'mar, what are you talking about?"

"A war is coming to your world, a war like the one that devastated your world in the past. We need to find a way to stop it. That's why I came to you in the first place. B'el must have felt you from before and followed you in your dreams casting a shadow across your awareness until he became real to you. When he had gain enough access to your world through your dreams and the dreams of others, he materialized and started to work behind the scenes. When I met up with you at first I thought you were just a conduit, a channel that I could take advantage of. Your ability to remember your dreams and work within them made you a much sought after portal. Instead, you became a …"

J'son's head was spinning. So many questions and the answers T'mar gave only raised other questions. What was real? He felt like he was living in two different worlds at the same time, neither of which seemed solid. Sons of God? That definitely sounded like something right out of the Bible. Why did he look physically different than he remembered himself looking? Why did his speech sound strange in his ears, even though he could understand what was said to him? Was he really supposed to believe that he was on a planet far away, deep in the universe and he got here because of some metaphysical doorway he had access to? And why was it that everything T'mar said sounded like she was making it up as she went? Something wasn't right. Looking at T'mar in the dim light of the cave and seeing the way the rays of the sun outlined her hair, J'son once again got the feeling that she wasn't telling the whole truth, that she was holding something back, that she wasn't telling him everything.

Suddenly, a shadow passed across the mouth of the cave, engulfing them in total darkness until their eyes adjusted. T'mar turned away from him and walked over to the opening, standing just inside the cave. She looked out at the gathering clouds and the blackness they brought. J'son followed her and approached her from behind locking his arms around her firm waist and pulled her close to him. He didn't know why he had done that, only that he was inextricably drawn to her, wanting to feel her warm skin against his.

His hand quivered as he fought the urge to reach up and cup her breasts. He decided against it and instead they watched the storm roll in, his chin resting lightly on the top of her head. The smell of her hair was a mixture of mountain air, various floral scents carried by the wind and a slight, musky odor that aroused his loins and filled his mind with thoughts that only two lovers would share. He wondered if she was feeling the same way. He ignored the energy enveloping them. What he didn't realize at the time was that his thoughts were the generator of her smells. He was the reason why her body was realizing sex hormones.

Dark, ominous clouds had moved in obscuring the sun and blanketing the sky and valley below in a thick darkness. The light of the sun was gone, but lightning flashed on the horizon streaking the sky in a violent, sporadic show of light. Thunder erupted all around them and the wind was starting to blow heavily. In the distance, illuminated by the storm, they could see dust and debris being sucked up into the sky, swirling up from the ground in a vortex of spinning debris.

"J'son, we have to leave this cave," T'mar said, looking back over her shoulder at him. She, too, was enjoying having his arms around her. It had been a long time since she had felt this way, but she knew what she was feeling and thinking was wrong. He was an earthling, an animal. She pulled away from him and the tenderness she had felt was replaced by a growing fear. "Prolonged exposure to the storm… Well, we just have to go."

T'mar brushed past him, heading towards the back of the cave. She disappeared within moments, hidden within the shadows. J'son could hear her footfalls as they scraped across the litter of loose gravel scattered around the floor of the cave. Her steps quieted and seemed to fade away, coming up to his ears from below instead of coming from the back of the cave. J'son followed her back into the dark, his eyes straining against the diminished light. The force of the wind had entered the cave and J'son could feel the electrical push of the storm against his back. The hairs on the back of his neck and arms stood up and he could see the discharge of static racing up and down his forearms. Raising his hands to eye level, the electrical current danced around his fingertips looking like a kirillian photograph.

Reaching the back of the cave, feeling around as best as he could in the dark and hoping he wouldn't slam his head against an outcropping, he discovered the cave narrowed down to a few feet wide, forming an inverted "V" shape. He felt a rock or something brushing up against his hair and he quickly ducked, instinctively lifting his hands up to protect his head. He couldn't hear T'mar anymore and he became even more disoriented.

It was dark in all directions, confusing him, and he wasn't too sure where he was supposed to go. He could still feel the wind on his back, but now he felt another breeze, not as violent or as electrically charged caressing his cheek.

"T'mar?" he called out.

"Down here," she said from below. "Take the passage to your left and watch yourself. The steps are a little steep."

Turning to the sound of her voice, he took a couple of tentative steps in that direction, holding out his hands to avoid slamming into a wall. A couple steps more and J'son could feel the gentle breeze blowing his hair away from his face. Groping his way through a rough opening cut in the rock, he almost tripped down the first step, coming down hard on his heel on the step below, sending a painful shock wave up his spine.

"Uhn," he groaned in the dark, rubbing the small of his back and arching it as best as he could in the cramped stairwell.

"Careful, sweetie," she called up again. "The stairs are hazardous in the dark."

Did she just call me sweetie? Cautiously stepping down to the next, rough-hewed step, J'son was surprised to notice sweat trickling across his forehead in spite of the coolness of the cave. He reached up and sponged his face with his forearm. The sweat stung his eyes and he closed them against further irritation. When he opened them again, blinking the sweat out, he noticed he could see a dim light filtering up to him from several feet below.

The steps rounded a turn and the light increased, but only slightly. J'son was now in what could only be called a tunnel at the end of which was an opening. The tunnel was about fifty feet long and barely three feet across. The ceiling was so low that he had to stoop just to enter it. T'mar had made it to the end of the tunnel and was standing at the opening looking back at him. She motioned for him to come then stepped outside and out of his sight. She seemed to be in a hurry and wasn't waiting for him.

J'son, bending over at the waist and moving as fast as he could, traversed the tunnel with little difficulty and approached the opening with hesitation. The wind was still howling outside and large branches could be seen flying through the air. Thunderous sounds of crashing and breaking accompanied the wind and he put his hands over his ears trying in vain to block out the noise. Looking at the destruction the storm had brought raging just outside the tunnel opening, he was starting to wonder why T'mar had wanted to leave the relative safety of the cave for the chaos of the open.

It didn't make much sense to chance getting hit by limbs falling from the sky, nor the biting sting of dirt impacting his bare torso. Seeing how he was dress in only a skirt-like thing that hardly covered his groin area, J'son really didn't want to brave the storm. What shelter could be better than this place? He wondered. Being this close to the opening, the hairs on his arms, chest and neck were standing at attention, vibrating slightly and popping like when he would put on a wool sweater in winter. In the darkness of the tunnel he could see tiny sparks flowing off of him.

The lightning flashed again, closer this time, followed a moment later by another riotous round of ear-splitting thunder. A lightning strike just outside the tunnel brought a nearby tree crashing down, falling just to the right of the opening. Limbs and branches stripped clean of any foliage littered the ground. The coverings of the trees were flying freely in the storm and occasionally he saw three foot sections of a fur-like substance similar to his tunic whip by at an alarming rate. J'son watched as one piece slapped into a tree, snaked its way around the trunk and disappeared into the storm.

There was the sound of a large explosion, very close, and the sky lit up. J'son lit up too. For every crack of lightning, he felt an electrical current rise up within him and saw a high voltage static discharge shooting out from the tips of his fingers. There was no pain associated with this phenomenon, just surprise and incredible feelings of power. It was the feeling of power coursing through his body that really surprised him. It seemed as if he were somehow connected to the storm itself. The lightning flashed and he glowed. The thundered raged and he experienced the popping of electricity.

J'son wanted to try something. Waiting for the next crash of lightning, he thrust his arm out in front of him, pointing at nothing in particular. The sky exploded in light and a high-intensity discharge leapt from his hand. A tree twenty feet away and as big around as a car splintered down the center from top to bottom. Staring at the palm of his outstretched hand and then at the broken tree smoldering a short distance away, J'son was nervously excited at the prospect that he had just obliterated something so large. It was like he had a ray gun in his finger. He really needed to speak with T'mar, wherever she was.

"T'mar," he yelled out into the storm, sticking his head out of the opening and cupping his hands over his mouth. The hurricane force wind carried his breath away and the sound of his voice fell dead, sounding flat in his own ears. Where are you! He thought to himself, feeling the force of his own mind.

(I'm over here, behind this boulder.)

He "heard" the words in his mind, crystal clear and full of information. He couldn't tell why he looked where he looked, but when he did there she was, poking her head out from behind a large boulder about a hundred yards down an embankment. He "knew" where she was as soon as she spoke to him. Somehow, they were in mental contact and J'son answered her the same way she had communicated to him. Forming the words in his mind and thinking about her at the same time, he released the words, consciously following them through the void of mental space.

(I'm coming!)

Chapter Three:

Poisoned

"We will speak with you, mortal. You have been given a great gift that must be used in accordance with our wishes."

The Transcendentals speaking
within J'son's hallucination

The ebb and flow of his headache seemed to pulse in time with the raging storm: a lightning strike, the release of energy, the stabbing pain behind the eyeballs. But wait. There was another step to the process, his heightened awareness informed him, but he couldn't explain how he knew that. It was only when he broke it down through reflection that he saw his part in what was happening outside the opening of the tunnel. He realized on some level just below conscious awareness that he was acting like a lightning rod. He was somehow in contact with the mind of the storm and was directing that consciousness toward them. He was the reason why the sky was on fire.

That realization brought with it a strange sense of calm and understanding. Closing his eyes, he flooded his mind with peaceful and gentle images, relaxing him, quieting the fear, doubt and confusion he had felt since waking up here on another planet. Even his growing anxiety over his inability to distinguish between the ethereal aspects of dream and the factual physical reality of this world seemed to fade into the background.

Outside, the storm quieted, the wind calmed down and the lightning flashed quietly in the distance, moving away. The clouds slowly parted and the sun was no longer totally obscured. Thick shafts of light shone down, casting large, irregular circles of illumination on the ground.

Sounds of small life forms scurried out from their respective hiding places, sniffing the air to see if the storm had passed. Looking down, J'son watched as a hairy, rat-like animal, maybe six inches long, moved about his feet having appeared out of a thin crack in the rock. It climbed over his sandal-clad feet on six, long, delicate legs, looking like those of a daddy long leg. Everywhere the animal stepped on J'son's feet left tiny, puffy puncture marks. Surprised by the stinging, bloodless wounds now covering both of his feet, J'son started to hop back and forth from one foot to the other trying to step on it or at least not let the creature touch him again. Jumping outside of the tunnel trying to get away, J'son stared down at the dozen or so whelps forming on his feet. The itching was unbearable and he lifted his foot trying to rub it up against the calf of his other leg. What the hell is that thing? He thought.

The air outside smelled wet and alive. The wind and lightning had died down considerably, but J'son could feel the potential hanging in the atmosphere. In the distance the sky was still a dark, swirling mass of clouds with occasional dull flashes and a rumble that he could feel coming out of the ground. Like the electric discharged he always felt whenever he used to play around the power cable towers back home, the air was filled with ionized energy.

"J'son, hurry up! We have to get off of this mountain before the storm comes back." T'mar had been hiding in the crevices between several massive boulders, but now that the wind had died down she poked her head up and was waving at him frantically. Moving away from the protection of the boulders, she started back up the slight incline heading towards J'son and the entrance to the tunnel.

Seeing her coming up the incline, J'son moved down in that direction to meet her. He had to climb over a large, fallen tree that was in his way and he tripped over the litter of broken branches scattered all over the place. His feet hurt and were starting to swell. They were numb, like when your feet fall asleep, and walking was becoming extremely difficult. The straps of his sandals were cutting into his flesh and he could see an ugly blue color mixed in with the red whelps. By the time he reached T'mar, he was hobbling and his head was pounding.

"J'son, your feet?" T'mar met him about half way between the fallen tree and the boulders and now had her hand on his slumped shoulder. She could see the strain in his face and knew that without immediate attention he might lose his feet. She had seen this before and knew exactly what had happened. He had been poisoned by a 'wat. It was a deadly poison that brought intense agony that lasted for days if not treated. But what concerned her about the infection at the moment were the hallucinations that would come soon.

"Do you think you can still walk?" she asked. "We have to make it to the bottom before that storm comes back. I should be able to find you some medicinal herbs down by the lake. It's all downhill from here, but we'll have to look out for roots and other vegetation sticking out of the ground. No need to have you breaking your leg and tumbling to the bottom."

T'mar's emotions seemed to be in check, but J'son could see the worry in her face: deep lines creased her forehead and there was a concerned look to her eyes. The deep pools of green that J'son had fallen for only a few hours before were now concealed behind nervous clouds of their own. His head felt like it was splitting in half and his feet had swelled to the size of footballs. His toes were normal size, but his feet were puffed up and indistinguishable as such.

"I'll try," he said dejectedly. His thoughts were falling and his mind was becoming unstable. Dark images flowed into his mind and took form blocking out all external visuals. Closing his eyes, cartoon-like figures in full psychedelic glory appeared. They seemed surprised to see him and turned to talk with him. There were two of them, tall and thin with long arms and legs. They were saying something to him, but J'son couldn't make it out.

"CRACK!" That was the sound of a lightning strike, hitting very close.

The sound reverberated around the mountain, startling J'son. He opened his eyes and stared around, eyes ablaze and alert.

"What was that?" J'son said, looking at the dark, ominous clouds in the distance. The sky had a fierce, turbulent expression, an angry look that reminded him of a tornado. But that wasn't what caught his attention. A strong breeze was blowing again causing the tops of the nearby trees to sway erratically in a twisting manner. Debris rapidly filled the sky again, twirling around, sending dust and small branches high into the air where they struck up against something invisible in the sky. The sticks and branches crackled and sizzled. Violent streaks of electricity arched up and scattered in all directions, following the curve of something incredibly large only seen when lit up.

Grapefruit-sized balls of glowing electricity rode the wind, emerging out of the dark clouds slamming up against that arch in the sky. Upon impact they exploded, splattering globs of plasmatic energy across the arc after which hundreds of jagged electrical tentacles fanned out and dissipated into the distance. Some of the blue/white, plasma-filled balls ran into the tops of trees, exploding there and raining super heated, pregnant globs of a jelly-looking substance down all around them, setting the grass and underbrush on fire.

"That's the roof of the Dome," she explained, raising her voice to be heard over the noise of the wind and static discharge. "It is part of the… protective field that surrounds this place. It keeps bad things from happening."

T'mar wasn't telling the truth and J'son knew it. What he didn't know was why she felt the need to lie to him. The fact that there was something high in the air that looked like some kind of force field was demonstrated by the sizable explosions of light. The storm, or whatever it was, was getting closer again. The wind had reached dangerous, tornado-like levels and was growing stronger, especially now that they were out from under the protection of the cave.

"Why are we out here?" J'son asked, yelling over top of the increasing noise. "I don't understand why we don't wait out the storm inside of the cave?"

"NO!" T'mar sounded panicked. "I mean, we have to get away from here and find shelter away from these trees. This mountain is off limits to us. We need to get down to a lower elevation, down by the lake. You need medicine and I don't want to take a chance of being hit by those falling gobbets. If they hit you, it will burn a hole right though you. C'mon. There's an opening through that stand of trees over there. Just below that is a small waterfall leading to the lake."

Before J'son could say anything, T'mar grabbed his hand and hauled him off in the direction she had indicated. Pinching his forehead together and fighting against the numbness travelling up his legs, he lurched along behind her as best as he could, stumbling every other step as she pulled him through the trees and down the mountain. The wind blew in circles over their heads and he found it difficult to breathe, the wind stealing his breath right out of his mouth. Moving by a combination of hops and slides, they passed through the large stand of trees and headed to their right, finding shelter behind some huge, black boulders. The gale force wind was momentarily buffeted away, creating a zone of silence within the middle of the storm. They rested there for a minute, trying to catch their breath.

"Where are we going?" J'son asked after ducking down and pressing his back against the nearest boulder. "This seems crazy being out here when we could have just stayed in the cave."

"We couldn't stay there. We were too close to the Dome. We could have suffered radiation burns if we were caught up there during this storm." T'mar was kneeling behind the jet-black rock and motioning with her head back the way they had just come.

Chancing a look, J'son stood up and peered over the top of his boulder, looking back and up, seeing the ledge he had stood on a few hours earlier. Dark shadows covered the mouth of the cave making it impossible to see more than a dark spot. Suddenly, a huge display of electrical fireworks lit up the sky; ball lightning exploded, followed by atomic blasts of thunder. Sounds of very large trees crashing to the ground erupted all around. The top of one tree broke off and fell to the ground, exploding against their group of boulders and covering them in a tangled web of branches.

"J'son, we have to go now before the lightning strikes again. Come on." On hands and knees, T'mar scurried out from under the broken branches, stood up and then made her way through another stand of tightly grouped trees. She slid sideways between two of the trees that had grown together, forming a low arch where they met, the apex merging one tree into the other. The trees themselves looked to be hundreds of years old, with a diameter reminiscent of the great Redwoods of California. By all accounts this was an ancient forest.

Following after her and passing under the arch, J'son considered the path they were taking and wondered if he could navigate down. With both feet now ballooned up to his knees, he felt like he was hobbling along on two delicate water balloons without so much of a crutch for support. It's not so much the pain that was troubling him, since his feet were too numb to feel anything. What bothered him was the downward slope the ground was taking. Even cutting across the slope going at an angle, sharp, jagged rocks jutted out of the soil at broken, razor-sharp angles. The trees were thinning out and it was getting much rockier.

The gurgling rush of falling water could be heard between wind gust and J'son could see the waterfall T'mar had mentioned. About a hundred yards directly in front of him, he could see the spray of water as it crashed against the rocks as it fell from higher up. The trees had thinned out considerably and the path between where he was and the waterfall had no cover. His vision was blurry and the pain in his head made it hard to think and he wondered if he could make it.

Preparing himself for the sprint to the waterfall, he leaned over with his hands on his knees and looked at his feet, taking in large gulps of air. His feet were scratched and cut and a sickly green color oozed out. Even if he could look at the bottom of his feet, which he couldn't, he was too apprehensive to discover their condition. The straps of his sandals had given way at some point and now he was treading around barefooted. Every step he took he could hear a sickly squish. His toenails had totally disappeared within the swollen flesh of his toes.

He felt dizzy and lightheaded, scatterbrained, almost as if his head was as numb as his feet. His stomach gurgled at him and he fought down the growing nausea. He stood up and closed his eyes, hopping to calm himself. Instead, his inner vision swirled around and then coalesced. In his mind, in his frontal lobe, he saw colorful and apparently three-dimensional shapes beckoning to him, waving at him to come closer. The reality of this world, T'mar and the storm raging all around him had faded to a dim memory. He felt himself pulling away, more like a tearing or a separation of some kind. The figures he saw drew closer and became more solidified, more clarified and somehow more real. Their fuzzy and diffused appearance which he had seen at first sharpened and J'son was taken aback by their reality.

The Beings were tall and thin and their eyes had a curious mixture of intense amazement and detached aloofness. They didn't have the mouth to smile, but that's the impression J'son got. They seemed friendly enough, but that might only have been curiosity, like how a person would be interested in a beetle he found underneath a log. Whether he lived or died was not their primary concern.

"J'son!" T'mar yelled over her shoulder. She was almost half way to the waterfall and had stopped to check on him. "We have to go. Now!"

J'son stumbled out from between the trees and was blasted by the wind, almost losing his balance and toppling over. He braced himself against the onslaught and half hopped, half slid down the side of the mountain, moving as fast as he could. T'mar had already made it to the falls and had disappeared behind some rocks. Moving was incredibly hard. The swelling in his feet and legs acted like ankle weights, slowing his movements. Struggling against the wind and his legs, J'son felt like he was in a snow storm battling the elements in movement-restricting clothing. Only this wasn't snow and the clothing was his body.

He reached the waterfall and came to a halt, puffing out of breath. The water started falling from high above him, tumbling down a sheer rock face and terminating at a large pool at the bottom. He was standing about half way between the top and the pool below, having approached the falls from the side. A natural trail running around the rocks lining the falls went down providing steps of sort to the bottom. The wind didn't blow so hard around down here and J'son took one tentative step down the stone steps. The next step was a little further down and he had to sit on one rock and slide down to the next.

Now at the pool, T'mar bent over the edge and put her lips to the water, taking a long drink. She lifted her head to check on J'son and then took another drink. Her thirst quenched, she stood up and started looking at the ground, turning her head this way and that, searching for something. J'son descended the remaining steps, breathing heavily, and sat down hard by the water's edge. He, too, was thirsty and rolled over on his stomach, plunging his head into the water. The cool water felt good on his aching head and after sucking some water into his mouth he plunged his head back under the cold water. The throbbing became a dull ache and for the first time since waking up here he felt the muscles in the back of his neck loosening up.

He pushed up with his arms and rolled to his back, his head pointing towards the water but not in it. He looked up at the sky and saw it was a deep blue the color of sapphire. The storm was moving away and the cloudless sky was luminous and dazzling. He didn't know if the radiance was because of the shield or not, but it was like looking at a jewel sparkling in the sun. Something resembling a large bird hovered overhead, riding the upward draft coming off of the falls. From the chaos of just a few minutes ago, it was easy to fall into a light sleep. Without any pain coming from his feet, J'son was oblivious to his situation.

As he was getting a drink and surrendering to the spell of sleep, T'mar was searching the ground around the pool, at times leaning over to brush aside the tall grass growing besides the water's edge. Not finding what she was looking for she moved to the next patch of grass and looked there. A small stream ran away from the falls and off into the distance, flowing downhill and disappearing around a bend formed by the roots of a large tree. She followed the stream and stopped after a few yards. She reached into the water and pulled up something resembling a plant, root and all. She stood up and made her way back to J'son who was lying on his back with his eyes closed.

The moment he had closed his eyes, he saw those same strange beings from before. This time there was no fuzziness, neither the momentary transition from a gaseous blob to a solid form. It was like walking into a room and seeing people there, only they didn't look like any people he had ever seen. They were communicating with him again, but this time he could actually hear them. What he heard, though, was more like singing than anything else. They were singing a song and just the sound of the melody was their language; it was almost like humming.

T'mar knelt down beside J'son and felt his forehead. He was cool to the touch and his rapid eye movements behind closed eyes was conformation enough to her that he was in the throes of a dark, twisted hallucinatory experience. She wasn't too sure if the poison would work the same way in a human as it did in them, whether the chemical would bind itself to the same receptor sites in his brain. For all she knew, she thought to herself, he may not be experiencing any mental aberration at all. Still, the swelling had progressed beyond his knees and would soon reach his groin area.

She took the plant that she had pulled out of the water and straddled him, sitting on his chest with her knees pressing against his biceps hoping to hold him down if he started to have convulsions. His breathing was deep and heavy and she could feel herself rising and falling with each breath. Sitting on top of him as she was the rhythmic movement was very arousing and she quickly lost herself, closing her eyes and slowly rolling her head back. It was only when she started to move her hips in time with his breathing that she caught herself. She opened her eyes with a smile on her face and stifled a laugh. That felt great, she thought.

The plant itself has six or eight spiny, orange, fleshy tentacles each the length and thickness of a finger. Growing in the water, the tentacles rose up from a central point, forming what looked like a cupped hand, with the fingers pointing up. The plant grew out of a thick root that connected to the base and was six inches long, about one inch in diameter at the base and tapering to a point. The root itself was covered with tiny sprouts about ¼ inch long and was more red than orange.

She put one of the tentacles in her mouth and bit down, severing the first knuckle from the rest of the plant. A clear gooey liquid oozed out and she dribbled it into his partially opened mouth. Whispering to him reassuringly, she milked the appendage between her fingers, saying, "Drink this, J'son. It's like an anti-inflammatory. It'll reduce the swelling in your legs. You'll be fine."

T'mar noticed some of the liquid had fallen on his lower lip. The liquid glistened in the sun, moisturizing his dry, chaps lips. Leaning over, she slowly parted her full lips and gently lowered her head. Their lips touched and a slight puncture sound, like that of cellophane, was felt more than heard. It was the sound of his aura, his ethereal body. It had weakened because of the state he was in, and it opened up to her. She lingered there for a few seconds, playfully caressing his tongue with hers.

"Uhmmm," she purred.

J'son closed his mouth reflexively to swallow and softly bit into T'mar's moist tongue. She pulled away startled and smiling and put her hand to her mouth, touching her tongue to see if it was still there. She thought about giving him another dose of the plant, but was concerned about how his metabolism would react. The leaves of the plant would help with his aching head, but he still needed to drink the tea made out of the root if he was to recover and nullify the visual effects. To make the tea would take some time and he would most likely remain in the grip of the terrifyingly psychedelic poison. T'mar knew the hallucinations weren't the real problem; it was the irreparable psychic damage that could be done.

She stopped straddling him and stood up still clutching the plant. She looked at his legs and thought that maybe she could see that the swelling had already started to go down. She walked a few feet away and dropped the plant on the ground in a little clearing by the stream. Either forgetting or ignoring the teaching about proper respect for all life, especially medicinal plants, she left the plant and walked over to a pile of broken branches and tree limbs that the wind had brought down. Breaking off several branches and smaller twigs, she brought them back to the plant and laid them next to it.

She moved away from the kindling and the stream and headed back toward the waterfall. Inspecting the rocks scattered all over the area and turning over several of the smaller ones, T'mar finally stuck her hand between two larger rocks. There was a gap about waist high made by the rocks and she had to stand on her tiptoes to reach it. She shoved her arm into the gap all the way up to her shoulder and groped around for something. Latching onto something, she yanked it out and held what she was clutching up to her face.

It was a dry, grey powdery substance that blew away easily in the gentle wind as it ran out between her fingers. Cupping both hands tightly around the powder, she made her way back to the plant and pile of sticks. Stooping down, she poured the dusty material on the ground and then proceeded to stacked the twigs and branches into the shape of a tiny pyramid over top of it. Pinching a tiny bit of the powder between her thumb and forefinger she sprinkled it into the palm of her hand. Slapping her hands together she began to rub them back and forth in a rapid motion.

Still rubbing her hands together, she bent over and blew into her hands, rubbing them faster and faster. After a few seconds she opened her hands and blew harder, showering the pile with superheated dust and flame. The dust under the pile of sticks ignited in a bluish flash, settling down to nice yellow/orange tongues of fire which slowly began burning the wood. She fed a couple of larger pieces of wood into the fire for good measure and then stood up. The fire was small and good for boiling water, something she needed to do. All she needed now was a container to hold water.

She walked back over to the stream and studied the water. Spotting what she was hunting for, she reached into the cool water and pulled something up out of the bed of the stream. The object was muddy and she washed it off under the swiftly moving water. The object was larger than her hand, encrusted and pock-marked like a piece of volcanic rock, and curved, having a dome on one side and flat on the other, like a shell. She ran a thumb nail along the edge of the object, scratching out mud and silt.

A visible groove ran around the circumference and she looked at it from several angles. Making a decision, she slammed the object down on a rock repeatedly until it broke in half. She tossed the flat side down and looked inside the domed half, scooping out something fleshly and dropping that into the water. She now had a bowl and she filled it up with water. She made her way back over to the fire, being careful not to spill any of the cool liquid.

The bowl held about two cups and T'mar carefully placed it on top of the fire, settling it down in the hot coals. She added more kindling to the fire and stoked the fire back into a flame. She picked up the plant and quickly separated the root from the leaves, tossing the leaves into the bowl of now boiling water. She took the root and placed it carefully on a flat stone she found by the stream. Taking a palm-sized rock, she proceeded to pound the root into a pulpy mass. Confident that she had exposed the inner flesh of the root, she took it over to the bowl of water and dropped it in. This may take a lot of water, she thought. I hope he can ride it out.

Sitting down by the small fire, relaxing now that she had the tea going, she looked at J'son for the first time since trying to hump him. She smiled at the memory, almost romantically so and giggled to herself for feeling so silly. The swelling did look to be going down and his breathing wasn't so deep, which was a good thing. She had known friends who had died locked in their own inner terror, suffering from oxygen deprivation and demented horror as their breathing slowed until minutes went by between breaths. If the extract from the leaves worked, the tea would completely neutralize the progression of the poison and return him to a state of mind that, hopefully, resembled his typical self.

She took the boiling medicine from off of the fire and blew on it to cool it off. The mixture had to be warm in order to work properly, but she didn't want to pour boiling liquid down his throat. Using one of her fingers to part his lips, she tilted the bowl and began pouring it in. He started to cough and she eased back, waiting for him to swallow. She poured some more of the liquid into his mouth allowing him time to swig it down. Emptying the bowl, she leaned back and waited.

Within a minute or so a murmur escaped his lips and T'mar's eyes locked onto his face. The small muscles around his mouth twitched slightly and his eyelids fluttered momentarily. Was he coming out of it so soon?

"J'son?"

Chapter Four:

The Lovers

"I've missed you. It's been hard being around him. He offers instant access to a source of awesome power. He may be the portal we have been looking for. I only hope he doesn't lose his mind."

T'mar to T'mer shortly after seeing each other

J'son was far from regaining consciousness and even if his eyes did flutter open he wouldn't have been able to receive external stimuli. However, while T'mar was running around finding bowls and boiling water, though, he was carrying on a conversation with the strange beings he now believed to be an integral part of ultimate reality: more real than real. They had been singing to him in a quiet, almost whisper-like manner and he had responded as best as he could. As before, the melody entered his ears as a waveform, but instead of "hearing" sound, he "saw" pictures. It was like the sound waves had dissolved in his ear canal into particles of light, each photon a fractal and holographic image of the original intension of the sound. They sang and he understood.

"We are so glad that you have made it here," stated one of the three beings standing before him. "You will learn many things here and they will come to you in the form of downloads. Do not be afraid and try not to speak with your mouth. Instead, focus on the images forming within your mind and project your consciousness into that. Think of it as a proto-language. It is conscious awareness before actual speech limits the meaning."

Their side of the conversation took no more than a second, a high-frequency stream of images pregnant with meaning. His response took a little longer and taking their advice made him dizzy and lightheaded. He saw images dancing around in his head but didn't know if he was transmitting or receiving. It was during his side of the conversation that he thought he heard a voice, a normal voice, coming from somewhere outside his present reality bubble. It was an actual voice and the sound of it conjured a mental image of a beautiful woman. She was in the throes of passion and calling out his name. He felt himself waking up and the beings standing before him misted over and the lines of their bodies softened, distorting them. "Wait!" they said.

T'mar watched J'son to see if he displayed any more signs of consciousness. After the facial tics a few seconds before, his face froze over again into a death mask, looking more like the plastic face of a mannequin. She looked back to the empty bowl sitting back on the fire and decided she needed to put more water in it before the root dried out and made the leaves inactive. She stood up and walked over to the stream, not seeming to be in any real hurry. Lying down, she leaned over the edge of the stream and touched her lips to the surface. She began to suck in the water until it filled her mouth. She walked back to the fire and spit the water out of her mouth and into the bowl, covering the root and leaves. The water returned to a simmer and then kicked back up to a boil as she added more wood to the fire.

"T'mar?" It was a male's voice, but not J'son's. It was deep and guttural mixed with happy surprise and belonged to a tall man of considerable mass. He had walked up to the clearing and saw her sitting by the fire with her back to him.

"T'mer!" Her excitement was noticeable and she could hardly contain herself, bouncing to her feet and running the short distance between them. She launched herself into his considerably large, muscular arms and threw her arms around his neck.

He held her close to his body, using his strong arms to pull her in. Their bodies molded together without effort, borne from obvious familiarity. He shifted his chin, lowering his head with eyes closed and parted his lips. In one simple, fluid motion their lips met and within moments they were kissing deeply and passionately, like two lovers long parted. Their enthusiasm grew and T'mar actually forgot about the tea, J'son, and everything else.

The sexual energy of the two lovebirds was rising. His hands were all over her: the small of her back, the back of her head, her waist. He slid his hand over the back of her skirt and roughly caressed her firm, round bottom. T'mer felt the fuzzy texture of her top and the dense flesh underneath pressed up against his bare stomach. He reached up with a free hand and locked a finger under the strap running between her shoulder blades. Without pausing he pulled down on the strap and met resistance. Trying again, he wrapped all his fingers around the strap and pulled harder, stretching the fabric before snapping and freeing her breasts.

"Ummmm," T'mar purred, moaning just like she did with J'son. Her uncovered breasts were pressed up hard against his body. They were still lip-locked and she smiled as she kissed him, feeling his growing warmth against her stomach. His hands moved simultaneously and grabbed the tails of her skirt and started to slide it down over her hips. She stopped him, placing one hand quickly and gently over his.

"No, we can't. Not here." Her breathing was slow and deep laced with slight moans and heavy sighs.

"Why not?" T'mer was hurt and backed away from her, holding her by the shoulders at arms' length.

"I'm sorry," she said, placing her hands on top of his. He dropped his hands to his sides and she move in closer, touching his lips with the tip of her finger. "I have to help J'son. He's been poisoned by a 'wat."

"Who is that?" he asked, noticing the prone, sleeping figure for the first time. "And what is he doing here? He's not one of us. Is he a residual, holographic projection from over there?"

T'mar dropped her hands to her waist and fitted herself back into her top. She turned away from T'mer and headed over to the fire still steaming with a strong, pungent smell. She knew T'mer would have questions that she couldn't answer. She had a lot of her own questions that she hope T'mer might help her with. But because he was below her in the hierarchy, she knew he wouldn't be a good source of information and his frustration toward her for not knowing would only get worse if she couldn't placate him with something.

"He's from Earth. He's the portal that I have been using. He has the ability to travel back and forth at will."

"That's not possible. No one can do that, not even your beloved B'el, regardless of what the rumors say. If he could he would be AB'el. It's not possible." T'mer followed her past the fire and stood looking down at the figure lying in the grass. He noticed the tiny marks on his feet and the swelling, which by now was only residing in his feet. No sign of torment or terror past across his composed face and T'mer wondered if J'son was still alive.

"He's a goner already. By the time you get that tea down his throat, he will be a psychological wreck. You've seen what happens when the monks try it."

"He's different. I've seen him do things that he shouldn't be able to do. Just his being here is peculiar. I don't know if he'll be sane when he wakes up, but…" Something T'mar didn't want to tell T'mer, or even acknowledge to herself, but J'son's ability to "portal" back and forth probably wouldn't be affected by permanent brain damage. That faculty is controlled at a deeper level and without access to the rational mind his ability might become enhanced. The monks that T'mer mentioned had found the way to portal, but at a cost too high for most to contemplate. They could portal at will, but they lack the clarity of mind to use it. Some have said that insanity is a gift, designed to protect the secret of the trans-dimensional world from the profane.

"How can he be here, T'mar? This has never happened since 'The Falling'. They can't come here. They lack the mental framework to even begin to understand how to materialize within the structure of the dream. Tell me what happened after you got here. I know you don't remember what happened before you got here."

"Actually I do! Not everything, but enough to talk about it. I think

J'son being here has helped me to remember. I was perusing B'el, following his energy signature, trying to find him so I could confront him."

"Or get seduced again." T'mer wasn't happy with the situation at all. Not only did she leave him to follow that devil, now she had brought back an insect for… what? All sentient creatures knew the prohibition and yet he bet she was keeping this bug around for reasons of her own. Still standing next to J'son, he turned to look over his shoulder at T'mar stoking the fire. She stood up slowly with her hands cupped around a streaming bowl of 'psi root.

"Damn this is hot," she said. She shuffled over to T'mer and J'son bow-legged, walking carefully, trying not to spill the tea. "Help me to get more of this down his throat.

T'mar set the bowl down on the grass next to J'son and then moved around to his head. She sat on her ankles, forming a pillow of sorts with her legs and then lifted and placed his head gently in her lap. She pulled down on his jaw, opening his mouth slightly. Moving up to his forehead, she brushed his hair out of his eyes, lightly fingering the thick, curly mane. She was nervous about what might happen next. The leaves had a soothing effect, but the tea made with just the root would have an immediate, terminating effect, stopping the hallucinations and brutally waking him. Depending on his state of mind, J'son may experience a wide range of side effects, anything from convulsions to screaming mania. She was glad T'mer was here to help her out.

"T'mer, pour the tea down his throat. And be gentle! We need him."

"Whatever." T'mer picked up the bowl harshly, spilling some of the liquid on T'mar's leg. "Is it cool enough?" he asked sarcastically.

"Just put it to his lips and be prepared to restrain him when he starts to come down."

"I'll snatch him up and snap his spine. Don't you worry about this 'slg." T'mer lifted his foot and put it on J'son's chest. He bent over, holding the bowl to J'son's mouth and tilted it, spilling lukewarm, dark brown almost black fluid up his nose and down his throat.

T'mar had placed her hands on either side of his head to hold it straight while T'mer poured. She watched as the dark fluid flowed into his mouth and looked up at T'mer when the liquid stopped going down. At first, there was no reflexive swallow, no choking or coughing. "I think that's all he'll take."

Suddenly, J'son sat up with such force that he flipped T'mer off of his one grounded foot, sending him sprawling on his back with arms and legs flying in the air. T'mar, surprised as she was, fell back from her seated position and extended her arms behind her for support. J'son was sitting board straight and perfectly still and she could see the muscles running along his spine tense and knotted.

"Damn," T'mer said while lying flat on his back. He sat up and stared at J'son contemptuously, scornfully looking at him, the way you would look at a pile of maggots on rotten meat.

"Leave him alone," T'mar said. "As long as he isn't running around screaming, I think he will be ok."

"Ok? T'mar, he's catatonic. His brain isn't anything more than mush. If the 'Great' monks can't handle it, why do you think he'll escape the terror? The fool! This is permanent." T'mer stood up and looked down on J'son again. He didn't understand T'mar's attachment to this worm. If it was a physical thing, he could appreciate that. The times he had gone back to Earth he had indulged himself. Once you get over the idea of having sex with an animal, it's easy to be aroused by these vermin.

But that didn't seem to be the case. She probably did have sex with him, but her affection for him was more like a pet than erotic stimulation. Still, he had needs and she was either going to help him with those needs, or he would have to help himself. He smiled thinking of the times he had done just that, with and without her. It was always more enjoyable that way. This grub, he thought to himself, will be cataleptic for hours, if he wakes up at all.

T'mar cautiously worked her way around J'son, and squatting before him, searching his eyes for awareness, she whispered, "J'son. Can you hear me?"

"T'mar, come with me."

T'mer's voice was gentle, but she knew what would happen if he didn't get the thing he wanted when he wanted it. He wouldn't like what she was going to say to him, but she had to make sure that J'son was stable first. He had to wake up, become aware of her, and then he could sleep for awhile. It would be a light sleep, not the deep, catatonic sleep of narcotics but restful and dreamless.

"Just a minute! Just let me make sure." She said that too short. He wouldn't like her tone, but she really didn't care about that right now.

"I said, 'Come here!'" He grabbed her hand and was now twisting her wrist trying to pull her up.

"No!" she thundered back, breaking his grasp and pulling away from him. "I said, 'Just a minute.'"

T'mer didn't like the way she was treating him, like he was nothing to her. So what if she was at a higher grade than him? After what he had done for her she owed him. Besides, she chose him, publically. After B'el, she was nothing, broken. She couldn't have cast a spell to save her life. And now she was blowing him off because of this brain-dead beetle. She did owe him and he would get what was his, one way or another. Let her take care of her plaything. She thinks I'm stupid because I didn't listen to his lies. I may be slow, but I'm strong. I can break them over my knee and crush their heads with my bare hands. Scowling as he looked at her, he turned around in a huff and walked away, mumbling under his breath.

"J'son. Can you hear me? Follow the sound of my voice." T'mar studied his face for any sign of cognition, any facial tic that would indicate he wasn't gone for good. Then a faint glimmer flashed in his eyes. His eyes widen momentarily and then closed, squeezed tight. His ridged body relaxed somewhat and his upper torso wobbled slightly. He opened his eyes again weakly and stared at her out of hazy, red-rimmed eyes.

"T'mar," he whispered. He fell backwards, slipping just out reach as she tried to catch him. He landed heavily in the grass and rolled his head back and forth, moaning a little but no violent outburst. His arms and legs twitched and shuddered, trembling on the ground. The spasms lasted only a few seconds and then he quieted down. He closed his eyes again, calmly and fell quickly into a light, restful sleep. His sleep would be untroubled for now and hopefully he would wake up later somewhat coherent.

"Ok, T'mar. Now that the 'mgl is tucked in, you have some explaining to do. And from the way I see it you can do all your talking on your back." He walked back over to her and met her as she was just standing up.

T'mer was leering at her and she saw that this time it was going to be even harder to rebuff him. She had to stall him and get his mind off of what she so desperately wanted, too. Even still, she wasn't going to do anything remotely sexual standing this close to J'son. He was aware that T'mer thought nothing of humans and saw them as nothing more than playthings to use and manipulate. But J'son was different, she told herself. He meant more to her than just physical pleasure or the hope of a possible portal. That thought stopped her cold. Was that true? Was it only because he possessed an ability that the priests would risk anything, even immortality, to have? Standing there, mere inches away from her husband, seeing the hunger in his eyes, she turned away and looked down at J'son.

"Damn it, woman." T'mer was furious and stormed away again, leaving T'mar, the stream and the mountain itself. Shouting over the roar of the falls, he said "Why do I always think it will be different. The Council said it wouldn't work."

"Wait." T'mar ran after him, pleased with the direction he was going. She caught up with him and grabbed his large, sculpted bicep, slowing him down and gently turning him around. They were now about twenty feet way from J'son, but T'mar wanted more distance between them. She guided T'mer over to a group of trees standing on the edge of a drop off. They were now about fifty feet away and T'mar felt it far enough to talk.

"T'mer, my love. I'm sorry about this. I want you more than you can know. It's hard being around them that way. Their minds are so simple and easy to control. Having unfettered access to their imaginations is intoxicating." Her eyes shined with a faraway look, the look of an addict remembering her last score.

"As intoxicating as B'el?"

"That was different. B'el was a mistake and I foolishly fell for him."

"Maybe that piece of meat is a mistake," T'mer said hooking a thumb toward J'son. "Look, you said he was different or something. What's so special about a 'vrn that can do tricks? Did you use him for personal gratification? Don't tell me you didn't. I never believe those monks that say they never indulge. It's like you said, it's like a drug."

"It is, isn't it? Do you ever wonder if we should search for a permanent portal, like the monks? Maybe-"

"You've been in their dreams. You know the power of possessing one of them. To be alive and have the power of will." He smiled at her, the lines and creases of his cheeks and forehead Xing across his nose, making his smile lurid and lustful. He reached out to her and caressed her breast with the back of his hand.

"We have to be careful," she said, allowing him to fondle her breasts. "I don't want him waking up and seeing us."

"Who cares?" He growled, dropping his hand and looking exasperated. "Who cares what they think, if he can think at all? We're a dream to him. He'll wake up in his bed with a great story to tell his friends. Just because we can feel him doesn't mean he's real. I've been thinking about it. Just like we are there, he is here. The fact he got poisoned was your perception of events. I think you are somehow still connected to him through the portal of dream. He isn't real."

"T'mer, I don't think it's that simple. If what you're saying is true, then how come we don't see this sort of thing all the time? Just like their dreams are haunted by us, wouldn't you expect our reality to be overrun by them?"

'Maybe, but you're the one who said he was different."

T'mar hated talking to T'mer because it always ended in an argument. She knew he had a problem with her choice to leave the hierarchy. Her knowledge of the black arts made her light-years ahead of him intellectually and her learned ability to conceptualize gave her an almost psychedelic clarity whenever she practiced the art. None of that mattered right at this moment. Without the tools of her craft, she was powerless over T'mer's brute strength. Nothing was gained by arguing with him except to enrage him.

"T'mer, I think he is the portal we seek. With him we could travel anywhere or any time."

She stepped in closer to him, slipping between his massive arms and throwing her arms around his thick neck. She leaned her head back and kissed him gently, then more passionately as he moved to embrace her. Her body melted into his and they stood that way together for a long time, mutually groping and fondling each other.

Her cares and concerns drifted away in his embrace and she let down her guard, mentally opening up to him in a way that left her very vulnerable to psychic attack. She knew that T'mer would detect her openness and reach out to her in the same way; however, he didn't have the ability to project himself out of himself in the way she could. For T'mar, letting down her psychic field to him was a show of passive submission to his clumsy, dominator guidance. She would have to project herself into his consciousness, once he lowered his field, as weak as it was, then metaphorically lie down and let him mentally take possession of her body as a willing spectator.

It was similar to what they do when called upon in dreams. Those who had the ability to manifest physically on Earth without the need of a "human" agent found it easier to pass back and forth through their portal. Those less fortunate, like T'mer, could only hope to possess the sleeping, unconscious mind of the dreamer and so forcefully dominate the poor bastard, inflicting all sorts of torture and mental anguish on the dreamer. The ecstasy of possession for the possessor is too much for most and soon a form of insanity eventually envelopes the traveler.

It was easy, T'mar knew, for those like T'mer to abuse the dreamer and cause them to do things they normally wouldn't do. Sometimes they would stumble across a human portal that had been opened by esoteric, occult methods, usually through ritual. Either the portal had been taught how to access that part of themselves through implanted dreams of personal power or the human accidentally discovered the ability through study of magical texts in their waking life. If the portal has the proclivity to use the Black Arts to call forth a "Demon", as they were called, then the portal had no one to blame but himself for any permanent psychic damage. However, to find and use a portal for personal pleasure and enjoyment at the expense of the portal was wrong, especially when using an inferior being, as all sentient beings knew.

Because of the savageness of the encounter, of being mentally raped and abused, it was usually more traumatic than most humans could handle, resulting in serious cases of mental disturbance, dementia and schizophrenia. Tales of ghosts, possession and the spirit world have sprung forth out of the fertile imaginations of humans in such numbers that for most travelers whatever the motif the portal embodies is the one they represent to the portal. If the portal has strong religious leanings, he may see the traveler as an angel or demon. If he has a sci-fi background, they appear as extraterrestrials. They almost always come through playing the dominator role, representing themselves as gods or devils, whatever the portal could understand. It was rare that one would come to Earth playing the part of slave, unless that role somehow enhanced the experience.

As T'mar and T'mer merged physically, their breathing heavy and their bodies sweating with desire, T'mer let down his field and she entered his thoughts, their minds connecting on a level above the mundane, joining as one. If he had the ability to project himself into her mind, the things that he was thinking now would be considered mental rape. As it was, she willingly entered his thoughts and let his growing lust ravage her. In this state, his primitive nature took over and he opened all the doors in his sub-conscious, creating sick, perverse mental images of violent acts that he wanted to do. T'mar was prepared for this onslaught, and opened herself more to his depraved desire.

She knew that if she allowed him this release, then their lovemaking afterwards would be sweet and gentle. She knew he didn't have control over his thoughts and the beast he'd become within the confines of his mind had to be satisfied. It was blindness, really. His inability to separate his thoughts from his actions always, eventually, led to horrible consequences.

Being on a higher level of awareness than him, T'mar had taken it upon herself to "educate" him in hopes of raising him to the next level.

The things she shared with him were not permitted, and she knew it. She was told before that by pursuing the higher teachings she would lose the objectivity of right and wrong and soon start to believe everything was relative. The ability to distinguish between what was good and what was evil had no meaning at the higher levels. She was taught that truth was a continuum between two polarities that were mutually contradictory and she would make better use of her studies if she would only grasp that one truth.

The morality of whether or not to manifest on Earth and use humans any way they wished was a point of mute discussion. Once one found a way to Earth and tasted the intoxicating power of the human imagination, all talk of morality was pointless. Maybe the monks had altruistic motivations, but as far as she was concerned B'el was right and had told her the truth.

As she fought to maintain her connection with his mind, reminding herself that the vicious attacks were not meant to be sadistic but a form of foreplay, she could perceive that his animal instincts had been satisfied by the changing spectrum of colors that made up their mental space. On the physical plane, the infrared end of the electro-magnetic scale was the lowest and the ultraviolent was the highest. The color of the mental space, or the color of their first manifestation on Earth, reflected the psychological structure of the entity. If red is the color of what you perceive, then a twisted mind was sure to be behind it. On the other hand, blue represented the higher realms and that realm was outside the domain of the profane.

Within T'mer's mind, red and shades of red were the dominate color, the color of blood and violence. Then, slowly, the colors began to change, lighten, becoming mixed with lighter colors. The red became orange which became yellow, topping out at that color and never going higher, mainly because he didn't have the ability to process that end of the spectrum. It was like explaining color to a blind person. You could relate it as shades of black, but not the degree of shade. The delicacy and subtleness of the higher end of the continuum was beyond his comprehension.

In the past, T'mar had tried to fill his mind with the otherworldly blue of her studies, the small glimpses of that higher reality B'el had demonstrated to her, but to no avail. There were lessons he needed to learn if he was ever going to grow beyond what he was. But those lessons were more like seeds planted in the psyche than actual memorization and rote learning. It was never what B'el had said or explained to her that convinced her, it was what he had proven to her through the practice of his teachings. He never said he could do this and he could do that. It was always him showing her what she could do herself. It was like when a great teacher speaks the obvious and you see confirmation of the truth echoing around within you.

The mental disturbances were balancing out now and T'mar could see a golden-yellow hue filling his mind-space. It was the afterglow bringing contentment and serenity. She knew it wouldn't last and if she stayed within his mind it was more than possible she could get trapped there. As his thoughts fell, he would close down his field in a defensive move, refusing to let anything in or out.

It had happened before. She had allowed herself to bask in the light of his higher self for too long. She had lingered within his mind, benefitting from the intimate connection and didn't realize that her way out would be harder than the way in. When one is a slave to the passions, finding a way within the mind of another is easy for anyone who has something to offer. Afterwards, though, when the ego re-asserted itself and didn't want to let go, it was like trying to find her way out of a labyrinth, a maze of psychotic imagery and demented fantasy.

She had learned her lesson then and since that time she had never allowed herself to enjoy the bonding experience too much. She couldn't afford to allow herself the luxury of intimacy. Love, so it seems, was not the domain of beings like her. She did care about T'mer, but loving him was beyond her abilities. They weren't equals, no matter how much she told him they were and wish it to be true. Communication is only possible between equals and for a long while she believed they were capable of that kind of relationship, but no more.

They redrew mentally from each other, returning to the reality immediately surrounding them. They were still standing close together, their arms wrapped tightly around each other in a passionate embrace. T'mar broke away first, easing her hold on him and looked into his eyes, smiling sweetly. She could sense that the aggression had past for now and he was in a "loving" mood. He gently caressed her cheek with the back of his hand, then placed it behind her neck and drew her back in, kissing her hard on her moist lips.

"T'mer," she whispered, breaking their kiss. "Here, let me help you with that. You've been so patient with me. And now that I have satisfied your fantasies, it is time that I satisfy your physical needs."

Quickly slipping out of her skirt, she stood there naked looking into his eyes, offering up her body as willing as she had her mind. She reached out and took hold of the hem of his tunic, yanking downward, freeing him from the confines of the material, allowing him to step out of it with little effort. Taking him by the hands, she sat down on the ground and pulled him down on top of her, inviting him inside of her. It would be rough and it would take some time before he could reach the point of release. Their lovemaking would resemble lovemaking on Earth, but much more intense and brutal, climaxing only after hours of painful intercourse.

They made the beast with two backs together, and several other animals not found on Earth nor could those positions be used on a human woman without agonizing consequences. He filled her and rocked her, owning her. She moaned in response to his actions, at times biting him on the shoulder and other erogenous areas on his body. He bit and fondled her, too, indulging himself in the delights of her flesh. They moved together in unison, each anticipating and willingly partaking of the other, gratifying every desire like it was a sacrament.

Exhausted, spent and covered with playful wounds, signs of their lovemaking, they rolled away from each other and lay on their backs staring up at the sky and the trees overhead. It had been nice, T'mar thought, and she wasn't too sore. She glanced over at J'son half expecting to see him staring back at them, awakened by the sound of their lovemaking. J'son still seemed to be sleeping and she looked away from him and back up at the sky. She didn't want J'son to know anything about them for now and she would have to convince T'mer not to say anything, either. She didn't want to risk her chance to escape by making J'son jealous, especially now that he might awaken with mental problems.

She glanced over at T'mer, quietly tracing the lines of his face with her eyes. He had a contented glow about him and the thunderous storm of shadow that usually covered his face was gone, at least for now. She would have to tell him soon about J'son and persuade him to keep quiet, but she didn't want to tell T'mer too much out of an intuitive suspicion that he would try to take J'son for himself. If she told him too much, she wouldn't put it past him to conveniently dispose of her and keep the portal for himself. Trust is for those who believe in love, she told herself.

"T'mer, we must keep silent about us. We can't let J'son know about our relationship."

Rolling to his side, T'mer lightly ran a rough palm over her breasts, coming to rest on her stomach. "Whatever you say. Never let it be said that I don't have compassion for the little ones. I'd hate to see what he would do if I made him jealous. Ha!"

T'mer lifted his head slightly to see over her, looking in the direction of J'son. She turned her head to look, too, and saw J'son lying perfectly still like before and resting peacefully. However, at some time during their lovemaking, J'son had moved his arms and folded them across his chest. She could see his chest rising and falling in an easy cycle of inhalation and exhalation. She looked at his face and admired his bone structure. He was so fair to look at and yet he wasn't handsome in the way T'mer was. Where T'mer's face was hard and sculpted, looking more chiseled and rugged, J'son looked softer, almost feminine. The lines of his face running along his jaw bone and around his chin were more curved than angular, delicate and flowing. It was that gentleness which was in such contrast with T'mer. Watching the easy rhythm of his breathing and the air of calm he projected in his sleep was very sensual and she found herself getting turned on again. They would make love again, but this time it was about what she wanted.

She rolled over and sat on top of T'mer, straddling him and grinding her pelvis into his abdomen. Looking down at him with a mischievous smile, the corners of her mouth curling up, she said, "I think I'm ready for you again."

Chapter Five:

The Hallucination

> "All things are related and of the same source. It is the recognition of this inter-relatedness that defines the parameters of existence."
>
> First lesson given under the power of the 'psi root

After leaving the presence of those strange, ethereal blue/white beings, J'son wandered out of body and out of time. He saw the birth and death of countless galaxies, the creation of light and the beginning of the universe. He was there the infinite moment before anything existed, a vast nothingness, the void, staring into the abyss. He drifted in and out of consciousness for eons without thought or reason, his awareness flooding with images too bizarre to describe. There were no words or sound, just pictures, some form of primordial symbolic language before verbal language came to be. In flashes of insight too lofty to comprehend, he nonetheless understood what he was seeing, intuiting it on a level beyond understanding, existing in a state of continual knowing rather than known.

His mind was wide open, enabling him to sense what was going on around him, on all worlds simultaneously, inundating his consciousness with conflicting and contradicting impressions. Fragments of memories both old and current took shape within him, twisting and turning into visions, illusions and delusions of what might be real. His human body had no meaning to him and he started to realize that all of life was a construct of belief. What he willed was what was real. It was his conception of the reality of the forces at work in the universe that brought the reality into existence. He was the generator and the sustainer of that creative energy known by many names.

He had no personal sense of self nor would he have cared to have lost his individuality and uniqueness. Characteristic qualities like those held little meaning to him and he would have looked on those terms as limiting and constricting. He would have identified with his ego and the terms of that reality if he had some kind of connection with his humanity, but at that endless moment he didn't. Having cosmic consciousness allowed him the objectivity to remove himself from the Karmic wheel of time and see life as a plan, an arrangement between chaos and order, winding down to the zero point, the beginning and the end. The shadow at the end of time throwing stabs of darkness back across history.

There was no central point in history that sent ripples into the past and shock waves into the future. Instead, the universe of experience derives from a conclusion in which waves of possibility swelled up and crashed, permeating the very fabric of existence, fleshing out the structure of propose. All of this, he knew, was created and control by the intensity of the will. All worlds were his and he was the god of the material universe. He could manipulate the very atoms of matter and take their charge to himself, raising their vibration into light or slowing their vibration down to bulk matter.

A kaleidoscope of colors raced across his awareness and he stopped their progressive flight out of the universe, studying the individual properties of each color, transforming the electrical current of each particle, raising its vibration and changing a simple yellow into an elemental force of tremendous power. The force possessed a personality, created from J'son's heightened awareness, although it was separate from him. It started to solidify and took on a shape.

The creature evolved out of the energized colors and stood before him. Fiery flames of electric potential flew out of the beast in a blistering discharge of high-voltage radiation. J'son studied it without knowledge of fear, but after awhile he grew bored with the creature and in a flash of thought it dissolved into countless specks of light, like a million fireflies hovering in the night's sky. Then, each little fragment streaked off in all directions, like the spokes of a wheel, with him providing the focal point, smearing tiny rays of light across the visible universe. The interval created by the outward rush of energy produced an emptiness that collapsed, forming an aperture, a doorway, a portal back to the reality of three dimensions.

Looking through the portal, he could see images of different worlds and different times reflected back at him. He knew he had the ability to enter into any reality of his choosing and could change and alter the destiny of all timelines. As the worlds raced by the opening, each pausing momentarily in the window of the portal, he detected images and scenarios that seemed familiar, catching his attention and slowing his thoughts. He focused on a particular energy, an essence that carried with it a feminine nature, but having the quality and disposition of a raging volcano.

The image intrigued him and slowed his thoughts even more, causing him to fall from that lofty abode of eternal contemplation. A delicate, ethereal ribbon of light flowed out of him, feeding the image, solidifying it and giving it life. Forms swirled and coalesced before him, drawing more energy out of him, pulling him toward the image. As he moved through the portal, he recognized another form that was his body lying beside a stream a billion miles away from Earth. He was drawn to his body out of some sense that he needed to return, that something wasn't finished, that the tall, bluish entities had a job for him.

That was the first connection he had with his body after returning from the realms of imagination, his first insight that he could become a limited being confined in a fragile vehicle of flesh. He experienced no thoughts related to that idea, no sensations, no feelings, only the persistent call of self apprehension complemented by the growing recognition of individuality. His awareness folded up, shrinking in dimension and spatial capacity. His essence, his fundamental nature, contracted and narrowed, adjusting to the confines of cranial capacity and brain size, placing voluntary mental and physical limits on what he would be able to perceive.

Human thinking came to him next, then his ability to reflect on that thinking. His thoughts explored the depths of his memory and what he had just experienced. He felt nothing, for he had not yet assimilated that part of his humanity into his increased awareness, making it personal and engaging the somatic systems of his body. Feelings would come with the return of sensory input and with it the micro-judgments everyone formulates trying to make sense of their particular world, but to say that one of his five senses came back before the others would be to misunderstand the nature of his awakened consciousness. The input from his senses transmitted their data all at once, fabricating sensual metaphysical impressions within him through a synthesis of feeling, confusion and the blending of these forms.

Where normally a breeze could be perceived with all the senses at once, their conscious awareness within the psyche would take descending steps from highest survival priority to unnoticeable or even subconscious. Instead of just feeling the breeze blow across his half-naked body, producing goose bumps and causing him to shiver, he simultaneously heard the breeze flapping against his eardrum, smelled the aroma of vegetation and dirt carried by the wind and even tasted the minute particles of pollen that stuck to his dry lips and found their way into his mouth. Although his eyes were shut, he had an image of a silver strip of cool, dense air waving and shimmering in the daylight and moving gently across his prone body.

The mental impressions caused by all the input stimuli hitting his awareness at the same time, demanding his attention and trying to elicit a proper response, created an almost holographic, three-dimensional object within his mind that represented all aspects of wind. He knew its speed and chemical makeup. He was aware of where the wind had been and detected delicate whispers of memory from everything the wind had touched. There were images of rocks and hills, mountains and deserts and the fragrance of trees and plants and animals.

All of these images, these forms battled for supremacy of cognition within his mind, demanding his attention. In the mind of a mortal, his personality would shatter and schizophrenia would result. A mortal would become lost in his own thoughts, a prisoner and victim of the very images his brain generated. J'son, however, had passed beyond the confines of mortality and had entered a new space, a place where he was the projectionist and not the screen. He knew he had the ability to change the flow and energy of the wind and even to become wind itself. All he needed to do was change the movie, but for now the experience was pleasing and he kept the wind as it was, soft and gentle.

The breeze chilled him slightly and he suddenly became aware that he had arms and could wrap them across his chest in an attempt to recover his body heat. He now felt the texture of his skin, the coarse hairs covering his chest, the cords of muscle and the slight raised outline of his rib cage. He also became aware that his stomach made noise and he felt hungry. The idea that he could feel delighted him and he observed, silently, the internal works of his body, smiling to himself at every new realization. He travelled throughout his body, carried along by the bloodstream, performing tasks and functions that normally occur below awareness.

His perception of all of these events came in waves, vibrations created by the movement of the infinitesimal forces all around him. He understood that all experience was nothing more than a string pulsating in empty space. He was a receptor of these energies and a transceiver. He knew that by just reaching out he could stop the universe, stop the thread of creation. Heisenberg had nothing on him.

Then fear gripped him. His body screamed at him, terrified at the prospect of having god-like power. He was conflicted and warred against his baser emotions, which were pulling him in all directions, making threats and promises. His emotion got the best of him and his mental state swung widely, producing a manic-depressive rollercoaster within his perception. Demons and angels appeared before him and then dissolved into nothing. He discovered his ego and watched helpless as it dominated and repressed the feelings running rampant throughout his nervous system. The need for an ego was evolutionary, nature's way of protecting the fragile personality of the unenlightened mind. He could sense his ego throwing up barriers with names like "Hate", "Anger", and "Jealousy".

Fully assimilated into his body now, identifying with his somatic functions, he became increasingly aware of his unprotected state, lying in the open, unsafe and fearful. His survival instinct, genetically encoded from the foundation of the universe, kicked in, scaring him awake. His eyes sprang opened and he twitched nervously, like when somebody "walks over your grave". Wide-eyed and rolling, his pupils dilated, he moved his head slightly from side to side trying to take in his environment, expecting trouble. His breathing was heavy and he could feel his heart beating out of his chest.

Sensing no immediate danger and falling under the spell of the soothing sounds of the stream trickling nearby, he closed his eyes again and tried to slow his breathing, taking deep breaths and letting them out slowly. He did this a few times, calming himself and opened his eyes again, hoping for a better start. He uncrossed his arms and laid them by his side, running his fingers into the cool vegetation growing all around him. He saw the trees overhead, swaying gently in the breeze, the limbs covered in a substance that looked very similar to his tunic.

Studying the foliage clinging to the branches, he noted the composition, recording several impressions at once. They were multi-color in that different trees possessed different colors. The trees themselves stood together in groups, although not every tree was of the same type. In each grouping, one color dominated and was expressed differently according to tree type. Shades of colors grew from the ground up, sprouting into leaf-like grass, small shrubs, flowering plants with thicket-like blossoms and thick brush. Color was everywhere in the form of reds, yellows and greens.

He rolled over on his left side and saw T'mar a short distance away. She was lying down by a group of trees covered in orange, obviously naked, and she wasn't alone. She was lying on her side with her back toward J'son, giving him an excellent view of her hind quarters. Lying next to her on her far side was the outline of a large male breathing deeply, his chest moving up and down. Her arm was wrapped across the man's massive chest and her head was resting quietly on his outstretched arm. T'mar's hip was positioned perpendicular to the man's body and the pleasing curvature of her body hid him from his waist to his upper thigh. Given their manner of dress, it was hard to tell from J'son's vantage point if the male was naked also.

Seeing them together like that should have bothered him immensely, but for some reason it didn't. In fact, he was smiling at them, happy for them and happy for her. On Earth, she had been his dream girl, someone untouchable and unattainable, the prefect fantasy. Here though she seemed more real and fragile, needing someone of great bulk to fight for her and protect her. Although J'son wasn't ripped and chiseled with thick, rope-like veins running all over his body, still he was fit and muscular in an athletic sort of way but looking nothing like the hulking figure lying next to her. They made a good pair together, he thought, her body complimenting his in every way. Where his legs where cut and powerful, hers were soft, smooth and supple, shapely.

The fingers of her hand were moving across his chest, playfully tugging and pinching his nipple and patting his chest. She moved her hand down from his chest, tracing the lower arc of his breast with one finger and then disappearing behind the curve of her hip. The male began to stir, pulling his arm in and wrapping her up, kissing her and maneuvering her on top of him. She straddled him and looked down into his face, smiling a strange Xed-out smile. The smile was more seductive and animalistic than beautiful, showing plenty of white teeth. She had the expression of a huntress about to pounce on her prey.

As he watched them, his impressions were those of one viewing great beauty which transcends all moral values. He had allowed the experience to wash over him, flooding his awareness in multiple, simultaneous streams of information, none of which carried any lustful or derogatory sentiments. He knew that all judgments and negative associations stem from an immature, emotional attachment to the flesh and the pleasure-enhancing/pain-avoidance circuits of his nervous system. To identify with those moods associated with the baser emotions only led to chaos and an unstable mind. Still, the cultural programming imparted to him from childhood onward was hard to shake and he heard a voice rebuking him, chiding him for watching.

It was only a small part of him, though, a tiny voice crying out from somewhere within him, an implanted cultural memory telling him that he was a voyeur and should feel shame for watching them. That voice and the thoughts associated with it sounded scared, mortified and self-reproaching, dripping with condemnation and guilt, accusing him and betraying the weakness of his flesh.

J'son rolled over staring up at the trees again and battled those thoughts which he knew didn't belong to him. The dark shadow of embarrassment and shame moving across his awareness lasted for only a moment and then he chuckled in spite of himself. He knew that he didn't feel any voyeuristic tendencies and that any thoughts of depravity came on the back side of judgment. Without judgment, there is no sin and the part of him that had judged belonged to an outdated mode of being.

Those unnecessary and self-deceiving thoughts drifted away from him as easily as they came and evaporated in the light of his mind, which had started to dim slightly. He knew he was coming down from whatever high he had experienced and the confines of his physical brain, coupled with the attachments of the flesh, were causing him some discomfort and distraction. Demands were being made of his awareness, petitioning him to leave the realm of ideas and imagination and pay attention to the necessities of survival.

He had examined the truth of existence, saw for himself the ballet of energy and how through focus of mind and will he could manipulate the very fabric of matter itself. It was all energy on a quantum level and he knew he was a sentient conduit of that energy. He had seen the whole of the puzzle, the riddle of existence and now the pieces were falling out, leaving cavities within his knowledge. He would remember, of course, but he would need to rediscover those pieces of illumination in order to remind himself that he already knew what had always been there. His mind was darkening and the lamp of understanding was going out. His everyday awareness was intruding and focusing on the mundane, but that level of consciousness was still attached to his highest self, giving him an almost Gnostic sense of perception, an intuition of what is good and what is bad.

He lay there, basking in the afterglow of illumination, feeling the bulk of his body and the sluggishness of his thinking pulling him down as he reengaged his normal nervous system. He was aware that T'mar was having sex on his periphery, but he kept on staring at the trees. He could hear them, too. As his thoughts fell, a violent turbulence was working its way into his mind, an emotional turmoil that needed expression. At first he didn't understand the cause of this new disruption in his thinking, but then he recognized it for what it was: The red-eyed dog of Jealousy. It hurt him that she would so callously engage in intercourse out in the open with him lying so close by, almost wanting him to watch them.

He looked over at them again, clenching his teeth, wanting to yell out to them to "get a room!" He didn't however and continued to stare at them, willing himself to accept the situation and with effort to submerge his feelings. Where a few minutes before he knew himself to be above the ego-enforced limitations of the baser emotions, now he was struggling with those same emotions like all sentient beings. The fire in his belly was still ablaze and the tension between his eyes focused his attention. An "X" formed across his face and hatred raged within him. He was so angry that he could spit, and was about to until he noticed the wind starting to pick up.

Still looking in their direction but higher up, he saw the tops of the trees they were under swaying aggressively in the gathering storm. The fur-like material making up the foliage peeled off the limbs and flew into the air leaving a pale white, unadorned skeletal carcass, like crooked, boney fingers stretching into the darkening sky. The wind blew harder and more furious in pulse-like precision, increasing in intensity and baring down directly on top of T'mar.

Noticing the gathering fury erupting all around them, T'mar rolled off of T'mer and stood up looking into the sky. T'mer stood behind her and wrapped his thick arms around her shoulders, trying his best to play the part of ego-driven male to protect her. T'mar was more surprised at the suddenness of the storm than its violence and broke away from T'mer, turning around to face him.

"This isn't natural," she said holding him at arm's length. "This storm was called down on us. Look, it's only affecting this area. Just like earlier before we met up. But that was because J'son…"

Looking around the bulk of T'mer's body, T'mar noticed J'son staring at them, his face pinched and shaded towards red.

"J'son! You're doing this. You have to stop."

Chapter Six:

Confrontation

"This world is where we first became 3-dimensional after leaving Earth. We no longer had direct contact with humanity because we didn't know where you were. We didn't even know where we were. It's only been in the last 6000 years of your history that mankind started to call out to us in dreams and visions."

T'mar trying to convince J'son who they are

As soon as he heard her voice, his face softened and the X cutting deeply into his cheeks and forehead disappeared. The ridge between his eyes flattened out and his temper cooled. In its place was a look of startled amazement. He realized that he was the cause of the change of weather and immediately started to control his breathing, calming himself. Gradually the wind dropped off to a quiet breeze and the treetops stopped their violent swaying. A few broken limbs fell crashing to the ground trailed by a multi-colored rainbow of foliage drifting gently to the ground. The end result was a vivid display of dazzling psychedelic color coming down like a curtain and covering the ground like a rug.

J'son was sitting up now, a dazed look in his eyes and he watched as T'mer bent over to pick up some blue-colored foliage off the ground and wrapped it around his waist. T'mar was walking in J'son's direction with a look of deep concern on her face mixed with a note of curiosity. She approached him slowly and stood looking down at him, a small, cautious smile turning up the corners of her mouth. She was standing there in her naked beauty without a hint of awkwardness or discomfort. Her flawless, curving body showed no sign of aging or sagging. She had a small amount of vegetation mixed in with her sexy, disheveled mane of scarlet hair. There was a slight sheen coming off of her skin, giving it an almost glowing quality. She seemed surer of herself, calmer than before and in her eyes was contentment.

"J'son?" she asked timidly. "Are you okay?"

"Well, considering ever since I woke up here on this planet I've been poisoned by a furry spider thing, swelled up like a balloon, got knocked senseless and passed out because I ate some fungus you told me to eat and, Oh yeah! had fire raining down on me, I think I'm doing okay. Where are your clothes, by the way? And who's that?" He looked past her to T'mer, who was now making his way over to them.

"Um, that's T'mer. He came to help us. Do you remember anything that has happened? Do you find it hard to think?"

"How come you're alive? How come he's alive, T'mar? Who are you?" T'mer approached them and stopped a few feet away, drilling holes into J'son with the look of his eyes, a look of intense hatred and distrust. His physicality and sense of domination scared J'son.

"No, T'mar," he said, trying to ignore T'mer. "And why are you both looking at me like that? He looks mad and you look … different. And where are your clothes?"

J'son stood up and found himself face to face with T'mar, standing just inches away from her. Her beauty was overpowering and the aroma coming off of her was very arousing. Her composure was like she had been given an energy boost. They stood that way, without moving, for several seconds. He was breathing her in, caught up in her scent, and then he looked down to discover he still had his covering on. He was thankful for that. He quickly glanced over at T'mer to see how he was taking the exchange only to discover that T'mer had turned away and was picking up some more of the fallen foliage. J'son hadn't seen T'mar wave T'mer off through the use of a secret hand gesture.

"Here," said T'mer, sounding a little less intimidating. "We might as well get new coverings before they die." He handed her two pieces of the strange furry foliage, green in color, which she took and proceeded to wrap around herself.

The trees produced an organic, fur-like substance of various colors that grew out of the branches like leaves, the fibers of which were strong as steel but soft as cotton. He watched as she took one piece and wrapped it around her back, touching the ends together across her breasts. The tiny fibers moved of their own accord, reaching out to each other, connecting and knitting together, forming a seamless garment. She took another piece, slightly larger but not much and wrapped it around her hips, bringing the ends together across her hip. The fibers did the same thing and sealed up the garment. The color was definitely flattering and caught the green in her eyes.

"Here," she said, picking up a brown piece that had blown up and got hooked around her legs, and handed it to him. "You might as well change yours, too. After a while the plant dies and the garment falls off."

The covering he had on was limp and somewhat matted. There were bare patches where the fur had fallen out giving it a leathery feel but spotted and mangy. The piece T'mar had handed him was lighter than he'd expected, seemingly alive and full of vitality, undulating in his hands and trying to wrap itself around his fingers and wrists. The way it wiggled around in his hands reminded him more of a furry snake than anything else. The fur was deep shag, soft and plush like the feel of a rabbit's pelt, a sharp contrast to what he was now wearing which had become coarse to the touch. J'son got the distinct impression that he was holding a life-form that had been genetically altered and was trying to perform its created function. He didn't know why he thought that, only that he felt like he was sensing it.

"If you don't hurry," she said, "it will bond with your hand and will be useless for a covering. It mates once, fitting over whatever you need it for and then it begins to die. If you want that to fit right you need to wrap it around your waist."

Taking the macrobiotic fabric from her, J'son turned and walked a short distance away. He looked over his shoulder to see if she was looking, which she wasn't, and slipped out of his old garment. He wrapped the new one around his waist like she had, bringing the ends together at his side. The fabric wiggled within his grasp, again as if alive, and joined together, becoming one. It started to shrink and tighten slightly, molding itself to the contours of his upper thighs and hips. The effect was creepy and J'son got the distinct feeling of fingers massaging the muscles in his backside. He cocked an eye at T'mar and said:

"That feels weird."

"Don't worry. You'll get used to it. Are you sure you're okay? Do you remember anything?"

"I'm not really too sure. I remember seeing these strange, blue-glowing beings and also thinking that I had somehow transcended time and saw the beginning of the universe."

"Who is he, T'mar! I don't like this. He should be dead or at least deranged." T'mer was now standing next to them with one hand hanging down by his hip clenched into a fist and the other one pointing an accusing finger at J'son. He was bending forward slightly, leading with his chest, playing the ego game of aggressor. That X that J'son was getting accustomed to seeing marked T'mer's face, and his almost black eyes were dim with suspicion and distrust.

"What's going on T'mar? What is he talking about? Why should I be dead?"

"Even the wise return changed, or maybe a better word would be damaged. You shouldn't be able to talk." T'mer was agitated and the tone of his statements sounded confused and scared, like the talk of a man with his back against a wall.

"Stop it T'mer." Again she moved her fingers in a twitching way and he immediately backed down and turned away, heading over to the stream.

"What T'mer is talking about is that the infection and antidote are often sought out by the different schools of deeper learning in order to see beyond in the hopes that the vision they bring back will show them a way to find and access a portal. It is a form of religion for them, although they wouldn't say so. It's also a form of sacrament and the ritual that accompanies it is a solemn practice. It is very dangerous and most who participate lose contact with their bodies and remain in the realm of pure imagination, a place full of hope and terror."

"Well that explains some of what I saw, I guess. But if you knew all of that, why did you make me drink it? Why did you take that chance?"J'son was a little apprehensive to say the least. All the talk about portals made him wonder if she was using him for her own purpose.

"It's not that simple, J'son. The storm must have driven the 'wat out of hiding. Usually we, I mean, they have to dig it out and can spend days trying to locate one. I've never seen a 'wat out in the daylight like that before. That's strange in itself. 'wats are normally caught at night and kept in a cage for repeated use. It's the venom that the monks need; that and the antidote."

"I don't understand," he said, eyeing her doubtfully. "You mean people actually infect themselves just for the experience and then take that other plant to come down? Why would anyone want to infect themselves and blow up like a balloon?"

"The 'wat doesn't provide the experience that they are seeking. It's the psychedelic properties of the antidote, the "'psi" that they seek. The 'wat would surely kill them and anyone who got infected within hours and their end is horrible, excruciating pain. However, just taking the 'psi alone destroys the nerve endings of the brain by overloading the synaptic membranes, which in turn creates a cascade of neuro-chemicals similar to the mood-enhancer dopamine making you chemically imbalanced." T'mar was speaking as if she were repeating a passage out of a science text book. "The result is a frying of the nerve endings leaving the mind of the poor, unfortunate fool unhinged, never to recover again. But they are the lucky ones. The majority never return to their bodies."

J'son was watching her with a sense of suspicion. Her almost rote recitation was discomforting and his perception of her body language took more of his attention than actually listening to what she was saying.

"The two drugs in combination form a symbiotic relationship within the bloodstream of the host, enhancing some qualities and cancelling out others. It is through conscious effort on the part of the monks that they chance consuming the sacrament. The only reason why I gave you the antidote and chanced harming you is because I didn't have a choice. You would have died if I hadn't given it to you."

"Hmmm, I see. So the blue guys were just a hallucination? They seemed so real and three-dimensional, solid, just like you do only there was a buzzing, vibrating effect and my head felt detached, like it was tethered to my body but somewhere far away."

"You were in the domain of the immortals, the Transcendentals, the gods of yesterday. You saw—"

"T'mar, shut up! What are you doing? Why are you telling this 'lav anything. Only the monks can interpret what they see. He didn't see anything. It's like he said he only had a hallucination, nothing else."

T'mer was having a hard time accepting what was happening. It was bad enough that he always felt inferior around T'mar. So what if she was schooled in the deeper things, the esoteric side of life. The way she used her abilities to control him, weakening him, subjecting him to the humiliation of female domination was hard enough. Now he had to contend with a human, a dreamer, here of all places, who said he had seen the gods. Impossible! The only thing humans had over him was their ability to dream, and even then they were too stupid to understand what they were doing, most of them completely ignoring what was going on inside of them. Every night they could journey anywhere they wanted, but they didn't have the mental faculties to comprehend energy transference and image projection and retention.

Although he had had been coached in the secrets of the various schools by T'mar, he never really had the chance to practice those secrets. At least he understood the concept .This moron, he thought, wouldn't know what to do with the knowledge even if he had it. And now T'mar is telling him about the gods? This has gone on long enough. Even if he did see the Transcendentals, they wouldn't have anything to do with him. Maybe experiment on him. They have no need of portals and would regard him only as a curiosity of study, nothing more. It's time I utilize my assets and brought order to this madness.

"Shut up, T'mar," he said again as he plodded over to them, stomping the ground like a raging bull.

"T'mer, we need to find out what happened to him."

"Stop it, and don't think your witch's ways have any power over me." As he approached them, he reached out and shoved T'mar violently, knocking her back and spilling her to the ground. She landed hard on her backside and elbows, expelling air as she hit.

"Oooooff."

"Get away from her!" J'son screamed. He instinctively threw his hands up in front of him, pointing his slightly bent fingers at T'mer in a kind of grabbing motion, not too sure what he hoped to accomplish.

"That's going to be a big mistake, 'uog. Here, let me—"

Everything happened so quickly that later J'son would have to think through exactly what did happened. T'mer had reacted to J'son reaching out to him by going for his throat. He slipped his hand between J'son's extended arms, grabbing his neck and squeezing his fingers into his flesh. The momentary contact brought a bright, static discharge and an audible "Zap!" T'mer fell back, howling out in pain and holding the wrist of his injured hand. A smoky emission wafted upwards from the tips of his fingers and his hand took on a bright ruddiness, like a sunburn.

A fierce, radiant crimson color encompassed J'son and misty waves of lower end electrical energy flowed out from him like steam off of a rock. There was anger in his eyes and he stood there trembling, buzzing from head to toe. The energy discharge continued to pour out from him and now moved toward T'mar, surrounding them both in a murky, semi-transparent bubble, condensing and solidifying, forming an outline of their bodies, providing them with a six-inch thick barrier between them and T'mer.

T'mar was lying on the ground, supporting the weight of her upper body with her elbows and stared up at J'son with a look of shock and surprise. His aura was pulsating now, keeping time with his heartbeat and growing darker and more opaque with each beat. She didn't like where this was leading and the rage which J'son was projecting at T'mer was dangerous. J'son was emoting without the benefit of advanced training. The passionate mind, unencumbered by a strong sense of morality and lacking the proper discipline was capable of all sorts of malevolence. That was a lesson she had learned firsthand.

"J'son, it's okay," she said. "Calm yourself. T'mer is here to help us. He wouldn't harm me. He couldn't touch me if I didn't allow him." She stood up and cautiously put her hand on his shoulder, hoping he had enough control to allow her to touch him.

The gesture produced an almost instantaneous reaction. The color of his energy field changed from red to a light blue and the contours of his face relaxed. He turned to look at her and saw she was smiling that sweet little smile he had fallen for back on Earth. His anger fell away, replaced by a look of uncertainty. His aural shield dissipated into nothing but a wispy fog. T'mer was calmer now too, and the three of them stood together in a rough triangle searching the face of the others for answers.

"T'mer, I think we need to take him to see the monks. What's happening here is beyond my training. We can use the ancient records in their library to see if this kind of thing has happened before."

"Why don't you take him to B'el's Castle," T'mer said sarcastically, a bitter bite to his words. "By the gods, T'mar! Don't you think we should take him to the City first and see what the Adepts have to say? He may be the weapon we need in our battle against B'el."

T'mer wasn't the only one having a problem with the situation. J'son was teetering on the edge of a knife's blade as far as his thinking was concerned. Even now, as T'mer talked about wars and weapons and T'mar talked about monks, J'son thoughts hadn't stopped spinning and he was trying desperately to integrate the mental experience he had under the influence of the drugs and the incredibly surreal, physical experience he was now enduring.

Was he dreaming all of this, or was his life back on Earth the dream? Was he still tripping from that root T'mar made him drink? Was she even telling him the truth? T'mer became very irate when she mentioned the "Transcendentals". Who or what were those beautiful blue beings and what was their connection with life on this planet. Was it true that the ancient gods of Earth were actually these creatures? Did that mean he had passed through the pearly gates of heaven and seen the Angels of God? And who were T'mar and T'mer really? A part of him had decided he was asleep at home in his bed and that he would soon wake up. But another part of him, a part of him that he identified with his true self told him that all of this was real.

"T'mer, we're going to take him to the monks to have a look at him. We need your protection. It wouldn't be safe or wise for me to use my power, even to defend us. As of now, we are the only ones that even know he is here; much less about his abilities. It wouldn't benefit us to draw attention to ourselves." She wanted to stroke T'mer's ego just enough to make him think he was needed. Although he didn't have the necessary training to manipulate matter in any meaningful way, still his physical strength could come in handy.

"You don't know that," he spat back at her. "I knew you had returned when I saw you in my thoughts standing in the opening of the cave. I felt your essence as it became visible within my mind, just like you taught me. How do you know no one else has seen him? You'd think something like that would have created an energy fluctuation or something that those sorcerers could pick up on. The Adepts can read that sort of thing."

"I'm sure you're right, but that's why we need your help. We can't chance him sending out such intense thought patterns again. It's true that the higher-level monks can pick up on passion-generated thought forms as they enter the grid. J'son, you need to control your thoughts and emotions, especially the negative ones. Your mental focus gives you the ability to create environments in which you are like the Immortals. The fact that you say you saw them confirms my suspensions."

"How do we know he won't turn on us, T'mar? I don't trust him."

"We have to trust him, T'mer. We have no choice. He's here and we are witnesses to what he can do. Remember the storm? It appears he doesn't even need a talisman to generate the focus needed to do what he can do. Only the high-level initiates can cast a spell of such intensity without the need of magical trinkets. Besides, you don't trust anyone above your level."

"I trust you, don't I?" The X was back across his face again and T'mar wasn't so sure that he did. "I still think we need to take him to the Adepts. They'll know what to make of him."

"I don't want anyone to do anything with me. T'mar, what do you think? I just want to understand what is happening to me and find a way back to Earth, in my own time. I don't want to be a portal for anyone except myself, if that will get me back home."

"You see, T'mar. He doesn't care about anything but himself, just like all humans. He doesn't even know that a war is coming that will destroy the majority of his people off the face of that world and enslave the rest. If he can be used as a weapon, then we must exploit that."

"A war?"

"T'mer, let's just drop it for now. We still have a ways to go through the forest before we make it to the crossroads. At that time we will decide which way to go." T'mar had already decided which way they were going, with or without T'mer, but she didn't see any point in forcing the issue before she had to. If it came down to it, she would use her mastery of the "Arts" to incapacitate him and take J'son to the monks herself.

"Whatever." T'mer walked away from them and stood by the edge of the stream. It flowed around a bend and disappeared under a grouping of rocks, travelling underground for several miles before re-emerging above ground and draining into a large lake at the base of the mountain. The trek would take them several hours. He knew that they had to get moving because the sun was receding. Wherever they went, time was against them. "Let's go, then."

Chapter Seven:

The Forest

"They would sit and chant the ancient verses, performing the rituals of their craft. Some would never awaken from their slumber; others would become raving maniacs, losing their minds."

T'mar describing the effects of the 'wat ceremony.

The three of them walked along the edge of the stream until it vanished down a sinkhole hidden between the hollow made by several megalithic stones that had fallen over and broken apart at some time in the past. Moss had grown in a semicircle around the hole and the sound of falling water could be heard in the depths. The stones were black and looked like they had been quarried and fitted together, forming a structure of some sort. The ruins were in an area devoid of trees and sat on an outcropping of black granite, giving the three of them a panoramic view of the valley and lake far below.

They looked out over the valley, seeing the tops of trees and a rough brown path working its way through the forest. The trees below them were tightly grouped together, growing in densely packed clumps of reds, blues, greens and purple. J'son couldn't see a way down from where they were and turned to look back at the broken structure wondering what it used to be.

"That looks like it used to be a building of some sort," he said.

"It was," said T'mar, without looking away from the valley below. "This is where, in times past, the monks would come and sit out the transformational effects of the 'wat ritual'. It used to be a covered square stone building surrounding a small pond. They would sit there for several micro-cycles meditating and taking the 'psi root, prolonging its effects and going deeper within themselves, hoping for the internal opening that would reveal a portal. Many a monk has died here in their pursuit for escape." T'mar was speaking once again sounding far away, lost in a memory somewhere.

"It was B'el who destroyed the building after he achieved 'Transportation', the ability to travel with just the power of his thoughts. It is taught that his release drew so much energy out of the rocks that where the stones came together the atoms dissolved and turned into dust, collapsing the building."

J'son studied the stones and noticed a combination of smooth and jagged edges with piles of a sandy material covering the ground. "How do you know what happened here, T'mar?"

"Yeah, T'mar. Why don't you tell him how you know that? I'm sure he would love to know what you did before you started stealing the energy of his dreams."

"That's enough, T'mer. He'll learn everything he needs to know when we talk to the monks."

"You mean if we go there."

The three of them turned away from the granite ledge and began working their way down the side of the cliff, following a stony footpath. Stepping on large, broken, stone-like steps, they descended slowly and carefully so as not to stumble and fall. The crude steps changed into a packed dirt path that was covered over by long, thin, needle-like vegetation and furry, multi-colored leaves from the trees overhead. The trail sloped gradually downward, snaking its way around huge boulders and the petrified remains of decayed trees that had fallen long ago. Slightly winded, they came to a relatively flat, open area surrounded by rings of several different kinds of trees, each bearing what appeared to be fruit.

"Let's get something to eat before we continue on down," T'mar suggested. "The blue ones are the juiciest, J'son. But the black ones have the texture and consistency of what you would call beef. Those are the only ones T'mer will eat."

"I'd rather kill and eat an animal," T'mer said as he reached up and plucked a dark, slimy, oblong object that looked more like a shriveled cucumber dangling from a branch just over his head.

The tree itself was strange, growing up like an inverted cone, the trunk a mere four inches in diameter and widening as it went, flatting across the top, with tuffs of liquorish-like appendages growing upward for a few feet and waving in the gentle breeze. Thick branches wider than the base of the tree grew out from all sides, bending downward, burdened with fruit. The stark white bark of the plant hid a soft, dark pulpy interior giving the tree incredible flexibility. It stood approximately fifteen feet high with the fruit -laden branches drooping down just within reach. The tree had a dull, ominous quality that J'son would have taken as poisonous.

He watched as T'mer crammed one piece into his mouth and grabbed another, gobbling the first one down before proceeding to the next. Dark, magenta-colored sap dribbled out of his mouth and down his chin before dripping to the ground. The fruit had a putrid smell and J'son wondered how T'mer could eat it without throwing up. He finished his second piece and tucked a third into the waistband of his garment. His hands and mouth were stained red and tiny, uneaten fragments of the fruit were lodged between his teeth, clinging to them, looking like bits of chewing tobacco.

J'son decided that he didn't want to eat of that tree and looked for another having a more pleasing appearance. Spotting a short, spiny, bushy blue tree bearing round green fruit a few feet away, he walked over and reached in, picking a particularly pleasant-looking plump berry. Screaming out in pain, he retrieved his hand to discover it covered with tiny splinters maybe two inches long. He pulled the needles out one at a time and tossed them on the ground, only then realizing these needles were what were covering the trail they were on. His hand sprouted blood from all the tiny puncture wounds and he looked at T'mar for reassurance.

"Is this okay?" he asked. "Or did I just get poisoned again?"

"You're fine, J'son. The best tasting fruit are always the hardest to get." She was eating fruit of her own, plucked from still another tree further away from where he and T'mer were standing. The truck of her tree was about two feet in diameter and tall, ending in a head of yellow fur. The top of the tree was bent over forming an arch, the leaves of which hung four feet off the ground and filled with heart-shaped orange fruit, looking more like strawberries, but larger, palm size.

She bit into hers and he heard a popping sound, like the release of pressure as the skin of the fruit was punctured. She slurped up the yellow juice, licking the fluid off of her fingers in a smacking sound reminiscent of a baby sucking on a bottle. She gobbled up two of them and bit into a third, chewing slower and relishing the taste. She was smiling a smile of contentment, almost girlish in its sweetness and was laughing quietly to herself. Some of the juice had fallen on her top and she looked down, wiping it off with the back of her free hand and leaving stains in provocative places.

"Here, try one of mine," she said, tossing a baseball -sized fruit at J'son.

He caught it low to the ground, bending over too far and almost landed on his head. Regaining his balance, he bit into the fruit, filling his mouth with the cool, tart flavor and his nose with a strong, floral fragrance reminiscent of honeysuckles. It was delicious if not sour and he held his hand up, motioning to T'mar to throw him another. She did, but he never caught it.

The sun was flickering between the trees overhead and a shaft of light struck him in the eyes, blinding him, and he adjusted his arm to block the rays. Without warning, the light triggered painful spikes behind his eyes and an overwhelming headache in the center of his forehead. He pressed his fingers to his head, scrunching his eyes shut and wobbled about on trembling legs. He felt sick to his stomach and his head swam. He was dizzy and then the images started, bombarding his senses in a kaleidoscope of color and transformational designs.

Still swooning, he suddenly stopped moving and his eyes snapped opened, staring and unmoving. His arms fell down to his sides and he stood there, stiff and trance-like, unresponsive and showing no sign of awareness. His heart rate slowed considerably and his breathing became shallow and unhurried. There was a slight flicker in his eyes, momentary and rapid at the same time, like the reflection of starlight bouncing off of the ripples of a lake, and then it was gone. There was a slight awareness that time had passed, but he didn't have any internal frame of reference to mark it.

Within moments clarity returned to his eyes. The milky-white of his eyes cleared, almost as if a cloud had passed over and he blinked several times, once again unsteady on his feet. He bent over, holding his hands to his stomach and vomited violently, spraying his bush with yellow bile and fruit juice.

"Blaaaa-hack."

"J'son, are you all right?" T'mar asked.

"I don't know. Blaaaa-hack. Uhhhh."

"He can't even stomach 'yog. What is he, gutless?" T'mer had moved from where he had been standing and was now eating from the tree that T'mar had eaten of. He was smiling between bites, chomping away and slurping up the yellow juice in spite of its similarity to the chunky bile dripping from J'son's bush.

Chapter Eight:

Power Leeches

> "They feed on your brain. They attach themselves to the base of your skull and burrow in, wrapping around the stem. You won't notice it until it's too late."
>
> T'mer explaining the danger of 'plcs

"What happened to you?" T'mar asked. "I tossed you the 'yog, but before it got to you, you just blanked out. You were just standing there, staring into space."

"How long was I like that?" J'son was still woozy and he was slurring his words.

"We were watching you for at least a few minutes before I walked over to you. I spoke your name a couple of times but you were expressionless. I was looking at you, trying to make eye contact. I thought I saw some recognition, but then you bent over and got sick. 'yog is usually pretty easy on the stomach."

"I don't think it was the fruit," he said, still bending over with his hands on his knees. "It felt more like I had been given a download of information. Everything vanished and I only saw interior visions."

"What's he talking about now? First the Transcendentals and now downloads. He sounds crazy, if you ask me T'mar. I say we ditch him and get back to the City. They'll want to know you're here." T'mer was eyeing him hard, Xing all over his face with two little bumpy knobs sticking out just under his scalp.

"I didn't ask you," she snapped. She knew he wouldn't like the tone in her voice and she was sorry for treating him so condescendingly. However, she was more interested in what J'son had just said than about hurting T'mer's feelings.

"Downloads, J'son?"

"They said it would come like that. They said they would communicate with me through downloads." His thoughts were clearing up and his speech quickened. "I'm still having a hard time integrating what I saw, or rather what they were trying to say to me. It was all pictures, a series of images flashing across my mind, each infused with so much meaning. I feel like I just sat through an 8-hour film festival without a break."

"Can you tell me what they wanted?"

"Who are 'They'? The Transcendentals? C'mon, T'mar. This guy is fried. By the time we get anywhere his brain will be mush. Remember when K'tum tried and his brains ran out of his ears? This parasite is a waste case."

"They want me to… I don't understand. I think I'm supposed to talk with someone. He looked old and bent over but somehow full of life, glowing. He has a braided grey beard and is wearing full clothing, a robe of some type. I was there talking to him, but we were somewhere else, like on the edge of the forest with the desert in the back ground. I felt like I had been talking to him for a long time, like we knew each other and had spent time together before. He was telling me things about himself and the Transcendentals, like he knew who they are."

T'mer and T'mar gave each other a funny, knowing look. They both realized he had just described a monk.

"J'son, do you remember what color his robe was?"

"This is garbage," T'mer said, jabbing a trembling finger at him. "T'mar, if you don't do something about this nut case, I will."

J'son felt a surge of energy growing within him starting at his stomach and spreading outward. A fuzzy, buzzing sensation filled his body and goose bumps sprouted across his arms. His fight or flight response had kicked in and he felt high-frequency energy radiating out of him, ultrasonic vibrations filling the space around him. He took on a defensive posture and his thoughts were turning toward survival. He was almost at the point of no turning back, almost willing to let loose on T'mer. His thoughts were extremely focused.

"I don't think you can," J'son said, sneering.

"J'son, calm yourself. You're glowing, warping the flow of energy around you. If you don't control your thoughts, they will control you.'" She said it like a mantra.

She was right, J'son thought. Through an act of will, he caused himself to relax, slowing his breathing and centering his thoughts. It came easier this time, like he had spent years practicing, and when he closed his eyes he saw vivid, three-dimensional pastoral scenes and quiet lakes. His face softened and a look of tranquility washed over him. Opening his eyes again, he saw T'mer and T'mar differently, knowing somehow that he was beyond them. He realized how silly it was to have taken T'mer's threat seriously. He knew he had a power within him that wouldn't let T'mer harm him in any way. He knew it, and now he was sure T'mer knew it too.

He straightened himself out, calmly observing T'mer and thinking pleasant thoughts. The sun popped back out and he searched the sky, noticing the remnants of dark storm clouds passing overhead.

"I caused that, didn't I?" he said.

"Yes, J'son. That's why you have to control your thoughts. It was you that brought the storm last time."

"Yeah! And I'm sure the priests and Adepts noticed it as well. If they didn't know he was here before, I'm sure they know now." T'mer quickly glanced around, looking into the spaces between the trees and apparently searching for something. "With him drawing off so much energy, I'll bet he has attracted the attention of 'plcs, power leeches."

"We don't know that, T'mer, so there's no reason to get excited. Besides, I would know if they were here."

"But by that time it might be too late. Look, I don't care one bit about him or his abilities. Portal be damn. When we get to the crossroads, I know what direction I'm going."

"Fine. Let's go then. I agree that the sooner we get out of the forest, the better." T'mar didn't show it, but she was just as concerned as he was that J'son's actions might indeed call forth creatures that she might not be able to defend against. Power leeches were dangerous, especially during the long night that was soon to come. It was then that one's life force could be sucked out of you without you noticing it, and by the time you did notice it would be too late. As long as the daylight held, she didn't think they were in too much danger. The energy of the sun would keep them at bay.

J'son had turned away from them during the discussion and was heading down the path alone, not wanting to wait for them to catch up. He was being led by some internal compass, marching to the beat of an interior drum that had no corporeal existence, at least as far as three-dimensional reality was concerned. It existed within his mind, a boney, apparitional finger looming large, beckoning him to follow. At times his inner visions, or the memory of them, dominated, but at other times a noise or a feeling brought him direct awareness of his surroundings, only deeper, more penetrating.

He was able to see normally, like the thinning trees and the increasingly openness of the sapphire-blue sky. But he also saw shapes and shadows, large, snake-like creatures with huge heads and long antenna-like appendages, clinging to the sides of trees, glowing eerily, almost florescent. He knew instinctively that they were the creatures, the power leeches, T'mer had mentioned. They didn't live in the here and now but somehow existed in two worlds at the same time, caught between realities, much like he was. These creatures didn't seem to notice him, or at least they weren't moving as he passed them. They were everywhere: in the trees, latched onto the branches, lying in the middle of the trail, wrapped around small plants and hiding under roots.

The creatures disturbed him, but at the time he didn't feel threatened by them. He was still ahead of T'mar and T'mer and didn't see the need to mention the creatures to them yet. Unless the creatures moved toward him, he said to himself, he wasn't going to say anything. Besides, T'mar had said she would know if they were around. But did that mean she could actually see them, or would she just sense them? Maybe she wouldn't notice them unless they moved more into the dimension of this world, more solid. Maybe it would be only when they began to feed on her energy stores that she would notice. That's what T'mer said about it being too late.

The creatures seemed to be feeding on the plant life they were attached to. He could see them drawing energy out of the plants, weakening their cellular structure and assaulting their genetic code, changing it, distorting it, leaving a physical black mark on the exterior of the trees and plants, killing it. He saw several rotted trees still standing but long dead with residual after-images floating in space, almost like a photo negative. He realized that unless T'mar and T'mer could see what he was seeing, all they would see would be dead plant life, never knowing why the trees and plants had died.

He was still calm and his thoughts were more reflective, being more of an observer to what was happening than actually participating in the scene around him. It was like he was on automatic pilot, simply walking along the trail, somehow knowing where they were going and how to get there. His energy level was high and closely contained, not disturbing the natural flow of energy around him. It was like he was moving along as part of a bigger whole, joined with it on a sub-atomic level, his particles merging with the whole, dancing, exchanging information and moving on. He was…

"J'son. Wait up for us." It was T'mar, of course.

The sound of her voice coming from behind startled him, and he stopped in his tracks. As waves of sound hit his awareness, he registered them as tiny vibrating particles of energy passing through him and striking the energy emissions of the creatures nearest to him. The collision caused them to move, absorbing the energy, slowing the vibration of their bodies to match the same sonic frequency of her words. Every syllable impacted the creatures, causing them to twitch in time with the sound. The more the creatures absorbed, the larger they became, swelling to twice their size and then shrinking back, pulsating, growing larger than before.

The sound of her words disturbed several of the creatures and now they were moving vigorously, drawn to a new source of energy of higher quality, a purer resource to tap. J'son watched as a couple of them moved down the side of a tree, leaving a ghostly trail of luminescence behind them, dimming from brilliant white to sickish yellow, reminding him of the slimy track of a slug in the moonlight. The creatures moved along lines of force sprouting out of the ground, like ley lines or something, energy patterns that followed the growth of the plants and grasses that grew along the trail. The creatures paused at intervals, coming across broken areas in the field, seemingly trying to negotiate the path that would take them closer to J'son.

He turned to look at T'mar and in a hushed tone slightly above a whisper he said, "They're everywhere."

T'mar stopped in her tracks, quiet and very still. T'mer was behind her and almost fell on top of her, colliding into her. "What the hell, T'mar."

"Shhhh," she said. "They feed off of our energy. Don't move or say anything. "J'son, do you see them?"

The question answered several questions J'son had. Obviously, she didn't see them the way he did nor did she seem to know exactly where the creatures were. She was standing a few feet away from J'son, turning her head left and right, peering into the shadows of the trees and searching the ground. She had a worried, defensive look on her face. Her hands were out in front her and she was waving her fingers around like she was testing the density of the air, probably trying to feel their presence. She closed her eyes and her lips started to move quietly, like in prayer. She slowly turned in place making a 360 circle, moving her arms and hands in a precise, ritualistic manner, looking more like a mime with each turn.

"J'son, I can't see them. It's too light out. All I can sense is the waves of energy pouring off the plant life. What can you sense?"

"I'm not too sure how, but I can actually see them with my eyes. They're in the trees, hanging on the lichen and slinking along the ground. They're actually glowing and I've got a couple of them moving in my direction."

"He can't see them. How can he see them?" T'mer spat that out, his voice definitely above a whisper.

"T'mer, be quiet. They feed off of—"

"T'mer, there's one right by your foot, a small one." J'son had watched, as if in slow motion, as T'mer's words radiated out from him and fell around him, waves breaking into particles and those particles raining down, striking the ground. As each energy-impregnated particle hit the ground, tiny, miniscule burst of light appeared and then faded, like tiny mushroom explosions. Now there were several small creatures all around T'mer, each feeding on the energy particle explosions, becoming bigger, their color swinging towards the red. T'mer was glowing also, emitting his own dark insignia from the lower end of the spectrum. To J'son, he seemed angry and was having a hard time of it.

"T'mar, he needs to calm down," J'son said. "He's emitting dark waves of energy and he's attracting several of the creatures."

It was true. Because J'son and T'mar were standing quite still, all the creatures in the area were making their way toward T'mer. The ones by his feet were about three inches long now, with one end swelling up, looking like a cherry attached to its stem. As T'mer's anger fuelled the energy radiating off of him, the creatures fed off of him, growing momentarily and then moving slightly closer before diminishing. One of the creatures had made it to his foot and was working its way up his leg.

The level of radiation flowing out of T'mer was increasing rather than decreasing and all the creatures within a five foot radius were now slowing their progressive march toward him, content it seems to bathe in the outpouring without expending their own energy to get it. They were growing larger, and the ones closest to T'mer were a very dark magenta, almost black in color. They were the size of baseballs with long, straight tails, mutating from fragile stick-like figures to something more substantial. Some, J'son noticed, were developing mouths of sorts filled with static, electrical teeth, blue to begin with and then turning darker as they grew. The one on T'mer's leg, larger than the others, lifted its head back with its mouth opened and sunk its teeth into the fleshy, inner part of his thigh just above the knee.

T'mer cried out in pain, clutching his leg, oblivious to the creature itself. Every creature within earshot started vibrating, matching the resonance of his voice, growing and multiplying. The one attached to his leg had grown larger, grapefruit size, and then split down the center, becoming two halves with tails of their own. The halves folded and undulated, rounding out their bodies. Their shape was very malleable, elongating and flattening as they move, no longer ball shaped, and they were working their way up his arm and over his shoulder.

They stopped moving once they had reached his head and they latched on to his neck, biting into the base of his skull on either side. T'mer showed a momentary recognition of intense pain and then collapsed on the spot, landing in a crumpled heap, striking his forehead hard on the ground. One of the creatures became dislodged by the impact and squirmed around on the ground as if disoriented. The other one was still attached and was burrowing its way into his neck, its trans-dimensional body partially obscured by T'mer's energy field. It was resonating at the same frequency, becoming the same color and then it disappeared, merging within him.

"T'mer!" T'mar couldn't control herself and very quickly found herself kneeling beside T'mer, cradling his head in her arms.

"T'mar, stop. They're homing in on you now." J'son was getting panicky and realized they were picking up on his change in mental state. Where before he didn't feel like he was a target, now he notice they were taking an interest in him and moving in his direction. T'mer and T'mar were covered with the creatures and J'son was at loss as to what to do. There were several of them approaching him and he back-stepped slightly, momentarily avoiding any of them getting on him. His movement, however, caused the creatures closest to him to stop moving. Instead, they lay there soaking up his energy expenditure and growing.

What am I supposed to do? He asked himself, standing without moving or even breathing. The creature that had entered at the base of T'mer's skull was completely absorbed under the skin and a huge bulged appeared right where the spine joined with the back of the head. It was pulsing underneath the skin, a painful, reddish whelp that was turning purple and growing in size. T'mer's face was a deathly shade of pale and his lips were turning blue, his energy field short-circuited and dropping off to a sickly pale yellow barely visible to J'son. T'mar had a creature of her own working its way around her neck and was about to open its mouth and bite, but then J'son did something that he hadn't completely thought out and wasn't too sure if it would do any good.

Just before the creature bit into the back of her neck, J'son narrowed the scope of his awareness. His eyes and nose pinched across his face, forming an X, and he directed a tight beam of highly-charged, concentrated light particles on the creature, sending mental energy toward the creature, hoping to overfeed it and kill it by gluttony. The silvery shaft of light came out of the center of his forehead and surged outward, striking the creature. The effect was momentary and rapid, occurring in the space of less than a second, a mental wink, a flaming projectile of thought energy, the release of which left him dizzy and unbalanced.

The shot hit the creature dead center and it swelled up like a water balloon on the end of a faucet, rupturing and splattering glowing, plasma-like bits of itself all over T'mer's face. The tiny bits of shimmering plasma sizzled and popped, burning his face and then fizzling out, dissolving into nothing, the energy dissipated. The other creatures, sensing what had taken place, scrambled away from T'mar and T'mer, expelling large amount of energy in the process and diminishing in size, seeking protection and the relative safety of the plants and trees from whence they came.

"T'mar, watch out! I think I've got it." Staring at each creature in turn, J'son focused his thoughts again and shot at the creatures closest to her and T'mer, blasting them into oblivion and scattering minute particles of disconnected energy everywhere. He wasn't too sure what he was doing, only that he imagined an intense white light and then released it.

As he thought and acted, J'son had the distinct impression of being a gunslinger squeezing off rounds, methodically and with precision clearing a space around the three of them. The barrage of thought projectiles left him drained and disoriented, weak in the knees, dizzy and partially blind. His energy stores were low and he felt himself vulnerable, not knowing if he could hold off another attack if it came to that.

"T'mar. We have to get out of here. I think I can create a clear path for us to take." J'son widened his mental focus, and just for good measure he stuck out one arm, pointing it in a direction devoid of trees. He took a deep breath, hoping to burn a path through. He exhaled and a flaming fire erupted out of his fingertips, and scorched the ground before them. Black smoke and fried vegetation three feet wide and ten feet long were all that was left. Moving quickly, he reached down to help T'mar to her feet. "C'mon."

"I can't leave T'mer," she said, refusing his help. "I think he's been infected." She placed her hand over the bulge on the back of T'mer's neck and began drumming her fingers lightly in a rhythmic manner, humming to the rhythm of her drumming. The humming created a vibration that ran down her arm, through her fingers and into the protrusion. Slowly, a tail emerged from the center of the bulge, wiggling like a fish caught on a hook. The tail jutted out a few inches and then stalled, not wanting to come out any further. T'mar wasn't aware of any of this, of course, and she just kept on humming a strange, repetitive tune, monotone and low pitched.

"Here, T'mar. Let me see if I can help," J'son said, kneeling down beside T'mer. Reaching out to grab the tail, shinning particles of energy extended from his fingers creating a shimmering appendage that matched the appearance of the creature. The tail stopped wiggling and became still, rigid. He pulled on the tail and more of the creature slid out of T'mer's neck. He grabbed it tighter, the particle appendage glowing in intensity, and he pulled more aggressively, dislodging the creature and finally removing it from his neck. J'son tossed the creature, now limp and lifeless, away from them, beyond the protected area. Before the shape of the dead creature disappeared completely, however, its electrical signature and all that it had been was absorbed by several of the smaller creatures still alive and outside the zone of burnt vegetation.

T'mer was still out cold and J'son helped T'mar to turn him over and raise him to a sitting position. T'mer's bulk was an issue and the two of them strained with his weight, trying to get him to stand up. They struggled together and managed to get him vertical; T'mer's massive arms were wrapped around their shoulders, each bearing part of his weight.

With T'mer hanging limply between them, they stumbled forward and followed the path J'son had blasted away, collapsing with their burden several yards away.

"We're not going to be able to stay here long and he's too heavy for us to carry. What do you think, T'mar?" J'son was breathing hard and scanning the area looking for any more of those creatures.

"Can't you keep clearing a path through all of this?"

"Maybe, but it wears me out. Give me a few seconds and I will try again. Is he in a coma or something?"

"No. The creatures feed on the pineal gland, working their way through the cerebellum. It is the seat of all higher visions. Some say it is the home of the soul."

"Visions? What do those things have to do with visions?" Something didn't seem right. The creatures were still all around them, but for the moment they were safe. The creatures seemed satisfied enough to feed on the residual radiation of J'son's blasting, not growing as big or glowing as bright, fading into the back ground, leaving just their silhouettes before disappearing completely. J'son thought they might still be there but they didn't have the energy to manifest bodies he could see. It was quiet again and the forest came back to life, like it had been hiding during the invasion.

"I think we're alone, for now. I can't see them anymore."

T'mar wasn't really listening to J'son, more concerned about T'mer than their collective safety. T'mer was still unconscious, but his facial features were softer and more relaxed, not the pained pinching he had shown when he was bitten. He was groaning quietly and his eyelids fluttered as he tried to regain consciousness. T'mar was cradling his head in her lap, stroking his hair and gently massaging his neck. The swelling was gone, but T'mar could feel the outline of what appeared to be a small tear that had been quickly fused together running just below his skull. The wound was hot to the touch and T'mar thought cooling thoughts, whispering words of reassurance into his ear.

J'son was looking around in a darting manner, squinting against his partial blindness, looking under the brush, up in the trees and on the ground directly around them. He was calming down, catching his breath and regaining his composure, not as dizzy and his physical sight was slowly returning to normal. He exhaled a heavy sigh more out of disbelief than weariness and looked down at T'mar and T'mer. He could see T'mer's eyes were half opened and glazed over and he was moving his arms and legs weakly.

"J'son, help me get him to sit up."

Once again J'son struggled to get T'mer into a sitting position, bracing him up by leaning against him. J'son could feel the pounding of T'mer's heart getting stronger and more rhythmic. His breathing was getting deeper and more representative of a conscious man. He was rolling his shoulders and moved one of his hands to his face, pinching his nose and rubbing the corners of his eyes. J'son felt T'mer supporting his own weight and he stood up, extending a hand to help T'mer up. T'mer peered at J'son out of bleary eyes, seemingly offended at the offer.

"T'mer, J'son probably just saved your life. He was the one who got the parasite out of you."

"Maybe, but he was the one who brought them," T'mer said indignantly. Still, he took the offered hand and practically pulled J'son down trying to stand up. "Thanks."

"Don't mention it," J'son said, releasing his hand and regaining his balance. Offering his hand to T'mar he said, "I think they are still here. I think they are always here feeding on low-level energy until they stumble across higher quality energy, like us."

"How do you know that, 'sec?" T'mer spat.

"J'son, what did you see? Did you actually see the parasites?" Now that T'mer was conscious and seemingly okay, T'mar was very interested at what J'son claimed to see.

"They were glowing balls of energy when I first saw them, a dark silhouette with bright centers. They grew larger as they fed, soaking up the radiation all around them. They looked like twinkling stars in the night's sky. The one that got on T'mer grew, divided in two, and went straight for his neck. What are they, T'mar?"

"I can't see them. I can only sense them when the air is right. Normally the sun's radiation is enough to feed them and they go unnoticed. They are believed to be thoughts forms from a higher dimension trying to access our dimension by feeding on our energy and manifesting physically. Some teach that they come from the Transcendentals; thought projections seeking expression. It is said they take their form from the thoughts of the sentient life around them. Without conscious thought, they don't exist in any way we would understand."

"You mean they get their identity from how we think about them?" That didn't make sense to J'son. "But I didn't know anything about them. How could I have created bodies for something I never knew existed?" J'son was puzzled by this as much as T'mar. Still, something about her explanation didn't sit right. Everything she said was prefaced by, "They believe; it is taught; they say." She spoke as if she had never really encountered them before and only spoke of second-hand knowledge.

"The Adepts, it is said, can call them forth and transform their energy into anything they want. This is how some of the masters find their 'tpo, and they bond with them for life, or until they need the energy that is bound up in the creatures. It is then that the Adepts will dissolve their mental constructs and channel the creature's essence toward whatever ends the Adept desires."

"I still think you sorcerers are full of 'dsh," T'mer said, still irritated. "And I think he brought those things with him, wherever he came from. I think you bring them here when you cast your spells. The only time I have ever had a problem with those creatures is when I'm around the monks. He's higher than you are, T'mar. Remember that. I'm moving on. The City's where we need to be."

T'mer stood up on shaky legs, frustrated that he had been attacked by something he couldn't defend against, but even more so about these mystics. They never acted like they seemed, secretive, always an ulterior motive, even T'mar. He was right about the creatures never bothering him. He didn't vibrate at the right frequency to attract their attention, his energy field radiating at a level that wasn't worth the creature's trouble. His vibration was "seen" by the creatures as sub-par and a wasteful expenditure of energy, costing more to retrieve it than what the creatures would get. It is only when the creatures are in close proximity to him that they can sense the energy output of his pineal gland.

By latching onto and devouring this gland, the creatures are able to become conscious and thus visible to the physical eyes. When this happens, the creatures become more like animals, with physical bodies and the corresponding appetites of such. If the Adepts are able to create and control a 'tpo, what the 'plcs become once "captured" by a host, the creatures were bound to them. Only a high level Adept would chance harnessing the power of a psychic vampire. The upside was portable energy storage, answerable to the one that bound it. The downside was to be devoured by that same potential.

However, if the creatures were extensions of the Transcendentals, thought forms generated for a specific purpose possessing intelligence, they were much more dangerous and should be avoided at all cost. The creatures they had just now encountered were nothing more than bugs in the grass, an inconvenience that normally would have gone unnoticed but for J'son. It was because of his energy output that they appeared to him and took notice. Three-dimensional life is a poor substitute for the purity of high-end radiation, the difference between a light bulb and a nuclear reactor. They could lie in the sun undisturbed, but preferred to dine on high-vibration emissions.

T'mer had returned to the original dirt trail and was disappearing down the gently sloping foothills. They were coming out of the mountains and would come to the crossroads shortly. Quietly, both with their heads down, each for different reasons, J'son and T'mar followed him, not in a hurry like T'mer, but also not lagging behind. The physical act of walking and the silence was good, comforting in a way. The mechanics of it allowed them to think about what had transpired and about what to do next.

T'mer, head held high, chest sticking out, scanning the immediate area in dominator mode, knew exactly what to do. There would be no discussion at the crossroads: no consulting of amulets, or praying with a talisman pressed between your hands. Those that can divine the fate of what's to come, to forecast the correct decision, live within the City gates.

It is the correct place to be. All reasonable knowledge was there, even the ancient knowledge taught by the Adepts. Who was it that told them when the darkness comes? Those found within the City. Those found outside the gates are fools without schools, pursuing and preying on the fantasies of lower life forms. It was all illusion, something they made up to beguile the gullible.

Never in T'mer's life had he a need for the "other" side of life, not even when he rescued T'mar from B'el. It was through sheer will that all things were accomplished, that and physical strength, his physical strength. The Transcendentals could send an army of thought projections at him. It was only when he was around T'mar that he found himself vulnerable to their attack. He had even been out in the Wastelands before and that couldn't defeat him. T'mar said he had been awakened by the experience, but all he knew was that he was as awake as he wanted to be.

The images he had seen in his head were not the worst of it, not by far. No, the worst was the void, the nothing. It was dark on the outside, in the Wastelands and he had become like nothing. He had broken down and dissolved into his basic atomic structure. He had become nothing but inert particles, devoid of energy and purpose. It was horrible, so much so that he has never told of his experience, not even to T'mar. It was only through the power of his will that he had survived. Even the power of B'el had failed to vanquish him. How B'el is able to survive the dark is one of the secrets of the Adepts, a secret told to very few. The City was where he was going. That's where there were people who had the answers.

T'mar was still several yards behind T'mer, struggling with her own thoughts. Why did the 'plcs attack? It was still daylight. They should have been able to pass without so much as a little fatigue. But for the fact that J'son had said anything, she wouldn't have known they were even there, wouldn't have known until it was too late. But T'mar didn't generate that high level of energy to be detected by them, not while the sun was visible. How could they have seen the three of them? They should have been blinded and unable to see anything more than the bright, pervasive radiance of the sun, trillions and trillions of minute, highly-energetic particles raining down on them. Or that was what she had been taught.

She searched her memory for any precedent, any footnote that mentioned daylight attacks without provocation. She hadn't been casting spells or calling forth the powers. They had been travelling undercover. They should have gone by unnoticed. T'mer had shown up at the cave because of their history together, their connection. As hard as it was for her to accept, it seemed that all questions and their answers pointed to J'son. How was he able to see them? How did he remove that creature with hardly any effort? She also had a hard time focusing and the chanting only made her awareness of the creatures indirect. He had brought the storms earlier without being aware of it, almost like it was a part of his nature. He had survived the 'wat, just like the monks and the Adepts. He was here, physically. None of this sat well with her.

Her memory was failing her and she couldn't quite remember how they came to be in the cave, only that she had found him there. She remembered she recognized J'son when she first saw him, but now she was beginning to mistrust him, and suspected that he might be an emissary from the Transcendentals. He claimed to have seen them and said they spoke to him. She found that hard to believe. Even B'el never claimed to have spoken to them, although he did claim that he was familiar with that dimension. J'son was a riddle that the monks would have to meditate on. They would want to see him to study him. She knew he would be as big of a puzzle to them as he was to her. She had been instructed by B'el himself and if anyone had answers, it would be the disciples of B'el. At the crossroads, she would turn towards the monks.

She knew T'mer wouldn't want to go, but she might be able to convince him. She knew he had already made up his mind about what he was going to do. It didn't matter. If he couldn't be persuaded to come with them, he could return to the City alone. That, however, bothered her. If truth be told, she didn't want him to go to the City and tell anyone anything, which would be the first thing he did. He always wanted to consult the Adepts in the City whenever he encountered something he didn't understand. She had tried repeatedly to get him to think for himself, but time and again he relied instead on the opinions of others.

She really didn't want to tell the monks anything, either. She wanted to keep J'son a secret to herself. If she had it her way, the only one she would speak of this to would be B'el. B'el would appreciate the significance of this find. He would know how to exploit it. The thought shamed her. She chastised herself over how easily she had thought about J'son as something to "exploit". But J'son wasn't a commodity, was he? No, he was a gift, a peace offering. Maybe then B'el's anger towards her would be cooled and the betrayal forgotten. She wouldn't tell the monks what she had observed. She only needed them to get a message to B'el. T'mer would have to come with them, or face the consequences. B'el may forgive her, but he wouldn't forgive T'mer. B'el wouldn't allow T'mer to speak of J'son.

Chapter Nine:

Not Alone

"When the air is still and a sound is heard, that's when you can be sure that you're being followed."

Ancient monastic proverb

J'son was hanging back and had lost sight of T'mer. He was staggering along, looking down at his dirty feet, when he abruptly looked up. T'mar was about fifty feet ahead of him. He had been lost in thought when suddenly he felt like he had been slapped in the face. His first impression as he was lifting his head in response was that T'mar had stopped in her tracts and turned around, slapping him when he got close enough. He would have sworn that she had done just that. He could smell her and had the impression she was standing very close. He could feel the warmth of her body and found himself becoming aroused. He thought that when he looked up that he would be staring into her eyes and asking her why she had hit him. Instead, in that brief moment between his head being down and head up, the illusion that she was standing in front of him shattered and he found that she was still walking down the hill, below him. It must have been the wind changing directions, blowing her scent towards him, he thought.

Puzzled by the experience, his thoughts sidetracked, he reflected on why he had the distinct impression that she had hit him. His face didn't sting like he had been slapped. In fact, the sensation was more like being surprised awake. Maybe he had. Maybe be he had fallen asleep while walking and was having a dream, except that it didn't feel like a dream and he didn't remember being sleepy. He had been thinking about those creatures and how he had been able to blast them just by thinking about it. He was thinking about fire coming out of his fingers when all of the sudden… What? It was like he flinched. Like he had been standing up to a bully and they had acted like they were going to hit him and he overreacted and jumped.

His heart was pounding, slowing down now, and he scanned the thinning trees, wide awake and alert to danger. But the only danger he sensed seemed to be coming from T'mar. There was something about her that he didn't trust. He knew she was keeping secrets from him. T'mer was simple enough to read and J'son picked up on his mistrust of her, even though they appeared to have a history. As they walked, J'son had seen faint, delicate ribbons of energy flowing between them, but he didn't understand their origin or purpose. She had said that T'mer was her husband, but there was obviously a power struggle between them. T'mer clearly had a problem with the delegation of duties and she had some type of control over him. There were so many questions and he didn't feel like he could trust either of them.

J'son continued walking and watched T'mar from behind, trying to pick up something, a thought, an image, something. He felt the hostility radiating off of her, could see waves of force hovering around her like metal filings around a magnet, but the wavelength was generalized and not focused, streams of energy radiating out and then collapsing back on itself. It appeared to J'son that T'mar was having a hard time about something and the power of her thoughts fed on the confusion all around them. Maybe it was better that J'son didn't know what was going on. Maybe it would be dangerous to everyone if he did understand what was happening to him.

Still looking at T'mar up ahead, watching her hips sway from side to side, J'son became distracted by a movement out of the corner of his eye. It was momentary, and when he turned to look in that direction he thought he caught a glimpse of something large moving between the trees and hiding behind the brush. He continued to stare, squinting into the shadows, his mind playing tricks with the lightly blowing vegetation, creating an assortment of imaginary beasts. Seeing nothing that looked predatory, he turned away and continued following T'mar again, but his attention remained fixed on the periphery, hoping to spot whatever he thought he had just seen.

He really didn't see anything, but he had the distinct impression that they were being stalked, hunted. He was sure of it. There was something just beyond the fringe, down in the hollow over the hill to his left, something large and out of sight, watching him. It was strange that he didn't feel scared or apprehensive and maybe that was what he was picking up from T'mar. Although very conflicted, T'mar was emitting anger and deception but not fear. He didn't think she was picking up on what he was feeling. He walked in silence, not really thinking but alert, hoping to get a clear look at whatever it was.

The trail they were on ran around one final fold in the hills and T'mar disappeared from his view. J'son rounded the same hill and came out into a meadow covered with blues, yellows and reds. There were several small, flower-like plants one to two inches high with blooms the size of his hand. The field was also full of tiny, flying insects with multiple, greenish appendages that acted as wings. They were jumping from flower to flower, stopping for a moment before moving on, like bees collecting pollen.

The flowers grew along the dirt trail and J'son kicked the nearest one, disrupting the insects and causing a cloud of bugs to rise up and swarm around his foot, not landing but hitting and bouncing off, attacking him perhaps. Without warning, the entire field erupted in a hazy cloud of insects moving as one, twisting and bending like fish in a school. They flew around his head and J'son tried swatting them away to no avail. The bugs were getting in his eyes and he swallowed about a dozen, choking up bits of them and spitting them out.

"Yuck!"

"J'son, you shouldn't have bothered them. As long as you stay on the trail they will leave you alone." T'mar had stopped and had turned around to face him, waiting for him to catch up.

"Fine. How do I get rid of these," he said, still swatting and waving his hand over his face.

"Just stop moving. You're a threat to them now. Let them swarm around you for a moment and think peaceful thoughts. They'll tire of you and go back to collecting their energy from the 'fbu."

J'son closed his eyes tight against them and lowered his arms to his side, keeping as still as possible. He could feel the bugs crawling in his nose and hear the loud buzzing in his ears. The warmth of the sun was bearing down on him and he lifted his head to let the light caress his face. The sound and the feel of the bugs drifted into the background as he cleared his mind and thought about his first view of this strange planet from the mouth of the cave. The image of seeing this world from high up was peaceful and transcendent, literally a world apart from his present location.

The buzzing faded away and the constant feel of their tiny feet covering his face and neck fell away, replaced with the sound of the wind rustling overhead. He then heard something that sounded like an animal walking across a pile of dry leaves, crunching and crackling. He opened his eyes and turned towards the sound, again to his left. This time he was sure he saw something, crouching low, the outline of a large predator hiding in the shadows. He was about to ask T'mar if she saw it when he was interrupted by the sound of T'mer's voice calling out a short distance away.

"T'mar, get up here. There's someone here at the crossroads who says he knows you, a monk I think."

Chapter Ten:

The Wizard

"Each particle, every speck of dust has consciousness of varying degrees. We speak to that consciousness and give it purpose and direction. We use that thought, that spark of intelligence and direct it, producing the physical manifestation of our choosing. In order to manipulate reality, you must learn to manipulate consciousness."

The wizard, C'ton, giving J'son a crash course on Magic

J'son and T'mar were standing within arm's length of each other when T'mer called out. He had disappeared around a small bend in the trail and was hidden by a large boulder jutting out of the ground at an extreme angle, forming a low-hanging covering across the trail. J'son and T'mar looked at each other, surprised at the declaration, and then continued down the trail, stopping under the overhanging boulder. The trail straightened out past the boulder and came to an intersection, a crossroad a few feet away.

The path they were on continued past the intersection, becoming wider and better maintained, wide enough for four men to walk side by side. It was lined with well-ordered rocks which outlined the path. To the right about fifty feet away was a small, arched bridge that spanned a narrow stream that bubbled quietly underneath it and flowed away into the distance, feeding a large body of water further below. To the left the road followed the curve of the low-lying foothills down into a vale of blue, carpet-like vegetation and disappeared behind a clump of small trees or tall bushes.

A low, flat rock that served as a signpost of sorts and a resting place for weary travelers sat at the juncture of this crossroad on the left. Seated on top of the rock was a man of indeterminate age sitting cross-legged with straight back, eyes opened and alert, his hands resting quietly in his lap with the tips of his fingers lightly touching each other. He was wearing a long, one piece tunic, furry and dark blue in color. His arms and lower legs were uncovered and the robe was wrapped loosely around his body and tied at the waist with a leathery rope that looked like one of the vines seen hanging from the trees.

He was smiling brightly at them, a curious and contented smile that made his face glow, the first genuine smile J'son had see in this place and lacking the "X" he had come to expect. He had a mouth full of teeth, the corners of which were hidden behind a long goatee', brown in color and tightly braided down to his upper chest. His didn't seem to be surprised at their arrival and acted pleased to see them, the light in his eyes almost bubbling over with amusement.

J'son, T'mar and T'mer were standing together now, staring at him, speechless; possibly waiting for this man to speak first. T'mer had a cruel scowl on his face, as usual. His eyes were close and beady with that malicious X marking his features and a look of intense mistrust. T'mar didn't look much better and she peered at him out of the corner of her eye, squinting at him and showing distinct signs of animosity. J'son thought the man looked familiar and immediately recognized him as the monk from his vision. He looked back and forth between them waiting for someone to speak, and then decided to break the stalemate himself.

"Hi," he said friendly enough. "I'm J'son and this is—"

"Shut up, boy," T'mer said harshly, not looking away from the man.

"That's okay," the man said. "I know who you are already, I think. I've been waiting for you. We're supposed to meet." And then looking straight at T'mar he said, "I know you, too."

"I don't think so," she said, not too sure if that was true or not. He did look familiar and she searched her memory to connect the face, but all that she could recall brought fear and suspicion.

"Well, I could be wrong, but I rarely forget a face, especially one as pretty as yours. You, though," he said turning back to look at T'mer, his bright smile fading a bit, "You, I don't know."

The two of them continued to stare at each other, their eyes locked and unblinking, the man's face growing more grave and contemplative now. After a few moments, T'mer's gaze wavered and he looked away, a shadow falling across his face. He was noticeably shaken and disturbed by the encounter and became fidgety, moving his stance around and changing the position of his arms from across his chest to by his side and back again. The shadow darkened as it passed across his face and the veins in his neck stuck out like thick, purple, pulsating ropes. His breathing grew rapid and shallow and his chest was heaving up and down. Whatever had past between them in that short moment had riled him and now he was tense and uneasy.

"Calm down, my young friend," the man said, unfolding his arms and legs and getting off of the rock. "I'm quite harmless and unarmed, as you can see. There is nothing for you to fear. My name is C'ton and I've been waiting for you to arrive. Or more specifically," he said, turning to J'son. "I have been waiting for you." He stood up slowly, stroking the braid of his goatee' with one hand. "I'm sure the Transcendentals made you aware of me, and now we have found each other. Do you have any idea why they wanted us to meet?"

"No. I—"

"J'son, don't tell this monk anything. He is a renegade from the proper schools, self-taught and more than likely insane. No one speaks openly about those that have passed on, and his master, if he has one, should have instructed him that it is a crime to do so."

T'mar didn't so much as recognize his face as his name. C'ton was a name that few would forget once they heard his story. She had indeed met him once, long ago, but he didn't look like he does now. Her memory of that time was fuzzy and she couldn't be sure that he was who he said he was. Her instincts told her to be wary and her fight-or-flight response began to stir up her energy stores, causing her to take on a posture of defense and mistrust. She understood precisely why T'mer reacted the way he did. This monk, C'ton, a name chosen for his supposedly advanced learning and an indicator of immense power, with just a look had peered within T'mer , saw the level of his training, dismissed it as trivial and by projecting a image into his mind had shown T'mer that he was no match for him. For someone like T'mer, being shown that he was powerless and easily manageable was infuriating. Nobody liked feeling vulnerable.

If what his name implied was true, she thought, even in her prime with the teachings she had acquired she had never reached his level of understanding nor his ability to manipulate reality. His hushed demeanor and calm confidence annoyed her and she didn't know if she would be able to defeat him, much less defend herself against him, if it came down to that. T'mer had the physical strength to break him in two, it was true, but it was T'mer's feeble mental strength that would make him a detriment to their plans. She knew she would have to expend some of her own power to prop him up, re-enforcing him, if she could, but she would have to do it without C'ton being aware of it. She would have to divert his attention somehow and then implant within T'mer the mental stability he would need.

"So," C'ton said matter-of-factly, his face reflecting tranquility. "Why don't you tell me a little about yourself, and don't mind them. With all of these wizards around everyone is a little jumpy. Come. Let's make our way towards the Temple. If it is training that you seek, then I'm sure you will find a good school among them."

C'ton was speaking mainly to J'son but kept his attention fixed on T'mar. He laughed as he spoke, smiling and winking at J'son in turn. He was assuming command of the situation and was trying to direct him down the right hand path.

"What's in that direction?" J'son asked, pointing down the road to the left.

"Well, that's where your large friend wants to go, I think. He finds comfort among the City-Dwellers where they appreciate his abilities. It was his race that built the massive structures that they are so proud of. Only in the City do they respect brute strength."

Even as C'ton spoke, T'mer was edging towards the left, making his way around the backside of the flat rock instead of walking around the front, avoiding moving closer to C'ton. T'mar wasn't moving at all, still on guard, and she darted her eyes between J'son and C'ton, searching for any sign that he might be trying to mentally influence J'son.

"C'mon, T'mar. I told you we were going to the City. This nut case looks like one of those simpletons who failed the 'wat rituals. There's no way he knew we were coming. He's just trying to take advantage of our situation. You know we have to take this boy to see the Adepts."

T'mer had now made his way around the rock and was several yards down the left hand road, walking backwards so as to keep his eye on C'ton. Being in such close proximity to him, T'mer felt strange, like he didn't have possession of his own mind. C'ton made him nervous and fearful, frightened like the time he had battled B'el, only that time it was the fear of physical annihilation. Now, however, he feared something else, something more remote and yet comforting. Around C'ton he felt his guard go down, whether willingly or not he wasn't sure. He felt like he was in the presence of a superior power that only wanted to comfort him, ease his pain and soothe the constant, burning anger that was always with him. Even when he was alone with T'mar, he never felt like this and he certainly didn't like it, not one bit. It was his anger that gave him his strength and courage.

"What about that way?" J'son asked, pointing straight ahead. "Where does that go?"

"That's the way we're going," said T'mar, finally moving forward and brushing past C'ton, purposely bumping into him. She crossed the road and turned around, facing the crossroad.

J'son was standing by the rock on the path they were originally on looking at the other three in turn. To his left was T'mer who J'son really didn't trust at all, wanting to go to the City. On his right was C'ton, wanting to take them to the schools of the monks, whatever those were. And standing in front of him across the road was T'mar, wanting to take him… Where?

"What about it, T'mar? C'ton said that there were schools in that direction. Maybe that's where we should go. Maybe they can answer our questions."

"J'son, we are going to the schools, the schools I attended. This path will take us to the only place that will have the answers you seek."

"I seek? I just want to know what I'm doing here."

"As one who has seen the Transcendentals, you do not want someone of lesser knowledge to instruct you," C'ton said over his shoulder as he continued to walk down the road. "Taking the path that your friend, T'mar, wants you to take will only complicate your confusion. Come! This is the way you should go, and we will talk along the way. Maybe I have some answers for you. Besides, just off the road, several miles ahead, another path branches off that will take you to the same place that she wants to take you. If when we reach it you still want to follow her, then I will take my leave and I will continue on my way."

"Is that true, T'mar? If this road will take us to the same place, I say we go with C'ton. Maybe he does have some answers."

Something about C'ton comforted J'son and it was easy to place his trust in him. Why T'mar wanted to separate from him was curious, considering ever since J'son found himself lying on the floor of a cave high up in the mountains she seemed to be nervous and fearful. This man, this monk, didn't seem afraid at all and by all appearances he genuinely wanted to help. And what about his vision and what the Transcendentals said to him? And who were they anyway. T'mar didn't want to talk about them and C'ton said he had been sent by them. Whatever T'mar had in mind, J'son wanted to go with this man, at least for awhile and talk with him about all of the strange things that had happened to him. He also wanted to ask C'ton about some of the things T'mar had already told him. The impression he got from this monk was one of confidence and trust, which was the exact opposite of what he felt coming from T'mar. She seemed to be filled only with fear and suspicion. J'son wasn't too sure if he trusted her and he really didn't think she was telling him the whole truth about some things. He felt, instinctively, that she was keeping something from him.

"Yeah, T'mar," J'son decided. "I think we should go with him."

"T'mar!" T'mer barked. "Let's go and leave these 'lugs to themselves."

"Just a minute, J'son," T'mar said, walking over to T'mer. "Let me talk to T'mer and see what he thinks about this. We'll need him if we go the way you want." T'mar already knew what T'mer thought, but she figured she could use this opportunity to persuade him to go with them anyway. Maybe this was the distraction she needed to reinforce his mental resolve.

It would be easy to change his mind, but she needed to do it without anyone knowing she was casting a spell over him. She would have to convince him that she needed him for protection and that they couldn't let J'son fall into the hands of this monk. She would convince him that together they could immobilize C'ton and hopefully take whatever power he possessed. With J'son as a portal and the power this monk must surely possess, together they could go anywhere. As long as T'mer played along, he was useful to her ultimate plan.

She came over to T'mer, smiling a secret, seductive smile that she knew would open T'mer up to persuasion and manipulation. It was the same smile she always used when she wanted him to do something that he didn't want to do. It was the smile of promise and the memory of sexual favors that she would bestow on him. For a man of his great strength, sex was his only weakness. It was the weakness of all men, and she used it to her advantage.

Her smile did caused T'mer's guard to go down slightly, by choice, and she passed within his defenses, merging herself with him and filling his mind with graphic, sadistic images of perversion and rape. Although she knew those images would hold him for awhile and he would do what she wanted, she also knew that simple, sexual re-enforcement wouldn't provide the mental structure she would need of him if things started to go wrong.

She would have to go deeper within his psyche to implant the kind of control over him that she would need to overcome any attack C'ton could device. It's one thing to hypnotize someone and implant a false idea; it's quite another to force someone to do something against their will. When push came to shove, T'mar would need T'mer to act without thinking about the consequences.

She had done this same thing previously with surprising results. She had done what she had to do in order to escape from B'el, she told herself, even though she still felt a tinge of guilt about it. Although he didn't know it at the time, she had implanted an overwhelming desire deep within T'mer to rescue her from B'el if the need presented itself, which of course it did. At the time, she had allowed him to think it was his great strength that saved her, but he was a mere pawn in her overall plan, a plan that had failed miserably at the time and almost took her life. He did come to her rescue and he did facilitate her escape, but the drawback was that she had bound herself to him, even changing her occult classification among the hierarchy. That was a terrible blow to her standing, not being able to fully reveal her abilities, but it was necessary. And now, it seemed, it would be necessary again.

As she filled his mind with corrupt images of debauchery and degradation, she spoke to him in whispers, creating the required and essential auditory vibrations needed to reprogram his mind so as to implant the controls she desired. She also moved her fingers in a way that would seem almost casual and conversational to observers, but in reality would open the doors within his mind and activate the controls that she had implanted earlier. The movements of her fingers acted as a distraction to his waking mind, pulling his attention away from what she was saying and allowing the sound of her words to reverberate within his mind, reaching deep into his sub-conscious.

The programming wouldn't take long and he would be left unaware that she had done anything except try to persuade him to go with them. Once she was done, he would think it was his idea to go with them in order to protect her from harm. The fact that he felt strong emotions for her made the programming that much easier. However, his increased sense of pride in his physical strength and the testosterone-fueled stroke to his ego telling him that he was needed would make him more hard-headed than ever and therefore harder to deal with, but it was the price she was willing to pay. He would conflict with J'son even more and quarrel incessantly, debating everything, but she knew she didn't have an option. She would just have to deal with it. As long as the controls held, she could handle his mood swings; she would have to.

C'ton had stopped walking and turned to face the crossroad. He watched as T'mar approached T'mer and she began speaking with him in whispers. He was looking at her back and so C'ton couldn't see what she was saying to him, but he did notice that she spoke with her hands a lot and he figured that she was manipulating him, convincing T'mer to do something, implanting thoughts within him. He tried momentarily to project himself into their conversation, but was hindered by her training. She was harder to read than T'mer, having learned, obviously, to block the mental intrusions of others.

He did recognize her and would wait for her to recognize him. They had known each other in the past, but she was more innocent then than she seemed now. She was naïve then, seeking skill and ability, full of passion and curiosity, unwilling to take the slower, safer path to initiation. She had wanted to be instructed by the best, no matter what the cost nor the consequences.

She had moved up the ranks rapidly, learning what she could from whomever and then discarding her teacher for one more advanced. It was this attitude, this uncompromising pursuit of knowledge, of gnosis, that had caught the attention of B'el. Although she had been a low-level novice then, a beginner in the occult arts, B'el had made her his apprentice, something that was unheard of at the time, which brought the envy and condemnation of some of the more advanced students.

Her time at B'el's Castle had been cut short for some reason and she had left, or as some had said escaped, from B'el before her training was complete. C'ton didn't know why she had left; only that B'el was furious and had sent out assassins to eliminate her. The entire hierarchy was thrown into disarray and for awhile B'el had retreated from view, disappearing completely. Some had said she had rejected B'el's advances and fled for her life. Others, and C'ton was a member of this school of thought, had suggested she had discovered a weakness in him and took that knowledge with her in the hopes of unseating him, possibly destroying him. Whatever the reason, her time with B'el had changed her from a fiery, quick tempered student of the nature of reality to a fearful, possessed enemy of all things occult. She had even changed her name, it seems, maybe in the hopes of hiding from B'el's assassins. What she had learned in the tall, dark towers of B'el's Castle was anyone's guess.

C'ton had heard that she had help in her escape and he looked more closely at her large companion, T'mer. It had been said that he had fought against B'el, and defeated him by exploiting whatever weakness T'mar had discovered. How a mere brute could have thrown down a Wizard as powerful as B'el, a Wizard who had no equal, a Sorcerer who aspired to claimed the title of AB'el, was one of the greatest mysteries of the present age and a source of constant, ever changing speculation throughout the schools.

Every small-time conjuror who had the mistaken belief that he could overthrow the Master, the Beast, soon found himself subdued, broken, enslaved and finally annihilated. Many a corpse, impaled upon tall shafts and stripped naked, had lined the corridor that led to the gates of B'el's lair. The images of that gruesome spectacle still burned intensely in the mind of C'ton, seared within his memory, an ever present reminder to never go against B'el.

T'mar and T'mer's exchange was lasting longer than C'ton expected and he grew bored of watching them. Instead, he turned his attention to J'son, the boy, who appeared to be something more than what he seemed. There was a vibe about him that intrigued him and J'son's aura was powerfully present at all times, radiating off of him like a current, affecting everything around him. The lines of force surrounding him bent all fields towards him, like he was his own black hole absorbing the energy around him, curving the space around him like a gravity well.

C'ton could feel his own energy, which he normally had such control over, flowing out of him and feeding J'son's field. It wasn't an unpleasant feeling, one that would have caused him concerned, but he started to wonder if it was possible that this boy had the ability to drain him of all his reserves. He wondered if J'son even knew that he was doing it. Was this why the Transcendentals wanted them to meet? Did they want C'ton to help J'son with this talent? He knew it was potentially dangerous to be around him, but C'ton didn't feel threatened by him.

Did T'mar understand and appreciate the significance of the power J'son possessed? He was sure she did. Why else was she so pre-occupied with him? But there was something else that he couldn't quite grasp at the moment. He felt there was another ability J'son had that she was interested in. There was something about him that she wanted; something that, C'ton sensed, she would fight for and possibly kill for. The Transcendentals wanted them to meet for a reason, and C'ton needed to find out what it was.

Chapter Eleven:

Magic Tricks

"Focus is the key. What you think about creates your reality and the harder you concentrate the more real it becomes."

C'ton explaining to J'son how to manipulate matter

As the Lovers spoke and C'ton ruminated, J'son was distracted by something just beyond his awareness, something in the shadows that was looming large and predatory. The feeling of its presence waxed and waned, like something alive that was watching them and then moved away, coming back at random intervals. At times, he thought he could hear something moving in the brush, rustling the leaves, and at other times he thought he heard it over head in the branches of the trees. He couldn't see anything solid, only an outline, maybe, a creature of some kind. The fact that he couldn't see it didn't bother him as much as the idea that they were being watched, studied.

T'mar and T'mer were coming back over to him now, having reached some kind of decision and the feeling they were being watched disappeared again. T'mar seemed happy, which was good to see, making her face glow a beautiful shade of attractive, but T'mer still had that X across his face, brooding. J'son knew by the look on T'mar's face that they were going to go with C'ton and that decision made J'son happy, too; relieved actually. He dismissed T'mer's expression as normal and he found his spirits lifting out of the dark, menacing cloud that had been overshadowing his thoughts. He was glad that they were going to go with C'ton.

"We will go with you," T'mar said, looking at C'ton with a confident smile. "At least for a little while."

"Good. Good. I am eager to converse with you and trade stories about the paths you have traversed. It isn't often that I get a chance to commune with fellow travelers, being a solitary monk and all. Come. You must tell me about yourselves and how it is that our paths have crossed."

The four of them started to walk down the road at a leisurely pace, with C'ton and J'son leading the way, T'mar right behind them and T'mer bring up the rear several feet behind. C'ton spoke mainly to J'son, but loud enough for T'mar to hear. T'mer, for his part, didn't care what they were talking about and spent his time debating with himself as to why he was going along with them. He scolded himself repeatedly for letting T'mar, once again, convince him to do something that he knew was against his better judgment.

It wasn't so much that she convinced him, he told himself. He knew she would be vulnerable out here away from the City without him and he consoled himself with that thought. He knew he went with them because he was her protector as well as her lover and he couldn't leave her to face the hard, cruel realities of life on the road without his protection. If only she didn't feel like she needed to look after J'son. Who cares about him anyway? Who cares if she thought he was a portal? T'mer didn't want to leave the planet of his birth anyway. All they needed was each other. Only the Wizards wanted to leave this world, his world.

As far as he was concerned, it was the Wizards that brought all of the problems and the wars. Except for a few Adepts they would need to rule in the City, all he needed was his strength and her sex. They didn't even need to live in the City if that was what she wanted. With her training, she could provide them with what his strength couldn't, which wouldn't be much. He watched the three of them up ahead pulling away from him and he scanned the thinning tree-line and shrubbery for any signs of trouble, hoping to prove to her once again that he was needed.

"So J'son," C'ton said, laughing as he spoke. "Tell me. How is it that you came to be here travelling this road with your companions?"

"Well, I'm not too sure," he began hesitantly. "I first met her on Earth, my home world. I met her in my dreams."

That remark caught T'mar's attention and she looked up from her thoughts. She had forgotten they had discovered each other on the other side. How could she have forgotten? That's right!

"You are from Earth. How intriguing. I didn't think you were from this world? How did you come to be here?" Ah. So that's part of the answer, C'ton thought. She thinks he might be a portal!

"What I remember is waking up here lying on the floor of a cave. I was wearing clothes very similar to this, but I don't know how I got them. I was already dressed when I woke up. At the time, I still had vivid impressions of my life on Earth and T'mar wanted me to try and return there. She wanted me to try and recall my life there and she was interested to know if I could see the present or was I just remembering the past."

This was very interesting to C'ton and now he understood why T'mar was interest in J'son. "Were you able to go back?"

"Yes, and I thought I could see my home town and some of the people I know, or knew. I think I was seeing the present, but an altered present. It was like in the future but not the too distant future. She wanted me to try and get back there again if I got the opportunity, but too much has been happening for me to try again."

"Well maybe we will find the time for you to try again as we walk along. Do you still have a good memory of your home?"

"I do, I guess. But your world is so different that it kind of pushes my world into the back ground, like a vivid dream that slowly disperses as you awake."

"I see."

T'mar didn't like the direction this conversation was going. J'son had already told C'ton more than she would have liked and she was sure that now C'ton knew that J'son was special. The search for the perfect portal was the goal of all learning. It was like the search for the philosopher's stone, but a stable portal was much more valuable. C'ton now knew J'son had the ability to travel back and forth and that he could remain three-dimensional throughout the process.

If C'ton thought he could wrestle J'son away from her and use him for his own purposes, he was sorely mistaken. She wanted to interrupt them to keep C'ton from asking any more questions and stop J'son from divulging anything else, but to do that would tip her hand. No, she would just have to let J'son talk and hope that C'ton would ask the questions that she wanted to ask. Maybe C'ton would have some answers that she could use.

She backed off from them, giving them some space in the hopes that C'ton would ask even more revealing questions. She knew that he knew she was listening to them and that the questions he was asking were very general, not wanting to appear intrusive. By distancing herself from them, she hoped C'ton would dig deeper and probe the mystery that was J'son. Any information that she could get would only benefit her and help her to find a way to exploit J'son's abilities. At least that was the plan.

"When I first got here," J'son continued. "The sky was on fire and lightening flashed everywhere. T'mar said I was drawing the storm to me, that my emotions were feeding it. I had to compose myself in order to calm the storm, which wasn't as hard as I thought it would be. I was also able to project my thoughts and emit a beam of energy out of the tips of my fingers. It took some concentration, but it seemed very natural for me to do so. Can you explain that?"

"Your finger tips are just a way for you to direct your thoughts. With a little practice, you should be able to just think about what you want to happen and it will."

"How can that be? Does this planet give me some special power or something?"

"No. Any special powers you possess passed over with you when you came through. You said that you first met T'mar in your dreams. Can you tell me about that? Do you have vivid dreams?"

"Well, I've always been able to dream. In fact, my earliest childhood memories are based on dreams. Sometimes they are so vivid that they are what I would call psychedelic, full of color and detail. It's almost like they are more real than real. And when I dream, I know that I am dreaming. Sometimes I can influence what I dream about. That was before I met

T'mar. Once I started to see her regularly, I began to feel like I could leave my body behind and I saw the world, I saw Earth, from a totally different perspective. I no longer thought of myself as a body of flesh and blood. I started to identify with myself as something more than physical. I felt like I was part of everything around me, but conscious and able to move within and through things."

J'son grew quiet and contemplative, lowering his head to stare at his feet. He felt embarrassed to be speaking so candidly like this to a total stranger, saying things that sounded crazy even to his own ears. But how could he think what he was saying was crazy after everything he had experienced here? Maybe this was a dream like all of the others. Maybe none of this was real and instead he was home in Hope, Alabama, lying on his bed having a very weird and lucid dream. Maybe all of this was a figment of his over stimulated imagination. Maybe he was schizophrenic, drugged up and lying in a coma in a mental ward. How would he know the difference? J'son's thoughts were falling and he was starting to get depressed. How could he trust anything if he couldn't trust himself?

"You're not crazy," C'ton said, reading the color output of his aura, picking up on his thoughts and deducing what he was feeling. "What you are is very gifted. Very few people on you world can see like you just described, mainly because your science doesn't recognize the importance of mental imagery, the power of thought. Your world concerns itself with Left Brain thinking and considers Right Brain thinking as fantasy and a waste of time, nothing productive in it and something you need to grow out of. And if you don't, you are slapped with a label as having a mental illness, only treatable with psychotropic drugs that further repress your intuitive side. What your science doesn't understand or won't admit is that they are damaging you and in effect bio-chemically re-programming you to experience reality the way they want you to see it. Through the use of pharmaceuticals, the elite of your world are enslaving your minds, mentally preparing you for the war that is coming."

"War! What war? C'ton, what are you talking about?"

"Let's not speak about such unpleasant things right now. Our time together would be better spent trying to find out where your abilities lie and how much control you have."

"Do you think that's such a great idea?" T'mar asked sharply, coming up from behind, startling J'son, making him jump. "I've seen what he can do and I don't think we need to be experimenting with that kind of power. I've been exposed to that level of learning. I mean I've seen the monks practice with the powers he seems to possess and I don't think even you could suppress it if he got out of control."

C'ton made note of her mistake, realizing that her name belied her true training. She was right to rephrase her statement. Someone with only a "T" level of learning couldn't possibly understand the forces residing within J'son. It was further confirmation that she wasn't whom she presented herself to be. But why the deception? She must purposely be trying to hide from someone or from something. Her tiny slip up strengthened his conviction that she was the student of B'el that he had seen many cycles ago. Now he had no doubt who she really was, and that knowledge could prove to be dangerous for all concerned.

"I can appreciate your concern," he said to her, stopping in the middle of the road and turning to face her. "But I have something just a little bit less risky in mind, something that I'm sure he can do without any trouble and would be no danger to ourselves. Let's see if I can find what I am looking for over here beside the road. It should be easy to find."

C'ton crossed to the left side of the road and started to kick at the grass and dirt with the toe of his sandaled foot, breaking up the ground and digging around in the loose soil. T'mer had caught up with the group and the three of them watched in silence as C'ton poked around in several spots. Finally, he stopped using his foot and bent over, reaching down with his hand, excavating down a few inches and wrapping his fingers around a palm-sized chunk of plant material, coal black in color, and stood up, holding it out to J'son.

"Here, take this J'son."

J'son took it out of his hand and was surprised at how light it was, almost weightless. It felt cool in his hand and he thought he could see it glowing slightly. He studied it, noticing the small pock marks and warts all over it. Bronzed-color dirt still clung to it and he picked at it with his finger, cleaning it off. The fungus, or whatever it was, felt spongy to his touch and he pressed his finger into it, smashing it down and compressing it into his palm. He released his finger and the material sprang back to its original shape, a small, dull blue bruise forming where he touched it. It was getting warmer now and he glanced at C'ton with a questioning look in his eyes.

"What is this?" He asked. "It's getting warm."

"Never mind that right now. What I want you to do is to think about it and see how warm you can make it."

"Well, that won't be hard. It's getting warmer by the moment, almost too warm for me to hold it."

"Then don't hold it. Think about it floating just above your hand and try to make it glow. Think of a color and try to make it that color. Close your eyes and concentrate." C'ton was impressed that J'son had said it was already getting warm without any direction. If J'son could get it to float and glow at the same time, that would be a good indication of his innate power.

J'son closed his eyes and tried to picture the object within his mind. Almost immediately he was able to imagine the object floating a few inches above his hand and he visualize it changing from black to red to yellow to blue and then to a brilliant white with spikes of light spreading out in all directions like the multiple rays of a star. He heard a gasp and then a loud, deafening explosion. He shut his eyes tightly against the sound and leaned away from his outstretched hand, only opening one eye slowly when he heard C'ton's jubilant laughter.

"Well done, my young friend. Next time I'll make sure to tell you not to imagine it going beyond blue."

Looking at his hand J'son saw that the fungus was gone and in its place was a dimly glowing, milky-white substance the consistency of water dripping from between his fingers, striking the ground by his feet, disappearing into the dirt and gradually losing its radiance.

"What happened?" He asked, his eyes wide and darting back and forth between C'ton and T'mar.

"You made it exploded, you 'mrn," T'mer growled. "Leave it to a human to screw up something as simple as lighting a glow ball."

"Yes indeed! And how wonderful that was," C'ton said with a big smile stretching across his face. "Not only did you make it float out of your hand, you were able to increase the intensity to the point of igniting."

"I'm sorry. I just did what you asked me to." J'son tried wiping his hand off on his tunic and smeared the still glowing liquid all over himself.

"Of course you did. Tell me, did you find it hard to do that?"

T'mar was staring dumb-founded and disbelieving. After C'ton handed the fungus to J'son, she understood exactly what he was trying to do. The ability to cause the fungus to hover without floating away was a measure of control and the intensity of the radiance indicted J'son level of concentration. To move upwards through the light spectrum like he did was a gauge of how much focus he had. To detonate it in such a short period of time implied a level of concentration beyond anything she had seen.

Unless one was using the glow ball as a weapon, no Wizard would dare show off their power so recklessly. It was a sign of vanity and therefore weakness. She decided then that she would have to be more domineering towards J'son, make him think that she was more powerful. If she could convince him that she possessed more power than he did, there was no telling what she would be able to accomplish through him. All thoughts of presenting J'son to B'el as a gift vanished and were replaced by visions of absolute power. Not even B'el could withstand an assault of such magnitude, and they were just getting started.

"Here, let's try this again," C'ton said, reaching down and grabbing a smaller piece of fungus the size of a pea. Handing it to J'son he said, "This time I only want you to imagine it glowing yellow, and try to project it over there against that tree."

"That fool will only manage burning the tree to the ground," T'mer spat.

"I don't think so," C'ton countered. "He's not the only one that can perform tricks."

J'son closed his eyes again and instantly the small toadstool floated out of his hand and changed color, becoming yellow. He opened his eyes, maintaining his focus and willed the golden orb to drift over to a nearby tree. It impacted the tree and flattened out, like a splattering mud ball. The fungus started to smoke and then a small flame appeared, burning a shallow depression into the tree. Within moments the fire spread and the side of the tree was engulfed in flames, burning furiously.

"What do I do now?" J'son asked dismayed. "I don't want to burn it down."

"That's okay. I'll get it," C'ton said, waving his hand in the general direction, producing a dense cloud of water vapor and directing it towards the tree. The flame was extinguished in a sizzling hiss of grey smoke. "I'll teach you how to do that later."

Chapter Twelve:

The Creature

"The flow of energy between the two of you has bound you with it. If you are to exert control over it, you must think controlling thoughts."

C'ton informing J'son on how to manage his pet.

"With everyone practicing witchcraft, I'm surprised we're not attracting... What was that?" T'mer was about to mention parasitic thought forms showing up to feed on their energy expenditures when he heard something moving behind them, coming up from the direction of the crossroad. He wasn't the only one to hear it, either.

"I heard it, too." T'mar said, spinning around to look behind them.

"I guess I should have said something earlier," J'son said. "But I think we are being watched. I've heard noises for a while now, sounds of movement just beyond my sight."

"Watched? More like hunted." T'mer was more excited than apprehensive. Drawing himself up to his full height and thrusting his chest out, he moved hastily in the direction of the sound, armed only with his clenched fists and his need to break something. Such willful ignorance of danger was a hallmark of his kind.

"Wait, T'mer. We don't know what's out there." T'mar was too late with her warning. T'mer had moved beyond her subtle control and he would meet the owner of that sound on his own terms.

About fifty feet away, T'mer stopped with his balled-up fists in front of him and his legs spread wide, ready for a fight. "Come out in the open. What are you, another Wizard? I'll beat you to a pulp."

Slowly, with deliberate intension, a large object, a creature of some sort crept out from behind a huge tree that had fallen on its side. The creature was invisible, or rather not solid, its shape only guessed at based on a glowing outline. Half of its body was still hidden behind the tree, but what could be seen of it indicated it was much larger than T'mer with two, tree-like stumps for legs supporting an enormous head covered in what could only be described as fluorescent fur.

It was radiating an intense violet color, but its head and upper body were transparent and objects could be seen through it, like looking through a window pane. It raised itself up on its front legs and moved out from behind the cover of the tree, the rest of its body following, revealing a long, snake-like torso with smaller and thinner back legs, ending in a tapered tail with more of that fluorescent fur covering the tip.

"T'mer, be careful. It feeds on energy, especially emotional energy like fear and hatred." T'mar knew he would resent her for telling him to be careful and implying that he might be afraid, but she also knew he didn't know what he was up against. "Just try to remain calm. I don't think we have the energy stores it would waste its time on. It's probably just interested in what we are doing."

"Don't be too sure that we wouldn't provide a nice snack for it," C'ton cautioned. "For it to be visible and expend its own energy would indicate that it is more than just curious about us. That is a thought form that has been called forth, and according to J'son it has been following us for a while." C'ton knew why it had become visible. It had sensed the possibly unlimited resources of J'son. And it was also possible that J'son himself had called it out without knowing it."

"Just back up slowly, T'mer, and don't turn your back on it. It's here for J'son, I think," C'ton continued.

"For me? What does it want me for?"

"It's okay, J'son," C'ton said reassuringly. "If it wanted our energy, we would be dead already."

The creature, swaying back and forth on its massive legs, lumbered over to T'mer, sniffed at him and then walked around him. Passing him, it wrapped its long tail loosely around T'mer's body and twitching it, spun him to the ground. Completely ignoring its helpless prey lying on his back stunned, the creature quickly made its way over to J'son, stopping before him and lowering its hind quarters into a sitting position. Its head towered over J'son and he found himself staring at its chest, or rather through its chest, and he saw T'mer slowly getting up off the ground a short distance away.

"Steady, J'son. I think I know what's going on," C'ton said. "See if you can imagine it having a solid body. Picture it getting smaller by reducing its radiance. Imagine it becoming increasingly more solid and dense. Use your mind, J'son and make it three dimensional."

Although J'son heard everything C'ton said, keeping himself calm was another matter entirely. He felt himself quivering with nervous energy and he thought he saw tiny particles of energy flowing out of him and being absorbed by this creature. Standing there, staring at its chest, he noticed a slight fluctuation in the color spectrum of the creature. His nervousness was feeding the creature and it was responding in kind. The creature stood back up on all fours and sniffed at him, smelling the fear coming off of him.

"J'son, calm down. It thinks it belongs to you, but you're scaring it. You're confusing it. Relax and think of it as a beloved pet. It only wants to bond with you. It's a part of you. Don't reject it!" C'ton was trying his best to sound unruffled.

A beloved pet? He could do that, J'son thought, and he had just the pet in mind. Forcing his eyes closed against his increasing fear, he pictured a dog that he had known long ago, a friend that he had grown up with and was a part of his childhood, a happy time that he dearly missed. The image that he conjured up was one that had been stored in his memory since the time he could remember and a smile came to his lips remembering that time. As he relaxed and his thoughts became reverie, he heard what could only be described as a deep, contented growl, a purring almost coming from the creature. Then he felt a large, wet, rough, fleshy tongue soaking his head and chest in foul-smelling slobber.

Opening his eyes and craning his neck upward, he found himself looking into the partially opened, fanged-filled mouth of a hideous looking, dog-like face with a nose as large as a 55-gallon barrel. Its thick, magenta-color tongue hung out at the corner of its mouth panting. Its black eyes were as large as J'son's head and they appeared happy and playful, bouncing around in their sockets with a curious depth to them. Its fur radiated out around its face like the mane of a lion and its ears were long and floppy. The rest of its body was smooth without any fur, except for the tail. Overall, it looked friendly enough and J'son reached out a hand to rub its chest.

"Don't touch it! Are you nuts?" T'mer was standing now, paying particular attention to its tail.

T'mer's voice spooked them both and the creature turned on a dime and was on top of T'mer before J'son knew what was happening. T'mer was floored by the massive beast and landed flat on his back, his large arms and chest looking like a stick figure compared to the creature's heaving chest. The low growl that sounded like a purr before was now a burning snarl filled with hatred. Its mouth was opened and large drops of spit fell out, drenching T'mer's face. The creature lowered its head, mere inches away from ripping T'mer's face off.

Instinctively, J'son said, "That's enough, boy. Come here."

The creature pulled back and looked over at J'son, an inquisitive expression on its face. Seeing J'son waving to it, the creature bounded into the air, arching its back, and flipped over, landing on all fours in front of J'son, waiting for approval.

"Good boy, good boy," J'son said thumping its chest with a balled up fist. "I think I will call you 'tok."

"Interesting," C'ton said. "I believe you have a new pet, created out of your memory and using your energy to sustain itself. Well done!"

"Well done?" T'mar said in disbelief. She had been quiet the whole time, more out of shock at what she was witnessing than fear. "J'son, you have to get rid of it before it drains you of all power and then comes after us. This beast is dangerous and you don't have the training to keep it under control."

"And you do?" J'son asked sarcastically. The creature, 'tok, had rolled over onto its back and J'son had moved around in order to scratch its belly. "I know this animal and he wouldn't hurt me or you."

"You don't know what you are talking about. This creature is just like the psychic parasites that we encountered earlier. That's probably where we picked it up. It will feed on you until you are used up and don't have the power to banish it. Do it now, J'son, before it is too late."

"She may be right," C'ton said thoughtfully. "How do you feel? Do you feel sluggish in your thoughts or physically exhausted?"

"Not at all. In fact, I feel rejuvenated and energized, like I just got a good night's sleep. Besides, I can see waves of force coming from me into him and back again. Actually, what I'm getting back is more than what I'm sending out. It seems that I am feeding off of him."

J'son did appear stronger and much more confident, something that bothered T'mar deeply. She had heard of self-perpetuating creatures, but never one that fed the host once it came into being. Never had she heard of such a thing that J'son had just described. Everything was about energy and it was crazy to think that a creature would give of itself to the benefit of the host. These energy parasites were just that: vicious vermin that would suck the life out of you if given the chance. What J'son was describing was some kind of symbiotic, mutually-beneficial relationship. This was unheard of, unless it was actually feeding off of them without their knowledge.

"It makes me nervous, J'son. I don't think you should keep it around. It's good for nothing, and soon it will need to feed."

"It's a 'Him' and his name is 'tok. I won't get rid of him unless he becomes a threat. Get up, 'tok. I want to ride you."

The creature, knowing exactly what J'son wanted, twisted its shoulders and sprang off of his back, landing on his feet. Kneeling down to one side and bending a leg to act as a step, 'tok purred willingly, rubbing his massive head up against J'son to direct him up on top.

"I'm not getting anywhere near that thing," T'mer said while walking around 'tok, giving him a wide margin.

"Yeah, I didn't think so. Besides, I don't think he would let you. What about you guys? We can make better time by riding."

"I don't think so," T'mar said, still skeptical and wary. "I'll walk with T'mer."

"Suit yourself. What about you, C'ton. He won't bite." J'son was having a good time with it all and he was starting to sound a little condescending.

"But of course, my friend. It has been a while since I rode a beast."

"He's not a beast. He's just an oversized puppy."

"Of course he is. I meant no offence." With a running start, C'ton jumped up on 'tok's still bent leg and landed on his back just behind J'son. He thought it was smart to take J'son up on his offer, to be seen by 'tok as a friend of J'son's and to bond with the creature, just in case things started to go bad. T'mar and T'mer rejecting the offer could only be bad news. What he knew of these creatures, loyalty was very rare and not something to be turned down lightly. These creatures could turn on you in a heartbeat, especially if they got hungry. He had to destroy one of his own creations a long time ago and he had only escaped certain death by convincing his creature that he loved it.

C'ton was also a little concerned about J'son's attitude. He could understand J'son's confidence at his ability to produce and handle a creature of this magnitude, but his confidence in himself bordered on arrogance, and the size of the creature he produced matched an ego that was untrained and inexperienced. No Wizard, no matter what level, would so readily exert such a display of power. J'son was tipping his hand, even if he wasn't aware of it, and making everyone around him nervous. T'mar was right to be so scared. What if J'son's character was such that he liked the idea of possessing so much power? What if he became a tyrant, a bully with a quick temper and lacking the training to cool himself? Not only would he be a danger to others, he could also become a danger to his own sense of self.

As they started to move along, a jerking, rolling stride that smoothed out as J'son and 'tok adjusted to each other, C'ton decided he would avoid delving deeper into the mysteries with J'son and instead, try to determine his state of mind and the strength of his character. C'ton turned in his seat to look over his shoulder at T'mar and T'mer to see what they were doing and if they were keeping up. Under normal circumstances, they would have left at the first opportunity; at least that was what T'mer would want to do. Instead, he was too sure that T'mar wasn't going to let J'son go without a fight, possibly through deception, something he would have to be on guard against. With enemies behind him and an unknown variable before him, C'ton knew he was in a precarious position.

"So J'son," he began. "How does it feel to be in control of this beast, I mean 'tok?"

"Well, it's not so much that I am in control of him as that we have a kind of agreement. It's hard to explain. I am in contact with him and he is in contact with me. I can feel his emotions, like he doesn't like T'mer. But instead of 'tok devouring him, I can apply a calming influence on him, convincing him that we're okay and to just ignore him, kind of like I do. When I asked you to join us up here, he didn't want you to at first, but I convinced him. He likes you now because you seem at ease and not full of fear. It is fear that drives him to do things that I wouldn't want him to do. He thrives on fear. But don't worry, he's loyal to me."

"Loyal to you, maybe, but what about the rest of us?"

'tok stopped moving and J'son turned around to face C'ton, a cold smile crossing his face. "As long as you don't try to take advantage of me you'll be fine. Let's go. It will be dark soon."

J'son really didn't know what he was saying, talking about it getting dark. What he didn't know was that the darkness would come, slowly and completely, but not like the way he thought. On this world, darkness came because the light receded, and then the monsters would come out to devour and destroy. The darkness was one of the reasons why everyone tried to find a portal to escape this world, that or a place of security, sometimes holing up with the monks in the Temple. But that decision mostly led to a servant/master relationship, and unless one had the proper training it could lead to all sorts of difficulties. C'ton was one of the lucky ones, not needing the monks or a portal, at least not now. He had spent his time in the oblivion of service and had managed to survive until the light had returned. He had been changed by the ordeal, of course, but he still maintained his sense of self, and the ability to love.

"I'm sure we will get there before the darkness comes," C'ton said.

"I guess so, but it seems like it has been daylight forever and I'm getting hungry. I think we will stop in a little while to eat."

C'ton didn't like how J'son just said that and his first impulse was to think about 'tok. Obviously J'son hadn't learned that he didn't need to eat anymore. With his ability to absorb energy from everything around him, eating was more of an instinctual, pleasurable attachment to a way of life that was now in his past. C'ton wondered if J'son even had a clue that he had been forever transformed by his experiences here on this world and would never be able to return to his old life, even if he wanted to. C'ton wouldn't explain this to him, of course, and he thought it would be a good idea to let him go on thinking he needed to eat.

Trying to see the lines of force emanating off of J'son to determine the source of his hunger, C'ton was troubled to see that 'tok wasn't giving back more than he was getting from J'son and that the energy exchange was leaving J'son with a deficit, a shortage that he would need to fill if he was going to maintain control of his "Pet." Normal food wouldn't be enough to replenish his energy stores, and soon 'tok would begin to feed off of them to maintain his physicality, only turning on J'son when they were depleted. It was hard for him to see how much raw energy J'son had access to, especially if he didn't understand the proper way to feed.

A monk fed on everything around them, just like this creature. But while a monk fed slowly, strengthening himself without draining those around him, this creature would gorge himself before anyone knew what was happening. T'mer would be the first to go. He would start to feel tired and weak, and then he would collapse in a heap, only to have his body dissolve into a billion particles of low frequency energy. If the creature became hungry and J'son wasn't aware of it, T'mer would be dead within minutes. C'ton didn't think T'mar would fare any better, even with her advanced training. Stopping to eat would be good, but convincing J'son to dissolve this creature would be even better.

They had been riding along in silence for a while when J'son spoke up and asked: "Those blue beings that I saw before. Who are they?"

"That, my friend, is hard to explain. They are everything that we are not. They exist in a dimension that is so alien to ours and yours that it would be accurate to say that they don't exist at all. In their dimension, their realm, the realm of light, there is no thought, for thinking is the wellspring of creation and a sinful mind would only create evil."

"I don't understand. You mean that they are evil?"

"Oh, no! They are pure and beyond the concept of good and evil. It is when we contemplate them that the potential for evil is formulated. To see them is to experience a phenomenon that is represented within the mind as appearing blue. What you saw, or more accurately, what you thought you saw was just a feeble attempt to make sense of the psychic impression that they left on your consciousness. Truly, it is easier to say that they don't exist at all."

"So it was just a hallucination?" This was getting confusing and J'son started to wonder if C'ton was doing it on purpose.

"I guess 'hallucination' is as good a word as any."

"So if I see them again, or experience them as you say, I should just ignore it?"

"It's not so much seeing as hearing. Their existence is based on vibration. It's what they say and how you react that gives them reality. For what is real is determined by how it affects us. One man's hallucination is another man's reality."

"If that's true, how do I know when they are talking to me?"

"If you silence yourself, you can hear them."

J'son grew quiet again thinking about what C'ton had just said. What did he mean by silencing himself? Was he talking about meditation or some yogic, blissful state that he needed to obtain? He just didn't understand. What he did know, though, was that by thinking and imagining he was able to create anything he desired, like 'tok. Even now, 'tok was a constant image within his mind, like a problem that needed resolution. J'son stopped himself. 'tok wasn't a problem and the fact that that analogy popped into his mind disturbed him.

'tok growled beneath him and shuddered slightly, pausing a moment in mid stride and then continued on. J'son wasn't sure, but he felt that 'tok had read his mind and 'tok didn't like being thought of as a problem, either. He was tired and his thoughts were falling, becoming dark. He tried to dismiss the feeling as fatigue, but it seemed more than that. They had been riding a long time and J'son looked up at the sky and noticed the sun was dimmer, redder, but not because it was going down. The sun was still in the same location it had been when he saw it the first time from the mouth of the cave. It was getting dimmer because it seemed to be moving away, becoming physically smaller in the sky.

Chapter Thirteen:

The Lake

"There's a Castle that sits in a blasted-out, devastated area, desolate and foreboding. There you will find the answers you seek."

The Transcendentals giving J'son direction

Turning away from the sun and blinking in spite of the diminished light, J'son exhaled an exhausted sigh. The path rounded a gently sloping mound and brought them into an open, level area. Before them was a large body of liquid, bright green in color, that J'son determined was a lake. It was oblong, egg shaped, with the smaller end closest to them and widening as it spread out. The lake was fed by a network of several small streams that seemingly appeared out of nowhere, literally bursting out of the ground and from under large boulders that surrounded the lake on the far bank.

The lake proper was at least a mile around, flanked by the low folds of the departing mountains on one side and a grassy blue meadow on the other. The surface of the water was still and reflected the sky like a mirror, giving it the appearance of great depth. The road followed along the edge of the lake, running the length of it and continued away to the right. The trees had all but disappeared, replaced by low lying orange shrubs filled with purple berries.

J'son leaned forward and patted 'tok on the top of his head. "Okay boy. This looks like a good spot. Let's stop here and get some rest and something to eat."

'tok left the road immediately and lumbered down to the water's edge, crossing a thin patch of grass and stopping once his front paws hit the water. Before J'son and C'ton could get off, 'tok lowered his massive head and plunged his nose into the water, lapping it up with great slurping noises. Except for his tongue, 'tok was stone still and J'son wondered if maybe 'tok had frozen in place.

C'ton was the first to dismount, sliding off of 'tok's back and landing on his feet. He stretched his arms high into the air and arched his back, popping his back in the process. "It's been a while since I rode for that long. Normally I just walk."

J'son was still sitting on top of 'tok, looking down at C'ton and watched him as he moved to the other side of the road, plopped down in the cool grass, crossed his legs and folded his hands in his lap. Although he was watching this, J'son wasn't really paying any attention. He was so exhausted from the ride and he felt the fatigue wash over his mind and body. He knew he should get down and see if those purple berries were edible, but he didn't think he had the strength or the motivation to do so. 'tok was still drinking deeply and J'son thought he could see a physical change in his pet. He appeared to be smaller, not by much, but enough for J'son to notice it. J'son also noticed that the waves of force he had seen before flowing out of him into 'tok and back out again had ceased. Instead, the flow was one way: out of him and into 'tok. There was no back and forth. 'tok was absorbing his energy without giving anything back, but the danger of the situation didn't register at the moment.

Slowly, and with considerable effort, J'son slid off of 'tok's back and rested for a few seconds with his back propped against his pet. He was struggling to catch his breath and J'son forced himself to move away from 'tok, staggering like a drunken man toward C'ton. He came to a stop inches away from C'ton and collapsed in a heap at the feet of the Wizard. His head was down and he tried to say something, but only a mumble came out.

"Mmmteble."

"J'son, I don't mean to tell you what to do, but you shouldn't be this tired. Your… pet is draining you. It's not safe for 'tok to be in such close contact with you. He is, after all, a beast; a wild, stray thought form that needs to be dealt with. It's like reading. Sooner or later you get tired and it's time to close the book. I guess you have noticed that he is no longer returning to you what you give him."

J'son didn't respond, too tired to even formulate an answer. However, after a few minutes of sitting on the ground, absorbing the energy of the grass, J'son was starting to return to normal. He understood what C'ton was trying to say, but some part of him didn't want to "close the book".

"I'm okay. I just need to rest and get something to eat. Are those berries edible?"

"They're suitable for eating, but you shouldn't need to eat. You're tired because 'tok is taking and not giving."

J'son looked over at 'tok and watched him still taking great gulps of the water. The waves of force had changed into particles and he could see tiny specks of lethargic light flowing out of him and impacting 'tok. He didn't understand why he couldn't stop the flow. It was like as long as he was connected to this creature he had to feed it. He closed his eyes and saw a vivid image of 'tok in his mind. He tried to replace the image with something else, but was unable to conjure up anything. His thoughts seemed to be consumed with 'tok and he was having a hard time even remembering what T'mar looked like.

"J'son?" It was C'ton.

"Huh? What?"

"I asked you if you were okay. You were sitting there with your eyes closed swaying back and forth. Were you trying to break your connection with 'tok?"

"Not break it, just put it to the side." Shrugging his shoulders, he added, "It's no big deal. I can do it any time I want to."

J'son didn't know why he just lied to C'ton. Maybe it was his own pride that kept him from telling him that he couldn't think of anything besides 'tok. Was it possible that he didn't want to believe C'ton and T'mar were right? He wasn't sure, but sitting here this far away from 'tok made him uneasy. He felt a tug in his head and a sharp pain just behind his eyes. Squinting through the pain, he looked and saw ‘tok was still drinking. J’son chuckled slightly in spite of the pain, imagining the lake drained of water before ‘tok had his fill. The thought drove the pain into the background and lightened his mood considerably. He stood up without saying anything more and walked back over to his pet.

Reaching out with a slightly shaking hand, he patted ‘tok’s side. ‘tok finally stopped drinking and turned his head to look at J’son. J’son gave him a tired smile and then made his way over to a bush that was located a few feet away, closer to ‘tok than where C’ton was sitting. The close proximity made him feel better, although he still didn’t feel quite right. He started to pick one of the berries off of the bush and got stabbed by a thorn, causing him to pull his hand away before grabbing the fruit. The pain in his finger gave him renewed focus and for the first time since encountering ‘tok his only thought was one of anger at being so foolish that he allowed himself to be pricked.

“Damn!” he said, sticking his wounded finger into his mouth. His blood had a metallic taste and he spit it out on the ground.

‘tok had gone back to drinking but raised his head again at the sound of J’son spitting. Smelling the blood, he turned away from the water’s edge and began sniffing the air.

“He’s attracted to the blood,” C’ton said, standing up and moving toward J’son. “Blood has the highest concentration of organic energy. He won’t do anything to you, but if that had been T’mer, especially in his present state, he would have attacked and killed him. J’son, it’s just not a good idea to keep him around, at least not at the size he is now. May I suggest that you make him smaller?”

“Smaller?” J’son was staring at the small bead of blood forming on the tip of his finger with a frown on his face. “What do you mean by smaller?”

“You can shrink his energy demands by making him smaller in size. You can still keep him around, but he won’t be as hard to handle and he won’t be such a drain on your resources. Just try to imagine him the size of a puppy and hold that thought until it becomes real. It won’t hurt him and, I think, it will make him happier.”

J’son nodded his head and closed his eyes. The image of ‘tok loomed large within his mind. He pictured himself standing besides 'tok, a minuscule boy next to an elephant sized dog. The image frightened him and he felt himself shaking, quivering. In his mind the image changed and now he saw clearly 'tok bending over and biting his head off. He screamed and his eyes snapped opened. He was staring directly into the eyes of a large, menacing creature that only slightly resembled his beloved dog. Its mouth was opened wide and filled with large fangs dripping with saliva.

"Easy, J'son. He's still your creation. You've just confused him. Try again, but without any doubt. Think comforting thoughts and try to convince him that you are trying to help him with his hunger. Picture yourself as the strong one who only wants the best for him."

C'ton was watching the two of them carefully, not too sure if J'son had the mental focus or strength to pull it off. It surprised him to see 'tok respond the way he did to whatever J'son had imagined. Although C'ton was keeping his distance, he knew that if 'tok turned on J'son, he would be the next to go. Preparing himself against such a possibility, C'ton raised his hands before him and moved them in a clockwise motion, one hand starting on top and the other down below, crossing in the middle. Normally, he knew, that motion would have caught the attention of 'tok, and more than likely brought the creature down on him in one fell swoop. Instead, he took the chance that 'tok was too pre-occupied with J'son to notice. Nevertheless, the energy shield he was creating would eventually attract the attention of this energy-starved beast.

J'son tried again, closing his eyes and forcing himself to remain calm. This time, he imagined himself as being larger than 'tok, hands on his hips and bending over slightly, like a loving master scolding a misbehaving pet. In his mind, 'tok lowered his head and his shoulders slumped, whimpering and looking ashamed. J'son projected warm, loving thoughts towards his dog, kneeling down in his mind and rubbing his face against the dog's nose. He wrapped his arms around 'tok's neck and held him in a tight embrace, just like he had done a thousand times before in his childhood.

"Well Done!" C'ton exclaimed. "You are indeed a mighty Wizard in your own right."

J'son opened his eyes and found himself, in fact, kneeling down beside an animal no bigger than a large dog, his arms wrapped around 'tok's neck like he had just imagined. He pulled away slightly and gazed into his eyes, seeing a loving, happy puppy, full of energy and in high spirits, glad that he had pleased his master. J'son, too, felt rejuvenated and full of energy, like a heavy burden had been lifted and he felt a delighted and cheerful spirit flooding his body and mind. He stood up and patted his chest, motioning for 'tok to jump up and rest his paws on his shoulders. 'tok responded immediately, licking J'son's face and neck.

"Okay boy. Okay. Good boy. I feel great," he said, turning towards C'ton for the first time. "What's that?"

C'ton had collapsed his personal security field when he saw that J'son had been successful. However, when J'son had just looked at him there were residual energy fluctuations still in the air surrounding him, invisible of course to the naked eye but still noticeable to J'son.

"Just a precaution. It's nothing for you or 'tok to be concerned about." A smile had returned to C'ton's face, giving it warmth and radiating kindness, just like when J'son had seen him at first.

"Who needs to eat now? Get down, boy. Good boy. I feel like I could pick T'mer up and toss him around like a rag doll. Where are they anyway?"

"By making 'tok smaller, you absorbed his energy. To sustain a creature as massive as 'tok takes incredible amounts of energy; he'll be happier now that he doesn't need to absorb so much energy to maintain that size. And he's much more manageable this way. As far as where the other two are, your guess is as good as mine. I suggest we wait for them here and enjoy the cool waters of the lake. You may not need it now, but those berries really are tasty."

Chapter Fourteen:

Some Background

"I really do care about you, T'mar. Why do you feel the need to manipulate me? I would never hurt you."

T'mer trying to encourage T'mar on their way to the Lake

As J'son and C'ton worked their fingers between the thorns of the bushes, probing for berries, T'mar and T'mer were making their way towards them at a leisurely pace. They had fallen behind, more on purpose than because of the speed that 'tok travelled. T'mar had wanted to keep some distance between the two groups in order to speak with T'mer in private and to continue to manipulate him into doing what she wanted. She knew he didn't like not being in charge, especially when wizards were around. She also knew that he was intimidated by J'son, not knowing what he or 'tok were capable of. She didn't like the idea of a 'tpo, a familiar of that size and strength running around loose and out of control. No matter what J'son may say, she didn't think he had it in him to subdue the beast if it came to it.

B'el had kept a creature like that around and allowed it to devour anyone it wanted to. Although he had said the creature was incapable of hurting her, still it had frightened her whenever it was around. She remembered a time when she had been walking down a wide, dark corridor in B'el's Castle when out of nowhere the creature appeared and stood in front of her, looking menacingly at her and growling, like a beast ready to attack. She froze in her tracks, unable to move, but she managed to speak to it, telling it to get out of her way. B'el had told her that it would obey her commands, if she wielded the authority to do so. It was cryptic in the way he had said it, almost as if telling her that if she didn't live up to her training the beast would sense it and destroy her for her error.

Summoning up all the courage she could muster and calming her mind, dispelling the fear that always waited in the shadows, she had spoken to it in a voice of command and power. The creature, whom B'el had never given a name, which was dangerous in itself, continued to stare at her, sizing her up, deciding if it recognized her authority, before it moved to the side of the hall, allowing her to pass. The memory of that time caused her to shudder at the thought and she stopped walking long enough to collect herself, trying to dispel the terror of that time. She took a couple of shaky breaths, blowing them out as quietly as possible to keep T'mer from noticing, but he did any way.

"What's the matter?" he asked gently, not sounding so harsh now that he saw she was upset about something. It was easier for him to lower his guard when it was just the two of them. Without having to concern himself with putting up a front and how he looked to others, he allowed his ego to be fully stroked and he wanted to come to her rescue.

"Nothing," she said, smiling sweetly at him for his gentleness and then she started walking again. "I was just thinking about C'ton. I think I know who he is. I've seen him before, but a long time ago."

"You were thinking about B'el again. I can tell. Don't lie to me. You always get like this whenever you think about him." He stopped her by putting his hands on her shoulders and looking intently into her eyes. "You don't ever have to worry about him again. I'm here to protect you from him or anyone else that would try to harm you. As long as we're together, nothing can break the bond between us." It was silly to talk this way, but he knew she liked to hear it.

T'mar smiled at him again, her face softening and growing more beautiful. The diminishing sun gave her features a warm, golden glow that went very well with her red hair and green eyes. She stopped shaking, feeling the strength of his hands on her round shoulders and liking the comfort that he was providing. It was so hard here finding that level of commitment and loyalty in another person. Everyone on this world had ulterior motives for everything they did, not like on Earth where love flourished. But all of that would change, of course, when The War came. Then love would die here, as well as there, never to be reborn again. Only the Transcendentals could change that. They were the originators and the generators of that life-changing force.

She reached up and touched his cheek with the tip of her finger, gently caressing the lines of his face, softening them, rounding them out and easing the pinched look that gave him that familiar X. Her touch was very alluring and it opened him up to her. She didn't have to probe his mind to get the desired effect. By being vulnerable and showing him her fears, his defenses dropped and the man that had risked everything for her came through. The way he was right then, it would have been too easy to implant more controls within his mind, but she couldn't bring herself to do it. This, she knew, was his true self, the one she had fallen in love with. To manipulate him felt like a betrayal, turning him into an automaton that only did what she wanted because she compelled him to.

There would be another argument between the two of them once they made it to lake where they would have to decide whether they were going toward the City or to stay with J'son. It would be so easy to take that argument away now and avoid the fight altogether, but every time she had to install blocks it weakened him, taking away his will to resist, turning him into someone she couldn't respect. No. She wouldn't do it, even if it meant he took the road that would take him to the City where there would be light and stability. There was knowledge among the monks, but not the type T'mer would accept nor appreciate.

He didn't like travelling back and forth through portals, and as far as she knew he had done it only once. He was too strong willed and, if the truth be told, narrow minded to make the transition from this world to Earth advantageous. Because of his lack of training, he didn't have the ability to interact with humans three-dimensionally once he got there. For him, it was a world of shadow where the voices of the lost were heard in psychotic clarity. She could make him go with her, but that wouldn't be fair to him. He would be more of a disembodied spirit under her constant control than her lover. In fact, she reminded herself, there had been others that had abandoned this world and all hope of finding love for the god-like powers that Earth provided.

She had the ability and the training to materialize on Earth, and she did enjoy the time that she had spent there, becoming almost like a god, having the power to create and distort their reality as she saw fit. Humans were her play things and she could have anyone she chose, sexually and otherwise, but the temptations were just too great.

She knew she could become like the Adepts of old, creating a religion around herself and demanding the worship of her subjects. She had access to the power, especially over there, to bring T'mer with her, allowing him to materialize, but then he would always be dependent on her, feeding off of her, weakening her. In the end, she would have to destroy him, scattering his energy particles throughout an unknown world never again to be reconstituted, except within her mind. The only thing that would be left of him would be her memory, a hopelessly flawed memory at that. She couldn't do that, not even for the possibility of obtaining a permanent portal.

She didn't even know if J'son would be aware enough to hold the door open once he made it back for her to come through. She didn't know if she would be able to find him again once he did go back. How they found each other before was by accident. That she was sure of. It was only luck that brought the two of them together. True, she had been pursuing B'el, but becoming three-dimension in the vicinity of J'son's hometown was a fluke. She had only latched onto J'son because of the strength of his sexual attraction to her, and the innate power of his dreaming mind. She was, after all, his dream girl, or at least she had been.

Things had changed so much since he came here. Even if he were to go back, would he still dream about her and open the portal into his world? She didn't know. Without realizing it, T'mar had just decided that she wouldn't coerce T'mer to follow J'son to the monks, nor without him would she go. The long dark would come and she would bare it out with T'mer at her side.

"I think the lake is just around that bend," T'mer said, taking the lead. "I can smell the moisture in the air."

"T'mer," she started, but then trailed off.

"What?" he called over his shoulder.

"Nothing. I'm just glad you are here."

T'mar followed after T'mer, her head down, feeling melancholy. The internal battle that she had been waging with herself had been won and she moved with the downcast motivation of someone that had accepted the outcome of defeat. In the end, it was her love for T'mer that had dealt the deciding blow. It was the same weakness, the blemish within herself that B'el had pointed out to her. It was that defect, or so B'el had said, that kept her from obtaining the coveted title that he had offered her. It was that error that caused her to fail the last test, the one that caused her to flee for her life and seek out the help of T'mer.

She admonished herself that she even entertained the idea of using J'son to beg B'el for leniency. She even contemplated using J'son to usurp the throne of B'el. What a ridiculous and dangerous thought that was, and fool-hearty. B'el would have read her emotions and her intensions the moment she came before him. He would destroy her and take J'son and there wouldn't be anything she could do about it. He would use J'son and open the portal to all of his servants, thereby filling Earth with all manner of evil.

The War may be coming as prophesized, but she wouldn't help B'el in that way. The only hope for Earth, and herself, lay in preventing B'el from entering in all his might. If she could only postpone what must surely come to pass, maybe for another age, then maybe the Transcendentals would forgive her and allow her entrance into the domain of peace. Maybe. Just maybe.

"There it is!" T'mer shouted, pointing a finger at the mirror-like surface down below. "And it looks like they are waiting for us. I don't see that beast anywhere around. What do you think happened to it?"

T'mar came up beside him and looked down at the water. She could see J'son and C'ton sitting on the far side of the road away from the water eating something, probably the berries that thrived and flourished along the edge of the water. She squinted into the diminishing light of the sun, cupping her hand across her forehead, straining to see if she could locate 'tok. Not knowing where he might be put them at a disadvantage and she could feel herself tensing up, preparing to defend herself and T'mer in the event of an attack. She was surprised that she couldn't detect the energy fluctuations that a creature of his size would inevitably produce. The life force of every living thing around should be flowing towards him like the spiral of light around a black hole. Everything should be drawn to his location.

"I don't know."

"Do you think it is still around?" T'mer had dropped his hand and was scanning the meadow below looking for anything large enough that might be 'tok. The X was prominent across his face, a sure sign of aggression.

"I don't know. Unless J'son dissolved him, dispersing his energy and reabsorbing his mental construct, I should be able to see something, but I don't."

"Maybe that's what he did."

"If J'son has that ability, then I'm really impressed. Once you let out a creature that massive and powerful, it is extremely difficult to put it back in again. Without proper training, trying to absorb that much raw energy would puncture his psychic membrane, destroying him in the process. But I doubt that has happened because he looks too comfortable and rested." She remembered what B'el had said about his creature, the one she had to confront in the corridor. He had told her that he would never chance dissolving it so long as it behaved itself. "Too risky."

"I guess the only thing to do is go down there and see what's up. Be on your guard, T'mar. I'm expecting that thing to materialize the moment we are within striking distance of them." T'mer started down the slope when he was interrupted by T'mar.

"What's that up there?"

Chapter Fifteen:

The Platform of 'vsn

"This place is sacred to the monks. It is a place of rest and reflection. It would do you good to close your eyes and allow the serenity to wash over you."

C'ton's suggestion to J'son upon reaching the Lake

J'son and C'ton had enjoyed their time sitting by the lake and eating berries, more for the refreshing taste than the need to rest and re-energize. 'tok ran around like a puppy, chasing his snake-like tail with the tuff of fur on the end and diving into the lake, hot on the trail of something aquatic. He swam to the other side of the lake and disappeared between the folds of the hills. J'son watched him for a while until he lost sight of him behind one of the larger mounds and then he fell on his back with his fingers laced behind his head, savoring the dim, cooling light of the sun on his face and chest, loving the feel of the furry grass caressing his back. The wind blew and the tiny, fleece-like fibers of the grass tickled him along his rib cage.

His mind started to drift off, not due to fatigue but because of relaxation. His thoughts floated away and he experienced a not too unpleasant buzzing sensation, a feeling of separation, like he was leaving his body and hovering above it. Images flooded his awareness, but he was too relaxed and carefree to hold any of them for too long. He saw scenes of him and T'mar talking with each other, but not from here. In those scenes he felt a longing for her that felt real, but only in the past tense. He saw himself as a young, naive man groping for her, his loins stirring and becoming excited at the thought of her. The skirt covering his pelvic region moved slightly and he felt his heart rate speed up, but he ignored it and fell deeper into himself.

Then from somewhere outside of his physical body he heard the sound of what could only be describe as a gargling, strangled, choked bark, like the sound of an animal dying that had been struck by a heavy object, its body crushed. The sound entered his ears while lying on the grass by the side of the road, but it registered within his consciousness floating a million miles away. The sound tugged on him and he felt the first stirrings of fear, thinking that either his physical body was in danger or that 'tok had been injured. He heard the sound again and that brought him back to the reality of the lake and the surrounding countryside. He was still out of his body, but now he was cognizant of the sights and expressions of the life around him.

From somewhere overhead, he saw his body reclining peacefully beneath him and C'ton sitting up next to him. C'ton was looking across the lake and up into the hills beyond. He was straining to see something that had caught his attention and he had an inquisitive, curious look on his face. Whatever he was looking at brought him amusement and J'son could see a broad smile forming on his face. C'ton looked over at J'son lying silently next to him and whispered something into his ear. J'son saw his body move in response before he registered what C'ton had said.

Somehow connected to the force of life all around, experiencing a form of cosmic consciousness and empathy for everything, J'son was able to sort and prioritize the jumble of images flowing through his mind and concentrate on what C'ton had said. In his mind, experiencing the words as a parade of symbolic vibrations, he "heard" what he had said.

"I believe I found your dog."

Guiding his thoughts in the direction of C'ton's gaze, J'son saw 'tok high up in the hills, standing on a natural platform that connected and was situated between two hills. The hills were among the tallest in the area and the platform gave them the look of a giant stool, with 'tok in the center barking out his location. 'tok was glowing like before when J'son first encountered him, but he was still small. The energy flowing out of him lit up the sky in swirling concentric circles, and instead of looking down on C'ton and J'son lying in the grass 'tok was staring up into the heavens, like he was talking to the angels, or more specifically, like he was aware that J'son was floating high above the lake and meadow far below. 'tok wouldn't stop barking, like he was beckoning for J'son to come join him.

Becoming more conscious of his surroundings but still detached from his body, J'son thought himself down to the platform, calming 'tok in the process but not so much that he settled down completely. As if responding to his presence, 'tok became semi-corporal, his head and front haunches becoming three dimensional while the back part of him remained ethereal. J'son stood next to him, his hand and lower arm solidifying and as he patted 'tok on his head he thought, "Good boy."

'tok was still bouncing around, more ethereal than corporal, trying his best to get J'son's attention, pulling on him and nudging him, directing his energy to flow out and down to the lake below. There, acting like a giant mirror, was the lake staring up at him, reflecting the static, hazy glow of the sky above and the dimming outline of the Dome, the energy field. The scene reminded J'son of a giant, visual echo, giving him the impression of a crystal ball able to discern the future. Nothing could be seen in the reflection except the sky above, but J'son thought he could just perceive the beginning of dim constellations.

Then, much to his chagrin, the constellations began to move and started to swirl around themselves, faster and faster, until they crashed into each other, falling toward the center, then exploding outward in a violent, blinding turmoil of disorder. All of this was seen as a reflection on the surface of the water and then the image changed, becoming milky white. Slowly, the pasty, opaque mirage separated, pushing the whiteness out to the sides, leaving a dark, blank slate without images. J'son was now staring into blackness, straining to make out anything. All grew dark and even the hills disappeared, leaving a singular void without movement.

J'son now found himself outside of the known universe, a shining ball of conscious energy floating alone in the void. Panic seized him and fear gripped his mind. Thoughts of death and destruction took hold of his thinking and his comprehension became cloudy and confused. The clarity of before was gone and he was left with just the sensory impressions of a body that had given up all hope of life. As he descended into this abyss of despair, the last thought that he could reasonably contemplate was the awareness of another ball of chaotic white light, immensely larger than him, floating nearby, self-contained and complete.

Reaching out with the last threads of consciousness he possessed, J'son willed himself closer to the gigantic mass that pulsated and crashed like an electrical storm. He didn't know what it represented, or even if the object had a reality outside his own mind, but something told him to merge with it, fearing obliteration if he failed. The object was so large that only its curvature could be detected in comparison to his insignificant ball of light. The surface of the object was flawless, like the surface of a marble, but deep within could be seen deformities and blemishes, the results of countless mortal choices that had gone horribly wrong.

He moved closer to the object and felt himself make contact with the leading edge. Instantly, he was bombarded with impressions of condemnation and static, a tempest of negativity and slander, a conviction of guilt and blame that now demanded payment in full. Without an advocate to turn to, nor the mind to comprehend the tragic character of the encountered, J'son struggled to penetrate the membrane of the universe that had unceremoniously thrown him out. He was a lost soul detached and alienated from the source of life. All was in despair and darkness took over.

Then there was a voice, a vibration that imprinted itself within the shadows of his psyche, turning the stones of his mind into fire, enlightening him once again. The vibration took the shape of one of the Transcendentals and it was reaching out to him in the darkness. It gave him purpose and meaning, telling him to ignore the disapproval of a dead world and instead to focus on the perfect living manifestation of existence. He was to continue on his journey and take his companions with him. Together, they would balance and harmonize life on all worlds. First, though, he would have to learn a secret that no one could teach him. He would have to be determined and have singleness of mind. Only then would he find and ultimately understand this secret, and with that knowledge he would return to his world.

The encounter was overwhelming and frightening, throwing his awareness back into the turmoil of the glowing orb, piercing its barrier, returning him to the realm of three-dimensional reality, moving within and through the chaos, driving out the criticisms and banality of the imaginary from before him. Once this was completed, several things happened all at the same time. Because of the ubiquitous state he now found himself in, J'son was able to register all these things simultaneously. However, as he observed them the order in which he perceived them had no linear meaning; he would have noted T'mar first regardless of the order in which they happened.

T'mar and T'mer were above the lake making their way down when T'mar stopped and pointed at the platform. She saw who she thought was 'tok, semi-corporal, squalling at the sky and then disappearing completely. Standing next to him was J'son, except he wasn't visible in the way that T'mer could detect. He was glowing brighter than the sun, radiating outward and filling the sky, obscuring the hills and the platform with his brilliance. Then his image changed and he seemed to be dissipating, like all of his energy had run out and he was dissolving back into the environment.

T'mar had seen this before during her time with the monks. Some of them, when they had grown tired of life and the endless pursuit of enlightenment, would seek release back into the arms of the universe, hoping to find comfort in another manifestation billions of years in the future, or so that was the belief. They chose death and eradication as the means of transforming themselves into a higher state. They would never be seen again in this age of the universe and so their decision couldn't be proven pragmatically. Whether they progressed up the evolutionary ladder, bypassing the hierarchy and sat in on the Council of the Transcendentals was a matter of faith that could never be confirmed.

B'el, as she knew, would scoff at the idea that perfection could be found in destroying oneself and hoping for a transfiguration into the higher life. He taught that this life was all that mattered and the knowledge one obtained here secured their place among the elite. Even the Adepts were wasting their time, he taught. No amount of study or meditation could promote one to the heights. Only the determined will could transcend this life and bring about the joy of eternity. She didn't think B'el even believe in the reality of the Transcendentals. He thought of them as mental projections of an unbalanced mind. Why progress towards the realm of the Transcendentals if they couldn't even affect the material plane? This life was all that mattered.

She thought of these things in the moments she saw 'tok and J'son high up on the Platform of 'vsn. Then in a blink of an eye, the light faded and she witnessed a glowing ember fall from the sky, striking the water below, disturbing the surface and sinking from view. The platform was now empty and the dark, still waters swallowed up whatever had fallen in. A wave of sorrow and sadness washed over her, like the feeling of tragic loss.

Sitting beside J'son's prone body, C'ton had a different perception. He had seen 'tok up on the platform and leaned over to whisper to J'son that he had found his pet. While he was speaking, 'tok had started to make noise, obviously keyed up and animated. C'ton turned his head to look back up at 'tok when he felt and saw a vibrant, pulsating electrical field envelope J'son's body. It covered his body like a glowing membrane, fully encasing J'son inside, humming and giving off particles of highly-charged packets of energy.

C'ton immediately realized what was happening and fell away from him, hoping to distance himself from what was about to happen. The energy discharge was a precursor of bodily diffusion, where J'son's body would be dissolved and be transported anywhere he chose. The consequence of being in such close proximity to his electrified body could easily disturb C'ton's own energy field, sending him across time and space without his consent. The procedure was especially dangerous in that if J'son wasn't in a protected place once his body materialized he would be unable to shield himself from the energy parasites that would surely come to feed off of his discharge.

Normally, travel of this sort was done in the privacy of a cave or some other shelter where your body was known to be protected and hidden from those who would take advantage of a mind detached from its body. Only after finding another protected place would one chance de-materializing his body and transporting it through the ether. If J'son was transporting himself up to the platform, as C'ton thought, he would be opened to the strange energy flux that surrounded the area. If J'son didn't have complete control and singleness of mind, he might lose his body and forever roam about searching for a suitable vehicle to store his mind.

Within moments after whispering to him, J'son's body disappeared completely and reappeared on top of the platform, standing next to 'tok. Neither of them, J'son nor 'tok, were fully corporal, and their bodily outlines faded in and out, finally disappearing altogether. C'ton didn't know if J'son was having trouble reconstituting or if he was fully aware of his situation. The sky lit up, filling the meadow and hilltops with a luminous intensity reminiscent of an atomic explosion.

C'ton shielded his eyes against the light, cupping his hand and squinting, trying to see what was happening. Then as quick as it started the light faded and C'ton observed what looked like a burnt-out cinder, an ember of rock, falling from the sky and striking the water, spraying a shower of water high into the air and raining back down again. The surface of the lake swallowed up the glowing piece of coal and then smoothed out again, regaining its mirror-like reflection and settling back down. The whole experience took no more than a minute.

As J'son became aware of his physicality again, the cold, dark water cradling his limp, lifeless body, he sank deeper and slowly came to recognize his situation and his inability to breathe. All was dark and cold and he found himself wondering if he would ever stop sinking. From high up on the platform it didn't look like the lake had a bottom, and now he was beginning to realize that if he didn't do something to reverse his descent he might not be able to make it back to the surface. He could see nothing and the pressure in his lungs was becoming unbearable. He felt the different currents buffeting his body, the warm, lighter water fighting its way to the surface while the cold, dense water pulled on him, drawing him down deeper into the abyss.

Somewhere above him he heard a splash and the waters separated. A warm current surrounded him and lifted him up, making him more buoyant. He was no longer sinking and the rush of water supporting him had a curious familiarity to it; smooth but furry at the same time. It was only when he started thinking that some type of fish had him in its mouth that he realized what was keeping him from sinking further. He wrapped his numb, lifeless arms around 'tok, holding him tight and pulling him closer to his chest. 'tok accepted his embrace and took off at an incredible rate, moving upward and breaking the surface within seconds.

J'son struggled to breathe, gasping for air and thrashing around, desperately trying to keep his head above water. His hold on 'tok broke once they reached the surface and his pet was treading water and swimming in circles around J'son. His matted fur made 'tok look like a water-logged beaver with just his head above the water. His snake-like tail trailed behind him and wiggled its way towards J'son, reaching out and wrapping around his waist. 'tok was smaller than before and J'son's weight was pulling them both below the surface once again. 'tok broke away from J'son and turned around, coming at him head first, diving underneath him and resurfacing , supporting J'son on his back before beginning to sink again.

"That's okay, boy," J'son said, choking back water. "Try to make it back to shore."

'tok dog-paddled and twisted his way towards the water's edge, with J'son holding on tight to his tail. The water was getting slightly warmer and J'son took that as a sign they were getting closer to the bank. He was falling in and out of consciousness, like a man trying to claw his way out of a nightmare. He heard voices, but discarded them as figments of his exhaustion. He didn't know what would happen to 'tok if he did pass out, considering they were connected as they were. He resisted the swooning urge to black out, fearing 'tok would disappear forever. It was only his concern for 'tok that got them to the shore.

"J'son! T'mer, help me. Let's get him out of the water!" C'ton was the first to reach him and he waded into the water up to his waist, reaching out to 'tok without thinking that the animal might consider this an attack against his master.

T'mar was the next one in the water; T'mer was too afraid of 'tok to be so bold. While T'mer waited by the bank, T'mar and C'ton grabbed J'son between them and hauled him out of the water. Once on dry land, 'tok immediately put himself between J'son and the others, fully visible but still shrinking. He was now about the size of a poodle. 'tok bared his tiny teeth and squalled, daring them to come too close to J'son. His audacious defense was only matched by his ferocious devotion to J'son, a very rare thing on this planet. The creature's diminutive stature and aggression spoke of a loyalty that went beyond his need to feed. 'tok was sacrificing himself in order to protect J'son. 'tok had enough residual energy left for one good assault and then he would be no more. Even T'mer knew 'tok couldn't do any real damage anymore. 'tok was just about spent.

Laying on his stomach, coughing up water, J'son tried, unsuccessfully, to push himself up on all fours, only to collapse under the effort. With his arms shaking and his chest hurting, he decided to rest, closing his eyes and letting his mind relax. He knew he was safe with T'mar and C'ton looking over him and he smiled to himself at their concern. Except for T'mar when he was poisoned, it was the first real show of compassion he had felt since finding himself on this planet. He felt T'mar's hand resting against his back and her touch communicated to him all the things that a loved one would say in a situation like this. Breathing deeply now and feeling himself drifting off to sleep, he mumbled something that nobody heard. He had told them, "Thank you."

"J'son, you just rest for now. Everything is okay and you're safe." T'mar was more than a bit alarmed, having witness everything and not too sure what it all meant. She surprised herself with her level of unease and confusion.

She had gone from deep sorrow and a sense of personal loss to frenzied apprehension and anxious uncertainty. When she had seen J'son falling from the sky and hitting the water, something inside her, some instinct, had clicked into place and she found herself wanting to risk everything if only he would survive. Later, she would tell T'mer that her only thought was what a waste everything had been. Now, however, she hovered around J'son like a lover hoping for the best in the face of certain death.

"Where's that creature?" T'mer asked, looking away from J'son's prone body and quickly glancing around him, half expecting 'tok to appear out of nowhere and devour them.

"I don't think we need to worry ourselves about him anymore," C'ton said, standing up and helping T'mar to her feet. "I believe J'son re-absorbed him once he was sure they had reached the shore. I've never seen loyalty like that before, and I wouldn't have believed it unless I saw it with my own eyes, but I think 'tok gave up his life force in order to save J'son. Believe it or not, but that creature sacrificed himself for J'son."

T'mar had noticed that also and the very idea frightened her. Why would a creature, even creatures such as themselves, purposely choose annihilation over self-preservation? Once freed from the control of a wizard and its mental link to him, all thought forms, regardless of origination, desired autonomy and free will. At the very least, 'tok should have taken off and found a place where it could feed and recover, becoming a predator and taking its place among the energy parasites like all the others that had escaped their masters and roamed the planet looking for an easy meal.

T'mar scanned the energy fluctuations in the area looking for any tell-tale sign that 'tok was still around. She should have seen his residual energy pattern no matter what happened to him, even if it was too weak to manifest physically. Instead, what she saw was a thinning line of flux radiating out from the forehead of J'son, indicating a leash that should have been connected to 'tok or any other thought projection J'son may have been creating in his slumber.

The fact that it wasn't connected to anything told T'mar, and C'ton, that he had lost connection and couldn't reconnect. Even in his slumber, J'son should have been able to retain a simple projection, a memory. What she saw, and feared, was the weak, thread-like precursor of a novice struggling to create just the rudiments of a mental picture. What she saw was the muddled visualization of every human she had ever encountered.

"Do you think he'll be okay?" she asked C'ton. "I mean, you see it, don't you?"

"Yes, I see it. But I don't understand it. He saw something up there and tried to merge with it. I don't know if he blew his psychic connection or if he has just retreated within himself, some kind of self-defense mechanism. How could he have just lost his abilities and still be corporal. I mean, it doesn't make sense."

"I agree. Nothing about him makes any sense. If he did see something, if he did see them, we have to find out what he knows." T'mar crouched back down beside J'son, rolling him over onto his back and stroked the side of his face, pushing the hair out of his eyes.

"He may not want to tell us what he saw. The Monks who receive a revelation or a prophecy seldom tell others about it."

"You speak like one that has been up there."

"I have, but in another life. I..." C'ton was about to say something else, but then stopped. He looked into T'mar's eyes and smiled, giving nothing away.

"Let me get you and the boy something to eat, T'mar." T'mer walked away from them the moment they started talking about "seeing" things. The speech of wizards always confused him and he neither cared nor wanted to know about what they were talking about. For him, all of this was the imaginings of those with unstable minds. Their fantasies, as he thought of them, were self-imagined and only brought problems.

"I remember you," T'mar said to C'ton cautiously, without looking directly at him, still kneeling beside J'son.

"I wondered if you would acknowledge our history, although that was a long time ago. You were no more than a girl then." C'ton smiled down at her, trying to look pleasant.

"I was a young fool, running after knowledge." She looked up at him and their eyes met. She was frowning and the creases in her face formed a shallow X.

"I hold no grudge against you," C'ton said. "I was just concerned that you were following the wrong path."

T'mar stood up with her head down. She was weary and disillusioned, not sure what she was feeling. "I won't say you were right, but it was a lesson I had to learn on my own. I lost faith in your teachings. You never explained things. You just wanted me to practice without telling me why I was doing what I was doing."

"Did B'el explain things to you?"

"B'el was… a mistake. He has knowledge, but he opened me up to things I don't think I was ready for. Look, I don't want you to instruct J'son in anything. I think it's best to let him discover his own limits without wizards screwing him up."

"That sounds like something B'el would say. He always lets you taste the poison first and then he lets it work on you, making you come back for more with the promise that he can take away the confusion."

"Why didn't you ever fall for his lies?" T'mar asked, looking at him now.

"That's another story for another time. Suffice it to say that we came up at the same time when the universe was different and right and wrong were more easily distinguished. Not like now where nobody trust anybody. It used to be that a smile meant nothing more than a smile, a display of friendliness, gratitude and peace."

"Those times are long gone, C'ton, and I'm not interested in some phony, meta-physical fantasy of the past."

"I know, T'mar. That's why you left. But to hope is more than just a fantasy. I believe in the Transcendentals and the work that they do. It is their will that J'son and I should meet. That is probably the only thing I am sure of. Look, J'son is coming around. Now we will see if he retains what he has been given."

J'son laced his fingers across his chest and was smiling to himself, enjoying the play of electrical fields dancing all around him. He had heard the two of them speaking and it pleased him to know that they knew each other and were speaking about the past. He didn't know the exact reason why T'mar had rejected C'ton as a teacher, but that didn't really matter. What mattered was that they both needed to come with him, beyond the Temple of the monks, and help him find the Castle of B'el. There, he knew, he would uncover the mystery and solve the riddle of his presence here.

He didn't understand everything the Transcendentals said to him, but he knew that they had something to do with maintaining equilibrium and giving stability to an unstable situation. C'ton would go with him no matter what the others did. T'mar would be harder to persuade, and T'mer would be absolutely against it. J'son had seen where the Castle was, but there was something about the air surrounding it. There was no life where he had to go, just death and those seeking death. The monks could point him in the general direction, but it would be T'mar who would show him how to enter.

Sitting up, feeling a slight buzz like adrenaline, his peripheral vision fuzzy, J'son looked up at C'ton and T'mar and said, "The way to the City is close. I saw where the road branches off to the left. It's just on the other side of the lake up ahead. Any discussion of where we are going must happen now. I am going to the monks and then I will pass beyond them."

"And I will go with you," C'ton said, reaching a hand down to help J'son to his feet.

"J'son, I don't know…" T'mar was torn. Seeing J'son fall from the sky had made her waver in her decision to go with T'mer to the City. However, she couldn't make T'mer go to the monks. She wouldn't.

"I'd understand if you want to go with T'mer," J'son said. "I think that's the best thing. I'm only a distraction to you."

J'son, it's just that… it's complicated."

"What's complicated?" T'mer asked, coming over to them with stained, bloody fingers and a handful of berries.

"We're deciding now who's going where," C'ton said.

"We're going to the monks," T'mer responded.

"What?"

"I decided earlier that I wasn't going to let you follow them without my protection," T'mer said. "Ever since I met this boy, we've had nothing but trouble. But if you feel you need to go with him, T'mar, then I'm going, too."

"T'mer. I can't ask you to do that."

"You're not asking me. I'm telling you what I decided and I decided I'm not going to let you follow them alone. I'm here for you."

T'mar smiled that bright, almost girlish smile that J'son and the others found so attractive and inviting, radically changing her look and softening the lines of her face. It touched her that T'mer would so willingly follow her lead without her having to manipulate him. She really didn't understand why she felt the way she did toward him. The word "Love" was bandied about so much here, usually as a preamble for a favor. All on this planet had heard about love from the humans and tried to mimic the behavior, but for most of them it was an exercise in vanity, showcasing their wants and desires rather than a true outpouring of emotion. Love was a term that defined a servant/master relationship, a way for an inferior to express their devotion and worship of their superior.

'tok had sacrificed himself for J'son, risking and receiving complete annihilation. The degree of loyalty it had shown went beyond her level of understanding. B'el would have told her that the creature got confused and frightened and that he was just reacting the way any thought creation would when confronted with the death of his creator. By saving J'son, or so B'el would argue, 'tok was hoping to save himself. The creature's actions were totally based on self-interest and personal survival, not out of some altruistic sense of nobility. Only the humans were so convinced and deluded. But her time among them had indeed changed the way she saw herself and those around her. Her feelings for T'mer were based on mutual respect and value. He filled some void in her and she gave him stability and affection. She used to think that her show of warmth and fondness toward him was based on advantage, but now she wasn't so sure.

When she had left him, after he had rescued her from B'el and she had rewarded him by taking his title, she gave no thought to him and didn't care one way or another if she ever saw him again. Once she had stumbled upon the portal that J'son provided, she had determined to never return to this world. Finding and pursuing B'el became her sole motivation, dismissing those feelings of longing and loneliness as something beneath her that needed to be expunged and eliminated. Her intellect was the only thing she needed. But now, here she was, smiling at T'mer fondly and glad he had decided on his own to go with them. She was beginning to believe in the reality of love.

"Outstanding!" C'ton exclaimed. "So the team stays together. We must be going. The sun is retreating and dusk will soon cover the world. We— J'son, are you okay?"

After announcing that he was going to the monks, J'son's reality started to swim and he was having heart palpitations. Fear and panic gripped him and he felt dizzy. His stomach churned and his feet felt like lead weights holding him in one place. He tried to moved, but found himself stumbling forward instead. He would have fallen over face first if it wasn't for someone grabbing him by the shoulders and pulling him back upright. Regaining his balance but still woozy, J'son turned to see who had grabbed him, surprised to find that the large, gentle hand on his shoulder belonged to T'mer.

"Hold on, boy. "I've got you. Are you able to walk, or do I need to carry you?" He asked sarcastically.

"No," J'son replied. "I'm fine, I think. I'm just a little dizzy."

"Do you need to sit back down?" T'mar asked, concern darkening her face.

"No, we can go," J'son said, pushing T'mer's hand off of him and stumbling forward several steps before needing to bend over.

"J'son, is it the vision you saw that is causing you problems?" C'ton was watching J'son closely, trying to read his aura, or rather his lack of one, but he couldn't read anything, like J'son wasn't really there. The impression reminded C'ton of the blank stares of those he had encountered in the dream world that exists between this world and Earth, like those caught within a portal, neither here or there.

"I don't know. It's like I can't see or something. Except for this thin channel of clarity, everything is blurry. It's hard to think straight." J'son was experiencing stimulation overload. Although he possessed some kind of ability that neither T'mar nor C'ton could rightly explain, he was still just a young man, a human struggling with the implications of everything he had experienced. It was a form of shock that caused his mind to close down to protect itself from the sensory assault.

Where normally the brain acted as a filter, distilling and ignoring irrelevant and extraneous sensory impressions, J'son's brain allowed everything to enter, clogging up his neural passageways with confusing and conflicting information. His experiences here were too much for his primitive learning structures. It was like taking a powerful hallucinogen and asked to operate a complex machine, that machine being his body. It felt alien and not his own.

Leaning over with his hands on his knees for support, breathing deeply and swaying on his feet, J'son insisted on moving forward, taking a few steps and then bending over again. It made sense to stop and rest again, but for some reason he felt compelled to keep moving. T'mer was standing beside him, reaching out tentatively every time J'son bent over to keep him from falling by placing a firm but compassionate hand on his shoulder. His head was still spinning and he felt drained, like he did back home the time he tried to run that marathon. His legs were rubbery and he was having a hard time keeping his eyes opened. But none of that mattered to him. He felt pressure to keep moving.

T'mer was following behind him, reaching out from time to time to prop him up and C'ton and T'mar were bringing up the rear, feeling uneasy and concerned. They walked along this way, mostly in silence, monitoring J'son's progress for any signs that he might be getting better. They reached the other end of the lake and passed the road that would have taken them to the City on their left. That road led around to the other side of the lake and disappeared behind the hills. The road they stayed on veered off to the right and away from the lake, the terrain eventually flattening out and becoming prairie-like, covered in wavy, multi-colored fur-like grass stretching out to the horizon.

The sun was directly in front of them and still shrinking in size, the mellow yellow becoming a darker, hazier red. In the distance just below the horizon a beam of intense, white light soared into the sky, disappearing into the dark, stormy clouds high above. The shaft of light seemed artificial, but from this distance it was hard to distinguish between the haze in the distance and the light itself. The only indication that the light was synthetic was the almost perfect vertical column ascending into the sky, rather like the beam of a search light, solid, concentrated and chalky white.

As they walked, the shaft of light remained before them, its source still hidden below the horizon. The road stretched out in a straight line, dividing the flowing, waving, graceful fields neatly in half. Tiny insect-like creatures covered the tops of the flora and danced around, bouncing from one stalk to another. At times the creatures rose in unison, forming a loose ball and moved closer to the group of travelers, seemingly watching them en mass as they passed, and then dispersing and going their separate ways. It was rare that the creatures came close enough to the road to actually leave the field and never did they cross the road to reach the other side. Although the road was only ten feet across, it appeared that it represented a barrier that they couldn't cross. J'son took notice of this and grew curious as to why they didn't socialize with the members of their own species on either side.

"Why don't they fly across the road? Are we somehow preventing them?"

"You would have to ask T'mar," T'mer said. "There is hostility between the two groups and occasionally, when the road narrows, some might chance crossing over. It's a mess when that happens and the road becomes littered with dead bugs. They crunch under your feet and their shells are razor sharp. You can cut your feet up if you are not careful. They are called 'ints."

"Oh." They reminded J'son of swarming gnats but bigger, more like wasps, with brightly colored wings, six of them and hard bodies that looked like they were made of plastic, almost artificial. They didn't seem to have any legs and he wondered if they ever landed or did they just bounced around. "Are they dangerous?"

"Only if you leave the road. You wander around out there for too long and you will be consumed before you know what happened. I've seen them pick the flesh off someone your size in seconds. He just stood there, covered in 'ints, then they flew away leaving just his bones. Just stay in the middle of the road and you will be fine. As long as it is still light they won't bother you. Once it gets dark, they multiply rapidly and the sky becomes filled with them. Travel becomes impossible."

"You talk about it getting dark, but the sun never goes down. It only appears to get smaller. I don't think I have seen the sun move from that spot since I got here. Doesn't this planet rotate?"

"No, it doesn't," T'mer said, his scowl returning to his face, showing disgust. "At least not this close to the sun. Soon, all you will see is nothing more than a dark, red star indistinguishable from the millions of other stars that fill the night sky. That is when the long dark comes and we must find sanctuary, either with the monks or within the City. My guess is we will spend that eternity huddled inside the Temple. It will be the passing of an age before the sun returns to its full strength. We are entering a time of danger and madness. Only the wizards would brave excursions into the night. But you don't have to worry about that. The light of the monks will keep you safe."

The way T'mer was talking had a distinct bitterness to it, almost combative, like the resignation of a warrior who knows he has been defeated but refuses to give up. What was so horrible about the night? J'son wondered. And what did he mean by "the passing of an age"? How long would it be dark?

"It's when the dark comes that all the parasites come out," T'mer continued. "The sun supplies most of the energy here and while its light continues to shine we are safe to roam around. But when it gets dark, that's when the closest of companions will turn on each other to feed. There is no loyalty when resources become scarce. I chose to come along because I am bound to T'mar, but if it came down to it I wouldn't trust her to sacrifice herself for me like your creature did for you. Energy is too valuable a commodity to be given away without benefit. Even your friend C'ton can't be trusted when the sun disappears. Remember that, boy."

T'mer stopped speaking, anger and hostility accenting his voice, giving it an edge of resentment and petulance. The X was deep in his face and his moodiness formed a tangible wall of resistance and defiance between them. His rapid change in mood scared J'son and he found himself looking back over his shoulder to see how far behind were T'mar and C'ton. There shapes were easy to see because the road was straight, but they lagged far behind and were no more than a couple of dark streaks bobbing down the center of the road.

Chapter Sixteen:

The Monks

> The Adepts couldn't manifest bodies until humans were created. We couldn't utilize Technology until you invented it. Technology came to humans to compensate for your fragility and lack of belief.
>
> A monk speaking to J'son in the grove

T'mar and C'ton had been discussing their differences, trying to maintain a sense of civility about them. It was hard because T'mar didn't trust C'ton's motives and C'ton didn't trust T'mar at all. She was too hard to read and what he could read about her was always deceptive. She had changed so much since he had last seen her; not so much physically -although her appearance had changed- but the depth of her intensity. He could see it in her eyes, cool and calculating, not like when she spoke to J'son, or T'mer for that mattered. She was purposely blocking him, keeping her emotions and thoughts in check. Their conversation had a decidedly guarded and restrained quality and it took several exchanges between them to get to a simple understanding. It bothered C'ton that she didn't trust him like she once did.

"I have no 'plans' for the boy, T'mar. I've told you that before. You're right, he is different, but I had always planned on passing the dark with the monks. I gave up on portals long ago. Their world is not our world."

"Yes, but what about the Transcendentals? You said it yourself they sent you to him."

"I never said they sent me. They only told me to expect him. How we came to meet is one of the mysteries of the Transcendentals. It was their will that we meet. I had nothing to do with it and unless something happens between here and the Temple I don't plan on evaluating J'son myself. It is the responsibility of the monks to investigate all deviations from the norm. You know that, T'mar, from your training. I stopped training apprentices long ago, shortly after you left."

That last part was only partly true. Actually, C'ton had stopped all teaching because T'mar had left. She was his last student, and her unfaithfulness had scarred him deeply. Her departure left him questioning his own beliefs and whether or not he should continue with his individual studies. When she turned her back on him that last time, leering back at him from over her shoulder, he felt indignant and offended that she thought she could learn more from someone else. It was that weakness, that flaw of his character that caused him so much guilt and shame, especially later when he found out where she had gone. He had pushed her to it, after all.

From his first awakening he had been drawn to the monks and he had many teachers himself before he took his first 'tyr. He never forgot the rush he felt the first time he opened the mind of one of his own students. The student's energetic show of warmth and gratitude flooded his awareness and strengthened him, lifting C'ton above his training, increasing his own understanding and infusing his body with power. It was extremely intoxicating, and dangerous. He wanted more. Soon, he discovered that the more powerful his student the more his own abilities increased. As long as he maintained his authority over his student, his 'tyr, the less likely the chance that his apprentice would turn on him, overpower him and subjugate him. That was what happened with T'mar. He had been too domineering with her. Instead of listening to her questions, he ignored them and discounted them as trivial. She was too powerful and too smart to practice the arts under the domination of another. He wanted her to grow in awareness slowly, absorbing the knowledge and creating a foundation anchored in truth, his truth.

She had accused him at first of not wanting to introduce her to the deeper things, then, later, she out and out denied his understanding and doubted his abilities. She had surprised him by manifesting something she had learned on her own, something that he had forbidden even to discuss. She had produced a thought form that feed on her own anger, much like the though form 'tok that J'son manifested, only much smaller and more aggressive. C'ton had forbidden practicing that type of manifestation because it fed on a part of the psyche that was better left alone. Once introduced to that part of oneself, it was incredibly hard not to be enticed.

He knew how to do it. He had learned it long ago when he had first began his studies from an unscrupulous wizard who had uncovered some of the secrets of the dark arts by ingesting a powerful hallucinogen, changing him forever. That wizard could indeed call forth strange and bizarre forces, but only of an inferior kind, mere illusions without substance. It was the type of illusion that wizards normally throw at one another to gage the other's level of competency, no more than a distraction. However, in the mind of a fool, or one turned towards evil, that distraction could create chaos and temptation, pulling them down deeper into the abyss. At least that was how C'ton saw it.

She had left him to learn the darker secrets from whoever would teach her. The only problem was that she was more powerful than most of the renegades she encountered and her abilities flourished because she found herself in constant battle with those so-called teachers. At some point, C'ton knew, she had crossed that line and decided that those teaching weren't so evil and that a stable mind could learn to control those powerful influences. Only someone who didn't fear the dark recesses hidden within his own mind and had worked through them would be in the position to teach her. That is when B'el had sent for her.

"C'ton, I'm telling you that I won't go along with handing J'son over to the monks. It's just that what do they know that we don't? Do you really think they can help him with his training? J'son is already beyond most of them and they wouldn't know how to control him. I'm afraid that they will do more harm than good."

"So you presume to just walk right up to the Temple with your arm wrapped tightly around J'son's waist without anyone knowing? They will see he is different the moment we enter through the gate. You can't hide him, T'mar. They will want to examine him and possibly test him, too. It is best if we tell them everything we know, holding nothing back. They'll know if you are being deceptive."

"And J'son doesn't have a say in the matter?"

"T'mar, you know where he is heading, don't you? He wants to go there and there's nothing we can do to change his mind. My concern is for the monks if they try to dissuade him. He is in contact with the Transcendentals and they are directing his steps. In my experience it is never a good idea to get in their way, nor to delay someone who is under their direction."

"I'm not talking about the Transcendentals right now. I agree we have to get him to the monks before the dark comes—"

"He'll not have the patience to wait out the age. He'll want to travel outside the Dome, in the dark."

"He's weak now. He needs to rest. I think you're right that he may have suffered a psychic break. We may not even have to worry about his abilities. He may be too ill to impress the monks with any show of power. I say that unless we are asked directly about J'son we should just pretend that he is a lower level Technician that has picked up some tricks during his travels."

"Picked them up from you, maybe?" C'ton was getting impatient himself. Because T'mar had changed her designation and was hiding her true identity behind it, he knew she could never tell the monks who she really was or how she and J'son met. There was no way a Tech could pass through a portal, find the source and return here with him. It was unheard of, although hints that it could be done flowed from the teachings of B'el. T'mar was right to suggest hiding J'son's abilities from the monks, but if they uncovered the deception it would be nothing for the monks to throw their little group out into the darkness. And without preparation, that would be disastrous.

"We'll just enter through the gates as a private party, seeking sanctuary.

They'll take us at our word and give us lodging. It's only as the dark deepens that they will start asking questions. Hopefully by that time we will be gone."

"T'mer has no idea, does he? He thinks we will be spending the age with the monks. He won't want to stay, but he sure won't want to go beyond the Dome."

"No, he won't, but that's the next hurdle. Getting through the gate is the only thing we need to discuss with him. Don't screw me over, C'ton." T'mar said that last with her finger pointed directly at his chest in a show of hostility that came very close to a threat. Her eyes were mere slits and the creases of her face cut deep into forehead and cheeks, forming an X. "I mean it."

They had been walking and talking like this for some time and slowly they were gaining on J'son and T'mer. The line of the horizon was no longer straight and unbroken. In the distance, the shaft of light could now be seen coming out of the top of a tall, spiracle structure and continued high into the sky. The clouds had broken revealing the termination point of the light. It struck the sky tens of thousands of feet over their head like it had hit an invisible barrier, exploding and spreading out in all directions, descending down, forming the roof and walls of a massive, semi-transparent Dome. It covered more than just the Temple, or the City, or the lake. Every living thing that moved or breathed on this planet was confined and protected under the Dome. It was the Dome that gave the sky that hazy look, diffusing the diminishing light of the sun and, in time to come, the blackness above.

"We'll wait here for T'mar," T'mer said. "Why don't you sit down and rest. They shouldn't be too far behind us."

J'son's legs gave way under him and he collapsed, hitting the ground hard and with a plop. He was still feeling dizzy and his head felt fuzzy. Although his thinking was fairly coherent and followed a logical form, still he found it hard to concentrate and the images which earlier flooded his mind were now concealed, hidden just beneath the level of his awareness. His inner lamp had gone out. He couldn't see anything when he closed his eyes and his head hurt, especially his forehead. He reached up with one of his hands and pinched his nose, digging his thumb and forefinger deep into his eyes. He was groaning within himself and he was relieved they had stopped. He wasn't too sure he could have gone on much longer if they hadn't stopped.

"I'm so tired," he mumbled.

"What? Oh, okay. Just sit there for awhile. And let me know if you start to do any wizard stuff."

"I'm fine. I just need to rest," he said, forcing himself to remain conscious.

The way he was feeling was beyond the need for rest, and J'son knew it. He felt like he had been depleted, like his very soul had been ripped out of him, crumpled up, trampled on and reinserted back into a broken and bruised body. He had no thoughts, nothing that inspired his thinking or motivated him to get up and keep moving. Nothing except a ghostly apprehension seared into his memory of the Transcendentals, a singular image that insisted he continue at all cost. That image, that feverish, iconic representation of purpose was the only neuro-chemical reality that he recognized, the only thing that kept him conscious.

He closed his eyes and tried to focus on the somatic sensations external to himself. He heard the wind rustling the grass nearby and the sound was soothing, making the pounding behind his eyes less prominent. He heard the buzzing of the 'ints flying around somewhere to the left and right and he tried to visualize their hard, plastic little bodies with their six wings flapping in unison. He tried to imagine what they looked like but drew a blank. He tried harder to see them, forcing himself to create the image. With his face pinched and his forehead creased, he narrowed his focus and concentrated until the pounding in his head became a sharp, cutting, stabbing pain.

"Owwwww!"

"Boy, are you okay?"

J'son was sitting with his legs crossed and his back straight when he toppled over, bent at the waist, hitting his forehead on the ground and blacking out. Blood from a deep gash near his temple flowed freely and spread out around his face. His breathing had dropped off to almost nothing, and the only indication that he was breathing was the tiny, swirling particles of dirt kicked up by his exhalation. Except for the blood, he looked like he was sleeping. His arms lay passively on either side of his body, wrist turned up in at an awkward position. Overall, he looked very uncomfortable, to say the least.

The sound of the 'ints increased and their buzzing became chaotic and aggressive, their presence closer than before. 'ints on each side of the road crowded up to the edge, forming a dense, animated wall three feet thick with their bodies and extending for several feet on either side of the road. The 'ints did all they could to prevent moving into the road, pushing and jostling each other to get closer without actually crossing the border, their collective bodies pulsating and undulating in line, moving forward and then falling back. The sound of their wings, each side buzzing in unison with themselves but at a different octave from each other, blocked out all other sound except for the occasional clicking.

The clicking sound was infrequent and erratic at first, coming from the left side only, like some form of communication. Then the right side started up, clicking at a different octave, a loud click followed by several quieter clicks. Then there was another loud click, more like a clock, low and forceful, coming from the left side, followed by intense silence. A few seconds past and then the right side responded with an even lower octave clocking sound, much more forceful, followed by more silence. The 'ints on the left side must not have like what they heard because all of them starting clicking and clocking uncontrollably. Some of them broke through the line and moved onto the road, crashing to the ground as soon as they left the protection of the grass.

The right side responded to the attack by raising a racket of their own and then entering the road en mass, falling to the ground almost as soon as they crossed the barrier, littering the road with their quivering, wing-flapping, plastic bodies. The left side moved in retaliation, swarming above the road and falling to the ground before making it half way across. Now, dead 'ints covered the road an inch thick on either side of J'son, creating a buffer zone of a few feet without touching him. The 'ints on both sides, embolden by the death of their comrades lying broken on the road, pushed the boundary again, moving their line further out, closer to the other side, and hovering over the dead carcass of the front line without crossing.

They hovered in that location for a few seconds more before each side decided to charged the other again, sending more 'ints to their death once they reached the leading edge of their advance. The dead 'ints created a wider forward area on each side and the live 'ints moved in, hovering closer to the middle, and closer to J'son lying near the center. All of this took place within a matter of minutes, wave after wave of 'ints entering the death zone only to be replaced by more 'ints entering the death zone, thus creating a safe zone for still further advance. In a very short amount of time, the 'ints were within striking distance of each other, and J'son as well.

T'mer saw what was happening as it was happening, but didn't know how to respond. Actually, he did know how he wanted to respond, but a sense of responsibility kept him from running down the road away from the deadly 'ints. When he saw the first of the 'ints move out into the road his instincts told him to get out of there and avoid them at all cost. He had seen how rapidly the 'ints could strip a man of his flesh while still standing and he didn't want to be anywhere in the vicinity. However, even as he was turning to leave, shielding his head with his arm, he heard T'mar's voice whispering to him to stay and help J'son. At the time, he would have sworn that she was standing right next to him. It was only when he jerked his head around to see if she was standing there that he realized he was alone.

He took a few hesitant steps closer to J'son, who was laying face down less than six feet away and then stopped. The blood from J'son's injured forehead ran outward toward the dead 'ints and flowed around them like a little stream, filling in the empty spaces between each dead 'int. The blood flowed mainly to the left and it was that side that attacked the road barrier first and more aggressively. Some of the dying 'ints, immersed in the blood, found renewed life, twitching and then rising into the air on sticky-wet, trembling wings and fluttering back into the protection of the tall grass. All the dead 'ints that were close enough to be able to partake of J'son's blood found resurrection, and that reassurance brought an increased brashness in the 'ints overall plan of attack. T'mer was at a loss as to how he could help.

The blood flowing to the left side of the road gave the 'ints on that side a strategic advantage, which they exploited fully. Those 'ints, instead of flying over the road and crashing to the ground, now snaked their bodies out from between the grass and wiggled over the dead 'ints, drawing closer to the fresh spilt blood. Blood from an open wound was a special treat for them, energizing them and increasing their size as they dined. It was rare that they had the opportunity to lap it up directly from the source: normally, any creature unfortunate enough to find themselves surrounded by 'ints died within seconds.

Each 'int would fight for the opportunity to take a piece of red meat, leaving very little blood behind. This time, however, their victim was still alive and his blood retained all of the vitality of the living, which meant the 'ints level of awareness could be raised merely by drinking it. That was the idea. In order to reach J'son, they would have to make it to his blood without dying and then consume it. The energy and awareness level they would gain would encourage them to cross the thin ribbon of blood connecting their dead comrades and J'son's prone body.

Like an army of legless ants, the first of the 'ints, the larger ones, slid their way over to J'son and followed the blood line up his face and congregated around the gash. There were only a few at first, but then others followed and soon J'son's head was completely covered in large, buzzing, flapping ant-like 'ints. A few of the larger ones started nibbling at his wound, cleaning away some of the damaged skin, peeling it back to get to the flesh underneath. J'son, at the moment, wasn't in too much trouble because the 'ints were more concerned with drinking than eating, but the number of 'ints were growing and the amount of available blood was limited. Within a few seconds the smaller-sized majority had given up on fresh blood and moved away from J'son's head hoping to find something to devour further down.

If it wasn't for the subtle controls T'mar had placed within T'mer concerning J'son's safety, J'son would have been eaten alive where he lay. However, the conditioning was too complete and T'mer moved without thinking of his own safety. Bending over and grabbing J'son by his arm, T'mer jerked him up off the ground and threw him over his shoulder, legs hanging in front with his 'int covered head and chest facing down and to the rear. T'mer sprinted back the way they had come, hopping to get to T'mar before J'son lost his face. His first few steps crunched beneath his feet, followed by the sound of clicking and clocking coming from the sidelines. Only by moving rapidly did he hope to dislodge the 'ints clinging to J'son's flesh and only vaguely did he think about the 'ints crawling on him.

He ran as fast as he could, holding J'son with one hand and smacking 'ints with the other. A couple crawled into his mouth and he bit down on them, cracking their bodies open like a shell. Spitting out bits of wing and shell from between his teeth, T'mer ran on, covering more than a hundred yards in less than a handful of seconds. Then two figures appeared and separated themselves from the landscape, stopping momentarily, and then rushing towards T'mer. Once he saw them running in his direction, he stopped, throwing J'son from his shoulder and proceeded to swat and smack the 'ints that now covered his head and shoulders.

The 'ints were much more aggressive than before, taking tiny bites out of him, leaving him spotted with open, bloody wounds, which in turn emboldened the 'ints even more. Once he dropped J'son to the ground, however, only the 'ints still attached to T'mer posed a problem and he clawed at them, ripping them from his flesh and ground them under his feet. The few remaining 'ints still drinking directly from J'son's wound had swelled in size, each bloated to about the size of a man's thumb. He didn't think too much about J'son except to acknowledge the hopelessness of the situation. Even if T'mar could remove the larger ones attached to J'son without killing him, his face must surely be half eaten away and hideous.

T'mar was the first to notice T'mer running towards them and she took off, hoping to cut the distance, leaving C'ton to make up his own mind. She arrived just a few seconds after T'mer had put J'son down and she stood there not knowing what to do. T'mer was busy ripping 'ints off his face and seemed oblivious that she was even there. There were only four 'ints covering J'son's face at this point, but they were as large as his hand, each one huddled next to the other around the gash, which had been peeled back and was now a one inch wide, three inch long tear running across his forehead. She reached down to grab one of the 'ints and then stopped short, balling her fingers into a fist to avoid touching them.

"Damn!" She spat. She knew that physical contact with them was a mistake and casting a spell would only draw them to her. They would feed off of her thought streams and gorge themselves before she could complete the spell. She needed to draw them away with an energy displacement, but she would have to deflect it away from her, distracting the 'ints with the intensity. Her focus would have to be narrow enough and the output high enough that the 'ints would willingly abandon their rare feast of live blood for the assurance of something more beneficial. That would be the hard part. There aren't many things better than fresh blood.

"You'll have to appeal to the logical side of them now," C'ton said as he approached the rest of the group. "They mutated too much to give up their victim willingly."

"That victim is J'son, you know." T'mar raised her hands face level, pointed a bent, twisted finger at J'son and mumbled something under her breath.

"Wait, T'mar. For now, J'son is safe. The only thing they are doing is drinking his blood. Since there are only four of them, they won't start to eat him until and unless he starts to die. Help T'mer first while I calculate the proper spell."

The 'ints on T'mer were smaller than the ones on J'son, making them easier to deal with. They could be removed either by the method T'mer had been using, ripping them out flesh, or they could be detached by simply feeding them energy burst and directing them away from their host. His face, chest and shoulders were covered with pock marks and painful-looking whelps. Tiny rivulets of blood flowed freely down his body, covering him in streaks of crimson. He looked like a man that had been beaten with a cat-of-nine tails and still he fought with them, pulling out hair, skin and muscle in the process.

"T'mer, put your hands down and stop moving. It will weaken their connection to you. Just hold still."

If she did this right, T'mar thought, they should fall dead on the road as soon as they separated from T'mer. Raising her crooked fingers back into the air and pointing them at T'mer, T'mar closed her eyes and tried to imagine a beam of energy streaming from the tips of her fingers. She was mumbling, using words like "pure" and "power", pronouncing them in a lower register in order to produce the required vibration necessary to create the illusion of unlimited supply. The words blurred together in seamless, rhythmic continuity, like chanting. Only the right aural frequency, coupled with the right mental focus, would allow her the clarity she needed to be successful.

"Purapowmayletura…," she said in a deep monotone.

T'mer lowered his arms like she said and tried to stay as still as possible. The 'ints dug into him like gnats and it was a test of his will to keep from swatting at them. Only the sound of the spell and the force of the words striking his ears gave him any relief to the intense biting. The vibration was right and the spell began functioning as intended. The 'ints stopped digging and burrowing and started vibrating, letting out a series of clicking more like a code, and flapping their wings, becoming increasingly agitated. The 'ints detached themselves from T'mer and swarmed around his head without landing, bumping into each other and getting louder.

The order of the words and their innate meaning, along with the correct mental focus and timbre produces a wave form that for the most part is invisible in the material universe but dynamic and vibrant one step above mundane reality. It is this wave, if broken down, that contains minute particles of pure and uncorrupted thought, which allows the manipulation of reality through the application of intention. T'mar's intention was to create an animated bridge of electricity that would entice the 'ints to land on it and encourage them to congregate there.

As she continued to cast her spell, speaking in hushed, mumbling tones, an imperceptible energy field took the form of an elongated disk between her fingers and moved outward towards T'mer, stopping just beneath his chin, acting as a platform. The 'ints, buzzing and clicking, landed on the disk a few at a time and began drawing energy from it. Soon, most of the 'ints were on the platform, with a couple of stragglers hovering around looking for a clear spot to land. All of this happened in the course of a few seconds after she began to chant.

"T'mer, step away from them as quickly and as quietly as you can," she said, breaking off from her chanting." I'm about to disperse the field. When you see them drop to the road, get away as fast as you can and avoid getting too close to the edge of the road."

As T'mar spoke, the field started to weaken, growing smaller and the 'ints became more agitated, bouncing around the platform and landing again. Most of the 'ints completely covered the platform, forcing the few, remaining stragglers to fight for room on the increasingly diminishing surface. T'mer stepped back as soon as the majority of 'ints moved away and he began scratching at his neck and running his hands through his hair to check for any that might have remained. T'mar back away from the 'int-covered platform and drew closer to T'mer, hoping to help him get out of the way when she terminated the spell and collapsed the field-generated platform. Because of the increased distance, the field wavered as she backed up and the 'ints became more aggressive, responding erratically to the energy fluctuation, attacking each other as the platform grew smaller.

"Run!"

T'mar lowered her hands and instantly the platform dissolved, sending dozens of 'ints to the ground in a dead heap. She turned her back on them and, grabbing T'mer by the arm, she ran several yards before stopping and looking back at them. Most of them fell in a pile, lying on top of each other, barely moving. Some had bounced off of the dead heap and tried to fly towards the protection of grass before falling back onto the road and dying. The grass running along the edge of the road was lined with buzzing spectators hoping to latch onto anything living and a few of them were able to feed on some of the 'ints that had the misfortune of just making it back to the edge of the road.

"C'ton!" T'mar cried. "How are you doing with J'son?"

"C'ton heard her but ignored her, instead trying to concentrate on the matter at hand. The four 'ints on J'son's face were now too large to drink without disturbing one another and they fought each other for a spot. There was one on the top of J'son's head and another covering his eyes, nose and mouth. The other two pushed and nudged the first pair trying to find room, tearing the wound open even more. Blood was flowing freely on the ground again and C'ton was starting to grow concerned that the blood would attract more 'ints. His spell had to work and he would have to be careful not to overdo it by coming at them directly.

As large as they were with the energy supply they had, it would be real easy for them to swim up any energy stream he produced and attack him before he could collapse the particle beam. He would have to cast a spell that appeared to come from another source, thus deflecting the 'ints away from him and J'son at the same time. His focus would have to be laser guided and quick, dispelling the particle beam almost as soon as he created it. He would have to form the platform within his mind, project it towards another energy source and deflect it away from him at the same time trying to lure the 'ints off of J'son. It would take an enormous amount of energy to dislodge them from their feast and difficult for sure.

C'ton closed his eyes and started to mumble, sounding more song-like than the drone of a memorized chant. His fingers were bent, but not at the extreme angle T'mar used. His spell developed more organically, the thought tripping the necessary triggers that came so naturally to him. He knew that to force the beam would create residual and extraneous energy bleed that could cause all kinds of problems: from thought parasites to attracting creatures worse than 'ints. Only by deflecting the energy beam away from him and creating the illusion that it came from some other location could he hope to dislodge them without getting infested himself.

A brilliant, white ball of light appeared between his fingers as he sang and quickly fell to the ground, floating away from him and settling down by J'son's head. The light was intense and pulsated, growing brighter and denser, solidifying. The two 'ints unable to find room around the bloody gash immediately bounced away from J'son and landed inside the glowing orb, trapping them. The orb fed off of the two 'ints and it increased in size again, releasing more energy in the process and growing more luminous. The 'ints inside the orb became harder to see, rapidly disappearing behind the intensity: a shrill, excited clicking the only indication that they were still alive.

The other two 'ints, responding to the ecstatic cries of their comrades, looked away from their feast and focused their attention on the glowing orb radiating energy a few inches away. They were more sluggish than the first two, more bloated and they moved slower, more hesitant to leave their easy meal unguarded. But the noise coming from the orb suggested an orgy of sensual delights that proved too much for their limited cognitive abilities to ignore and they moved in unison, gradually backing away from the wound, clicking at each other, first one and then the other. They were either going to leave at the same time, or they wouldn't leave at all.

They were too large to fly, their six wings mere flimsy, transparent, useless appendages that didn't respond adequately enough to lift them up. Their bodies were bloated past physical definition, more like a gelatinous blob, an overfed tic, than the plastic-looking hard shells they had. They moved by rolling their body in a particular direction, like slime running downhill. They slipped off of J'son's face and landed on top of the orb, slowly sinking into it, crying out in happiness and disappearing inside within moments. Inside the orb, the energy field produced an illusion that caused the 'ints to experience a rapture of sorts, satisfying their insatiable hunger and blinding them to the reality of their situation.

Once they were secure within the orb, C'ton sang another song and the orb rose off the ground and moved across the road, stopping just short of the grass. C'ton snapped his fingers and the orb ballooned up, glowing increasingly brighter until it became almost transparent before it evaporated into nothing, dropping the 'ints by the side of the road, away from the protection of the tall grass. Within moments, all of the small 'ints that had been watching by the side of the road swarmed the four fat, bloated 'ints and devoured them, leaving a dark-grey, bloody stain soaking into the ground.

C'ton knelt down beside J'son and put his hand, palm side down, on top of his wound, mumbling in sing-song with his eyes closed. His hand began to glow a dull yellow and the blood surrounding the wound dried up, crusting over and flaked away. The gash was still visible between his fingers but the torn skin was now lying flat against J'son's head and appeared to be healing, the edges softening and becoming pink and flesh colored. J'son was still unconscious and C'ton placed his hand on the side of his face tenderly, like a father looking at his sleeping son. He was quiet and thoughtful, closing his eyes again and barely moving his lips.

J'son's color started to look better and C'ton took that as a sign of encouragement, concluding that he was at least stable enough to continue on towards the Temple. He would need to be carried, but not as roughly as T'mer had carried him. They needed help, possibly from the monks. He looked up and saw T'mar and T'mer standing a few feet away. In the distance behind them, coming from the Temple, he saw several monks moving rapidly in their direction. The Temple was still quite far off and C'ton wondered if they would need a stretcher of some sorts to carry J'son.

"Is the boy going to make it?" T'mer asked. "That gash doesn't look so bad now."

"It's not the wound I'm worried about," C'ton said. "The 'ints were only attracted to him after he passed out and hit his head. It's his psychic wound that I'm more concerned about. I detected brain activity but I don't know if he has any cognitive abilities. I believe he will recover, considering he is still in his physical body, but I'm not too sure if he will retain any of his special qualities."

"Maybe that's a good thing," T'mar added. "If when the monks get here he is still unconscious, then we won't have to explain who he is. They will want to take him to the House of Healing where mental intrusion is unlawful. They won't ask too many questions about him until he recovers. By then, we will be ready to leave."

"Leave?" T'mer said, flabbergasted. "What do you mean leave, T'mar? I thought we were going to pass the age with the monks." He looked up at the diminishing sun and continued. "We are running out of time. Soon it will be dark and we must find shelter. If we are going to leave, I say we leave him with the monks and try to make it to the City. It will be dusk before we even get to the Temple. It will be pitch-black before we can set out toward the City."

"We're not going to the City, T'mer," T'mar said. "And we're not going to be staying with the monks."

"T'mar, I'm not going to Earth, even if he wakes up and can open a portal for us. You know I have no ability there. I would rather spend another age in the dark before I return to Earth."

C'ton stood up and looked at T'mer, speaking slowly. "I don't think that's where she wants to go."

"If we don't go to the monks or the City, and it's decided we won't travel to Earth, then where do you propose we find shelter?" T'mer was getting anxious, although he would never acknowledge it. The monks would be here within minutes and the mere sight of them brought back memories of his time among them. It was long ago and he hated it. He didn't have the freedom of choice there and he was made to do things that he thought was beneath him. The monks were monks for a reason. It was part of their training. That was the life they had chosen for themselves and to impose their belief system on him was more than just an inconvenience: it was a prison sentence.

He cared for T'mar, but now that he was this close to the monks he didn't know if he could stay with them again. The City was where he really wanted to be. There he was needed and valued. His physicality brought respect and his strength was something to be feared. Not like the monks that depended on the manipulation of others to prove themselves. He never trusted the monks or any wizard, for that matter. He was getting use to C'ton, but that was probably because he hadn't really been around him that long. Besides, C'ton wasn't all that threatening and he didn't act all full of himself. There was something humble about him, something that T'mer actually liked about him.

"The monks will be here in a minute," T'mar said. "We don't say anything about J'son or our plans. We're just travelers passing through hoping to find shelter from the dark."

"Whatever you say," T'mer said.

Four men, leaning on long staffs, dressed in a full-body, brown tunic belted around the waist with several pieces of knotted grass, approached the group and walked through them, stopping at J'son's prone body.

"This is him," one of them said.

"Prepare a carryall. We must get him to the priest," another one said. He was older than the others, and based on the deference paid to him by the others he seemed to be their leader. The other three dropped their staffs on the road, ripped the top half of their tunics off, baring their skinny, hairless sunken chests and proceeded to fold the material around two of the staffs.

"Uh, can we help you with something?" T'mer asked indignantly.

"T'mer," T'mar cautioned.

"We are here to help the one that we were sent to help. We saw him in a vision," the leader said. "We are going to take him to the High Priest. We are on a mission from the Transcendentals."

"The Transcendentals?" C'ton was amazed that the leader mentioned them openly and even more shocked that he said they saw J'son in a vision. That means they were already aware of him and probably knew of his abilities. Whatever plan T'mar had for their group, it seemed the Transcendentals had other ideas. Now, there would be no way they could hide J'son from their scrutiny.

As the monks finished with the stretcher, they lifted J'son off the ground and place him gently between the staffs, laying him on his back with his arms folded across his chest. Then one of the monks ripped more material from his tunic and covered J'son's bare upper body with it. The other two monks, one kneeling by his head and the other by his feet, grabbed hold of the staffs and lifted J'son off of the ground. They proceeded to walk away in the direction of the Temple.

"Wait a minute!" T'mar didn't like how the monks had come up and taken J'son without even asking permission. It was just like the monks to assume that what they were doing was more important than everyone else. Standing there, her hands on her hips in a show of open defiance to what they were doing, T'mar looked toward C'ton, trying to gauge how he was taking this.

"We know you, C'ton," the leader said. "But that was long ago. The brute is familiar to us also. He is a mere Technician, hard-headed and quite combative if I remember right. The woman who chooses to speak before spoken to is unknown to us. Although it is known to us that she isn't who she claims to be. You, C'ton, we will speak to."

Just a handful of words out of their mouths and the monks had managed to irritate T'mar, and judging by the deep cut Xing his face, infuriate T'mer as well. The monks saw themselves as guardians of the sacred fire, the sole protector and generator of the "Blessed Light". Without them, it is said, the Dome of heaven would collapse and the Wasteland would move in and devour all life on the planet. They carried with them a sense of importance that not only bordered on arrogance but crossed the line, deeming all those not affiliated with the Temple as inferior beings lost in a lost world. It was only through their teachings that their world would continued to be saved. It was an on-going processes, they claimed, to ensure the harmony and synchronicity of the planet. Theirs was the law and all dissenters were lawbreakers.

It was that attitude that first persuaded T'mar to leave the order in search of true knowledge beyond the restrictions and limitations of living in the Temple. She had broken with C'ton, her teacher, mainly because he refused to answer her persistent questions concerning the truth about B'el. In the annals which were held within the heart of the Temple stories were told, legends mostly, about the time before time and the part B'el and others like him had played in the building of the Dome and its real purpose. The stories concerning B'el directly were cloaked in metaphor and allegory, myths that had taken on a dark and sinister tone, transforming one of the founders of the world into a byword for evil.

T'mar had a different designation then and a different name. She had been brought up in the Temple after being found alone wandering around in the dark between the ages. She was young and beautiful, full of life but scared and alone. She had been cast out into the dark for reasons unknown to all, except T'mar, and she only said that she didn't remember how she came to be abandoned in the dark. C'ton had found her on his way back from the City while travelling with a group of monks.

She had been hiding under a rock formation, watching them, too scared and distrustful to move. She watched them pass by holding her breath so they wouldn't hear her, but C'ton did hear her. He had stopped a few feet away from her, staring into the dark, and began casting light spells in her direction, trying to illuminate her hiding place. Seeing the light, she feigned tears and came out of her hole in the ground, running towards C'ton and throwing her arms around his neck, trembling with fear.

C'ton took her in and comforted her, spurning the displeasure of his colleagues and took her as his apprentice on the spot in defiance of the law of succession. She was no more than a girl and he treated her like a daughter, teaching her the art of energy transformation and training her to distinguish the subtle difference between using her knowledge for good or evil. She had been his student and had learned so much from him about the nature of reality and how to develop her innate abilities. It was only when she started to question the status quo and B'el's true identity that she began to pull away from C'ton's teachings and seek answers elsewhere. It was a decision that would take her outside of the Dome and lead her to the Castle of B'el.

"It has been a long time since we had the pleasure of your company, C'ton," the leader said. All of them were walking now, following the two monks carrying J'son.

"Indeed it has, D'nan. It is strange that I didn't know of your coming. You said you saw J'son. Did you see me, also?"

"No. We were just as surprised as you to see you again. We were sent by the Council to retrieve the boy." D'nan looked at C'ton and then turned away. "What do you know of him?"

C'ton didn't really know how to answer him. If what he said was true that the Transcendentals were involved, then why hadn't he known about it? He himself had seen J'son in a vision given to him by the Transcendentals. Why they hadn't bothered to inform him about this chance encounter he didn't know. How much did D'nan really know and how much was he just trying to get out of C'ton? As far as he knew, they didn't know about his vision and so they were partially blind to J'son's future. He knew where J'son wanted to go, but how did the monks fit within the plan? Were they trying to manipulate the situation and bend it to their will? Only time would tell and he decided in keeping with T'mar to keep secret what they had experienced together.

"Probably not as much as you do. I was out on one of my last outings before the dark comes when I ran into T'mar and T'mer. They were coming from the caves at the border and had J'son with them. He wasn't feeling well and they thought it was a good idea to bring him to you for healing." Because of her perceived low level, C'ton knew that D'nan wouldn't question T'mar about anything that he said and hoped that they would be too caught up in their own mission that they wouldn't care to probe him for more information.

"So they were together when you first saw them?" D'nan asked. "It seems very convenient that you should run into them. When was the last time you conversed with the Transcendentals? Things are happening in which this boy takes part. It is being taught that the war will begin at next light, after the passing of this age."

"Mind your designation, D'nan. You shouldn't be speaking openly about them and you really shouldn't speak about what is being taught inside the Temple to those without." Normally, those of a lesser designation would never presume to speak to one of a higher grade with such open contempt for the law, especially to someone as high ranking as C'ton. To speak of the Transcendentals openly and among strangers was synonymous with heresy and subject to banishment from the Order. C'ton was of such a rank that if he had the mind to he could seize command of the monks and direct them to do whatever he demanded, even releasing J'son if he thought that was in his best interest, and D'nan would have to obey.

Since D'nan had recognized him immediately, normal protocol would have been for D'nan to defer to him and inform him of what was going on. Instead, D'nan acted as if C'ton was nothing more than a mere Technician, speaking to him and questioning him like an officer speaking to a subordinate. That didn't sit too well with C'ton and he debated with himself to do something that wasn't officially permitted and was frowned upon by all. To read the mind of another monk without their expressed permission was considered an invasion of their personal sanctuary, defiling it and, possibly, casting it down. To read another's thoughts was vulgar and offensive, disrespectful and boorish, something beyond bad manners.

A City-dweller was different. It was assumed that whatever was in their minds was of no importance and to read them was considered doing them a favor and most monks refused to engage in such sideshow antics. City-Dwellers, like T'mer, were easy to read. Their auras radiated the chaos of their minds and manipulating them was just a matter of implanting suggestions and allowing the City-dweller to think he came up with the idea on his own. It wasn't considered an intrusion because the monks didn't think anyone except them understood the sacredness of life and whatever thoughts the doubter had were the thoughts of a child. They were deemed unimportant.

C'ton turned away from D'nan, debating with himself whether he should demand information or just take it without D'nan knowing. The morality of it bothered him, but he didn't like how they had taken J'son without first advising him of the will of the Council and what they had foreseen. It had been a long time since he had visited the Temple, but that didn't mean he was out of the loop. By the right of his designation he still sat on the High Council and would be justified in demanding knowledge from D'nan. But that's not what he wanted to do, for in demanding what they knew he would be compelled to divulge what he knew, and unless the Transcendentals spoke to him specifically concerning J'son he wouldn't chance telling the monks anything that they could use to their advantage.

C'ton causally waved his hand across his face, distracting D'nan and capturing his attention momentarily. It was a subtle trick that all initiates would recognize as preparation for a spoken spell and they would brace themselves against it, putting up mental barriers, closing down vulnerable parts of themselves and retreating within. The only problem with that type of defense is that it left wide regions of their awareness unguarded and unprotected, like someone deep in thought oblivious to the fly crawling around his face. He might swat at it absently, but his conscious awareness wouldn't be bothered by such a distraction.

Having drawn D'nan's attention for a moment, C'ton peered into his surface thoughts, the radiating cellular memory that all sentient beings shared, reading the lines of his face and picking up the subtle clues that would tell C'ton where D'nan had been and possibly, hopefully, what the Council had said to him. Seizing the moment, he quickly glanced into D'nan's eyes, seeing their mirror-like quality and the light burning brightly behind them. Only those so trained could interpret the reflection and determine what it meant.

Passing air between his lips to create a low decibel vibration, something akin to a hum but more melodic, C'ton produced a wave pulse directed towards D'nan that enveloped his eye and mapped the recent contents of his mind like the reflection of a steel marble. C'ton saw glimpses of images skirting past him, a chaotic jumble of light emissions that lacked coherency or time frame. Then the images became static and he saw a landscape of descriptions and illumination filling his own mind, and in that split second he perceived their strategy and knew why they wanted J'son.

It wasn't true that the priest had been told by the Transcendentals to retrieve J'son, or so that is what D'nan understood. The Council had discovered a strong variance in the energy field that produced and supported the Dome and had gone into deep meditation in order to uncover the source of that variance. While in that state, the Council sought out the guidance of the Transcendentals in the hopes that they would show them the cause of the fluctuation and how to resolve it. What they had been shown was the face of J'son. D'nan and others had been sent out by the Council to find J'son and bring him back to the Temple.

Their purpose was to discern the meaning of the fluctuation and J'son's part in it. D'nan's orders were to retrieve J'son at all cost and bring him back. There, he would have been questioned and read to determine if he was friend or foe. It would appear that J'son didn't have a choice in the matter. C'ton didn't like this at all and even with his rank within the Council he knew he would have a hard time getting answers. It was best, he decided, to follow them to the Temple and request an audience with the High Priest, C'aad.

It had been a long time since C'ton got mixed up in the politics of the priesthood, and could have gone for the rest of the age without engaging them. If it wasn't for J'son and the vision he had been given by the Transcendentals, he would have liked to have spent the dark in a refuge on the far side of the Dome in deep meditation. Obviously, that wasn't going to happen. Soon they would pass through the sacred tree grove surrounding the Temple and come before the gates. There they would be separated: J'son would go to the House of Healing before being taken to the sanctuary; T'mar and T'mer would be led to the House of Labor, forced to expend their energy supporting the Dome; and he would be left to fend for himself.

T'mer would balk at the idea of service and T'mar won't be able to conceal her true identity from them for much longer. It was taking more energy for her to maintain her ruse than what they would demand from her as a mere Technician. C'ton knew she didn't have the discipline or the refinement to remain undercover indefinitely and his concern was more for the welfare of T'mar and T'mer than for J'son. If J'son had suffered a psychic break, like he feared, J'son would be no use to them. On the other hand, if J'son recovered and awoke with full possession of his abilities he might prove to be more than the Council could handle. The fate of T'mar and T'mer was more uncertain.

C'ton dropped his hand to his side and smiled at D'nan, wanting for the inevitable response.

"A spell then, C'ton?"

"Oh, no. All this time wandering around separated from the Temple has deprived me of a connection powerful enough to cast any spell, much less one that could manipulate someone such as yourself."

"Why take that which is freely given. You could demand anything from me and I would obey, as is the custom of the enlightened. We have nothing to hide. You are right, C'ton. You have been away for too long. The High Priest has said you should have taken the test. Maybe then you would know what has happened."

The glint in D'nan's eye, the sign of confidence and secret knowledge that betrayed his designation, caused C'ton to wonder if D'nan had access to knowledge, or experience, above his rank. "Shouldn't you have moved up by now, D'nan?" C'ton asked acerbically, becoming more annoyed by D'nan's insolent attitude.

"Things have changed a lot since you were last here. The tests are still being given, but due to a disagreement over the direction we should take all promotions have been temporarily suspended and I am one of those that are caught between designations unable to claim my rightful position. So mind yourself when you enter the Temple. The Council will not tolerate a lapse of discipline and all offenders will be dealt with the upmost of severity. These are trying times."

D'nan stopped talking and moved past C'ton, walking quickly and catching up with T'mar and T'mer. They were a few feet behind the monks carrying J'son, walking side by side, the fingers of their hands lightly touching, conveying tenderness and also comforting support, one for the other. D'nan broke through them, pushing them away from each other and proceeded to the front of the formation, whispering something to the monks with the stretcher as he passed. His disruption caused T'mar and T'mer to stop in their tracks, watching J'son and the monks move away, then they turned towards each other in dumb silence.

C'ton came up between them and put a gentle hand on their shoulders. He smiled feebly at them, hoping to convince them not to retaliate with violence but to accept the situation with patience. "The gracious formality of the monks has lessened of late. There are things happening here that we are unaware. I suggest we proceed with caution showing kindness and reverence. Their lack of respect may be endemic of what we may find in the Temple. We can't tip our hand, not yet. We must find out what they know concerning J'son."

"I could crush him and his mindless automatons. If he only knew—"

"Careful T'mar," C'ton cautioned. "I suggest you to bury that knowledge down deep and keep on guard against divulging that information. Keep it secret. I have a strange feeling about this. If they find out who you really are that would be disastrous. They would take you, sentence you and put you to death."

"That was a long time ago," T'mar said caught up in reflection. "I have since renounced my affiliation with B'el and have spent the last age trying to defeat him."

"Are you sure whom you serve, T'mar?" C'ton asked. "The monks believe they have the right of worship. We must be respectful and unassuming of their position."

"That's easy for you to say," T'mar shot back angrily. She was getting frustrated. "I won't work for them, C'ton. We need to be with J'son until he gets better to protect him. Then we need to get out of here."

"If any of them try to put their hands on me or T'mar again, T'mer growled, "I will snap their spine and yank their hearts out."

"It's that type of violence I want to avoid, T'mer. We have to remain undercover in order to depart without incidence. They will find it incomprehensible that we will want to leave after the darkness is complete, but I will suggest that Technicians in the Temple will only cause trouble. They will remember you, T'mer and recommend that you leave. But T'mar they will want to know more about. Already the heat of your anger is lighting up your aura and your connection to an energy source beyond their control is troubling to them. D'nan senses that you are hiding something, but he assumes all will be revealed once inside the Temple. It is up to you, T'mar, to keep your identity secure."

"Is this another lesson then, C'ton?"

"No, no lessons, T'mar, just words of caution. I am as curious about

J'son as much as you are. He is an oddity for sure. The Transcendentals seemed to have taken an interested in him, also. If what D'nan said about The War beginning at the beginning of the next age, it is important to find out what part J'son might play in it."

"That's what you think, isn't it?" T'mar asked incredulously. "You think J'son's presence here indicates the start of The War. You believe he fulfills the Prophecy!"

"What prophecy?" T'mer asked.

"Nothing that needs to concern you, T'mer," C'ton said. "It is just the High Priest's analysis of an ancient document. T'mar knows that such manuscripts lend themselves to different interpretations depending on astral alignments. 'Prophecy' is the wrong term for what is happening here. A more correct term would be 'Utterance', more of a self-fulfilling prophecy. I do not subscribe to specific utterances, no matter who might make them. There is too much room for confusion. I find it hard to believe that the Council is teaching such expressions as fact. It isn't for the Council to be activists. That might be why the Transcendentals are involved."

"Transcendentals! Prophecy! All of it is nothing but imaginary creations used to manipulate the weak." That X was deep in T'mer's face and he narrowed his eyes, staring at the backs of the monks. "I don't think you wizards are capable of telling the truth. Everything you say and do is designed to further your own agenda. Lies are your foundation and deception the building materials."

"That's not true, T'mer," T'mar said sadly. "At least not for all of us. I have learned that lies are harder to remember and therefore not beneficial. As far as being deceptive, we use deception as a cover to protect the mysteries surrounding this world. Not everyone should have access to those mysteries. Those truths given to someone without the proper training and context can cause all sorts of problems, like mental illness and psychosis. Only the strong willed can tame and wield the power inherent within all of us."

She shouldn't have said that, not to T'mer. It was true that it took cycles of training to stretch the mind of the initiate, to prepare them to accept the ideas presented to them as real and only those with superior mental discipline managed to progress up the ranks. Technicians rarely possessed the mental strength or the plasticity of mind for such rigorous instruction. T'mer's fragile ego would rebel against the notion that he didn't qualify for higher learning because he was mentally weak. It was a slap in his face to suggest that in a battle against a wizard he would be defeated because of a mental weakness.

"That's not what you would have said in times past," C'ton replied. "I remember a hard-headed girl once who believed all knowledge should be freely given for the betterment of world. I tried to warn you then that certain knowledge must be kept secret."

"I didn't show mental weakness when I rescued you from B'el," T'mer spat back. "You're no smarter than me and your illusions are mere shadows to frighten children. I don't believe any of it."

"And that's why you fail," C'ton said quietly.

D'nan and the other three monks had each taken hold of the stretcher and were now running towards the Temple with J'son between them. C'ton, T'mar and T'mer glanced at each other without saying anything and proceeded to chase after them, breaking into a full sprint in order to close the gap. They settled down into a fast jog and maintained that pace, keeping only a dozen feet between them and the monks. The road widened considerably as they approached the Temple, which had before it several structures. They could also see monks and other travelers like themselves just entering the sacred grove and moving towards the gates of the Temple.

Chapter Seventeen:

The Grove

"Our chanting produces a vibration. That vibration is controlled and directed upwards towards the top of the Dome. If we were to stop chanting, this planet would become a wasteland."

One of the priests describing the importance of what they do

The spire coming out of the top of the Temple dominated the sky; its luminous shaft of light broke through the clouds overhead and touched the roof of the heavens. The Temple itself was all white, polished like marble and surrounded by a high, thick wall made of a black rock with only one entrance. The main road, made out of a quartz-like material that sparkled in the sun but would glow deep red in the dark, led out from that gate in a straight line and passed through a forest of artificial, perfectly aligned metallic obelisks. The obelisks were silver in color and a thousand feet high, as thick as trees at the bottom but tapering towards the top and forming a point, looking more phallic in construct and mimicking the spire coming out of the top of Temple. This grove of metal spikes surrounded the Temple hundreds of rows deep, evenly spaced one behind the other.

It was hard to determine at this distance, but in between the rows could be seen figures, individual and small groups, moving through and around the obelisks. Some of the figures, robe-covered monks mostly, appeared to be sitting down in a circle around a central figure with their head down, like in prayer. Their number could only be guessed at because the obelisks dwarfed them and gave one the impression that they were more like insects than people. Only the ones that were nearer the road and farther away from the Temple could be made out clearly. There was also another road that ran in front of the grove of obelisks perpendicular to the main road on both sides. On this road could be seen other travelers pushing overloaded carts and carrying their personal belongings, all of them heading toward the Temple, seeking the front gate, hoping for sanctuary against the dark.

Coming to the juncture of this road and the main road, the monks carrying J'son stopped running and settled down into a more unhurried pace, leaving the 'int-infested road behind. They entered the grove, nodding in respectful silence to those they met and continued down the main road towards the gate barely visible deep within. Some of the monks and other travelers heading towards the Temple left the main road and made their way through the obelisks, moving deeper into the grove and halting when they came upon a group of monks sitting on the ground in a circle chanting and singing. The new comers were immediately welcomed into the group without comment, where they sat down and started chanting also. The monks carrying J'son didn't stop to participate or even seem to be aware that others were leaving the road.

C'ton, T'mar and T'mer entered the grove moments after the monks and did take notice of the activities going on all around them. It could now be seen that the grove was filled with people in all manner of dress and appearance, some of them leaving the main road heading for the small groups scattered throughout the grove, but most of them staying on the road, heads down. C'ton and T'mar didn't pay too much attention to them, instead keeping their eye on the monks with J'son.

T'mer, however, having only been to the Temple once before, was very attentive to what was going on. Although the obelisks were placed using precision and standing behind one kept you from seeing the others beyond it, T'mer was able to see that in certain places the obelisks formed openings devoid of these structures. It was at these places that the monks and other travelers sat down and chanted. These open areas were situated all over the grove with no apparent rhyme or reason, at least not at ground level. Some were larger in circumference, some smaller. Some of the openings were grouped together in twos and threes while others were located by themselves and had one or two monks sitting by themselves. These were located deeper in the grove and were harder to see, disappearing behind the obelisks surrounding them.

The chanting of these groups closest to the main road increased in volume and T'mer tried to make out what they were saying. Their words were repetitive and monotonous, only a handful of low, guttural sounds repeated over and over again. The words, or at least the sounds, were incoherent and jumbled together, only the ups and down of the rhythmic cadence could be discerned. The vibration produced by their precise, musical synchronization created a sonic force that could be felt by all and only seen by few.

As they continued to chant, a vague illumination enveloped these groups, more like a haze or a mist, and increased in intensity whenever they came to the end of their chant and started over again. If T'mer knew what he was looking at, he would have known that the mists forming around these groups were particles of a wave-form that lacked the energy needed to unite with the shaft of light coming out of the top of the Temple. To unite in this way was the sole purpose of their chanting.

As they travelled deeper into the grove and closer to the gate, more and more groups could be seen between the obelisks and the sound of their chanting grew louder, a low drone that produced a constant vibration that could be felt like an undertow carrying them towards the gate. At these groups, unlike those further away, a bright, shimmering dome, almost opaque, enveloped them, obscuring those inside. A shaft of light came out of the top of these small domes and slanted upwards, over the gate, towards the top of the Temple, joining with it and seemingly helping to produce the protective Dome that covered the habitable areas of the planet.

"What are they saying?" T'mer asked.

"It is an ancient language and only the elite know the translation. But it's not so much what they are saying as the vibration they produce," C'ton said. "Vibratory waves are much denser than light waves. More energy means more power."

"How much do you remember from the time you were here?" T'mar asked T'mer, her eyes still locked on J'son and his stretcher.

"I remember they made me sit in one of those groups and gave me a sound to hum. It was so repetitive and nonsensical. I had to sit like that for hours on end and then they made me do manual work in the Temple, like serving them food and cleaning tables. It was humiliating!"

"They may have you do it again, T'mer," C'ton said. "They take service very seriously."

"I have no problem with physical work, but I won't sit on the ground and hum for them. It's a waste of my time."

"You do realize, T'mer, that if it wasn't for those groups the Dome would dissolve and the Wasteland would move in and cover the world." C'ton noticed T'mar was quiet and reflective and took her silence as an indication that she either didn't mind C'ton instructing T'mer or she didn't care. Either way, C'ton hoped he could impress upon T'mer the importance of the chanting.

"The chanting takes on the form of actual words as we get into the Temple. Those smaller groups that we saw at the perimeter of the grove are for practice. They are where the apprentices start before they become initiated; also City-Dwellers and others will come to fulfill their vows there. Those groups don't produce the right quality vibration needed to help support the Dome, but they are still used for training purposes in the hope of discovering those with the gift of chanting. It is not until they know how to chant before they are given the actual words. It's the words that are important in order to produce the right quality vibration. I am sure they put you with the neophytes."

"T'mer was a rather difficult student, weren't you? Wait! C'ton, do you see that?" T'mar stopped walking and pointed at the monks carrying J'son up ahead. J'son was lying still on the stretcher looking relaxed, but he was covered in a glowing red veil of mist, dim but getting brighter. She could see shafts of light radiating outward from him and connecting with the closest of the groups out in the grove, merging with them, branching out further and connecting with other groups farther out. The monks carrying him either didn't notice the energy fluctuation or didn't deem it important.

"Why is he glowing like that?" T'mer asked.

"We have to catch up to them, C'ton," T'mar said. "That shouldn't be happening. He is still unconscious. They shouldn't allow that to happen. Only in the House of Healing should they do that. They should be protecting him."

"Calm down, T'mar. I'm sure they—"

T'mar took off and closed the gap between them and the monks in a moment, seizing one of the staffs of the stretcher and knocking that monk violently to the ground, causing the other three to stop. The glowing ceased immediately and the shafts of light faded away.

"What are you doing, woman?" D'nan snapped. "It is forbidden for you to touch him. You don't have the proper training. Or do you? T'mar. I know you, don't I?"

"What you are doing is wrong," she said, yanking on the staff trying to pull the stretcher out of their hands despite the consequences.

"T'mar," C'ton said gently, putting his hand on top of hers. "D'nan, we are just concerned about his well being."

"For a mere Technician to be so presumptuous and to interfere, especially within the grove is grounds for punishment. If she would have done this inside the gate, she would have been taken away instantly to be reprogrammed."

"Nobody is going to take her anywhere," T'mer said, scowling with that X crossing his face.

"T'mer. T'mar. Please."

"It's okay, T'mar," J'son muttered, trying to lift his head up off the stretcher and failing.

"J'son? How are you, son?" C'ton took his hand off of T'mar's and placed it on J'son forehead, like he was checking on a fever. "You need to lay still. Can you talk?"

"So you see, T'mar," D'nan said, lowering the stretcher down in the middle of the road. "What we were allowing was actually helping him. You shouldn't have interfered."

"I'm okay, T'mar," J'son said. "I was drawing strength from the Dome Preservers. They were helping me to regain consciousness and didn't even know it."

T'mar let go of the staff after placing it on the ground and reached out to help J'son up into a sitting position. J'son was woozy and slightly nauseous. His vision swam before him and his eyes were glassy and cross. He squeezed his nose between his thumb and forefinger, digging them into the corners of his eyes. Removing his fingers and blinking several times, he looked at T'mar and then up at C'ton standing above him. "I guess we're almost to the gate."

"Can you stand?" C'ton asked, reaching down with an opened hand and pulling him up off the stretcher. He found it odd that J'son seemed to know exactly where he was.

T'mar stood up with him and had her arm around his waist, helping to support his weight. T'mer moved over to them and grabbed J'son under his arm, also helping. J'son was standing now, although on wobbly legs and his eyes still didn't look right. They were dilated and full of veins, blue and red in color. He looked ragged and exhausted, but T'mar thought it was good to see him standing again and conscious. The monks, without saying a word, broke down the stretcher, took up their staffs and the clothes used to make the stretcher, and continued towards the gate, leaving D'nan behind with the others.

Chapter Eighteen:

The Gate

"Once within the gate, no one will be permitted to leave. Travel between the Temple and the lands beyond will be restricted until the age has passed."

D'nan cautioning the others of their present situation

"You are hiding more secrets than your friend T'mar, boy," D'nan said. "I was hoping the power of the 'dprs, the Dome Preservers would help draw you out of yourself, but I never assumed you would have the ability to enhance the overall frequency strength of the Dome. We have been told that you would be beneficial in balancing out the energetic fluctuations in the transmission, but we believed that would have something to do with your untapped, unconscious abilities, not through any cognizant effort made by you. This is indeed a pleasant surprise."

D'nan turned towards C'ton and for the first time he bowed down low before C'ton and mumbled words of reverence and respect. Standing upright once again, he stared directly at C'ton, ignoring the others and not bothering himself with the formalities of rank. As far as he was concerned, they all had secrets and he wanted to clear the slate and start again to illicit any pertinent information that they were willing to give. In order to build their trust, however, he knew he would have to divulge information that the High Priest wouldn't approve of. Nevertheless, D'nan needed to know what they knew. Information was power, and in the political realm of the Temple in order for D'nan to advance he had to have leverage.

"D'nan, we know this is a bad time for you," C'ton said, speaking first. "We can see by the laborers in the grove that the time is fast approaching that you will need all available inhabitants to help in Dome generation. We are here to help you in your necessary and vital calling of maintaining that which keeps all of us alive. Our primary concern at the moment, however, is for J'son's safety."

"That depends," D'nan said, glancing over at J'son and then back at C'ton, "on whom he claims to be and where he got his training. Although I see certain tendencies in him reminiscent of your teachings, it is obvious to us that he has come about his abilities naturally. An analysis of his aural spectrum, his special memory, indicates that he just appeared here and has no history tract that we can study. Was he shielded from us on purpose?"

There were several things that stuck out in C'ton's mind all at the same time. He was comforted to know that the Council had no idea who J'son was and where he had come from. That was logical enough in that never before has there been verifiable evidence of anyone using himself as a portal and crossing the barrier between worlds, much less a human. But D'nan didn't mention anything about portals. He only said that they needed J'son to stabilize the energy fluctuations in the Dome. C'ton looked up into darkening red sky beyond the haze of the Dome, took one last look at the receding sun which was no bigger than a pin prick amid a sea of brightening stars and then looked at the comparatively bright shaft of light bursting out of the top of the Temple. He could detect the fluctuations in the beam, seeing the light bending towards the red and falling away from the blue which was characteristic of its normal illumination.

A glowing red Dome at this early stage in the age cycle wasn't good and should only turn red towards the end of the darkness. C'ton understood now why they needed J'son, or rather the energy he seemed to possess. The monks were having trouble with Dome production and instead of being a light in the long darkness it now looked like the Temple itself was running out of energy. He looked at the groups in the groves chanting and humming, trying to produce the vibratory acoustics necessary to merge with those within the walls of the Temple. There weren't enough of them nor were the ones present able to generate the quality needed to keep the Dome in operation.

If the priests thought that the Transcendentals had sent J'son to help them with the Dome, then his history wasn't as important to them as his abilities. If the Transcendentals didn't feel a need to tell the Council J'son was from Earth, then C'ton certainly didn't want to complicate things by divulging that information. However, D'nan also mentioned war coming at the start of the next age. Is that war going to begin over energy? Will the monks still be able to retain power if the Dome falls? And what of the City? If the monks fail to keep the Dome intact, will those in the City completely deny the sacred and fully embrace their Technology? Is the era of the gods coming to an end?

"We will not be staying with you or any of the monks," J'son said, feeling stronger and more clear-headed. "We will continue on our path until we reach our destination. I will help you with what I can, but the answer to your problem lies beyond the Dome. Only the one who has created the Dome has the ability to keep it from collapsing."

"J'son, I think it is best if we speak to the High Priest and see what he has to say," C'ton said. "If D'nan were to tell the truth, he would tell you that we have lost the power of pre-cognition. It started to slip away as soon as we entered the grove and I began to hear the chanting. Their poor quality noise production interferes with proper mental focus. I am sure all on the other side of the wall are experiencing the same disruption. We can't see the unperturbed reverberations from the future, so making the right decisions becomes less obvious. We need information. The more counsel we obtain, the more we can see with clarity."

"So now we all know this boy has abilities and his steps are directed by the Transcendentals," D'nan interrupted. "He was sent to us at our greatest moment of need and he comes to us now to help us. I don't know what you mean by continuing on your path for all roads lead here. Outside of the Temple is nothing but death and misery. The science of the City-dwellers leads to confusion and distraction and hoping in those who live close to the boundary will take you in their folly. They don't have enough of anything and don't share. Only here is there the promise of life and transformation. The Dome will not fall and unless the High Priest has released you personally, you will not be permitted to leave. Once you entered the sacred grove, you came under the authority of the Temple. My directive is to return to the Temple with the boy, alone."

"That's what you think," T'mer growled.

"You're not taking him anywhere without us," T'mar said, stepping forward and forcing her way between C'ton and D'nan.

"We're all going, T'mar," J'son said. "I will speak to their High Priest and explain to him what is happening. Then we shall go out into the dark."

The five of them started walking again with D'nan and C'ton in the lead, J'son in the center and T'mar and T'mer bringing up the rear. J'son had his head down and closed his eyes against the incessant chanting, which was growing into a deafening clamor that could be felt rising and falling against his chest, drumming out a pulsating rhythm that made it hard to proceed. Each step he took forward was met by resistance as the pressure of each syllable crashed into him. The flow of sounds was becoming less jumbled, more coherent, and actual words were starting to emerge, although he still couldn't make out their meaning.

He wasn't as clear-headed as he would have liked. So much had happened to him since he arrived here and much of that time was spent either in an altered state of consciousness or knocked out. His head was spinning and whisks of memory darted around in his consciousness. His recollection of the events was vivid, but somehow he didn't feel like they had happened to him personally. It was like an overriding presence had taken up residence in his head and was showing him things that were, that are, and things that would come to pass if he stayed on his present course.

He heard the voice of this presence as one heard the echo of childhood: it was there but transient, lurking in the recesses of his mind and providing occasional guidance when needed. J'son knew he had to help the monks with the Dome, but he also knew that the time of the Dome was almost over. He had been shown that. He had also been shown why the Dome was collapsing and that the war the monks were so concerned about would start sooner rather than later.

The Council had failed in their mission by allowing transit between worlds and so poking holes in the very fabric of their reality. It was through these holes that precious energy had leaked into the world of the humans and destabilized energy production on this world. The Council didn't seem to know or understand that passage between worlds was a matter of give and take. When J'son passed through from Earth to the planet of the Elohim, a doorway, a portal was left opened, serving as a conduit for energy to pass back and forth with J'son acting as the doorman.

The grove they were moving through was created to generate an artificial energy field that kept waves of force moving in a particular direction and all those found within its circle of influence discovered through observation tiny pulls of energy coming out of their bodies, kind of like a magnet pulling on metallic filaments. However, the magnet only draws out the highest quality of energy, leaving the dross for personal consumption. Anyone living behind the walls of the Temple for any length of time lost all sense of personal identity and found themselves conforming to the rituals of the priesthood, yielding over their distinctiveness to the overwhelming demands of Dome support. J'son knew they couldn't stay at the Temple for long without losing all of their individuality and freedom.

As the wall of the Temple grew closer and the gate loomed large, J'son noticed that the walls weren't as linear as they seemed before they entered the grove. Instead of a high, straight wall running the length of the Temple, it took off at an angle leaving the gate nestled in a niche. The walls ran along a diagonal in opposite directions from the gate and extended deep into the grove of obelisks. It was those remote corners, pushed to the extremes to the left and the right that they encountered first. Using the gate as the apex and crossing the imaginary line made by connecting the two outermost corners, the road split the wall into two right triangles.

The wall was darker and more ominous up close, casting a gloomy blackness on the obelisks closest to it. Where the obelisks were maybe a thousand feet tall, the wall towered over them twice as high. Running along the wall close to the top at regular intervals were several windows or openings and several robed monks could be seen busying themselves and occasionally looking down on the different groups of chanters far below. Central in each window was a round, concaved, reflective disk that the monks kept polished and free of dust and blemishes. Only rarely did the monks up in the wall look in the direction of the main road, seemingly more interested in adjusting their mirrors and watching those in the grove chanting than in those approaching the gate.

As the light from their receding star diminished it was getting easier for everyone to see the shimmering, iridescent mini-domes surrounding the groups of chanting initiates and novices. The tone and quality of those chanting closer to the gate was far superior to those further away, but J'son could see that the character of the sound was still inferior and far from obtaining perfection. Each mini-dome produced a shaft of light, a beam of concentrated energy that materialized at the top and slanted upwards towards the wall, making contact with the mirrors located in the windows. The beams hitting the mirrors were weak and diffused, having a yellow/orange tint. The monks seemed concerned with the color of the beams and adjusted the mirrors accordingly.

In the blackness of the openings, J'son could see the beams of energy entering the front side of the mirrors in a slow-frequency wave, condensing and changing color and then exiting out the back side in a tight, brilliant stream of photons. The photons struck another disk further within the wall and were absorbed. The effect produced tiny, humming packets of yellow florescence striking the mirrors, followed by a tight radiant beam of photons coming out the other side and ended by being absorbed by a non-reflective, black disk. The sound that could be heard above the chanting was a humming, a popping, some buzzing and then a low end vibration chased by a pulse. It was the quality of the pulse that the monks wrestled with and they kept busy adjusting mirrors trying to produce pulses of the greatest benefit.

"These haven't been trained right," J'son said, pointing at groups on the ground. "They need to concentrate harder and create a beam of energy that doesn't have to be altered. You're losing too much energy in the transfer."

"How do you know that, boy?" D'nan asked. "As long as we get a pure beam within the Temple, the Dome will sustain itself."

"That's not true! I can see the distortion in the beams now. If these people are representative of whom you have behind the wall, then I see the Dome failing before this world reaches the periphery of its orbit. Your star will not return before the Dome collapses."

"J'son, how do you know these things?" T'mar asked from behind him. "The Dome and the sacred rituals have stood since shortly after the beginning. What do you know about Dome production?"

"He is right," D'nan said. "The Dome is failing and the workers are too few. Many that would have come from the City have decided to ride out the night there. There is rumor that the City-Dwellers have developed an independent source of energy and there is even talk about them working on an artificial portal. Our... ambassadors there have sent conformation that a permanent door is being constructed and will soon be opened within the City. Although we believe such endeavors are fruitless and will come to naught, our concern is that it is because of these rumors that the people have failed to come to support the Dome."

"J'son," C'ton said. "I have noticed that the chanting bothers you. Some claim that the chanting is a calming influence and inspires them into selfless service, but I can see by the tiny stress indicators on your face that the chanting is disrupting your inner mental state. Is there something I can do to help?"

"I don't think so. It's the quality of the sound that's not right. It's like the words and the sound are out of step, out of harmony. I don't think it has anything to do with the words. I can see the quality of energy they are generating is low, but not because they are doing it wrong. It is almost like they are purposely trying to alter the consistency of the vibration. It's subtle, but those on the ground are producing a vibration that is one step down from what is required. It's like they are singing off key."

C'ton and D'nan looked at J'son with a look of surprise and amazement. J'son was right about the chanting being out of harmony with what was required. Because of the unsatisfactory and inadequate workers that those in the City represented, the Council took it upon themselves to alter the actual wording of the chant in hopes that the change would be easier for the novice to replicate and thus their output would increase. However, the poor quality of the sound produced created a transient, counter-vibration that had to be filtered out and neutralized. That was the function of the mirrors. This hi-tech device was borrowed from those living in the City in the beginning when Dome construction was new, but had become inadequate for their demands once all the bugs of Dome production got worked out.

The mirrors had been in storage for several cycles and were long forgotten until just recently when the Council made the decision to re-incorporate Technology into their rituals. It was a decision based on need rather than desire, and several high-ranking monks were totally against the use of the Technology that came from the City, fearing that it would be interpreted as a sign of failure and confusion on their part, making them look vulnerable and putting their religion into question. They were supposed to be the light of the world and it was their beliefs that sustained and maintained all life on the planet. Some had decided they would rather live among the humans with diminished powers than accept that theirs was a bankrupt system.

C'ton knew all of this and it was one of the reasons why he left the Temple and refused to sit in Council. For macro-cycles he argued for the inclusion and assimilation of Technology into their rituals in the belief that over time their own mental dexterity and competency would drop off leaving them in just such a situation as they now found themselves. He argued that those in the City should use their knowledge to help in Dome support and that a new period of cooperation between the two belief-systems should prevail. However, C'aad, the High Priest resisted overt assistance from the "heathens and heretics" and pulled the mirrors out of storage, installing them in secret without telling the City-Dwellers about it. "That's all we need," the High Priest had said. "Let them think they have the answer. We will never hear the end of it and our positions will be taken away from us. Without the trust of the population, we have nothing."

It was true that the monks feared those from the City and what their Technology offered. "Take a pill or institute a program and all your wildest dreams will come true," was the common belief within the City. It was easier to sit at a keyboard and punch out your wants than to imagine your wants into being. To become a monk, or at the very least an initiate, took discipline and serious study to reprogram oneself to accept the teachings which brought about personal transformation. Those that continued with their training found themselves, over time, unable to think in terms that contradicted their new programming and that programming produced within them an aversion towards everything remotely Technical, thinking it was beneath them and profane.

It was because of this strenuous and demanding discipline that most monks, unlike C'ton, considered themselves superior to others and their enhanced abilities established that fact. "The more precise your understanding of the mysteries, the more power you had available to manipulate." In truth, it was more a determined belief in their sense of self that gave them any power at all, but that power was weakening and growing stale due to a lack of belief in the old ways.

Their power was peaking at the beginning, but started to deteriorate shortly after B'el left, which left a power vacuum. In the grasp for power that proceeded after the founding of the Dome, old and young initiates battled each other for superiority and position, hoping to seize the more powerful positions on the planet. It was an unstable time and many young initiates promoted themselves into positions they weren't properly trained for. D'nan was one of those. It was because of that inexperience D'nan hadn't been able to advance and continue developing his abilities.

Young and ambitious, D'nan was motivated by the promise of personal power rather than the obtainment of power for altruistic ends. It was one of the disagreements C'ton had with D'nan, arguing from his experience that the drive towards personal enrichment only led to the mistake of B'el. The accumulation of knowledge was supposed to be for the improvement of all, C'ton and the Adepts believed, but for the younger generation that hadn't been around at the beginning knowledge was static and what you did with it determined whose side you were on. The Temple was filled with too many of those young, inexperienced initiates that never had the opportunity to study under the masters. Their learning came from the fragments of war and the dictates of those that rule. Only a few like C'ton still remembered the original teachings of the Ancients and how far those within the wall of the Temple have fallen. It was no wonder that the Dome was failing.

The gate was right before them and the obelisks had thinned out considerably. A large, triangular area had opened up in front of the gate, having neither obelisks nor shrubbery of any kind; only a gem-embedded road fanning out to fill the space before the gate. The gate itself was pushed back, like a sliding door, into the recesses of the wall. Fully opened, the opening in the gate would have been one hundred feet across, but due to the lateness of the age the gate was almost shut and only a gap of about ten feet was made available for their entry. The gate was thick, made out of the same black stone of the wall. When closed, one would be hard pressed to detect the seam between the gate and the wall and it has been debated by those on the outside that the seam is made invisible by a spell cast by the High Priest.

The gate and wall are so thick that as they walked through it took several micro-cycles to reach the inner wall. J'son, impressed by the thickness of the wall, counted his steps as they went to determine an approximate measurement. He stopped counting once he reached five hundred steps. By his estimation, the wall was over one mile thick without a single line or crevice to indicate the stacking together of blocks. By all appearances, the wall was constructed out of one piece of stone hundreds of miles long and at least ½ a mile high. Except for the precision, angular cut of the stone, the wall surrounding the Temple could have been part of the ridge line of a small mountain range. But wall construction was a mystery that had been lost to the general public a long time ago. Only the library located deep within the Temple, books only the High Priest and a few others high up in the hierarchy had the privilege of studying, had the true tale of how the wall was constructed and why the manner of manufacturing was kept secret.

J'son didn't concern himself with wall construction and only entertained the thought of how something this massive could have been built for a moment. He was more interested and increasingly preoccupied by the clarity of the chanting coming at him from inside the wall. The noise coming from the grove faded into the background as they moved through the gate, only to be replaced by the pleasant-sounding, precision chanting emanating from the other side of the wall. Although slightly muffled because of the wall, the sound was purer and had a clarity that allowed one to discern the actual words, if not the meaning behind them.

It was easier for J'son to bear the sound, finding it more in harmony with the constant buzzing he detected within his own mind. The vibration was also different, and better. The discordant thumping that he experienced earlier pounding him on the chest faded behind him into a Doppler-effect wave-form that ceased to be disturbing and off key and became progressively more acceptable and easy to bear, like listening to the noise of a live rock concert and then afterwards turning on the radio to hear the same songs played with a certain amount of skill and production. The sound coming from inside the wall was music to his ears.

"Lasset uns beten zum Grossten Gott, der Allmachtige, der Schopfer von Alles." The chanting was low, mono-toned, monotonous and repetitive, over and over again, the tone rising and falling but maintaining that same vibratory frequency. It sounded like the humming of a power line with words thrown in for good measure.

"What words are they using?" J'son asked. "They seem different and it's obvious that the quality of the vibration has increased. What I am hearing now is almost right. The pitch is still off slightly, but that might have something to do with the wall. It's creating a dampening effect with minimal sonic deterioration, keeping all available energy behind the walls. I perceive very little energy drain coming from within."

"Once we pass the gate," D'nan said, "you will see the purity of the power generated in support of the Dome. It used to be that we took all outside the gate of the Temple and allowed them to bask in the glow of proper Dome creation. Nowhere else on the planet can you participate in the holiness and sacredness of power generation. However, because of their irreverence and complete lack of the sacred, we had to limit access and now we only take those who can perform adequately. The grove, once a source of energy storage has now become almost useless. Even the highest-ranking among us can barely traverse the road leading away from the Temple without experiencing fatigue. The obelisks, so long without proper maintenance or the energy necessary to convert low-quality sound into high-level power, have become more of a power drain than we can spare."

"So those on the outside are out of luck," T'mar said, sarcastically. "They won't be allowed in, will they?"

"You are 'lucky' to be let in," D'nan said. "I know you are not a Tech, T'mar. You are hiding your true identity from us using a powerful spell. I can see your energy levels rising in response to the chanting. T'mer, on the other hand, is locked in confusion and frustration and also fear, too, I think. That is what I should be reading from you, but you are reacting like one trained in the arts. C'ton, I know you aren't helping to conceal her identity because I would be able to see the spell trail flowing from you, which means she is either generating the cover, or she had one place on her that is so seamless that I doubt she even knows who she is. Even so, once we cross over into the Temple, all secrets will be revealed and woe to you, T'mar, if there is something important or clandestine you are keeping to yourself."

Chapter Nineteen:

The Courtyard

"I won't let them take me to the lower chambers, C'ton. I am more than just a sex toy."

T'mar voicing her disgust at the treatment of females

Passing through the gate, the wall and road were emitting a harsh, radiant red in response to the dark closing in on them. J'son and the others found themselves having to shield their eyes against the increasing ruddiness coming from within the wall. Moving away from the gate and the wall, finally entering into the courtyard of the Temple proper, J'son saw countless groups of differing size, each containing at least a hundred or more monks, stationed along the wall from end to end. Each group had a chant-generated dome over them of the purist white, and translucent with twin shafts of light slanting upwards in opposite directions. These domes were receivers of the energy that was being generated from the outside.

High up within the interior of the wall were openings just like those on the outside, but instead of being concave these mirrors were convex. The energy received from the outside and converted to a purer form was beamed down from high up in the wall and contacted the Domes at an angle. The energy of the beam was absorbed by the domes, causing them to change color frequency slightly before readjusting, and then combining with the energy of the chanting monks another beam of light shot out of the domes and angled off in the opposite direction towards the Temple rising in the middle of the courtyard.

Those beams, and hundreds of others coming from all over the Temple wall, came together, striking some type of device mounted at the apex of the Temple. The beams striking the device from all angles and locations were absorbed, and then in one tight, intense shaft of light it erupted out of the top like a volcano, jetting into the sky for miles until it terminated and arced over, forming the one Dome that protected the inhabitants of the planet.

The chanting continued without ceasing, without a pause or interruption. The energy level within the Temple was thick and full of static. Lightning flashed in some places where the power level wasn't the same, travelling up and down the primary shaft of light and arcing across the Dome, creating an opaque, white star-burst shape directly over head. Occasionally, the center of this star shape opened up revealing a dark circle, a literal hole in the Dome, filled with tiny points of light and an increasingly reddish, retreating star in the middle that was their sun. The appearance of this hole was sporadic and of different size depending on fluctuations in the quality and quantity of the energy supply. It was this hole that bothered the monks and they busied themselves trying to even out the surging fluctuations. The hole was the reason why the monks needed the mirrors because they couldn't close the hole and stabilize the fluctuations through directed meditation alone.

The Temple was directly before them and the main road ran straight into it without any diverging trails or cross passages. All who came through the gate made their way to the Temple without exception, unless prior arrangements had been obtained. The Temple was constructed out of one massive, black, naturally triangular-shaped rock with a white spire jutting out of the top. The rock of the Temple was of the same material as the wall and was carved in the image of a stony phallic symbol. Columns of windows ran up the white, conical structure facing the four points of the compass, thirteen to a side.

Above the windows, the Temple narrowed and became rounded off, forming a spherical space containing a room. This sphere was enclosed with additional windows, giving it the appearance of an observation tower. The windows, however, were tinted to only allow a particular frequency of light energy inside. It was in this room at the top of the Temple that another machine had been installed to manage the hundreds of energy streams coming from the wall and from those within the wall.

This device was more like a transformer, an ancient machine that converted all wave forms to the same vibrational frequency and then discharging that energy by use of the shaft of light exploding out of the top. The device also served as a surge protector, preventing the unauthorized use and/or indiscriminate access to an almost unlimited power supply, stepping down the power if it detected an energy spike, a problem that could conceivably blow the top of the Temple apart. It also acted as a power reserve, channeling energy back down the Temple shaft and re-distributing it back to the obelisks outside the wall for times of need. During the height of energy production, when the sun was at its closest, those that need healing or were struggling with doubts would be able to seat themselves within the Temple, in meditation, and absorb the therapeutic and restorative properties of Dome production.

Now, however, with energy in such short supply, even the House of Healing had nothing to spare. The monks might lay you down on one of their rehabilitation beds and even pray over you, but the truth was that they didn't have the belief structure necessary to transmit the healing properties of the energy into the body of those that were hurting. It was a problem that started at the beginning of the age and had increased in complexity ever since, so much so that most of the monks rejected the very idea of medicinal use for the energy. Over the span of time, those on the outside, those from the City, came to doubt the teachings of the monks and their ability to help, heal or even lead. The doubt of the City-dwellers was just one link in a long chain of events that had brought about the serious crisis of total Dome collapse that now faced the monks, and the planet.

D'nan and C'ton had stopped walking shortly after entering through the gate and waited for J'son, T'mar and T'mer to catch up. The three other monks that had accompanied D'nan earlier were nowhere in sight and the road leading up to the Temple was starting to fill up as some of the chanting groups broke off, disbanded and made their way towards the Temple. These groups were replaced by other groups of monks that had either come from the Temple, or came from outside the wall closest to the gate. The groups from outside that replaced the monks within the wall were mostly City-dwellers and dressed as such: short tunics and bare-chested. These groups closest to the wall were making their way through the gate to take their place chanting within the wall. They were lead by monks of stern countenance possessing that X that is so common on this planet.

The groups further away from the gate at the periphery of the obelisks were still yelling out their chants, screaming in hoarse voices, hoping for the chance to be found worthy enough to be allowed entry. But that was not meant to be for them. They were farther out from the gate for a reason. The dissonance of their chanting and the unstable wave fluctuations they were helping to perpetuate would only add a burden to those within the wall. While the monks promised all who came to help with Dome generation would be protected from the horrors of the dark, the truth was that the monks, for the most part, were stealing energy from them for personal use.

The monks were doing exactly what was forbidden but justified it by saying they were doing the heathen a favor. It was too late for them to make their way back to the City and unless they were allowed in they would perish. Taking their energy stores was a matter of convenience and conservation. Those further out would never see inside the walls of the Temple and would probably, eventually, storm the gate, demanding entry, throwing their weak and useless bodies across the road, only to die there.

As those from outside began to make their way within the wall, much to T'mar's dismay, only a very select few were female, the monks believing most women lacked the mental discipline needed to maintain the focus necessary for correct spell formation and creation. Women weren't allowed within the wall normally and the decree of slavery was the standing law for those women that were allowed entry. The basis of the law was that they would cause disturbances in the established order and disrupt the energy exchange through un-tethered, emotional desires feeding off of the power of the Temple.

Women were too physically attractive and arousing to properly serve in Dome production and so were regulated to the humiliating status of mere sexual playthings existing solely for the pleasure of the monks. Women could be found within the Temple, but they were usually kept out of sight and below ground in a labyrinth of passageways and caves resembling bed chambers. The women never saw the light of the sun and were only used by the monks to help them get through the long night. Most of the women never lasted long, however, dying because of physical abuse and neglect. Any male child born to these women was given over to the Temple monks as soon as he exited the womb. All females were raised in these chambers and taught how best to please men. From the time they could walk they were taught what to do with their hands and other body parts and only later as blossoming young women would they take their place among the other slaves.

Women like T'mar, though, were an exception. When C'ton had found her so long ago, his first instinct was to take her on as his sex companion as was common among the monks and for a short time that is what she was. It was only after C'ton came to know her and her ability to understand the mysteries that he initiated her as his student, teaching her the things she would need to know to keep her from being dominated by the power of the monks. When C'ton had returned to the Temple after finding her, he resisted the law which stated she became the property of the monks once inside the wall. She had become a free agent, or so C'ton argued, and insisted they evaluate her based solely on her knowledge and abilities. It had been done before by others professing the equality of the female species and some of the women had overcome the challenges, becoming androgynous and asexual in the process by physically changing their appearance once they learned the correct spell.

T'mar had braved the challenges and rose above them, but refused to change her physicality to that of a man. She enjoyed being a women and felt that her feminine nature was her greatest asset. At first she rebelled against everything the Temple had to offer and all except C'ton turned against her. What bothered the monks the most was that she debated with them, exercising her superior mental abilities and embarrassing them in the process. The turmoil and chaos that came about because of her stubborn refusal to conform soon settled down and the monks started to warm up to her, finding themselves distracted whenever she was around and even fantasizing about her while in the bed chambers with other women.

She deduced this by the coy and uncomfortable way they looked at her when she walked by and then turning away as if they weren't interested. She discovered that she liked flirting with the monks, disrupting their meditation and causing them to lose focus in such a way that they couldn't cast any spell as long as she was near, and she used it to her advantage.

C'ton had taken a lot of heat over her initiation and defended her right to be treated as an equal in front of the Council, arguing that T'mar and those like her were the will of the Transcendentals and that not to accept her was a mistake. The Council agreed that she did possess innate abilities, but her training should be limited to low level spells and she would be put on a program to help her strengthen her mental focus, in effect making her male. Basically, she would be trained as a monk, but would spend most of her time in deep meditation to purge herself of her willfulness and more importantly her femaleness. She would live within the Temple and carry out all duties assigned to her, without exception. If she didn't agree to this, she would be turned out after being drained of all her energy. C'ton didn't like it but he knew he didn't have much of a choice, and neither did she.

When C'ton approached her to inform her of the decision of the Council, he knew by looking at her face that she wouldn't like what they had to say. Still, C'ton was able to persuade her to do what they wanted, arguing that she could learn so much if she would only follow the wisdom of the Council. It was hard at first and T'mar had to learn the meaning of patience before she was able to live among the monks without controversy. C'ton was her constant companion then and he kept her safe from the insatiable lust of the monks, protecting them from her more than the other way around. T'mar was as hot tempered then as she is now and her angry outburst brought embarrassment to those that thought it would be a fun exercise to provoke her. Those monks found themselves in need of counsel after messing with her and some of them even left the order.

It was during this time that T'mar first heard about B'el and even met some of his disciples, back when the disciples of B'el and the monks were united in vision. She had been enticed by their stories of power away from the Temple, in a place that could only be reached by going through the Wastelands. She was told that B'el possessed a portal and could teach any who had the mental discipline how to use it. This knowledge prompted her to ask questions that were above her designation and she demanded access to what was written in the sacred library located within the Temple. It was these demands that brought her into conflict with C'ton, deciding that it was time for her to leave the Temple and search for answers outside the understanding of the monks.

All these memories and others flooded her awareness, awakening within her a sense of dread and peril. T'mer was feeling it, too, judging by how nervously he shifted his weight back and forth from one leg to the other. He had been okay outside of the wall and was keeping himself in check, pressing forward and keeping his memories from overwhelming him. He had come to the Temple long ago before he ever met T'mar but after C'ton had found her. He came to the Temple as a delegate of those living in the City, back in the days when there was still trust between the monks and City-dwellers. He had come with a companion and the purpose of his visit was for an exchange of ideas and Technology. The monks would provide the ideas and they would provide the Technology.

In the City, where T'mer felt most comfortable and useful, he was considered one of the smartest of the Techs, achieving that reputation because of his understanding of how things work. Those within the Temple thought everyone except them were ignorant, lacking common sense and devoid of all practical knowledge, but from T'mer's perspective he was very bright and understood more than the monks, or even T'mar knew he knew. It was because of his aptitude that he was sent to the monks in hopes they could help with their own energy problems. The Technology the City-dwellers were using didn't produce enough energy to power the machines that kept them alive. T'mer was sent to the monks with a plan to physically wire the City to the Temple and buy the energy they needed from the energy-rich Temple.

It was supposed to be a simple proposal that explained the procedure and how it would benefit the monks. The City would get all the energy they needed in exchange for labor, food, crafts and women, especially women. T'mer and his companion were to spend several macro-cycles at the Temple, using the power of the monks to create the equipment and machines necessary to establish a direct connection with the Temple. The schematics for these machines were provided by the Adepts from the City, plans which T'mer knew by heart, having built a similar device for the City-dwellers. T'mer and his companion installed and tested the components, ran a diagnostic to confirm it was operating within normal parameters and then flipped the switch.

As per the agreement, T'mer and his companion were recruited as laborers, performing whatever job the monks assigned. T'mer and his companion were split up, with T'mer helping in the fields and chanting for endless amounts of time. His companion was taken into the Temple where he worked for the High Priest. The instructions T'mer received from the monks on the ground was different than the education his companion received in the Temple and it was because of that difference that T'mer was allowed to leave when their service came to an end. Where T'mer was used for manual labor, his companion was used for breeding purposes, living mainly underground in the bed chambers. The High Priest also used him to examine, analyze and repair the device that converted all thought into energy and shot it out of the top of the Temple. Where T'mer labored and preformed tasks that he believed were beneath him, his companion lived as a Sultan enjoying sex with different, multiple partners and having his every male fantasy realized.

When his service came to an end, T'mer searched for his companion around the base of the Temple, shouting out his name and demanding that the monks return him. It was at this time that T'mer saw T'mar for the first time. It was a quick glance, like out of the corner of his eye and then she was gone. She was coming out of the Temple and passed him on the left, smiling a secret smile. She moved away quickly without saying anything and disappeared down a passage in the side of the rock base. His first thought of her was that she was a sex-slave of the monks, but she was walking around outside without an escort and she seemed different, strong and confident. T'mer was there to get his companion, but he caught a long enough glimpse of her to make an impression.

In the few moments that he was distracted by her, T'mer's companion came out of the Temple and stood above T'mer on hand-carved, black stone steps which rose out of the rock and disappeared inside the Temple. He had a large smile on his face and his hands were on his hips. He was shaking his head and trying to explain to T'mer that he wasn't going back to the City. The High Priest had personally selected him to be a continuing liaison between the City and the Temple. The monks needed him and he was starting to believe what the monks were telling him. He wouldn't leave the Temple, but he did guarantee that as long as he was there he would make sure that the connection between the two capitals would remain opened.

T'mer had known his companion, his friend, T'tan, his whole life and there was something not right about him. The look in his eye, the secret smile that all the monks seemed to wear, his expression of superiority and arrogance; T'mer almost didn't recognize his friend. That look, that smile like they knew something you didn't. It infuriated T'mer to no end and after he grew tired of debating he left T'tan on the steps of the Temple and made his way out the gate, swearing he would never return. That was his first time within the walls.

This was now his second time here and fear was rising up within him. The first time was bad enough, but that was long ago and he had grown older. T'tan had fallen under the spell of the monks and it scared T'mer to admit to himself that he might not have the will to resist them again. If he had been chosen to serve in the Temple, would he have made the same decision that T'tan did? Would he have the strength to oppose them again? He looked at T'mar and noticed she seemed tense and lost in her own memories. Would she be able to defend herself against their attempts to convert her into a sex-slave a second time? Would she be able to maintain her cover and remain loyal to him at the same time? What if his thoughts weren't his anymore? At what point would his thoughts grow quiet only to be replaced by the voices of the chanting monks?

"Globe transport has been approved beyond this point," D'nan said to the group as they huddled together, intent on keeping themselves together.

"Bout time," J'son said, throwing his arms out to his sides. A crackle of energy jumped from his finger tips and blasted past the group. The streams of energy flowing from his fingers spread out and stopped, forming a ten foot long shaft of energy with J'son in the center. The energy started to creep upward and downward at the same time, curving around the group, enclosing them in a shimmering ball of static electricity. The energy stopped flowing from his fingers and the ball of energy, which was brilliant white at first, changed colors. The bottom half of the ball solidified and became opaque, concealing everything from the waist down. The top half of the globe was clear with a tint of blue, like it was polarized. Inside, J'son, T'mar, T'mer, C'ton and D'nan stood staring at each other.

J'son moved his hands over a console that was partially hidden below the lower half of the globe. He closed his eyes and tilted his head back, like he was staring at the top of the globe. The bottom half of the globe turned bright orange and the globe lifted a few inches off the ground, hovering. Then, in the blink of an eye, the globe disappeared and reappeared several feet in the sky, hovering delicately in the air, floating and bobbing like a balloon tied to a piece of string. Everything happened so fast that the only one startled enough to respond immediately was D'nan.

"What are you doing?" He asked, furiously. "You are not authorized to use Globe Transport within the walls of the Temple. Put us back down, now!"

"Whether or not he is authorized to fly a transport globe is immaterial," C'ton said, enjoying the break in protocol. "It appears you don't have a say, unless you can materialize a globe that will encompass his."

"Put us down. That is an order. I am a representative of the High Council and will not tolerate insubordination. Put us down at once."

"I think you better enjoy the ride, D'nan," T'mar said, also enjoying herself at D'nan's expense.

The globe hovered about twenty-five feet above the ground for about a minute before it disappeared again and reappeared hundreds of feet in the air. The Temple was before them in the distance and the gate was behind them. They were now almost to the height of the wall, floating in their globe and observing their surroundings from ¼ of a mile up. J'son was being careful not to run into any of the energy beams that formed a lattice of sorts around the Temple.

"We are supposed to report to the High Priest without delay. The use of Globe Transport is only authorized for that purpose. Return us to the ground so that I may take us to see the High Priest." D'nan was more than a little peeved. What J'son had done –creating transport without permission—and what he was doing was beyond his designation and only those with a designation of "D" and above had the authorization to generate and fly a transport globe, and then only if the situation required it.

Normally, to produce a vehicle to use in globe transportation required tapping the resources which were so much in contention. To be granted access to the power streams necessary to create a globe transport meant much debate and discussion, usually ending in compromise. It's like politicians on Earth arguing over a limited amount of money and each one believing his need was greater than the others. Energy distribution decisions were made by the High Priest and all unauthorized energy uses were forbidden. For someone to steal the limited resources of the monks was tantamount to heresy and punishable by slow, energy-draining death. If J'son had done what D'nan thought he had done, J'son would have put himself and his companions in extreme peril. But J'son didn't take any power away from the monks. What he was able to do was to produce a globe using his own resources, which is why D'nan had no control over J'son's creation or his ability to pilot it.

"D'nan, I think you need to settle down a bit," C'ton advised. "It seems pretty obvious that you or the Council have nothing to do with this. J'son, how are you maintaining this transport?"

"Well, when D'nan said we were approved for transport I saw his thoughts on what he had in mind and I created it before he could. I knew he wanted to take us to see the old guy, the High Priest, but I wanted to get a better look at those mirrors. I can see minute fluctuations coming out of the energy beams on this side, up in the wall there. But I don't think that's the problem. See how the fluctuations spread as it is beamed down to the monks on the ground and then that same fluctuation is introduced into the Temple, where it is magnified. Here, let me show you."

J'son turned the globe around to face the wall and maneuvered carefully around the shafts of high-intensity energy that were being beamed to the chanting monks down below. The globe pulsed and shimmered as it moved closer to the shafts, but J'son acted like the energy streams weren't there. He moved rapidly along the wall: first in one place and then, instantly, in another until he came upon one mirror that was emitting a distorted waveform. The energy flow coming from this mirror was slightly out of phase with the others, causing an interference wave, which was then absorbed and integrated into the system. The counter vibration was only detectable by observing the angular velocity of the electron discharge, something that only the very sensitive could detect.

"You see that?" J'son asked, pointing at a dull spot on the mirror. "Right there you can see a subtle difference in the way that the energy is processed. The distortion is channeled down toward the monks where it is reabsorbed and discharged into the Temple device. I can't see where it goes from there because the distortion merges with all the other beams."

"If the problem is just one mirror out of sync," T'mar ventured. "Then why don't they just replace it? I would have thought your people could have handled this problem before now. Even I can see the distortion, now that J'son has pointed it out. Why can't you just refashion a new mirror?"

"It's not that easy, T'mar," T'mer said. He had taken an active interest in the situation once J'son started flying around the mirrors. He was one of the ones that had installed those mirrors and was curious as to how the mirror could have gotten out of spec. They had used mirrors just like this in the City since the founding and never had a mirror produce the wrong vibration. Unless the mirror was physically damaged, the material used was almost self-correcting; like a rubber ball, once squeezed, will return to its original shape.

"Even if they replaced the mirror," T'mer continued, "that still won't fix the problem. I'm sure, D'nan, that your people have already looked into it and have found the problem to be one of replication. I can see even without your wizard eyes that that mirror has already been replaced. It is not the same one I installed."

"You are quite right, T'mer," D'nan said, recovering his composure and acting as if he were the one in charge. "We discovered the power fluctuation almost at once and proceeded to manufacture and install new mirrors. Only the new mirrors did the same thing. We even took mirrors that were malfunctioning and exchanged them with ones that did work. The malfunctioning ones corrected themselves and the ones that worked started to produce that counter wave. We don't believe the problem exists in the mirrors."

"D'nan, are you trying to tell us," C'ton said, "that you believe the problem lies with the monks?"

"We have always had to deal with fluctuations in the energy grid because of inferior and inadequate mental focus, but we have been able to balance those out using the clarity of our meditations. This is something different. Every time we re-align the mirrors or replace them the energy distortion increases to the point that we are going backward. We are expending more energy trying to maintain the grid than what we are generating."

"How can that be, D'nan?" T'mer asked. "The obelisks are used to store energy during the light so that the Temple can have power over the long dark. What happened to the energy stores?"

"They have been drained," C'ton said cryptically.

"Who could have drained them?" T'mar asked. "And where would they have hidden the energy. A power drain that massive would be impossible to conceal."

"That's why D'nan believes it is a monk or a group of monks," J'son said. "You're talking about a conspiracy within the walls of the Temple, you know."

"What do you know about this, J'son?" T'mar asked.

"I know… I know that the problem can't be solved by producing more energy. If what you say is true, then all those chanting monks are wasting their time. They are generating negative energy transfers. In effect, by chanting they are decreasing their own energy stores. The chanting does not replenish them. What about those outside the wall, D'nan? What will happen to them?"

"They will be locked out. And as long as they remain within the obelisk grove they will slowly die. We will take their life force until there is nothing left for them to give. It is better that the heathens should die than allowing those within the walls to perish. If we can make it through the long dark, it will be us leading the world back to the light."

They had been hovering in one place for a while, looking at the mirrors lining the wall. The globe was slightly above the height of the wall and they were able to see the obelisk grove below them. The gate of the Temple had finally closed and the people in the grove were rushing to the wall. From their perspective high above the ground, the crowds of people looked like ants scurrying about. Some of them had already made it to the gate and were pounding on it with balled up fists, shouting out in hoarse voices for the monks to open up.

They had been promised sanctuary if only they helped with Dome support. Now, it turns out, after they had spent themselves dry, thinking they would be given refreshments once they were let in, they were left instead empty and wasted, a look of horror on their faces as it dawned on them that they had been tricked.

"J'son?" T'mar said.

"Yeah, T'mar," he said sullenly, watching as those poor wretches beat down the gate. "Let's get back down. I think the High Priest wants to hear our report. He will be especially interested in what you have to say, T'mer."

"Me? Why?"

"You are not the only Tech that has observed this first hand, T'mer," C'ton said. The Council will be very interested in your input. The monks are very good at illusion and manufacturing images, but when it comes to machines we tend to turn a blind eye towards it, believing Technology to be beneath us and not worth the effort to master. Only now do we see how shortsighted we were. You're right, J'son. It is time for us to have an audience with C'aad, the High Priest."

"Yes," D'nan interjected. "We have had enough play-time. I will take responsibility for your insubordination as long as you agree to follow my lead and allow me to explain. Do you understand me, J'son?"

"Yeah, J'son," T'mar said with a tiny smile forming at the corners of her mouth. "D'nan wants to make sure you won't 'wrt him out in front of the Council. Ha-ha."

T'mar's sarcastic laugh ended abruptly, followed by a strange silence, like when everybody knows that what you just said wasn't appropriate. She had used the term "'wrt" off the cuff, but it impacted D'nan to his very core. He looked at her in the ensuing silence, a far-away glint in his eye like he was remembering something from long ago. That term, 'wrt, is the expression used when describing a heretic or one who has left the Order and decided to live among the City-dwellers.

They are considered 'wrts because the only form of currency a monk has is his teachings, which are forbidden by law to be taught to those outside the walls of the Temple. In order for a fallen monk to survive in the outside world, he must market his wares in exchange for material goods. To speak to those outside the Temple of things within is to 'wrt out the whole Order.

T'mar had been called a 'wrt once by the monks when she left the Temple to pursue the teachings of B'el. She didn't go to the City and whore herself out as they thought. In fact, when she departed she left the protection of the Dome and wandered in the Wastelands, forsaking all companionship and contact with those living within the Dome. The monks didn't know this at first and assumed she went to the City, betraying their trust and divulging the secrets of the Council. She became anathema to them and C'ton took the brunt of the criticism and condemnation. Because of her betrayal, he was made to stand before the Council and explain himself. His defense turned into an accusation against the Temple over their inability to see that their way of life was coming to an end and that the monks needed to embrace the difference and uniqueness of women.

It was D'nan, who was lower in the hierarchy then and named G'nan, who stood up in the Council as an observer and denounced T'mar as a 'wrt before all the members, then he stormed out of the proceeding declaring that C'ton should be severely reprimanded and striped of his designation for bringing a female into the Temple in the first place. Stripping a high-level monk of his designation and removing him from his seat on the Council was something that the High Priest refused to do, not wanting to set a precedent. In reality, C'aad, the High Priest, didn't want to preside over proceedings that could work against him. If it were possible to remove a monk from office, then it was possible to remove the High Priest himself.

T'mar was named G'mra then and was equal to or slightly above G'nan in her training, although he had more respect within the Council. He wasn't one of the monks that finally warmed up to her, keeping his distance and loathing her in secret. Because she was so beautiful, possessing all the feminine qualities of the sex-slaves below the Temple but nowhere near as submissive, G'nan thought about her all the time, fantasying about her every time he went to the bed chambers, at times hurting the girl he was with out of frustration that he couldn't possess G'mra for himself.

The few other females that had been accepted into the Temple had no problem with the regulation which dictated that they change their physical appearance to that of a male once they had learned the proper spell. G'mra (T'mar), however, had refused to transmute her bodily image into that of a man and G'nan (D'nan) took that act of open rebellion as an excuse to defile her within his thoughts. If she would have changed her appearance to that of a man, he never would have lusted after her in the first place.

In that few moments of silence that followed T'mar's remark, D'nan looked at T'mar and for the first time he caught a glimpse of who she really was. Memories flooded his awareness, and even though T'mar didn't look like she did back then she was still very easy on the eyes and she had cast a spell that gave her body even more bumps and curves, making her leaner and sexier than before. If his memory was correct -and he was certain that it was- she had lost about twenty-five pounds from her face, waist and hips. Her breasts were rounder, firmer and more erect and her cheek bones more angular, but she still possessed that intoxicating look to her eyes. Yes, she still had the same effect on him now as she did back then and D'nan took those moments to settle his thoughts and beat down the raging lust that was building up within him.

"J'son," D'nan said, breaking the silence. "I think now is the time to get to the Temple."

Without saying anything, J'son lowered his hands over the console and closed his eyes. Immediately, the globe disappeared from its location near the top of the wall and reappeared at the base of the Temple, the globe disintegrating into a flash of light as soon as they touched down. Before them, the Temple rose out of a foundation of black rock, with one hundred or more steps cut into it, rising from the base and terminating at the entrance to the Temple proper. At the top of these steps stood several monks waiting to greet and accompany the group into the interior of the Temple. The monks were looking down on them, smiling their secret little smiles, waiting patiently.

Chapter Twenty:

On the Steps of the Temple

"We must convince the boy that he is needed and use every means available to ensure that he stays with us. C'ton will be helpful in this if we can depend on him. Surely he knows the importance of what we are doing.

C'aad, the High Priest, discussing
his plans with the Council

"So C'ton," D'nan said sarcastically. "Did you really think that the two of you could fool the Council? I know who she is, don't I G'mra? Did you think that you could just waltz into the Temple without anyone knowing? We will wait here for the Temple guards to apprehend the heretic and take her below. You, C'ton, will join us before the High Priest along with J'son. T'mer, you will be needed up in the power room. Someone will be down to take you there, someone that you might remember."

The monks up on the top stair began to make their way down the steps, walking two by two, a dozen of them at least. One of them was taller and physically larger than the others and looked out of place. He had chiseled features and long, blonde hair resting on his broad shoulders. He was dressed in a short tunic and was bare-chested. He had bumps and cuts everywhere and walked down the steps in a side to side motion because the size of his thigh muscles kept his legs too far apart. Although incredibly muscular and resembling T'mer in appearance, he was fatter and softer than T'mer and he didn't have the menacing look that someone of his genetic inheritance should have.

This monster of a man and another monk were the first ones to the bottom step and they stopped short of running into D'nan and the others. The other monks, once reaching the bottom, fanned out around the group and enclosed them within a circle. Recognizing the out of place monk for whom he was, T'mer was the first to speak.

"T'tan? Is that you?"

"It's actually S'tan and yes, my old friend, it is me."

"S'tan has been very useful to us and he has studied hard to gain the "S" designation," D'nan said. "You could have stayed with us too, T'mer and moved up in rank. S'tan is our Chief Technician and he has done very well."

"Thank you, Master D'nan," S'tan said, bowing low to the ground." I only live to serve the Council."

T'mer saw his old friend bowing to the monks and the action made his stomach turn. His old friend, the boy he grew up with and entered the Tech-field with, the companion that helped him build his reputation and rise to become assistant head Tech and then later Tech Supervisor, was now groveling at the feet of wizards and paying them reverence. And now T'mer was being told that his friend had been trained by them? He had said that he would never return to the Temple because of his hatred of the monks and their controlling ways, but his real reason he swore to never return was because after he had seen what had happened to his friend it scared him that he might lose his individuality, too. Looking at S'tan now only made him long for the days before all of this, even before the days of T'mar, when to be a Tech was a thing to be proud of and the Adepts had all the answers. It saddened him to think that his friend had gone over to the monks and that S'tan didn't even seem to notice what they had done to him.

"Come, T'mer, my old friend. Let's get up to the power room and see if, together, we can solve the energy production problem. Don't worry about your friends. They will be well taken care of, I can assure you."

As soon as S'tan finished speaking, several of the monks, playing the role of Temple guards, grabbed T'mar from behind and physically restrained her, twisting her arms behind her back and placing a rough hand on the back of her neck, forcing her head down. After that, several things happened all at once. T'mer reacted immediately, reaching out with one hand to grab the monk closest to him, but found himself held back when S'tan grabbed him by the shoulder first. C'ton, caught off guard by both the monks and by T'mer, looked at D'nan, expressing his displeasure with a pinched face. J'son, knowing all along that the monks would want to take T'mar but not knowing exactly why, spoke up in hopes of dispelling the rapidly growing hostility he felt coming from T'mer and T'mar.

"D'nan, if you want my help you will have to release T'mar. We all go together or we don't go at all."

T'mar was struggling in the grip of the monks, fighting against them. "Get your callous, bony hands off of me or I'll cook your brain and feed it to you."

"Shut up, whore," one of the monks holding her arms said. "Shut your trap before I put something in it to make you shut up."

At that, T'mar grew quiet and stopped resisting them, closing her eyes and mumbling something under her breath. It was a simple spell that didn't require much focus, one that novices were taught very early in their training in order that they might create light and heat on their own in the event they needed it. She thought about how her body felt when the sun was shining, how warm and relaxing. She imagined the sun warming her and she concentrated on the temperature, raising it by degrees until her skin was hot to the touch.

Normally, when using this particular spell the initiate would point to a pile of wood or other flammable material and a flame would shoot out of his fingertips, sparking a fire. But starting a fire wasn't what T'mar had in mind. Instead of releasing the growing heat within her, she retained it until she couldn't stand it any longer. Within moments, T'mar's skin was as red as a furnace and the monks holding her let go, screaming out in pain and holding up the blistered and scorched body parts that had been in contact with her. Their clothes, too, became burnt and were hanging off of them, smoking.

"Ahhhhhhhhhhh!"

"My hands!"

"You whore!"

After the monks released her, T'mar jumped back into a fighting stance with both hands out in front, fingers extended. T'mer broke away from S'tan, prying his hand off his shoulder and stood next to T'mar with his back to the steps and the monks in front of him. C'ton, realizing that he had absolutely no control over the situation and saw it getting worse before it got better, made a motion to speak, hoping to diffuse the increasing tension. He was cut off, though, before any sound escaped his lips, leaving him with his mouth open and a finger pointing towards the sky.

"Is this what the Temple has become?" T'mar asked still in a defensive posture. "Are we reduced to fighting before the door of the Temple?"

"We will not be separated," J'son said, stepping in between the monks and T'mar and T'mer. "At least not until we meet the High Priest. Everyone in our party is here by the will of the Transcendentals, something C'aad knows to be true. T'mar, it is obvious to me that there are some unresolved issues concerning you that the monks would like to unravel. For some reason I can't see what it is. It is more than just your gender that bothers them. There is so much distrust here. They don't even trust you C'ton. In fact, D'nan believes himself to be your superior and that you are more of a danger than help."

"J'son, these fools are deluded by their own teachings but are too close to it to understand," T'mar said, relaxing a little but still on alert. "C'ton, it was your suggestion that brought us here. Do you still believe we made the right decision?"

Except for D'nan, all of the monks surrounding them were low-level novices without the training to do mental battle, and the spells they had were simple subsistence spells that could only produce food, water and fire. But unlike T'mar, they didn't know how to use those spells as a weapon, as she had done. The only weapon they possessed was their physicality. But unlike T'mer, they were skinny and lacked definition, making them not much more than annoying. Only S'tan had the bodily strength to withstand and repel a brute attack. But it wasn't corporeal battle that concerned the monks.

Standing around nervously, looking back and forth between D'nan and T'mar, the monks were at a loss as to how to respond. Nobody had ever challenged the authority of D'nan, knowing that he could crush them mentally, turning them into incompetent and senseless sex-mules destined for the bed chambers. To witness D'nan, their master, submit to the threats of a female was more than their poor, brainwashed brains could handle. One of the first lessons a novice must learn is to be aware of his mental state and acknowledge when he is losing focus. Doubt was the kernel of destruction within the mind of a novice, leading him to question the teaching of his teacher. Watching as the confrontation escalated all around them, the monks allowed doubt to enter their minds, like a splinter.

"It appears your monks are in a state of confusion, D'nan," C'ton said. "They haven't been trained correctly, probably because there are no more teachers that teach the ways of the Ancients. They shouldn't even be in the Temple; they should have been out in the obelisks grove improving their mental abilities through meditation and chanting. Without proper training, they serve no useful purpose. Why are they allowed in the Temple?"

"Things have changed since you sat on the Council, C'ton," D'nan said.

"I sit on the Council still!"

"Really? Then why haven't I seen you in the Judgment Hall? We have had much discussion over the past age. One of the decisions those on the Council have made is to form a defense force against the heathens. These you see before you are the Temple Security Force. They have been trained in combat, used to repel those that would storm the wall."

"You have never needed a security force before," C'ton said. "Why do you think you need one now?"

"I told you. Things have changed since last you were here. C'aad himself has foreseen what will happen to us throughout the long dark." Standing fully erect, his eyes glassing over, D'nan began to speak cryptically. "We will be attacked and the wall will be breached. The obelisks will be torn down and only those locked up behind the door of the Temple will survive. Before the sun returns, the walls of the Temple will be destroyed and all energy stores will be depleted. With the fall of the Temple walls, the only light in the world will come from those within the Temple."

"The only light?" T'mer spat out. "Those in the City are sitting on a reservoir of energy. What do the Techs need of your light? If what you say is true, then it will be the City-dwellers that will be the light of the world." T'mer was angry and the X was deep in his face. Those two knobby protrusions in his forehead above his eyes were red and throbbed in time with his pulse. They appeared to be growing slightly larger in height and diameter, looking more and more like tiny horns. He reached up and massaged the bumps, rubbing them like they were causing him pain.

He shouldn't have mentioned the reservoir. The plans that the Adepts had been working on for the past age, ever since T'mer first installed the mirrors in the City, was being carried out covertly, outside the knowledge of the monks. They had come to the monks with feign humility hoping the monks would help them with their energy production, although that was a ruse. The Technology they had installed in the City and in the Temple were performing in according to specifications, helping those in the City to produce an unlimited energy supply. But what those in the City didn't tell the monks was that they wanted access to that kind of power so they could develop a device that acted like a portal, which needed incredible amounts of energy. When all was said and done, their portal would have been energized and a doorway to Earth would have been opened. The plan was to abandon the City during the long night and spend the passing age on Earth. The only problem was that once they went through, unless someone stayed behind to keep the power on, the portal would collapse and they would be stuck on Earth.

Those in the City have known for awhile that the monks were having trouble producing energy and it was also known that the monks had reinstalled the mirrors and were using them to recharge the Temple. Using the electrical connection that T'mer and S'tan had laid down long ago to channel energy from the Temple to the City, the Techs began to steal energy from the monks using a feedback loop that was programmed into the grid of the mirrors. The energy flow was slight and undetectable at first and the Temple energy monitors had no idea they were losing energy. The feedback loop measured the amount of energy in storage in the reservoir and reflected that amount back to the Temple monitors, misleading the monks into believing that they had more energy than they really did. It was a trick, an illusion, but one done using Technology instead of spells.

It wasn't until the Techs fired up the portal to test it that the monks first became aware that they didn't have the energy stores that they thought they had. The Techs knew that powering up the portal would cause a voltage drop system wide, detectable by the monks, but they thought it would be a momentary drop and then the system would return to normal. What the Techs didn't know was that the obelisks grove wasn't operating correctly and the momentary dip became a disastrous plunge that wiped out all reserves and shut down the portal before it could be fully tested. Since then, the Techs have been diverting all available energy to their reservoir, hoping to energize the portal one more time and keep it opened long enough for the Adepts to pass through.

The monks never discovered how the Techs were involved, concerning themselves instead over the disappearance of their energy stores. How the obelisks lost their power and why was of utmost importance. Since the portal test and energy depletion was done during the height of energy production, the monks still had time to investigate the matter and decided to reinstall the mirrors, confident that they had enough time left to fully re-energize the obelisks. What they didn't count on was that the obelisks weren't drained because of a short, but because the energy was going somewhere else. Even as they struggled to recharge the obelisks, the energy they were collecting was disappearing faster than they could replace it. They have been in negative energy production ever since. The monks knew they wouldn't have enough energy to provide for all those who came to help and so the decision was made to use them up and then abandoned them outside the gate.

T'mer knew all of this and yet he never mentioned it to anyone outside the offices of the Adepts, not even to T'mar, which is why nobody in his group knew about the artificial portal. Up until now, he had been found loyal to the Adepts and their plan, not even allowing the idea to filter into his conscious thoughts. He slipped up, though, by mentioning the reservoir. He knew with wizards around that his faux pas wouldn't pass detection and that he might have just jeopardized the entire program. As far as he knew, except for a few rumors passed back and forth on the road between the City and the Temple, the reality of the portal was still secret and the energy problem was a separate matter.

Once he had authenticated the rumors of large-scale energy storage within the City and the ensuing, awkward silence that followed, T'mer noticed one of the monks break ranks and take off running, disappearing around the back of the Temple, heading for someplace on the far side. The movement caught the eye of everyone. C'ton and D'nan looked at each other and then towards T'mer, who was looking at S'tan. The four of them looked at each other and then at T'mar and J'son. The six of them stared at each other for a moment and then turned in unison to watch the feet of the running monk. D'nan, a puzzled look on his face, turned around to face another monk. He didn't say anything to the monk verbally, but communicated visually, placing images into the mind of the monk. The monk acknowledged the order by bowing slightly and then took off up the steps of the Temple, taking them two at a time until he reached the top, disappearing into the dark entrance.

T'mar didn't like all the monks running around and was on high alert, expecting ambush or worse. The monk that ran up the steps didn't bother her as much as the monk that headed off around the base of the Temple. When he had come down the steps with the other monks, T'mar thought she might be acquainted with him, but not from when she was here before. This monk she recognized from her time spent with B'el. She wasn't sure it was him at first, but when he ran off immediately after T'mer betrayed the Adepts, or something she registered in her awareness as betrayal, she sensed veiled contact with a force that was coming from outside the walls of the Temple. The contact was strange in that since they had entered the Temple the only thing she had been able to sense clearly is the all pervasive, background electrical discharge which is Dome support.

This feeling, growing stronger as the monk moved farther away, cut through the mental fuzziness that was the discharge and stood visibly in her mind's eye, viscerally affecting her, making her feel sick and excited at the same time. The feeling made her want to follow after the monk and she had to restrain herself to keep from chasing him down. The last time she had felt this way was in the presence of her old teacher, B'el.

The feeling was intoxicating and she found herself almost swooning as she lightly touched and caressed her face, neck and breasts at the memory. She was sure now that the monk was a disciple of B'el and she had known him from before. In fact, that particular monk had served in B'el's Castle and even waited on T'mar. She looked different now and wasn't sure if the monk had noticed her, like D'nan had, or if he was contacting B'el to inform him of the reservoir kept by the Techs. Either way, B'el would know about their group and J'son's abilities soon enough, if B'el didn't know about them already.

C'ton had noticed both monks moving in different directions and knew instinctively that the monk who ran around the Temple left without permission and was on an errand separate from the Temple. The running monk startled D'nan for a moment, C'ton thought, but he recovered quickly enough by sending the other monk into the Temple. C'ton, like T'mar, didn't know why the first monk ran off or where he might be running to, but he was pretty sure he knew why the second monk went into the Temple.

T'mer did reveal the depths of a plan that nobody knew existed, or if they did it was only believed to be in the idea phase. T'mer's assertion that the Techs had a reservoir of energy on par with the obelisk grove would make any first-grade initiate perk up their ears. The monk was sent into the Temple to apprise C'aad of that situation. C'ton didn't think, though, that D'nan would let a low-level monk, a Temple Guard of all people, inform the High Priest of the identity of T'mar. That was a gift that D'nan wanted to present personally, and for now her association with B'el was still somewhat secret.

Like T'mar, C'ton felt something disturbing and yet familiar coming from the running monk. In the split second that C'ton opened himself up to the running monk, he was able to see into his mind and yet C'ton saw nothing, implying that the monk had resources beyond his limited training, or he had been programmed by a high-level initiate to hide in plain sight, wiping his consciousness clean leaving only a blank slate. C'ton wasn't aware and didn't have much use for what had happened to T'mar once she left him to find B'el, so he wasn't as attuned to the subtle influences of B'el's power. Where T'mar was fighting with herself to stay present and not fall into some erotic reverie of her time spent with him, C'ton was merely pondering the feeling he was getting with the clean slate that was the mind of the running monk.

"Having your monks run off like that without comment does a lot to stir up distrust," T'mar said.

"I didn't ask you to trust me, G'mra," D'nan said. "It is only because of your abilities that I haven't had you washed and bound and thrown into the bed chambers."

"I'll rip your head off and feed it to you if you so much as touch her again," T'mer said, spitting the words out.

"T'mer, calm down-," S'tan said, putting a hand on T'mer's shoulder.

"Get off of me! I've had enough of you wizards. J'son, why don't you conjure up another transportation globe and get us out of here."

"Where would you go, back to the City?" D'nan asked. "You know as well as I do T'mer that the Adepts have guards on the wall of your City to protect you from the madness that the dark brings. To enter the City in a transport globe would get you imprisoned for practicing sorcery. And approaching the City without proper identification will get you shot. You are here for the duration of the age, I'm afraid."

"D'nan," C'ton started, trying his best to reduce the tension in the group. "Instead of fighting on the steps of the Temple, why don't we go in and see what wisdom C'aad has to impart? I know he will want to hear what J'son has to say about the Dome."

"You're right, C'ton," D'nan said. "All this bickering is a waste of time and gets us nowhere. S'tan, take T'mer with you and show him what you have discovered. The four of us will proceed to the Council Chambers after I take J'son on a quick tour of our power production facilities. Report to the Council once you have anything of note to report. Come."

Chapter Twenty-One:

Sexual Tension

"There is nothing down there for me. The girls will be more interested in the males and I will be view as completion."

T'mar trying to reassure T'mer of her motives

D'nan turned towards the steps and started walking up, pausing once after a few steps to look over his shoulder to see if the others were following. J'son was the next one to take to the steps, followed by T'mar, C'ton, T'mer and finally S'tan. The other monks remained at the base of the steps, observing the others until they reached the top step and stood on the platform leading into the Temple. Looking down on them from above, D'nan, with barely a motion to indicate that an order had been given, dismissed the monks on the ground. He then proceeded into the Temple, walking along a long, straight passage cut into the black rock of the base. After about one hundred feet, the passage came to an end and they entered a circular room with two doorways to their left and right.

"The door to the right leads to the higher levels," D'nan said. "The door on the left leads down into the bowels of the Temple. There, J'son, you will see something that might impress you. Not all of our energy comes from chanting."

J'son was starting to experience doubt and the growing inability to choose the next path. Ever since he entered the Temple grounds he felt like a passenger riding around in his own body. That other presence, that other expression was there, in the background, waiting, not saying anything. It was the silence that bothered him the most. His time here had been more like a trip to the library than an actual education. Whenever he needed to make a decision, like when he created the transport globe, all he had to do was think about how to do it and in the amount of time it took to think about it, he created it. Now, however, his librarian was silent and he couldn't read any of the books floating across his awareness, couldn't grasp the meaning of the images assembling and dissolving within his mind.

The cause of this confusion was because of his feelings for T'mar. J'son had a good idea that D'nan wanted T'mer to confer with S'tan about the mirrors and he really thought he was going to go with them to see what he could uncover. But when D'nan suggested that J'son was going with them, he found himself elated at the idea. That other part of him urged him to go with T'mer and became silent the moment J'son decided not to go with T'mer, even though J'son's insight could prove to be crucial. It was the first time J'son, the young man from Earth, resisted the guidance of his spiritual other.

There was something coming up from within the bowels of the Temple, a vibe or an energy that was purer than the energy created by chanting monks, but the energy had a strange effect on those that came into contact with it. Just as J'son was able to detect subtle influences that others would have a hard time accepting as real, he was able to pick up on the peculiar forces swirling all around them coming up from below. These erotic waveforms are what caught his attention, pulling his thoughts out of the depths of his consciousness and stirring up his primal nature by displaying graphic images of sex and desire.

The thoughts embarrassed him, causing his short tunic to move slightly and his cheeks to blush. He looked over at T'mar, who was anticipating T'mer's reaction that she wouldn't be going with him, seeing her in profile. His thoughts were still being influenced by whatever was below the surface and he smiled at her figure as his mind began to fall into a daydream that included him and her doing things to each other that would make any red-blooded male stand at attention. The vision only lasted a few moments, coming to an abrupt and unsatisfying end, the second S'tan spoke.

"We are taking the door to the right, T'mer," S'tan said, putting his hand on T'mer's shoulder again.

"I'm not going anywhere without T'mar."

"It'll be all right, T'mer," T'mar said, feeling the same energy surge coming from below and secretly wanting to be alone with J'son. "Because of their power restrictions, they don't have any leverage over me, so I don't fear them. They have already done to me all that they can do. My concern is for you. Will you be safe with your friend?"

"He'll be fine," S'tan said. "It has been a long time since I had another Tech to discuss things with. He will be safe if only for his knowledge."

"Yes, quite safe," D'nan said. "Come, we are wasting time, a commodity we don't have enough of."

It was true that they were running out of time. It was completely dark outside the Dome with only tiny, pin pricks of starlight to cast any shadow. Within the Dome, all took on the dim, reddish hue of the glowing road, obelisks, wall, Temple and Dome.

From deep within the entrance to the Temple, the light filtering in down the passage made the walls and floor glow like a flame, giving the inner room the look of a setting sun, only it wasn't the sun giving off the light. In broad daylight, the inner room was dark and cast in shadow, a rectangle of light marking the entrance into the Temple, but now all was red and the entrance shimmered blurry, like looking through the flames of a fire.

Under normal conditions, the Temple would have been lit up bright, a beacon in the night. All light came from Dome production and it wouldn't be until late in their planetary orbit around their sun that energy depletion would cause the Dome and everything under it to glow red. By that time, their star would have returned in the sky and a countdown of sorts was begun. As their sun grew bigger and brighter in the sky, the red Dome illumination mixed with the yellow of their sun to the point that the

Dome glowed orange before returning to its fully charged state of white. The fact that the Dome was glowing red at this early stage was a clear indication that the present level of power production wasn't going to get them through the dark.

Also, because of their limited energy supply all power use within the Temple had to be approved in advance, meaning for the most part that no one had the authorization to cast any spells and so tap into the resources of the Temple. Without the expressed permission of the Council, no one, not even D'nan or C'ton, had any power to do anything, and a wizard without power was just a crazy eccentric mumbling words that had no meaning.

That's why everyone was so surprised by J'son's ability to generate a transport globe outside the dictates of the Council. Without approval, J'son shouldn't have had access to the energy stores used to create the globe. Instead, much to everyone's astonishment, he was able to generate one using his own energy supply. It was that personal and separate energy store that D'nan and the Council was interested in. They had the capability to monitor their own energy consumption, but didn't have a clue as to how much energy J'son possessed or had access to.

The six of them stood around for another minute or so looking at each other, then S'tan and T'mer walked over to the right hand door. S'tan reached out for the gold-colored latch and opened it. Stepping through the thick doorway and closing the door behind them, they disappeared from sight, leaving D'nan, T'mar, J'son and C'ton standing alone in the room.

"So now we go," D'nan said. "This should be a welcome treat for you, J'son. I think you will enjoy yourself and help with our energy needs at the same time. It is a customary sacrament that all monks requesting entrance into the Temple must pass through the bed chambers and leave a deposit of their essence on file. How long has it been since you visited the bed chambers, C'ton? Not since you left the Council Chambers in a rage, I would expect."

D'nan moved to the left hand door and opened it. Stepping through the doorway, he turned left and immediately started walking down a steep flight of steps that took him out of view of the others. T'mar was the next one to go, moving down the magenta-colored steps by placing her hands on the rough-carved walls of the stairwell to keep from falling head first down to the bottom. J'son came next, followed by C'ton, who hesitated for a few moments watching the others disappear down the stairs before bringing up the rear. He was having issues with the energy coming up from below just like T'mar and J'son, but unlike them he knew exactly why he was having trouble because he had been here several times before when retiring to the bed chambers was a natural part of the functioning of the monks.

Back then, he had no qualms about the females they kept or their place in the service of Dome production. The energy generated through sexual intercourse was one of the primary ways in which the monks expended their own energy to produce a purer energy signal that would be directed towards the Council Chamber for the exclusive use of those sitting on the Council. It was this sexual energy that provided most of the raw energy used to maintain the Dome and the Council controlled who was allowed to enter the bed chambers and how long they had to remain. Only those who took advantage of the pleasures of the females and could recover within a short amount of time were allowed to stay for extended periods. All others, those that were spent and those who had lost their ability to enjoy women, were asked to leave so their shame wouldn't affect those that wanted to do their part.

C'ton used to visit the women regularly as part of his responsibility as a sitting Council member and had enjoyed himself with all the females had to offer. It was not until he met and adopted T'mar that he stopped going to the bed chambers and used T'mar for personal energy creation. She was just a girl then and C'ton taught her everything that a woman was good for, showing her what to do and watching her as she practiced. Her innocence and sexuality merged in such a way that captivated C'ton and he had a hard time keeping his hands off of her, even when he didn't need to generate energy. He felt guilty that he was using a female that hadn't been brought up in the Temple, but she was more than willing to help him and she genuinely seemed to enjoy their love play, not like the vacant, drug-induced stares he got from other females in the bed chambers.

They made love constantly and C'ton's abilities skyrocketed, proving that City women could be used for physical gratification as well as helping him to focus on the higher spells available only to those at the top. It was because of her sexual energy that C'ton was able to persuade the Council to let her initiation stand. He had promised those on the Council that they could taste the fruits of her body if they wanted further proof of her service and support, a promise which most of them had taken advantage of. It was only after she was accepted into the Temple and refused to change her appearance that the other monks began to despise her, thinking of her more as a tease than a help. It was soon after this that C'ton stopped having sex with her, telling her that she needed to take ownership of her body and only give it to a male if she wanted to, a radical idea at the time to say the least. C'ton hadn't had sex with another person since then.

The steps leading down were narrow and uneven, cut right out of the rock. The air was thick and warm, carrying a strong, musky scent that smelled like seawater. The pungent smell was offensive at first, but once they got used to it they found themselves pleasantly intoxicated and sexually aroused, like walking into a strip club. After stepping down thirteen steps and reaching a platform the stairwell turned at a right angle. Then the stairs continued down another thirteen steps to another platform and again turned to the right. The only light in the stairwell was the dull, reddish glow coming from the rock and the hazy, flickering, scarlet light coming from below, which was glowing more intense and redder and hotter. The temperature had to be somewhere around 100 degrees and everyone was sweating.

C'ton was sweating as much as anyone and he noticed what J'son had noticed about T'mar; but instead of allowing himself to enjoy the view he was struggling to maintain his composure. He lifted his head up occasionally just to check out where they were and his eyes kept on falling on T'mar, watching her as she worked her hips back and forth stepping down from one step to the next. Her figure held his attention for only moments at a time and then he forced himself to look away, the image of her sweaty, swaying hips seared in his mind.

Seeing her like that, hot and sweaty and smelling like sex, was hard for him, considering he had stopped thinking about her like that a long time ago. Still, he heard himself say, it had been a long time and she didn't even look like she did back then. To take her at this point and in this place would be only natural. Besides, they did enjoy themselves and making love to her was very pleasant and easy. It was he, after all, that had ended their sexual relationship. She had wanted to continue and even pleaded with him, sometimes coming up to him in the most inappropriate places and reaching for him. He never could resist her once she put her hands on him, though.

Although it had been many macro-cycles since he had made love to her, he knew that if she reached out to him now he wouldn't have the clarity of mind to deny her. The thought made him smile in a self-conscious way and he had almost convinced himself that he should make himself available to her. He even thought about applying some of the mental and physical constraints the monks used to control the women in the bed chambers. He wouldn't use drugs like many of them did. Instead, he would tweak her already stimulated libido by using subtle massage spells designed specifically to create within the unsuspecting recipient the feeling that they were being felt up in all of her erogenous zones.

He was just about to cast such a spell when he caught himself. It was only because of her sensuous sexuality and the overpowering draw of her scent that he had become partially blinded to what he was planning to do. It was only through concentrated effort that he was able to lower his hand and stop the words of the spell from coming out of his mouth.

He felt ashamed and stopped on the steps, letting the others continue down. He was shaking and the blood in his veins throbbed, causing him to bend over at the waist to catch his breath. He grabbed his member tightly in one hand, twisting and squeezing it like he was trying to apply a tourniquet, hoping to fight back the indomitable lust rising within him. He groaned at the feeling of the pressure his hand exerted on his genitals and sighed once he released it, pumping his hand like he was squeezing a tennis ball. Groan, sigh. Groan, sigh. Over and over again rapidly until he felt he had gotten his lust under control.

One of the practices of the Council, in times when the sun shined bright, was to masturbate while holding oneself back from reaching orgasm. They were trained to masturbate for hours at a time, never seeking release and holding on to their power for as long as possible. This practice was frowned upon once you were in the bed chambers, for the sole purpose of the bed chambers was to release your load as soon as possible and then recover as quickly as possible. If you were able to continue after a few minutes rest, then it was permitted for you to remain in the bed chambers until you were spent. On a good day, a regular monk may have sex with up to ten different women.

C'ton stopped squeezing himself and supported his now limp member in the palm of his trembling hand. He was shaking less visibly now and was composing himself, closing his eyes and bringing his breathing under control. He scolded himself for even thinking about T'mar that way and tried to reinforce his mental focus, suppressing every sexual thought that entered his mind. It was hard, but he was determined to resist his primitive instincts and not participate in the orgies in the bed chambers. D'nan would have a big problem with him if he refused the advances of the females. He would insist that the females would become unruly if C'ton rejected them and that might lead the females to abandon phallic worship and practice their skills with each other. He would also be challenged by the Council for his deliberate refusal to participate and a charge of heresy might be imposed. He didn't think the Council would go that far, though. As an original member his opinion carried the same weight as anyone on the Council. It didn't matter. He knew that what the Council did with the women under the Temple was wrong and once he stopped having sex with T'mar he hadn't so much as touch a female with lust in his mind.

After thirteen flights of stairs, they reached the bottom step. D'nan was the first to get there and he moved off to the side waiting for the others to enter the outer hall. T'mar was the next one to enter the hall, her body glistening with sweat and her clothes sticking to her body. J'son was right behind her and almost fell on top of her stumbling on the last step. He was still aroused and was pointing at her, embarrassed but having a lustful grin on his face. T'mar turned around slowly when she heard the noise he made and stood in profile with her head looking over her shoulder. Her deep, auburn hair, reflecting the fiery red of the rock and the hall, fell across her shoulder and down to about the middle of her back. It was wet from perspiration and looked like she had just stepped out of a shower.

J'son was standing directly behind T'mar, physically more aware of the temperature than either C'ton or D'nan, mainly because he was watching the streams of sweat trickle down T'mar's back, soaking the waist band of her skirt. The material clung to her, outlining the supple curve of her butt, the fabric slowly slipping down her hips, giving him a good idea what she would look like naked.

Several times he wanted to reach out and run his fingers down the arc of her spine, to feel the heat of her body and taste her sweat, but he stopped himself, knowing that to touch her would cause trouble. He didn't really know what to expect down in the bed chambers, but he knew there was a growing part of him that wanted to take T'mar on the steps right then and do things to her. There was no way now that he could hide his growing, physical excitement and he stood there with his hands cupped over his groin.

Standing there, staring at her with his member as stiff as a javelin, the material of his tunic forming a tent of sorts, J'son saw the shape of her breasts straining against her tight, clinging top and her hard, erect nipples standing at attention. She smiled pleasantly at him, her eyes looking up and down his body, pausing at the area below his waist and between his thighs. A sly grin materialized on her face and a look in her eye told him she appreciated his attention. He felt stupid standing there, wanting to touch her and caress her body. He wanted to kiss her and lick the sweat from her body, paying special attention to her breasts. He wanted to wrap his hands around her firm ass and slide into her.

He wanted to do so many things to her but found himself unable to move. It was like the only thoughts running around in his head were filled with sexual imagery and trying to resist those thoughts caused a malfunction in his motor skills. He knew if he moved, he would pounce on T'mar, tackling her to the ground and performing the beast with two backs with her, knowing he would be unable to control himself. It was getting to be more than he was able to handle and he felt himself building up to an explosive release. He was shaking and his hips rolled forward unconsciously in a rhythmic, humping motion. He felt like a school boy infatuated with his teacher, not knowing exactly what he should do to relieve himself.

"I wonder what's keeping C'ton," D'nan stated, leering at T'mar lustfully while he slowly took off his wet clothes, dropping them to the floor. "T'mar, this is your first time down in the bed chambers, isn't it? Since you refuse to participate in the rituals by transforming yourself into a male, I'm not too sure how much fun you will have. We do have some females that are transsexual, possessing both male and female equipment. They were bred for the more deviant monks that need homosexual stimulation to perform adequately. I hadn't thought about it until just now, but you might want to avail yourself of one of them. We haven't done any test to determine the energy output of a sexual union between a transsexual and a female, so you can still help us."

"Why would she need a female with a dick?" J'son asked incredulously, coming out of his sex-induced stupor, surprised at D'nan's suggestion. "I mean… Because if she… I can…"

"J'son, my dear boy," D'nan responded. "It is not for us to have sex with each other. That would be unseemly. She must pick a female and retire with her into the bed chambers. Her sexual exploits will be monitored to determine if she is expending the proper amount of energy. Our hope is that her love making will generate more energy than expected. It is already known that when two females engage in sex with each other while the monks watch their lesbian activity enhances the overall sexual output of all involved. Maybe with a transsexual T'mar will heighten the experience for all of us. The sexual tension rising between us and especially that which I sense coming from the boy, is feeding the grid even as we speak. It makes us wonder how much energy you could produce if we left you here for awhile."

"No one is going to be left here, D'nan," C'ton said as he entered the hall having finally made it to the bottom. "Because of the situation with the Dome, I find our visit here to be totally unnecessary and a waste of our time. I, for one, will not participate."

Even as C'ton spoke, from the far end of the hall several young women appearing to be just out of their teens came running down the hall, laughing and singing, buck naked. They were moving toward the group, running and skipping and dancing, the look on their faces one of naïve simplicity and an open willingness to play with the monks that had just entered the bed chambers. Some of the women were holding hands, swinging their arms in time with their skipping while others twirled around by themselves, smiling the smile of the young.

As the companions watched the women making their way towards them, a slightly order women, mid twenties, appeared at the far end of the hall and started following the other women. She was indeed built like a mature woman, with huge, perky rounded breasts and wide, shapely hips. She had large, pouty lips and long, blonde hair that framed her breasts and spilled down her back. She was also completely nude and cleaned shaven, her pelvic region as bare as her breasts.

She was walking slower than the others and she moved by swinging her hips back and forth seductively while at the same time caressing her breasts and touching herself. Where the other women would play with the monks without really knowing the moral consequences of such play, this woman knew exactly what she was doing and what men wanted. The look in her striking, almost violet eyes told of sexual pleasures awaiting all who would welcome her.

"Whatever you say, C'ton," D'nan said. "Why you wouldn't want to take advantage of the pleasures of the Temple I don't know. Maybe G'mra still takes care of you. I never did believe the rumors that said you had given up on sex. How do you expect to replenish your energy supply? Taking energy from the environment is one thing, but there is nothing like the taste of the power you receive after participating in an orgy."

"These practices were set up long ago as a form of relaxation, not for energy generation. You have perverted the purpose behind the union between a man and a woman."

"The Great C'ton, defender of the whore and the champion of the harlot! What? Did you fall in love with G'mra's vagina? Females exist solely for our benefit and enjoyment. Only you, G'mra, of all women, have been given the right to indulge in the pleasures of our females. My suggestion to you is to not fight them and allow them to pleasure you. You might not have the equipment that they crave, G'mra, but they still know how to satisfy you orally. Again, we must get you paired up with a transsexual. I am sure your attitude will change once you drop your guard and permit our grown females to kiss you all over. Look! The young women are almost here. You can either take off your clothes yourself, or you can wait for them to undress you. The experience can be quite pleasant."

"No problem," T'mar said. Crossing her right leg over her left, narrowing her hips slightly, she slipped effortlessly out of her skirt, which landed in a wet bunch on the floor. Stepping out of her skirt, she reached up with one hand and grabbed a breast, tugging on the material of her top until it came loose and then dropped it on top of her skirt. She was glistening with her own sweat and the look of her wet, naked skin caused a whimper to pass between J'son's lips.

J'son was having real difficulties. His hips were still humping the air and he moved them around, first pointing at T'mar and then pointing at the older woman approaching from the rear. He saw the way she moved, and just watching her mouth was enough for some to blow their load before even being touched. Remembering what D'nan said about not being able to have sex with T'mar, J'son now started to focus on the older woman in the back. Physically she was younger than T'mar, but the way she carried herself spoke of someone with plenty of sexual experience pleasing men. Seeing T'mar standing there naked, along with D'nan, J'son took no time ripping his tunic off of his sweaty body, accidentally getting the material caught on his member and pulling it away roughly.

"Are you going to join us, C'ton? Or are you going to let the women do it?" D'nan asked, a broad smile stretching across his face.

"I'll do it myself. It disgusts me to think of what we have done to these innocent young women, and what you will do to them."

"Innocent?" D'nan said laughing. "They are bred for just such a purpose as this. To take away their function in our society would be cruel. Look at the smiles on their faces. They want to please us and you want to refuse them. Do you want them to suffer? What would they do if they didn't learn what was expected of them in a few short years. Don't be foolish, C'ton. Don't you know we still joke about your ideas about woman equality? Would you have us masturbate and release our essence into our hands only? That, I think, would be ridiculous and wasteful. The energy created during masturbation is lost once you release it, unless you have a proper receptacle. Don't fight tradition or you may find yourself battling all those that trust in the wisdom of the Temple."

C'ton dropped his clothes in a pile and stood naked like the others. However, his member was soft and limp, hanging between his legs like a shriveled up worm. It didn't embarrass him considering most monks at this stage in the bed chambers needed the stimulation of females to get erect. In times past he remembered monks that needed a hand wrapped around them at all times and others that remained flaccid until the very end when they left the company of the regular women and proceeded to another area of the bed chamber that housed women that were different. This was where the transsexuals lived among others that were either physically deformed in some way that was considered sexually exciting or mentally deranged in such a way that performing perverted, deviant sexual practices was pleasurable to them.

The older woman in the back, C'ton knew, was one of those women and would have no problem taking all of them on at the same time. It was said that time spent with one of these women would turn all who tasted of her forbidden fruit away from the natural use of a woman, even going so far as to do things that they found personally shameful. The Council didn't have a problem if some of the monks wanted to participate in deviant sexual practices because their participation radically increased their energy output. Whatever it took to produce energy was acceptable to the members of the Council, their attitude being the more deviant the practice the greater the return.

The first of the young women reached the group and immediately began dancing around D'nan, forming a chain by clasping their hands, singing and laughing. There were about half a dozen circling around him and laughing, playing little games with him and each other. The rest of the women came by ones and twos, about twenty of them total, stopping first at D'nan to offer up their services and then moving over to C'ton and J'son, ignoring T'mar for the moment. C'ton was truly disgusted watching the women touching and grabbing on him and he tried to gently push them away from him.

"No, ladies. Please don't touch me. I'm not here for this."

"You don't want to play with us?" One of the women asked, looking up at him with sweet, innocent, trusting doe eyes.

"No! No I don't," he said too harshly. "You are not needed." He knew that by saying that he would crush the spirit of that woman and throw her into confusion. His hope was that by showing them another side to the monks they would begin to question their station and maybe finally stand up for themselves, withholding the only thing they possessed. Just as T'mar had come to know the power her sexuality held, C'ton was hopeful that maybe this generation of women would begin to understand the power they wielded.

The women that swarmed around J'son, seeing his excitement and feeling very comfortable with his predicament, started giggling when they saw his stiff member. He wasn't paying too much attention to them, however. In fact, they were more of a distraction than anything else. Instead of paying attention to what they had to offer, J'son was transfixed by the older woman who was still walking down the hall, smiling a secret, seductive smile. Since he wouldn't be able to have sex with T'mar, he had decided that the older woman would be more than just a pale stand-in. The way she looked, the way she walked, and her lips and breasts and that sweet spot between her thighs. He was more than willing to let her do whatever she wanted to him.

The older woman reached the group, ignoring the throng of young women running around, pushing them out of her way and made her way past D'nan, C'ton and J'son, stopping in front of T'mar and proceeded to kiss her hard on the lips. At first T'mar pulled her head back trying to resist the advance, but the woman placed her hand on the back of T'mar's head and forced her head forward. The woman's other hand was on T'mar's ass, squeezing it and digging her fingers into her flesh. T'mar's resistance was short lasting and she finally surrendered to the passion she felt flowing within her.

T'mar's hands were down by her side when the woman first approached her and she raised them to her chest, palms out, forming a buffer between them as they kissed. Once she had yielded to the temptation of her flesh, she moved her hands out of the way and wrapped her arms tightly around the woman's waist, pulling her in closer and pressing her breasts against the woman. It was only a matter of moments before the two women were locked in a full embrace, their arms, hands and lips roaming all over the body of the other, their tongues licking the hot, dripping sweat off of each other.

D'nan was panting and laughing quietly to himself, a kind of giggling reminiscent of teenagers in the back seat of a car late on a Friday night. He had a dreamy look in his eyes and he stood there holding himself while a couple of the young women ran around him. C'ton had plainly ostracized himself from the women and was standing there naked looking at the ceiling, continuing to ignore the soft-core porn going on all around him. J'son, on the other hand, was starting to lose his erection and his lust. Not only was T'mar off limits to him, but now it appeared the older woman was more interested in T'mar than him.

Watching the two women go for it, totally uninhibited and oblivious to those around them, the encounter was having the opposite effect on him than expected. Instead of watching them with voyeuristic intensity, J'son started to lose hope that he would have any chance of having sex with two of the most sexually stimulating women he had ever met, or dreamt about. His libido cooled along with his thoughts and he found himself thinking about the Temple and the Dome. Where only a few minutes ago he was about to bust, dry humping the air around him, now he was feeling a little queasy and the idea of sex seemed repulsive to him.

T'mar had backed the other woman up against the wall and had lifted her off the ground by grabbing her ass to support her. The woman wrapped her legs around T'mar's waist and was rolling her hips into T'mar, moaning as she rocked. They were still kissing and the woman was fondling one of T'mar's breasts. None of this seemed out of place or out of the ordinary for those present, even though T'mar was a woman. When it came to sex, all was permissible. The heat the two women were generating caused the walls and floor to glow orange and increased in intensity the longer they pleasured themselves. Just the sounds of their sucking and moaning caused the color of the walls to pulse with each groan.

C'ton was somewhat surprised by J'son's reaction and wondered why he was sexually turned off by the activity of the two women. Not only was T'mar a gorgeous woman, fully proportioned in all the right places, the other woman could have been T'mar's younger mirror image, except she was a blonde and T'mar a red head. He turned away from them again and looked at J'son. C'ton could see anger rising in J'son's cheeks mixed with mental confusion and frustration. J'son was watching the women, but his thoughts weren't on sex. Instead, he seemed like he was about to say something, his mouth opening and then shutting without any words coming out. J'son put his hands on his hips and bore holes into the back of T'mar's head with his stare.

"T'mar," C'ton said quietly. "I think J'son has something to say."

As soon as T'mar heard her name, she jerked her head back and let go of the woman's ass, almost dropping her to the floor. T'mar's hips and pelvis were still pressed up against her and the woman grinded her hips forward slowly, taking T'mar's movement as a sign that she wanted the woman to do something else. Feeling the pressure in her loins, T'mar stepped back and pushed herself away from the woman, pressing the woman's shoulders back against the wall. T'mar looked into the eyes of the other woman, seeing the lust and sensuality there, and a longing. The sight of the woman looking at her like she was a male, bent on satisfying her and bringing her to orgiastic pleasure, caused T'mar to question exactly what she was doing.

Hearing C'ton's voice embarrassed her, reminding her how he used to whisper to her while they were making love. It was that same tone, the one she remembered, that caused her to pause. As horny as she was, it wasn't a woman she wanted to satisfy her. T'mar looked over her shoulder at J'son, caught a glimpse of him staring at her and then she turned away, the blood rushing from her lower regions to her checks. Seeing the look that J'son gave her, she came to the rapid realization that none of them were going to participate in the sex rituals required of them. Ordinarily, they wouldn't have had a chance to back out because they would have been locked in the bed chambers as long as it took for them to engage in sexual activity that would produce the optimal amount of energy. However, if J'son refused T'mar didn't think D'nan would lock them in. With the Dome structure dangerously close to collapse, making an enemy of the one person that may be able to help wasn't an option.

"This practice is disgusting," J'son said, forcing back the bile that suddenly filled his mouth. "This can't be what the builders intended. I came here to help you balance out the energy fluctuations in your Dome. I thought I would be able to detect the source of the disturbance by observing how unchecked sexuality contributes to power generation, but all I see is the manipulation of the sex impulse, a clouding of the mind so severe that we can't think straight. You can do whatever you want, but I'm going to look at the apparatus that converts perverted sex into pure energy. It's down that hall, isn't it, D'nan?"

With that, J'son gave one more look at T'mar, feeling his lust for her rising again, and then turned away in a huff, heading off down the same hall that the women had come down earlier, knocking some of them out of the way and forcefully pushing them to the side. He stormed off down the hall mumbling, throwing his arms up over his head and shouting out occasionally. J'son's attitude was one of frustration and anger, most of which he directed at himself. Seeing the naked young women and T'mar locking lips with another female caused more confusion and complicated his feelings towards T'mar. When he was looking at the world through lust-filled eyes, any naked body would have been good enough. But now sex was the last thing on his mind.

The others watched J'son storm down the hall, pushing the women away harshly, causing them to cry. The older woman, reeling from T'mar's rejection of her, reached out to some of the women and put her arms around them, holding them tight against her the way a mother might try to protect her children. The lust in the older woman's eyes was gone, replaced by a look of anxiety and fear. Confusion was registered in every eye and soon all of the young women were bunched together around the older woman, huddling close and hiding behind each other. There was true terror in their eyes, like the look of a child that had done wrong and was now awaiting punishment. The young women refused to look up at anyone and the older woman, catching glimpses of D'nan staring at them, tried to soothe them, telling them it would be okay and that they did nothing wrong.

The reaction of the women to J'son's behavior occupied the attention of the others causing them to almost miss the glow that J'son cast as he walked down the hall. It was an eerie sort of glow, more bluish-purple, surrounding him and radiating out all around him. His glow mixed with the pulsating orange color of the walls and floor creating a blend of darkness and hinting at violence. The glow followed him down the hall, casting vulgar silhouettes of him against the walls. J'son kept raising his hands and pointing them towards the ceiling, mumbling and cursing under his breath. Everywhere he pointed, a flicker of electricity jumped from his fingers, hit the wall or ceiling or floor and exploded in a shower of radiant embers. Tiny, molten pieces of rock fell from the ceiling and formed on the floor, looking like little BB's, glowing red but cooling to a dull grey. Sparks, pops and crackles followed J'son all the way down the hall.

Chapter Twenty-Two:

The Three Chambers

"We may have to detain the boy for his own good. We can't risk letting him go and taking his abilities to the Techs, or worst yet to B'el. If we don't provide him sanctuary, he will be hunted by everyone: B'el, the Techs and anyone who desires unlimited power.

C'aad the High Priest to D'nan

T'mer and S'tan didn't have to walk up a bunch of steps to get to the power room. Instead, once they entered the transport shaft and closed the door, they found themselves encased in a sphere of translucent blue similar to the transport globe they had used outside the Temple. The sphere remained in place as S'tan punched in the proper clearance code and designation route number on a transparent, colorless keyboard mounted at chest level. He struck three buttons simultaneously using the tips of his fingers and pulled down on a lever, clicking it into place and causing the keyboard to light up. The sphere began to hum slightly and then with a whooshing sound they were rocketed up the shaft at incredible speed. The rose-colored light filtering in from the windows located on each floor of the Temple flashed by as they rose higher and higher, illuminating the transport tube in a sunset orange glow. They shot passed the floor housing the Council Chamber and came to a stop near the top of the Temple.

The keyboard grew dim and transparent, the humming ceased and the sphere disappeared. A door appeared in front of them and slid opened, revealing a large, circular room with a metallic, semi-spherical disk located in the center. The disk was enclosed within a glowing orb of red light and sat on a rotating pedestal made out of the same black rock as everything else. The concaved aspect of the disk pointed straight up towards the ceiling and had a thin wire or antenna coming out of the center. The rotation of the disk was rapid and all along the perimeter could be seen a smudge of color, a solid line of deep blue about four inches thick.

Every so often, though, without provocation or occasion, the band of blue broke for the moment, revealing a strip of white, a minute fluctuation just below the threshold of sight. It was hard to notice just by observing the blue line spinning round and round, but T'mer detected it almost at once. Walking around the sphere and studying the blue line, T'mer was able to see a slight wobble in the line, also. With only a quick glance, T'mer thought he saw the problem, but he wouldn't be able to prove that he had seen it until he could measure the magnetic resonance of the entire device.

"Your harmonic stability equalizer seems to be out of whack," T'mer said after completing one rotation around the disk. "I'm sure you have measured, tested and adjusted the synchronizer before now. Why won't it stay in balance?"

"That's what I would like to know," S'tan said, stepping up next to his old friend and putting his hand on T'mer's shoulder. "Every time I readjust the synchronizers, a fluctuation enters the grid and re-scrambles the default settings. We have thought about fashioning a new ring, but that would mean shutting down Dome production until we can get it installed. If the Council would have heeded my advice the first time I brought it to their attention, then we wouldn't have to concern ourselves with the prospect of total Dome collapse. Between you and me, T'mer, I don't think the ring is the problem. The fluctuations come from outside the Temple, or under it."

T'mer was still walking around the disk, looking at the various connections and following the thick, massive cables running all over the floor. One of those cables, larger than the others, ran from the disk away to a large booth that sat against the far wall. The booth was jet black and rectangular, about the height of a man and ten to fifteen feet long and four feet wide. There was a section of thick glass maybe 3X5 feet in size embedded into the wall of the booth that acted as a window allowing a two-way view. The window was smoky grey and polarized, like the look of welder's glasses. A dull radiance could be seen spilling out from behind the window and the light gave the interior of the booth a strange, greenish hue. A door was located on the end of the booth facing the transport shaft with a small, numeric keypad serving as the lock.

T'mer knew what function the booth served and understood that during times of full Dome production the only way a Tech or anybody else could observe the operation of the disk was behind the protection of the booth. Because of the reduced energy flow, the two of them were able to walk around the disk without the use of special gear, nor did they have to worry about a radiation cascade. At this low level of output, they could remain in the power room indefinitely, but that wasn't their intension: they were there to observe, diagnosis and report their findings to the Council as soon as possible.

"We'll need to power it up in order to test it properly," T'mer said, looking at the booth and then at S'tan. "Will the Council give you permission to boost output so I can see what the readings are?"

"They don't have much choice, do they?" S'tan said walking over to the door of the booth and punching in a set of numbers on the keypad. "I informed the Council that I would need to power up the Dome once I realized it was you among the wizards. I explained to them that if anyone could help explain the fluctuations it would be the one who helped designed the grid. I told them that I would need unlimited access to the power grid, free from the dictates of the Council."

"Yeah, I'm sure they agreed to that willingly. Why would they let a mere Tech have control over the power supply without endless discussion and high-level meetings? Since when did the monks decide Techs had any value outside brute strength?"

"I have been given many opportunities here and I have taken advantage of every one. At first they treated me like I was a child; ignorant, unaware and untrained. That was right after we installed the mirrors and you left. But then they started to experiment with my sexual output. They allowed me access to the bed chambers and gave me a whore all my own. She stayed down in the bed chambers, but I was allowed to visit her whenever the monks needed more research. Soon, I was spending most of my time in the bed chambers, even impregnating her. The baby she delivered was a female and the last I heard about the child she was getting along well with the males, but the females shunned her. They thought she was too self-important because she was the offspring of a Tech who worked in the Temple. I have never seen it."

"You're a father?" T'mer said laughing. "Since when does sperm donation make anyone a father? And why would a sperm donor even care about the sex? Even in the City children are taken from the female shortly after birth, some brought up to become Techs and others we give to the monks for barter. Personal attachment is counter-productive. You know this, T'tan. I'm surprised you would speak openly about something as shameful as paternity."

"Please, T'mer. My designation is S'tan. It is what I answer to. As far as paternity, I have often thought about having a man child of my own. In the 'gly, the Great Library, it has been written that in times before, in times before the Ancients, men and women came together to create life and raise it to maturity."

"That's blasphemy!" T'mer chided his friend good-naturedly. "And now you're telling me that the monks let you read out of one of the sacred books? Why would you want to? Old books of wisdom and tales of the beginning days that couldn't save those who wrote them are only good for burning. Why would you keep books that contained no mathematics, no science, no instructions or practical information? I would like to see how those books benefit a monk lost out in the dark. Ha! Maybe he could burn them to provide light so he could read it. I would much rather know how to survive the trails of life than speculate about the existence of Transcendentals."

T'mer's reproach, although made in fun, bothered S'tan but he didn't show it. In fact, facing him, he placed both hands on T'mer's shoulders and smiled brightly. T'mer's words troubled him because he understood where T'mer was coming from. But he had learned so much from the monks about how to silence his thoughts and focus his intension on the matter at hand. In most ways he was more knowledgeable than T'mer concerning the things of the monks and had grown to appreciate their paradigm. Where Techs like T'mer could create machines and gadgets that promised freedom, the effect was spiritual stagnation and degeneration.

S'tan and T'mer had seen that stagnation first hand while training to become Techs. Their instructors, instead of being the leading light of knowledge, insisted that the younger Techs needed to prove themselves by doing or creating something that those who came before had never dreamed of. It was because of this insistence that T'mer and S'tan had volunteered to go to the Temple and set up the mirrors in the first place.

They had stood above the others in their training and the instructors had high hopes for the two of them. It was only after they left the comforts of the City and entered the Temple that S'tan started to doubt the wisdom of Technology. Sure, machines provided for everything you needed, but S'tan was sure something had been lost. Once he had entered the Temple, and especially after T'mer had left, he felt like something had awoken within him, an awareness that his thoughts had changed because his external stimulus had changed. The silence of the Temple blocked out all the noise and busyness of the City, releasing the deeper thoughts residing within him.

T'mer's comments were standard defense against the persuasion of the monks, but what the Techs didn't understand was that by studying the Ancients and reflecting on their words one would never become lost and the light of gnosis would ever shine around you. He had become an initiate and had experienced the life-changing clarity of illumination, but didn't have the vocabulary to express the encounter in terms that someone like T'mer could appreciate. If only T'mer would read the words for himself, he thought, he, too, would experience the peace the monks offered. T'mer, S'tan knew, was too hardheaded to sit patiently at the feet of a monk and would never, ever think that he could learn from someone like C'ton. C'ton would be a good instructor, but T'mer's unexplainable attachment to T'mar would only impede his illumination, inhibiting him, making him feel less independent.

S'tan still care about his old friend and didn't want to argue with him about disputable matters. Instead, he decided to concentrate on T'mer's insights in the hopes that by working together he could rekindle that same camaraderie and trust they had known before. If he could revive that trust then, maybe, he could persuade T'mer to just listen to the words of the Ancients. For those following the path, the dark has no power over you. Even the potential collapse of the Dome was nothing to dread. S'tan knew and believed he was exactly where he was supposed to be and that seeing T'mer again was the will of the Transcendentals. That was what C'aad had told him personally. It was up to him to convert T'mer and he wouldn't fail the High Priest.

"You're right about that, T'mer. But still I find that the Ancients speak about things that are relevant for us today."

"Oh really? You mean to say that the answer to prevent total Dome collapse is written down somewhere? Then why don't we make our way to the 'gly and start reading before all the light goes out."

"I can see you still possess that same sarcastic, antagonistic attitude towards anything remotely spiritual. 'The answers to life', T'mer, 'lies not in the work of your hands, nor in your vain imaginations, but in the pursuit of gnosis.' With gnosis, all problems are seen in their proper light and melt away like butter in the sun."

"Yeah, and what is left is a slippery mess. Try practicing your beliefs in the face of immediate danger and see where it gets you. You know what it gets you, T'tan, S'tan, whatever. I'll tell you: Doubt and division. The greatest threat of our age is the resurgence of B'el, who by the way studied the same books you are quoting from. It was because of his interpretation of the texts that he came into conflict with the Council and was expelled. Are you trying to tell me that B'el is the pattern on which you base your beliefs? No, he is an abomination and his words are lies, the same as the monks. If there was life in the wisdom of the Ancients, why did they pass away? Where are the fathers of old if their teachings had any merit? It will be up to those who possess the real knowledge of science that will lead us out of the dark and into the light. The wisdom of the Ancients is for those who are dead and dying."

T'mer and S'tan had been walking around the disk and checking cable connections, a simple visual diagnostic that's usually perform before powering up the projection beam, the luminous power source structure on which the Dome depends. Their discussion was distracting to T'mer and he felt his blood rising, blurring his vision slightly, which made it difficult to detect any tiny discrepancies. His eyes ached from the strain of examining the disk and the spinning blue ring. There was nothing more he could do this side of the booth. It was time to seek the protection of the booth and power up the beam.

The door to the booth had slid out of the way and T'mer looked within, smiling to himself as he remembered the last time he had been inside. S'tan had entered ahead of him and was standing in front of the large window looking out at the spinning disk. He placed his hands on a transparent work station located beneath the window and his fingers sank into the glowing consol up to his knuckles. He wiggled his fingers slightly and the room lit up in bright green, followed by a loud click and then a low grade hum which produced a vibration that could be felt through the soles of their feet.

"If the monks are going to give you full access to the power grid, then let us 'brighten up the night and raise the mood of the lost hoards' outside the Temple," T'mer said mocking the words of the Ancients. "Don't you have to contact the Council or something before we go full power?"

"Yes, and I am in contact with them as we speak." S'tan had his eyes closed and his head tilted back. He was breathing slowly and deeply and his fingers were still. "I am being told to bring the power generator up to 25% production and hold it there until we receive further instructions. There's some confusion over bringing it up beyond that. There seems to be a problem in power generation coming from below in the bed chambers. I'm not too sure what the problem is. Maybe D'nan is having some difficulty with the power coupling. Or maybe the monks are measuring the sexual output of your friends and want to wait before they integrate the two power sources."

"They can decouple the power transmission from there? How does the Council control the output if those in the bed chambers can stop the flow of energy?" The door to the booth closed automatically as soon as S'tan placed his hands on the consol and T'mer was standing just behind him looking over his shoulder trying to detect any irregularities in the readouts splashing across the left side of the window. The readouts were displayed in red and included graphs, dials, meters, some kind of scope showing wave variations plus other assorted gauges revealing information pertinent to the stability and consistency of the energy going into the disk.

"They don't really disconnect from the Temple. After you left, the High Priest summoned me and asked if I could run a separate cable from the bed chambers to his command center in the throne room and from there to the power room. I didn't ask questions then and I installed a transformation device on his Dais, giving him the ability to divert and/or cut off the sexual energy produced in the bed chambers from the power room. It was explained to me at the time that they had all the energy they needed stored in the obelisks and that the monks were experimenting with the negative vibrations that came out of sexual intercourse."

There was a bar graph highlighted in the lower left hand corner of the window that showed, in red, a bar growing taller incrementally, approaching the midway mark on a scale that started at zero at the bottom and reached 100 at the top. A dial to the right of that graph showed a needle sweeping left to right, slowing as it neared the quarter mark. A digital readout located underneath the dial indicated the needle was registering RPM's and the number it gave was 10,000. The hum had settled down into a sub-audible vibration that was felt more than heard. The booth was washed in green and red, giving the spinning disk an eerie orange glow. The disk was spinning so fast now that T'mer couldn't detect the white stripe he had seen earlier when the disk was rotating slower.

Although S'tan and T'mer wouldn't have been able to see the actual color of the beam the disk produced because the glass in the window distorted it, what those outside the Temple saw was an intense, bluish-white eruption exiting the top of the Temple and merging with the substance of the Dome. The increase in power production lit up the ceiling of the

Dome and slid down the sides, like milk poured over a glass bowl turned upside down.

The energy coming up to the Temple from the mirrors lined all along the top of the wall changed colors as well, like a drop of food coloring added to water changes the tint of the water. Normally, filters which are built into the mirrors would clean the tint out, releasing a purer but diminished form of energy directly into the grid. In this case, however, what S'tan and T'mer were doing was producing the opposite effect, sending the energy back down the support beams where the power was held unfiltered in a storage receptacle.

The power increase wasn't enough to affect the obelisks, but the glow of the Dome, spreading out to cover all of the habitable places on the planet increased from deep red to dull orange and would stay that way until they either increased or decreased power production. At twenty-five percent power production, the glow of the Dome was brighter than it had been, but still a far cry from what it should be at this stage in their orbit around their star. Those in the dark would see the glow of the Dome like the setting of the sun, and some of them would again try to make it to the Temple, thinking that the light of the world was once again shining. But they would be mislead once again and perish outside the gate.

S'tan and T'mer weren't thinking about this, though. All they saw was the polarized radiance of the disk rising out of the power room. They knew that even if they got permission to increase energy production to 50% or higher, it wouldn't last long enough to give anyone hope. At the present rate they knew the Dome could only burn for a relatively short period of time. They didn't have the resources to maintain that level for very long. Even if they connected the bed chamber output to the power room, they could only hope of maintaining the Dome at 25% capacity for a very short period of time. Without the power storage of the obelisks, it was common knowledge among the Council that they wouldn't make it through the dark even at 10% capacity.

The fluctuation in the energy grid had produced a counter vibration that decreased output by as much as 50%, but it wasn't constant and varied from source to source, making it impossible to balance it out without injecting the system with a clean energy source and purging the distortion from the grid. If they raised the output above 75%, then because of the fluctuation they ran the risk of blowing the power room apart and incinerating everything within a hundred miles of the Temple.

"Everything seems to be in working order," T'mer said, looking down at the readouts and up at the spinning disk. It was hard to make out any of the details of the disk and it looked more like a solid orange ball sitting quietly on a pedestal than a parabolic disk spinning at over 10,000 rpm's. Only the readouts in the booth gave any indication that the ball was actually a disk spinning incredibly fast. "At this rate of spin, it is getting harder to pinpoint the location of the discrepancy from moment to moment. The inertial dampeners keep making minors adjustments to compensate, but there doesn't seem to be any discernable pattern that I can detect."

"Maybe when we get the okay to take it above25% we'll be able to recognize the discrepancy and trace it back to its source. At this level, the fluctuation is merely a background echo and too hard to isolate. We'll need to kick up the output before we can send out a diagnostic tracer, or maybe we will never be able to see it; it will get gobbled up in energy transfer. I have been instructed to maintain this level and prepare for a sudden increase in output. They are about to reconnect the lower level energy supply, infusing the grid."

The problem that the monks were having with the energy transfer had nothing to do with experiments or power couplings and everything to do with J'son's blatant refusal to participate in the sex rituals. After he had blasted down the hall, throwing out electrical discharges from the tips of his fingers and scorching the walls, he stopped at the end and disappeared, turning to his left and following the direction of the hall. This shorter corridor opened up into a large, circular room with passageways cut into the black rock at various intervals.

Connected to these passageways off to the side were rooms with large, plate-glass windows displaying females in various stages of dress lying on beds, some of them in the act of copulation. Other windows showed women of different ages dressed in what appeared to be shiny, black straps that covered minimal amounts of skin. They held electrically charged whips in their hands and they cracked them over their heads, ionizing the air. Still other windows were filled with women playing with an assortment of sex toys and devices that the women displayed in a sexually and demonstrative way.

There was noise all around J'son, but none of it was coming from the disk. Sounds of giggling and laughter and moaning filled the chamber and naked females of different sizes and ages packed the spaces between the passageways, speaking with the other monks that were present and playing with their manhood. The air was saturated with the smell of musk and sweat and sexually erotic scents and most of the monks had a dazed smile plastered across their faces. The girls were everywhere and several of them approached J'son, reaching out to him, trying to be the first one to grab hold of him and lead him into a bed chamber of his own. He chased them off just by looking at them, scowling at them and showing open contempt towards their advances. He didn't want to be taken in by his own lust and tried to focus on the power couplings he saw running all over the floor.

Thick cables ran out of the passageways across the floor of the massive room and met in the center, looking like the spokes of a wheel and joined up with a device that looked very similar to the disk and pedestal in the power room. This disk was surrounded by a translucent ball of bright red, but it wasn't rotating like its twin high above. Instead, it sat motionless and tranquil on top of its pedestal. The antenna was pointing up from the center of the disk and was glowing red, like a poker resting in a fire. Another cable, thicker than the ones running across the floor, was attached to the side of the pedestal and rose vertically to the ceiling, paralleling the shaft tube that would encase the energy beam once the power coupling was engaged. The other end of the cable disappeared into a rough hole hewn into the rock above.

A trap door of sorts made out of a dark wood with a round, metal handle attached to one end sat closed on the floor next to the disk. A hole had been cut into the door and a thick, black cable similar to the others ran through it and down under the pedestal. A bright, red light could be seen reaching up from the depth, flickering like a fire. Down there was where the main power coupling was located. Only D'nan was authorized to enter that chamber and link up with the power room, but that was exactly where J'son knew he wanted to be when the connection was re-established.

Ignoring the clamor around him and focusing on the task at hand, J'son walked over to the wooden door and reached down, grabbing the metal ring in this hand and pulling up. The door opened easily without a sound and locked into place, standing open perpendicular to the floor. Steep steps descended downward into the fiery light and hot air rose up, striking J'son in the face like a steaming hot towel. He recoiled from the heat and wiped newly formed sweat off of his forehead.

J'son heard a noise coming from behind him like the shuffling of feet and he looked back across his shoulder to see the cause. C'ton, D'nan, T'mar and several young women came out of the hall and exited the corridor, stopping in front of the first passageway and blocking the view of those behind the window. This chamber was almost always the first stop of the monks that came to visit. Down the passageway were several smaller rooms holding more young women. Usually the sound of laughter and giggling and music could be heard spilling out of the chamber as they played. Now, however, the females were all gathered in the front room looking out the main window at J'son, wondering why he had rejected them and worried that he represented a change to the established order.

D'nan was the first to speak, sounding whiney and frustrated, calling out to J'son above the din and commotion J'son's was causing everyone in the bed chamber.

"You are not allowed to go down there!" D'nan commanded, his high-pitched voice cracking like a school boy going through puberty. "You are required to participate in the rituals. It is mandatory and essential that you drive out your negative, pent-up frustrations, converting that energy into something more useful, draining yourself of all selfish desires. You must leave those desires here in the bed chambers with the women. You're rebellion will not go unpunished."

Seeing them, he smiled weakly at T'mar as she stood there dressed in nothing with her hands on her hips and her breasts up front and prominent, looking at him hungrily. He ignored D'nan and stepped down the first step, pausing for a moment before venturing down into the gloom.

D'nan was frowning, with red, flustered cheeks and moving around nervously, throwing his arms into the air while simultaneously grabbing his crotch. The look in his eye was one of extreme disappointment and panic, like an addict who is shown his drug of choice but not being able to indulge. Nothing was going like he had planned. What was supposed to happen was that he was to lead them down to the bed chambers, allow them their choice of perversion, couple that energy exchange to the power room and let them power up the Dome while they, especially J'son and T'mar, engaged their lust.

D'nan would monitor their output and at the moment just before release, he would make the connection that would send a large jolt of energy up the transfer shaft, diverting it towards the throne room first before sending it to the power room. Nobody in the bed chamber but D'nan knew that the cable running up to the ceiling went directly to C'aad and not the power room. He was ordered to re-connect the power the moment J'son had entered a bed chamber with a female, but J'son wasn't cooperating.

D'nan was tense and jumpy almost beyond his ability to maintain his mental stability. His mind was infected with the thoughts of sex and his loins were about to bust. The term "blue balls" floated into his awareness and he fought the urge to masturbate right there. He had been holding off sexual release, working himself up mentally and holding the release of his fluids just for a time such as this. He had fantasized about the flavor of T'mar's output and what it would be like to participate in an orgy where he could watch and feel the sexual energy. T'mar was standing in front of him and he wrestled with himself as he tried to pry his eyes away from her achingly beautiful body, physically restraining himself from reaching out to her by tucking his hands underneath his arms. But the temptation was too great.

He removed his hands, cupping them out in front and quietly walking up behind her. The tips of his fingers were almost touching her firm, round butt cheeks, twitching as he reached out. She must have sensed something for tiny goose bumps appeared on her ass and the cute, little hairs in the small of her back stood at attention. His fingers tips just brushed her soft, supple skin before he flinched, jerking his hand away. The action caused T'mar to look around, but she was unsure whether she had been touched or not.

"Huh? What are you doing back there, D'nan?"

"Nothing," he said, recovering his composure and acting like he expected what was happening. "You're friend, J'son, has a lot to learn. He is rebellious and unschooled, unable to do what he is told. No matter. C'aad has already foreseen this and has made the proper calculations to compensate. Whether you all participate in the rituals is not important. It was our hope that you would enjoy indulging your desires. Sometimes, only the females can scratch that itch."

"And sometimes the females can steal your vitality," C'ton said, moving out in front and making his way towards J'son. He was still struggling with his desires, not only those that came from watching naked women willingly throwing themselves at him and the warm, musky smell that filled his nostrils and mind with thoughts of sex, but also with the desire he still felt for T'mar rising within him. It was fairly easy for him to ignore the other women running all over the place, but T'mar, the woman he had enjoyed in his youth, was much harder to overlook.

He knew the thoughts of D'nan and had seen within his mind the image of him grabbing T'mar's ass and wrapping his arms around her waist, bending her over and entering her from behind. None of that happened, of course, but he notice that D'nan actually did touch her: He saw a minute blue spark, like the flash of static electricity on a door knob, jump from the tips of his fingers, imprinting T'mar with a slight discoloration resembling a five-pointed star. That star was D'nan's mark of ownership.

J'son reached the bottom step and saw a large, comfortable recliner upholstered in that same furry material that their clothes were made of. It was sitting in the center of the small, twenty-feet in diameter, circular room. A rectangular console sat before the recliner, opaque except for a round, flashing light. To say the light was red would be to assume the room was lit using normal ultra-violent luminescence, but that wasn't the case. Everything in the room and in the bed chambers blazed with a ruddiness that saturated the very air with a glow like a fire with different shades of red spilling out from every corner. Seeing the light flickering on the dark control panel, J'son got the impression that the button attached to the light was some sort of power switch that needed to be flicked before he could couple the bed chambers to the power room.

Leaning over the console, he reached out with one finger and pushed the flashing light until he heard a slight click. The light stopped flashing, settling down into a steady purple, and then he removed his hand. Immediately, a silvery screen full of wavy lines of static appeared at the foot of the stairs, sealing the lower room off from the bed chambers above. The light inside changed and a calming green filled the room as the console powered up, revealing dials, gauges, meters and a key board, all produced digitally and with light. Except for the actual frame of the console and the recliner, nothing lit in the room had any solidity beyond the codes of a computer program.

J'son lifted up one of the arms of the recliner and slipped into the seat without having to move the console out of the way. Seated comfortably behind the console, the arm of the recliner came back down automatically clicking into place. A restraining harness made out of beams of pure energy emerged from four slots: two located in the seat on both sides of him and the other two coming down over his shoulders.

The beams made an X across his chest seamlessly preventing him from any unwanted movements. His forearms rested easily on the arms of the recliner and his hands hovered lightly above the now illuminated console. He moved his fingers slightly, applying downward pressure on the console, his fingers sinking down up to his first knuckle and he closed his eyes, trying to see the wave pattern within his mind, coming up with nothing. He opened his eyes and spotted another flashing light in the lower left corner of the console. This light was glowing yellow and appeared to be in stand-by mode; it wasn't flashing as persistently as the first light.

Taking the fingers of his left hand out of the console, J'son reached out to the other flashing light and pushed that button, hearing a click and returned his hand back to the console. A shaft of intense white light shot out of the center of the console and struck J'son between the eyes, holding his attention momentarily like a deer caught in the headlights before he was able to close them again. Images flooded his awareness and he felt like he was in contact with something alive, something just on the edge of his consciousness. He saw images of T'mer and his friend talking in a booth somewhere, arguing about something having to do with the monks. That connection was slight and not very discernable, the image wavering within his mind and throwing out wave patterns that he couldn't comprehend.

There was someone else he was picking up, someone of extreme power and seemingly unlimited resources. At first the clarity of the image was worse than the connection he had with T'mer and he concentrated on that image until it revealed itself, showing the contents of the mind of C'aad. C'aad must have been connected to the power room because as soon as J'son was able to see C'aad clearly the interior landscape of C'aad's mind changed and now J'son could see external events, like the members of the Council conferring with each other. He couldn't hear what they were saying, but judging by their body language it was heated and no one was in agreement. It had something to do with connecting the bed chamber.

The beam of light coming out of the console dimmed considerably and J'son opened his eyes again, blinking several times trying to remove the images circling around in his head. A palm print glowed just beneath the surface to the console on his right and he sunk his hand down into the console, aligning his hand with that of the glowing imprint. His mind instantaneously filled up with long lines of computer code with breaks coming at intermittent intervals. J'son took these breaks as some kind of password protection. It would only take a quick thought to input the password and re-connect the bed chamber to the Council Chamber.

But it would have to be the correct password or J'son risked locking up the system. He would only have one chance to get it right before his just-now-assigned personal identification number would be locked out of the system, preventing him from accessing the grid. He saw the gaps in the code visually within his mind and he tried to determine the length of the gaps, hoping that an obvious pattern would emerge. If this room was keyed only to D'nan's genetics, then J'son wouldn't be able to couple the lower power supply to the power room.

"Get out of there at once!" D'nan commanded, pounding on the electrified door now separating the lower room from the rest of the bed chamber. "You must not engage the power coupling. You are not qualified nor authorized. The…, what are you doing?"

As soon as J'son had placed his hand on the palm print, a visually dense, apparently solid wall of magenta rose out of the bare rock floor of the bed chamber rising to the ceiling, filling in the gaps and imperfections and completely cutting off those members enjoying the pleasures of the females from the quiet and motionless disk in the center of the room. The wall was thick but still see through, allowing all to experience the intensity of the power transfer without having to endure any of the negative effects.

D'nan was still pounding on the security screen separating J'son from the rest of the room. The energy of D'nan's vocalizations and movements were being absorbed by the electrical field frustrating him even more. T'mar and C'ton were at the top of the steps looking down silently watching D'nan rapidly losing his composure. C'ton knew from prior experience that only one person was supposed to sit in the seat that J'son now occupied. What he didn't know was whether J'son knew he couldn't re-connect the bed chamber to the power room with the door opened and them standing outside the protection of the lower room. The system would read their life forms and automatically shut down, preventing activation. The system could be bypassed as long as the right code was entered into the computer, but unless J'son knew the password there was little chance that they would burn up in the intense, fervent heat of power transfer.

"If I let you in," J'son asked, his voice coming up from the depths of the room sounding like the tinny voice of an intercom, "Will you play nice and allow me the opportunity to engage the grid directly?"

D'nan stopped pounding on the screen. Sweat beaded on his brow and rivulets of moisture flowed down his chest, covering his upper body in a slick, reflective sheen. He was having a really hard time of it. It was bad enough that the impetuous boy was uncontrollable, but now he was sitting in the very spot designated specifically for his rank and level. Where regular monks enjoyed themselves with the females, it was the responsibility of D'nan to control the output of those engaged in sexual activity. The plan had been to watch the others participating in the orgies while he sat in the command chair monitoring the energy output of their lust. Then at the moment of peak output D'nan would re-connect the power cable, sending the heat of the bed chambers directly into his body and acting like a transistor. He would hold the power build up as long as his training allowed and then release it into the power grid.

Being fully integrated into the system, like J'son now was, would allow the operator to experience the rush of sexual release coming from the hundreds of monks and females so engaged. The effect of such a powerful jolt hitting the mind and body of one not prepared was capable of overloading the emotional centers of the brain, scrambling the neural network and reprogramming the belief structures of the unfortunate initiate who happened to connect himself to the power grid. D'nan had been waiting patiently ever since the Council informed him that he would be needed as an operator to guide and direct the outflow once the Dome was powered up. The thought made him physically excited and he had been feeding the lust of his mind ever since he left to meet J'son outside of the Temple.

Seeing J'son sitting in the chair that was specifically coded to his DNA, D'nan's mind warred against him, telling him that he wouldn't be able to participate in the power transfer and that thought made him even crazier. He couldn't let J'son engage the grid and he thought quickly about how he could take the chair back once he was inside, but first he had to get inside.

"Of course, my boy," D'nan said. His voice was quivering somewhat as he tried to hold back the growing anxiety building within him. "Just let us in before you activate the power grid. You don't want to fry us, do you?"

With his back facing the screen, ignoring the growing signs of anxiety betrayed in the sound of D'nan's voice, J'son moved his hand to the right, embedding his fingers up to the joint in another location and pressed a button, holding it down long enough for the screen to dissolve. The sound in the lower room changed vibrations and a slow hissing could be heard, like air rushing out a hole in a tire. The hissing stopped after a few moments, followed by a strong sucking sound. The sucking sound came from somewhere above and J'son, following the sound, became aware of tiny particles of energy flowing out of him and swirling around him creating a current of spinning particles of light moving towards the ceiling.

The sucking sound continued and grew louder as D'nan entered the room. J'son looked over his shoulder at D'nan and saw similar particles flowing away from him and into the ceiling. C'ton and T'mar came down the steps next and entered the room a few seconds after D'nan. The noise in the room increased because of their presence and became more chaotic, the particles forming a swirling vortex of energy with the chair and console serving as the focal point. The three of them were standing back against the wall of the small room looking at J'son to see what he was going to do.

"Don't worry, D'nan. I am only going to connect the power couplings long enough to balance out the fluctuations and give them some stability. Then you can have your chair back and power up once I am done. I'll need your password to re-connect the power couplings."

"How do I know you won't take the power for yourself?" D'nan asked sounding harsh and accusatory.

"I have no need of it, D'nan. I will re-connect the power coupling and only allow enough energy to be transferred to complete the re-alignment. I promise." J'son said that last part with a bright smile on his face.

"J'son, are you going to be able to resist the onslaught of power once the transfer starts?" C'ton asked hesitantly. "The amount of energy flowing through the power coupling is like the pressure of water spilling out of the sluice of a dam. Once the power is reconnected, there's no stopping the flow. It could seriously damage you, burning out the pleasure centers of your brain."

"I think I can handle it. I plan on diverting the majority of the flow to the Dome, bypassing this chair in a kind of energy loop. I'm not too sure how I am supposed to do that, though." Pressing the same flashing button on the console as before, the screen blocking the door materialized again, sealing them inside from those on the outside.

"Give me your password, D'nan."

"No! I am the only one authorized to sit in that chair. Get out of it before you damage the grid."

"Give him the password, D'nan." C'ton didn't know for sure if J'son had the ability to control the flow of energy to the Dome, but he did know that if D'nan connected the power coupling they would be held hostage by him, trapped in the room until he came out of the hallucinogenic trance that usually accompanied power transfer.

"It's not right," D'nan shouted, slamming his hand down on the back of the chair. "That chair is mine."

D'nan almost touched J'son, reaching out with his hand to grab hold of his neck, but pulled it back at the last moment. To touch an operator connected to the console without permission could cause the offender mental disharmony, creating a disturbance that could cascade across the grid, triggering a bottleneck in the system and another fluctuation.

It was here in the lower room that J'son thought was the source of the initial fluctuation and he wondered if D'nan was aware of how much his dependence on the bed chambers affected his ability to master his own energy output. "Only the pure of mind can produce purity of power". It was another mantra of the monks. Negativity of any sort, more so sexual negativity, was a great problem throughout the power grid and the monks were diligent in their monitoring.

"That's not what C'aad said," J'son said. "I am in contact with the Council at this moment and it has been decided that I will re-connect the bed chambers with the power room. See for yourself."

J'son leaned over slightly, allowing D'nan access to the palm print embedded in the console. D'nan was uncertain and hesitated, but after a moment of indecision he thrust his hand down on the imprint. The program identified him as D'nan immediately and took the pass codes out of his consciousness and inputted them without need of authorization. Just his imprint was all that was needed to activate the system.

Once activated, the beam coming out of the console brightened again and splintered, branching out, striking both J'son and D'nan between the eyes. They closed their eyes and together they were thrown into that other environment of mental and electrical thought transfer, a venue only existing in the collective minds of those so connected. It was a locale where thoughts moved at the speed of light and whole conversations could be held within moments.

D'nan's connection to the console was short, direct and to the point. He was advised to step aside for the good of the Temple and possibly the whole of the planet and that later he would be permitted to indulge his fetishes without hindrance and possessing an unrestricted chip. It was the last word that caught his attention and he finally renounced his claim to the chair for the time being. The key word, "Unrestricted", meant that he would be allowed to engage in any activity for any length of time. He just had to be patient and hold on to his lust a little longer. It was hard for him to bury that burning fire consuming his loins, but the promise of unspeakable delights persuaded his body to obey the will of his mind.

With D'nan's pass code properly imputed, the sucking sound ceased and the humming sound returned, followed by a whirling sound as the disk above them began to spin. A monitor on the console showed several views of the bed chambers from within the magenta wall and from outside of it. The view outside showed the monks and the females finally getting back into their regular routine, filling up the rooms and windows surrounding the spinning disk and engaging their sexual appetites.

The field separating the spinning disk and room below from the bed chamber proper was transparent like cellophane, radiating a brilliant, multihued red, like the color of a sunset coming through the clouds. A hush had fallen over those participants engaged in sexual practices as the red light of power transfer flooded the rooms and beds. The only sounds were the faint erotic moaning of flesh enjoying the pleasures of sexual contact.

The view from within the field showed the disk and pedestal encased in a purplish orb. The disk was spinning faster than the eye could make out and only a reddish outline of a ball within the purple orb gave any indication that there was anything inside. The antenna coming out of the top of the spinning disk looked like the stem of an apple, pointing straight up with a slim beam of light coming out of the top and disappearing into the ceiling. This was a tracer beam intended to mark out the path the beam would take once they had re-established the connection. The spinning disk developed a slight wobble visibly perceived and the beam of light coming out of the top traced a small circle in the rock above.

Chapter Twenty-Three:

Powering up

"Do you think he can handle the output?

T'mar voicing concern about J'son's mental stability

"I believe we are ready to re-connect the power couplings," J'son said speaking to them in a voice that seemed like it was coming from far away. "At my count, we are going to power up to 10%. Ready? Three, two, one…, now."

A connection was made on the console and the room exploded in a sudden, intense, deep hum that rattled their bones and sent a vibration around the room counter to the direction of the spinning disk. With his hands fully embedded into the console, J'son closed his eyes and saw in his mind a gauge that went from 0 to 100. He concentrated on the gauge and watched as the needle moved up from zero to ten. A digital readout next to the gauge oscillated between 9.8 and 10.5, an acceptable variance at this level of output. A variance of less than one percent wasn't a cause for concern, but as they increased output that deviation could increase by more than 10-20%, enough of a variation to cause the disk to go out of balance and detonate.

The small room was humming, producing a sensation that raised them above the mundane reality of sound and allowed entrance into the realm of psychic sensation. The chair on which J'son sat was vibrating to the point that he looked like the solitary image in a blurred picture. The floor of the room buzzed with the power buildup, acting like an echo chamber and amped up the output. As the disk continued to pick up speed, tremors in the system grew and faded, creating an oscillating wave of equal strength and intensity that helped cancel out minor fluctuations as they approached operating levels.

"I'm just about ready to send it up stairs," J'son shouted over the din, sounding far away and tinny. "All I need to do is release the conduit power stabilizers to allow for unobstructed energy transfer. As long as I keep it at 10%, we should be alright."

"Please be careful, J'son," T'mar said, barely above a whisper, knowing he didn't hear her. It was a real concern of hers that this experience, unlike the others he had to endure, could very well scramble his brains. To absorb that much raw power coming into his body, especially the quality of that power, could alter his basic genetic programming. This experience could turn his mind to mush, a grayish blob of pleasure-seeking, addictive behavior.

J'son, staring blankly straight ahead at the area above the console, his eyes opening and closing randomly, inhaled deeply and he held it while he moved his hand to another location on the console and pressed down. The room erupted in a volcano-like shower of string-like particles which flowed out from the chair and console and disappeared into the ceiling, following the tracer beam. A reddish-green shaft of light appeared from the center of the console, splintering into spiky shards of angled light which crisscrossed around the room, sending multi-colored illumination throughout the small chamber.

The figure of J'son sitting in the vibrating chair was dissolving, merging with the energy in the room and becoming one with everyone connected to the grid. J'son was tingling all over and he felt himself lift up out of the chair, like he was having an out-of-body experience. The view in the room faded into a blank nothingness, devoid of color; even physical sensations seemed to grow fainter and more remote, like he was just an observer and not a participant. He found his thoughts travelling away from him, acknowledging the fact that the impressions and opinions forming within his mind were coming from another source beyond the confines of the lower chamber. It was getting harder for him to distinguish the sound of his own thoughts from the noise all around him and he kept getting distracted by the other voices he heard floating on the current of the ascending particle beam.

Within moments of re-connecting the power coupling, J'son found his awareness becoming conscious of itself within the confines of the Council Chamber. He saw C'aad, the High Priest, sitting in his chair up on its Dais, his face and eyes radiating a state of total bliss. There were others in the Council Chamber connected to the power supply in the same way as C'aad, with a thick cable running out from C'aad's chair into a black, semi-metallic box sitting on the floor between him and the others.

Coming out the other side of the box were a dozen thinner cables that ran to the chairs of the others. Their chairs were situated around the outside of the Council Chamber in a half circle with C'aad in the center facing them. All of the monks had a pleasing appearance about them, smiling without awareness and willingly ignorant of exactly who was responsible for the bliss they now participated in.

Moving higher up the beam, J'son saw the interior of the power room, a brightly glowing ball of energy spinning incredibly fast in the center separated by a wall of translucent blue-white. Beyond the wall running along the outer perimeter was a booth with black cables connected to it. Inside the booth T'mer was standing next to S'tan, who was sitting in a chair before a console that looked very similar to the one located in the lower chamber. S'tan was connected to the grid in the same way as J'son and C'aad, receiving the same amount of energy as the other two.

T'mer, because he wasn't connected directly to the grid, being one step removed from the source like the other monks on the Council, only existed within J'son's mind as a shadow and an outline in the blinding intensity of power transfer, lacking any corporal substance that could be called tangible. The others, also, existed as a thought within the grid and could, depending on the strength and training of the operator, become disembodied, lost within the system, unable to escape without the help of a sympathetic, authorized operator. T'mer and the others risked their very lives by being connected to the grid like they were. By participating in powering up the Dome in the way they were, they walked a thin line between bodily reality and mental reality, their materiality dependent on the whims of the one sitting in the chair behind the consoles.

"I guess they got the problem worked out," S'tan said to T'mer in a dreamy voice that sounded more drugged than sober. "We'll hold it at this level for a few minutes to check out the integrity of the system. Once the diagnostics come back with positive verification, we'll be authorized to bump it up to 25%. At that level, we'll all bliss out for a while. It will be up to C'aad to minimize the downtime and bring the Dome up to full power. Just a few more minutes."

The smile on S'tan's face had a dopey, serene look with the corners of his mouth turned up and the lids of his eyes partially opened, like slits, glowing red. It was getting hard for S'tan to remain conscious and a fleeting thought floated across his awareness stating that maybe he should get up out of the chair and let T'mer enjoy a direct connection. But the moment the thought was found fully formed within his mind, another thought, harsher and more self-seeking, responded that he, S'tan, had every right to be sitting where he was and he didn't owe T'mer anything, much less the pleasure of being an operator. Besides, T'mer was still able to partake of the overspill and that should be enough for a mere Tech.

All three chambers were vibrating like the very foundation of the Temple was under attack. Under normal circumstances, with the power set at 25%, the Lower Chamber, the Council Chamber and the Power Chamber would hum and a slight vibration could be felt coming up from the soles of their feet. Their fingers embedded in the consoles would tingle slightly, but nothing more than that. Now, because of the misalignment and the inerrant fluctuations running rampant throughout the grid, the vibrations were harder to control and compensate for. Unless J'son could balance out the fluctuations before sending it up the power conduit, power levels above 25% could conceivably tear the Temple apart and bring the Dome down on their heads. Anything that happened next would be determine by J'son's ability to control the fluctuations and stay conscious, an act made harder due to the intensity of the psychic ecstasy he now indulged in.

The pleasure centers of J'son's mind were on overload and the dreamy smile stretched out across his face spoke of delight beyond measure, like a man caught in an orgasmic loop, his lower body below the waist fruitlessly humping the air against the belt restraints in a spasmodic twitching that had no rhyme or rhythm. His thoughts were consumed by images of sex and sexual indulgence. Except for the occasional pelvic spasm, his body, unable to keep up with the demands of his over-stimulated brain, sat flaccid and limp in the vibrating chair.

The power level was increasing incrementally and the hum in all three chambers was reaching a climax of sound and vibration above which the inertial dampeners would engage and shut the process down to avoid self-destruction. It was just below that level that the three operators tried to reach and maintain. It was a procedure that required strenuous mental focus and was growing increasingly harder the higher the output.

In a voice coming at J'son from somewhere outside his conscious awareness he heard the command given to increase the output to 25%. Feeling dreamy, his thoughts unhinged and flowing effortlessly through the cables connected to the grid, J'son regained just enough conscious mindfulness to move his hand across the console and engaged the power coupling that would allow the power flow to increase. He closed the connection, had a moment to reflect on the impact of the power flow on his body and mind, and lost consciousness, his head falling forward until his chin hit his chest, the belt restraint supporting his upper body.

The small, lower chamber had become a vibrating mass of electrically charged particles that filled the room in a brilliant maroon light, obscuring the image of everyone in the room. T'mar, C'ton and D'nan, leaning back against the curved wall of the chamber, slid down the wall, their legs giving way once the power level reached 25% and collapsed in a heap on the floor, the mental impact shutting them down physically. The pleasure centers in their brains, however, were still active and would record the experience for later recall and replay. When the three of them eventually awoke from their hyper, sexually-induced coma, the feelings of physical well being and sexual satisfaction would encase them in a womb of bliss and serenity.

The same type of experience was available to all connected to the grid and those so connected throughout the Temple and even those up in the windows high up in the wall with the mirrors would lose consciousness temporarily, falling into a dream of sexual encounters and delight. During this time, the Temple and everything within it fell silent as if someone had flipped a switch that instead of turning everything on, turn everything off. All chanting had stopped and those outside the Temple on the grounds of the Temple were lying down, some in a prone position while others were piled one on top of the other where they fell. The only sound that could be heard throughout the Temple was the low-grade hum of the power conduits converting the sexual energy of the lower chambers into something more useable.

By the time the raw energy of the lower chamber had passed through the Council Chamber and reached the power chamber, the purity and quality of the energy continuing on to the top of the Dome had been filtered down to a single point of light, striking the Dome, outlining it in yellow. At full power, that line would have been a shaft of light ten feet in diameter, white and large enough to create a Pleasure Dome that would cover all of the habitable places on the planet. But because of the distortions and vibrations, that shaft was only a line, not large enough to deliver the power necessary to sustain the Dome, nor did it have access to the power stores needed for full power. If J'son couldn't balance out the power coming from the lower chamber, the Council had decided to limit the area the Dome would have to cover, lowering the height thereof and bringing the walls of the Dome within the walls of the Temple. The consequence, if they couldn't balance out the fluctuation, all who lived outside the Temple would die, including those who lived in the City.

C'aad was the last to lose consciousness, having built up a tolerance to the anesthetizing effects of the power transfer through countless cycles of training and close contact with the source. The others in the Council Chamber had lost consciousness at about the same time as everyone else, their heads either falling back against the wall of the Council Chamber or their chins down resting against their chest. Although C'aad was still conscious, his eyes were closed and the silly smile stretched across his face had the dopey look of a man basking in the afterglow of great sex. His lips were trembling, moving of their own accord, a simple expression indicating that he had lost control of his body and was only vaguely aware that he was still sitting on his Dais.

The bliss was at its peak and his mind was growing dark in the narcotic-like ecstasy. The thoughts of everyone connected to the grid had fallen off to just a distant echo, followed by an intense, creepy silence, a void, an empty space within the collective consciousness of the Temple. If C'aad allowed himself to drift off into the abyss of nothingness that power transfer represented, there wouldn't be anyone left with the training to redirect the power flow back into the grid and away from those so connected. He was hanging on to the tiny shred of consciousness still available to him, hoping to push his consciousness to the limit and even beyond in a mad endeavor to retain consciousness for as long as possible.

He was slipping into darkness and he programmed himself to awaken once the last of his consciousness had departed. He had done this before, during training assignments, going under completely long enough to increase his tolerance to the power transfer, but it wasn't something that all on the Council agreed. If C'aad went under completely without programming himself to wake up, then all within the Temple would fall into a deep, dreamy, catatonic stupor, unable to awaken themselves, their minds and finally their bodies succumbing to the inevitable progression of entropy and death, their energy being re-absorbed into the grid.

C'aad thought momentarily of doing just that: retreating into the mental bliss of power transfer never to wake again, his energy and that of the others, cycling through the energy conduits between the Dome, the lower chamber, the Council Chamber and the power chamber continuously until all grew dark. If he would just let go, cut the silvery thread that connected him to the reality of the Dome, the last thing he and the others would experience would be the impression of a flame blowing out and the slow dissolution of their life force like smoke trailing off the end of a smoldering wick.

It would be pleasant and the thought of death comforting. If it wasn't for his belief in the mission of the monks and his unwavering faith in the rightness of their religion, he would have let go and followed the path of bliss, hoping to reach the domain of the Transcendentals. He would have just slipped away for good if it wasn't for another voice riding within the grid pleading with him to "Wake up!"

The voice startled him awake, his mind filling with the light of consciousness even if he didn't open his eyes. No one but the High Priest should be able to communicate through the grid at this level of output. His should have been the only consciousness aware of its surroundings, much less have the mental energy to form impressions within his mind capable of refocusing him on the task at hand. The voice disturbed him, recognizing the owner immediately. It was too timid to be D'nan, and C'aad knew C'ton, connected indirectly as he was, would never presume to break the silence of power transfer. Other than those two, whom C'aad knew about and participated in their training, no one but he should have the ability to speak while connected the way they were.

The only other operator connected to the grid was J'son and it bothered C'aad that he didn't have a firm grasp on what J'son could do nor the limits to his power. Even connected the way they were, C'aad had a hard time perceiving the thoughts and motivations of J'son, finding himself mentally battling the command given from below to disconnect from the power transfer directly and allow the energy to flow freely up the power shaft into the Dome. With C'aad attached to the grid, his body acted like a gateway separating out the low level energy from the higher quality power needed for Dome support. By stepping out of the way, figuratively, all power would flow towards Dome production and he would emerge intact, his batteries recharged, possessing more personal power than anyone living under the Dome.

It was now too late for him, however, to continue down the path of oblivion that he had just contemplated; his mind was too alert, too awake. He had been ripped out of the bliss of power transfer like a man sobering up as he consumed more caffeine. He had been denied his release and deep rapture, holding back the waves of lust for so long that now he was unable to return to the mental state that would benefit him the most. He felt like he had gotten caught with his pants down just on the verge of discharge, and now had nowhere to relieve himself without experiencing the embarrassment such a situation produced. He thought momentarily of D'nan, who also had built himself up for release only to be denied that very release. C'aad would have smiled at D'nan's discomfort if it wasn't for the fact that C'aad was experiencing and having to deal with some of the very same annoyances.

Feeling let down and under-powered, tired, C'aad turned his resentment and sexual frustration into a "teachable moment", telling himself that if they were able to stabilize the power output he would have access to all the power he would need and missing out on this one power transfer wasn't too much to ask of the High Priest. What he didn't allow himself to think about was what would happen if they couldn't stabilize the output.

Instead of not being allowed release, he wouldn't even have access to the power stream necessary to achieve release. For someone of his rank and responsibility it took more than a trip to the bed chambers for him to find release. What he needed had to be much more stimulating. Maybe if he could persuade T'mar into sitting with him on the Dais once J'son stepped into the power tube. Her physical beauty plus her own energy reserve, mixed with the flush of 25% power could very well help C'aad achieve release. But she would have to be willing and not resist his mental advances.

Moving his hands slowly but deliberately across the face of the console before him, C'aad slipped his index finger over a flashing, yellow-orange light to the left of a dial indicating power levels. He completed the connection and his hand fell back into his lap. The separation was fast and the disconnection relatively painless. His mind was freed from the grid almost immediately and he gave out the command all across the grid:

"Those without prior commitments are welcome to continue in your own private fantasy. Enjoy! S'tan. D'nan. I want you here in chambers. Don't bother to clean up D'nan. You will have opportunity to indulge later. We all must make sacrifices. That is all."

And that was all. The energy coming up from the sex chambers and entering into the Council Chambers had been diverted away from the Dais and was now flowing directly into the dish assembly. To say the energy had been diverted is a misstatement. When the Temple was originally constructed, the power flowed through the dish up towards the power room. It wasn't until much later that the High Priest C'abl installed the cables running to the Dais, thus diverting the power flow away from direct Dome support and funneling it off to be used as purposed by the High Priest.

Sitting in his chair high up on the Dais, his console pushed back and out of the way, a faint, translucent glow surrounded C'aad, comforting him, the serene, passive afterglow of power transfer. His mind, however, wasn't quite as still as he normally experienced it. Usually, his thoughts drifted around lazily, unhinged and disconnected from the mundane, superficial problems that typically occupied his thinking.

But now, he was distressed, unable to enjoy the full after-effects of power transfer, his thoughts consumed by J'son's ability to communicate within the grid during power transfer, his own lack of release and the image of T'mar's exquisite body seared into his mind, an image he lifted out of D'nan's mind while they were still connected. His loins burned in lust for her as he contemplated the feelings and emotions surrounding this woman and he waited for the others to meet with him in chambers, considering ways in which he could manipulate her into giving him what he wanted. She would have to be willing.

The others would be in chambers soon and then he would impress them with his ability to manipulate the energy of everyone in the room, shocking and surprising his underlings, hoping to blind them to the truth of what was really happening in the Temple. C'ton might understand the situation but he would never agree with how C'aad implemented his strategy. Nevertheless, C'ton wasn't his main concern. It was J'son, and everything he signified. Some of those connected to the grid had made mention of the "Prophecy of the End", referring to the One whose energy J'son embodied.

C'aad didn't subscribe to the interpretation of prophecy that was part of their doctrine and had over the last age refined the standard interpretation, taking some things out and spiritualizing the meaning of other key passages, twisting the sense of the prophecy and reinterpreting the message that had been passed down throughout the age as a guide for future generations. It was this reinterpretation of scripture that C'aad felt was necessary to compensate for and explain their present situation. He didn't believe C'ton would question his interpretation publically, but if C'ton could convince the others that C'aad was misguided in his thinking, it was possible, however improbable, that C'ton would make a claim to the title of High Priest. C'aad didn't think C'ton would do this, but still he wasn't sure.

Chapter Twenty-Four:

The Council Chamber

> "We only need to convince the boy to enter the energy beam for the good of the planet. Once he is in, we will have all the energy we will need to make it through this crisis."
>
> C'aad speaking to the Council

T'mer, who wasn't connected to the grid directly like S'tan, was the first to regain his composure. The silly smile plastered across his face, a physical marker of the chemical cocktail coursing through his veins, faded into a look of grave misgivings as he recovered. S'tan was still hooked into the console and he turned to look at T'mer, his face a mask of asinine simplicity with eyes partly opened and glassy. With a dopey grin on his face, smiling the smile of the mentally incompetent, S'tan tried winking at T'mer but only managed to scrunch up his cheeks, making him look even more stupid.

"I guess we should make our way to the Council Chambers," S'tan said, smiling brightly between slurred words, his eyes glossy and watering. "C'aad will want to hear our report."

Steady on his feet, T'mer moved over to the console where S'tan was still sitting and lifted the armrest, moving it out of the way. Reaching down, he wrapped his massive arms around his friend's upper torso just under the arm pits and lifted S'tan into a standing position, steadying him as he wobbled around on shaky legs. Although the graphic, sexually-stimulating aspects of power transfer had for the most part been filtered out through the Dais, the mental impressions of the others were still there, residing within S'tan like a vivid dream. He didn't feel sexually excited or even have the mind set to engage in sex, but he did feel like he had spent some time in a sauna, relaxed and quite content.

The power chamber was awash in light, the disk was spinning incredibly fast, and the energy pouring out of the top of the disk flowed towards the ceiling, bursting out of the top of the Temple, striking a point high in the air and spreading out and down, enclosing all those living within the protection of the Dome. The color of the Dome was yellow-orange, holding stable at that wave length, but T'mer knew that it wouldn't stay that way. Once the initial brilliance of power transfer faded, the Dome would return to a deep red, staying that color until all available energy had been bled way, then the Dome would begin to collapse, shrinking down in size and volume until only the Temple was protected. After that, the Dome would collapse completely and the cold chill of the Wastelands without would begin to take over. Without energy, all life ends.

With the Dome still running at 25% power and the protective wall up, the only way T'mer and S'tan could leave the booth was to exit out a different door than the one in which they had entered. That door was at the opposite end of the booth but back against the wall, as opposed to being situated on the end like the other door. The door had no handle, only a series of nine buttons arranged in a square resting where the handle should be. There weren't any hinges, either, and if you weren't looking for it the door appeared to be just an aesthetic line providing contrast to the bleak walls.

Helping to support his weight, T'mer half walked, half dragged his friend over to the door. Stabbing the keypad with his finger, T'mer keyed in a default code, hoping the combination hadn't been reset. A tiny light switched from red to green and the illumination within the booth decreased in intensity. The console powered down and locked into an automatically-controlled and monitored sub-routine. The door opened, sliding into the wall, revealing a brightly lit, curving corridor running off in opposite directions. This corridor was located up against the inside of the outer spire of the Temple and followed the curve around, making a complete loop. The yellow light spilling into the corridor came from the outside and filtered in through one of the four windows located on this floor.

They followed this corridor for a short while, curving around the power chamber until they came to the transparent door of the transport shaft. Punching in the pass code on the keypad to the right of the shaft, again hoping the monks hadn't reprogrammed the system, the door, very similar in construction to the screen in the bed chamber, faded away in a wink of light, revealing the interior of the transport shaft. S'tan, stumbling forward and breaking away from T'mer's support, practically fell into the opening, hitting the rear of the transport shaft with his fore head.

"I think I better key in the designation code," S'tan said, slurring his words but standing on his own now.

"You mean to tell me they wouldn't trust me to use Temple transport accordingly? Where would I go that they couldn't shut me down? With all the problems they are having with power generation, you'd think any unauthorized use would be locked down immediately."

"So you would think. Still, unless I receive instructions from the High Priest allowing you direct access to the power grid, I'm afraid there aren't any default codes that would give you admittance."

Punching the keys on another small console within the transport shaft, S'tan entered the four-digit designation code for the Council Chamber. The transparent screen reappeared, sealing them within the shaft. A sub-audible buzz filled the small shaft with tiny, crackles of light, like the spray of color one sees coming off of a sparkler. There was the slight feeling of falling, like sitting down in a chair too fast, followed by an abrupt finish. The screen disappeared again and the transport shaft opened up to a hall just outside the Council Chamber. Before them was another door, black and appeared to be made from the same rock as everything else. The door was opened ajar and bright yellow light streamed out from the crack, filling the hallway before the transport shaft and the Council Chamber with a warm, inviting brilliance.

S'tan and T'mer were the first ones to make it to the Council Chamber not having to travel as far as the others, considering the power chamber was only one floor above the Council Chamber. Also, they weren't as sexually charged as those in the bed chamber or Council Chamber, considering C'aad had diverted the majority of the sexually-charged energy through his console and filtered out the more physically stimulating aspects of the energy, leaving only the mental expression, of which mental exhaustion being the primary residual aftereffect.

They entered the Council Chamber looking fatigued and a little out of sorts, their minds still swimming with images just beyond consciousness. T'mer was the more stable of the two and journeyed further into the Council Chamber before stopping before the Dais of C'aad. He stood at attention, like he had been taught in the past, with his hands clasped behind his back. He stared up at C'aad, sitting on his throne, waiting patiently for the High Priest to speak, ignoring the other members of the Council who were slowly returning upright in their chairs and trying to look more dignified.

They sat in chairs, twelve in all, which surrounded the disk sitting in the middle of the room. Directly behind the disk, with six seats on one side and six on the other, connected by a thick cable running to his chair, C'aad sat on his podium in a state of tension and distress, mentally fighting back the lust rising from his loins and physically readjusting himself in his seat, trying to find a spot that was more comfortable.

"Come forward, S'tan," the High Priest ordered. "I appreciate your discretion in this matter, but I think we will dispense with the formalities. Soon, T'mer, your female will be here, something that hasn't happened since I was made High Priest. Her presence here would normally be prohibited, but everything that has been happening is beyond our experience. Perhaps allowing her entrance into the Temple is the will of the Transcendentals."

The Transcendentals! C'aad had long ago departed from the path that had been laid out by the Transcendentals, spiritualizing their teachings in such a way that what the Transcendentals had to teach was taken apart, re-evaluated and re-introduced in such a way that the original prophecy and the correct interpretation of such was lost. Only by studying the original Autograph, which was located in the vaults of the 'gly, could one hope to unravel the mess that generations of High Priests had managed to create. The only problem with studying the original was that all subsequent readings were based on the interpretation of the previous High Priest and how he understood it. It was expected of each High Priest to bring a new reading to the prophecies and direct his administration accordingly.

The first High Priest, chosen for the part shortly after B'el left for the Wastelands, was the only one not to bring an interpretation to the original Autograph, holding fast to the literal meaning of the text and using the original to define terms that he wasn't familiar. His supremacy didn't last long, though, less than a few macro-cycles. His fall was due to subversion and conspiracy, brought about because of his refusal to reinterpret the prophecies in order to match the situation with which they had been faced. It was because of that refusal and his subsequent weak rule that the first murder of a High Priest was the first High Priest.

C'aad sat on his Dais looking down at T'mer and watching as S'tan staggered closer to the Dais, trying desperately to clear his mind and refocus. Standing next to T'mer now, S'tan looked up into the smiling, bony face of the High Priest. The X, which is discernable on the visage of all on this planet, cut deep into the face of C'aad, giving his smile a sinister, insincere expression that spoke of mystery and malevolence. His head, sitting heavily on top of a thin neck, small shoulders and a tiny frame, was larger than normal with eyes that were large, when they were opened, fixed and dilated, bugging out of his head like two light bulbs. He didn't blink as he stared down at them, but held his gaze steady. His eyes shined bright yellow and seemed to glow like a harvest moon on a crisp, autumn evening. It was this expression that made it hard to look at him without bowing your head and acknowledging his superiority and rule.

C'aad had finally found a comfortable position in his chair and was resting calmly, if not menacingly, at least on the surface. He knew it would progressively get harder to deny himself, especially once T'mar got here, and his demeanor would change accordingly. His wit and wisdom, so praised among the lower echelons of the monks that they made songs out of his sayings, would become harder to access the longer he endured the tedium of his office.

What he wanted at the moment was to enter into deep meditation and find his way back to the bliss of power transfer, but that wasn't going to happen any time soon. First, he needed feedback from his personal Tech and was very curious to hear what T'mer had to say. Then, he needed to examine J'son closely to see how he reacted to C'aad's authority. He appreciated T'mer's show of respect, but he wasn't sure how J'son would behave or whether he would continue to help them. C'aad knew that J'son's intension was to leave the Temple as soon as possible, and short of physically restraining him C'aad didn't know if he would be able to manipulate J'son into doing what was needed.

"S'tan," C'aad began in a voice dripping with contempt and sounding aloof and superior at the same time. "Report!"

"The disk is rotating within specs and holding steady at 25% power. The injection rate ratio is now 75/25. Pushing the energy transfer rate higher than 25% will deplete the bed chamber stores. In order to increase the total output above 25%, we will have to enhance the quality of the signal coming up from below and push the injection rate above 80%. At that level, the signal will consist mostly of the negative aspects of power transfer, making your job extremely dangerous. I recommend increasing the rate coming out of the Council Chamber to maybe 35-40%. That will decrease the fluctuations and produce a cleaner signal. Do you concur, T'mer?"

"I agree. You will need to up the output from here and lower your dependence on the energy coming from below. To inject any more negative energy into the grid at this point will cause an increasingly unstable condition. You think you had fluctuation problems before, just wait and see what happens if you jack up the output without combining a comparable influx of higher quality energy. Anything above 75% would be unwise."

"You presume to instruct me in wisdom, a mere Tech? I am fully cognizant of our situation and I appreciate your input, but perhaps you don't quite understand the threat we face. Without the reserves that the obelisks are supposed to provide, we don't have the available energy necessary to increase Council output much above 25%. If we hope to keep the Dome up and operating at present levels, we will need to risk boosting the output coming from below. It was our hope that your friends would have participated in group sex, enhancing the overall output. However, -"

"Don't you get it?" T'mer asked, astonished at the seemingly naive attitude of the High Priest. "Just because you add more people to the mix doesn't mean that output will increase. It's like wax to a candle. No matter how large the candle, the flame will only burn so hot. Sending people down to the bed chamber will only add to the length of time that the Dome will stay lit, but it won't boost the intensity. To increase intensity you will need vast power reserves. Nobody you send down there for any amount of time will be able to replenish the reserves, not to the level you need. The most you can hope for is a short continuation of the Dome at this flow rate."

"At that rate," C'aad responded, "we won't be able to function. A twenty-five percent power flow won't be enough to sustain life across the planet. We will be forced to limit the Dome's coverage to a smaller area in order to survive."

"I know what you mean," T'mer said angrily, removing his hands from behind his back and placing them on his hips. Tilting his head back in an open display of aggression, he continued. "You mean to limit its coverage to only include the Temple. What about the City? How are they supposed to survive if you take away the Dome? I thought the old alliances still held true. How can you even think about limiting the coverage?"

"Do you think I am playing games with you?" C'aad fired back, disrupting his calm demeanor. "What choice do we have? Already the glow from the Dome is diminishing. There are those here present that believe the Adepts already know what they are going to do. They believe those living in the City are responsible for the missing power reserves and have stolen that energy to power up their own power generator. It is true, isn't it? I can read it in your eyes. You accuse me of plotting to remove the Dome from over the City, plunging it into darkness, at the same time stealing from us and conspiring against us. What would you have us to do once the Dome fails completely? Make the journey in the dark, begging the keepers of the gate of the City to let us in? Don't you know that I am the possessor of the Sacred Fire and have been granted all authority? Before I bow down at the feet of the City-dwellers, I will sacrifice myself and delete my personal energy reserves in a vain attempt to maintaining the Dome. I will set the example and all will follow my lead."

C'aad was getting aggravated by T'mer's disrespect. That and the constant throbbing located right behind his eyes. He had been able to keep the sexual frustration to a minimum by focusing on the energy flow coursing through his body, but hearing the truth coming from a mere Tech caused him some irritation. If C'aad couldn't persuade J'son to connect directly to the power grid, then the Dome would fail and all would be lost. C'aad knew he needed a contingency plan in case he had to make the decision to decrease coverage. Those within the Temple wouldn't be too much trouble at first; it was those on the other side of the wall, finding themselves outside the Dome probably for the first time that would cause the most trouble. Valuable resources would be wasted early in a feeble attempt to repel the heathens as they tried to breach the outer wall.

C'aad had regained his composure through a series of short, discrete breaths, holding them long enough to deprive his physical body of oxygen. Connected the way he still was to the power grid, he really didn't need to breath in order to remain conscious. All his bodily needs were met through the thick, black cable running to his chair. Where the other two operators, S'tan and J'son, had disconnected from the power grid once recovering from the rush of power transfer, C'aad was still connected, filtering the signal coming up from below through his chair.

Sitting stoically upon his Dais, his hands folded loosely on his diminutive lap, the weight of his bulbous head supported by a headset device that gripped him around the back of his head, C'aad stared out at them with blank eyes, like he was in a trance. Instead, his consciousness had detached from his body and floated almost effortlessly through the cables running all over the Temple. The affect gave him continuous, semi-clairvoyance so long as he was in physical contact with his chair.

In times past, long before C'aad had come to rule the Council, the High Priest spent relatively little time connected to the power grid, but that was before the Dais was wired directly into the grid. The first High

Priest, C'abl, had taken over the title and responsibility from B'el for Dome support and was required to sit within the spinning disk, connecting directly to the power grid without the benefit of any filtering devices. At that time, the majority of energy production came from the chanting of the monks within the walls of the Temple, creating a signal almost 98% pure. Sitting within the spinning disk was an act of veneration so complete that to lose oneself within the energy transfer was considered obligatory.

The rapture of that action was orders of magnitude beyond that of the sexual bliss of power transfer as it exists now. Then the High Priest emerged from the experience shinning like the sun, their skin almost translucent, their eyes possessing a far away twinkle and glowing. That glow would last for an entire cycle and the Dome would continue on in its full strength. The High Priest only entered the field of the spinning disk once a cycle. It was that action that would signal the end of their dependence on the sun, while acknowledging their dependence on the mystical teachings of those who came before, the wisdom of the Transcendentals.

Now, however, every High Priest since the death, or murder, of C'art had to use a filtering device and was unable to enter directly into the light of the spinning disk, the energy transfer rate being too high to compensate for any negative aberrations. With such a high flow of negative energy coming from the sexual contributions of those in the bed chamber, to enter into the energy flow without a filter meant either sudden psychosis, their minds having been overthrown by the graphic images generated within the grid; or death as the mind, unable to control the mental onslaught, drifted away unattached to his physical self, his energy reabsorbed into the grid leaving his body a lifeless cadaver.

During the interim between the death of C'art and the installation of the cable, others tried to merge with the spinning disk, some claiming the title of High Priest, proving their claim by stating they had been given a vision by the Transcendentals. Many a monk tried to tame the surge of power released during power transfer only to end their lives in horrible pain as the energy consumed and dominated the will of those unprepared. After several deaths and the mental chaos of those who "survived", fewer and fewer monks made a claim to the title of High Priest. It wasn't until they had connected the filtering Dais to the disk that the next High Priest was chosen, and that by default. Since then, no one had attempted to sit within the spinning disk during power transfer.

C'aad would never willingly give up his chair, especially to a rouge variable like J'son, but how could he convince J'son to take the position where even he dared to sit? And C'ton would warn him of the danger, he was sure. C'aad would have to appeal to J'son's sense of morality, so strong in word but weak in deed. He would have to convince J'son that sacrificing himself for the good of the planet was an obtainable goal that he should commit himself to. But C'aad knew that J'son held no allegiance to them nor did he have the sense of duty so inbred in the rest of the monks. Would he show C'aad the appropriate respect due the position? Or would he continue as he had been, ignoring the rules of the Temple? C'aad wouldn't allow a showdown within the Temple. Instead, C'aad decided he would feign confusion and ignorance at J'son's presence, bowing to his suggestions and act as if J'son was the sole representative of the will of the Transcendentals.

Just as C'aad was about to reintegrate himself back into his body, giving him more a sense of physical reality than the distracted, mental pleasures of power transfer, he received a mental impression coming from within the disk showing J'son and the others standing just outside the transport shaft before the door to the Council Chamber. They were speaking to each other, C'ton and J'son, with T'mar and D'nan standing behind them, quiet and preoccupied. D'nan lips were pursed and he looked stressed and distracted, like he was dealing with an issue that had nothing to do with the High Priest or the Council. The four of them were still naked, but they didn't show any sign of embarrassment or even recognition that being naked was something to be ashamed of.

Standing before the closed door of the Council Chamber, J'son was just about to knock when D'nan reached between them and touched a rectangular pad beside the door. The pad lit up, revealing a glowing palm print, and D'nan placed his hand squarely on top of the print. The pad changed colors from a gloomy red to a languid green, followed by a tiny chime indicating that D'nan's palm had been read and he was allowed entrance into the Council Chamber. This was actually just a formality, as if D'nan hadn't been expected and was requesting an audience with the High Priest. It was a show of respect to wait patiently for permission.

S'tan and T'mer didn't go through such a formal procedure because the magnitude of the situation dictated a suspension of such formalities for them. D'nan followed the rules governing entrance into the Council Chamber for one reason only: He was bucking for a promotion. What D'nan didn't know was that C'aad would have rather had D'nan walk on in instead of standing on convention. Time was of the essence.

"They are finally here," C'aad said, blinking for the first time, looking towards the door and watching as they entered. "Come in, D'nan, master of the guard and inheritor of the sacred fire. Welcome most trustworthy and faithful servant of the Transcendentals! What news do you bring?"

It was all pomp and circumstance C'aad addressing D'nan in such a way, but the formality was a herald of what was to come.

"My lord," D'nan said, moving towards the Dais and bowing low before it. "High Priest of the priests: Monk of monks: Inheritor of the Sacred Fire. I salute you and speak the name of the great Lord of the world: Cerotincalipharpinatum' Andrypromoussocumluantius Amorfosteronity Dianosteriositus!"

The full name of C'aad was stated in a sing-song voice that registered in the higher octave and produced a counter wave that bounced off of the far wall of the concaved chamber and rippled the air, causing a resonance that reverberated around the room, fading into an echo which garbled the clarity of C'aad's name. The tone and quality of the declaration was nearly flawless, producing the essential intonation and modulation necessary to invoke a state of mental submission and compliance. The silence that followed was one of reverence and deep respect. The other members of the High Council left their seats and bowed down reverently and then returned to their seat looking aloof. One of the chairs on the far end, however, was empty, lacking a Council member.

"That's very nice, D'nan," C'aad said, smiling, waiting for his full name to take effect. "Take your place and let's see if the boy has anything useful to say."

D'nan took up his position in the empty chair, walking slowly and deliberately. It only took a few seconds, but that was long enough for C'ton to measure C'aad's reaction and he watched C'aad watching him. That empty chair belonged to C'ton as an undisputed member of the Council and was left vacant the day he decided to travel the planet as a transient wanderer. That seat wasn't supposed to be filled by anyone except by a member of the Council. Until and unless C'ton died or renounced his claim to the Council, that seat shouldn't have been filled by anybody, and especially not by D'nan, who didn't have the proper designation to begin with.

When C'ton had sat in Council long ago, he was the next one in line to become High Priest and sat closest to the Dais. Once he departed, his seat was taken up by the next one in line and so on down the line, leaving the last seat on the left empty. D'nan taking up the seat wasn't what bothered C'ton, however; it was expected. C'ton understood why D'nan had taken a seat on the Council. Without C'ton there to offer his opinions and exercise his wisdom, there would only be twelve members, an even amount that would more than likely lead to division. The seat had to be filled in order for the Temple to operate according to the will of the Transcendentals. What reality troubled him was that upon seeing him enter the Council Chamber the other members of the Council didn't move down a seat to accommodate him.

By Temple decree, C'ton's place on the Council was determined based on his designation, a title he had been given at the initiation of the Temple to distinguish between those that were here at the beginning from those who came up after. D'nan was an example of one of those who came after. D'nan's title was imparted whereas C'ton's title came with the territory. Once he had entered the Council Chamber, the other members, in a show of deference and respect for his higher authority, should have stood up from their chairs, the utmost to the least, and bowed low before him, each in turn offering up his seat to his superior, forcing D'nan out of his seat and back to his position standing behind C'aad. But that's not what happened.

"Your munificence and goodwill have fallen as of late," C'ton said, speaking to C'aad. Although C'ton and the others were still unclothed, C'ton knew that C'aad had manipulated the condition of their nakedness in order to cast a shadow of humiliation and mortification on them, the idea being that a naked man wouldn't have the certainty of his convictions to argue over ceremony. "Since when is it reasonable for a member of the High Council to stand on this side of the disk, especially when his inferiors are seated and advice is sought. Do you deny my claim to a seat on the Council?

"C'ton, my old friend." C'aad adjusted himself in his chair and smiled brightly at C'ton's dilemma. "We mean you no disrespect and were only thinking of our situation. It has been so long since you joined us that we didn't make arrangements for you to sit in Council. D'nan, please remove yourself from the Council and allow the others to return to their intended positions."

D'nan stood up immediately, followed by the other eleven members. Standing behind their chairs now, they each bowed their heads slightly towards C'ton and then those on the left side moved one seat over, leaving the chair to the right of C'aad empty. The Council members returned to their proper chair without a word and sat down in unison. The empty chair next to C'aad was pushed back and to the side in a haphazard manner like it was cast aside, like it was now held in contempt.

"If you must insist on occupying your position," C'aad continued, "then please take your seat so we can discuss what can be done."

"What must be done is obvious," J'son said, speaking for the first time, breaking with protocol. He was standing next to T'mar watching the proceedings. His mind still wasn't right and he felt lightheaded and a little nauseous. The presence that he had detected within him from before was unexpectedly quiet but also surprisingly in attendance, like a court reporter whose presence is only known after the fact. He knew what had to be done, at least for the time being.

There was no correcting the problem at this point. The damage had gone on for too long unchecked and the missing energy reserves were the least of their problems. Someone or something had drained the reserves, making it impossible for the monks to keep the Dome operating at full capacity. But with their dependence on a mixture injection rate of 75/25, even with full reserves the internal fluctuation and instability would be too great and the power transfer would reach a toppling point where the power stream would begin to flow backwards, bringing the Dome down on top of them.

What had to be done to prevent total Dome collapse, at least for the foreseeable future, was to correct for the instability. Someone would have to act as an in-line filter by connecting directly to the power stream. What was needed was for an operator to sit above the disk while it was spinning and separate out the negative aspects of the energy transfer, using his body as the filter to redistribute the incoming energy. J'son knew that as High Priest, C'aad should be the one to take the risk, but he could tell C'aad had no intension of sitting within the spinning disk. J'son would be the one to offer up a solution and he would have to be the one to carry it out.

He would have to risk sitting in the place that all feared to sit. He was more than a little concern, though, about whether or not he would have the ability to hold back the flood of negative energy that would inundate the Council Chamber. Without C'aad sitting up on his Dais operating the filtering controls, J'son would be subjected to the full force of the energy coming up from the bed chamber. Where he and the others had trouble controlling their emotions once they had descended down into the bed chamber, sitting within the spinning disk would cause him to lose his sense of control. He didn't know if he had the mental focus or strength to maintain consciousness while his electrons flowed independently throughout the power grid.

When he was connected to the grid as an operator in the lower chamber, J'son was able to stay somewhat conscious and even followed C'aad around the power grid, acting like a tracer signal and marking his location within the grid. Without C'aad's experience with handling the subtle energies of power transfer through the use of the Dais, J'son wouldn't have had the mental anchor to stabilize his thoughts. At one point during that first transfer, he found himself following C'aad's lead only to discover C'aad going down an energy path that would have brought dissolution and annihilation. Using the force of his own consciousness, J'son was able to communicate with C'aad, reminding him of his duty to the Temple. J'son didn't think he had gotten through at first and only realized that he had succeeded when he heard C'aad give the command to reintegrate.

Would the light of his consciousness be bright enough to allow him to remain mindful to the conditions within the grid? He really didn't know. But even more confusing, the Transcendentals had told him that his mission would take him outside the Dome in search of B'el's Castle. He didn't know if he would be able to survive the procedure that would bring some stability to the Dome and he found his mind sifting through ominous warnings and hidden dangers waiting just outside his awareness. There would be a point where he would be totally detached from his body and his thoughts could just as easily flow up and out of the power room instead of remaining within the grid. If that happened, he would lose consciousness, possibly destroying himself in the process.

He would need an anchor, someone he could trust to bring him back into awareness once he had slipped away from the confines of his physical self. It would have to be someone other than C'aad, though, because J'son didn't trust him to call him back from the void. C'aad, given his position and filtered access to the grid, could detain J'son within the grid perpetually, keeping his consciousness a prisoner within the grid while at the same time annihilating his personality. It was a great risk and J'son felt for the inhabitants of the planet, but repairing the power generator wasn't why he was here, of that he was sure. His presence here was determined, fixed and encoded into the very fabric of existence, like a set of mathematical equations which explain the proof. He felt like a spectator having no say in the outcome.

Chapter Twenty-Five:

T'mar's Secret

"She is not what she seems. I can't put my finger on it, yet. But I will eventually."

C'aad ruminating of T'mar's identity

"If it is so obvious," C'aad said, his voice dripping with haughtiness and self-importance. "Then why don't you enlighten us, human. Yes, I know where you came from. And I know you, too, don't I G'mra?"

"You must take up your seat within the disk," C'ton said. "Now is the time for you to substantiate your claim to the title of High Priest."

A short gasp came out of the closed mouths of the members on the Council at C'ton's audacity.

"Don't be a fool, C'ton. You dare to challenge me before those on the Council? No one has sat within the disk since the beginning. And now you speak about validation? Only a fool would even suggest sitting within the disk. I am sure that isn't the advice you would give, is it boy?"

"Never mind J'son," C'ton countered. "All here know that now is the time for true leadership and sacrifice. If you won't discharge your duty and take your place within the disk, then I will."

The other members of the Council winced again, recoiling at the outrageous suggestion C'ton had just made. To stand before the Council, accusing the High Priest of being a coward, then presenting himself as the rightful successor to the throne was an act of outright belligerence that demanded disciplinary modification. The chamber grew quiet as the members of the Council settled down, curious to see how C'aad would handle this act of open rebellion against the Temple.

C'aad had closed his eyes as soon as C'ton started speaking, willing his emotions into check and trying to maintain his composure. To lose his poise and self-control at this point would only demonstrate C'ton's claim that C'aad was unfit to lead the Council. C'ton had to be admonished in a way that diminished his standing while at the same time reminding the members of the Council of C'aad's importance to the administration of the Temple, securing his position.

"Go, if you must," C'aad said to C'ton. "I will direct the platform to be positioned over the disk and you can step into it at once. Of course, your destruction is assured and your energy will be released into the grid. Only I have the training to enter into the disk and filter out the instability, but now is not the time. I will only enter the disk when all else has failed and only the Temple is left. To risk my life force when there are other options on the table would be foolish."

"What options are you referring to?" C'ton asked, not understanding C'aad's reference. In order to stabilize the fluctuations and correct the energy imbalance, merging with the system was the only option available and no one except C'aad possessed the knowledge. Even if C'ton did mount the steps that would take him above the disk, he knew that he might not have the energy reserves necessary to breach the energy wall surrounding the disk. And even if he did breach the wall, he really didn't think he could balance out the flow before he lost consciousness. Also, he feared the same thing as J'son. C'ton didn't trust C'aad to anchor him to the here and now. If C'ton entered the field and survived the merger, there was no assurance that C'aad would allow him to return to his body. Like J'son, C'ton was afraid his conscious energy would become trapped within the grid.

"C'ton," J'son spoke again. "Although the Transcendentals appreciate your deliberate and noble intensions, I have been informed that your abilities will be needed elsewhere. This is not for you. I will sit within the spinning disk and perform the necessary adjustments. Remember, I have already been connected to the power grid and I have an idea what to expect. I will need you to pull me back once the fluctuations stabilize."

"J'son," T'mar said, her voice shaking slightly. "You and I already have a connection that goes deeper than the connection you have with C'ton. It is true he has the greater power, but it won't be special training that will get you out of there. You'll need our special… attachment."

"T'mar! Don't think I don't know what you are talking about." T'mer was angry that she would so openly discuss her involvement with J'son, much less suggest that she would put herself at risk. He had participated in the design and construction of the hardware associated with Dome maintenance and he was conscious of the extreme dangers that merging with unfiltered energy presented.

In theory, the energy beam was like a crystal clear stream carrying bits of floating debris on its current. The floating debris represented distortions, fluctuations, rogue vibrations and other abnormalities. The operator within the disk had a metaphorical net that he scooped up the debris, leaving the stream clear and uncluttered again. By entering into the stream, one had to be very careful not to let the debris touch you.

If the operator made contact with the debris, the abnormalities would cling to him, concealing him behind a web of negative energy that would eventually turn on the operator. Under ordinary circumstances, the distance between the floating debris was great and the High Priest, using his direct connection to the grid via the filtering instrument of his Dais, had no trouble avoiding them. Now, however, the concentration of negative influences was too great and all who entered the metaphorical stream risked being pummeled immediately with high-energy, particulate negativity.

It was assumed that someone with the knowledge that the High Priest possessed would be able to compensate for the negative energy flow, but that was before they increased their dependence on the negative aspects of energy transfer. Now, all feared to enter into the field of the spinning disk. If C'aad didn't take his place within the disk, and he wouldn't let C'ton try, then T'mer was more than content to let the Dome fail. T'mar didn't have the designation to be an operator and she never should have put herself up like that.

"I'll need you, T'mar, to get back out," J'son said, smiling at her concern. "But you will need to make yourself available once I enter the beam and sit within the disk. You know what I intend to do. Once I am inside, I will need you to anchor my thoughts so I don't get lost. We won't have much time."

~

T'mar turned away from J'son and looked up at the spinning disk and the peculiar shield-generating wave-forms that made up the energy beam. If she remembered her ancient studies correctly, what J'son suggested would have them rise up on an oblong, energy-generated platform created by the powers of the High Priest. Only the High Priest could authorize saucer transport that close to the energy beam, and only for what C'ton accused C'aad of not doing.

Looking at a spot several feet above the disk, the place where J'son would pass through the energy shield, disappearing from this reality, T'mar contemplated what would happen on the inside of the beam. Would she have the courage to walk through the shield when the time came? And once inside, could she trust C'aad to bring them both back after they completed the adjustments? It was suicide and T'mar knew that's exactly how T'mer would see it. She didn't put it past him to bring the whole Dome down on top of them to stop her from doing something he would characterize as reckless and stupid. If J'son entered the light of the beam, then she would be compelled to follow him. If she didn't, then his fate was already determined.

"You boy? You think you can just step right into the beam without harm and then balance out the fluctuations merely by your presence?" C'aad was playing the role of critic, mainly because it was expected of him, but also he wanted it to seem to the others that he found J'son's proposal to be the pointless rambling of the mentally deranged. In reality, J'son volunteering to enter the beam and merge with the power grid without the security of a filter was exactly what C'aad was hoping for and would later claim he engineered.

He really didn't think J'son could stabilize the beam. No one but B'el could absorb that amount of negative energy without destroying himself. What C'aad had planned was to abandon J'son within the grid and use his untapped resources to power the Dome for as long as possible. J'son would cease to exist as a tangible manifestation, but his essence would be felt for as long as the Dome remained.

Other consciousnesses had been lost within the grid over the ages, and from time to time their fundamental nature, their soul, the Ancients taught, would appear, a vibration that has the "flavor" of the departed monk. C'aad was always in touch with such subtle vibrations within the grid and at times had found himself communing with the spirits of the dead, either pleading their assistance or manipulating their energy. Yes, he would have to make a convincing argument against J'son sitting within the disk, but he would only go so far to prevent it. He would need D'nan to make the unprecedented suggestion of allowing J'son to sit within the beam.

"It's not just my presence; it is my human genetics that will act as the counter balance," J'son continued. "If I understand correctly, the idea is to allow the negative debris to pass through me, convert it and channel it out of here. I believe I have the ability to act as a conduit for part of the negative energy. If I can apply what I learned while connected to the grid down in the lower chamber, then I think I will be able to flood the power chamber with purified energy. However, if I can't your dependence on the bed chambers for the bulk of your energy production will only bring the Dome down on top of you. The reservoirs need to be replenished and I don't have the energy to do that. It would take the sun shining for a thousand years to refill the reserves. All I can hope to do is correct certain misalignments in order to sustain the Dome over an extended period."

"So you say," C'aad said with a hard smile Xing his face.

"I will need you to pull me out when the time is right. Can I count on you to do your part?"

"You dare to inform me of what will happen in my chambers? Do you really think I would hold you in bondage? If you survive passing through the energy beam, which I sincerely doubt, your mind will be mush."

"Maybe it would be wise to let the friend of the Exile risk his life, D'nan suggested. "Even you, lord, have spoken openly of the will of the Transcendentals concerning this boy. Maybe the lord, in his most highness will—"

"Oh shut up, D'nan. Don't you think I have given that interpretation at least some consideration? But yes, perhaps you're right. Is that what you want me to say?" C'aad was speaking harshly to D'nan, but secretly C'aad was delighted that D'nan used the opportunity given to him and spoke up exactly when he should have. "Very well, I will salvage what I can for as long as I can. You did strengthen and reinforce the polarities coming up from the lower chamber, but I have severe reservations about letting you so willingly sacrifice yourself. You do possess incredible reserves of personal energy, though. If I allow you to enter the disk and I find your mental processes to be deteriorated beyond recovery, I will dominate your will and abandon you within the grid where your essence will be used according to the needs of the Temple throughout the rest of the age. There will be no discussion."

That last part he said looking down at C'ton, knowing he would be a problem and the only other one in the room who had the ability to determine the existential reality of a post-transfer fusion. C'aad had no intension of ever letting J'son out of the grid once he had merged fully and he knew the debate that would ensue could disrupt the hierarchy, bringing C'aad's reign to an end even before the Dome collapses. No, C'aad would have to be patient and allow J'son to merge and integrate with the system, holding on to him long enough so as to convince J'son that C'aad could be trusted. Only after completing whatever J'son though he could do, would C'aad feign trouble, calculating the odds of full re-integration without mishap only to give up in exhaustion, claiming he had travelled too far away and the mathematics to retrieve him too delicate and limited to be useful.

"J'son, you don't have to do this," T'mar said in a worried-filled whisper.

"Yeah," said T'mer. "Let these wizards worry about things wizards worry about. All of us here have survived living outside the protection of the Temple during the dark. I say we make for the Dome boundary and find company with the 'dbys, those living at the outer reaches of the Dome. At one time I had companions among them."

"They are heathens, T'mer," S'tan said, speaking for the first time since entering the chamber.

"You will be allowed to leave the protection to the Temple only after you have completed the tasks assigned to you," C'aad said. "If, as you say, you must leave us and follow after the "Heretic" in accordance with the will of the Transcendentals, then I will help you on your way, once you have helped us, but not before. I will allow you to throw away your physicality, boy, in the hopes that your uniqueness will be useful to us. If not, I promise you that I won't bring back the mentally deranged, especially one who has such inexplicable abilities as yours. It would be too dangerous. So go, my brave, young human. Walk the steps to your assured dissolution, after which we will not mourn you and we will commemorate your vain sacrifice by upping the power transfer rate."

T'mar, still caught up in deep reflection on the very possibility of her own dissolution, turned her eye on C'aad, staring at him, blanking her mind as she had been taught, hoping that he couldn't enter her thoughts.

"Not only did I allow you to train under C'ton, breaking protocol out of respect for him," C'aad said, speaking directly to T'mar. "You stole from us, leaving your teacher and taking your spoils to the Heretic. What, may I ask, did your merchandise afford you? Entrance into his Castle, that much is known. Why did you betray us, G'mra? There are those here who have a long memory and the others have read about your treason in the histories. If it weren't for your attachment to the boy and your hold over him, I would have you arrested, bound and thrown into the bed chambers. There you would learn to be submissive and not so belligerent."

"She didn't betray us, C'aad. She herself was betrayed." C'ton spoke slow and quietly, allowing his words to sink in. He of all those on the Council knew what happened to T'mar once she left the Temple long ago and where she went. The memory of that time was still painfully etched within his mind. Guilt flashed by his awareness, with shame following a close second. Hatred was there, too, accompanied by suspicious, cynical thinking.

"No? What do you call taking one of the sacred books out of the library and handing it over to B'el?"

"What she took was out of ignorance. Besides, the book she took was just one of the occult histories of B'el's involvement in the creation of the Dome. The more legitimate histories are still here and provide a greater overview of those times. There was nothing in that book that could prove detrimental to the order of the Monks. Most of that book was written under the direction of B'el himself. From his perspective, she just returned to B'el something that belonged to him anyway."

"And that's your excuse for her crimes? Don't be naïve, C'ton. You were just as shocked and horrified by her betrayal if not more so. I asked you at the time if you knew she was going to defect and you said you had no idea. Does your answer still hold true today, I wonder?"

"Yes, C'aad, I was disappointed, but not in her. I was disappointed in myself for not being the teacher she needed me to be. I didn't take into account her rapacious curiosity and so didn't calculate the effect the lies of B'el would have on her. There is none here who can stand toe to toe with B'el. He is too powerful and we are either too aged for open warfare or lacking the experience to even understand how to prepare. T'mar is here of her own free will. She knew the dangers of coming here and decided on her own what path she would take. Since she has been within the walls of the Temple, she has done nothing to bring shame or mistrust on herself. She is willing to help us in this present crisis and I say we should accept her help willingly. It may be that something she learned at the feet of B'el will help us."

"It is that knowledge that I don't trust, C'aad said. "How do I know she won't do something that will bring B'el here clamoring for the throne?"

"He was offered that position long ago and he renounced it, abandoning the Temple and us as well. He has no claim to the Temple, nor do I think he desires it."

"Especially not a Temple without energy reserves."

"T'mer!"

T'mer's comment dislodged T'mar out of her introspection, causing her to lose focus momentarily. Her mind opened up for a second, reaching out to T'mer in hopes of calming the tempest intensifying within him. C'aad, seizing the opportunity, barreled into her consciousness, retrieving some precious nugget that T'mar had hidden there. T'mar, realizing her error, quickly shut her mind off from C'aad, but not before he had taken something from her worth more to her than all the energy of the sun. What he took from her made her flinch; sucking the air out of her like it was something tangible. Closing her fingers around nothing, T'mar stood there with her balled-up fist out in front.

"What's the matter, T'mar?" J'son asked, feeling a sense of great lose coming from her.

"So now I have the answer that has eluded me since the time you entered the Temple," C'aad said. "C'ton, how were you able to recognize your old student in the body she now possesses? Were you able to pick up on some old program that you had written? Or perhaps it was her smell. What I find when someone takes on a new personae is that they forget to change their diet. They may look different, but they smell the same, especially when they are as fragrant as G'mra, or T'mar to match the new look."

"I was able to recognize her because of the connection we have."

"Does your connection tell you that the woman standing here is wearing a disguise to protect her true identity?"

"We all conceal our identity to preserve our individuality. To show oneself openly outside the walls of the Temple is foolishness defined. All of us here know that you have the gift of Spectacle, the ability to see through the masquerade and witness us naked, as it were."

"Yes, this is true. However, not all here possess a veil that they can hide behind. J'son, the boy, for one. He looks just like he imagines himself to be. There is no hiding with him. T'mer, of course, has never needed to hide his identity. You, C'ton, go back and forth so much that I don't think even you remember what you looked like originally. But T'mar, my dear girl. What was that I saw within you, hiding? Would you like me to reveal your secret or do you want to tell C'ton yourself?"

"What is he talking about, T'mar?" C'ton asked, looking hard at T'mar, trying to see what she was so afraid of. He knew she was wearing a disguise but couldn't detect the identity seam, not when he first met her or even now. At the time he found her, he just assumed that what she looked like back then was her true appearance. Once he ran into her again back at the crossroads, he recognized certain qualities and quirks of her original personality, ignoring the change in appearance.

"I… ah."

"We are wasting time here, G'mra. C'ton, look at her. Can you not see her identity seam? It's not where it should be, is it? Even if you had taught her how to hide her identity I should still see your fingerprints all over her. I can't, and for a while I didn't understand the properties of the spell that had been cast, concealing her. It bothered me at first because I thought you had discovered a spell sequence that was beyond my ability to ascertain, but now I understand why I couldn't see beyond her veil. You see, C'ton. The beautiful form you see standing before us is what she actually looks like. She isn't using a spell or any other mathematical sequence to conceal her identity. In fact, now that I can laugh at my own folly I can see that the figure standing before us is T'mar's actual physical representation. She is hiding herself behind herself."

That statement took everyone by surprise. Almost in unison, C'ton, J'son and T'mer all turned to look at T'mar, their mouths hanging open. It was hard to believe, but the dazzlingly beautiful, perfectly proportioned body of T'mar belonged to her and not her imagination. All of their eyes were locked onto her, sifting the information coming into their brains via the visual cortex. It was one thing to stand next to a beautiful woman knowing she wasn't exactly what she seemed but enjoying the view anyway. It was another thing altogether to know that the soft curves and the generous, rounded scoops of flesh were real and not some mental or surgical enhancement.

She stood there, her arms falling down to her sides, exposing her naked body to them without shame and holding her chin up a little bit in a display of indulgence, taking pride in her own features. "I'm sorry C'ton," she said, turning away from C'aad and looking affectionately at C'ton standing next to her. "The girl you found so long ago hiding in the bushes was a trick. I deceived you that day by hiding behind a pretense. There would have been no way for you to know."

"But how were you able to mislead me for so long?"

For the first time in a long time, T'mar blushed, her cheeks turning deep red. She dropped her head, allowing C'ton's question to sink in, keeping quiet out of embarrassment. The reason why he was so easy to mislead was because she could manipulate his sex drive in order to distract him whenever he brought up her past and why she was hiding outside the gate of the City. They made love over and over back then, falling into each other arms out of sheer physical exhaustion. The sex act, she knew, helped to quiet his questioning mind until he had finally forgotten the question and had grown to trust her.

"How did you come to possess such a powerful transformation spell? Who taught you?" C'ton asked hesitantly, not really wanting to know where she got the concealment spell.

"One can come into possession of many things with the right contacts," T'mar responded coldly.

"You mean B'el?" J'son asked, becoming more confused in his thinking by this revelation than by the possibility of his complete dissolution within the energy beam.

"I didn't know B'el back then. I didn't know anything about the monks or the Temple, having been sheltered for most of my childhood up to that point."

"Then who taught you how to conceal your real identity?" C'aad was angry now, accusatory, displaying open aggression towards T'mar.

T'mar thought herself quiet, a calm passing across her face and she stood her ground before C'aad, refusing to answer his question. He may have taken away her secret, but he still didn't know who gave her the spell.

If she didn't learn the spell from B'el, C'aad thought, the only one who could possibly possess a spell as powerful as the one T'mar used was either in this chamber at the moment, or had died and merged with the grid. It was known to him that certain spells could be retrieved from the grid and this was where C'aad believed T'mar had received her instruction.

Somehow she had been able to merge with the grid, find a departed monk of sufficient rank, and convince the disembodied consciousness to share with her the secrets of identity concealment. C'aad didn't know how she would have been able to do that, but he was sure now that she had somehow made contact with the departed.

"Your Holiness," S'tan said. "The state of the power chamber when we left was stable at 25% with an injection rate ratio of 75/25. With that much negative energy holding at 75% capacity we don't have too much time left before we will experience a destructive feedback loop that could blow the top off of the power chamber, incinerating the disk. We must move quickly if we hope to maintain the Dome at present levels, much less increase the output."

"Yes, yes, S'tan. Very well. D'nan, I need you down in the lower chamber to access the grid from there. You are assigned there until further notice. Go and relieve yourself. The chaos of your thoughts is distressing. I thought you had better control over your lusts. Go! Merge with the grid and find your release."

D'nan, hearing the command that he so longed to hear, broke ranks immediately and stumbled towards the door, bending over at the waist and grabbing his crotch roughly. The pressure was building again, but this time he wouldn't wait so long before he allowed release. His eyes began to roll back in his head as the pressure ebbed and flowed. He couldn't see clearly and the only images haunting his awareness were ones of sex and orgasmic release. A sardonic smile formed on his lips at the thought and a chemical wash of testosterone flooded his brain with aggressive, pleasure-seeking impulses. Reaching the door, D'nan passed through, heading to the transport shaft.

"And you, S'tan. Take T'mer with you back to the power chamber and prepare to merge with the grid. I will commune with you shortly."

"No!" T'mer said, moving closer to T'mar and farther away from S'tan. "I won't leave T'mar here alone without any way to defend herself."

"Why do you think she would need to defend herself against the Council? If it was our intension to detain her, then we would have done it already. She has nothing to fear from the Council as long as she remembers her place. Besides, as long as C'ton and J'son are here with her she doesn't have anything to worry about. After all, she isn't the one that will sit within the beam. Her personal safety is guaranteed as long as she does as she is told."

"Yes, T'mer," T'mar said, gently placing a hand on his broad shoulders and ignoring C'aad's warning. "I'll be fine so long as I got C'ton and J'son looking out for me. Go and help S'tan stabilize the energy beam."

"Let's go, T'mer," S'tan said. "We need to get up there and plugged in before J'son can do what he is going to do. He'll need us in case something goes wrong. C'aad will anchor him here, but if he travels up the beam without someone there to guide him he may very well get stuck. It shouldn't be too hard distinguishing his signature from anything else that we might find within the grid, considering the uniqueness of his energy pattern."

S'tan and T'mer turned around and exited through the same door as D'nan, making their way to the transport shaft, heading towards the power chamber. Once there, the door slid open and the two of them emerged, walking at a fast pace around the outer corridor, heading to the door that would take them back inside the control booth.

Sitting behind the console, S'tan strapped himself in and placed his fingers on top of the glowing board and pressed down, engaging the grid for the second time. He closed his eyes and lowered his head, trying to find the right mental space for him to proceed. His hands hovered over the console, rapidly pressing his fingers down in selected areas and releasing them, changing the vibration in the booth. Everything was in place. All that was needed was for J'son to take his seat within the spinning disk.

"So now my foolish, young friend," C'aad said looking down at J'son from his perch high up on the Dais. "Are you ready to perform your duty to the

Temple and so ensure the safety of all living under the Dome? Then mount the platform that will take you to your final destination."

J'son moved over to the disk and stood on an etched out, oval area directly to the right of the spinning disk. T'mar followed after him, stepping in close to keep him from falling over the edge of the platform once it rose into place. The static hum of the disk combined with the electrical discharge of the protective retaining wall caused J'son's and T'mar's hair to stand up straight, dancing around like grass in a gentle breeze.

"Be careful, J'son," C'ton said, moving away from the spinning disk.

"I may need you, C'ton," J'son said, swallowing hard. When he first suggested that he would sit above the disk performing the duties of the High Priest, he said it like one who was going to the store and would be back in a few minutes. But now that he was about to enter the energy beam he was having second thoughts. The reassuring presence that had been with him up to this point was now strangely absent. Even that place within his mind that seemed to house the presence was missing, or at the very least blocked off from his awareness. Standing on the platform, he wondered where the presence that had been guiding him was.

Chapter Twenty-Six:

The Grid

"By allowing him direct access to the grid, there's no telling what he may be capable of."

A Council member expressing the thoughts of all concerned

J'son and T'mar were holding tightly on to each other as the platform, changing color from an ugly grey to a bright, translucent shimmering blue, levitated off the floor approximately twenty feet and hovered above all of the members of the Council, all except C'aad, who was sitting almost eye level with the platform. The platform was solid under their feet, but seemed to join and fuse with the energy beam of the disk upon contact, leaving a seamless connection between the beam and the platform. They were standing only inches away from the beam and J'son could feel his energy reserves flowing out of him and towards the beam, blending his energy with that of the beam. T'mar was standing just to the side of him and he could detect the anxiety surging out of her, making him even more nervous.

"You don't have to do this J'son," she whispered to him, trying to hide her doubts from C'aad. "Even if you are successful, the only hope of maintaining the Dome is to have the one who designed it come and recalibrate for the fluctuations so that the system can stabilize itself. Even if you can maintain your identity throughout, the best we can hope for is a reprieve from the inevitable."

"You don't have to do this either, T'mar," he said, touched by her obvious concern. "You will be just as much at risk as I will be once I enter the beam. Because we are connected the way we are, your energy will mingle with mine and so you will be in danger of losing yourself within the grid without even merging with it. There won't be any room for doubt. Promise me that when you start to feel your essence slipping into the grid you will pull out, saving yourself. Remember, if C'aad doesn't want to bring me back, I will need you and C'ton to find me again and draw me out. If both of us are absorbed into the grid without an anchor, then we'll both be lost."

"I know. I..." What T'mar was going to say was that she loved him and she had a bad feeling that she wouldn't see him again. She wanted to tell him that she cared for him and that if he didn't come back she would squeeze the secret of resurrection out of B'el himself to find him. Only B'el had the ability to disperse his energy anywhere in the universe and reconstitute himself. It was an act of will that was orders of magnitude stronger than producing transportation globes or creating energy bubbles. The knowledge in B'el's possession was beyond anything taught in the Temple and she privately formulated a plan to convince B'el to come to their rescue if J'son failed to return.

J'son and T'mar were holding hands, twisting their fingers together, totally immersed in their own nervousness. The energy field crackled and buzzed, sending out tiny sparks of electricity, popping with static discharge. Slowly pulling his hands out of hers, he raised one of them up, palm out, thumb down, and held it against the energy field until his hand began sinking into it and disappearing into the electrified field. He turned around to look at T'mar, smiled weakly at her, hoping he didn't appear worried and then turned to face the field. Pausing for a moment longer, he took a deep breath and stepped into the field, vanishing from view.

As J'son emerged into the space just behind the shimmering energy field, he felt his body dissipating, like the atoms that made up his body had lost their nuclear connection and were bouncing around without any coherent form. Once his body, acting as the only physical anchor he possessed linking him with 3-dimensional reality, started to dissolve, his consciousness was torn away from its physical moorings in a jarring, violent tearing of the immaterial from the material, separating his thoughts from his mundane bodily processes and sending them out across the vast network of the power grid.

Within moments, J'son was connected to every cable and mirror, every mind that was plugged into the grid. He saw the confusing, web-like spokes of the grid spread out before him like the colors of a prism, each thread locking and crisscrossing each other forming more complex patterns. The darker colors in the web represented the negative aspect of energy production which dominated the purer, lighter colors produced and generated by the chanting of the monks. If things had been working properly, there wouldn't be any differing shades of color highlighting the energy source because all colors would be blended into one: White.

J'son no longer had a sense of a body or even knowledge of why he ever needed one. His state of being at the present was beyond the limiting aspects of verbal language and he noticed his thoughts taking on a mathematical formulation where numbers appeared within his mind instead of words. The numbers symbolized concepts that his material mind wouldn't be able to conceive and he found his mind imaging long, intricate equations expressing the properties of the energy field, some of those equations trailing away from him, following a path beyond his ability to traverse.

He was thrown into a vortex of swirling energy that took him up through the top of the Temple, where he collided with the break at the apex of the Dome, spreading out and down. His consciousness was disconnected and jumbled. Every energetically-charged particle that crashed into his self-generated mental projection altered his thought processes making it hard for him to remain cognizant. The different vibrations produced by the differing velocities and energies coming from the unrelated and conflicting energy sources made recognizing and neutralizing the fluctuations extremely difficult.

The inconsistent, contrasting energy flowing throughout the Temple and over all those living under the Dome produced a visceral, semi-conscious living entity, more akin to the chaotic release of a volcanic explosion following geological processes than possessing a clear intelligence. This creature, the accumulation of all knowledge and powered by the thoughts of everyone who had ever merged with the field, lacked any stabilizing or guiding influences and rested within the grid waiting an initiating force to awaken it. That influence was supposed to be the High Priest, who would subject it to the will of the Temple.

In theory, the creature was nothing more than a rogue, animated, programmed projection created by the grid as a sort of contact port to allow communication between the computerized interface of the grid and the Council. Over time, the High Priest of the age had changed the programming to allow more intimate connection without total dissolution. The result is that the grid now had a form of consciousness that was more analogous to the intelligence of a wild animal than a computer interface. Only through the use of filters built into the Dais would anyone have the control and focus necessary to maintain their identity while travelling throughout the grid. Without the use of the filters, as J'son was now discovering, losing yourself was a matter of acquiescence, like his consciousness was just along for the ride.

But that wasn't why he had decided to enter the energy field. From somewhere far away, coming up to him like the sound of an echo from the depths of a deep well, he heard an electronic sound ("chink"), followed by the image of a floating, disembodied head, the mental projection of the creature based on information contained within the grid. The head had a familiar look to it, but was created out of the contrast and shading between the negative and positive energies. The head had a fierce countenance and emitted a harsh, reddish glow whenever J'son's energy interacted with it.

J'son's energy signature was foreign to it, something beyond its experience and the grid was having a hard time incorporating J'son's energy into that of the grid. The entity didn't like the flavor of J'son's energy signature and shortly began avoiding all attempts at merging with him. It receded away from J'son, fleeing the strange energy signature, and headed into the labyrinth of the grid, seemingly trying to avoid detection.

J'son, using the last bit of his consciousness to determine a direction, followed after the creature, moving along the electrified strands of the grid. The impression he had before losing complete contact with the outside world was that this creature had more to do with the depletion of the energy reserves and the fluctuations than acting as any type of interface.

The creature left energy signatures that were easy enough to read and J'son continued after it, losing all sense of direction or spatial coordinates, seeing himself from the perspective of a million eyes all looking within, pinpointing the glowing flicker that represented the creatures' presence racing along the fibers of the grid. Following the creature was like watching the blips on a radar screen: First the creature appeared here, within the grid, disappeared and then reappeared again somewhere else. The creature was the only other entity within the grid besides J'son that had semi-autonomous movement.

The creatures' programming language was different than the programming used by the monks, and that was J'son's first indication that the entity might have been initially programmed by someone other than the builders. Why else would the creatures' programming be fundamentally different than the programming used to sustain the Dome? Any item within the grid was assembled through the use of intricate, mathematical formulas that corresponded and interacted with other programs within the system so they all worked together. The creature's programming, however, was too different to work in harmony with the other systems, like comparing Microsoft with Apple. Each could be made to run in the other's environment, but problems with compatibility would always occur. It was this difference in compatibility that J'son was now starting to believe was the real problem, the one causing the fluctuations and the increasingly more unstable grid environment that the Dome was constructed on.

He didn't understand why the builders would have created an interface having a completely different programming language, unless this creature was programmed by someone other than the monks. But who would write a program that ran counter to the best interest of the planet? And why did this entity flee from J'son as he tried to merger with it? Did the energy coursing through J'son's body create instability within the programming of the creature? He had so many questions that had no answer and no frame of reference to objectively assess the situation correctly.

J'son discovered the creature hiding in the lower levels of the bed chamber, having attached itself to the energy beam coming up from below. It was feeding, apparently diverting a portion of the negative energy through its programming and releasing its waste in a form of a fluctuation. J'son watched as the fluctuating waste rose up the beam, changing the color and vibration of the beam, decreasing the interval between fluctuations and creating instability as it went, travelling up the beam heading towards the power chamber.

J'son now had enough information to diagnosis the problem and formulate a possible solution, at least temporarily. He didn't possess the knowledge nor the power reserves to obliterate the creature and he really didn't know what would happen if the creatures' programming imprinted on him. After all, in his present state he was nothing more than a series of 1's and 0's held together by a program. Instead, he would have to fool the creature into thinking that it was full and needed to retreat back into the grid until interface was needed again.

What activated the creature initially J'son didn't know and began to wonder how long it had been interfering with the output of the Dome. This creature, J'son was now sure, was a product of industrial espionage, programmed by either the Adepts living in the City, or someone else outside of the Temple. The programming was so unlike the programming of the Temple, which they inherited from the Adepts, and contained a string of symbols that reminded J'son of ancient hieroglyphics. The symbols were unreadable but showed a finesse and aptitude beyond anything he had seen since coming here. It was that refinement of a program, the simplicity of the arrangements that made J'son realized he was seeing the handiwork of B'el.

J'son watched the creature from a distance, observing how it ate and noticing it only had a taste for the negative aspects of the grid. It had a voracious appetite, sucking long and hard on one of the wispy tendrils coming out of the bedchamber. Its need to feed constantly kept it below the Council Chamber, where the bulk of the positive energy was stockpiled. It was there where J'son would need to establish a center of operations if he were to battle this entity. He would need to maintain contact with the positive energies while avoiding the negative ones.

If he could convince the entity to remain in the lower levels by threatening to use the positive energies defensively, then he believed he could balance out some of the instability and increase output without endangering the integrity of the Dome. This wouldn't be a fix per se, but more like an inferior repair that would only last for a short time. Unless J'son was able to take on the creature directly, driving it from the grid and erasing its energy signature, there was no possibility of returning the grid back to its original state.

The creature was too strong now that it was attached to the negative energy supply coming from the bed chambers, embedding itself within the grid, almost taunting the energy signature that was J'son to follow it down into the lower chamber. Finding himself more attracted to the positive energies than the negative ones, J'son was content to remain as close to the source of the positive energy as possible. He knew that to follow the creature down into the lower chamber would be the end of him.

The grids program parameters, which allowed him to think 3-dimensionally about things other than the grid, gave him the clarity to assess the situation with detachment. As long as he had connection with the positive energies, he was able to maintain some semblance of consciousness. If he were to venture down into the lower chamber, the negative aspects of the grid would overwhelm him, obliterating his consciousness and stealing his energy reservoir. If that were to happen, J'son would cease to exist.

He knew he needed to create an energy weapon of some sort, one that he could use to weaken the creature without recharging it. He would just need enough energy to push the creature back, hurting it enough that it would think twice before moving up the energy beam again. To do that, however, J'son needed to change the direction of the energy flow. Instead of negative energy coming up the beam, he would need to send positive energy downward, hoping it wouldn't become too diluted with the negative energy. He wouldn't be able to do it alone, though. He might be able to focus enough to direct the positive energies downwards, but he knew he wouldn't be able to maintain his own mental projection at the same time. He may very well succeed in creating a barrier separating the creature from the rest of the grid, but in so doing he would lose his tentative grip on the anchor of his reality. He needed help if he was going to try and stabilize to grid.

Then the image of T'mar appeared within his thoughts as a mathematical equation and he remembered she was standing just on the other side of the energy beam. He called out to her, using his mind to transmit his thoughts out to her.

"T'mar!"

Outside of the beam, standing in the middle of the floating platform, T'mar watched as J'son entered the energy beam and disappeared, leaving a crackling, shimmering silhouette imprinted on the beam. The shape faded almost immediately leaving behind an opaque curtain of iridescent blue, the color of the energy beam once J'son was inside. She closed her eyes, trying to reach out with her mind and make contact with J'son on the other side. She blanked out her mind and started to mumble a chant under her breath. The chanting helped her clear her mind so she could see what images might be found there, but only drew a prolonged blank. It scared her to think that she might have lost contact with J'son permanently and she redoubled her efforts, dropping down through meditation into a mental state that prevented the flow of physical stimuli and shut out any thought related to 3-dimensional reality.

Her mind had become as still as a deep, mountain lake looking for and waiting on the thrown pebble that would cause a ripple across the water of her mind, signifying J'son's presence. It was only because of their other-worldly connection that she was able to focus to the point that only J'son's signature would be allowed to enter her thoughts. She couldn't detect him as yet and that bothered her more than if she had seen him die from the 'ints. She should have been able to detect something if he was still conscious. But if he had fallen victim to the illusion of the grid, then no amount of searching on her part would find him.

It was a risk that all were aware, but T'mar really didn't believe J'son could be imprisoned within the grid. Because of his abilities and his connection with Earth, she didn't think he would be in danger. However, not being able to contact him directly caused her distress and the stillness of her mind was disturbed, like turning over a cup full of water and watching helplessly as it slid across the table and splashed onto the floor. Her eyes flung open wide and her mouth dropped down. She stared at the energy beam before her, boring her frightened eyes into the beam, trying to see beyond the veil.

"J'son!" she screamed.

"T'mar, are you ok?" C'ton asked, moving away from the Dais and closer to the platform. "What's happening?"

"I can't find J'son. His consciousness is somewhere within the grid, but I can't find any trace of his energy signature. C'ton, I'm scared."

"Such doubt," C'aad said sarcastically. "Did you really think that boy could withstand the onslaught of unfiltered energy? Everything that he was is gone. The only hope we have now is to use his energy and see how long he can power the Dome."

C'aad finished speaking and move two fingers across the console like he was pushing a sliding switch. Instantly, a deafening hum filled the chamber and the energy beam changed from blue-white to hotrod orange. C'aad had momentarily decreased the purity to the signal, throwing the Dome support structure into disharmony but increasing the output. By making the connection, C'aad was able to run the energy J'son's disappearance created through his filters and back into the grid. It was like taking the energy of the sun shining on photo-electric cells and converting it into a power source capable of running a light bulb.

The Dome would hold at this level temporarily for as long as C'aad allowed the energy to flow through the filter of his Dais. Eventually, the filter would become saturated with negative energy and he would have to back flush the filter with a purer power source coming down from the power chamber thru a back connection. The filtered black waste would find its way back to the lower chamber where it would be recycled and reused.

Normally, all energy flowed up and out of the Temple with tiny, parasitic drains a typical consequence. These parasitic drains flowed into the maintenance program that supplies everyone living under the Dome with enough power to carry out day-to-day operations. It was this energy that the High Priest had complete control over and he would dole it out in insignificant amounts to his favorites. This arrangement kept the Council in order and firmly under his domination. He was just about to close another connection on his console when he was interrupted by the combined protests of C'ton, T'mar and T'mer all at the same time.

"What are you doing?" C'ton snapped at C'aad.

"C'ton, he's cut us off from finding J'son. You meant to do this all along," T'mar said, screaming at C'aad.

"Stop what you're doing right now," T'mer said, throwing his chest out in a threatening manner towards C'aad. "You want me to take out his chair?"

"Don't be foolish, T'mer. I would humble you to the ground before you even made it to the first step. Enough with this silliness! C'ton, you knew this was going to be a failed attempt even before he ever entered the beam, and we need his energy to help us make it through the long dark. Now, if you will let me do what I have to do, we will increase Dome output by changing the injection rate ratio to 65/35. The Dome will be much more stable and we will be able to save more life because of his sacrifice. I salute the young man, but now he is gone. It is the Dome which takes priority."

"But by blocking the flow of energy, you created a situation in which we can't search out J'son's energy signature," C'ton said. "The energy coming into the filter is fundamentally different than the energy exiting. By redirecting the energy to flow through the filter, we lose the ability to reconstitute him. What goes into the filter comes out different. Disconnect the filter immediately and let us try to find J'son before it's too late."

"It's too late already," C'aad said coldly.

"T'mar!"

Chapter Twenty-Seven:

Battling the Creature

"Want to play a game?"

The energy creature taunting J'son and T'mar

It was an impression, not really a sound, but T'mar recognized it at once. "J'son! C'ton, I've made contact."

"Step back from the beam, you foolish woman, unless you intend on sacrificing yourself as well. Already I can detect his influence within the grid. He has indeed corrected several system and has somehow isolated the, ah, abnormality, although deep within the grid. That is why it is too late and he is lost. He lacks the energy to keep the problem under control for much longer. He has lost his connection with this world and now travels at the speed of light in worlds beyond our imaginations."

"But that's why we have to help him," T'mar said sounding very anxious. "I hear him. I am able to hear him. We must go in and rescue him. I'm going in."

"T'mar, wait."

"No you're not going in there. He turned to atoms the moment he entered the beam and so will you T'mar." It was T'mer.

"Just wait a minute, T'mar. Hold on." It was C'ton. "C'aad, what right do you have to re-engage the filtering system without informing the Council?"

"You are now informed."

"Dammit T'mar. Get down from there. He's gone. He knew what he was in for." Now T'mer was getting anxious. He didn't trust her not to enter the beam and believed she was foolish enough to do it.

"You don't deserve to sit on the Dais, C'aad," C'ton said." You never intended to bring him out of the grid and now with just a flick of your finger you plan on wiping out any chance of bring him back in any cohesive form, even as an interface. You need to stop what you are doing and step down."

While the other members on the Council were astounded at the open challenge of the High Priest, C'aad allowed C'ton his impertinence. Long had C'aad wanted C'ton to rise up in the Council and oppose his rule. Long did he want to test his abilities against C'ton's, forever banishing the idea that C'aad was unfit to rule. But to step down without engaging in battle, what was C'ton thinking?

"You can't be serious, are you? C'ton, would you really set yourself up as High Priest in my stead? Go back to your wandering. Maybe you can find another companion more suited to your predilections. I think—"

"T'mar! Stop! Don't."

Too late. As the others were arguing over who would sit in C'aad's chair, T'mar scoffed at the idea that the one who demands obedience was the very one too afraid to take up his position within the beam. Watching them argue, seeing the blood rise in C'ton's cheeks, T'mar turned away from the scene and without further hesitation stepped into the beam, vanishing from sight.

As soon as T'mar entered the beam, she could feel the atoms of her flesh dissolving their nuclear attachment, scattering the moment she fully emerged within the beam. The organization and structure of her thoughts were chaotic and confusing, lacking any concrete anchor on which to rest. Holding the image of J'son paramount within her mind, though, she cast off the limitations of physical existence and plunged deep within the grid, following a weak, wispy trail that T'mar took to be J'son's energy signature. It was the only thing producing wave-forms that was in direct opposition to the rampant fluctuations that were now flooding the system.

T'mar sensed his precarious situation and locked on to the only thing stable enough to anchor her thoughts. She reached out to him in a manner that resembled a jumble of numbers within her mind; in actuality what she was doing was writing the beginnings of a search program. J'son had called out to her in a similar way, creating the image of her name through the use of mathematical formulas. Now, T'mar was writing her own program, using a search spell alongside a recovery spell. The idea being that if she could locate the center of his consciousness, she could retrieve it and bring it, J'son, back with her. It was a complicated spell and she relied on her training to get it right.

"I'm here, T'mar," J'son said, responding to her spell. His response, though, was weak and disconnected; he was aware she was looking for him, but lacked the programming to communicate more directly.

It seemed that whatever J'son was doing was causing the entity considerable discomfort and irritation. Using its connection to the grid, the entity used variation and instability as a weapon, attacking J'son and the grid at the same time. J'son's existence was dependent on the stability of the grid and any volatility disrupted his cohesion and attachment to it. Without that attachment, J'son was as good as gone. Like a soap bubble clinging to the side of a tub as the water is let out, J'son's consciousness was just a hair breath away from total dissolution.

The entity was indeed trapped within the lower chamber and the energy creature found it increasingly hard to branch out. Its negative power input had been diminished through the use of increased positive energy, thus diluting its useable energy stores. The positive energy allowed the actions of the entity to become more visible without giving it any more power. The positive energy only highlighted what it was already doing, like a spotlight in the dark.

That increase in visibility made it easier for T'mar to distinguish between J'son's energy signature and the damaging effects of the entity. J'son was doing a great job of keeping the entity separated from the rest of the grid, but its influence was still being felt. The barrier program which J'son had written to separate the entity from the rest of the grid was full of mathematical holes due to his lack of training and the entity was working on a plan to slip thru one of those holes in the program.

The barrier that J'son had erected was similar to a firewall, in that without the proper pass code no unfiltered energy could pass thru without consent. However, with C'aad sitting on the Dais filtering the energy as it came up the beam, he inadvertently gave passage to the entity, exacerbating J'son's efforts to detain the creature within the lower chamber. C'aad's actions were in direct opposition to what J'son was doing, hampering him and throwing more confusion into the system. The mathematical holes within the barrier widened and narrowed, depending on what particular program the entity wrote to overcome the barrier. For the most part, the entity was fenced in and isolated, but unless C'aad disengaged the filter, the entity's influence would continue to be felt.

"J'son. I found you! Hold still so I can formulate the proper commands to absorb your essence into mine," T'mar said using mathematical constructs. "I will have to rewrite part of your program to make it compatible with mine, so you might experience a strange sensation rippling thru your program. Just let my instructions permeate your consciousness. If I can remember the correct sequence, it should help with our integration. Don't resist me, J'son. If I can't pull you out, then both of us will be lost."

T'mar knew the danger of what she was about to do, but she was out of options at this point. To rewrite J'son's program in order to incorporate his signature within hers was like adding additional flavors to a recipe lacking basic measurements. Most of the elements were there, but in the wrong proportions or lacking the cohesion to maintain any internal integrity.

By writing a retrieval program in such an environment as the grid without the benefit of a computer interface, T'mar risked being incorporated into the grid as a permanent visitor, like the ghosts of past Council members who were now an integral part of Dome production. If she couldn't write a program that kept her anchored to the reality of the Temple at the same time incorporating the best parts of J'son with his barrier, she ran the risk of losing her own individuality, in effect becoming a part of the grid without hope of retrieval.

T'mar travelled deeper into the grid, taking notice of miniscule energy fluctuations lying within the crisscrossing web-like network as she went. These particular fluctuations had more of a positive influence on the grid reminiscent of J'son's energy signature than the otherwise negative impact of the creature. She followed this path of positively charged influences, moving to the extreme outer edge of the grid, which was located deep under the lower chamber. It appeared to her that the entity was hiding in an unused electrical conduit that ran away from the interface of the lower chamber to someplace under the Temple, disappearing from detection but waiting just on the edge of the grid.

J'son's barrier was still holding, keeping the entity separated from the rest of the grid, but T'mar detected a slight variation in the energy signature of the creature causing her to wonder if, in fact, the creature actually wanted to infiltrate the power chamber. It seemed too patient to be waiting for an opportunity to escape, and its actions belied its true intension. Instead of attacking the barrier directly, the creature roamed out of sight, appearing at the entrance of the conduit as a tiny spark of high-intensity interference. Its presence at the mouth of the conduit sent waves of disruption out into the grid only to withdraw when the disruption broke against his barrier.

Hitting the barrier, the entity was able to send simple, elementary equations through the holes in J'son's barrier, rewriting basic programs, opening and creating files. The entity diverted rudimentary systems into these files and hid them from the security program by use of a basic encryption code. What these files contained and their purpose was beyond T'mar's training to decipher and analyze. The encryption code was written in a language familiar to T'mar, but possessed a flexibility and plasticity not found in any known programming languages. The skillfulness and beauty of the equations reminded her of some of the spells B'el had developed and taught her.

The equations were very similar to the ones B'el used, but she didn't understand why the creature would waste its time rewriting basic programs.

The multifaceted simplicity of the new programs outweighed their intended function, like the programs were written more for show than actually performing any defined function. It was that lack of defining function that bothered T'mar the most. If B'el had broken into the mainframe and was rewriting basic maintenance programs, what was his intension? Buried this deep within the grid, T'mar didn't think anyone had the slightest idea that B'el might have established a foothold within the grid.

The entity seemed to be playing with J'son the way a computer might load a game and wait on the player to continue, only instead of playing against pre-set defaults J'son found himself having to counter whatever problem the entity threw at him. His barrier was weakening, but it wasn't due to an assault against it. It was weakening because whatever program the entity was using allowed it to analyze the construction of J'son's barrier and offer upgrades. The barrier, because it existed within the grid, accepted the upgrades automatically without scanning for compatibility, giving the entity, once the program had been installed and updated, a backdoor into J'son's program, like it was hacking the system. The intension was to open up a channel through the barrier without destroying it.

The longer J'son and T'mar stayed within the grid, the more likely they wouldn't be able to escape. Since their consciousness was attached to the electrical aspects of the grid their reality was based on the quality of the energy they were using. Because they were located deep under the Temple, anchored to the energy output of the disk in the lower chamber, the quality of the energy keeping them alive and animated was mostly negative energy. They were able to maintain their unity and stability within this environment, but it was filling them up with destructive negative ions. If T'mar couldn't merge with J'son within the next few nano-seconds, his positive qualities would disappear and the barrier would be rendered useless, probably taking his electrical imprint, his signature, along with it.

The negative energy coming from the disk was intense and overwhelming, but at least it was confined to the lower levels. The entity, seemingly uninterested in J'son's barrier now, retreated back down the conduit and hid within a simple maintenance program, disguising itself and lying low, watching as a new energy signature joined J'son and helped him close some of the more obvious holes in the barrier. The new signature was T'mar and the entity gave off an erratic discharge in response to her arrival.

The electrical discharge coming from the entity doused J'son and T'mar in a flood of negative energy, like the system was conducting a cleansing program and the discharge was just backwash from clogged filters. The negative energy stream came up from the lower levels and flowed into the disk, overloading the safety programs, slipping through the barrier and striking T'mar and J'son in such a way that dislodged them from the anchor of the disk. Floating free, not connected in any way to the grid, T'mar and J'son recovered from the shock of being hit by the blast of negative energy and groped around in the empty space between programs trying to reconnect with anything that could hold their essence in one place.

J'son had accumulated so much negative energy that he was increasingly conforming to the likeness of the creature. T'mar still had a large reservoir of positive energy, but her time within the grid was drastically altering that balance. J'son's positive to negative ratio was about 60/40 and changing rapidly, setting up a situation that would soon make him incompatible with her. As long as she was able to maintain a higher ratio of positive energy in contrast to his increasing negative output she believed they would be able to merge by using the negative aspects of his energy like a magnet and couple it with her positive aspects.

Her main concern at the moment, however, was whether she had enough positive energy to compensate for his negative energy. She was bleeding positive energy away at an alarming rate and soon she would be more negative than positive, repelling him instead of attracting him. She knew she would have to act fast before J'son became nothing but negative energy.

Using their mutual attraction, T'mar began to mentally write a compression spell in hopes that she could create a space within the grid separate from the hardware and software but still allowing her to access to the consoles in each chamber. She accomplished this by freeing up space on the main frame and creating a simple, open file and dropping the spell into it. Since T'mar was the one to write the program, she alone knew the file name and was the only one that could open it once she closed it. Together they retreated from the attack of the entity and hid within the program file she just created all the while overwriting J'son's signature with parts of hers.

Their electric currents flowed towards each other and met in the file where they joined together, her zero's matching up with his zeros and his ones merging with her ones. The file kept them hidden from the entity, but they were powerless to maintain the barrier. The holes were wider now, more like gaps. They were on the other side of the barrier and could see the gaps and the entity flowing thru it, but could do nothing to prevent it. They would have to leave the protection of the file in order to create patches to seal the breach, but that would leave them defenseless against another assault, and T'mar knew they wouldn't be able to withstand another blast from the entity.

Their only hope of keeping the entity confined to the lower levels would be if C'aad back-flushed the filter with positive energy, wiping out the negative influence and possibly flushing the entity out of the grid for good. But she didn't trust C'aad to allocate that much energy, and even if he did she didn't believe he would divert enough positive energy away from the Dome and send it down to the lower levels. He would think it a waste of energy, and without a sure sign that they were still cognizant he wouldn't authorize it. They had done all they could do and now it was up to those outside the grid to do what must be done.

Chapter Twenty-Eight:

C'aad's Death

"What has been will be again and what was lost will be found. We mourn the passing of a brother but celebrate his resurrection."

A prayer for the dead

Standing outside of the grid, before the members of the Council Chamber, T'mer had just shouted at T'mar not to enter the beam, feebly wiggling his fingers in the air like he was trying to grab her. A loud zapping sound was heard as she disappeared behind the beam, increasing the luminosity of the chamber momentarily, then it faded back to a reddish glow. The room was silent for several seconds after T'mer yelled and everyone in the room stared at the empty platform that only a moment before supported J'son and T'mar.

"C'aad, she won't last long in the grid," C'ton said, the X prominent across his face. "Already her essence is being disassembled and reintegrated into the grid. You have to back flush the filter and allow them more access to the positive energy coming out of the Council Chamber. If we don't act soon, J'son will be nothing but a ghost in the machine and T'mar will be reduced to a maintenance program."

"Oh, I don't think the grid would waste her experiences by turning her into a simple repair construct. It seems more probable that she will be rewritten as a sexual aid to improve the girls' mating prowess. I'm sure she will be a good addition to the programming library."

"Get out of that chair now, C'aad. You never had any intension of trying to bring them back no matter what they were able to accomplish. Back flush the filter now while we still have time."

"What time do you think we have? Even if your friends can contain the abnormality to the lower levels, the conversion rate down there is too high. I wouldn't be able to bring them back even if it were possible to isolate them within the grid. It has already converted much of J'son's essence, making his retrieval unnecessarily dangerous. Can you guarantee me, C'ton that if back flushing allows them to float to the upper levels that what emerges won't trip the safety programs? I won't allow a negative energy beast to roam freely around above the lower chamber. I won't chance rescuing a trapped, unknown variable out into the Temple. Energy creatures are notorious for being completely out of control."

C'ton thought briefly about the energy creature J'son had created by the lake and how it obeyed his every command, even dissipating back into a thought form within J'son's mind when directed. If he could be retrieved from out of the grid, would there be anything left of J'son to salvage? And what about T'mar? She had the proper training to maintain consciousness within the grid for awhile, but her essence was rapidly being replaced by the negative ions coming up from the lower chamber. If reclaiming J'son was out of the question because of the danger involved, he knew he only had a few seconds left to pull T'mar out. Flooding the grid with positive, filtered energy would create a magnetic repulsion against what was left of T'mar's positive energy. The resulting affect could propel her out of the grid, thrusting her back through the beam and landing her on the platform.

"Run the filtering program, now! Do it or I'll…"

"Or you'll what, my dear friend? Your challenge falls flat. No one here has any attachment to those poor souls who sacrificed themselves so we may continue on for a little while longer. They will be remembered for their sacrifice and a program will be written to preserve the best parts of them both. Everything he has done since he came here has been recorded and will be used to recalibrate the beam once he has been absorbed. Even in his dissolution he has helped us. So now, C'ton, let's dispense with these pointless challenges and rather concentrate on how we can benefit from the repairs that the two of them have carried out."

"I've heard enough," T'mer said, turning away from the empty platform and approaching the Dais, placing one foot on the first step leading up to C'aad's chair in a show of open contempt for the position of High Priest. But instead of stopping at the first step, T'mer mounted the stairs, taking them two at a time, reaching the top in a heartbeat and grabbing the collar of C'aad's robe before anyone could stop him. T'mer lifted C'aad out of his chair and threw him down the steps he had just ascended, breaking C'aad's contact with his chair for the first time in more than an age.

"T'mer. No. Don't!" Too late.

T'mer stood high up on the Dais looking down the steps he had just thrown C'aad. The High Priest lay twisted and broken on the bottom step looking up at T'mer, a trickle of yellow fluid spilling down his face. He looked to T'mer like a tiny rag doll from his vantage point. Suddenly, the thought occurred to him that he could take the seat of power for himself and no one would be able to stop him. By sitting in the chair, connecting to the grid directly, he knew the transition would be painful and he could possibly pass out before making full contact.

His experience with the Technology of the Techs allowed him access to the grid, but he didn't know if he could handle the energy flow without some kind of partition separating him from the negative aspects coming up from below. He would be useless in this position and a moment of doubt entered his awareness. He didn't know what he had accomplished by removing C'aad from the Dais, but he knew he could never sit in that seat of power.

"T'mer?" It was C'ton, speaking softly, not too sure what T'mer was doing. C'aad lay crumbled on the floor at his feet, unable to move anything except his eyes. "You have been removed, C'aad. It is over. Let us call the medical personnel to help you. You can do nothing more now. You have lost your connection to the grid and you know as well as I that you will never reach those heights again. An agonizing dissolution awaits you, I'm afraid."

T'mer was still standing up on the Dais contemplating his next move, but C'ton already knew what had to be done. The thing he had avoided for the majority of the age was now before him, beckoning to him, reaching out to him. The call of the High Priest was now his and he closed his eyes meditating on the path he now must take.

"C'str. C'mem," C'ton said to his fellow Council members. "Help make him more comfortable. There's nothing more we can do for him other than ease his passing. Withdrawal from the grid is incredibly painful and torturous. The mind slowly closes in on itself, feeding off of the last remaining traces of positive energy leaving his body. I am sorry it had to come to this, my old friend, but the time of the monks is over. The light of the Techs will lead us."

C'ton and the other two Council members leaned over and straightened C'aad's body. C'ton placed a cold hand over C'aad's forehead and mumbled something barely audible. C'aad's body, lying prone at the base of the Dais, seemed to relax at C'ton's touch and then it fell quiet again, but more peaceful. His breathing had slowed and the lines on his face soften, the prominent X was now buried beneath the folds of his limp, doughy skin.

C'ton's prayer had the intended effect but it did something else that he didn't expect. By touching C'aad on his forehead and opening himself up to the flow of healing energy, C'ton inadvertently created a channel through which C'aad's consciousness was able to traverse and lock on to. All C'ton had to do was take the seat of the High Priest and C'aad's consciousness would flow back into the grid without a physical body to anchor his thoughts. In effect, C'aad would become a disembodied entity himself.

With his intimate knowledge of the grid, C'aad would be able to reintegrate and reconstitute himself into the grid, the very thing he had contemplated earlier. C'aad wasn't cognizant of his plan, for it was happening on a level beyond the ability of consciousness to comprehend. It was a safety program that was built into the Dais for just such a moment as this. It worked covertly using sub-routines and maintenance programs to house the spark that was the High Priest energy signature. Once contact was made with the console, the safety program downloaded the assorted variables necessary to reconstitute the mental fluctuations and deviations that represented the thoughts of C'aad.

"T'mer, you must come down from there," C'ton said quietly, not too sure if T'mer had presence of mind to distinguish between wisdom and folly.

T'mer, hearing C'ton speaking to him, turned to look at the chair one more time and then, with his head down in a show of defeat, he started slowly down the steps, taking each step one at a time, fully aware of what he had just done. Reaching the bottom, he looked C'ton in the eye, searching his face for some reassurance that T'mar wasn't lost, not yet. Seeing only doubt and uncertainty, T'mer turned away, stepping over the prone body of C'aad without giving it a second thought. For T'mer, C'aad represented nothing more than a pile of crumpled up rags needing to be burned. Fear of the power of the Temple had vanished and T'mer no longer showed any regard for the institution.

"T'mer, go over to the platform and wait on my signal," C'ton said, mounting the stairs of the Dais and climbing the thirteen steps to the top. Placing his hand on the back of the chair, he closed his eyes again but this time his lips didn't move. Finishing his meditation, he turned around to face the glowing, spinning disk and sat down quickly without preamble, adjusting himself to the contours of the chair before pulling the console across his lap. He was just about to place his hands into the console when something made him hesitate. Once connected to the grid, C'ton didn't know if he would ever be able to leave the Temple again.

One of the two Council members standing beside C'aad knelt down and cradled his head in his lap, stroking his bald head and praying over him. The other Council member was placing his hands all over C'aad's body, searching for damage and casting healing spells over his broken body. The medical personnel entered the Council Chamber and rushed to C'aad's side, covering him with a blanket and trying to make him as comfortable as possible. Because of the proficiency of the monks and their ability to manipulate three-dimensional reality, the medical personnel were, like the Temple Guard, more show than substance. They didn't have the high level of training as the members of the Council, so their presence there was more out of concern for his comfort than actually being able to help him.

C'ton had already done about all anyone could do to relieve C'aad's agony. The pain coming from his broken body was secondary to the mental anguish he was experiencing due to withdrawal from the grid. The safety program was operating silently waiting for the opportunity to engage its programming and download the mathematical equivalent of C'aad's consciousness.

C'ton watched them making C'aad more comfortable, then without further delay he thrust the fingers of both hands deep into the console and instantly he was connected to the grid in the same way that C'aad had been. Sitting straight back, his eyes wide and lost to the inner landscape of his mind, C'ton felt an electrical current flowing into his body through the contact made with his fingers. The change in perception was puzzling in that what he was experiencing seemed foreign and out of place. For a moment, he thought there was another presence with him but then he put it out of his mind in order to concentrate on the task at hand. Assuming control of the grid, he immediately rerouted the energy beam to flow through the filter, coming out the other side transformed and purified.

Taking the sanitized, positive energy, C'ton transmitted it back down the energy beam, following a tracer program that would take it into the lower chamber. Injecting the chamber with positive ions changed the way the energy ascended back up the beam. The color of the beam going down was golden in stark contrast to the red of the ascending beam. The idea was to flood the lower level with enough filtered energy to regulate the output towards a more suitable level. What he hoped to accomplish was to dilute the energy coming up from the lower level to make it easier to handle. He couldn't see T'mar's energy signature and his fear was that she had already been transformed into a maintenance program hiding in the negative shadows of the energy grid. He didn't bother to look for J'son's energy signature, believing J'son was already lost, absorbed within the grid.

He continued to send positive energy down to the lower level, searching every nook and cranny for any discernable indication that T'mar was still cognizant and able to be reconstituted. If the majority of her energy had already been converted into mathematical sequences heavy on negative integers, he knew he wouldn't be able to locate her. If that was the case, she would fail to stick out within the grid and become nothing more than a mating program used for the pleasure of the monks. He knew that would be something she couldn't stand and he silently prayed that her program would be wiped clean instead of being used for sexual gratification. Her integration into the grid, however, would be stored in the memory banks to be pulled up and used whenever the need arose.

All was white as C'ton merged deeper into the grid, the light of his positive energy illuminating the three chambers with his presence within the grid. His conscious mind rode the current down into the lower level, searching the web-like conduits for any sign, any indication that she was still conscious and complete. Reaching the place within the grid where J'son and T'mar had gone, C'ton saw the tattered barrier they had erected and noticed an energy source flowing through it.

It was disguised as a sub-routine, but its energy signature was very strange and not one that should be found within the grid. The abnormality appeared to be re-writing a basic program using a programming language far above the programming language of the grid. Only an initiate of high rank had the ability to re-write programs within the grid, and C'ton feared the worst. If, as he was starting to believe, the grid had been compromised, there was no telling who was writing the programs, but he was starting to have a clue.

He was just about to leave the area when he noticed an energy fluctuation reminiscent of T'mar but weak and containing another element he didn't recognize. The fluctuation oscillated back and forth between the positive and negative poles of the energy beam, spiking on the positive side and flattened out on the negative, over and over again. Each spike failed to reach the height of the one before and falling created a depression which deepened with every rebound. It wasn't the depressions that bothered C'ton, though; it was the decreasing spikes that caused him concern. If the fluctuation was the last remnants of T'mar's energy signature, he knew he had to act fast if he was going to save anything remotely resembling T'mar.

Even with his connection to the grid as it was, C'ton was beginning to have difficulties maintaining his own integrity. Time was running out, and at the speed of light it was going quick. He had to move now before it was too late, but he didn't really know what he could do other than providing an energy signature she could follow up and out of the grid. However, if her cognitive abilities had already been compromised and degraded, she wouldn't be able to follow him anywhere.

The flow of positive ions coming down from above had penetrated deep into the lower chamber, looping back on itself and flowing back up. The vibration of the barrier and what C'ton took to be her energy signature took on a lighter shade of red, bleeding into the ultraviolent as it progressed upward. The light of the conversion made it easier to recognize T'mar and C'ton was now sure it was her. However, he noticed her signature appeared to encompass another presence very similar in construction, the mathematical sequences complementing each other and he held on to the hope that maybe some form of J'son was still present.

The ions excited the area surrounding the lower chamber, flooding the space and dislodging the mathematical equivalent of T'mar out of her position next to the barrier. C'ton saw her floating up the current, quietly staying afloat of the rising force pushing her up into the Council Chamber. She appeared to have some autonomous movement and managed to remove herself from the rising current once she entered the area of the Council Chamber so as not to become a part of the Dome.

Seeing that she had indeed retained some semblance of consciousness, C'ton chanced removing himself from the grid in the hopes that she would see him and follow him out. His consciousness returned to the Council Chamber, and seeing the conduit he had originally taken out of his body, C'ton entered it again and merged with the chair. His limp and sagging body became physically conscious, twitching slightly as he slipped into it. His eyes regained the look of attentiveness and he blinked a couple of times like someone trying to wake up. He was back in the Council Chamber sitting on the Dais with his fingers still embedded into the console. He quickly removed them and stood up in a clumsy way, knocking the console out of the way, his legs unsteady beneath him, breaking all contact with the grid.

"C'ton, what happened?" T'mer asked as soon as C'ton stood up. "You just engaged the grid a moment ago. Did you find her? Is she alright?"

C'ton, still fuzzy headed from the experience, looked down on T'mer, feeling his concern but unable to articulated exactly what happened. "I... She... Look there!"

A sound of tearing, like a bed sheet torn in two, filled the chamber, followed by a hard thud as an object was ejected out of the grid and onto the platform. The disk was spinning at an incredible rate, absorbing the filtered energy coming up from below and sending it up to the power chamber where it would continue its course up to the Dome. A crackling followed the thud as the conduit remained open, spewing ions out into the Council Chamber, illuminating the chamber in an intense blue-white light. The conduit had to be shut before anyone could see what had come through or whether it was still alive and cognizant.

C'ton leaned over the console again, plunging two fingers deep into it, closing a connection and sealing the conduit. The bright light disappeared once the conduit closed and C'ton could see from his vantage point that the platform contained the prone body of a naked female figure lying face down on top of another body, a male body. T'mar's head was resting in the crook of J'son's neck with her arms wrapped gently around his head, almost cradling it. Her legs were bent at the waist and spread out, her knees touching the floor of the platform, straddling J'son in a way that was sexually provocative.

As T'mar was trying to integrate J'son's energy into hers within the grid, she knew she didn't have enough programmable memory to retain all aspects of J'son's personality and physical dimensions as a separate individual; and so she made concessions, merging his body into hers whenever she could, removing all extraneous perimeters and even eliminating the space between them. Parts of his body needed their own corporal reality, like hands, legs and a torso, but other parts she decided to take within herself to save space, namely his sexual organs. As long as he was inside of her, the two of them were joined in a way that they shared the same space. Even the air molecules which normally form a sweaty moisture barrier separating two bodies so entwined were missing and like Siamese twins they shared the same skin as one organism.

T'mar had just enough awareness to follow C'ton up the beam and when the grid spit her and J'son out she landed on top of him, fully filled with his maleness. In the reality of the Council Chamber, T'mar was now able to draw upon the positive energy circulating around the room and she mentally cast a separation spell, giving J'son his own skin and individuality. She then removed her arms from around his head and placed her hands on either side of his prone body, pushing herself up into a sitting position on top of him. The change in posture brought a wave of feeling and she threw her head back as she rocked her hips forward, smiling in spite of herself. Not only were they successful in getting out of the grid, she just had an orgasm to finish it out.

Rolling off of him, T'mar landed on her back next to J'son, their bodies barely touching, like two lovers resting quietly together after copulation. The electricity passing between them warmed their bodies, causing them to tingle. T'mar turned her head to look at J'son, smiling, but the smile quickly faded as she realized that J'son wasn't conscious. His body was stiff, his color pale and T'mar couldn't detect any respiration. She sat up quickly and placed her hand on his chest, hoping to feel his heartbeat. He appeared lifeless and T'mar screamed.

"J'son! Can you hear me? C'ton, he isn't breathing."

"Bring them down, immediately." The platform, sitting motionless up to this pint, vibrated slightly and then began its slow descent, reaching the floor and disappearing, like the platform was nothing more than a mental construct. J'son was lying as still as the dead and T'mar got back up on her knees and was straddling him again, but definitely not in a sexual way. She placed her hands on his shoulders and began to shake him violently, trying to wake him up.

"J'son, wake up. Please."

C'ton made his way down the steps of the Dais on shaky legs and reaching the bottom he practically tripped over the monks and C'aad lying in the way. Regaining his balance, C'ton moved quickly over to J'son's side, placing his hands on his chest and forehead and mumbling, his lips moving rapidly and repetitively, like he was chanting the same thing over and over again. He glanced over at T'mar as he was chanting, seeing the concern in her eyes. With his lips still moving, he turned back to J'son, raising his hands a couple of inches off of his body. A dim glow could be seen in the space between his hands and J'son's body. The more he raised his hands, the brighter the glow became. Within moments, the glow of C'ton's energy started to mix with a different kind of glow, a glow possessing the color characteristics of J'son energy signature.

"You're drawing him out," T'mar exclaimed, the look in her eyes changing from helplessness to hope.

"Is he still alive?" T'mer had moved over to the platform as soon as T'mar and J'son emerged from the grid and was now standing helplessly by as C'ton prayed over J'son.

What C'ton was trying to accomplish by placing his hands above J'son's body was to pull whatever remained of J'son's consciousness to the surface. The hope was that J'son would awaken from his blackout a little beaten up but cognizant. The fear was that J'son was nothing more than a vegetable without the means or mental awareness to awaken to anything. Seeing J'son's lifeless body unresponsive to his efforts, C'ton looked back to T'mar. He wanted her to help him draw J'son out, but because of the situation and her special attachment to J'son, he feared she wouldn't have the mental clarity J'son needed.

"What do you want me to do?" she asked in a quiet voice, her nerves betraying her.

"I need you to remember the teaching you received from B'el. He must have taught you how to retrieve a lost soul."

C'ton's statement brought extreme condemnation in the form of riotous vocalizations coming from the members of the Council. To mention the name of B'el in the Temple was bad enough, but to request that one should practice the heresies of the profane was more than the Council members could take. With their High Priest lying broken on the floor at the foot of the Dais, the Council members were at a lost as to how to proceed. By right of ascension, according to the dictates of the Temple, C'ton was the next in line to assume command. However, because of his apparent lack of respect for the sacredness of the position the Council members didn't want to give him the title.

C'aad might have been a condescending, narcissistic leader, but he was their leader. The devil they knew, as they thought, was better than a devil they didn't know. For them, C'ton was a rebel not to be trusted. At least C'aad would dole out energy chits as a reward for obedience. With C'ton, he might very well bring the Dome down on top of them.

"No one is going to practice blasphemy in the Temple." It was D'nan.

Chapter Twenty-Nine:

The Library

"Leaving him alone in the library without a guardian isn't wise. He may stumble across some things that are better left undiscovered."

A Council member expressing his concerns to D'nan

Due to his inexperience, of all the Council members D'nan was the least prepared to take charge of the Council, but the most vociferous and influential in matters relating to the functioning of the Temple. D'nan had been standing out of the way watching the scene unfold and was just biding his time, waiting for the perfect opportunity to seize command. Seeing confusion and doubt reflected in the eyes of his fellow Council members, D'nan presented himself as the obvious choice for leader being the only one arrogant enough to speak out against C'ton in open chambers.

"I was C'aad's personal secretary for the past age and I am privy to his counsel. Get away from the boy, C'ton. He has performed the function his programming has enabled him to do. He has brought a measure of stability to the Dome. Already the readouts are showing a slight increase in positive energy production. Leave him on the floor next to C'aad's body and we will inject the energy remaining in their bodies back into the grid. And bring the woman. The Council will determine what will be done with her. C'ton, choose now where your loyalties lie and whom you serve:

The Temple and its rightful heir to High Priest, or the riffraff who have no hope. Choose now!"

C'ton heard everything D'nan had said, but didn't pay too much attention to it. If D'nan wanted to wrest control of the Council away from him, C'ton was more than willing to let him have it. If they didn't unlock the mystery of the depleted energy stores and the resulting imbalance, there would be nothing left to reside over and D'nan's rule would come to a short end. The rule of the monks had come to an end and the ways of the Temple had become corrupted beyond measure.

The collapse of the Dome had been predicted since the beginning, ever since B'el had told them about the weaknesses in its construction. B'el had predicted this very situation would happen and he used that excuse as the reason why he left and made for the Wastelands. According to the Council's interpretation of the sacred books, J'son was a self-correcting anomaly within the grid created specifically to perform the function he had just carried out. Based on the most fashionable, modern analysis of the prophecy, J'son was created by the Transcendentals as a way to balance out the fluctuations endemic in the original programming. This present crisis was predicted and the solution worked out long ago.

Only that's not how C'ton read the prophecies. In his study of the original manuscripts, read in the chambers of the Great Library located two floors below the Council Chamber, J'son, if indeed he was sent by the Transcendentals, wasn't mentioned in connection with Dome support. His reading indicated the Dome would fall because of the degradation of the precepts of the Temple. But by reaching out to the one who first constructed the Dome, B'el, the Dome would continue for another age, although in a different, lesser form. It was that different form that the priests sought to control and use to their own means in the coming age.

Before J'son entered their world, the prophecy had been interpreted to mean that B'el would return from his self-imposed exile, take up his position on the seat of the Dais, proclaiming himself High Priest and correct the imbalance. Once J'son's presence was known, however, it was said that he fit the pattern in the prophecy better than the one previously held by B'el. With C'aad's consent, J'son energy signature had been placed on the template of prophecy, and according to the new interpretation J'son was now the mathematical equivalent of a counter spell designed specifically to stabilize the grid. But J'son, as far as C'ton was concern, was more than that and he believed J'son was working directly with the Transcendentals to correct a problem that the original designers hadn't expected to encounter. It was this belief that caused C'ton to take command of the situation.

"No, D'nan. As long as I can still breathe the air of this world, J'son's body will not be regulated to the refuse bin. There is life in him yet. I think the calming atmosphere of the library would be the best place for him to recover. If his essence, his consciousness has indeed been lost within the grid, the only thing we can hope for is that he can find his way back. If we destroy his body, the vessel he has chosen to use in this manifestation won't be any hope for him, or any of us, for that matter. There are couches in the library. We will take both J'son and C'aad there and make them as comfortable as possible. T'mar, I'll need you to go with them. By the command of the Temple, I am authorizing you to practice the teachings you learned from B'el to try and retrieve the spirit of J'son."

"What about C'aad?" She asked, looking at his crumbled, broken body lying twisted on the floor below her. T'mar had despised everything having to do with the religion of the monks and knew firsthand the depravity they engaged in. Seeing the lifeless body of C'aad lying a few feet away, she repressed an intense urge to kick him in the stomach. "Why should we care about that power addicted parasite? His time has come to an end and now we should pay our respects? I say good riddance."

"You… You are not allowed to speak that way about the servant of the Dome," D'nan said, stuttering in shock that his claim to the Dais was challenged and his command was being ignored.

T'mer bent down next to J'son's body and gently lifted him up, cradling his head in the crook of his arm. "I've got the boy. S'tan, open the door to the transport shaft and help me get him down to the library. C'mon S'tan, let's go. It's time to choose. Are you a monk or a Tech? The Dome might last until the beginning of the new age, but once a decision has been made concerning the boy's future I plan on going back to the City. The Adepts will have answers to the mysteries of the missing energy reserves."

"That's because they are probably the ones who stole it in the first place," D'nan said heatedly.

The accusation stung, but the truth of the matter was T'mer really didn't know for sure if the Adepts hadn't taken the energy reserves to power their own portal. For all he knew, those living in the City had already opened a portal, passed through and sealed the breach before being detected. He didn't think that was the case, considering nowhere else on the planet except in the obelisks was storage of that amount of raw power possible. If the Adepts had taken the reserves to power up the machinery capable of tearing the very fabric of space, its operation would be instantly known throughout the planet.

"No, D'nan. I don't think so." It was T'mar. "C'ton, I saw something down there that I recognized from before. I think B'el is responsible for the missing energy reserves. I think he was able to somehow infiltrate the grid and now has established a presence within it. The energy signature I saw was very close to the one emitted by the psychic creature he created to guard his Castle. I think he may have managed to open a portal within the grid in which he, or rather his creature, travels back and forth between the Temple and his Castle. I'm almost sure that's the identity of the entity that J'son and I battled to keep contained. But what I don't understand is why would B'el have need for such massive amounts of energy? What could he be doing with that much raw power? And where could he contain it that would be hidden from the view of the Temple?"

"These are questions that need an answer," C'ton said, "but J'son must be our first priority. His physical self has encountered a terrible shock and won't allow his consciousness to re-emerge. He will need a calm setting in which to return, and someone reassuring there to help him. I haven't given up hope on him yet."

Two of the Council members, following T'mer's example, picked up the limp, boney sack that was C'aad's body and carried him out of the Council Chamber, heading towards the transport shaft in the outer hall. C'ton watched them go in silence, following them with narrow eyes, not too sure why he felt such apprehension. Something told him that C'aad wasn't as gone as his lifeless body indicated. He was also torn between the title he just took up and all the responsibilities associated with it, and wanting to go with T'mar to the relative peace of the library. With the Council in such a mess, lacking direction for the first time in recorded history, C'ton knew he had to remain there and readdress the situation, appointing new custodians and somehow manage to keep D'nan away from the Dais and taking a position he wasn't prepared.

"Take them to the library and I will follow you shortly. T'mar, you will find help in some of the manuscripts B'el left behind. I have examined several of his writings and I can assure you that if used properly some of his spells can help retrieve J'son's missing essence. I have seen it done, from before." C'ton left off speaking and fell quiet, as if in reverie, then his eyes cleared and he smiled sadly. "I'll meet you there as soon as I can get things organized here. Don't be afraid to speak the words of B'el, regardless of what the monks say. On the strength of the Temple and my right to swear by it, I give you permission to utter the unspeakable. Make J'son as comfortable as possible and spend your time in meditation. Go quickly."

C'ton turned away from T'mar and stared up at the Dais sitting thirteen steps above. He would have to mount the steps again in order to exercise command over the Council, plugging himself back into the grid and taking up his position as head of the Council. There would be much disorder and confusion, but he didn't think he would encounter any resistance from the other members of the Council. D'nan would be a problem and C'ton would have to move quickly if he was going to appease the ranking hierarchy by forgiving D'nan and allowing him to return to his position as secretary to the new High Priest. He would have to be on his guard, however, against the machinations of a jilted pretender to the title.

"The profane shouldn't be allowed access to the Holy Scriptures!" D'nan thundered once the doors to the Council Chamber closed. "Who are you to take the Dais and the power it entails? Where have you been for the last age? Out wandering around befriending the untouchables? What right do you claim to the sacraments of the Temple? You are nothing more than a usurper, taking what isn't yours and presiding over us whenever the mood strikes you. Guards! Follow them down to the library and prevent them from entering. If you must, take them into custody and confined them in the foyer. They must not have access to the restricted learning of the Temple."

The Temple guards, who were nothing more than low-level initiates destined to the subterranean ranks of the Temple Rites, had entered the Council Chamber, a half dozen of them, looking more like a band of bumbling misfits. The order had been issued by D'nan, but they recognized C'ton as the immediate successor to the title of High Priest. Being low-level initiates, part of their training had been in chain-of-command and the order of ascendancy in the event that there might be a vacancy for the position of High Priest. It had been known for many cycles that C'ton, even though he wasn't a seated member of the Council, still retained the title and authority as Viceroy. Seeing C'ton standing at the foot of the steps leading up to the Dais and D'nan positioned immediately behind him, the guards looked back and forth between them hoping for a resolution to their dilemma of who to follow.

"Don't go anywhere," C'ton said turning away from the steps to face them. "What we need now is continuity and a smooth transition, not a lust for power. Never before has there been recorded a dispute between who would lead us. I do not seek this position out of some vain attempt to lord it over you, D'nan. I have no interest in heading a Council that is doomed to repeating the same mistakes. We are still not safe from the Dome collapsing. What J'son and T'mar accomplished only extended the inevitable. If what T'mar said is true, then B'el has brought this down upon us and is only waiting for us to contact him for a solution. I have to find out what J'son knows, providing that we can revive him. That settles it, then. I will go to the library and help T'mar with her task. You, D'nan will assume the seat of the High Priest, if only in title. You will be denied the power of that position until after we have left the Temple."

"You can't deny me what was promised me. You don't know what C'aad has said to me, nor the spells he has taught me. How can you deny the power that comes from the correct recitation of the mathematical equations?"

"It takes more than a familiarity with the unseen workings of this world in order to rule it. Take the seat, D'nan, but don't be surprised if the forces residing within the grid reject you as being too impetuous. Your time for power has not yet come." C'ton turned away from the Dais and stormed across the court in a huff, busting through the group of guards and exiting the chamber.

As C'ton passed, one of the guards said: "But who do we follow?"

"Follow him," he said, stopping for a second, pointing at D'nan, who was even now placing a foot on the lower steps of the Dais. "If you want business as usual, there is your man. Bow down to him." And with that, C'ton entered the transport shaft and disappeared behind closed doors.

The transport shaft dropped the two floors quickly without any sensation of moving. Unlike the entrance to the Council Chamber, the door of the transport shaft opened onto a large, spacious room without a hallway or connecting corridor. The library was circular, as consistent with all rooms on each of the thirteen floors of the Temple, possessing an open floor plan with a central passageway dissecting the room into two halves. On the right and left side of the passageway were long rows of shelving that ran the length of the room and curved around the back of the far wall, coming up the other side like a horseshoe. In between the rows of shelving were several, comfortable-looking couches and chairs with helmet -shaped headsets.

The shelving itself contained several long, narrow boxes filled with stacks of small square plates organized by category. Embedded in the shelves at shoulder height were several rectangular viewing screens spaced at various places around the Library Chamber. Most of the screens were blank, but one was displaying a distorted, encoded image playing in some kind of loop. It had been left on and was running by itself, projecting images onto a screen that no one was there to observe.

The images came from an info-plate that was sticking half way out of a spherical device with a slot in it. Expect for the buzzing whine coming from a loose headset, all was quiet and C'ton wondered who had departed so suddenly that they left the viewer on and the plate out. Only a monk on the order of the Council had permission to enter the library and he spoke out loud concerning this.

"Someone was just here and they were retrieving information."

T'mer and T'mar had set J'son down on one of the couches, gently propping him up against the back to give J'son the appearance of resting while sitting up. The other two Council members carrying C'aad's body had placed him on a couch next to J'son, stuffing him into the fold between the seat and the back, placing him there like a bag of trash, without concern to his comfort. His arms were twisted and bent under him and his head hung down against his chest. He looked uncomfortable but no one gave him a second thought, thinking C'aad was now gone and his body useless.

C'ton saw the careless way they handled his body and he found himself somewhat disturbed at their lack of respect shown to someone who had been here since the beginning. T'mar might not have fond memories of her time spent among the monks and seeing his body so casually tossed aside might bring her some level of vindication, but C'ton respected the position enough to know that C'aad's body deserved more reverence than what he was being given.

"T'mer," he said. "Can you please straighten out C'aad's body and make him look more comfortable? As High Priest, he deserves a better ending than this."

T'mer reached down and pulled on C'aad's legs, adjusting his position and straightening his crumbled body. He then laid his arms across his chest. C'aad still looked lifeless and T'mer shook his head at the futility of making a dead person comfortable. It was hard to take seriously because T'mer had never known another High Priest and he wasn't sure how he felt seeing such a great wizard with so much presumed power lying dead on a couch. Until just recently, T'mer believed all monks were immortal and couldn't die, but now thought otherwise. Looking at the withered, misshapen appearance and sunken features of C'aad lying silently on the couch T'mer turned his nose up like he was smelling something unpleasant and twisted his lips into a sneer.

"You'd think that the death of a High Priest would bring more sympathy, but I guess sympathy is for the less fortunate," he said.

"You are right, T'mer," C'ton said coming over and placing a friendly hand on his shoulder. "Let us hope that we don't face the same end. Still, something tells me that we haven't heard the last from C'aad."

"What do you mean?" T'mar asked. "I was taught that involuntary disconnection from the grid could cause irreversible psychic damage. C'aad died from withdrawal. You don't mean to suggest that his essence is still hanging around, do you?"

"I'm not too sure, but C'aad was very wise and I can't believe he would have left himself vulnerable and open to destruction in the event he was forcibly removed from the Dais. No, I believe C'aad has transcended the physical bonds of this world and now exists as a phantom in the system. I gave the Dais to D'nan, but I don't think he will be able to access the grid in the way a High Priest should. If C'aad's essence has somehow managed to merge with the grid, he will use D'nan for his own ends, a mere puppet without the power to properly lead the Council. Who was using the info-plates?" He asked again, changing the subject.

"We don't know," T'mar responded. "Everything is just like we found it when we got here. It appears the librarian didn't clean up after their last visitor."

"I don't think that's the case. These records are considered sacred and shouldn't be out without proper security. This is extremely unorthodox. The viewer running without a host can only mean that you surprised someone by coming here; surprised enough that they left or went into hiding. In fact, they may still be here and if in hiding it means they were doing something unauthorized."

T'mar turned away from the small group and moved in a bee-line towards the running viewer. She reached out with one hand and touched the screen. The wavy, distorted images cleared and for a moment the picture on the screen became coherent, only to distort again once she removed her finger. The image broke up and closed down, becoming a tiny white point and then beeping off. The screen popped back on after being rebooted, revealing a dim green background with a yellow cursor blinking in the upper left hand corner. Touching the cursor with the tip of her finger and dragging it to the opposite corner, the screen became animated and brought up a listing of every category listed alphabetically and cross-referenced by priority, the higher levels of learning encrypted and inaccessible to those unauthorized to use it.

C'ton, being one of the last ones left alive from the beginning, had access to the encryption codes and previously had given them to T'mar in their earliest training days together. This knowledge allowed her access to the system to bring up anything stored within the grid. Punching C'ton's PIN into a keypad, she was given instant access to the vast knowledge base of the grid and within a few keystrokes had brought up the records she was hunting for. They were hidden under a label denoting heretical thoughts and beliefs, and by selecting that category the name of B'el topped the screen, showing another listing of spells and a short description of what to expect once they were cast.

Tapping the screen above the category she wanted, the screen flickered and a dialog box opened stating that the information she requested was beyond what her PIN allowed. Puzzled, she closed the box and tried the same category again receiving the same result. Closing the dialog box again, T'mar selected a different category under a different subject heading.

She was still cued up under heretical beliefs, but requested access to a rudimentary search engine, taking the long way through the file. Selecting "Guide" as her preferred method of search, a brightly flashing blue cursor appeared at the lower right hand side of the screen. Tapping and dragging the cursor towards the listing, she dropped it on top of the original category and waited access. The cursor disappeared behind another dialog box stating she didn't have authorization to access the files requested.

"Something's wrong," she said over her shoulder. "The system won't give me access. It's says I'm, or rather you, aren't authorized. How can that be, C'ton?"

C'ton walked over to the screen and T'mar stepped back out of the way. C'ton tapped on the same category as T'mar and got the same result. A PIN reset button was located on the keypad and C'ton tapped it. The screen flickered and a dialog box opened asking for a PIN. C'ton punched the 7-digit alpha/numeric code into the keypad and pressed "enter". The category listing came up again and he selected the file relating to unorthodox spells, a subdivision not as blasphemous and profane as the strictly heretical spells. The system, refusing him access, caused him a moment of confusion before he understood what had happened.

"There are only two reasons why I can't gain access to the files. The entire system has been reprogrammed, something I highly doubt; or I am being prevented from gaining access by an unknown entity."

"You don't think B'el's energy creature is keeping us out of the system, do you? How can a thought projection prevent us from accessing the grid from the outside? I could see it preventing J'son and me from gaining access to the grid while we were within it, but how can it affect what we do outside? All we are trying to do is access a file. What kind of encryption code can keep you out of the system?"

"That's just it," C'ton said, sounding more annoyed at the now obvious deception. "Look at the screen as I try to access the file. See how the screen flickers just before the dialog box opens? The file is being displayed right now, but it is hidden behind a distortion. It's not that we are being kept out. We are made to believe we are being kept out. Actually the deception is quite ingenious in its simplicity. Instead of taxing the system with unwieldy numerical equations, the perpetrator placed a window over the pertinent information. I'm sure we would have trouble accessing any information dealing with B'el. The system's been breached and a cleaning program has been set up to filter out any and all requests."

"But who could do that? Who has the ability to write such a program? Surely you don't think B'el did this?" T'mar was getting excited and a little scared. Without being able to access the files they needed, all hope for J'son's survival was rapidly receding.

"No, this isn't the work of B'el. He of all people would want us to have access to his files. This is the work of a monk of high competency. Either some member of the Council or…"

"Or what? Who do you think is keeping us out of the library records?"

C'ton turned away from her and didn't answer. Who he thought it was defied the logic of the system. A program could be written in two different ways. Either a programmer would sit behind a keyboard and punch out an endless series of zeros and ones, or he had to be connected to the grid like C'aad was when he sat up on the Dais. Being connected to the grid in such a way allowed one to become a conscious program within the system while at the same time maintaining the awareness of his body sitting outside the grid. But that level of programming was only permitted through a direct interface, by sitting on the Dais. With the body of C'aad lying in a lumpy mass on a couch and no one to take his position, C'ton feared the obvious conclusion.

"I think the essence of C'aad is still viable and inhabiting the network of the grid. I believe he is still conscious and hiding within the grid. I think it was he that accessed the library and left the viewer up and running. He was looking for something before you caught him. Now he is writing simple programs as a way to trick us. I think I can access the files we need by bypassing the security features." C'ton tapped on the screen several times as different dialog boxes opened and directed him to various sub-routines. His manipulation took him to a basement file, a backdoor which he installed in the beginning and left unlocked. It was a trick all good programmers employed as a means to enter the system undetected in the event he had become locked out of the grid.

The basement file was still located where he had originally hid it and all indications suggested that it had been left undisturbed. C'ton selected the file and opened it, revealing the contents. There was only one link in the file and he activated it. Instantly, the system recognized him and a dialog box opened welcoming him back after so long an absence.

"Why did it say that?" T'mar asked, looking over his shoulder. "It acts like you haven't had access since before you wrote that file."

"In a sense I haven't. When I wrote the file I used a different energy signature than the one I now possess. I was a different person back then. I almost forgot what it felt like to be that other person. That part of me hasn't been awakened since that time. The energy flow is a bit higher than I like and more rapacious, harder to handle. Ah, the impetuousness of youth! Here now, I think we will be able to gain access to those files."

C'ton brought up several files all at once and had them on display in a couple of different windows. An energy bar indicating memory consumption appeared at the upper left hand side of the screen. A warning symbol stated that he was approaching the energy consumption limits for that particular search and the system would redirect him to the Council Chamber to get approval for further exploration. He selected the "close dialog box", smiling slightly at his ruse.

"There, while the system spends more energy trying to keep me out we will slip in unnoticed by any of the security features C'aad may have set up. If I'm right, C'aad will think I am trying to infiltrate the system through force. All we want to do is read a file. And so..."

A smaller window opened up on top of the other windows displaying a blinking search cursor. He entered his search request into the keyboard and the desired files began downloading. Accessing the same file as before, C'ton was granted admission. Choosing the proper listing, a catalog of spells, all of which were heretical and extremely dangerous, appeared. He opened the file containing the spell he wanted and read the contents silently to himself. T'mar watched from behind, trying to make some sense of the shifting lines and squiggles that represented the spells.

These spells were cloaked in symbolism and allegory, making it almost impossible to decipher the true source of their power and rendering the user, the one who would cast the spell, impotent, not knowing if the spell was cast correctly until it was too late. B'el had designed his spells to backfire if they were used by someone other than those authorized. And considering he wrote them for his own use, without proper training those same spells could very well destroy them all.

T'mar, knowing the danger of casting such spells, was hesitant as she quietly meditated on the images that began swirling around in her head. The images were too intense and she backed away from C'ton and the screen, closing her eyes and calming her mind, trying to focus on what the images were saying and not on the rising fear lurking in the dark recesses of her mind.

"I probably shouldn't be reading that," she said after a moment, sounding tired and a little depressed. "As soon as I saw the symbols I was taken back to my time with B'el. The sound of the spells awakened within me the manner in which B'el used to speak. I'm having trouble with the images, C'ton."

C'ton had been bent over the keyboard studying the spells and straightened up after hearing T'mar speak. His fingers relaxed in mid stroke and he looked at her over his shoulder, seeing the strain in her face and eyes. He understood exactly what she was talking about because he was having the same problem with the spells. The manner in which one was to speak it captivated the mind of the one casting it. C'ton was struggling with his own images, battling the inner luring of power that the symbols represented. It frightened him to think that B'el had full command of his senses whenever he casted these spells. The strength of his focus and the drive of his will, the singleness of purpose was the state that all monks strove for and yet B'el had managed it by pursuing his own path, the path of the profane.

Enticing as the promise of power was, C'ton had spent his entire life avoiding going down that treacherous path. T'mar, he could now see, was being enticed to follow the same path that she once tread, a path that would overthrow her mind and turn her once again into a slave of B'el. She may have escaped from him before, but it wasn't of her own choosing. The memories were still there and vividly alive. He could see T'mar wasn't up to the task of stilling her mind from the onslaught. C'ton hadn't thought about how viewing the spells would affect her; he was only thinking about how not to lose his own mind.

"I'm sorry," he said at last. "I shouldn't have let you see this. I should have warned you. Turn away from the screen."

"Do you really think I would have listened to you?" She asked pinching her face as waves of confusion creased her forehead. "I haven't been your student, your 'che, in a long time. I am my own woman. Now cast the spell, C'ton and retrieve J'son's soul before it's too late."

Knowing she spoke the truth, C'ton dismissed the growing guilt and turned back towards the screen to look at the spell one more time. His mind burning bright with the symbols, he got out of the chair and knelt down besides J'son, who was resting comfortably on the couch. He placed an uneven hand on J'son's forehead and began to cast the spell.

Instead of repeating the Soul Retrieving spell verbatim, as most monks did when trying out a new spell for the first time, C'ton closed his eyes and concentrated on the symbols within his mind. At first the symbols were just images swirling around in his head; then his mind captured the individual images and froze them in place, solidifying the images into three-dimensional representations of the symbols. The symbols had a severe modulation, a vibration which produced varying shades of color depending on their nature. Since all the spells in B'el's library were considered heretical, the symbols took on a dark grey, almost black tone.

The white slate that was the mind of C'ton became dark and his training fought against him to return his mind to the relative serenity of its white state. As he mentally battled the dark forces that were arising within him, he parted his lips to speak the words of the spell before the darkness overtook him completely. The verbal expression was strange and very guttural, the words more like foul sludge dripping out of his mouth than any discernable language.

"Alles gooten freizen cumbana sebalten rosa, J'son. Alles gooten freizen cumbana sebalten rosa, J'son. Alles gooten freizen cumbana sebalten rosa, J'son!"

C'ton spoke the spell thrice, which was typical, adding the name of the intended recipient at the end as a way of directing the energy of the dark forces. Because of the intensity of what J'son had been through, C'ton feared that his soul had indeed fled, leaving is body behind as a shell. If what C'ton believed was true, that the essence of C'aad had somehow survived his disconnection and was now running around the grid, then it was a very real possibility that J'son's body could be taken over and used by C'aad. The spell would work, he knew, but whose soul would return to the body? Seeing J'son's body still immobile and vacant, C'ton was about to cast the spell again, something that was more dangerous than casting it the first time, when T'mar came up behind him again.

"I need to do this, C'ton. I know what forces you battle and the danger of resurrecting a lost soul. I can't guarantee that I can cast the spell as skillfully as you, but if the vibration is tinged with my energy signature hopefully it will make it easier for him to recognize. Let me try.

You shouldn't cast that spell more than once anyway. B'el explained to me what would happen and then he showed me, using one of his initiates. The result was a mess and the initiate was left to perish in the Wastelands. J'son's body didn't respond to your call, and maybe that's a good thing. Let me try, C'ton."

C'ton stood up and moved out of the way without a word of protest. He really didn't want to press his skill a second time. "Just be careful."

Taking C'ton's place beside J'son, T'mar thought back to the time when she was with B'el and tried to remember the manner in which he spoke the spell, the inflection and tone of his voice. Everything was about vibration, and if she was going to succeed in bringing J'son back from the abyss she needed to cast the spell correctly without mistakes. Doubt entered her awareness and she secretly wished C'ton wasn't here to see her weakness.

She saw the symbols in her head the way C'ton had, but because of her energy signature they took on a softer, more diffused appearance. The vibration was different, not as dark, and the lighter aspects allowed her to enter into the language of the symbols. Her feminine qualities gave the spell more fluidity and variability, allowing more room for flexibility. She repeated the same words that C'ton had spoken, but coming out of her mouth the spell took on a sensual quality that sounded like the hot, breathless communication expressed between lovers engaged in foreplay. The result of her specific qualities raised the sexual tension in the library, giving C'ton and the others a sense that she was casting a binding spell, her to J'son.

As she finished speaking the spell for the third time, accentuating J'son's name with each repetition, his body began to move. At first his eyes fluttered and his fingers, resting across his chest, clinched and then released, falling to his sides. His arms and legs began to twitch and he appeared to be experiencing a seizure. Then he inhaled deeply and held his breath for a few seconds, letting it out forcefully and inhaling again, holding it for several seconds more.

J'son looked like a man struggling to breathe, like someone who had swallowed water and now wasn't too sure if the air he was taking into his lungs was fit to breathe. He let out his breath again, more slowly this time, sounding like air coming out of a leaking tire.

"Eeeeeeeeeeeh!"

The sound stopped and J'son inhaled again, only this time he turned his head towards T'mar kneeling next to him and opened his eyes, smiling as he saw on her face a mixture of concern and relief.

"I was back there again," he said weakly, his voice cracking and sounding dry. He was starting to breathe normally again. "I was back on Earth, lying on my bed. At home."

"What is he talking about?" T'mer asked. "He wasn't anywhere but unconscious. His body was right here the whole time."

"Have you forgotten he is a portal, T'mer?" C'ton was just as puzzled as to what J'son just said as T'mer, but he didn't doubt what he had said. Whether or not J'son's body was here in the library was a moot point. If J'son believed he was back on Earth, at least mentally, then surely he was. "What do you remember? Was it as vivid as this world?"

"More so. I just woke up a moment ago in my bed with the remnants of a strange dream bouncing around in my head. I was lucid and the dream was vivid and had substance."

"You mean you dreamed a dream about your world?" T'mer asked incredulously.

"No, I dreamed a dream about this place. I woke up in my bed thinking everything here was a dream. Only now do I see this place has a reality all its own. I don't know if I'm in my bed having a dream about this place, or if my bed is just a memory of a dream." J'son sat up slowly and rested up against the back of the couch. "C'ton, I was there. I was back on Earth and this place was nothing more than a dream. I heard you calling out to me from the dream, but I didn't want to listen, thinking it was just sounds out of a fantasy. I was about to get out of bed and go to the bathroom when I heard another voice, sweeter and definitely feminine, like the voice I used to hear from before."

"That would have been T'mar casting the spell," C'ton commented. "It's the same spell, but she..."

"You called out to me with the sounds of cooing like a lover," J'son said, grinning weakly at T'mar. "The imagery I was receiving was very sexually stimulating and I found myself falling back asleep wanting to lose myself again. It was only a few seconds ago that I felt myself getting aroused, and then I saw you. Trust me when I tell you that I am very surprised to find myself here in the library, sitting on a couch on another planet. I still don't know whether I believe in the reality of your world or not. How do I know if you're not the reaction to a bad slice of pizza?"

"A slice of what?"

"How are you feeling now?" C'ton asked. "Does this place feel like a dream now? I can assure you that I am very real and the things we've experienced together have meaning. What are the images you are seeing now?"

Chapter Thirty:

Sexual Appetites

"I have done my part and now J'son owes me. Maybe T'mer will join us."

T'mar fantasizing in the clothing booth

C'ton heard how he sounded and hoped J'son and T'mar were too preoccupied to notice the doubt that had slipped in. It was a great debate of most import among the higher initiates whether or not life on this planet was real in the sense of actually having an independent existence outside and beyond the influence of those dreaming minds on J'son's world. From the very beginning the monks of the Temple seemed to have a symbiotic relationship with the shadows from the other realm. But unlike shadows that disappear in the light, C'ton, among others, was keenly aware that unless his mind was fixated on encounters with J'son's world, he didn't have any memory of his existence prior to that time.

The memories flooded in once he was able to hold the idea of Earth as a real place, almost as if his reality depended on the dreams of humans. It was only in the light of their planetary orbit could those on C'ton's world even remember the light of J'son's planet. And only during their relatively short daylight cycle could those on Earth see them. It was only during the long dark that the light of gnosis kept C'ton's world from falling back into barbarism.

"Nothing now," J'son said. "The feeling that I am in a dream is gone. This world is now my reality, although my head still feels fuzzy."

"You are still integrating. But if you close your eyes right now," C'ton asked, getting more animated than he should have allowed himself, ignoring the wisdom of allowing J'son to fully integrate. "Can you take yourself back there again? J'son, do you think you could take someone with you if you thought about them?"

"C'ton, what are you doing?" T'mar asked. "We just brought him back from the dead and now you want him to return? This isn't right. Has the spell got a hold of you?"

It was a legitimate question, considering C'ton was wide-eyed with inquisitiveness, a not too subtle sign that the dark power he had wielded was working on his consciousness, changing it, and offering up to him unlimited possibilities. B'el's spells worked that way. They opened up the mind to its own potential and added a level of curiosity that would, sooner or later, become insatiable. The questioning was the first indication that maybe C'ton was travelling down a very slippery slope.

T'mar saw the look in his eyes, the wide, piercing gaze searching J'son's face for answers, and she had to ask: "C'ton, are you okay?"

The spell didn't affect T'mar in the same way as it did C'ton, mainly because he had cast the spell from a position of deep knowledge, aware of the dangers but confident that he could control the mind-blowing forces that the symbols represented. T'mar, on the other hand, had cast the spell from a position of want and sexual desire. The spell worked on her psyche differently, stirring up lustful thoughts that could be satiated very easily by a vigorous session of lovemaking. The spell, looking for an anchor within the mind of T'mar, latched onto her primal, hyper-sexual instincts and used that energy as a focal point, her lust acting like a lens, concentrating her impulses. She was as curious as C'ton as to where J'son's mind might have gone, but her thoughts focused mainly on how she could satisfy her ravenous lust.

She was sitting next to J'son with C'ton kneeling on the floor below them. Where C'ton's look was intense and penetrating, beads of sweat collecting across his forehead, T'mar was just the opposite. She had a leering look to her eyes that lingered back and forth between J'son's naked, slim but muscular chest and his exposed, lower torso. She was having a hard time maintaining her composure and several times she stopped herself from reaching down and grabbing him. At times she twitched nervously, like a schoolgirl about to engage in sex for the first time. She wanted to touch him, but she knew that the power of the spell, the symbols that still circulated around in her head, would overpower her and she would be at the mercy of her over-stimulated libido.

"Yes, you are right, T'mar. The spell is working its evil within my mind. I can see the truth of B'el's pursuits and how one could be taken over by such thoughts. My thinking is foul and my curiosity unrelenting. J'son, you must ignore my questions, to help me. I will want to know everything about your time spent on Earth, but you mustn't instruct me. The power of B'el's beliefs is all intrusive, reshaping the mind according to its own needs. Right now I am being inundated by questions concerning your ability to pass from this world to yours. The goal of all monastic pursuits is to create within you a two-way portal, a way to escape the long dark of the mind. B'el would have wanted to ask these questions and I fear that his influence has already begun its work. I can feel my mind changing to accommodate this new-found power."

C'ton hung his head down, turning away from J'son, and stood up, moving a few feet away from the couch. Looking at the floor, unable to lift his head and meet J'son's gaze, C'ton appeared diminished somehow, ashamed by being caught doing something wrong. The images in his head were extremely powerful and vivid and closing his eyes took him far away from the confines of the library. Even with T'mar and J'son sitting only a few feet away, C'ton became oblivious to his surroundings and instead delved deeper into the source of his questions. He was lost to the outside world until he felt a firm, warm hand on his shoulder. It was J'son.

"C'ton?"

The sound of J'son's voice penetrated the dark fog C'ton was in and he opened his eyes. The reality of the library filled his senses and for a moment he forgot that he had cast the spell. It was like he had a split personality and from one moment to the next he slipped back and forth between his own thoughts and those forced upon him by casting the spell. In his moments of clarity, C'ton raised his eyes to meet J'son's and found stability there, an assurance that no matter what was happening everything was going to work out fine. J'son's eyes didn't waver and C'ton discovered that by holding his gaze he was able to calm himself enough to block out the immediacy of the symbols. His mind relaxed from a state of hyper-awareness and the cool, white slate that was his mind returned to its former condition. By keeping his eyes on J'son, C'ton was able to keep his mind under control.

T'mar was having a harder time controlling her impulses. When J'son stood up and reached out to C'ton, T'mar watched him from behind, appreciating his lean but well-developed back and tight, muscular ass, so unlike T'mer in proportion but still sexually pleasing. She stood up, throwing her ample, rounded breasts out and slipped up behind J'son, brushing her hard, erect nipples against his shoulder blades.

At any other time what she had done would have been taken as nothing more than a causal, friendly, chance encounter where the parties concerned would have laughed it off as a joke, nervously laughing together and playing it off as an auspicious faux pas. Instead, once her nipples touch his skin an electric current passed between them and her body became covered in goose bumps so much so that her already hard, stiff nipples felt like two pebbles against his back. She didn't retreat from him and instead reached her arms around him and grabbed him about the waist, just inches above his loins. T'mar, losing herself to the sensation, thought nothing of what she was doing; only that she had an itch that only J'son could scratch.

J'son, for his part, was pleasantly surprised to feel warm, firm breasts pressed up against him, but he was even more startled when she wrapped her arms around his waist. Her fingernails played gently over his stomach, twirling the tiny, light brown hair running to his loins between her thumb and forefingers. She was just about to wrap her hands around his rapidly swelling member when C'ton, realizing what was happening, spoke up.

"T'mar! Stop what you are doing this instant. The spell is affecting you on a different level. Your present behavior is the consequence of the spell on your pleasure centers. Do not do this thing. You will wind up in the bed chambers a slave to your lust."

C'ton's protest was like a slap to the face and she removed her hands in a quick gesture that left them dangling nervously by her sides. She was still standing behind J'son and she brushed herself up against him in one last vain attempt to appease her appetite before forcing her hands between them to push herself away. Her hands rested softly against his back and she resisted the impulse to spin him around and drop to her knees; and if C'ton hadn't been there she probably would have given in to the temptation. Instead, she dropped her hands again and backed away.

"I'm sorry," she said. "I don't know what came over me."

"Yes you do," C'ton responded harshly, struggling with his own demons.

J'son turned around and looked at her thoughtfully. He had a smile on his face and a hint of lust played around in the reflection in his eyes. What she had done had definitely gotten him sexually aroused and he stood there facing her with a powerful erection, feeling fully energized from within. His smile remained fixed and plastered shamelessly on his face as he looked at her body. His mind was rapidly filling with sexual images that were being transmitted to him psychically by T'mar. All thoughts about the reality of Earth and his possible dream state here faded as more of his resurrected mind accommodated her delightful and highly enjoyable invasion of his thoughts.

Seeing his comfortable smile, her expression softened and she almost gushed like a young girl, feeling feminine, attractive and desirable. This was the same way she felt, she now remembered, whenever she was in B'el's presence, a helpless slave to her own desires. She knew her strong physical attraction towards J'son was wrong, especially so soon after reviving him, but her body wouldn't listen to her training. J'son hadn't reached out to her, as of yet, and secretly she was grateful for his restraint. If he would have touched her, anywhere, the erogenous zone that was her body would have exploded in waves of orgasmic ecstasy.

"J'son," C'ton implored. "Don't let her fill your mind with thoughts of a base nature. Through resurrection your mind was made pure, clean. You are allowing her to reprogram you to respond as a carnally directed, sexual creature instead of the spiritually uncontaminated being you should have become. You are falling into the mistake of B'el. You must show restraint even if we don't. Do you understand?"

"Yes, I do," he said, his body relaxing as his sex organ softened. His smile and the leering look in his eyes changed to those of waning desire mirrored with a slight sadness. "I feel as though I have a split personality. Part of me wants to explore the sexual promises T'mar awoke in me, while another part, a deeper, driving force wants to seek out B'el and the secrets of his power. For some reason, I feel compelled to search him out, like I am an integral part in some cosmic play. C'ton, I need information. I need to fill my mind with facts and data, to occupy it with something other than forbidden pleasures. You are so beautiful, T'mar."

T'mar was beyond embarrassed and left J'son and C'ton standing alone together. She walked away quickly, covering her breasts and pelvic area with her hands as she went. She slid into a private viewing booth a few feet away and disappeared behind a thick, dark curtain made out of the same furry material as their clothes had been. Inside the booth, hidden behind the curtain, she touched the lower, right hand corner of the viewing screen and brought up a simple attire program from the library database. The screen filled with holographic, three-dimensional representations of various garments of different colors and varying degrees of coverage. Her first impulse was to choose the most sexually revealing outfit that would accentuate her obvious physicality, but she knew that would defeat the purpose of her coming into the booth in the first place. Instead, she tapped the screen next to a very modest, two-piece ensemble and activated the proper spell.

Clothing spells were available to all, regardless of rank, and many a monk took advantage of the simplicity of the spells to change their look. The material was created out of a program that used Dome energy to convert pure electron flow into base, material objects. For the uninitiated, the grid produced whatever was requested of it, within reason. However, for those acquainted with the higher levels of learning the recitation of the proper spell was all that was needed. Holding the thing that was desired within consciousness allowed the innate power of the initiate to create at will. It was this skill that T'mar now employed, giving voice to the symbols to produce the correct vibration and holding the image of the outfit in her mind. A slight luminosity filled the small booth, the light shooting out of the tips of her fingers and the ends of her hair. Her eyes shone with a strange brilliance and she stared at the screen, not seeing it.

The light engulfed her for a few seconds and then diminished, leaving T'mar clothed in a tight, dark blue brazier that cupped her breasts and pushed them together, putting her ample cleavage on display, and a short, blood-red skirt that barely covered her posterior end. The viewing screen showed her a picture of what she looked like, kind of like a three-dimensional mirror, and she smiled sadly at her reflection, the clothes cooling her passion as well as covering her feminine qualities. Her appearance saddened her because she didn't know if J'son would still find her attractive with all those clothes on. Except for special, ritualistic and sacred occasions or to keep the elements away when one found themselves outside the Dome, clothes were normally optional for women and rarely worn.

"Why would anyone want to wear such constricting garments?" She asked her reflection, frowning at herself and then turning sideways to admire her profile. Her nipples were no longer erect under the material, but their outline could still be seen. Her shoulders slumped slightly, depressed that she couldn't control herself enough to enjoy the feeling of nakedness. The clothes were restricting and she felt hot and confined. She thought about removing the top and emerging from the booth dressed only in her skirt, but the more rational part of herself, the part of her that recognized the training of her youth, prevented her uncovering herself again. She wanted J'son's attention, needed his attention but knew she had to resist that impulse, for all of their sakes.

She emerged from the viewing booth to see J'son and C'ton talking quietly together. C'ton seemed to be doing most of the talking, which was good. It meant that J'son wasn't answering any questions and C'ton was busying his mind with other things. J'son had his chin in one hand stroking the slight stubble growing around his mouth. He was shaking his head in agreement with whatever C'ton was saying and T'mar felt a sense of saneness returning to her mind. The clothes, it seems, reduced her passion for him by offering a thread of protection between her body and his. She was more under control now and the sexual thoughts whirling around in her head were becoming more of a distraction, a daydream.

"We need to get out of the Temple immediately," C'ton said once she stepped out of the viewing booth. "I don't need to remind you of the danger involved in what we have just done. Now, all the initiates will want to explore B'el's path, to their detriment I am afraid. B'el's spells should never be made available to the initiates much less the profane. My greatest concern, though, is the very real possibility that B'el has penetrated the Temple through use of a sub-routine. It was the vibratory frequency of the lower chamber which allowed him to gain access."

"Well, what's to prevent him from taking over the whole grid?" J'son asked, showing an intense curiosity toward the whole matter.

"That's what I'm not too sure about," said T'mar. "Why would he stop at the lower levels if he had access to the entire grid? I never felt like B'el's psychic creature was trying to penetrate the power distribution network, only that he was there to keep us from seeing where he came from. The energy levels were already depleted when we were in the grid, so I'm not too sure what it was doing there other than guarding his exit."

"B'el has already taken what he needed and only left his thought creature as insurance that his backdoor would remain open it would seem."

"But we corrected the imbalance, the fluctuation. Shouldn't that have closed off the leak?" J'son asked. Suddenly, the lights in the library dimmed noticeably and the background hum of the power chamber dropped off considerably. Whatever J'son thought he and T'mar had accomplished was proving to be a short lived. The power levels were dropping fast, too fast for the grid to compensate and the brightly lit library changed back to a dull red color. Several of the view screens flickered on and off and then blanked out. Sounds of automatic doors opening and sliding closed could be heard all over the library. Strange hissing and sucking sounds erupted all around them as hermetic seals were created, sealing them inside.

"The system is trying to reboot," C'ton pointed out. "We just experienced a power drop greater than 50%. The backup sequence has been engaged. We won't be able to get out of here until power is restored or we are rescued by someone from outside. The transport tubes will be useless."

"What happened, do you think?" J'son asked, moving towards the sealed library door and trying the handle. "It's locked. What happened? Did the fluctuations return?"

"I don't think so. Do you feel a presence in the room, like someone is watching us?"

"What do you mean, C'ton? We are the only ones here." T'mar quickly jerked her head around scanning the library for anything remotely resembling another person.

"I'm not talking about being here physically. When the power dropped, I thought I detected a familiar presence, an energy manifestation that left the grid and is now free roaming. I feel like I have lost contact with the ethereal forces of nature, like I am being blocked, like someone is monitoring my thoughts. When I open myself up to the grid, I feel like we are being watched."

"I'm not too sure what you are talking about, C'ton. Everything is always being recorded. Everything we have done since passing through the wall of the gate has been documented," T'mar pointed out.

"Recorded but not monitored. Nobody should feel like someone is looking over their shoulder. I can't place it, but I'm sure I recognize the presence."

"It's C'aad," J'son said with complete confidence. "You were right, C'ton. C'aad entered the grid the moment he was removed from the Dais. That empty husk lying there on the couch is all that remains of his material life, but his consciousness has taken up residence within and without the grid."

"And you know this how?" T'mer asked, sizing up the sealed doors.

C'ton didn't say anything, just nodded his head in agreement. He knew C'aad had entered the grid but had assumed he didn't possess the wherewithal to become cognizant this early after his removal. C'ton didn't think C'aad was the one who caused the power drop, though. Instead, he feared that the power drop was caused by another source. If D'nan had taken his position up on the Dais, without the proper training he may have caused a conscious power drop by trying to integrate himself into the grid. C'aad would try to reprogram the grid to accept his energy signature as High Priest, but the grid might have responded to the unauthorized intrusion by running a protection program designed to keep everyone out of the grid by limiting access.

C'ton's main concern, if he was right, was the unbalance D'nan would cause trying to penetrate the grid without the sanctioned endorsement of the members of the Council. The power drop signified D'nan's attempt to enter the grid, but that didn't tell C'ton whether he had succeeded. If both C'aad and D'nan were in the grid at the same time, the resulting conflict could bring the grid and the Dome crashing down around them at any moment.

"We need to get out of here and away from the Temple," C'ton said. "The power struggle that will ensue is sure to cause more problems than the missing energy reserves. Our path lies elsewhere."

"They aren't missing, C'ton," J'son said. "I think we all know who took it and where it went."

"Yes, but what we don't know is why he needs so much energy and how he was able to hide the drain behind power fluctuations. But that's not our immediate concern. B'el took what he wanted and left the grid, leaving behind only a psychic impression to tell us he was there. It is not B'el, or even C'aad that worries me, but D'nan. He is too inexperienced to sit up on the Dais. If he has entered the grid by connecting himself to it, then all of us are in danger. He will have absolute control over everything and everyone confined under the Dome. You see what B'el's spells did to our consciousness, how it changed our thinking. Imagine what it would be like to have access to all the spells and the power to wield them. D'nan already doesn't like me and may see J'son as a threat to his authority. You, T'mar, represent nothing more than a sexual plaything to him. We need to get out from under the Dome and his influence before we become trapped here."

At that moment, the door to the transport tube opened with a loud hissing sound and a young Council member, followed by four Temple guards, entered the Library. The guards held long, thick, white poles with red balls on top in their right hands while their left hands reached around their backs grabbing something. Their look was tight and stressed. X's covered their faces and they were scowling at C'ton and his group. One of the guards removed his hand from behind his back and produced a weapon of some sort, pointing it at C'ton while using his pole to keep T'mer and J'son at bay.

Chapter Thirty-One:

Escape

> "The path of enlightenment lies between the split of wood, under a stone, in the way a blade of grass bends in the wind. You must master the art of perception in order to truly see."
>
> First Axiom in the annals of B'el

"We have been commanded by the High Priest to take you back to the Council Chamber," a Council member said. He was much younger than C'ton, newer to the Council. C'ton didn't recognize him and assumed he had taken his position on the Council only after C'ton had left. "The others will remain here until further notice."

C'ton had been standing next to a silent viewer when the Council member came in followed by more guards and now passed a hand over the console, activating it. The screen flickered on and a glowing search cursor blinked in the corner. C'ton moved his fingers rapidly across the keyboard and brought up a restricted file. He opened it using his backdoor and the view screen filled up with strange symbols and geometric shapes. He tapped on one of the shapes and a three-dimensional info cube appeared before him, indicating download was complete. He grabbed the cube and placed it against his forehead, where it disappeared and then turned away from the screen.

"And who gave that order?" C'ton asked.

"W-what did you do there, C'ton?" the same young Council member asked nervously. "Step away from that view screen and follow us up to the Council Chamber. D'nan, the High Priest has summoned you."

Two of the guards moved past J'son and T'mer and made their way over to the prone body of C'aad. They gently picked up his limp body and carried it between them, one of them holding his legs and the other one held him about the chest. They carried his body back to the now opened library door and entered the transport tube. Two other guards held J'son and T'mer back with their long, glowing staffs in a threatening manner. C'ton moved away from the viewer and towards the young Council member, who raised a sharp, pointed weapon upon his approach. C'ton had his arms held wide and smiled easily at his fellow Council member, moving closer.

"Stop right where you are, C'ton. You are ordered to return the memory file you just now stole from the library immediately." The Council member, C'zag, was visibly nervous and his weapon shook in his sweaty hand.

T'mar looked at C'ton, her eyes growing wide as she tried to communicate with him about what to do. She raised her hand and ran her fingers thru her hair, brushing it away from her face in a very causal but determined way. She knew T'mer could take out the guards without too much problem and that C'ton appeared to have a plan. She saw that he had taken something from the hard drive but didn't know what file he had brought up, only that he must have felt it to be important.

"Not now, T'mer," C'ton said. "We will follow our brother C'zag back to the Council Chamber and see what trouble D'nan has stirred up."

"That wouldn't be wise, C'ton," T'mar said. "You said so yourself."

"I thought we were going to get out of here," T'mer said, gritting his teeth, wanting to grab the staff out of the hand of the guard closest to him but resisted the temptation once he heard C'ton.

"Follow them into the transport tube. We will see what D'nan has in store for us," C'ton said.

The guards holding C'aad entered the transport tube, stepping to the side. The guards holding the staffs lowered them and pointed towards the open doors. J'son and T'mer moved past them and entered the transport tube, stepping towards the back. T'mar was nudged towards the door by the waving of C'zag's weapon. She walked past C'ton, looking at him with questioning eyes.

"Don't worry, T'mar. Everything will be ok," he said to her.

Everyone except C'ton and C'zag were now in the transport shaft waiting for them to enter. C'zag turned his weapon on C'ton and he spoke more forcefully now that they were alone in the library.

"Now, return whatever file you took and join the others in the transport tube."

"I don't think that will be necessary," C'ton said as he moved towards the opened transport tube, stopping just outside the door. "This file is of no concern to you. Now, T'mer."

T'mer, not really knowing what C'ton had in mind, took the opportunity that C'ton's distraction provided and grabbed the two armed guards behind the back of their heads and slammed them together, knocking them out cold. Their staffs fell out of their hands and clattered on the floor. J'son picked up the staffs and gave one to T'mer. The other one he pointed at the two guards holding C'aad, forcing them tight against the wall.

T'mar, not wanting to be bothered, took them out by punching them in the face with a left and a right, breaking their noses. They dropped the body and put their hands over their bloodied faces, crying out. Taking advantage of their unprotected mid-section, T'mar jumped up in the air and delivered a twin, flying kick to their groin. The guards folded over and fell to the floor, now cupping their manhood. Standing over them, straddling their bruised and bloodied bodies, T'mar looked at C'ton to see what he had been doing during the short assault.

C'ton had managed to make his way behind C'zag and now held him by the neck, immobile, his thumb and forefinger just under C'zag's jaw, squeezing the fleshy part of his throat. C'zag had dropped his weapon to the floor, startled at C'ton's speed and was now standing with his arms held out to his sides with a look that suggested dreaded uncertainty. C'zag had come to take C'ton into custody, but now it was he who was held captive.

"Now, C'zag," C'ton said. "Why don't you tell us what happened up there that caused the Council to send you down here."

Gagging, struggling against C'ton's tight grip on his throat, C'zag began to speak, responding more out of basic training than a show of respect. "It was D'nan. As soon as you left, he mounted the steps of the Dais and took his place on the throne sitting in the seat of the High Priest before anyone on the Council could object. Once we heard you renounce your rightful position, D'nan wasted no time in taking it for himself. The grid accepted him as the legitimate successor to the title and integrated him. That's when the power level dropped."

"That shouldn't have happened, C'zag, and you know it. The power drop was a defensive measure to counter unauthorized access. For the power to drop like it did would take a high level of volatility greater than the fluctuation caused by B'el's energy creature. A power drop that immediately recognizable wasn't caused by the elevation of D'nan to the position of High Priest. Something else was happening to cause it drop. What else did you see, C'zag?"

"D'nan took the seat and closed his eyes and for several seconds he was silent. Then he opened his eyes and we could see a glow, like sapphire, radiating out of him. He looked to be in a daze and he spoke, sounding distant and detached. He reminded me of C'aad in that one moment. Even his voice had the same inflections, a looping of the syllables that made his speech sound absurd and sing-song like."

"What did he say? What words did he use?" C'ton asked, relaxing his hold on C'zag's throat but still battling an overwhelming desire to know.

The young Council member and the four guards were moving around freely now, licking their wounds, but they didn't offer any resistance nor did they seem to mind that they had failed to apprehend C'ton and his group, actually looking somewhat relieved. It wasn't in them to question the intelligence of someone of C'ton's rank and being told what to do was much better than having to make decisions without the approval to the Council. The more C'ton kept asking questions, the more C'zag and the others felt at ease. They really didn't want to bring C'ton to the Council Chamber through the use of violent force, but had hoped he would have come along quietly. Obviously that didn't happen.

"He was smiling when his eyes were glowing and he spoke some words,

I think it was a spell, but I didn't recognize the cadence or the rhythm. Even the vibration seemed wrong. It was only after he stopped speaking that the power level dropped. I couldn't tell you what he said, only that the language was dark and left me feeling filthy, soiled, like how I feel after I visit the bed chamber. Dirty."

"He was casting a retrieval spell similar to the one we used to recall J'son's soul," C'ton said. "The only reason why D'nan, or anyone for that matter, would cast such a spell while connected to the grid would be to either commune with a High Priest that has passed, or he was made to articulate the spell by an unsettled life force."

"You're talking about C'aad, aren't you C'ton?" T'mar was leaning back against the side of the transport tube, shaking her head like she was suffering from a headache. "What D'nan did amounts to necromancy, a practice forbidden by the Council and only used during times of confusion when the path has been lost. You don't think D'nan tried to communicate with C'aad so soon after taking up his position? Why would D'nan seek the counsel of C'aad in matters relating to the function of the Council?"

"He wouldn't T'mar. I fear C'aad has done something that only B'el has tried before: Resurrection of his consciousness by possessing the body of a willing initiate to gain some advantage. In this case D'nan cast the spell in the hopes of gaining C'aad's knowledge, but I'm afraid D'nan has been deceived. Somehow C'aad was able to maintain his consciousness and used the focus of his will to trick D'nan into surrendering his will for that of C'aad's. D'nan may still be conscious trapped inside a body he no longer has ownership of, or he may be somewhere lost in the grid. I don't believe D'nan would want me to return to the Council Chamber. Only C'aad returning from the energy grid would want me placed under guard, for his own sake. Only I would know what C'aad has done. C'aad would want that knowledge hidden. Better to hide and accomplish his task unawares than trust D'nan's pathetic attempts at ruling those living under the Dome. This way, anything that goes wrong will be blamed on D'nan and not his predecessor, C'aad. The records will show that the Dome collapsed under D'nan's rule and that he was the one responsible."

"C'ton, we have to get out of here," T'mar said. "It's bad enough to think that D'nan now has control of the Council, but now you are telling us that C'aad still exists and has taken over D'nan's body, possessing it. An un-tethered soul with unlimited access to the grid is dangerous for all living under the Dome. C'ton, if what you say is true, then D'nan acting under the influence of C'aad has access to the spells of B'el. He will have access to those powers just by thinking about it. He will be able to cast a spell faster and with more accuracy than either of us. You won't be safe in the Temple."

"None of us will. What you say is true, T'mar. J'son might be spared, but you will be given over to the lower chambers and I will be locked away having to face the great dark in isolation."

"No one has ever made it through the dark in isolation. You will be destroyed!"

"I know, T'mar. That is why we have to leave now," C'ton said, sounding firm like he just made a decision. Speaking to the four guards and the young Council member, C'ton said: "You have a choice. You can either return to the Council Chamber empty handed explaining that we overpowered you and escaped, or you can remain here in the library, pretending that we knocked you out before you could apprehend us."

"I don't think that is a good idea," T'mer said, casting a suspicious eye towards C'zag. "If we let them go, the Temple guard will be alerted and prevent us from leaving. I say they don't pretend to be knocked out and I knock them out for real."

"T'mer," C'ton said, lifting his hand up in a gentle way. "They didn't do anything wrong. They are just following orders, but I agree with you. We've changed our minds. Your choice now is to have T'mer restrain you either here in the library or in the transport tube. If you stay in the tube, we will be going down, not up and I am afraid that we will have to confine you inside. Which is it?"

"C'ton, what if D'nan needs your help?" C'zag asked before he was cut off by a blow to the side of his head.

"Enough talk," T'mer said standing over the now unconscious C'zag. Then punching another guard in the face, he said, "Two down and three more to go."

The three remaining guards back peddled their way out of the transport tube, leaving C'aad's body where it lay, tripping over themselves and crashing to the floor just inside the library. C'ton kicked their feet out of the way and tapped a button on a display, closing the doors. A swooshing sound was heard and the tube dropped down several floors, stopping at the base of the Temple within moments. The doors slid opened and C'ton, T'mar, T'mer and J'son came running out even before the doors had fully opened.

"Run for the outer wall!" C'ton shouted to the group. "This way."

They rounded the base of the Temple, sure-footed on the slick black rock and followed the same path that monk had taken earlier. On the backside now, they headed in the opposite direction from the main gate, crossing over uneven ground in the open, hoping to make it to the cover of the forest located on the far side of the Temple complex. There didn't appear to be anyone pursuing them yet, but the dark glow coming from the Dome made it hard for them to distinguish anything in the shadows. Before them was nothing but a blurred, black line representing the tree-line, and behind them the Temple stood alone, stoically, the dim light streaming out from the windows, piercing the darkness like fireflies.

"They'll know we left before too long, if they don't know already," T'mer said, running beside C'ton. T'mar and J'son were out in front of them about ten feet ahead. The ground was hard under their falling feet, mostly short grass now and patches of dirt. There were no roads on this side of the Temple, only small walking paths used for meditation by the wandering monks. Worn, brown trails ran in all directions in a crisscrossing, zigzagging manner, all of them looping back around to the entrance of the Temple. They took none of these paths and cut across them, stumbling occasionally on the uneven ground.

"Not before we make it to the tree-line, I hope," T'mar said from up ahead. "Will they send the Temple guards out after us, C'ton?"

"I doubt it," he responded slightly out of breath. They were about a couple of miles away when they slowed their pace to a quick jog. "They have their own problems to worry about. They will think we won't be able to survive outside the walls of the Temple, if they understand that's where we are headed. They might send a security force to keep us from coming back but I doubt it. Only C'aad would want us back, especially J'son. I don't think D'nan will use his new position to hunt us down, if he still has any autonomy. It's C'aad we have to concern ourselves with. Resurrected within the grid like he is, he will be able to manifest in any form he desires at any time. We must be on the lookout for anything that seems out of place. I don't think we will be hunted; as long as we remain under the Dome C'aad will be able to see us. He can use the roof of the Dome like a lens. He may be looking at us at this very minute."

That thought gave J'son the shivers as he looked up at the Dome glowing dimly overhead. He tried to see the stars, to see if he recognized any constellations, but the opaqueness of the Dome blocked out their light. Electrical storms raced across the roof of the sky, illuminating different patches of the Dome. At times the electrical glow centered above them, pausing, spinning around in a sort of vortex of showers and sparks, then the storm moved off, stopping over another place and performing the same fireworks show. Was that C'aad up there searching for them?

"It's no good to be out here in the open," T'mar said as they came to a halt besides a small grouping of trees. "One lightning bolt could vaporize us."

"What if I create a transport globe?" J'son asked. "We could get to the outer wall in no time."

"J'son, don't you remember what happened to us in the cave?" T'mar reminded him. "Your abilities attract the storms. Even if you were able to create a transport globe, providing there was enough available energy to do that, the storm would lock on to your energy signature and your globe would become a focal point for power distribution. The closer we get to the outer wall, the closer we get to the side of the Dome. None of us will be able to cast or use any spell. We will be powerless until we reach the outside of the Dome, and then who knows what waits us."

But T'mar did know what awaited them because she had made this trip before. It was a wasteland with an unpleasant, noxious smell resembling sulfur; cold, hurricane force winds and small, venomous, flying insects that can cause paralyses just by touching the skin. No one could survive for long exposed to the environment outside the Dome and T'mar wondered what they were going to do once they made it to the outer wall. The way she had travelled to B'el's Castle in times past was blocked and had become sealed off after T'mer had rescued her, and as far as she knew there wasn't another way. All those who had tried to find their way to B'el's Castle by a different route perished beyond the wall and their dead, twisted bodies littered the apron on the other side, a sure sign that all who continued would face the same fate.

"Do you think you can create a transport globe to carry us some of the way?" C'ton asked with a hint of intellectual curiously.

"Would that be wise?" T'mar asked, scanning the dark for any sign that they were being followed. "We need to keep moving."

"I think so," J'son said. "C'ton, I don't think I am limited the way you are. My power reserves come from another…"

"Dimension." It was T'mer getting restless standing out in the dark with only a couple of low trees for cover. "Transport globes or not, we have to get moving again. Are you ok, C'ton?"

"Just a little winded is all. I'll be ok once we reach the main tree-line."

Chapter Thirty-Two:

Globe Transport

"We'll get zapped out of existence if that draws too much energy. You know what happens when the energy levels get too low."

T'mar uncertain of the wisdom of their actions

C'ton was looking a little pale and the slight X that normally crossed his face was now very pronounced. His face carried a look of deep contemplation and stress. He had exerted an incredible amount of energy over the last few time cycles without the opportunity to replenish his reserves and now it was starting to show. He was unsure of himself and every time he raised a question the X deepened and his mood darkened. Silently he wished J'son would create a transport globe regardless of the consequences. He doubted that the Council would waste resources tracking them down, but still there were other dangers that they would encounter lying up ahead, outside the relative safety of the Dome.

"Let me try. There is enough residual energy floating around here that it might screen out our position. I'll use the energy signature of these bushes as a source of power. If I'm right, all that will show up is the glow of a shrub blowing around in the wind. Here..."

J'son raised his hands above his head in a manner similar to a touchdown sign and then spread them out to his sides, tracing the upper arc of his transport globe in the air. He brought his hands all the way down until they were pointing at the ground and began mumbling something that sounded like "I need a globe this big."

A subtle glow flowed out from the tips of his fingers and struck the ground, illuminating the surrounding area with ten, tiny circles of light. Nodding to the group, he motioned them closer together without saying a word. The others stepped inside the small circles of light and huddled close to J'son without touching him. He turned his hands over with palms out and then brought them back over his head, clapping his hands together in a loud, smacking sound. The outline of the globe solidified and enclosed the small group within a hazy, blue-green shell barely transparent enough to see through.

The energy signature of the globe resembled that of the surrounding vegetation and blended in well with the dark, casting a gloomy shadow all around them. Without the light of the sun shining down on them, the globe looked more like a fat flowering shrub. J'son was pretty confident they wouldn't be detected. All anyone from the Temple would see is a black blob in the midst of a dark field releasing residual energy, nothing to distract them from looking for actual life forms.

"I think we will be safe from their probing eyes as long as we remain within the globe," C'ton said after a few moments of quiet. "They won't be able to see us as long as we remain close to the ground. J'son, do you think you can move the globe without raising it into the air?" Another question. "It will be difficult to control; maybe we can roll it."

Without pay too much attention to what C'ton was saying, hearing the questioning doubt coloring his voice, wondering why he sounded so bewildered and unsure of himself, J'son closed his eyes and imagined the globe rising a few inches off the ground. It didn't move as easily as it did before and J'son found himself fighting his concentration in order to keep the globe off of the ground without flying into the air. A strong wind buffeted the globe, pushing and pulling it in different directions at the same time, causing it to spin. J'son felt like a boat captain piloting his craft through rough waters.

"Where did all of this wind come from?" he asked over the noise of the wind.

"It's what happens when we leave the gravitational pull of the sun and began streaming energy out of the atmosphere," T'mar said trying to maintain her balance inside the globe. "As long as we are under the Dome we will be forced to deal with these changing conditions. We need to get to the outer wall and the cover of the tree-line before these winds rip us apart."

"Isn't it strange that we didn't notice the wind until after J'son created the globe?" C'ton asked. Every time he asked a question, the X deepened and held that position until the question had been answered to his satisfaction and then the X softened. The look disturbed the others, but they ignored it once his face relaxed, thinking it was just the stress.

"Why do you think that is?" T'mar asked.

"I'm afraid that C'aad's reach has made it out this far. I don't think he knows where we are. I think the wind kicked up as a response to the consolidation of energy J'son's globe created. As long as we allow ourselves to be carried along by the wind, I don't think he will be able to detect us. Hopefully the wind will drive us in the right direction. Do you understand, J'son? Don't steer the transport globe like before. Allow it to move freely with the wind. Make minor course corrections a little at a time. As long as we move closer to the outer wall, allow the wind to drive us."

The globe was still bobbing a few feet off of the ground, like a piece of cork caught in an eddy. J'son fought with the controls to keep the globe upright and moving in a direction heading towards the outer wall. It was hard going and he felt his energy stores straining against the strong headwind. No matter what direction J'son guided the globe he couldn't seem to avoid or counteract the power of the wind. For every foot forward, the wind seemed to push them sideways two. They were moving parallel to the tree-line and not getting any closer.

"Maybe if we rise above the wind we can make better time," T'mer said. "The curvature of the Dome will keep the wind down to a minimum up towards the top. Raise this thing up above the wind, J'son. Even if they can make a mark on us, we will be under the cover of the tree-line before they can locate us. The tree-line will break the wind once we are back on the ground."

"That will take us too close to the Dome," C'ton responded. "The way J'son attracts energy we will escape the wind only to be vaporized by a bolt of lightning. No, the best way to go is low and as straight as possible. A ball of energy floating towards the top of the Dome will bring too much attention. C'aad, or even D'nan for that matter, would try to re-absorb the globe with us in it just for the energy. Without proper authorization, all objects are subject to annihilation and re-absorption. It is the primary law of Dome production. It is imperative that we stay below the tree-line and off of the ground. Do you best J'son to keep us moving in a straight direction."

"I'm going to try something. Hang on. You might get a little dizzy." Using the wind-induced spin of the globe like a gyroscope, J'son positioned it at an angle to the wind, increasing the spin. The whirling globe buffeted the wind, glancing off of it at an extreme angle. Like wind caught up in a sail, J'son was able to use the centrifugal force of the spinning globe to push them over the ground and headed in the right direction. He angled the globe in such a way that the harder the wind blew against them, the faster it spun, and the faster it spun, the faster they moved forward. The globe was almost impossible to steer. Only by keeping his sight fixed on a point on the floor was J'son able to keep from getting motion sickness.

"If we... don't... get there soon," T'mer said, pausing between syllables to swallow the bile rising up his throat. "I'm going to blow chunks. Burp."

The spinning increased to the point where they couldn't speak anymore, the whirling globe taking all of the air out of their lungs. They were making headway, though, and the tree-line rose up before them, a dark, wooly, vague shadow that increased in height until it blocked out all signs of the Dome. The going was nauseating and they all had vertigo. J'son was just about to be sick when they approached the trees.

The wind was dying down and the globe slowed its spin, hovering above the ground a few yards away from the first grouping of trees. The spinning slowed to a stop, and after regaining their equilibrium J'son sat the globe down hard, misjudging the distance and hitting the ground with a hard thump.

"Sorry. I'm about to collapse the globe," J'son said. "Watch out for the flying debris." Small sticks and furry leaves smacked up against the outside of the globe, impacting the globe and sizzling out of existence upon contact.

"I'm as ready as I will ever be," T'mar said. Then, "C'ton, are you ok?"

"I'm fine. I just need to catch my breath and recharge. Go ahead and collapse the globe, J'son. I'm having a hard time keeping focus, but that's probably because of the spinning. Get me on solid ground and I will be fine."

J'son raised his hands above his head again, clapping them and then brought them down to his sides, mumbling something that sounded like, "Go away!" His fingers were pointing straight down and the radiance of the globe seemed to crawl back into his fingers where it was re-absorbed. The globe disappeared as quickly as it was created and the four of them found themselves standing out in the open trying unsuccessfully to shield their faces from the flying debris.

"C'mon," T'mer said, racing towards the cover of the trees.

They covered the short distance to the trees within seconds. T'mer and J'son were in the lead as T'mar helped C'ton along by wrapping her arm around his waist and practically dragging him. A lightning storm developed over head, swirling in a counter-clockwise direction. An opening appeared in the center of the storm revealing a gaping void that seemed to go on forever. The opening collapsed in a thunder of noise like the slamming of a great door only to open back up before the echo faded, releasing a bolt of lightning and sending it down towards the small party.

"Look out!" T'mer saw the lightning before the others and leaving the cover of the trees he ran out, diving towards T'mar and C'ton, knocking them over and covering their proportionally smaller bodies with his. The lightning struck the ground in a fiery blast, barely missing the three of them, leaving a sizeable crater in the ground a few feet away. Scrambling to his feet T'mer picked up C'ton around the waist and carried him away quickly, depositing him under a large, old tree besides J'son before looking to see if T'mar had made it under cover.

They were now protected from direct exposure to the storm, but the electricity in the air was palpable, causing the hair on their arms and neck to stand out. Tiny balls of electricity popped all around them, biting them like gnats whenever their bodies touched. The discharges stung like the jolt one gets on a dry, cold winter day. It was more annoying than painful and they kept their distance to lessen the shock.

"We're getting close to the outer wall," C'ton said, sounding indifferent and slightly depressed. "It will be hard to make it to the other side. All of this electrical activity will act like a barrier preventing us from crossing the border. Do you still think the way is open to us, T'mar?"

"I don't know about the way out, but the way back was closed off after I… escaped. The cave may still exist, but the passageway may prove to be impassable. We will need the help of the Dome-dwellers. Somehow they have managed to survive the elements by living within the sight of the outer wall. They would know if the way is still blocked."

"Those people are crazy," T'mer replied angrily. He was extremely frustrated and was starting to wonder why he was here in the first place. "T'mar, the 'dods left their minds behind in the Temple and now they live as nomads, avoiding all contact with the Temple. They won't help us. In fact, more than likely they will try to capture us. J'son should be advised against using whatever tricks he has learned from you wizards and maintain a low profile. If the Dome-dwellers find out about his abilities, we may end up in a worse situation than the one in the Temple."

"Don't worry about that, T'mer," C'ton said. "I have spent some time with them in the past and they aren't as nutty as their reputation implies. They possess abilities that would surprise most of those on the Council. Living so close to the Dome has changed their chemical and electrical makeup; it has changed their energy signature."

"They may be watching us right now," T'mar said.

"They wouldn't be out here in this storm, would they C'ton?" J'son asked.

"That depends. It was you who brought the storm. They may come out to investigate. Of course, they may already know we are here. It is my guess that we aren't the first travelers to come this way. Our situation may already be known." C'ton was breathing heavily but his color was coming back. He still looked fatigued and the lines crossing his face were very intense and intimidating. He tried smiling as he spoke, but his thoughts were dominated by an endless stream of questions all demanding answers. The constant barrage of questions, like an interrogation, clouded his thinking, allowing doubt to confuse his thoughts.

"What do you mean?" T'mar asked in a distracted tone. She was pulling furry leaves off of the lower hanging branches of the nearest tree, collecting an armload and then handed them over to J'son, purposefully avoiding looking below his waist. She had been trying unsuccessfully to ignore his hanging member since casting that spell back in the library, but any void in her thinking was rapidly filled by thoughts of sex. She continued to pull down more of the vegetation, dropping it to the ground without thinking how much she was getting.

"I don't think I need this much material just for a tunic," T'mer said, kicking the large pile of multi-hued, furry leaves out from under his feet.

"The monk that ran behind the Temple when we first got here; did he look familiar to you, T'mar?"

"I'm not too sure," she responded, sounding defensive, thinking the others knew what she had been thinking. Her words came out quick and severe, like she was being asked to explain herself. She was caught off guard by C'ton's question because she had been watching J'son lustfully as he fitted the material around his waist, attaching it on the side. She heard his question, but her mind rejected the intrusion, having nothing to do with her simmering lust. "I mean, I thought I did when I first saw him. He reminded me of someone I knew long ago."

"If I'm right," C'ton continued, "that was one of B'el's disciples. I think I recognized his energy signature from before. It's been known that B'el's agents have infiltrated the ranks of the hierarchy, but for one of them to break their cover could only mean that he had information, meaning us, which would prove to be useful for B'el. I'm sure our presence here is known and B'el will be expecting us. I wonder how he will receive us."

The sky lit up in the distance a dull red, the storm having moved off. C'ton looked intently at the shadows between the trees, searching for any signs of movement. He dressed slowly, covering his private parts behind a thigh-length tunic and covering his chest with a thick shawl that crossed over his shoulders and fell to his waist. He was starting to shiver against the blowing chill and he wrapped his arms across his chest, trying his best to hold in the heat. It would get colder than this once they were outside the Dome and C'ton was having doubts whether or not he would be strong enough to make the trip. The prospect disturbed him, making him anxious, a feeling he hadn't felt in an age, and he contemplated other alternatives, other paths they might choose.

The info cube was still embedded in his forehead and he reached up to pull it out, hiding his action from the others. The cube, the size of a die, was inert and he closed his hand around it, looking about to see if he was being observed. He had hoped that by removing the cube his doubts and insecurities would subside and he slipped it between the folds of his tunic, close to his heart.

"If that's true," J'son said, flattening his tunic and then placing his hands on his hips, his smaller but well-defined, chiseled chest protruding out in front. "Then wouldn't that suggest the way to B'el's Castle is open? How could B'el have agents in the Temple if they didn't have a way out and back? Maybe B'el's energy creature can travel back and forth over long distances using the grid, but I can tell you from first-hand experience that travelling that way isn't for those whose thoughts are bound to a materialistic worldview."

"That's true," C'ton said, turning around to face the others. "When I saw B'el's agent making his way around the backside of the Temple, I thought that maybe the way had been opened after all this time. We must locate the entrance to the cave of 'loh and then decide what we must do. If luck is on our side, those dwelling near the outer wall will either help us or leave us alone. I don't think they will be interested in capturing us. They try to avoid contact with monks at all cost. My guess is that they will monitor us from a distance to see what it is we are up to, but that is all. Come! Let's get moving while the storm is away. I think we can make it to that hollow within the trees without attracting too much attention."

Without another word, C'ton took the lead and raced away from the cover of the old tree and made a bee-line through a natural opening in the undergrowth, a path used repeatedly by the indigenous life-forms inhabiting the area by the outer wall. He followed the path until it rounded a small hill at which point C'ton disappeared from the sight of the others.

"Wait a minute!" J'son chased after the old wizard and disappeared like C'ton behind the small hill.

T'mar and T'mer looked at each other for confirmation and then followed after them. They rounded the same small hill and almost stumbled down the steep incline the path made, falling forward and tripping over their own feet trying to slow their descent. T'mer jammed his toe against a large rock embedded at the bottom of the hill, striking it hard and splitting his nail, drawing blood. T'mar was too close behind him and ran into his back, her breasts pressing against his shoulder blades, providing minimal cushioning against the impact.

The two of them stood there front to back collecting themselves, allowing their eyes to adjust to the deepening dark. Scanning the area for the other two, they saw C'ton bending over at the waist gasping for air while J'son was standing beside him with his hand on C'ton's back. They had made it this far but none of them really knew what direction they should take. For the first time since entering the gate of the Temple, the four of them were at a complete loss as to what to do.

Chapter Thirty-Three:

Sand Trap

"It funny the things you remember once in a familiar place. I haven't thoughts of these things since before I left the Order."

C'ton remembering a time before T'mar left him

"I think I can remember the way to the cave if we get to the Dome," T'mar said after a few moments of silence. "A small chain of mountains separates this side of the Dome with the Wastelands. We can follow the curve of the Dome until we find the right mountain. The entrance is hidden behind the fold of two arms. I only hope we don't get lost in the dark. But even if the way is still open, once we enter we will only have the dark for a companion. The only light we will see outside the Dome will be the creepy radiance of B'el's Castle."

"C'ton, are you ok?" J'son asked, helping C'ton to stand erect. "You don't look so good. Your color is almost grey and your face… Well, you look scary."

"I'm sorry, my friends. I'm just winded and the trees in this forest are packed tightly together. It's hard to get a breath of fresh air."

"C'ton, you were breathing like that when we were out in the open. I've never seen you like this. What's going on?" T'mar, looking at C'ton really for the first time since leaving the Temple, noticed how deep the X penetrated his face. She saw him trying to smile, but it was obvious to her that he was struggling. Avoiding sexually stimulating thoughts was hard for her, but she guessed avoiding all questions was even harder. How could one think without asking questions?

"I over-exerted myself in all of the excitement. I haven't been able to replenish my energy stores, and with the light of the sun almost fully extinguished it is getting harder for me to maintain my energy levels. Hopefully, we will chance upon an energy conduit where we can all recharge. They are closer to the surface near the outer wall. Maybe the one that was located in the cave of 'loh is still available. Maybe there we can renew our energy reserves."

The hill they were standing behind offered a zone of relative peace and quiet enough to talk without having to shout. In the dark, in the distance, as their eyes continued to adjust to the increasing dimness, they could see what looked like light-forms dancing between the trees, shadows that emitted radiation in the infra-red end of the spectrum giving off a crimson glow. They looked like fireflies grouping together, flickering on and off as they moved behind the trees. They lacked any clear shape or definition, playing tricks on the eyes of those watching them. The four companions were each staring at the strange display of red dancing light when the lights flicked off and stayed off. The four of them listened intently for any perceivable sound coming from the direction of the lights, but the only sound they could hear was the strained breathing of C'ton as he sucked air into his lungs.

"Those are light mites, C'ton said between breaths."They are microscopic energy projections which feed off of the residual radiation coming off of the Dome. They have a tendency to congregate around energy bleeds. That's the direction we need to go."

"You mean that's the outer wall?" J'son leaned into the dark like he was trying to discern the curvature of the Dome. The lights didn't come back, but the afterglow made focusing on any one point extremely difficult.

"I don't like just standing here, " T'mer said showing agitation at just standing around. "We may be protected from the wind and cold here, but we need to get deeper into the forest before we are seen. "If that's the way you want to go, then the sooner we head in that direction the better. Come on."

T'mer took off in the direction of the phantom lights, plowing through the underbrush and making a path for them to follow. C'ton was the next to go, taking a deep breath and pushing forward, putting his arms up in front of his face to protect it from the broken and hanging branches that T'mer left in his wake. J'son and T'mar brought up the rear, stepping lightly on the new-made path to avoid snapping any more branches and making any more unnecessary noise. The four of them still felt like they were being watched, but unlike T'mar and J'son who were trying to be quiet T'mer was making his passage through the forest known to whomever would listen.

T'mer became lost to the dark, but the others could still hear him crashing around, stepping on fallen branches, cracking them, and rushing sounds. C'ton, who had taken the second position behind T'mer, had fallen back and was now struggling to keep his feet moving in a forward direction. T'mar caught up to him and was now walking next to him. She put her arm around the old wizard, trying to comfort him, not really knowing what to do for her old teacher. J'son had moved past them and was doing everything he could to keep up with T'mer. J'son imagined the thorns and briars he saw lying broken on the ground digging and cutting into T'mer's flesh as he passed.

The party was now separated: T'mer was somewhere up front crashing around; J'son was by himself following by sound alone, occasionally leaving the path T'mer was making by mistake and finding himself caught in a briar patch. C'ton and T'mar brought up the rear, but they were falling further and further behind.

The wind wasn't as heavy here deep within the forest, but the blowing made strange sounds as it raced through the trees and around the large stones found littered all over the place. It was obvious the stones had been here long before the trees as the latter grew up and around them, some of the trees growing out of splits in the rocks. The random dispersion of rock and stone gave them the impression that a massive boulder, possibly a comet, had exploded over the area before the Dome had been installed and fell haphazardly to the ground. The stones had a burnt-like odor to them, although that was hard to see in the dark.

In times past, monks of all levels would make the journey to the outer wall for the solitude and a tangible reminder of what the Dome represented. C'ton had passed this way before, approaching the Dome from the north and making his way south following the eastward curvature of the Dome. He had climbed the mountains and stood at the summit, gazing out across the Wastelands on the other side of the Dome. Nothing but a hostile environment greeted him and he remembered, as he walked, how he had wanted to brave the climate of the Wastelands and make the trek to B'el's Castle. But that was a long time ago when communication with B'el was still open and the secrets he had to teach weren't regarded as heresy.

C'ton didn't make the journey then. Something had warned him against going, a growing uneasiness that he couldn't shake. He came down out of the mountain, by-passing the cave of 'loh and continued his way around the curve of the Dome, making his way back to where he started, close to the City. It was during that trip, he now recalled, that he first met T'mar, hiding in the brushes just outside the main gate to the City, on the road that would take them to the Temple. C'ton tried to keep his thoughts focused on the memory, reliving the experience, not having to question himself about where they were intending to go.

For the moment, and for the next few micro-cycles, C'ton's mind was at rest and he smiled to himself remembering the times and adventures he and T'mar had had. Those were good times and the memory softened the X crossing his face. He fell in love with her then, or what makes for love with a wizard. She was just a child and he remembered wrestling with himself over whether or not he should sleep with her. It was expected, especially amongst lone travelers, to partake of the female wherever she may be found and C'ton had had several sexual partners before meeting T'mar. But she was different and he avoided physical contact with her until much later.

In fact, it was T'mar that came on to C'ton, something unheard of coming from a female. She made the decision for him when she had asked him why he didn't enjoy himself with her. She had told him that she felt unwanted and ashamed that a monk of the Temple didn't want to sleep with her. She asked him what was wrong with her that he rejected her body. It was the look in her eye, the accusatory and yet innocent look that told him he better do his duty or risk her leaving him and joining up with another monk looking for sexual gratification.

That query, he remembered, was the first time they shared each other's bodies and C'ton drank deep of her beauty, doing what was unwise for a monk to do. He fell in love with her then, and a part of him now chimed up to remind him that he still loved her like a man should love a woman, not as a sexual plaything only kept around to satisfy his needs. He jealously guarded his relationship with her, even at first preventing other members of the Council from partaking of her fruits. All women were meant to be shared and C'ton's refusal to allow her to be taken and used by the members of the Council brought severe reprisals and condemnation from the hierarchy, the first of many official reprimands.

"I can see a background glow coming from somewhere up ahead," T'mar said, still with her arm around his shoulders. "That's going to be the residual blush of the Dome as it releases its energy into the atmosphere. We are getting close to the outer wall. The tree-line stops before the mountain range and opens up to a dusty area full of pits and sand traps. Very dangerous!"

C'ton smiled up at her, leaning over as he was. The memories he had been reliving brought lightness to his expression and the x softened away almost completely. Hearing her voice after the silence of the dark made him smile brighter and he continued to look at her, his countenance changing to that of a man in the throes of romantic love, a foreign concept here on the Planet of the Elohim.

"Yes," he said. "But the sand traps won't be as difficult for those who have made the trip before and know about the dangers."

"But I never made the journey in the dark, C'ton. There is only a very small path that takes us through the sand and I fear we might miss it. C'ton, we need to catch up with J'son and T'mer before they enter the sand. T'mer gets so hardheaded at times that I fear he might continue towards the mountains without waiting for us. That would be dangerous for all of us. We need him."

"I know. Come then. Let's pick up our pace and cut the distance. I believe T'mer will wait for a short while before venturing across the sand. We both know how impatient he is."

With that, C'ton took off at almost a sprint, weaving in and out of the briars and ducking under the low-hanging, broken branches that stuck out at all angles. He seemed possessed with a youthful agility that T'mar hadn't seen since they made their escape from the Temple. He seemed full of life and vigor now, a look that T'mar liked and it reminded her of their time together. She missed that time they had spent together.

The background radiation of the Dome became easier to see as the trees thinned out and a small mountain ridge could be detected in the distance. A jagged, fiery red line traced its way across the horizon outlining the mountain and showing the Dome's connection to the rock. By climbing the mountain pass, as C'ton and others had done, one had the opportunity to come within feet of the Dome, to almost touch it, something that was not only forbidden, but deadly. Standing in the radiance of the Dome at full power brought immediate disintegration. Only during times of low power needs, like when the planet returned to her sun, was it safe to journey that close to the Dome termination point. At all other times the energy output was too intense.

To say that the Dome terminated at the top of the mountain range, as it appeared to, would be a wrong assumption, and many who have lodged in the smaller caves and tunnels littering the top of the mountain like a maze found themselves living too near the Dome and they suffered for their error. The Dome penetrated the solid rock down to a depth almost equal the height of the mountain down to the bedrock. Even if someone could carve out a tunnel directly through the mountain they would encounter an impenetrable barrier emerging out of and blending with the rock. The depth of the Dome was pre-planned in order to completely seal off those living under the protection of the Dome from the harmful effects of the Wastelands.

The cave of 'loh was discovered, or as some have suggested, created shortly after the Dome went up. The entrance was hidden and buried under fallen rocks that contained an unusually high level of a quartz-like substance. This substance, an element coveted and used by the monks to focus their thoughts when casting a spell, has the ability to deflect the Dome's energy signature back on itself and re-direct it. Because the entrance contained such a high level of this material a cavern was created that allowed one to pass under the Dome and out to the other side. That was before the way had been sealed off. This is the way that T'mar took when she answered B'el's call. She was able to make the trip to B'el's Castle underground, avoiding the noxious, sulfur-like fumes that dominate the Wastelands.

There was only one point where one had to leave the safety of the tunnels and continue the journey above ground. Only those who had reached a certain ability level could generate a protective shield powerful enough that would hold long enough to get them into the Castle. All others perished, either living out the rest of their lives huddled around the exit, too afraid to venture out, dying due to exposure, or they dragged themselves away from the exit, broken and defeated, never making it back to the Temple and dying along the way, littering the passageways with their skeletal remains.

T'mar remembered the day the exit was sealed off, preventing passage either way. T'mer had just rescued her and they were making their way across the Wastelands, desperately trying to locate the opening that led underground. Their energy bubble, created by T'mar using occult devices, was almost spent and T'mer had been showing signs of contamination and radiation sickness. His energy reserves were too low, drained from the battle and eventual escape, and T'mar remembered with a shutter and shame that she almost left him there, to die, even after he had liberated her.

Her thinking back then had been warped and selfish and her only motivation at the time was to regain her freedom and practice what she had been taught. Her escape was proof that she was ready to take her place among the members of the Council and the nagging thought that B'el had let them go evaporated as her arrogant mind convinced her that she had escaped based on her own intelligence and shrewdness. She hid from the world then, changing her appearance and waited for the appropriate time to reappear.

An explosion occurred shortly after she and T'mer had entered the tunnel on the other side of the Dome, managing their escape but sealing off that portion of the tunnel and blocking passage. It was said that she had been the last to travel that way and her betrayal had so angered B'el that he vowed to never take on another apprentice. Since that time, rumors had run stating that another way had opened up and B'el was training monks to take up positions on the Council.

It was known by the Council that at least one, if not more, members might be double agents for B'el, but it was too hard to discern the mind of a monk simply by looking at him. Instead, the Council tolerated the supposed infiltration and waited for the spy to make his move. He never did, and until just recently all thought about the possibility of a mole was forgotten. It was only when C'ton saw the monk running around the back side of the Temple that the idea of a spy returned.

T'mar and C'ton came out of the forest and paused, coming up to the edge of a sandy expanse. Wild grasses grew up sporadically in small groups, coloring the dull, burnt yellow sand with patches of dull, overcooked green. The wind had completely died down on this side of the forest and the sandy ground lying before them was devoid of any imperfections, looking more like scorched glass than a beach. Their feet made slight impressions in the sand, feeling more like they were stepping on rock. The sound of their footfalls was more like a slapping as it echoed away from them and bounced off of the mountains in the distance.

T'mer and J'son had walked a short distance out onto the sand and were standing fully out in the open, talking to each other while they waited for the others to catch up. Although the wind was non-existent, the air was chill and getting colder, falling down on them from above. The material T'mar had collected for their clothes wasn't going to be enough to keep the cold away and J'son was asking T'mer if they should collect more furry vegetation from the rapidly sparse trees existing near the sand.

"If the temperature keeps dropping, we will need more clothing. Will the cave be any warmer?"

"How am I supposed to know," T'mer responded angrily, not liking where they were or where they intended to go, especially being out in the open. Because of the size of his upper body and torso and its ability to create massive amounts of body heat, T'mer wasn't as affected by the temperature drop as J'son and basically ignored J'son's call to get more covering. Instead, T'mer was scanning the area right before them for any sign of danger, looking at the sand beneath them and the straggly green-brown grass. It was only when C'ton and T'mar came up out of the forest, pausing at the sand line that he turned around and seemed to take interest in the needs of those around him.

"C'ton, you and T'mar might want to grab more material. The temperature is dropping and J'son says he's cold. I'm going on. The mountain isn't getting any closer."

Before anyone could respond, T'mer took one step forward, stepping on top of a patch of grass and he felt the ground give way. The sand was softer, less compacted where the grass grew and he sunk up to his ankle in the mushy soil; and the more he tried to free his foot the deeper his leg slipped into the sand.

"T'mer! Watch where you are going," T'mar called out to him. "This entire, sandy apron surrounding the mountain is one large death trap. The depth of the sand has never been discovered. One wrong step and you could find yourself buried up to your neck."

J'son had moved over to T'mer and he attempted to help him free his leg, being careful to avoid that particular patch of sand T'mer had just stepped on. It was like pulling a stick out of mud and J'son's efforts only managed to produce slurping, sucking sounds while driving T'mer's leg deeper into the sand. T'mar came up behind them and wrapped her arms around T'mer's waist, trying her best to power lift him out of the quicksand. J'son was kneeling down by T'mer's leg and had his fingers of one hand tightly wrapped around his lower thigh, just above his knee while the other hand dug around in the sand by his foot. They pulled at the same time, T'mer digging the heel of his free foot into a shallow depression in the ground for leverage.

"Sluck, squish, pop!" were the sounds made as they tried in vain to free T'mer's leg from the vise-like suction of the sand. There was a secret to removing your leg once it was stuck and that entailed doing the exact opposite of what common sense told you. The more they pulled up on the leg, the deeper and tighter stuck his leg seemed to get.

When T'mer first stepped on the patch of grass, only his foot got stuck, but now with the help of J'son and T'mar his leg was buried passed his knee. It was hard for him to stand erect and as he lost his balance he plunged his stuck leg deeper into the sand. Falling over, T'mer reached out with his hands to keep him from landing on his face, only to have his hands sink into the sand up to his elbows. Now T'mer had both hands and one leg embedded in the sand, trapped. He looked like he was trying to do a pushup, holding his upper body up and away from the sand, but he only managed to sink in deeper. T'mer was now practically lying prone on the shifting ground with his face just inches above the sand and he was sinking fast.

"C'ton! Help us. Please."

"J'son," C'ton began. "Stand on the right side of the grass, assuming the mountain as forward. The grasses need rock to anchor their root system, but can only grow in loose sand. You will need to pull T'mer out from your left. Here, let me show you." C'ton covered the short distance in a moment, walking deliberately on the right side of the various grasses growing beyond the tree-line. His foot slipped once and his big toe sunk into the sand, burying the nail, but instead of pulling it out like T'mer had, C'ton plunged his toes and his foot deeper into the sand.

Hitting up against something hard lying just below the surface, more than likely a rock, C'ton used that anchor to push up instead of pulling. His foot, covered with sand and a mucus-like substance, emerged from the sand with a slipping sound. He held his foot aloft, wiggling his toes to get the sand out from between them. Planting it back down on a hard spot to the right of a grassy patch, C'ton looked at the group struggling with T'mer's leg and arms and said: "Just like that."

"So I should just push his leg deeper into the sand?" J'son asked incredulously, still lying next to T'mer with his hands buried up to his wrists. "That doesn't make sense."

"He's right, J'son," T'mar said, releasing her grip on T'mer's waist and allowing him to sink down slightly. "I'm going to push down on his shoulders and when I do, I want you to yank up on his leg at the same time. Just relax, T'mer. Don't you try pushing or pulling. Just let the sand take you down for a moment."

C'ton had freed himself and made his way over to the group, marking his steps. He was hunched over at the waist and walked like an old man, shuffling his feet and occasionally poking his foot at the sand to test for solidity. Reaching the group, C'ton grabbed T'mer's forearms, allowing them to sink deeper into the sand as T'mar pushed. Then, just as the sinking slowed and before it stopped, J'son and C'ton pulled up quickly on their individual body parts, freeing first the leg and then the two arms, which came out with a loud "slurrrrrrp!"

T'mer fell over on his back in response and then bounced up into a sitting position. His leg and arms were freed from the sand and he wiped the debris away in a rough manner. The tiny, glass-like particles of sand were embedded in the hair on his arms and leg and it frustrated him that he couldn't get rid of it. The wiping motion scraped his arms raw as the sand particles bit into his flesh and burrowed into his skin. The sand was ice cold, numbing his arms and leg, feeling like he had lain on then funny. He tried to stand up, but needles of pain raced up his leg as soon as he put weight on it. He fell back down on his rump with an audible thud, throwing his arms behind him to break the fall. Pain raced up his arms like an electrical shock and he shouted out loud his displeasure.

"Damn, that hurts," he said, lying on his back with his arms across his chest.

"It will pass soon enough," C'ton said. "You need to get up and move around. That will get the poison moving. Right now it is concentrated in your arms and leg. Just walk in circles until you begin to feel them again. But stay on this side of the grass. It seems pretty solid here."

T'mer stood up on his own, throwing off J'son and T'mar's help with a shrug and steady himself on his one good leg and the wobbly other one. "How are we supposed to cross the sand to get to the mountain if we don't know where to step? T'mar, I don't remember this sand from before. How did we get back across the sand once we made it out of the cave?"

"We didn't come this way after leaving. We came out north of here and separated once the City came into view. You wanted to continue into the City, but I left you on the trail. I'm sorry for that." She didn't leave him to die in the Wastelands, but she did leave him once they made it back to civilization. It was after leaving him that she changed her looks and disappeared out of his life. She didn't know it at the time, but T'mer followed after her for several cycles, trying to find her again, failing and finally giving up all hope of seeing her again. "This way was deemed too dangerous, too open. We would have gotten captured if we came this way before."

"We will be okay," C'ton said, "as long as we stay to the right of the grass going in. They grow around rock, but the area immediately surrounding the grass could be several yards deep, maybe more. This place used to be an opened hole at the base of the mountain. There were lakes and animals and every kind of green and living thing. Once B'el left the Temple to set up his Castle in the Wastelands he came this way and created a trap for all those who tried to follow him. It is said that the sand is the powdered remnants of those who did follow him. It is said that these sands are possessed by the spirits of the dead."

"But why would anyone want to follow him?" J'son asked. "All I've heard since arriving here is talk about how evil and powerful he is and how he holds heretical secrets to the mysteries of this place. Why would anyone want to follow him if there wasn't at least a 50/50 chance of survival? How could all of this sand be the skeletal remains of those who followed him? For what reason?"

T'mar's head was down, a look of shame crossing her face turning her cheeks bright red. She had followed him like so many others, but unlike the others she was able to make it to his Castle using all of her training as a guide. Her sole focus was on physical and spiritual survival then and that was the only thing that kept her on her course, through all the dangers and deceptions. She knew, though, only after arriving at his Castle that what she went through was necessary in order to open her up to the secret teachings of B'el.

By the time she reached his Castle, she was extremely self-centered, defiant and hostile, and more than a little introverted. She rarely spoke once she entered his Castle, fearing her thoughts would betray her. She had reached the end of her quest only to discover that her torment was about to begin. She had a moment of doubt then, but dismissed it as being an inferior emotion not necessary for her further growth. She regulated that doubt to the dark recesses of her mind and had forgotten it until that very moment. J'son had asked why anyone would venture across the planet to face certain death and she was too ashamed to give him an answer.

She had an answer once, long ago, but now that answer seemed too condescending, too conceited and full of self-importance. In her mind she heard B'el's voice speaking to her, lifting her sense of self above and beyond her fellow travelers, making her think of herself as better that the others, even better than C'ton. She shook her head to clear out the voice and the accompanying feelings, but she became confused as to whether the voice in her head was a memory of before or something new. The teachings seemed right, but they also seemed new, like he was standing there speaking to her. The effect caused her to look behind her and then forward into the distance, seeing the top of the mountain ridge blending in with the cold of the Wastelands on the other side of the Dome.

"C'ton, I…"

"What is it, T'mar? Are you okay?"

"Yeah. I just thought I heard someone speaking to me. It was just a long lost memory jarring thoughts from before."

"Are you sure that's what it is?" C'ton was quiet now, looking at T'mar, trying to read her thoughts like he used to do. He didn't like that she was hearing voices. It was one thing to take the sounds of the wind and make a conversation out of it, and an entirely different matter to imagine voices in your head. But she had said she thought she heard someone talking to her. A strong memory could make one believe they were back in the past, but he didn't think that was what it was. He knew the closer they got to the mountain range and the Wastelands beyond the more likely hidden memories and, more forbiddingly, hidden teachings would come to conscious recollection.

To know the power of B'el's teachings was different than actually hearing them. C'ton had a lifetime of knowledge swirling around in his head, but he rarely entered that mental space which allowed the formation of spells. You could know the proper spell to cast in times of practice, but to hear those spells verbalized within one's own mind was one step away from casting them. If T'mar couldn't control her thoughts to keep her mind clean and clear, C'ton feared that the enemy might become a member of their own party.

Chapter Thirty-Four:

Another Secret

"Trial and error is the pre-requisite for formulating proper spells. True perception comes only after one believes in the reality of the imaginary. It is in that mind-space that worlds are created and destroyed. Belief, then practice will reinforce your perceptions. Believe that you will make it and you will. To doubt is to murder the reality of your mind."

Dome-dweller giving advice to J'son

The four of them made their way across the sand, walking to the right of the grasses with C'ton leading the way. Their going was slow but safe. C'ton's growing feebleness and mental instability caused the group to move slower than T'mer and T'mar would have liked, but at least they were all still vertical and moving forward. The grasses began to grow more sporadically and the space between each clump grew wider. Now, instead of winding their way around the grassy patches, each member of the group had to pause at the last clump of grass and jump to the next one, hoping to land on solid ground. The space between each clump grew increasingly wider to the point that C'ton was having a hard time closing the gap.

"C'ton? Are you ok?" J'son asked. He was right behind C'ton, sharing the same clump of grass, waiting for C'ton to hop over to the next grassy patch. T'mar and T'mer were behind them standing on their own clumps of grass, also waiting for C'ton to move so they could take his spot and keep moving.

"I don't care if I don't see anyone watching or not," T'mer said, sounding sarcastic and irritated. "We need to keep moving. I don't want to make it across only to be ambushed by the Dome-dwellers. We're too vulnerable out here in the open."

Rivulets of blood from the sand ran down T'mer's legs and one of his arms and he sucked in air between his teeth holding back the searing pain every time he inadvertently touched his arm or legs. He was bring up the rear and was consciously aware that he, right now, was their greatest liability. C'ton may be slowing them down, but the smell of his own blood filling his nostrils was a constant reminder that even if they weren't being watched, their presence was known by every predator downwind of them. Even the tiny sand creatures that made their home just below the sand had managed to make their way to the surface and were crawling their way towards him. The small pool of blood gathering under his feet was attracting them and he knew if he stood in one spot for too long the creatures would find him and begin to penetrate his skin.

Crushing some of the bugs under his feet as he alternated back and forth from one leg to the other, not too sure how much solid ground he had to work with, T'mer looked up from the wiggling, animated sand and hollered out: "We have to keep moving!"

"He's right, C'ton. Can you continue?" T'mar was dealing with her own set of problems, most notably the increasingly familiar background voice that she kept hearing. The voice came from a place within her that she recognized and was habitually accustomed to visiting, but it was working through her lust circuit, creating sexual impressions that were hard to ignore.

Her mind was filled with thoughts of sex and every blade of grass that rose up before her reminded her of an erect phallus. As the wind twirled around the open sandy desert, it kicked up tiny dust vortexes that reminded her of ejaculation and the release of seminal fluid. It was these thoughts, and the assorted images formed around these thoughts, that were the origin and source of all occult power, according to the teaching of B'el. B'el, she thought, would be delighted to know that his teachings were still having that effect on her.

J'son for his part was more concerned about C'ton's welfare than their current situation. C'ton didn't look right and J'son could almost feel the anxiety coming off of him. His burden, whatever it was, made C'ton look like an old man suffering the pangs of advanced maturity. J'son, standing right next to him on their tiny clump of grass, put his hand on his bent shoulder in a show of reassurance and support. The feel of his hand on C'ton boney shoulder brought a shudder over J'son's body as he realized the physical fragility of this particular monk. If C'ton didn't have the physical strength to continue on his own, J'son wondered if T'mer would be able to carry him and jump from clump to clump at the same time. They were almost half way to the mountain, and looking ahead he saw the distances between clumps were getting wider. If C'ton couldn't make the next distance, he surely couldn't make the one after that.

"T'mar, I think we need T'mer up here. I don't think C'ton can make it to the next patch."

"I'm fine. I just need to rest a little."

"No, you're not. T'mer, get up here!"

"Just get out of the way and I will carry him. I'm tired of just standing here." With that, T'mer hopped past T'mar, stepping on her clump of grass and landed on unsteady, wobbly legs on top of a smaller patch directly between T'mar and J'son. He almost lost his balance, pin-wheeling his arms in the air as he landed but regained it by bending over at the waist, placing his hands on his knees. "Alright kid. That patch isn't going to be big enough for the three of us. You'll need to jump this way as I jump that way. Ready?"

"T'mer, please be careful. You don't want to knock C'ton into the sand. He won't be able to support your weight if you lose balance."

"No, I'm fine. See. I can make the next jump now." C'ton stood up straight, cracking his spine by placing his hands in the small of his back. "It's just a little jump. I don't need anyone to carry me."

"C'ton, wait a minute," J'son said, but too late. C'ton dove forward, leaping into the air like a man diving into a pool of water, arms out in front. J'son tried to tighten his grip on the old monk, but his grasp slipped, causing C'ton to veer off at a funny angle. He wasn't going to land on the next patch of grass where he intended and J'son called out to him in a state of fright.

"C'ton!"

"Look out!" T'mer said, as he jumped off from his patch of grass, landing on the patch of grass J'son was standing on with one bloody leg and then bounding off of that one and stretching out to grab C'ton in mid air. He managed to snatch C'ton's tunic, altering his path slightly and nudging him back towards the next patch of grass. They both landed safely, standing chest to chest with their arms wrapped tightly around each other, waiting for their forward momentum to subside. T'mer slowly pulled away from C'ton and smiled at him for the first time, the X that normally crossed his face easing, revealing an almost beatific expression foreign to his customary demeanor. T'mer was very pleased with himself for his daring act of selflessness.

"I think I will take the lead from here," T'mer said.

T'mer did have to carry C'ton occasionally, picking him up roughly and practically throwing him over to the next clump of grass. The gap between the patches of grass did widen, making their passage more difficult, but then after a relatively short distance they grew closer together again, becoming close enough to form a narrow path that the group could walk on without too much trouble.

The mountain rose before them to encompass the whole sky, blocking out the shield where it connected to the rock high above. A slight hum could be heard echoing off of the mountain and the occasional cracking of the Dome overhead, but they were too far away from the side of the Dome for J'son to attract any electrical discharges.

The sand, becoming more compacted as they approached the foothills, ran up to the base of the mountain, where it stayed within its bed, packed down and flattened, forming a winding path around the foot of the mount.

The grass had thinned out considerably here and only grew between the cracks and crevices in the rock face. Great arms of the mountain fell out before them, impeding their forward progress, leading them south and parallel to the mountain. They walked along the parapet in silence, hoping to blend into the dark shadows cast by the dull-red illumination of the Dome against the mountain. The sky had the look of a smoldering fire, like the glowing embers of a spent bonfire. The tree-line on the other side of the desert had disappeared completely into the distance and the area they had just traversed looked like a sea of bloody glass. The group was glad they had made it across and their spirits seemed to lift once they had started moving south.

"C'ton," J'son asked, hoping to gauge his condition by his answers. "How far down does the Dome penetrate the mountain? I can't imagine it going down too far."

"When the Dome was first installed over the Temple area, and later over the rest of the inhabitable planet, the lip of the Dome pierced the mountain all the way down into the roots of the mountain itself, ending several miles below the surface. Before those of the Temple discovered the entrance to the cave of 'loh, it was thought that if one wanted to reach the other side of the Dome one would have to tunnel deep underground, but even that might not guarantee success."

"It is said that there exists a passage which leads from the lower chamber under the Temple complex and runs directly under the Dome." It was T'mer. "It is said that you monks have been using that passage to visit B'el's Castle for the past age, trafficking in his heresies."

"If a tunnel exists, I was never made known of it," C'ton said, slightly perturbed, as if he were being challenged. "There used to be a time before the Dome came down and passage between the Temple and his Castle was common. It was B'el, after all that came up with the idea of the Dome. Back then, heresy was just a word denoting improper training. All knowledge was permissible and we had a good relationship with those who chose to study under him. It was only after the Dome came down, blocking the passage to the east, that travel was lessened and B'el's actions were soon ignored and forgotten."

"You remember the cave I found you in when you first woke up?" T'mar asked J'son, looking to the west across the sandy desert, remembering that time like it was an age ago. "That became the only way to leave the protection of the Dome. The Dome had sealed all of us inside but left a small opening in the west, in that cave. B'el said…, well, that opening was part of the program; a hundred cubic foot space that the Dome developed around. We could leave the Dome from the west, but to reach B'el's Castle one had to traverse the circumference of the Dome, coming to his Castle from the outside."

"But why would he create a Dome that only left one opening? What was the purpose?"

T'mar and C'ton looked at each other, seeming to speak volumes with just a look in their eyes.

"That's how we… I mean." T'mar stuttered over herself.

"It was how we were able to reach your world," C'ton began for her. "Once the Dome went up, we were cut off from your world, unable to see you and you unable to see us. The Dome blocked your transmission. B'el said he knew that would happen and wrote into the program that opening. It is only in that cave we were able to project ourselves into your world."

"I was on a spiritual quest, holed up in the cave for several cycles before you started to dream about me, J'son. I had sealed myself in and was trying to transmit myself into your realm, not too sure if I was going to make contact, when I saw you for the first time. I was only a remnant of one of your dreams, some vague memory of a girl you use to know, but it was enough. I had made contact just like B'el—"

"Once we made contact with your world," C'ton said, picking up the story by cutting her off, the conversation moving causally back and forth between the two of them. "The search for a permanent portal was on. The area was too small to accommodate all those who wanted to spend the age over there, on your world, and so only a few of us were permitted to spend any amount of time in the cave. We only had a few micro-cycles to find someone, anyone, from your world who could come through clear enough for us to occupy, latch on to. T'mar was one of the few to retain her identity while over in your world. What we needed was a portal, a doorway, a permanent opening to your world that could be accessed without needing to leave the protection of the Dome. That's what you are, J'son, a portal."

"The Adepts say that B'el has created a portal of his own and some say he has left our world behind, living as a … human! Can you believe that?" T'mer asked, snickering.

"Is that possible, C'ton? Is it possible to leave our world and exist independently on theirs? I thought it was only possible to materialize on their planet with a host. Without the mind of a dreamer, how could we maintain any kind of cohesion? We would be just vapor without a host."

"That is what B'el set out to do. It is considered heresy to practice the arts which would free us from this world. In the distant past, we were cast down on this planet and abandoned here due to a moment of indiscretion on the part of the Council. We used to live on your planet, J'son, before the fall. There was a time when your people and our people worked together. You served us and we provided for all of your needs. Then there was war and the Dome came down and all contact with your world was lost. We even forgot you were there. It was only after we started to study under B'el that we remembered you even existed. B'el was the first one to re-establish contact while living in the east, the birthplace of the sun. He was the first one to use the opening in the cave to pass over to your side. After that, a whole stream of monks and others made the trek out west, some of them waiting their turn outside the cave for several cycles. The mouth of the cave became like a transportation station, some leaving for a few micro-cycles while others, unable to make the transition, started to take up lives living too close to the Dome, searching the perimeter for other openings, seemingly to no avail."

"Those became the Dome-dwellers, the 'dods. They're crazy monks, mostly nutty and out of their mind; drug users all of them." T'mer's contempt for them was more than obvious." Why do you monks think you can open up a portal within yourselves? It is only through Technology that a portal can and will be found. Imagining a mind-space that can project you out of our world and into theirs is an exercise in futility, the domain of the lunatic fringe. If we are real and their world is real, just imaging them won't allow you to travel to their world. You would need a machine that can create a tear between our world and theirs. It's physics."

What T'mer knew about the occult could fit in the palm of his hand, but the physics involved in trans-dimensional travel came easily to him. His people, the Techs, hadn't perfected the device, not yet, but travel between the worlds was already theoretically possible; all they needed was the co-ordinates to J'son's world. For that, the Adepts needed an anchor, someone like J'son, who could travel back to his own world while carrying a tracer. The Techs could lock onto the tracer thru trans-dimensional space, and if the physics were right, punch a hole through the fabric of space/time.

They knew they needed an incredible amount of energy to power up the device and had hoped to use some of the power reserves of the monks to test it unawares. But now, because of the problem with the Dome and the lack of accessible power distribution, T'mer knew the device wouldn't be powered up within the next age, probably not even in his lifetime.

"The cave of 'loh, on the other hand, was discovered by one of those 'Dome-dwellers', as T'mer likes to call them." C'ton was getting into the conversation about the past and a slight gleam entered his eyes, almost an ocular sneer like he was relaying ancient mysteries. He had spent time among the Dome-dwellers, known as the 'dods the planet over, regardless of where they maintained their residency, and found life among them to be extremely calming and trouble-free.

While he was speaking, he slipped one of his hands into the fold of his tunic and seemed to be clutching at something just out of sight. The info-cube he had taken from the library and had hidden from the others until they forgot about it was now moving slowly, almost tenderly between his fingers, kind of a gentle rolling of the object. Every time the tips of his fingers touched two corresponding corners, the cube downloaded giga-bites of information from whatever file he had opened. The longer he held the cube thus, the more info he received. He was using the cube like a drug addict would use his own supply. He thought he could monitor his soon-to-be insatiable curiosity consumption by administering himself minute quantities of knowledge, like injections, over a period of time. What he didn't consider, or more properly didn't want to consider, was the degree to which his addiction would impair his judgment.

"It was discovered by C'ber, a dear friend of mine and high ranking member of the Council before he left to become a 'dod. As he told me the story, personally," C'ton said, looking hard at T'mar like she might challenge his interpretation of the facts. In fact, C'ton wasn't recalling a conversation at all but merely reciting recorded history. "He was resting at the foot of this very mountain, reclining in the cool shade of a shallow cave when he felt a slight breeze blowing across his face. He traced the puff of wind to a tiny crack in the back of the cave, crawling on his hands and knees to find it. Pulling at the loose rock and digging into the soil with a stick from the 'jun tree he managed to open up a hole through the rock wide enough for him to crawl through. The short tunnel opened up into a large cavern, the cavern of 'deh, adorned with the red crystal of 'nco. It was the radiation coming from these crystals that blocked the Dome from lowering into the cavern, instead converting the energy of the Dome into an electrical vacuum, creating a passage through to the other side.

"Once in the cavern, C'ber began to mediate perceiving that the large, rock hall was conducive to mental projection. After an unspecified amount of time, C'ber experienced a spontaneous energy transformation. His energy signature left this world and united with yours, if only for a few moments. For the first time in the recorded history of the Council one of us was able to directly project himself into your world without needing you as a host. He appeared as one of you before he was pulled back."

"B'el tells a slightly different story, claiming he was the first one to cross over," T'mar added, looking back at C'ton from the corner of her eye. "When asked about the cave of 'loh, so named after the fact, he said it was part of the unpredictability program that stabilized the main frame. There was no way to predict its forming, nor the concentration of red crystal. No amount of detection would have found it. According to the base program, even now, the only opening in the Dome is the western opening. The library doesn't contain reference to the cave of 'loh. Only in the mythology of the Temple monks can allusion to its existence be found, although it is known to many."

The mention of the library brought C'ton's mind to the fore as he mentally searched the info cube's memory for the first formal reference to the existence of the cave. T'mar was right concerning its location within the library. The official account makes short mention of the cave shortly after C'ber's return. He had given the cave its name, although the meaning was a little obscure. The next mention came as a declaration from B'el after breaking several cycles of silence. He made the claim that he had found the cave and had practiced "soul transmutation" in the crystal cavern. He hadn't made his discovery known to the Council until then because he didn't want to be accused of heresy again. To pass to the world of the human was in direct conflict with the standing Law of One, and he didn't want to be accused of trying to tempt the monks away from their practices.

There was a string of zeros in the memory cube associated with the discovery of the cave. Normally such a sequence of negation denoted the insertion of new material, like a splice, like when the High Priest communes with those who have past and returns with fresh interpretations of the sacred texts. Only this time the zeros seemed to be hiding a deletion, like someone had erased something but didn't eliminate the magnetic signature. C'ton could detect B'el's influence all over that particular reference in the way the program was written. Although not part of the "official" Temple records, T'mar's occult recollection of the cave's discovery was probably more accurate.

"That's right, J'son. It is known that the records have been altered, but those of us who remember the beginning remember the true account. I was there," C'ton finished abruptly.

"B'el was an original member of the Council," T'mar said, looking at C'ton still with a guarded eye, wondering how much occult history C'ton was willing to divulge to the profane present. T'mer should never know about the mysteries, considering his kind turned their back on the esoteric to embrace the exoteric. They had access to some of the breakthroughs made by B'el and his occult discoveries, though. After all, the Technology of the Adepts was based on those same discoveries. And J'son, who's to decide what he should and shouldn't know? At another time C'ton could be trusted to reveal the secrets to those found worthy, but considering his obvious recent mental and physical deterioration she determined B'el was the only one qualified to show J'son the truth.

"That was before. But it was because of his counsel that—"

"C'ton, maybe we should take a break and get our bearings. You looked fatigued." It was J'son.

They stopped walking and huddled down on their haunches, trying hard not to look so much out in the open. The mountain towered up from them blocking all view except the black, dully-radiating rock face. Littered across the face of the mountain at different locations and levels, some higher up than the others, small opening appeared here and there. The depths of these opening were hard to determine and in the dark they looked like shallow scoops in the rock face.

J'son stared at one particularly large cave opening located about twenty feet above them, set back about fifty feet. Pointing in the general direction, he asked: "Is the cave opening we are looking for at ground level or up higher like that one?"

"Don't do that!" C'ton screeched, batting J'son's arm down with a stinging slap. "Those are the dwellings of those who live here. That larger opening is probably a main entrance to their honey-combed complex of tunnels and passageways. We have been under their surveillance since reaching the mountain, I am sure. Pointing at them could be interpreted as an act of hostility."

"C'ton, I'm not too sure why you are showing so much suspicion and distrust." T'mar looked up at the cave briefly and then back at C'ton. "I have also spent time with the 'dods and I always found them to be friendly and hospitable to strangers and weary, fellow travelers. Even you said your time among them was good, but now you speak like if we were spotted we would be in danger. I say we seek out their help. They may have information we can use. They of all people would know if the way has been opened and could tell us if anyone else has passed this way. We shouldn't fear them."

T'mar was right, of course. They shouldn't have to hope to subterfuge and deception in order to clear the Dome. What they needed right then was a friendly face that could take them to the cave of 'loh. The 'dods might even have access to energy vents, cracks in the surface of a rock that allows sub-strata energy transmission, a place where C'ton and the others could recharge. These vents were found throughout the Wastelands and crept up on the Dome at various places, mostly deep underground.

Occasionally these vents were found on the surface for whatever geological, plate-tectonic reason and covered the surrounding area with radioactive fallout. The nuclear particles are harvested out of the ground using a device that looks very similar to an oil rig. To harness that raw power was a priority of the Adepts. With that energy at their disposal, the Adepts thought, they would be released from the dictates of the Temple monks, a shaky allegiance at best. The Adepts dependence on the High Council for power needs was more than frustrating; it was exasperating.

"My only concern is whether they are on our side, the Temple's side, or B'el's side. All will turn against us if they believe it benefits them," C'ton said. "Remember T'mar, no one outside this group knows who we are. For all they know, even dressed as we are, we're just a group of travelling monks looking for shelter against the dark night. No need to mention our contact with the Temple unless we half to. Our cover will be that we are 'dods from the west with news about the Dome. That should ease our passing. Dome news is always interesting."

C'ton straightened up, looking more like himself, but with a creepy glow in his eyes that was very disturbing. His eyes had an eerie, glowing confidence to them, but they blazed with a reptilian intensity, more like the eyes of a snake. He seemed more energetic and took off from the group, moving quickly to the south with his head down, like he had made a decision without informing the others.

J'son pursued after him before the other two could process what had happened, widening the gap between the two groups. When J'son finally caught up with him, C'ton wrapped his arm around his shoulders and speaking in a low tone, almost a whisper, said:

"J'son now is the time for you to choose whom you will follow. Once we enter the cave of 'loh, they will change, T'mar and T'mer. T'mer will get more belligerent and possibly hostile. It is not his physical size that concerns us at this point. A tiny spell will keep him under control, at least for awhile. But don't you cast it! I will do it when the time comes. It is T'mar that I am more concern with. It isn't her teaching that we need to look out for, but her thoughts."

"I don't understand," he said, looking back over his shoulder at them. They were several yards behind and huddled together like he and C'ton were with their foreheads almost touching and their lips moving rapidly. They were talking in hushed tones and a deep X crossed both of their faces, splitting their features into four sections. Their countenance frightened J'son and he turned back around as quickly as he could to avoid eye contact. He drew quiet for a moment re-evaluating what he was going to say. Maybe he did know what C'ton was talking about.

"J'son, you are dealing with things here that you have no knowledge of." C'ton voice was sharp and he spit out the words, sounding hateful and conspiratorial. "Things will change as soon as we make contact with the 'dods. You'll see. They'll have questions and T'mar won't know the answers, not answers she can divulge. She is increasingly being led by the most basic of her emotional programming. Her connection to B'el will prove to be too overwhelming. I expect she will turn on us before it is all said and done. She may have left him, but his teachings has influence her thinking and actions for all time. She is bound to him."

"Bound to him?" The revelation shocked and floored him, stopping him in his tracks with his eyes wide open and full of incredulity.

"Yessss. That is the secret T'mar refuses to share with others, and with good reason. He called out to her and she responded by making the trek to his Castle. Once there, under his tutelage, she became initiated into his brand of sorcery. The initiation consisted of an elaborate ceremony where she recited the ancient, binding spells that bound her to him for the age. It is now at the end of this age and the beginning of the long dark that T'mar would have been released from her vows, free to reign as a god, an equal to B'el and far superior to all the other monks, even those on the Council. He would have let her go too, once the terms of the contract had been satisfied. But that's not what happened, is it dear T'mar?" C'ton said the last looking back over his shoulder at her, knowing she couldn't hear him but cluing her in to the idea that she was being talked about.

"I don't understand. Why would she bind herself to someone like B'el? What did she hope to gain? Why would she even be attracted to him? I remember what he looks like from my world: sinister, evil, full of deceit." J'son's mind was whirling. All this time, here and also back on his world, she never led him to believe that her interest in B'el was anything other than to prevent him from exploiting those on J'son's world. Never did J'son think that her pursuit of him was the result of some sort of twisted stalker scenario.

Did J'son follow T'mar into her world under the mistaken assumption that he was acting chivalrously, chasing after his dream girl so that he could stand by her side when she confronted her adversary? Was she using him to get to B'el? If she left, as C'ton and T'mer alluded to, was she just trying to soften her return by offering B'el a gift? Was he that gift? All that talk about him being a portal, was that the real reason why they were risking their lives, so she could present B'el with a doorway into J'son's world? Was he being used? But was it his idea to go to B'el's Castle, or rather the Transcendentals. Maybe T'mar was nothing more than a pawn in a larger game that he couldn't understand. Maybe she was making this up as she went along, hedging her bets, using J'son and probably C'ton as hostages, bargaining chips, a form of trade to negotiate in the event B'el didn't want any uninvited guest.

Chapter Thirty-Five:

The Vent

"I don't have fantasies. My life is one uninhibited fantasy."
T'mar under the influence of the 'vjc

"The question why she married him can be answered simply enough," C'ton said. "B'el is very charismatic and his power over females is legendary. She married him out of lust. He turned her into a virtual whore, keeping her in a state of constant sexual stimulation while she learned his secrets. The method is called tantric learning. The effect of his behavioral conditioning on her was one of open, sexually-uninhibited suggestibility while at the same time needing that level of sexual energy in order to cast his spells in the proper way. The result, as you can see, is a heightened sexual libido that activates every time she thinks about casting a spell. Her need for sex is constant and she will turn on anyone she believes might keep her away from satisfying her sexual hunger, getting it from wherever and from whomever she can. Avoid all physical contact with her. Don't even touch her. You can very easily fall prey to her sexual advances. It's what she excels at."

J'son fell quiet again, following close behind C'ton but not really paying too much attention to what C'ton was saying now. He was rambling on about the difference between a wizard, like himself, and a sorcerer, like B'el. C'ton even said something about T'mar qualifying as a sorcerer instead of a wizard. J'son looked back at T'mar and T'mer again. They weren't talking anymore, but were gaining on them with grim expressions.

"How do you know so much about what happened to her? T'mar doesn't seem like someone that would talk openly about that part of her life. Is it a part of the official record?"

"Not so much. Some of my knowledge of her comes from my time with her; part from her time with the Techs; part from the Council records; and part from the stories surrounding her. I didn't know that she wasn't using a disguise until it came out in the Council. Her history is complicated and wrapped in mystery. Even now I still have questions concerning her whereabouts immediately before I found her on the side of the road. I didn't question it at the time because females were just playthings, distractions. It wasn't until much later that I started to notice something different about her and her perchance for remembering and casting simple spells."

"But I thought she didn't go to B'el until after you met?"

"That is true, but now I'm not so sure she didn't meet him before that time. The spells she knew could be bought with money, or in T'mar's case with her body, but it was how she wielded the spells and the sexual slant she always gave to each vocalization. Hearing her cast a spell, as long as it wasn't directed specifically at you with evil intent, brought up sexual fantasies and filled your mind with overwhelming images of lustful satisfaction. Whatever the spell cast, the air surrounding her became sexually charged and intercourse would commence shortly afterwards, regardless if those engaged in sex were aware that they had been manipulated or not. I think that is what happened to me."

"You're saying she manipulated you? She forced sex on you without your consent, is that what you mean?"

"Once one reaches a certain level of knowledge, no matter how they obtained it, they are accepted into the ranks of the Initiated. We give them that opportunity in order to flesh them out, to see if they might be unstable or prone to emotional outbreaks that could be hazardous to the normal functioning of the Temple. T'mar was given a lot of space, and distrust, especially by the older members of the Council who rarely accept females into their ranks. The Council was aware of her existence but properly ignore her presence."

"C'ton, up ahead!" It was T'mer pointing at something, a shadow hiding between the folds of the rock. "I thought I saw something. Wait for us to catch up." Grabbing T'mar by the elbow, T'mer picked up his stride and trotted over to them, closing the gap in a few seconds. The four of them moved together, slowly but cautiously towards the boulder T'mer had pointed. Two arms of the mountain folded over themselves, creating a passageway of sorts that ran deep into the mountain itself. Looking into the opening of this tunnel, T'mer thought he could see a dim light coming from the back of the den.

"Come out of there now and show yourself!" T'mer shouted into the opening, sounding commanding, demanding and authoritative.

"We have no influence here, T'mer," C'ton said quietly. "Remember that the next time you decide to speak for the rest of us."

T'mer drew back from the opening feeling livid and embarrassed. C'ton had openly reprimanded him for his thoughtless belligerence without so much as raising his voice. T'mer tucked his head down and brooded, a dark cloud of shame descending down around him. There was nothing he wanted to do more right then than rip C'ton's throat out, but he denied that impulse and pined about in steaming semi-silence, kicking at small rocks on the ground and pounding his hands against the walls of the opening.

T'mer's action echoed down the throat of the passageway, sounding like a gong or the fading sound of a mono-syllabic meditation mantra. The sound died away, and as the four of them strained their ears listening to the ensuing silence, the sound of pebbles scratching across the rock floor came out to greet them. Something was coming out of the passageway, preceded by a scratching and scraping sound, metallic. Something within the cave reflected back at them and then faded away, like the flickering of a blade. It was moving towards them, slowly, the shiny item, but then it stopped, coming to a rest about waist high hovering in the dark. It looked like a disembodied, floating smile, curving upwards and shining.

"We need light," C'ton said, bending over and picking up a slick, round rock lying partially buried in the sand. He brushed the sand off by rubbing it between his fingers and then he held it in the palms of both hands, cupping them. He blew into his hands for a few seconds until the rock began to glow a dull orange. Normally this trick was a weak source of light, but in the dark of the opening it turned into a blazing radiance. He tossed the glowing rock into the mouth of the passageway, illuminating the interior.

The glowing rock surprised the figure in the cave, catching him off guard. The now obvious male figure threw his arms up across his eyes to block out the light and looked between them trying to see who it was that had just lit up the world.

"Only a wizard of high initiation has the ability to create light out of solid rock. I mean no harm to you and only have myself so armed against the wildlife found in these parts. My name is F'bol, a peaceful, meditative monk like you, looking for a way out of this world."

The man lowered his arms as the glow from the rock diminished. He held a long, sharp thin dagger in his right hand, pointing down. His fingers were clutching a handle made of tightly-wound rope that had the color of dirty sweat. It looked very ancient, chipped like an arrowhead but more delicate. Its appearance made it look more like a play-time knife than a real weapon.

F'bol was dressed in clean, brightly colored foliage that covered his waist and groin area. He was barefooted and his nails were painted in a bright, almost florescence green. His face and chest were dirty and smeared the color of coal; and his long, black hair stood out at all directions, thick and matted. He had a quiet smile on his face, and after his initial surprise seemed quite friendly and welcoming.

"You are quite right in assuming that we are high level initiates of the Temple," C'ton said, ignoring his own words of caution and speaking for the others, taking command. "We are here with news about the Dome. Where is your 'cfr, your chief mediator? I have a need to speak with him concerning something of vast import. The Dome will collapse before the return of the sun unless we may continue with our mission. We are looking for the opening to the cave of 'loh. News has reached the Temple that the way has been reopened. Is this news accurate? Has the way been opened?"

"Yes," F'bol said slowly, observing the group closely but especially the older monk. There was something familiar about him that F'bol couldn't put his finger on. The larger of the other two males was obviously a Tech from the City. But the woman, who looked like a sexual pleasure model, didn't carry herself like she was at the beck and call of the males. She looked more like the leader maybe, radiating awesome powers that moved just below the level of conscious awareness.

He could see the energy flowing though her, enveloping her in a safe, protective cocoon that kept her separated from the others while still maintaining a close connection. She wasn't at all what she appeared to be. Tiny, wispy, ghost-like tentacles extended out from her touching the boy on his forehead and mid-chest, gently caressing those areas. A special connection to the boy, then! F'bol tried to read J'son, but he was veiled behind a translucent energy projection that masked his abilities. F'bol wasn't sure, but he didn't think the boy was from around here.

"Yes, the cave of 'loh is still being used to transmigrate from this reality to the world of the dreamers. It was rediscovered by a member of my group several cycles ago."

"You can pass under the Dome, then?" T'mar asked, too abruptly, giving away their intension.

"Pass under? Oh! You are interested in making your way across the Wastelands. You wish to study under B'el? It has been said that he has taken on another apprentice. It is said that you can see his Castle glowing once more on the horizon."

"How did you come by this knowledge, F'bol? Have you ever journeyed to his Castle yourself?" J'son was very interested in F'bol, considering his whole demeanor was in complete opposition to the standard J'son had gotten use to. F'bol's smile implied simplicity and serenity, peace without the distinctive, characteristic X. He appeared to be in harmony with his surroundings and his place in it. Even the light dust that he kicked up walking across the floor of the den fell down around him, swirling around his bare legs in an almost effortless dance of free-flowing energy particles, glowing and bouncing off of him, floating around him, hovering where they were. The reflecting debris made it hard to keep a straight eye on F'bol and J'son was coming to the realization that the man before them was something more than a half-naked monk mediating in a dark cave.

"I have travelled there, once, shortly after the way was found again. I didn't enter his Castle, but I saw it on the horizon, glowing so black that it reflected the stars overhead like a crown and the glass-like sand beneath it like a hole in space. The tunnels end before you get there and you have to move over ground. Very dangerous! The air is toxic, but a way has been made for the wise. I didn't take the path overland, but I have seen it glowing in the dark, black and red and burning like lava, with smoke rising from the pinnacle like a volcano. It is an impressive sight, to say the least, but too dangerous just for the curious. I turned back after losing a close companion to the ill winds of the Wastelands."

"So you can take us to the cave of 'loh?" T'mar asked, sounding a little frantic and impatient. "You've passed the boundary of the Dome? You took the tunnels to the end?"

"I have made the journey before, but now I prefer the relative safety of life by the Dome. We are called 'dods by members of the Temple council, a rather derogatory term, but one that adequately describes us. We live here because we refused to cope with life under the terms of the so-called sanctuary. The secret of how to contact another world shouldn't be kept locked up in the sacred vaults of the monks. All should have the opportunity to travel into other dimensions, even if it is just an illusion."

"An illusion? What do you mean? You mean you believe my planet is an illusion?" J'son blurted out, revealing his place of origin. He was just starting to get comfortable with the idea that he was dreaming this up, even though everything seemed so real. But now, even his dream creations were telling him that nothing was real.

"I was sure a companion of such a high level initiate as he," F'bol said, pointing at C'ton, picking up on J'son's blunder. "Would understand the nature of the things I am saying. You and I and everything else are nothing more than the gossamer of an exotic dream, a figment of someone's overactive imagination. None of this is real, your world or ours.

Nothing exists except you and The One and you are just a figment of his imagination."

"Whose imagination is making this up then? The One, whatever that is?" J'son asked, shaking his head. Was he the One? If anyone possessed an imagination active enough to dream up this world, it was J'son. But was all of this just the result of indigestion? How is it that F'bol is aware that he is the figment of J'son's imagination? How could he be aware of that unless F'bol was himself outside the influence of this dream, an outsider to this planet, kind of like J'son? Was F'bol a fellow dreamer like J'son, creating this reality as they spoke, or was he just another illusion lacking any independent existence?

This was too much to handle and J'son closed his eyes for a few seconds trying to re-imagine the scene before him, trying to alter the appearance of the opening and the man standing before him. If this was part of his dream, then just by wishing it he should be able to change the scene to whatever he wanted. Wasn't that one of the advantages of dreaming, being able to wake up when the situation demanded it, or being lucid enough to change the direction of the dream? J'son opened his eyes again and was greeted by the same setting as a few seconds before, only now the glowing, floating particles had lost their radiance and the passageway lacked any brilliance or novelty.

F'bol was still smiling at them, looking like a young Buddha, peaceful and tranquil. J'son tried to change F'bol's appearance, the color of his eyes or the length of his nose simply by thinking about it, but only managed in giving himself a slight headache located around his temples. He closed his eyes again, squeezing them shut until tears formed in the corners, blocking out all illumination. He opened them again and noticed F'bol had moved away from the four of them and had travelled deeper into the passageway, pausing for a moment to gesture with his head that they should be following him. He disappeared around a black corner in the back, although the sound of his feet could still be heard scraping up against the floor, echoing away from them.

"Come! Let's go, J'son," C'ton said, patting him on the back and then venturing ahead of them. "We should be safe in these passages as long as we don't lose sight of F'bol. These tunnels twist around and run into blinds easily enough. I have known of monks that have died, lost in these tunnels."

T'mer took off next, followed slowly after by J'son and then T'mar. The tunnel turned into a cave proper after turning the corner and J'son and T'mar found themselves at the beginning of a massive grotto whose heights reached up into the belly of the mountain, disappearing into the dark, and multiple passageways running off in all directions like the strands of a web. Embedded all along the walls of this cavern were tiny, radiating jewels, like yellow quartz but twinkling, like stars. The light they gave off illuminated the cave just enough to give J'son and T'mar a good view of the interior and they could see F'bol, T'mer and C'ton on the far side, waiting for them.

J'son and T'mar crossed the floor of the cave, trying to ignore the uneasy feeling they had of being observed. J'son thought he saw dark shapes huddled around the openings of some of these other passageways, but he turned away from the imagined, watchful eyes, keeping his head down, listening.

T'mar marched along showing extreme confidence in her footfalls, keeping her head held high and her eyes alert, scanning the passageways but not holding her attention there for too long. She knew where she was and who these people were. They were outcast, like herself, leery of those from the Temple but friendly enough to those who show them kindness. It would be expected of the 'dods, T'mar thought, to be a little apprehensive of those wandering around the base of the Dome in the dark. They would want to know about them and their so-called mission. But why did C'ton divulge they were from the Temple? That admission would put them at an extreme disadvantage. It wouldn't be hard for them to determine their actual identities.

"F'bol was just telling us," C'ton said as the other two approached them, "that we will rest for a few moments in a sleep chamber just beyond this cave. It is there that we will get our bearing and be shown on our way to the cave of 'loh."

"The cave of 'loh can be reached by following a secret channel that takes you through the mountain," F'bol said. "It is a long and dark tunnel, but I am sure your wizard can generate the light you may need."

"We need to recharge our… batteries," J'son said, smiling at his own joke.

"There is an energy vent located in the sleep chamber. It isn't strong, but it is enough to make you happy. The vent appears to be from a pure source, but it's too small to follow it down. A few micro-cycles on top of that vent and you should be feeling no pain."

"That would be wonderful," T'mar said, letting her guard down a little, sounding relieved and run down but smiling all the same at the thought of a pure energy bath.

T'mer wasn't saying anything and was extremely distrustful at the hospitality of their host. Why would a 'dod show them any compassion or empathy? Why would they be willing to help them out if it wasn't for some ulterior motive? What did they hope to gain by helping them? And how would they know if the vent F'bol mentioned was even a pure vent? Just because he said it was? Maybe it was noxious, toxic. If the boy was so important, maybe they knew about him and wanted to take him for themselves. When you have spent the majority of your life living with distrust and in constant competition, never knowing if the relationships you had were for personal or private gain, you understood that all relationships were based on favor and T'mer wanted to know what favor they were going to ask of them.

They continued down a narrow passage barely wide enough to walk one behind the other. The slight glow from the grotto lessened to nothing and the passage became pitch black and hot, stuffy and humid, almost claustrophobic. There was no sound except the scraping of their feet against the floor, and that was muffled. They walked along with their hands out in front of them to avoid running into each other. At one point J'son, following in the forth position behind F'bol, C'ton and T'mer, ran into a low-hanging outcropping, smacking his forehead hard against the rock, cutting his head and reopening the wound made by the 'ints. A small trail of blood ran down the bridge of his nose before pooling into a large, heavy, bead of sweaty red, which fell in great splat-y splashes on the wet, stone floor.

"Holy Crap! Sonofabitch that hurts." J'son gently touched his wound with the tip of a finger, pushing down on the gash and then releasing it when it began to hurt again. "Ouch."

"Are you okay?" T'mar asked, coming up from behind with her hands out. Her arms slipped around his chest, massaging the muscles and then let go, abruptly. Reaching up, she patted the outcropping staring her in the face. The distinct sound of her long, very feminine nails scrapping lightly across the rock sounded muted and yet crystal clear. "You should have bent over. Try to be more careful, 'lvb."

She knew J'son wouldn't be able to see it, but she was smiling brightly at the entire exchange. She loved the feel of his flesh under her fingers and touching him she felt the muscles in her pelvic region loosening up and getting moist. The lust was almost unbearable in these close quarters and she was having a hard time controlling her stoked, fiery libido. The hot passageway only brought the musky smell of the four men to the fore and she found herself analyzing the different pungent scents trying to place each with its proper owner.

She was able to distinguish between F'bol and J'son mainly because F'bol's order was fragrant, almost flowery like a bouquet but possessing a slight undercurrent of something rancid. She recognized the smell as the outcome of a purified life: The outward shell cleansed of all impurity, while the inner man, slowly dying, releases the toxins of daily life. A monk nearing the time for his departure from this existence will produce a smell that is both aromatic and scented and putrid and rank. The former is the aroma of departure and the latter the stink of decay. The combination that she now detected coming from F'bol caused her to wonder if he was very close to leaving this world for good.

J'son's scent was distinct in that he didn't really have a scent. Although they were all sweating profusely, his sweat lacked the biological component. She could smell the salt and the water squeezing out of his pores and the blood dripping off of his nose, but that was all. It was almost as if his body lacked any biological reality. She could detect nothing uniquely his in the different odors hovering in the thick air. It wasn't until the two of them started walking again that she realized what his scent reminded her of: He smelled freshly bathed.

The passage came to a halt, ending at what seemed like a dead-end. A thin crack separated two large boulders blocking the way and the five of them could feel a cool breeze coming at them from the crack. F'bol reached his hand in between the two boulders, sinking his hand in all the way up to his forearm. He twisted his arm, turning it 90 degrees and a metallic click could be heard, followed by a buzzing, humming sound. The sound stopped and then a sliding, grinding noise was heard as the two boulders slowly pulled away from each other revealing a smallish cave with a low ceiling.

The interior was lit by a bright bluish glow coming out of a crack in the floor of the cave. A misty vapor could be seen rising from the vent and the moisture of the vapor collected on the ceiling directly above it. The moisture had crusted over and hung from the ceiling in flat, fungi-looking flakes. Several pieces of the flakes had fallen to the floor around the vent and were in the process of reverting back into a liquid.

"Here, let me help you with that," F'bol said when he saw the blood running down J'son's face. Leaning over, he picked up a small flake lying close to the vent, one that was more like jelly in consistency, and smeared it onto J'son's injury, pressing it deep into the wound. The feel was cool on his forehead and the pain eased almost immediately. The jelly-like substance, mixing with the blood, took on the look and texture of putty, covering the wound and blending in with the rest of his face. The blue light cast by the vent gave his wound the color of a deep bruise, painful to look at but for the most part pain-free.

"The four of you can rest here for awhile and regain some of your former strength. I will leave you here to recuperate and discuss your plans. I will return after a few micro-cycles to hear of your decision and help you along your way, if that is your destiny. The boy, though. He doesn't appear to need the rest like the rest of you do. What would you say if I wanted to take him with me while the three of you rested? I would like to get to know him better. There is something different about you, isn't there, and the fact you claim to be from the world of the dreamers is interesting in itself."

"There is no way we are separating," T'mer spat, sounding aggressive and possessive.

"My name is J'son and you're right. I'm not—"

"J'son!"

"It appears your wizard doesn't want you to divulge too much. Don't worry Servant of the Temple. I only meant to converse with him without bothering the rest of you. My intensions are pure." F'bol finished speaking and smiled at them. His teeth were a florescent blue in the glow from the vent.

J'son felt no hostility coming from F'bol, only curiosity. J'son himself was also very curious and part of him wanted to leave his companions and follow F'bol, to ask him questions and to be given answers that J'son knew would be different than the answers C'ton and T'mar would give. He looked at the four of them in the glow of the blue illumination, scanning the stressed faces of his companions in stark contrast to the look on F'bol's face.

T'mer and C'ton looked very distrustful and their X's never left their faces. T'mar, on the other hand, looking tired but intense, seemingly possessed of an energy that the others didn't have access to. Her eyes burned with a hunger, a desire and she didn't seem to want to stay in one place for long. He knew if he said he wanted to go with F'bol that T'mar would want to go too. And if they went, then C'ton and T'mer would want to follow them. Seeing the weariness in C'ton's face and his obvious need to "recharge", J'son made the decision to stay with his companions.

"Thanks anyway, F'bol. But I think I will stay here with my friends until you come back for us."

"What does friend mean?" F'bol asked surprised by the strange-sounding word and the context in which it was used.

"They are," J'son said, sweeping his arm in the general direction of his companions, smiling at F'bol's ignorance of something as basic as friendship. But then he thought twice, staring at the others, realizing that they might not understand the concept either and that their fellowship was based only on self-benefit, nothing altruistic. Companionship on this world, it seems, was based on profit. A friend was a liability that could cost you your life if the price was right. Dog eat dog and all of that. The thought made him sad and he felt his energy stores slowly ebbing away. It was a mental function and not an actuality, but he felt rundown nonetheless.

"Rest here then," F'bol said. "I shall return once you have bathed in the light of the vent. Hopefully when I come back we will be able to converse and maybe those two won't be so hostile towards those who would give them shelter in the dark." He turned away from them and left the small cave the same way he came in. He paused at the entrance and turned back to face them. "Normally I would seal the opening so you could get the most benefit from the vent, but under the circumstances and the amount of distrust already engendered I will leave the entrance opened. Please remain here until I return. There are many passages leading away from here and not all of them go somewhere. It is easy to get lost in the dark."

"Well, what do you think?" T'mar asked C'ton after F'bol left them.

"I think we need to take advantage of that vent and replenish our reserves. We will need all the energy we can absorb if we are to continue towards the Wastelands."

T'mer moved over to the vent and placed his hands above the rising vapor, wiggling his fingers in the blue mist. Within a few moments his fingers were dripping wet and glowing. He placed one finger into his mouth and licked the moisture off, like someone testing the temperature of a soup. His finger emerged from his mouth clean, dry and lacking the florescence glow that his other fingers had. Smacking his lips like he was rolling the flavor around in his mouth, the corners of his mouth turned up slightly, forming a sly grin. His eyes opened wide and he had the look of someone possessed, wild and way too intense.

"This is definitely a pure source!" He said. His bizarre, mischievous smile grew larger, made more creepy looking as the X cutting into his face gave him a hideous expression. This was T'mer's version of a smile and the vent had made him very happy and relaxed. He forgot about his misgivings for the moment and plunged his entire hand into the vent, pulling it out a second later and cupping it to his mouth. He drank deeply of the florescent blue liquid, plunging his other hand into the vent and drinking from that hand as well. As he drank, the hair on his head began to stand out straight and tiny points of blue light streamed out from the ends. The effect made him look like he had a head full of candles, brightly lit and lighting up the small cave.

"You might want to slow down on that, T'mer," C'ton said, moving closer to the vent and sitting down next to it. "It is more beneficial to absorb the energy indirectly. That way the body has more time to adjust."

"Why don't you mind your own business, old man?" T'mer snapped back at him. He knew what energy vents were and what they were used for. They had energy vents in the City, including one much larger than the tiny vent now before him. Time could be scheduled for personal rejuvenation within one of the vents and he had spent much of his free time bathing in those vents. A large one was located within the City proper and rested at the bottom of a shallow depression, forming a pool, like a bathtub.

When scheduled he would spend several micro-cycles lying in that pool, drinking the cool liquid and submerging himself completely under the blue fluid. It almost always made him pass out in a state of extreme bliss. Afterwards, he would awaken totally renewed, possessing the still vivid memory of the bliss he had found. That feeling of well-being would stay with him for awhile, usually until he had associations with others of his kind. Then the feeling would leave him, replaced by his typical demeanor of distrust and skeptical suspicion.

It was said that at such times, before the feeling of well-being left him, it was possible for a Tech, much more so for an Adept, to pass the boundary of this world and transmigrate to the world of the dreamers. The ecstatic afterglow of consuming 'vjc, "vent juice", allowed the girders of the mind to loosen, bend and reform, permitting thought patterns to emerge that possessed a transcendental nature. There were oral histories that gave rise to such beliefs and the official archives mentioned Adepts that had passed beyond the confines of this world, but the names of these Adepts were not known. Drinking the waters of the vent as he just did could make lesser men mentally unstable and psychically damaged, but T'mer's ego wouldn't let him dwell on the misfortunes of the profane.

"T'mer, I think C'ton was just trying to be cautious. I'm surprised you jumped on the vent as fast as you did. Earlier I thought I detected reservations coming from you. The fact that you trusted F'bol and took him to his word shows there is hope for you yet." T'mar smiled at him, teasing him, feeling pretty good now that they had been in contact with the vent. It didn't take long for the vapor to take effect.

T'mer continued to drink in the liquid, using both hand to fill his mouth. He was starting to feel loopy and his body wasn't responding to his commands in the normal way. He sat down hard on the cave floor, crossing his legs and laying his hands in his lap. His grin made him look ridiculous and he swayed back and forth, seemingly following the rhythms of an unheard melody.

It was very uncharacteristic of him to become so intoxicated around others and that could prove to be dangerous. If T'mer wasn't lucid enough, his overwhelming temper could break free of his partial control and who knew what could happen. An out of control T'mer was a danger to himself and everyone around him. It wasn't good to have a drunken Tech in your party. Techs knew just enough of the physics involved to cast spells, but as intoxicated as T'mer was getting without the normal inhibitory restrictions that a sober Tech would possess it was possible that he could cast spells in his drunken stupor that would be hard to counter.

"T'mer, I think you've had enough. T'mer?"

T'mer had slipped one hand into the vent, keeping it there until his chin hit his chest and he nodded off. T'mar gently pulled his hand out of the vent and laid it in his lap. The hand radiated a violent blue but began to fade now that it no longer was in the vent. T'mer had passed out and was now in the land of psychedelic dreams.

Everyone sat around the vent, reclining as best as they could and waited quietly for the intoxicating effects of the vapor to work its magic. Nobody else put their hands into the vent directly, but C'ton and T'mar were kept busy rubbing the moisture collecting on their bodies into their skin. Everywhere they rubbed, the fluid glowed and streaks could be seen running down their arms and legs. T'mar was rubbing her neck and cupping her breasts, coating them and pinching her nipples until they stood up hard and erect. She smiled to herself as she looked down on her perfect bosom glowing in the dark like headlights.

"Look at me sweetie," she said to J'son, pointing her illuminating globes at him. The vapor was starting to take effect and she giggled like a schoolgirl, feeling the lust in her belly rising to the fore now that her inhibitions were lowered even more than usual. She was horny as hell, but she didn't have the mental capacity to perform any sexual acts. In fact, as she began to fall under the sway of the vapor, she found herself in a sexual fantasy where she was lying on her back with her arms and legs splayed out to her sides. She couldn't move her hips but she didn't care. Instead, she fantasized about being raped over and over again, her body yielding to the men, and women, who tried to enter her. After her fourth orgasm, she lost consciousness.

Chapter Thirty-Six:

F'bol's Seduction

> "It is used to meditate, a place where one can fine peace and transcendence. But that is not your final destination. Don't be fooled by the lights or you may become lost within yourself. Take my advice and only meditate on one star at a time."
>
> F'bol's suggestion to J'son concerning the Cave of 'loh

While T'mar was masturbating and T'mer was in an ecstatic bliss, C'ton and J'son were having quite different experiences. C'ton was having considerable trouble keeping his mind in check. Although he sat quietly by the vent, absorbing the mentally stimulating vapor, he was locked in a bitter battle with his will. Needing to feed from such a pure source, he nonetheless was resisting that impulse. The longer he sat by the vent, the more active his mind became to the point that his thoughts were whirling around on their own accord. The images filling his head spoke of power, showing graphically visual representations of different spells and the outcome of casting them. It took all his training to keep from opening his mouth and casting those spells.

The burden to know was growing too great for him to cope. It was a catch-22 situation where his need to replenish his energy reserves outweighed his desire to remain focused and in control of his thoughts. He wouldn't sit there as long as T'mer; he couldn't. If he were to pass out, without the inhibiting force of his mind to quiet the noise, any and all images that entered his head would be re-created in the material world. Someone with a good disposition, with good thoughts wasn't a problem, and at times could be very entertaining, like a happy drunk. The images coming out of that kind of mind were usually very funny and amusing if not sloppy and unhinged. But C'ton's mind wasn't focused on happy thoughts and his fear was that while passed out all of his inner demons would come to the surface. It was a truism that one never abolished his demons, only subjugated them.

J'son, on the other hand, was experiencing profound revelations, seeing the Transcendentals but not being able to interact with them as before. They seemed to be oblivious to him, or maybe they were just ignoring him. He also saw grotesque, distorted caricatures of everyone he had met while on this planet. These faces, twisted and seemingly melting off the bone, were pleading with him, asking him to do something, but he was unable to understand them. The more he tried to perceive their meaning, the more distorted and perverted the creatures became. He knew instinctively that the creatures lack any objective reality and their presence there was just a product of his imagination. But those images were trying to tell him something.

When F'bol returned much later the four of them were scattered around the small cave lying up against the rock walls. T'mer had fallen over backwards and had hit his head causing a deep gash. The blood had mixed with the slick moisture and coagulated there, turning syrupy and gooey. T'mar had snuggled up against J'son, spooning him from behind and had her hands wrapped tightly around his groin, possessing it like the hilt of a sword. He was flaccid and quite incapable of producing an erection, but the pressure there kept bring up sexually explicit material for his mind to chew on. C'ton, who had kept his distance away from the vent as best as he could, never lost consciousness but stayed in constant opposition with himself. Where the others would awaken refreshed and full of energy,

C'ton had spent his time depleting his resources battling his growing fatigue.

"How are we feeling? Well rested I hope. But no! Your wizard appears more stressed than when he entered. Why would that be?"

"I have been wrestling with some issues concerning our mission and didn't have the time to allow my body rest. My mind is sharp, though and that is what's important. I will be fine once we reach the Cave of 'loh. There I will truly recharge and regain my former prominence. All will be well as soon as you show us the path that will take us to the cave."

"Then we shall leave immediately. I have spoken with other members of my company and you have been recognized, C'ton. It has been a long time since you last came here. I would ask the identity of the other two in your party, but the Tech has no meaning to us and the woman is only good for one thing, as the boy found out."

"We didn't do anything. We just—"

"Yes, yes. I'm sure. I can smell her above the vapors and all the way down the passage. It is because of her… scent that the others refused to meet with you. It would be too much of a distraction for us, possibly causing some of our weaker, less experienced brothers to lose their way and to find transcendence between the legs of a female. I will only take you so far and then I will have to leave you to your own destiny. I wish I was strong enough to join you, C'ton, for I would enjoy meditating with someone of your experience, but the pressure associated with travelling with your female would be too great. Even now I feel my lust welling up in my belly, stirring my member. I will have to purify myself as soon as I leave your presence. I only hope that the image seared in my mind of you will not be my undoing." He stared at T'mar for a moment, looking at her hard, but then softening he turned away from her, never to look directly at her again.

"You are not the only one who has passed this way recently," F'bol said as they followed him out of the small cave.

"Really?" C'ton said, feigning surprise. He was right behind F'bol, puffing along and moving too rapidly, practically pushing F'bol through the dark tunnel. The ceiling was low and the five of them were bent over at the waist with their hands touching the sides of the passage. There was nothing but blackness up ahead, giving the tunnel a sense of endlessness. C'ton knew the thickness of the mountain, how far one would have to travel in order to cross the Dome barrier and emerge on the other side, and he tried to keep his mind occupied discerning exactly how far they had come and how much farther they still had to go. The activity helped a little, as long as he didn't have to speak.

"Yes. About three half-cycles ago. He came from the Temple judging by the way he was dressed. He was still wearing his Temple tunic and the insignia of a Temple guard. He came to us just as the Dome began to grow dark. He said he was on a special assignment, too, just like you. He said he had a need to meditate in the Cave of 'loh as part of a purification ceremony. I know as well as your wizard that mediation in the cave does nothing to purify your thoughts. He knew the way, it seems, and we let him go. I didn't recognize him, although that doesn't mean anything."

"How much longer do we have to go before we are out of this tunnel? It feels like a crypt." J'son sounded like he was coming out of a deep fog. His voice rang out distant and lonely, depressed, having a quality that sounded like someone calling out in a dream. As he walked, he kept his eyes at half mast, concentrating more on the images still flashing across his awareness than on watching where he was going. He stumbled along third, right behind C'ton, bumping into him occasionally and then falling back a step or two and stepping on T'mar's toes.

"Ouch! Just keep moving, sweetheart," she said, grabbing his hind quarters with her hands and squeezing him roughly. She couldn't keep her hands to herself. Her mind, unlike C'ton's at the moment, had been overthrown by her growing lust and now she walked along the dark tunnel fantasizing. Her mind brought up sexual images from her past and present and she fondled herself as they continued. Her body allowed her physical release as they walked and the odors coming from her, mixed with the sweat and grim and close quarters of the tunnel, filled the air with a strong pungent aroma that turned the thoughts of J'son, T'mer and F'bol towards sex.

"The entrance to the Cave of 'loh is just on this side of the Dome," F'bol said, answering J'son and trying unsuccessfully to control his own growing lust. "The cave proper passes below the Dome wall and through it to the other side. It is the one place on the planet where one can truly be outside the Dome and still under its protection. It is known to us, C'ton, that your coming here is a herald that portends the end of the Dome as we know it and that your journey will take you beyond the Cave of 'loh. It has been prophesized. Only a wizard of high initiation would chance the journey to B'el's Castle in the hopes he may learn how to stabilize it. What makes you think the Heretic would help us?"

C'ton was taken out of his mental calculation at the mention of B'el's name, throwing his mind temporarily into a state of confusion. His intension was to keep their ultimate plan hidden from F'bol until the very last moment, if at all possible. F'bol had already said he would leave them once they had made it to the entrance to the Cave of 'loh and C'ton had hoped he wouldn't have to divulge the purpose of their final destination.

"Why would you believe we are going to cross the Wastelands and seek the counsel of B'el? We are but fellow travelers, such as you, looking for shelter against the long dark. Our desire is to experience transcendence and pass beyond the confines of this world. We hope to utilize the Dome failure to project ourselves into the world of the dreamers. Our personal light should be enough to cast a shadow into their world with enough force that the dreamers will begin to dream about us. I would rather be held captive in the dark recesses of the mind of a slumbering dreamer than spend the dark here, experiencing decay and entropy. Now is the time for all to escape into the magical realm of the dreamers."

C'ton's response surprised T'mar and took her out of her own sexual fantasies. The slight smile she had been wearing disappeared, replaced by a look of concern. C'ton had just revealed a deep secret of the monks, a teaching only available to the highest level of initiate. The purpose of all mediation was to bring one into a mind-space without boundaries or pre-conceived notions of what is real. It took the total domination of the will over the rational part of your mind to accomplish this task. Only through belief could one hope to reach out to the world of the dreamers and so connect with them, transporting them psychically into another realm.

The procedure was known to the elite, as well as to the Adepts of the City, but its secret was guarded above all. If the profane came to know how the monks traversed the cosmos, as had happened in the past, the world of the dreamers would become filled with the ghosts of the mentally incompetent, the undeserving and the violent. T'mar had run into the distorted reflections of some of these blasphemous heathens before during her time on that other world, but the images lacked cohesion and direction. Without the proper training, even if one found themselves on the other world they would lack the awareness of mind to do anything there and so would remain trapped between worlds, an energy that slowly dissipated, causing chaotic vibrations in the physical grid of that other world. Poltergeist was a label they used on that other world, if T'mar's drug-enhanced memory served her right.

But why should she have remembered that, considering she had no memory of anything else from the world of the dreamers. The mental fuzziness induced by the 'vjc made it hard for her to remember anything. Even J'son's presence here refused to conjure up those memories. Looking at him from behind, she couldn't remember how they came to be in that cave on the far side of the Dome. The only thing she could remember about that time was that J'son was her partner and they had to make it to the Dome before darkness fell. Where did she meet up with him? Was J'son from the City?

It was obvious to her that he wasn't a monk, but he had power nonetheless. It radiated out of him and she was sure F'bol noticed that illumination. J'son already told F'bol that he was from Earth, didn't he? Why couldn't she remember? J'son's ability to act as a portal, a doorway to that other world, if it were known to the 'dod's would be an ability all would want to possess. Did F'bol already sense that?

T'mer was bringing up the rear, rubbing the back of his head and moping. He could smell T'mar's sex as it filled the atmosphere with her delicious scent, and walking behind her, seeing what he could of her hips as they swayed back and forth seductively, caused him more than a little discomfort.

He was jealous of the boy, knowing she wanted him more than she ever wanted him. He couldn't say anything to her and tightened every time he saw her touching J'son. He didn't give one whip to where they were going or how they expected to cross the Wastelands. His only concern at the moment was relieving himself of the mounting sexual pressure building inside of him. The bliss of the vent had aroused his libido and now he was ready to explode.

Techs had a different sort of arrangement with their females, considering males and females held the same title. Theirs was a mutual understanding, a common need that each shared, giving and taking as the situation required. The sex palaces located in the City were always filled with males and females, each negotiating and bargaining with the other, promising ecstasy if only the other would do assorted, perverse acts designed to bring about a heightened sexual response. The males had certain things they liked having done to them and likewise the females, also. T'mer knew exactly what T'mar liked, and if they were in the City he wouldn't hesitate to give it to her, renting a sex room for the two of them and not leaving it until they were spent. The thought increased his frustration as he remembered how she used to take him into her and slowly milk him dry.

"T'mar! I… I mean…"

"What is it, T'mer?" T'mar asked, turning around in the dark and standing before him, her breasts barely brushing up against his massive, heaving chest.

"I…" T'mer reached up in the dark and out of familiarity placed one, callused hand on her breast, squeezing the nipple between his fingers and playing with it with his thumb.

"T'mer. Not now, you silly boy." She smacked his hand away a little too harshly but stood up on her toes to plant a long, slow, wet kiss on his hard, dry lips. She knew exactly what she was doing and enjoyed the power she had over not only T'mer but the others as well. She relished her sexuality and her mind flowed with sexual thoughts and imagery. She was playing a game with T'mer, stroking his insatiable libido, trying to bring him to the point of explosion. Her kiss, along with her soft tongue, was a conscious act designed specifically to bring him into a slave/master mentality where she was the master and he was the slave. It was an easy spell to cast and she did it deliberately, first with T'mer and then, later she would want to cast it on the others as well.

She knew F'bol wouldn't be a problem, since he was about to break his vows at just the smell of her. J'son, her lover boy play thing, wouldn't even need a spell. He was more conservative, though, than the males she had been with in the past. Normally, she would have to fight the males off, sometimes drawing blood; all specific acts of foreplay. By the time she got around to having actual, physical sex, their bodies were so bruised and bloodied and covered in sweat and seminal fluids that the act itself was more like a cooling off period. Sex with T'mar could go on for several micro-cycles at a time, leaving the men, and some women, physically spent and exhausted. J'son, on the other hand, she was discovering, needed a slower, less intense sexual adventure.

Sex with the dreamers was always accompanied by feelings of guilt and embarrassment on their part. Nocturnal emissions, while enjoyable, were something to be avoided and discouraged, they believed. For the dreamers, dreaming about sex was second rate to actually having a physical partner. T'mar really didn't understand their guilt and found waking up with an orgasm one of the highlights of mediation. Imagine feeling guilty about sexual pleasure, no matter how it came about. Masturbation was just one of the ways one gave and received pleasure, and to deny oneself that simple pleasure just didn't make too much sense. It was funny, she thought, how she could remember that particular aspect of that other world.

C'ton would be more difficult. They had a past, and sex with him was decent if somewhat strained, considering at first she began calling him her AB'el during intercourse. But he didn't seem to need sex like the rest of the males. He had told her back then that he had all the sex he needed as a young monk and only participated so as not to offend the females. She wanted to cast her spell against him just to see if she could without his notice, but the vibrations she was receiving from him gave her pause. There was something about C'ton that frightened her. Her fear was that the spell would backfire and trap her into the role of a mindless sex slave, like the ones found in the bed chambers. The garden between her legs was drying up and growing cold and she allowed doubt to enter her instead. C'ton would have to wait.

"The Cave of 'loh should be just up ahead," C'ton stated, coming to a halt in the small passageway, breathing heavily.

"And so it is. Your wizard has the gift of 'cvd, the ability to map distances without any available markers. That art comes from cycles of wandering our world. But come! We must turn a corner up ahead and then you will begin to see again."

F'bol moved ahead and disappeared into the dark, a shadow slipping into a shadow. C'ton followed after him and almost ran into the bend in the tunnel, striking his bare foot up against an outcropping. Turning to the right, the tunnel opened up into a larger room that possessed a diffused light coming from high above them through a crack in the ceiling, a crack which led to the outside world. In times past, when the Dome was at full power, the crack allowed enough light into the chamber to fill it with a soft, white light. The effect was very soothing and after the long walk in the dark was a welcome sight. Here the monks would wait before entering the Cave of 'loh, allowing in only one contemplative at a time. Normally such a journey was undertaken as a solo venture, no distractions.

Now, however, the light of the room was very dim and offered no comfort. T'mer, coming into the room last, fell against the wall and slide down to the floor. His legs were spread wide as he sat, accommodating his huge penis as it rested against his leg. He was still moody and extremely sexually frustrated. Knowing his release was long in coming, T'mer pleased himself in a darken corner of the room, totally ignoring the situation before him and the others. He felt no guilt or reproach over what he was doing and stroked away watching a fantasy unfold within his mind.

T'mar barely took notice of T'mer in the corner, only looking at him to see if her spell was working its magic. She smiled to herself and then looked at J'son. Her thinking was sexual, as her mind now had no foundation for anything other than sex. Like an addict looking for the next score, her thoughts revolved around getting sex, having sex and recovering from epic sex. She knew T'mer would be pre-occupied for a time being and seeing J'son's form in the dim light she decided to act. Hoping to instill in J'son the same level of sexual frustration as T'mer, she projected herself into his open and waiting mind. She directed her sexual energy into him, concentrating on his pelvic region, causing it to itch.

J'son moved around the room, twitching and rubbing his groin. He didn't know why, but for some reason he was horny as hell. His growing member started to embarrass him and he tucked it between his legs to hide it from the others. He stared at T'mar standing on the far side of the room, who was looking the other way, and he smiled to himself, a secret, seductive smile that mirrored the rising burning lust blazing away in his belly. He started to walk over to her but stopped when he saw the look on F'bol's face. It had the look of horror and shame, mixed with yearning and desire. His peaceful, almost angelic countenance was gone, replaced by one displaying confusion and doubt. F'bol had turned away from the others to face a wall. His lips were moving rapidly and he seemed to be praying, eyes closed.

"I must leave you now, before it is too late! Alas, but I think it may be too late already. Your witch has possessed me and even now my mind is overthrown, filling it with images that I can't bring myself to defend. Help me if you can, C'ton. My purification has been ruined and now my mind is bankrupt. I must leave you. Just beyond is the entrance to the Cave of 'loh. No! It is too much."

F'bol bent over at the waist and grabbed himself, squeezing his eyes shut. Without looking up and to the surprise of everyone F'bol raced out of the room, heading back the way they had just come. His footfalls echoed loudly down the passageway, sounding in a rush. A whimper, a sudden intake of air and emotion was the last sound the four of them heard coming from the passageway.

"T'mar, what did you do?"It was C'ton and he sounded angry. "It's not enough that you drive us crazy with lust by your smell, but now you are casting spells on us so that even our own minds deceive us? You are passing too close to the will of B'el. You must keep yourself in check. I pity F'bol. Because of you he may never find the mental focus needed to find transcendence."

C'ton knew what she had been doing but ignored it up to a point. His thoughts were in confusion as he battled himself over many things, his thoughts never giving him rest. He was besieged with jealousy concerning T'mar's sexuality and her attention to J'son. He was struggling with his own desires and his ego spoke boastfully to him, reminding him that he already had drunk from the cup of her fruit and had worn it out cycles before. The memory of that time drove him even nuttier. He was also wearied by the constant questioning of his mind and his need for answers. The info cube he took from the library provided him with any answer his probing mind asked, but having the answers at the tip of his fingers brought with it the crushing realization that he wouldn't be able to function properly without it.

And now T'mar was casting spells, trying to imprison them. Poor F'bol, he thought. He didn't know what he was getting into with T'mar. The spell she cast at J'son had rebounded toward him and so infected him with perverse, sexual thoughts. He knew F'bol must be having difficulties. In some respects, F'bol's mind was purer and more pristine than C'ton, even before he had cast that spell of B'el's. C'ton, through experience and his initiation, normally had the mental constructs to keep someone like T'mar at bay. Only when he allowed her entrance into his mind did her witchcraft affect him. It was always pleasant when he allowed this, but extremely dangerous. F'bol didn't have a chance.

"I was bored," she said indifferently, acting naive. "Why wouldn't one wish to fill their mind with such ecstasy?"

"It is ecstasy as long as it is you who is in charge," T'mer said, coming away from the wall feeling less frustrated for the moment. T'mer had dealt with his sexual energies concerning T'mar many times in the past and he liked how she would come to dominate him, possessing him. Someone as physically powerful as he enjoyed her dominatrix personae and would willing let her do whatever she wanted. There had been times that he didn't even gain release, being too exhausted to perform adequately but still glowing in the aftermath. Sometimes it took him several micro-cycles to recover, his body beaten and bruised, and he had hidden out in the sex palaces to regain his strength.

Thinking about those times with her brought his lust back up to a simmer and he felt his mind turning back towards sex. He also felt sorry for F'bol. If she did infect him, then he would never be able to get her out of his mind. His life as a monk was officially over. He knew the 'dods didn't have females of their own, like in the Temple, and that sexual matters were dealt with on a spiritual level. Still, he didn't understand why someone like F'bol would ever want to deny themselves of the fruit of the female. If F'bol felt as frustrated as he did, T'mer didn't know what he would do if even masturbation was prohibited. How could one live without sex?

"T'mar, I don't think it is wise for you to continue. I won't go into the Cave of 'loh with your mind under the influence of B'el."

"What about you, you hypocrite? You spoke out loud one of B'el's spells. I can feel the confusion within you now. Yes, when I was with B'el he opened me up to another way of thinking and living and so those memories of that time fill my mind, but do not think that I can't control my thoughts. They are just memories. I have at least as much knowledge as you, C'ton, probably more but I haven't tested myself against you."

It was true that T'mar had similar training, if not the initiation being different. Once one reached a certain level of training, the knowledge was the same. It was how that knowledge was obtained that determined your mindset. It was only her own admonishment that she might not be his equal that kept her from attempting to captivate him. If he detected her thoughts within him, even for the moment he would be forced to defend himself. But like all monks and wizards alike, when two come together to battle the only victor would be the one left with conscious awareness. If she attacked him, he would either have to send her packing to the sex chambers in the Temple where she couldn't do any more harm, or he himself would have to take up residence within the Temple.

A monk of his understanding would prove to be too dangerous out in the open. Even if his mind had been overthrown, he still possessed the knowledge but in a faulty mind. Neither option was appealing; he decided right then that in the event of an attack he would use the information contained in the info cube to project into the world of the dreamers. It was a dangerous retreat, throwing his consciousness into the void in hopes that a dreamer would see him and begin dreaming about him. Failing to find a dreamer, C'ton would be lost in the ether between this world and the world of the dreamers.

Collecting himself and regaining his composure, C'ton spoke softly, trying to diffuse the situation. "T'mar, there is no reason to challenge me here or anywhere for that matter. I am not your master and I have no say in how you exercise your abilities. I was only reminding you to take caution and to remember B'el is the enemy. Those thoughts which create disharmony within you are not your thoughts. Regain your tranquility and return to self-possession. You will need that mind-space for you to continue, as we all will."

Chapter Thirty-Seven:

The Cave of 'loh

"I'll take her when the time is right. She won't know what hit her."
T'mer fantasizing while pleasuring himself

After F'bol's hasty departure, J'son stood quietly against a wall watching T'mar and C'ton arguing. T'mer had moved forward in the room and was standing by a large gap in the rock wall, apparently the entrance to the Cave of 'loh. J'son thoughts were filled with visions of sexual conquest but also curiosity. It was this curiosity that kept his mind semi-free of T'mar's influence. He lusted after her like a schoolboy having an infatuation, but his inquisitiveness nature and highly-developed imagination kept him centered and aloof from the sexual energies floating around the room.

"Enough of this," T'mer said, snapping off his words like he was issuing a command. "I'm going in." With that he passed through the opening, turning sideways to do so.

The gap spread out and turned a corner, opening up into a large, cavernous room filled with glowing, jewel-like objects embedded into the walls. They looked like the red crystal 'nco or some other mineral and the glow coming from them gave the impression of a star burst. But instead of the rays of light streaming away from the center they gave the appearance of radiating inward, like they were drawing you in.

Staring at them and meditating on the nature of the light brought one into a mind-space that took you out of your physical environment and plunged you into a netherworld of pure imagination. It was from this launching pad that monks of all time projected themselves into the void. It was rare that one was able to accomplish total transference and most emerged from the cave refreshed, energized but still present in this reality. The effect of meditating produced incredibly vivid hallucinations and if one didn't have the experience to understand what they were seeing it was all too possible to become lost within your mind. Everything came down to training.

The others followed T'mer through the gap and entered the Cave of 'loh, coming to a halt right behind T'mer. The glowing stars embedded in the rock walls were a sight to behold and the four of them stared at the lights like in a trance. The radiance was hypnotic and instantly produced a mind state that was very similar to a dream. Each jewel possessed a doorway unique to itself, and staring at one in particular opened the mind to worlds unimaginable. Each jewel created a characteristic vision, different from the others but also distinct from the perspective of each individual viewer. Two people could look at the same jewel and have two entirely different visions. The character of the vision was based on the refraction of the jewel, which, in turn, produced a similarity in content but the symbols used were different. Whatever the mind of the seeker needed to open up his consciousness was given to them by the jewels.

C'ton was the first to speak, breaking the silence in the cavern. "This is the launching pad that will take you into the outer universe. Already our minds are filling with destinations beyond the confines of this world. I can see the stars of the constellations and a map laid over them showing the direction to another world. It is written that the walls of the Cave of 'loh mirror the sky of other worlds. It is my belief that those stars are familiar to your world, J'son."

"Yes! That one is Sagittarius and that grouping there is Orion the hunter. And there's the Big Dipper!" J'son was pointing at different groupings of jewels, drawings imaginary lines between them, connecting them into star groups.

"How can you see the stars as C'ton sees them?" T'mar asked, coming out of her own trance, seeing nothing but graphic, sexual imagery instead of constellations. "How can you see that?"

"I'm not much of an astronomer, but the walls are filled with star patterns that remind me of the night sky on my world."

"Your world?" A light dawned in T'mar's awareness. She had forgotten again. It was so hard to stay focused. He was a portal. J'son wasn't from this world. "You think the jewels embedded in the walls of the Cave of 'loh are a graphic representation of the night sky on your world?"

"That makes sense," C'ton said, sounding preoccupied.

"We use the jewels to travel within in hopes of encountering a disembodied dreamer from your world. It is difficult work deciding on which jewel to focus on out of the countless ones here." T'mar was trying to distinguish patterns on the walls but could only recognize the sexual imagery patterns taught to her by B'el. She had only ever seen their stars once, considering the daylight normally obscured their location. Only as the long dark fell, as now, did the stars come out. Her familiarity with the stars in her sky was due to her training and the sacred books handed down from the primordial past. Knowledge of their constellational representations only came through study of the ancient texts.

"See those two jewels up there and the three running at a diagonal? Those two are the shoulders of the hunter and the three are his belt. His knees are the two below that. And those that form a box with a tail, is what we call the Big Dipper."

"You see your night sky reflected up on the walls? How very interesting." C'ton was pawing the info cube searching for the labels "Orion" and "Big Dipper". Then the realization hit him. "Of course! It has been here all the time. Your world is hidden within the patterns on the ceiling. Where is it? Show me J'son. Which constellation holds your world?"

What C'ton had just asked was the question all monks of all times had asked. Knowing the location of the dreamer's home world would make mediation a lot easier and passing into their world as simple as walking through a door. All high-level monks had the training and mental focus to transcend their world, but without a place to go their mental wanderings could very well get them lost out in the void. It was only during the daylight when the world of the dreamers could peer into their world that the monks could be sure they had made contact and so pass into the mind of a dreamer.

To know the location, and to meditate on that grouping alone, would open the door to their world and allow passage back and forth without the need for extensive training or mental discipline. The way would be opened for all to use, and abuse. The reason why the location of the dreamer's world was kept a secret, unknown to all now alive, was to keep that world separate from their world.

It was written in the annals of the monks that in the distant past a decree had been made that forbid contact with that world and the location was hidden. It was written that a great war had cause the formulation of the decree prohibiting that knowledge. It was a punishment that has been handed down throughout time. But now here was J'son pointing out constellations that he recognized. So the location hadn't been lost after all and was embedded in the ceiling of the Cave of 'loh. C'ton was getting excited thinking that the goal of the ages was embedded in the ceiling of a cave.

"But who would have known the location, much less possess the ability to hide that location within the placement of the jewels?" T'mar asked, following C'ton inspiration and realizing the implications of what he said.

"There is only one who could have known, only one with the ability. I would think you would have known, T'mar. But I see in the color of your aura that you have no idea, or at least didn't know."

"B'el!" J'son said, echoing what the others were thinking.

"That knowledge wasn't part of my training. In fact, the location of their world was taken as a passé form of study, not worthy of consideration. B'el taught that stars could be seen on their world and he even tried to pinpoint those stars in the old books. He felt the Ancients knew the location, but that travel between worlds was forbidden and only the mind of a dreamer could call one out of our world. I didn't waste my time searching the ancient texts for the location of a lost world. My time was spent perfecting transference. Meditating on a dreamer was the goal of

B'el's training. His teachings centered on creating a mind-space that was conducive for transference to occur. He taught he didn't need to know the location, only that his mind could reach across the universe and capture the mind of a dreamer."

"You mean to possess him," T'mer said, being the last one to come out of his trance and join the conversation. "You know, T'mar, the learning of the Adepts centered on using Technology to create a portal of their own. They believe that passage to their world would allow them to manifest physically. The ultimate plan was to inhabit another world in their star system and make it their own, separate from the humans so as not to break the prohibition."

"Yes, T'mer. Is that why the Techs stole the power reserves?"

"We didn't, C'ton. We were going to, but someone else beat us to it. We were going to open a portal for the world to use. But that didn't happen."

"I'm not too sure, but it looks like the jewels were placed where they were from the perspective of someone looking up from my world," J'son commented. "It's like the floor of this cave is the Earth and the ceiling is the heavens."

The mention of the word, "Earth", a word not heard in the Cave of 'loh since the very beginning caused a rumbling sound accompanied by a deep vibration. The light of the jewels faded and then winked out. There was a moment of complete darkness and then several jewels lit up at the same time, forming star groupings that emphasized the known constellations in the sky above Earth. Then a ring of light enveloped the four of them and turned into a blue-green globe with oceans and landmasses. The constellations faded again and were replaced by another grouping of stars, ones that were familiar to the monks. A line was drawn between the globe and the second grouping of stars mapped out a grid that showed the location of the globe within the second grouping. Finally, the first grouping reappeared and a line was drawn between the globe, the first group and the second group, forming an inverted triangle, the symbol of union of male and female principles. There before them was a map showing the location to the world of the Dreamers.

"Where is it, J'son? Tell us."

"Well, I…" Something was keeping J'son from responding to C'ton's question. He wasn't sure, but from what he could determine from the map it appeared that the stars of his world were superimposed upon the grid of their star groupings. The triangle shape that connected the globe with the two star groupings mirrored themselves like polar opposites. The various magnitudes of the different stars didn't correspond with its counterpart, giving the false impression that they were different stars. But upon closer inspection, if the stars on this world were made the same size as the stars of his world, then the alignment would be almost exact, but on a smaller scale.

It reminded J'son of points painted on a balloon and then blown up. If the Earth was located in the center of the balloon and the constellations of his world were represented by the painted points before the balloon was blown up, then the stars of this world were represented by the fully-inflated balloon. They stretched out on a grander scale with more space between them and different magnitudes of brightness. By mentally contracting the one star grouping, J'son was able to see the two groups as one. The location of Earth, by this method of interpretation, was within this very spot. They were standing, as J'son saw it, in the middle of the universe, but on a different level.

"J'son?" T'mar asked quietly. "Do you know where it is? Can you point it out to us?"

"Well, like I said, I'm no astronomer. Maybe if we could see your stars I might recognize some similar patterns."

"No one sees the stars. Only fools like us would venture outside the Dome once the dark had fallen."

"Fools like us, T'mer?" T'mar attention returned to her burning, sexual predilection as soon as she realized that J'son didn't, or wouldn't, tell them the location of his home world. Like B'el had taught her, the physical location of Earth was of unimportance, only the meta-physical location, which was in the mind. He taught that the physical Earth didn't exist in the same form as their planet existed. The world of the dreamers was just a psychic manifestation of their own psyche, lacking solid reality. B'el likened the physical reality of Earth to the gossamer of dreams. It's real when you are there, but disappears as soon as you return.

"Never mind, J'son," C'ton said, sitting in the middle of the floor with legs crossed and the back of his hands resting in his lap, palms up. He was about to enter into a meditative state in the hopes of stabilizing his growing discomfort and mental unbalance. His subject of focus would be the new configuration of lighted jewels and he began to concentrate on which one might hold the key to Earth's location. Within a few moments he was breathing deeply and rhythmically and his body took on a curious, fiery-yellow radiance within the globe. He looked like he was consumed by a glowing fire, but by all outward appearances he was calm and peaceful. He would meditate this way in silence for many micro-cycles.

"Well, I guess we should do the same," T'mar said, sitting down on the floor directly in front of C'ton, closing her eyes. She, too, entered into a deep state of meditation almost at once and left T'mer and J'son staring at each other.

"Are you going to do that, too, T'mer?"

"Are you kidding?" Those monks and wizards are all nuts. I've a good mind to take T'mar as she meditates and have sex with her. She needs to know the difference between a real sexual encounter and her imaginary ones. What do you think boy. You want a piece of that first? I may take awhile so you're welcome to go before me. Trust me. Having sex with T'mar when she is in deep mediation is beyond anything you can imagine. While her mind might be lost out among the stars, her body is here and very responsive to all forms of physical contact. It's like having sex without having to deal with her mental manipulations. Look at her, boy. She is nothing but a plaything like the monks of the Temple insist. What do you say?"

T'mer was looking back and forth between J'son and T'mar, spending more time staring at T'mar than J'son. His lust was growing to the point of unmanageability again, and even if J'son did want to take advantage of first come, first served, he now wouldn't have let him. Seeing J'son unresponsive and hesitant to the invitation, T'mer moved over to T'mar, standing to her left, his pelvic region level with her seated position. Reaching out with his hands, he grabbed her head roughly and turned it towards him. "Why don't you busy yourself trying to find that location they're so concerned with? I'll be awhile."

J'son turned away from the three of them and backed up against the wall of the cave. He stared up at the glowing jewels and contemplated their construction. It was obvious that the cave had been designed by someone for a particular purpose. While T'mer used T'mar as he would and C'ton sat as a silent observer of the perverse scene before him, J'son studied the jewels in more detail. The closer he got to the jewels, the more he realized the jewels weren't jewels at all. They were points of light for sure, but the location of their glow seemed to come from deep within the rock, like a flashlight shining through a long tunnel. He wondered if one were to dig out one of the jewels, one of the optical reflectors, would he come to another cave deeper in the rock. He got the impression of a cave like this one with a huge light source in the center and holes drilled into the walls through to another cave. He felt along the rock walls touching the different sized jewels and found his fingers slipping into holes, passing through some sort of electric field that gave him a jolt like static electricity.

"Ouch! T'mer, what's on the other side of this wall?" The question stuck in his throat even before he got it out. T'mer was too involved in what he was doing to T'mar and was oblivious to anyone else in the cave. J'son was slightly horrified by what he saw T'mer doing to T'mar. It was so violent and brutal, like a starving animal devouring his prey. It was shocking to see her unresponsive and yet being used like a piece of meat. He turned away and then rubbed his eyes. The smell of sex filled the cave and the jewels, or whatever they were, seemed to pulse with energy, reaching maximum illumination in time with T'mer's movements. By watching the light increase and decrease, J'son had an idea whether T'mer was in or out. The pulsating lights disgusted him at their implication, and mixed with the sounds and smells of the place he was starting to become nauseated.

He sat against the wall and tried to imitate C'ton's posture and breathing, closing his eyes and unsuccessfully ignoring T'mer. His mind wandered but he remained fully conscious and aware of his surroundings. Every time he heard T'mer grunting, his eyes popped opened and then slowly closed again. He had practiced meditation before but never seriously. A girlfriend from his hometown had got him into it as a form of foreplay and he participated wholeheartedly, if not ignorantly. He couldn't remember the girls' name at the moment, but he did remember their lovemaking: awkward and way too quick. She had wanted him to practice mediation as a way for him to control himself, but if he lasted more than a minute that was considered marathon sex.

With these thoughts whirling around in his brain, suddenly he felt a tingling at the base of his spine and he wiggled his butt around thinking it was growing numb. The sensation increased and moved into his groin area causing an erection before rising into his abdomen where it burned like a small fire. The sensation wasn't unpleasant and felt like the rush of adrenaline: slightly nauseating but exhilarating at the same time. He felt his heart rate increase and his breathing became rapid. Then in a burst of intense emotion, he felt as if his heart was about to come out of his chest. Feelings of profound love directed outward filled his breast and he experience "Agape", universal love, cosmic consciousness. Just as he was about to become overwhelmed by the intensity of the feeling, reeling on the edge of consciousness, the sensation rose to his throat, causing him to speak out to the shadows in the cave.

"Gibba lato makato simbulatcy eirodo demsinti!" The sounds didn't make any sense to him and yet he continued to repeat them. Once, twice, three times.

The words did, however, make sense to C'ton and T'mar. The ancient sounds jarred C'ton awake and he sat staring at a blinking, jewel-encrusted wall trying to regain full consciousness as his mind first registered the sounds and then tried to understand the implication. T'mar eyes flung opened at the first syllable and stared up into the heaving chest of T'mer, who was lying on top of her. She lifted her arms and pressed them against T'mer, looking like she was doing a reverse pushup. The suddenness of her reaction lifted T'mer off of her and threw him to the ground next to her. She pushed herself up on one elbow and turned in J'son's direction.

J'son had finished his third repetition of the sacred mantra and the flame within him rose to his forehead where it filled his mind with an intense tingling that produced a sense of power and deep wisdom. He saw the past, present and future as one continuous eternal now and all the questions were answered with one thought. The truth was there and his mind began to formulate the proper sentence structure in order to express it. But before he could visualize a reply the blue flame within him rose to engulf the crown of his head, sending a fuzzy, tingling sensation throughout his entire body.

He was now beyond his mortal senses and the confines of his physical body. He was racing down a long tunnel that was illuminated by a bright white light at the far end. He passed the realm of ghosts and specters, hurled past the domain of the gods and came to rest before the celestial blue-white Transcendentals. He had transcended the confines of this world and all worlds. He was one with the universe. He had found the beginning to time and saw its eventual end, a closed ring that had no beginning or end. He had become a Transcendental. He had reached to goal of the monks.

"J'son!" C'ton was near panic and he practically flew from his seated position to stand beside the radiant, translucent shell that used to be J'son's body.

"He has said the mantra," T'mar said, crawling over to him. "What does this mean, C'ton? Has he left us?"

"I don't know. His body is still here, but that may be his ethereal, dragon body. It will be up to him if he returns to us. It was his attachment to you, T'mar that has kept him here on our world. But with your unbridled lust and willful manipulation I have no doubt that he may never return. Shame on you! You alone will have to carry the implications of this."

"And reap the rewards." T'mar was hoping that what they both believed had happened did indeed happen. To have an advocate in the realm of the Transcendentals was more than to be wished for. With her connection to J'son, she was thinking, speaking to and coming into contact with the Transcendentals would be profoundly simplified and she could travel throughout the universe and beyond with nothing more than by thinking about J'son.

Using him as a focal point in her meditation the doors to the higher realms would be thrown opened and she could pass between without restriction. She would possess a power greater than any monk, greater even than B'el himself. The thought excited her and she turned toward T'mer, a dark, seductive glean in her hungry eyes. The energy she was radiating filled the cave, blocking out the glow of the jewels. Her power was at full force, causing C'ton great concern and for the first time, frightening him.

"You need to calm down, T'mar. What's wrong with you?" T'mer asked, sounding fearful.

"He's right T'mar. Settle down. Remember your training. Don't let the promise of Transcendence overtake you. Return to us before it is too late."

The cavern began to rumble, a low, deep growl that came from somewhere beneath them. The illumination of the jewels grew in intensity and seemed to suck the energy out of the room. Even T'mar was taken aback and she found her newfound confidence waning, fading as quickly as her own illumination. She was brought back to herself within moments, bewildered and dazed, like waking up with a hangover. It startled her and she did feel shame at what she had been thinking, selfish.

"C'ton, what's happening to me?"

Before C'ton could respond, J'son opened his eyes, his radiance not as bright but still glowing, almost as if he were part of the glow of the jewels and not competing with it. He was still seated in the classic posture of a mediating monk and when he spoke it was softly and his words were filled with wisdom and patience. He hadn't fully integrated back into his body and his words held a dream-like quality, like he was speaking from a vast distance. He was smiling and the other three felt at peace, like they were listening to the voice of a god.

"We are all okay. Do not be afraid. I will return to you shortly with much guidance. Rest now for we will leave this place soon and journey above ground. We must stop B'el before it is too late. And you, T'mar will be the linchpin on which the fate of all worlds will be held. They have faith in you, that you will make the right decision, when the time comes. You, C'ton will see them sooner than you think, but your part isn't over yet, not yet. Have patience, my friend."

J'son stopped speaking and closed his eyes again. His breathing was slow and rhythmic and he appeared to be sleeping. Even his glow had diminished to a subtle radiance, like the glow of someone content and happy, at ease with himself and the world around him. What could only be described as a holy silence filled the cavern and the four of them rested quietly for some time, not wanting to leave the tranquility of the Cave of 'loh.

They stayed this way for an indefinite period of time, not even knowing if an age of the world had past or only a few micro-cycles. J'son was the first to awaken, back in his own body, alert and surprisingly back to his old self. He had a faint memory of his transcendence and he remembered the eternity he spent with the Transcendentals as one of them. It was a strange memory, almost like a past-life regression when view through the lens of hypnosis. He had complete clarity of the event but his mind lacked the mental vocabulary to describe it even to himself. Intuitively he knew what they had to do and saw the ramifications if they failed, but it was beyond him to articulate it.

He looked around the cave, seeing the others gathered around him in blissful states of repose. He smiled gently at them, not wanting to wake them, absorbing the peace and serenity that saturated the cave with a loving, benevolent tranquility. It was the first time since coming here that he felt safe. Even T'mar's uncontrollable lust was abated and she looked gorgeous, not an object of sexual desire but of unabashed beauty. Her appearance reminded him of his dreams and the longing he felt just to be near her. He reached out to touch her, to wake her but was hesitant to break whatever spell she was under. He didn't want her to return that that lustful, using creature she had become.

"T'mar? I think it is time that we get moving."

"What? Oh, ok."

"That was the best rest I have had in many cycles," T'mer said reaching up into the air with raised hands, stretching, popping his back. "What did you do?"

"He didn't do anything," C'ton said sounding cranky with a hint of jealousy. "It was the Transcendentals that allowed this to happen. He was merely a receptacle for their will, nothing more."

T'mar turned to look at C'ton as he stood up, holding his back. A dark scowl had formed across his face, coloring his X, deepening the lines, splitting his face into violent quadrants.

"He did nothing."

"C'ton? What…"

"Let him alone, J'son. He has his own issues to work out. Let him go."

T'mar knew better than any of them that C'ton was having a hard time accepting J'son as it was. But to acknowledge that J'son had transcended the confines of his body and this universe to become one with the Transcendentals was beginning to be more than he could handle. The peace that had a few moments before filled the cave was gone and T'mar could sense the rising tension. His knowledge base was wider than hers and so the attacks came faster and more directed. T'mar wondered how long it would be before C'ton lost all control and used his power in ways that wouldn't be acceptable. She had never tested herself against her old master, but now she began thinking of strategies to use against him in the event that possibility presented itself. The idea frightened her.

C'ton moved away from the group and stood by the back of the cave running his hands over the rock walls looking for something. He stopped by a crevice in the rock and stuck his fingers in up to his palm. Pulling it out, he followed the crack down to the floor, where it ran in two directions along the base. Following the crack to the left, he stopped at a pile of small and medium-sized boulders and began moving the smaller ones out of the way. As he moved them, sand and gravel could be heard sliding down behind them, like the first signs of an impending avalanche.

"Be careful, C'ton," J'son said, coming up from behind. "Here, let me help you. What are we looking for?"

"The way up," T'mar said joining in. "There used to be a passage leading to the surface, but it has been filled in, and by the sound of it just recently. Look!"

C'ton ignored her but J'son followed T'mar's pointing finger, seeing a pile of larger rocks that didn't carry the same age as the rest of the cave. It looked like they had been dislodged from somewhere higher up in the cave, falling to their present location. They were covered in a fine dust and looked to be recently fallen.

"C'ton, I think the passage we are looking for is over here," T'mar said. "T'mer, come here and help us remove these larger boulders. I… Oh my C'ton. Look there. I think that's a finger. But it still has the flesh on it. One of the 'dods you think?"

T'mer removed a large rock revealing not only the finger and the hand it was attached to but also an arm extending to the elbow. Another rock covered the rest of the arm and, presumably, the rest of the owner. Dried blood covered the ground in front of the rock and had formed a rusty pool underneath it. After removing several smaller rocks and a couple of the larger ones, the form of a flat torso could be seen, the legs of which extended back under even larger rocks. Judging by the position of the body, it looked as if the owner was moving in their direction when the cave started to collapse.

"I think he was trying to get in rather than out," T'mar said. "Who would have been coming in to this cave from that direction?"

"That is our monk from the Temple," C'ton said. "The one who took off in such a hurry as soon as we got there. It doesn't appear he made it to B'el's Castle after all. Poor fool. The cave came down on him before he could report to his master. We may still have anonymity on our side. Our presence here may still be undetected by B'el. Now if we can only find a passage up to the surface."

"I feel a slight breeze coming from over here," J'son said, running his hand up the face of the wall closest to the body. "I can feel a breeze and I can smell… something."

"Don't inhale too deeply, my young novice," C'ton said casually. "The air is poison and I don't think you can convert that even with your abilities. Move out of the way and let me see. T'mar, we will need a breathing spell from this point onward. Do you have the training to encompass all of us, or do you need my help?"

C'ton was sounding increasingly sarcastic and uncaring, which bothered T'mar and the others a great deal. For their entire time together they had come to depend on and even take for granted C'ton's protection, wisdom and leadership. But now he seemed aloof from them and coldhearted. J'son noticed this especially and he questioned his motives. Had they lost C'ton to the lure of B'el without their notice? J'son had been so pre-occupied by T'mar's lustful advances that he hadn't bothered to pay attention to C'ton's growing resentment and irritability.

Without responding to the dripping sarcasm, the others began to remove the rocks and boulders surrounding the dead body, opening up a small, narrow tunnel of fallen rocks which led back into the wall. The walls of this tunnel seemed stable enough if not precarious. It was tall enough to crawl through and J'son was the first to go in, tossing smaller rocks out into the larger cave as he moved along. Again, sand could be heard sliding down and dust rose out of the mouth of the crawlway. J'son started to cough, which caused T'mar great concern.

"J'son, come out of there. You need to be protected. Let me cast a spell so we all can breathe." She closed her eyes and started to mumble something, her fingers twitching in the dust-filled air. J'son didn't come out but continued on, his coughing sounding stifled and distant. "J'son! Come back here."

"The presumptuousness of the naïve," C'ton intoned.

"T'mer. Help me clear more of the rocks away. J'son!" The concern in her voice surprised even her.

T'mer moved a couple more boulders out of the way and then stopped. "Any more and I'll bring the tunnel back down on him. We'll just have to go on our hands and knees."

Chapter Thirty-Eight:

The Wastelands

"There was a war here, long ago, that destroyed the ecology of the planet. The idea of constructing a Dome was first brought up for discussion by B'el. He knew what he was doing even before we agreed. The moment we signed that agreement and Dome construction began was the moment we surrendered our freedom.
C'ton cryptic answer to why the Wastelands existed

The three of them followed after J'son with T'mar in front and C'ton bringing up the rear. The spell T'mar had cast enveloped the four of them in a static-y, light-green haze, an oblong bubble of breathable air that offered no protection other than keeping the noxious fumes from entering their lungs. The glow of the bubble illuminated the cramped tunnel, giving J'son a fairly clear view immediately in front of him.

The tunnel was obviously formed by the collision of falling rock, giving the floor and walls a rough, jagged texture. Crawling hurt their hands and knees, scraping them and causing them to bleed. It was slow going and they only managed to move along a short distance before J'son stopped, trying to catch his breath. Surprisingly, the air he took into his lungs was cool and refreshing in contrast to the hot and confining tunnel.

"How large can you make this bubble?" J'son asked, sitting up against the side of the tunnel with his head tucked down between his legs.

"What's the hold up? Keep moving!" It was C'ton pushing them from behind.

"The bubble is generated by the energy from our own bodies. It takes the oxygen already within us and swells it to cover the size of whoever cast it. I have extended it to include all of us, which is about the extent of its size. Anything larger and the bubble would burst. That could be potentially dangerous, especially in the Wastelands. Just momentary exposure to the atmosphere up there and we would be dead. The danger lies in the lack of available energy to work with. I'm not too sure if I can—"

"No need to concern yourself with that, T'mar. If it comes to it, I'm sure the boy has all the power you'll need. T'mer, get out of my way. No time to rest."

"Where do you expect me to go, C'ton? The tunnel isn't large enough for me to let you pass."

"It's ok. I'm moving again, J'son said. "T'mar, how long do you think we need to go before we- you know- find a way up? This tunnel feels like we are going downward and not up."

"That's about right. Before the cave collapsed, a passageway led down into another large cave that ended at a staircase, carved out of the rock. The stairs led up from there and entered the Wastelands on the other side of the Dome. There used to be a, ah, guardhouse that was permanently staffed by the worshipers of B'el, providing a way station for wandering monks and the like. It has since been abandoned, long ago when the way between the Temple and the Castle was severed. Now, I'm not too sure what we will find, or even if the stairs still exist. I never came back this way so I don't know."

"But you knew about its location!" Again, C'ton sounded condemnatory and accusing, like he was blaming her for something. He had become inscrutable and enigmatic to T'mar, closed off and the tone of his voice was disturbing. It was an attitude that was causing T'mar growing concern. If he was acting like this now, how would he react once they made it to the Castle, if, in fact, they did make it?

A heavy sigh. "C'ton, I'm not too sure what going on, but I've got my… lust under control, for now and I wish you would do the same, for the good of us all."

The tunnel had widened slightly and the roof extended away from them, allowing them to stand. C'ton brushed past T'mer in a rather rude fashion, pushing him to the side and causing T'mer to restrain himself momentary. He didn't care what C'ton's problem was. Wizard or no, he wasn't used to being treated like a rag doll. And respect was one of the things that T'mer had issues with. Many a times he had run issues with T'mar over her apparent indifference to his need for respect.

"Watch it, Wizard," he growled.

"T'mer, it's ok." T'mar placed a warm, tender hand on his shoulder and smiled up at him, a smile that said she cared for him; it was a smile he hadn't seen in a long time. That smile disarmed him and the irritation left almost immediately, leaving him feeling humbled.

"I see something up ahead. I think it is the staircase." J'son took off, breaking away from the group and severing his connection to the bubble. He sped off without the benefit of protection and disappeared in the gloomy dark, his footfalls sounding muffled.

"J'son, wait," T'mar said, but too late. The remaining three stood in the dark of the tunnel glowing from the bubble. Up ahead was total darkness and J'son couldn't be seen.

"Relax," C'ton said. "We'll catch up to him. He'll be waiting for us, either dead or alive."

"How can you be so callous?" T'mer asked. He then took off after J'son, foolishly breaking his connection to the bubble and disappearing in the darkness.

"Those fools!"

"C'ton, help us. Please." T'mar looked at him, seeing the indifference and then took off after the other two. Even though she had cast the spell, the bubble split in two and fully encased him. Because of his training he was able to appropriate that spell and incorporate it into himself. He stood alone in the tunnel; and the color of his bubble radiated a dark green, the color of envy.

The floor of the tunnel fell off sharply a few feet beyond where they had just stood, and T'mar almost stumbled down the incline, coming to a halt at the bottom. Before her was J'son and T'mer, glowing a bright blue, surrounded by an energy field created by J'son that was more protective than the one surrounding T'mar. They were staring up at a lengthy staircase that reached up into the gloom of the ceiling, disappearing from sight. Rocks and boulders littered the uneven floor and all around were signs of a recent cave in. Several steps had been broken and the way was blocked by huge protruding rocks sticking out in all directions. They would have to crawl their way across the larger ones, but the way up was still passable.

"I think I see tiny points of light up there," J'son said. "Are there more jewels like in the cave of 'loh?"

"I don't think so, J'son. If you're seeing what I think you are seeing, then those points are the stars of our world. Remember, it will be totally dark on the outside. To see the stars with my own eyes is… well." T'mar broke off reflectively and musing to herself.

"So! The stairs are still here," C'ton said coming up from behind, breaking the silence, sounding almost triumphant, like he was the one who found them. "All that is left to do is to journey upwards and then out, which may prove to be more difficult than the way here. If the access is blocked and sealed, not even the gods will be able to move it. But maybe B'el wants to be visited and the way will be opened."

"I think I can see stars up there, C'ton. At least that's what T'mar thinks."

"Stars?" C'ton moved alongside the others and looked up, squinting into the dark. The glow from his bubble hindered his ability to see much further than a few feet away.

J'son's bright blue allowed him increased vision with clarity and now that he knew what he was looking at he was sure that they were stars. "Can you see them, T'mar? Here, let me show you." With that, the bright blue bubble reached out to encompass them, but it failed to capture C'ton wrapped up in his dark green, pulling away from him as if reacting to a fire. The three of them, J'son, T'mar and T'mer stood looking up at the tiny pinpoints of light shinning above. Just discernable in the dark, J'son thought he could see a shadowy ring surrounding a group of stars. The effect reminded him of looking through the eyepiece of a telescope.

"I think there is an opening up there, a way out."

"Of course there is a way out, you fool. This place was made to have a way out. Come, I will lead us out. We have wasted enough time here." C'ton moved J'son forcefully out of the way and mounted the first, high step, then the next, pausing just long enough to keep his balance on the rapidly rising stairs. After a few steps, the stairs had been obliterated leaving a gaping hole where several steps should have been. Ignoring his instincts to stop and let T'mer help bridge the gap, C'ton flung himself over the breach, clawing the next available step and pulling himself up. Turning around to look down the chasm he watched as pebbles and small rocks fell into the dark. His heart was pounding and he was on the edge of panic, but he had made it across without the help of the others. That knowledge gave him renewed confidence and he beckoned to the others to follow him.

"Nothing to it," he said breathlessly.

The others looked at each other, fear and suspicion filling their eyes. T'mer put a hand on J'son's shoulder, holding him back, and approached the gap, looking down. Without saying a word he jumped over and landed solidly on the next available step, pin-wheeling his arms for balance. Maintaining his equilibrium he extended a hand to J'son, indicating his assurance that they could make it across. T'mar was last to span the gap, and watching her jump the chasm was like seeing a gazelle bounding over a hedge. She almost floated across, landing lightly and pulling herself into T'mer's waiting arms.

C'ton's glowing dark-green bubble could be seen bouncing on up ahead taking the steps a little too fast for the comfort of the others. He didn't seem to care that there were others in his party and that they saw him as their leader. What seemed more important to him was that he would be the first to reach the top, regardless if the others made it or not. He still had a long way to go and he estimated the surface to be more than

1000 feet above, or five hundred steps to go. He counted silently to himself every step, pausing occasionally to look down on the others to see their progress, with a self-satisfied grin on his face.

"Why is he acting like this?" J'son asked. His growing concern for C'ton's mental stability was silently echoed by the others in the expressions they carried. What was happening was totally out of character for C'ton, at least the C'ton he had come to know.

"It was the spell he cast back at the Temple to help resurrect you," T'mar explained. "The words of B'el are poison, especially to those of a pure heart."

"But didn't you cast a spell, too?"

"Yes… I did. I was trained differently, by B'el himself, so I have a better understanding of what those spells can do. For me, the spell works on my natural inclination and in some circles it is expected for a female to act the way we do. C'ton, on the other hand, as the spell started to work on him, it captured the part of his mind that could be most easily affected, namely his insatiable curiosity. The spell has been intensified for some reason that I can't quiet put my finger on. It is almost like another force is adding to the influence of the spell, like it is being fed by something other than the echo of B'el's words. I can't explain it."

The bouncing dark-green bubble had all but faded away in the gloom and T'mar wondered if C'ton had made it to the top. "Whatever is feeding it, his curiosity, I hope it run out of food soon. It will be hard enough to cross the Wastelands without having to worry about C'ton abandoning us. His eternal quest for answers will drive him ahead of us. He has always wanted to meet B'el on his own terms, to test his knowledge against that of B'el's. My fear is that he will be bested and become a willing slave of The Master."

"A willing slave, T'mar?"

"Well, yes. Once in his power, all come under the sway of his black promises and would willingly sell their soul to learn at his feet."

"Like you T'mar?" T'mer was bringing up the rear keeping an eye out for possible dangers as well as looking behind them to see if they were being followed. "I'm more concern for you, considering what happened to you."

"T'mer!"

"What is he talking about? I know you were a student of his and T'mer had to come rescue you when B'el wouldn't let you leave. What else is there?"

T'mar was silent, debating whether or not she should tell J'son the truth about B'el and her. She had hoped that divulgence wouldn't be necessary and she was anxious of how that truth would affect J'son. "Well..."

"Tell him, T'mar. He needs to know what he is up against. If C'ton had turned, he won't know who to trust unless you tell him the truth."

T'mer's logic was sound and she began to relate the story in part. "I was more than just a student of B'el's. When he called to me and I heeded that call, I was looking for power over the priesthood in order to bring it down. I was angry and full of venom, wanting nothing more than the total destruction of the Temple and everything it represented. I was angry, J'son and young, naïve. The secrets he promised to reveal, and did reveal, showed the truth about this world and how the priests had twisted that truth to perpetuate their positions of power. He told me the truth about your world and our connection to it.

"By possessing this truth, one had access to a power that would shake the foundations of the planet and dissolve the stranglehold that the hierarchies here held over the laity, those without knowledge or power. Your world, J'son is also under the domination of the priests even though they depend on you for their power. At its best it is a symbiotic relationship that weakens the host while creating a bond that has become impossible for you to break. Your world is enslaved through a series of lies and deceptions that has made you the slave of a dictatorial master. Religion has become the tool of the priesthood to control you and was in fact created by them. All religious dogma has come to your world from this world. What B'el teaches is to see religion for what it is and release you from its suffocating grasp. He freed me, J'son."

As she spoke, T'mar became entranced by her own monolog, reliving the teachings and sermonizing, proselytizing, preaching the "truth" to an increasingly bewildered J'son and agitated T'mer. She was making B'el sound like a savior of sorts instead of the deceiver he was. It was intoxicating to hear her speak and the very air within their bubble drew on the occult power such proclamations generated, changing the color from the bright blue of J'son's bubble to a dark red resembling the ruddiness of lava. The walls around them seemed to close in and the shadows seen in every nook and crevice took on a life of their own. Her speech was drawing out the supernatural forces embedded in the rocks themselves. Soon their location would be easily noted by B'el, but they didn't think about that at the moment.

C'ton was moving along above them at a good pace. He felt energized and sure-footed. He was taking in vast quantities of air, gulping it down, but he didn't feel winded or tired. He was drawing energy out of the rock surrounding him, virgin energy, as no one had come this way in a long time. The energy was pure and unpolluted, easily used and manipulated. He felt strong and confident, that is until T'mar started to speak. He didn't hear her or even recognized the nature of her speech, but he could sense the power that was being drawn to her.

Pausing on the steps, feeling a change in the energy field around him, he saw small, multi-legged creatures emerging out of the rock, working their way downward. He could hear hissing and the howl of some beast coming from somewhere far below. His dark-green bubble became almost opaque to the point he couldn't see beyond it. The air within the bubble energized him with an evil intent, reinforcing his already negative feelings, causing him to think black thoughts directed at the others below him.

Enveloped as he was in his dark bubble, unable to see where he was going, he thought briefly of hiding in the shadows until the others caught up, surprising them and sealing them within a caging spell. That would be one way to neutralize T'mar without the probability of open battle, but J'son would be another story. With his bright-blue energy bubble, C'ton didn't think he would be able to hide from him. For all C'ton knew, J'son was able to see like it was daylight, burning away all shadows, mental and otherwise, and revealing his intension.

He would have to be careful with J'son from here on out. He would have to bury his true intent, even his very thoughts if he wanted to take advantage of J'son's abilities. C'ton closed his eyes and spoke a mantra to himself that he had learned long ago to calm his increasingly chaotic mind. He wasn't capable of clearing his bubble or the troubling influence of T'mar's speech, but the negative voices were gone and he found a mind-space that allowed him the peace he normally possessed. He would wait for them, out in the open until they caught up with him and then he would allow J'son's bubble to envelope him, giving him clarity of mind and vision.

He didn't have to wait for long. Shortly after T'mar's discourse, the three of them continued upwards in a strained silence. T'mar's words had startled them, especially J'son, and he was the first to continue climbing the steps even before she had finished speaking. He was starting to suspect many things and he could sense she was still holding something back. He couldn't put his finger on it, but for some reason he was starting to believe she had become something more than just a 'che.

He had many questions, like why did T'mer come after her and why did she need rescuing? She had mentioned being a willing slave and that willing part bothered him. They were going into the heart of the beast, as it were, and both T'mar and C'ton seemed to have an ax to grind. T'mer didn't seem to be as greatly influence by B'el as the other two, and that gave J'son a little comfort. Maybe it was his scientific background that didn't allow him the luxury of the free association necessary to become influence by B'el. People like T'mer, the Techs, needed concrete proof of the validity of something before they could embrace it, especially a belief system based on esoteric philosophy.

But T'mer had seen the effects of that philosophy and had known T'mar over an extended period of time. He had seen what belief in the occult could do. Maybe it was something else that prevented T'mer from falling under the influence of B'el. His attraction to T'mar was obvious, boarding on strong emotion. He cared for her, maybe even loved her, for what that meant to people like him. And J'son could see that she cared for him, too. Together the two of them formed a bond that, maybe, protected

T'mer from that influence. But shouldn't T'mar benefit from that same bond? She had been trained as a Tech, also, and so had the advantage of knowing about the occult and the grounding in science to understand what the secret powers could and couldn't do. Maybe that was why she was able to overcome her lust where C'ton was still possessed by his.

These thoughts stayed with J'son as he climbed the stairs, keeping his head down and eyes on the next step. Part of him was oblivious to T'mar and T'mer following closely behind him. He could hear them breathing and the echo of their steps, but if they were to stop suddenly he would have taken little notice so pre-occupied as he was by his own questions. Even C'ton's location above them was out of his mind, and so when he did reach C'ton's position it was a surprise, literally scaring him and causing him to cry out.

"Ahhhhhhhh!"

T'mar and T'mer, also deep in thought, were just as startled and T'mar instinctively held her hands out in front preparing to cast a protection spell, even though such a spell would rebound back on her in the confines of J'son's bubble, proving to be mostly ineffective. T'mer responded by balling up his fists, ready to pound them into whatever caused J'son's outburst. They had momentarily forgotten about C'ton being ahead of them and so their reaction was truly one of alarm. The dark-green of C'ton's bubble was hard to see in the dark and when he spoke his voice came as a shadow within a shadow, a cold whisper floating in the stifling air. Its character startled them more than J'son cry.

"I'm so sorry J'son. I didn't mean to frighten you," he said, sounding comforting in spite of the icy tone.

"That's okay. I was just… we were… the climb has been so exhausting, but I think that may have something to do with this field I am generating."

"You're right about that. You shouldn't go so bright, conserve your energy. You'll need it. We'll all need your energy reserves once outside. Here, let's not work against each other. There is no reason why we need two energy bubbles. I'll drop mine if you will extend yours around me. I will help feed you and take some of the load off."

Immediately, C'ton's dark-green bubble disappeared, evaporating from an opaque shell to a transparent mist to nothing in a matter of moments. C'ton began to cough, breathing in the toxic fumes of the stairwell. His face became distorted and he truly needed J'son's help if he was going to survive for more than a few seconds. Collapsing his bubble took the others by surprise, giving them no time to consider C'ton's offer, an offer T'mar took to be a bad idea under the circumstances. The only thing that J'son could do at the moment was to do exactly what C'ton suggested.

C'ton had fallen to knees on the narrow step he had been standing on, and J'son instinctively envisioned his bubble extending outward to encompass C'ton. Now, taking deep gulps of fresh, cool, clean air C'ton turned to look up, seeing the stars for the first time. The ring of black surrounding the stars was clearly an opening and the way out. They were almost to the top and the stars were like bright crystals embedded in deep, dark velvet, shinning like mini spotlights, casting shadows around the mouth of the stairwell.

The florescence of J'son's bubble kept the shadows at bay but only for as far as his bubble extended before them. The shadows and the lights were easily seen by all and they stared up at the beauty of the stars as their pure radiance rained down on them. It was mesmerizing, the light, and they stood there for an indefinite period of time, marveling over their loveliness. Tears came to J'son's eyes as he remembered the stars of his own planet.

"They're beautiful," he whispered.

Continuing their upward climb, the mouth grew in size until the stars filled it up and the opening disappeared completely. They reached the top slightly out of breath and stood out in the open. There was a brutal wind and black sand pinged against their bubble. The guardhouse T'mar had mentioned was off to the left and made of black rock like the Temple. Most of it had fallen and lay broken on the ground. Two walls still stood intact, though, if somewhat scarred, and the roof which had covered the opening in the past was lying shattered and ruined before them. Large chunks of it lay buried under a thick blanket of the black sand that stretched out in all directions, hiding the horizon to the left, right and before them.

Turning around and pointing in the direct of the Dome, C'ton was excited to mark its location. "There! Can you see it, J'son? Do you see that dark-red line curving upward obscuring the stars? That is the outline of the Dome. Under normal circumstances, it would be glowing bright, a beacon in the dark. Brilliant and as intense as the sun residing high in the sky, it would beckon all to its light and protection, a shelter against the long dark, a hostel of comfort where learning could be obtaining and fears would be banished. Now, alas, it is dim and soon it will be as dark as the night,"

"C'ton," J'son began. "If the Dome is always lit, as you say, as bright as the sun, how would you know about the stars? Wouldn't its glow block out their radiance?"

It was a good question, and one which the monks had discussed over the age. As beautiful as the stars were, one wondered why anyone would want to stay within the confines of the Dome. Imagine never having a night and never being able to see the stars. Why would you want to subject yourself to that requirement? Did anyone ever venture outside the Dome once the dark fell? And why did B'el have a Castle out here in the so-called Wastelands? There were two schools of serious thought on the manner and C'ton and T'mar looked at each other regarding his question, silently debating whose story should be told: the monks or B'el's?

"The Dome was constructed," T'mar began, taking the initiative, assuming now that they were outside the Dome what the monks had to say held no meaning. She started walking towards what would have been the horizon in the direction of the largest star in the sky, a sparkling jewel lighting up the night. If directions had any meaning here, it could be said she was taking an eastward route. However, her sense of bearing was based on memory, considering the last time she had come this way the sun was high in the sky and had provided direction. Now, however, she was going forward based on an intuitive sense of where she thought the sun might have been. It was fool-hearty to wander around out here without some sort of signpost or marker and that was why she chose that particular star to follow.

"...at the beginning of the last age, all was chaos and knowledge had been lost. The Wise were nothing but fools dressed up to look wise, wearing tattered robes and pompous headdresses. We were barbarians and pagans, worshipping the sun and the nature spirits, even the creeping things. We were no better than your race, before you were granted civilization."

Granted?

"B'el was the first one to stand up before the primitive priesthood and declare an end to ignorance. He—"

"That's not exactly true, T'mar," C'ton interjected. "We all belonged to the priesthood then and it was decided in committee, before the Council was formed."

"I think J'son has a right to know, C'ton. If you interrupt me even before I get to the good stuff, he'll never hear the truth."

"The Truth! Hah. The way B'el sees it, maybe." She was right of course and C'ton decided to bide his time and let her unravel the mystery in her own way. It wouldn't matter anyway. The "Truth" would never be known so long as B'el held sway over the minds of those seeking the esoteric way of knowledge.

The sand stretched out before them without interruption, an unbroken sea of undulating dunes and bottomless sinkholes, with no signs of life. The burning heat that was daylight had rapidly turned into the freezing cold of open space. The atmosphere of the planet had vanished long ago and the toxic fumes that made up the air were the results of radiation of a nuclear type. A mass destruction had rained down on the planet's distant past, it was said, as a punishment for crimes committed by the gods. The Dome was the result of the survivors, a pact made between B'el and C'ton, plus others that were part of that group. C'ton knew the truth of the matter, of course, but from a different perspective than B'el, the deceiver.

B'el had managed to protect some of the knowledge from the past, although he never revealed how he came to preserve it or why he was the sole possessor of it. His possession of the sacred knowledge made the priesthood nervous, but they couldn't deny his right to guardianship. He had convinced them that they needed the Dome in order to prevent the lost of that knowledge once the sun had left the sky again.

"To speak of the sun leaving the sky again was considered blasphemous, even after they had been witness to it, or rather their memory of it. We were animals, J'son, without a leader or clear direction."

"You said 'we'. Were you here at that time? I thought C'ton said—"

"No she wasn't; much to her annoyance," C'ton interrupted again. "It is a fact that she needs to accept. Just because you are taught a thing doesn't mean that you were there when these things occurred. She has melded teaching with memory."

"That may be so, C'ton. But remember that is was B'el who came up with the plan that saved us all. Without his foresight, none of us would be here." C'ton's interference angered her but she understood why. He had change over the course of their journey and his insistence on being first went against his character but also complimented it in a way. He used to be patient and uncomplaining, but now he was challenging and provocative. It was almost like he was trying to wrest J'son away from her through subtlety and innuendo. She was only trying to enlighten J'son concerning the nature of their foe. They should be working together, not quarrelling over disputable matters.

The sand was endless and the going slow. The wind pushed against them from all sides making their progress sluggish and time-consuming. Their energy reserves were up, though, thanks to the vent back in the smaller cave. J'son didn't seem to be bothered by the discussion nor the back and forth between T'mar and C'ton. T'mer was quiet in the rear of the party ever on the guard, only partially listening to the exchange. He had heard T'mar's report before, and the training he received at the Academy practically mirrored C'ton's beliefs. The two systems of thought had been fused within his school, with the monks' interpretation gaining the more orthodox acceptance. The only point of details, so the school taught, was for equations and graphs. To speculate on the distant past and the plethora of "facts" stemming from that time only led to confusion and bickering among the power elite, and T'mer had little patience for it.

As they continued their march across the flat areas, avoiding the movement of the rolling dunes and the deep pockets left in their wake, they crossed the desert in a winding, zigzagging direction, keeping the bright star foremost as a beacon. The other stars shone down all around them, but the radiance of the main star encircled their party in a halo of sorts, a field of light that merged and blended beautifully with the bright-blue of J'son's bubble. The combined effect gave them clear visibility within that halo but also diminished their ability to see into the distance. Just beyond the glow of their bubble all was dark except for the pinpoints of lights that dotted the sky.

T'mer felt the tension in T'mar and he reached out a cracked and dry hand and placed it on her shoulder in a show of comfort. He didn't know why, but she seemed so small and vulnerable right then and he didn't like the way C'ton kept challenging her. These discussions had been going on since the beginning, or so he had been taught. Who cares what the truth was! They were probably going to die out here as it was without ever making it to B'el's Castle. And even if they did make it to that black, towering fortress, he didn't think he had it in him to face that fear again. It had taken all that he was to face it down before and without his strength and courage he didn't believe they had a chance. What good were Wizards in the face of such destructive power and malevolent wisdom? Only time would tell.

"So he teaches," C'ton said. "It was B'el that came up with the idea to steal the energy of J'son's world in order to build the Dome. He enslaved a race that had nothing to do with us and only lately came to seek us out. He dangled the world of imagination before them and so stole their dreams, offering only empty promises."

"He gave them civilization and Technology, C'ton. They were hiding in caves fearing the lightening, living like beasts. He awakened within them their innate ability to dream and grow as spiritual beings. Without his intervention, they would still be lost in a lost world. He brought them religion and the idea that there was something else, something sacred. He gave them the concept of the One."

"Yes, by making them believe he was that One."

"You mean, God?" J'son asked, becoming really interested at this point. The talk at first centered on this world but now had turned to a discussion of religion and the foundations of such.

"In the parlance of your world, yes," C'ton said, talking control of the discussion once again. "Before that time, before the time of your enlightenment, you had no concept of a higher power. Your world was filled with violence continually. Not a very conductive place to contemplate spiritual matters. We needed you to see us, but with your innate abilities slumbering, so to speak, we couldn't reach out to you or you to us. We needed you to search us out, to call out to us. We didn't know of your existence until the first dreamer called out to us. It was just a coincidence that happened when our sun was bright in the sky. We conjectured that the light of our sun allowed you to see us. Up until that time, we were invisible to you, possessing no discernable form or reality. And with your ability to dream out of your conscious awareness, and no sense of the One, you wouldn't have dreamed about us at all.

"At first your dreamers considered the visions running through their primitive minds were the results of the mentally ill and derangement. We were considered monsters and, later, demons. It was only after we realized our mistake that we came to you in the form of ethereal beings."

"You mean Angels," J'son said making the connection.

"Yes. That was one form that we took. But later, as your Technology progressed, we appeared to you as you wanted to see us: Angels, demons, alien creatures from other worlds, which, I guess is the closest to our reality. The greatest of us were able to manifest physically, bodily as well as in crafts which you dreamed up. It was confusing to us, jumping around from one belief system to another, but we managed to adapt. Some of us, even now, are on your world, living and... well..."

"Tell him, C'ton," T'mar said. "He needs to know what we have done. We are your leaders and the people of power and industry and authority. We control your world like never before. It is the goal of our people to transport ourselves to your world, to avoid the dark of this world. It is believed we will not survive another cycle of dark. You won't be able to see us and we won't be able to travel to your world. We will become lost to you once again, as is happening right now. J'son, I can't stay here. The Fear! We need you as a portal to return to your world. Help us. Please!"

Chapter Thirty-Nine:

B'el's Plan

"The will to power is the only power. A strong mind can overcome all obstacles except doubt. Without the willful focus of intention, the mind can do nothing."

From the annals of B'el

"T'mar, that's enough for now." C'ton was quiet and reserved. She had said more than he was willing to reveal. The secret, the goal of his people, was to travel to earth, and if possible find a host to which they could join and so stay there indefinitely. Possession was what they called it on J'son's world, and the people of C'ton's world had found many willing subjects to possess. It wasn't always the plan to possess these mortals, but their willingness to step aside and allow one of them to inhabit them became too irresistible. To possess a body that had the spark of the divine residing within them, a power that could literally turn them into gods was more than the ethics of C'ton's world could account for.

Morality was relative among them and the lure of unlimited power caused many of them to fall within the bodies of the unenlightened, trapping them within the chaos of a mind unprepared to handle the implications. It was dangerous to possess a human in this way and the higher initiates of C'ton's world practiced self-control to avoid such a scenario. They learned to be patient, residing within a particular family, biding their time, quietly instructing people of a certain persuasion over the course of generations until finally they could manifest among them without fear of rejection or derangement.

T'mar had done this under the tutelage of B'el. She had become so proficient coming and going that she was held up as an example of how to navigate the world of the dreamers. C'ton, too, possessed that ability but rarely used it, so concerned was he that he would fall victim to the overwhelming temptation to stay and live out his life on their world in the body of another. It was a practice that was strictly forbidden and the Dome and the Wastelands were the primary reminders of that prohibition.

The red glow of the Dome had faded away behind them. Looking back C'ton didn't know if it was because they had moved far enough away that the Dome fell below the horizon, or if the energy had finally run out. Either way, it didn't matter. He knew within himself that this was a one way trip. Even if they managed to reach B'el's Castle and found he still had enough power to make it through the dark, where would they go after that. He knew they could never persuade B'el to give up his reserves for the good of the monks. B'el may consider a trade, if he had the reserves. But that trade, that deal would be one C'ton wouldn't want to make. J'son had different ideas about why they were going there, something having to do with the Transcendentals, but that was knowledge C'ton wasn't privy to.

J'son had said something about stopping him, but stopping him from doing what? Was B'el responsible for the missing power reserves? Is that why the Transcendentals had sent J'son to them? Was J'son the missing key to the lock of this mystery? C'ton didn't know and as much as he fumbled with the info cube searching for that answer, the more strained his thinking became. J'son did possess a strange ability. Here was a dreamer that could pass between the worlds, and according to T'mar he could take them with him, as long as he could maintain a residual impression of them within his consciousness. But maybe he could only hold one of them at a time. Who would J'son take with him when that time came? C'ton was pretty sure that during a time of extreme crisis J'son would automatically cross the barrier between worlds and "wake up" on his home world.

He had seen that kind of effect personally, when the dreamer was startled awake. It was a practice that the monks taught to force a dreamer to remember them, and so bring them into the waking consciousness of the dreamer. The longer the dreamers could remember their dreams, the more time the people of C'ton's world had on their world. If the reaction was strong enough, pleasant enough or frightening enough, the higher initiates could materialize and remain as a physical entity. T'mar had done this on many occasions using her sexuality as the motivating factor. Sometimes it failed to keep the dreamer awake, so delicious was her presence in their dreams that the dreamer would spend most of their time in dream states. That could be pleasant, but there they would remain in a world of dream, and depending on the predilection of the dreamer the monks would find themselves at the dictates of that particular mind.

Some of the monks would try to scare the dreamer, creating a nightmare scenario in which the dreamer would be haunted and so carry the monk with him with frightening clarity. Those particular monks employing that type of stimulus would invariably create an environment in which the dreamer became twisted, slightly neurotic if they possessed a strong personality or psychotic if they were weak. Either way, so the monk would argue, they got to stay in that world manifesting as "familiars" or "spirit guides". That type of manifestation wasn't what C'ton wanted or thought ethical. Instead he, like T'mar, wanted to materialize physically, independent of a dreamer and live out an immortal existence, becoming a god for the betterment of man.

His time here was up and C'ton knew that whatever happened once they reached B'el's Castle he wouldn't stay, couldn't stay. He couldn't face the long dark, not again. He had taken the info cube with his plan of escape in mind. It bothered him that he would use the knowledge contained within the cube to transport out of this world, leaving the others behind, but reason dictated this course of action. He would wait until the very last moment, then without preamble or discourse he would simply leave. And now that he had an idea of where J'son's world was, based on the star chart found in the Cave of 'loh, he could safely and somewhat confidently do just that. It would pain him, this deception, but the outcome would override any remorse that he would have.

"T'mar, what is that?" J'son said cupping his hands over his eyes like binoculars, shielding the glare of the energy bubble, giving him a view of the landscape in the distance. "I think I see a glow or something."

"Out here? That's not possible," T'mer responded.

"Wait! I think I see it, too," T'mar said mimicking J'son's posture. "It can't be. C'ton?"

C'ton, who had been deep in thought, looked up, startled out of his contemplation. His eyesight wasn't as strong as T'mar's, but using subtlety he cast a seeing spell that the others didn't notice. The brightness of the bubble diminished slightly because of the spell, making it vaguely more transparent, but its transparency wasn't what allowed C'ton to see with more clarity. The spell allowed him to see through the eyes of any living thing that he chose. In this case, he saw through the eyes of J'son, quietly entering his mind without so much as a stray thought. J'son wouldn't sense it except for a momentary flash of double vision. Instinctively blinking his eyes would clear that up.

With the bubbles' intensity slightly dimmed, all of them could clearly see the glow far away. It was faint and the radiance of the stars made it difficult to discern, but the glow was there nevertheless. It looked like the beginnings of a sunrise, J'son thought, but the glow was white more than blue, yellow or red. The glow diffused the radiance of the stars lower on the horizon and blended with them, causing them to lose their individuality.

C'ton began to cough and that tore his awareness away from J'son. Immediately the bubble regained its full strength and the glow on the horizon faded from view. He coughed again, holding his chest trying to breathe in the purified air within the bubble. He had taken too much energy away from the bubble and allowed some of the radiation to filter in. The bubble seemed smaller, like it had shrunk, forcing them to bunch up, and closing them in. J'son looked slightly weaker, tired, as did the others. It seemed C'ton's spell had taken precious energy away from the bubble, weakening them all.

"T'mar, is that what I think it is?" T'mer asked showing the least effects of the radiation and energy reduction.

"It couldn't be. How could we see it, in the dark?"

"See what?" J'son asked turning away from the horizon to look on the others. He felt his energy slumping as soon as C'ton started to cough, but didn't pay too much attention to it.

"B'el's Castle," C'ton said.

"There's no way we could see it. How could we see it? We would almost have to be on top of it before we could see it. It's nothing but a black spike in the night. And that glow!" T'mar felt a warm tingling enter her belly coming up from her lower regions. The thought that they could see B'el's Castle excited her, but she kept that exhilaration to herself, or so she thought. At the moment of her realization, the bubble expanded without losing intensity. The others didn't notice except to move away from each other, pre-occupied as they were.

"That may be our missing energy reserves," C'ton commented. "I think we have found where those power reserves went."

"That's not possible," T'mer said. "We would have noticed the drain moving in this direction. The Adepts would have seen the power increases out here; there would be nothing to hide the transfer."

"You monitor the Wastelands?" It was a statement that took C'ton by surprise.

"We've never trusted B'el and have always kept an eye on his Castle."

"And you never picked up the power increase?"

"Maybe that's because he only just now released it," T'mar said. "Maybe he was waiting for the dark to fall."

"But why would he need so much power? He must know that he was being monitored and releasing that much power would surely give him away," T'mer was dumbfounded at the obvious implication of the extreme power expenditure.

"Maybe he wanted us to know," J'son said. The others turned to look at him and saw on his face what they were too afraid to contemplate. "If C'ton is right and that is the location of the missing power reserves, what if he powered it up only now as a beacon to all on the planet that now he was the sole possessor of power. It would call us to him, in a way, wouldn't it? If the Adepts are monitoring him, they would see and send envoys to investigate, wouldn't they?"

"Yes, they would," T'mer said, agreeing with the logic of the boy. "You're right about that. He wants us to know he stole the power reserves. "

"That much is easy enough to figure out," C'ton said, purposefully trying to annoy T'mer, hoping to cloud his thinking. C'ton's need for information was setting him up to be the exclusive dispenser of that information. It bothered C'ton on a vain level that he didn't see the implication first. "He wants to set himself up as the sole provider of knowledge, and in this case power and knowledge are the same things. He's trying to attract the whole world to himself."

They continued to walk along in silence, moving closer to the glow on the horizon. The star they had been following had grown smaller in the night sky, like it was moving away, as if it were a guide showing them the way to B'el's Castle. The star became irrelevant as a directional beacon as the glow on the horizon increased in intensity. Most of the light from the smaller stars had been bleached away and only the two remained: the original star that they had followed, and the flat, shining glow that was now becoming more vertical, reaching above the horizon.

The shape of the object was still hard to discern, but it was becoming more obvious that the glow rested on top of a structure. It reminded J'son of a lighthouse. The structure below the light appeared to be cylindrical, rising perpendicular to the line of the horizon, a black object illuminated by its lack of color. The glow sat on top of the object and rose like a star rising higher in the sky as they moved forward. If that was B'el's Castle, its height was truly impressive, even at this distance.

"How far away do you think that is?" J'son asked.

The four of them were walking in a straight line abreast of each other. T'mer and C'ton had the ends with T'mar walking next to T'mer and

J'son between her and C'ton. The more C'ton pulled ahead, the faster the others walked. Each one wanted to be in front to be the first to witness the spectacle. The bubble had adjusted to accommodate this arrangement and its protective strength had increased in intensity the closer they moved toward the object. The clarity level of the bubble had also increased and was now more transparent, like a clear glass lacking color. Soon the bubble was more like the Dome in construction instead of a wrap.

They moved freely within it, sometimes close together and at other times further out. The rolling, undulating dunes had smoothed out and resembled the sands of a beach: hard, packed and flat. The wind had died down considerably and only occasionally blew against them. They were making good progress now and the object was taking on a definite shape. It was cylindrical at the bottom and tapered as it went up, conical. The peak was obscured by the light and blended in with it. The shape was reminiscent of the Temple, and it was hard to tell, but it appeared to have windows or openings running up the side. Tiny points of light streamed out from these openings giving the object a sense of perspective. It was massive but its height was still too unpredictable. Without anything to compare it to, the object could be anywhere from a few hundred to thousands of feet tall.

It seemed to be made of the same black rock of the Temple but on a larger scale. The absence of any other rock or mountain range gave the object, the Castle, the appearance of having been dropped out of the sky. Its presence there looked artificial and created, but its size stretched the imagination that such a thing was possible. What was it doing out here in the middle of nowhere and how did B'el come to find it? J'son had many questions and he spoke looking forward, not too concerned who responded.

"Did B'el create that?"

C'ton looked across at T'mar and she did the same. The two of them spoke volumes without saying a word, staring intently at each other. The silence was almost embarrassing and T'mer cleared his throat about to answer the question when T'mar touched his hand, stopping him. This was one of the great secrets that only B'el and his initiates knew. Revealing this knowledge, it was said, would render the speaker mute, as the spell cast and the pledge made became the token of secrecy. Why this was so no one but B'el's initiates knew. Even C'ton couldn't give a true account of its foundation and looking at T'mar only re-enforced his frustration of not knowing. He knew of the binding spell that prevented her from speaking and he fumbled with the info cube searching for the answer.

"Well, it sure is impressive," J'son said breaking the silence.

"It is very old," T'mar finally said. "It is possibly the foundation stone of the world. It was here before recorded memory and that was where B'el made his fortress, preserving the knowledge of the lost age, the time before this time, when gods roamed your world, before they were cast out and sent to this world. All of that knowledge would have been lost had it not been for B'el. He collected that knowledge and stored it for the coming night. He has offered that knowledge to the few, those of special qualities and abilities in the hopes that there wouldn't be a return to the chaos. I was one of those chosen to receive that knowledge and its dissemination is strictly controlled through a series of initiations. Many are invited but only a few are selected."

The information T'mar was relaying could be found in C'ton's info cube and wasn't banned. It was common knowledge that B'el took recruits and that those recruits became initiates, if they proved themselves worthy of receiving that knowledge. But to speak openly of that knowledge was prohibited and its distribution prevented. Nothing of what T'mar had said was forbidden and C'ton's impatience was growing exponentially. It was like a drug addict who was in the presence of his dealer but that dealer refusing to deliver, even though the addict had the money to pay. It was maddening and he found his self-control losing waning.

"Dammit, woman! Tell us what you know. We are the only ones here and soon that knowledge will be lost again. You may be the only one left who possesses that knowledge. Most of the others have already crossed over. B'el hasn't been seen since shortly after the Dome went up. He taught a few of you and then vanished. No one has seen him or been to his Castle for most of this age. You were the last, probably because you were able to hurt him like no other."

"What's he talking about, T'mar?" J'son asked, startled by C'ton's outburst and open aggression.

"Tell him, T'mar," T'mer said.

"I was… Well how can I say this? I was his greatest student. He taught me things that he never taught anyone else."

"You were also the only female to learn his secrets," C'ton spat out, accentuating the word "female", sounding bitter.

"Yes, I was the only woman he ever taught, and that is why I hurt him so."

"Tell him, T'mar. Tell him now or I will."

"You see J'son I was his… companion, his confidant. He had a need to share his knowledge with someone and I was that someone."

"You were more than that. You were his—"

"Don't say it, C'ton. Let her tell it her way." T'mer had grown angry by C'ton's seemingly pointed acts of aggression and was equally keyed up by his behavior. He thought C'ton was bullying her and he moved down the line to stand before C'ton, halting their progress. His massive size was threatening and he stood chest to nose with C'ton.

"J'son, I was what you would call his bride. I had bound myself to him in a very esoteric and personal way. I melded myself body, soul, mind and spirit to him and his teachings. I did it to learn the secrets, the mysteries. I wanted to bring down the priesthood and the suffocating grasp they held over this world and yours. I wanted to learn how to pass back and forth at will to escape the dictates of the Temple and how to destroy the monks and all they stood for. It's a sham what the monks teach. It is a series of blinds and a method of brainwashing to capture the souls of your people. Religion was introduced to your race as a form of control. I wanted to break that control and bring enlightenment to your people. But I failed miserably."

Most of what T'mar just said went in one ear and out the other as J'son had heard bits and pieces before. What did stick was the word "Bride". The fact that she had been wedded to B'el, and she did it for knowledge, was definitely a shock. In effect, she had sold her soul to the Devil for the secrets of existence. It was the archetypical story of Eve and the Serpent. But who was her Adam? Was it T'mer? C'ton? Or was it J'son? Had he tasted of her fruit out of a desire to unite with her? He tried to remember that time that seemed like ages ago when he first started to dream about her.

The recollection was foggy and he closed his eyes trying to force the memory. He pictured his home back in Hope, Alabama and his bedroom. He saw his dog, Tonka, and the memory brought tears to his eyes. The tears cleared his mind, though, refreshing him and it brought up pleasant memories. He could see her, T'mar, in his mind's eye, remembering the first time he encountered her in his dreams. She was beautiful and intoxicating and she beckoned to him within the dream to come to her. That was the first time he left his body, experiencing what he was to later learn was an OBE, an Out-of-Body Experience. She had told him that first time, "This is how it is." The experience frightened him but also left him wanting to know more, to KNOW more. Had he been her Adam?

Somewhere in the depths of his mind, picturing his room and his dog and the scene of her standing by the edge of his bed, he heard a faint voice, sounding a lot like T'mer. It was a panicked voice calling out to him. It implied danger and warning and it wanted him to come back. They needed help, and he heard coughing and gagging. Something was wrong and even his memory of T'mar grew to look distressed. She was fading and fear played out across her beautiful face, distorting it. She was almost gone, faded from memory, before he remembered that this was just a memory. The voice became more urgent but sounded weaker. T'mer was coughing and his call came out muffled.

"J'son… help us… come back."

J'son opened his eyes, not too sure how long he had been lost in reverie. The three of them, T'mar, T'mer and C'ton were face down in the sand. T'mar and C'ton were lifelessly still and T'mer was barely moving. The protective bubble had shrunk and was now only surrounding J'son. The others lay outside the bubble and their skin was starting to turn blue, covered with painful-looking red scales and peeling away.

They appeared dead or close to it. What had happened? Instantly, J'son spread out his hands in their direction, god-like, and the bubble expanded, enveloping them. A steam of sorts rose from their bodies and he could hear a sizzling sound. The smell was terrible, pungent and foul, and he fought against it by holding his breath. Kneeling down he placed his hands on them in an alternate pattern, first on T'mar then on C'ton and T'mer.

The bubble got smaller as energy flowed out of his hands into the bodies of his three friends. It took awhile and the bubble shriveled up to a thin covering, but eventually their color came back and their skin stopped flaking away. Sores and boil-like blisters still covered their bodies, but their breathing returned to that of a deep sleep. They were resting now out of danger and J'son sat down besides them, occasionally laying his hands on them when their breathing became erratic. They stayed that way for a long time before they started to move in obvious pain. The star they had been following had disappeared completely leaving only the brightly glowing Castle still in the distance.

"Where did you go, J'son?" T'mer asked. He had been the first to stand, helping J'son with the others.

"What do you mean? I just closed my eyes for a few seconds and then I heard you calling out to me. I must have lost concentration and withdrawn the bubble. I'm sorry. I didn't know that would happen."

"I didn't call out to you. You weren't here. You disappeared."

"I… What?"

"J'son, did you return to your world?" T'mar was the next one to get up. Her beautiful skin was now pock-marked and pus-y red blisters covered the exposed areas. Portions of her gorgeous red hair had fallen out in clumps and she now sported patchy bald spots.

"I was just trying to remember the first time I met you and I tried to imagine what my bedroom looked like. I saw you there, and my dog. Then I heard T'mer calling out for help."

"I did not!" T'mer's vanity was showing.

"But I heard… then I opened my eyes."

"You transported back," C'ton said. He was slow to get up and the sores were extremely painful, causing him to remain bent over at the waist as he winced against the pain.

"Here, let me help you," J'son said reaching over to straighten him out.

"You fool! I don't need your help." Forcing him to stand erect caused the boils to rupture and now C'ton stood oozing pus.

"I'm sorry. I wish I knew what happened."

"I told you. You transported back to the time of your choosing. You re-entered your body as it was then. Why didn't you just stay there and leave us here us die. We would have been better off."

"Speak for yourself, you old wizard."

"T'mer. This isn't helping the situation. Is it true, J'son? Did you go back home?"

"If C'ton thinks I was, then I must have been. But if I was back at that time and T'mar was there, shouldn't she have come back, too? I saw her there."

It was a good question and C'ton picked up on it immediately. Through watery, slit eyes he glared at T'mar wondering if she did go back with J'son but wasn't letting on. He didn't trust her. He didn't trust anyone at this point. Speaking to T'mer without taking his eyes off of her he said: "Did she disappear, too?"

"I don't remember. We were walking and I was thinking—"

"I don't give a damn what you were thinking. Just report what you saw."

Continuing but peeved at C'ton's audacity, he said, "I was thinking that the air was getting coarser. Then I heard you cough and I turned to look at you. I was concerned about your health. That was the first time I noticed J'son wasn't there. The bubble had also disappeared and you had fallen to your knees. I… I don't think I even noticed if T'mar was there or not."

"You stupid Tech. You can remember a string of equations but can't remember what happened moments before."

"It was longer than a few moments, C'ton. Look at our skin. We must have been exposed to the outside for at least five short-cycles. We're lucky to even be alive."

"That still doesn't answer the question, T'mar. Did you go back with him?"

She thought about it, longer than C'ton's patience could bare but he remained quiet. She tried to piece together what did happen and the sequence of events. She had been walking like T'mer said and then she collapsed on the ground. No, that wasn't right. Why didn't she hear C'ton cough like T'mer did? They were walking and she remembered feeling tired, sleepy. They were quiet and she remembered telling J'son "This is how it is." She couldn't remember why she had said that, but she had a distinct memory of pointing that out to him.

The question weighed heavily on her and she could feel C'ton's powerful mind boring into her. He was trying to enter her thoughts but lacked the available energy necessary to cast the proper spell. He had been in her mind before, but it was always gentle and somewhat comforting. Now, however, he was trying to pierce her defenses, cutting into her psyche like a blade. If he had the resources available and hadn't been weaken she was sure that he would have ripped her consciousness to shreds to get at the answers. She almost let him in, thinking that he could bring to the surface the missing time. But in his present state she didn't trust him to protect her, not like a lover would, and she would only allow such an intimate invasion of her mind at the hand of a friend.

"Well, were you there or not?" C'ton's impatience was growing beyond his capacity to control, and in his weakened state he was explosive.

"Shut up, C'ton. I don't care if you are a Wizard or not. I'll rip your throat out if you speak to her like that again."

"Guys, it's okay," J'son said trying to make peace." We're all on edge and we want answers. T'mar, I remember you being there. Was that you, or just my memory of you?"

As she searched her recent memory, the only thoughts residing there were of her speaking to J'son. She didn't have a clear view of anything and had, until a few moments before, written it off as just boredom of seeing an endless sea of sand. But the light of B'el's Castle should have kept her mind from wandering. It had excited her when she first saw it and she felt that excitement rising. It comforted her and had helped keep her lust in check. Her thoughts had turned back toward lust, however, clouding her mind as she fantasized about seeing B'el again. Her mind was fixed on that Light and she had felt the arousal deep within. Then she…

"Oh my! I was back there. I was in your bedroom and your pet was just lying there at the foot of your bed. It didn't notice me and I remember smiling. I called out to you and you emerged from your body. That's when I communicated to you verbally. I had finally found a conscious conduit."

The four of them remained quiet. The revelation brought different responses from each of them. J'son was perplex about how he was able to travel back in time; T'mar became excited over the fact that J'son took her back with him; T'mer was distraught that he didn't notice she had left them and her reaction to having left; and C'ton was angry that J'son didn't take him with him and left him to die. His physical weakness kept his anger in check, though and instead of acting out he contemplated his next move.

"I think we have wasted enough time here," T'mer said, sounding more like a leader than the others. "Let's get moving. The star is gone from the sky and if B'el cuts off that light we may get lost out here."

"It's the sun."

"What?"

"That's was the sun," C'ton repeated, quieter, more mellow. "We have been following the receding sun. The orbit of this planet takes us close to the sun and then far out into space. The time-cycle of that orbit is vast and like I said before it was just a coincidence that we were close to our sun when the dreamers reached the point in their development that they were aware of their dreams. Without the light of our sun they never would have been able to see us. The dark would have prevented that."

"B'el knew that. He knew the time was coming and that all contact with the mortals would soon be over. That's why he stole the energy reserves." T'mar was talking fast, excited. "He needed a concentrated source to be seen. Once the dark took over, we would have been lost again." Finally the ultimate secret, the one B'el never told her, was coming to fruition. He desired passage between the worlds without having to wait for the beginning of the next age. He convinced the monks to build the Dome knowing all along that he would steal their reserves, leaving them in the dark.

"He must not have had a storage battery large enough," T'mer said, weighing the implications. "That's why he didn't build it himself."

"Also he would have needed workers. Knowing B'el, he wouldn't trust them to keep his secret." C'ton felt a fool. It was so obvious now and the Council never had a clue. He got them to build the Dome as a way to generate and store energy with the intension of taking it when the time was right. The Dome was never meant to protect the citizens of this planet. It was a ruse, and a highly effective one at that.

Chapter Forty:

The Castle

"Those are the artifacts of an earlier age, before the gods fell. B'el is believed to be the sole possessor of that ancient body of knowledge.

C'ton, after seeing the treasures of B'el

Different thoughts went through the minds of all. The revelation that B'el had deceived everyone, including T'mar hit the group hard. The Techs had expected B'el was busy doing something locked away in his Castle, but they didn't have a clue to its magnitude. T'mer was despondent walking along without any sense of mission or purpose. The Techs had been building their own portal, or at least a proto-type that they thought could possibly be used, if they had the power reserves. They had planned on approaching the Monks to offer them a partnership once the device was ready to be activated. The plan was to have it operational just before the sun had left the sky, but the Dome started to lose power even before the planet had swung away. They were the first to notice the power drain and had sent emissaries to the Temple to discover what was going on. T'mer had been on his way the Temple when he felt T'mar's presence. Of course B'el had beaten them to the power reserves. He was always the first, and the last.

As he looked at the glowing Castle, and the energy streaming out in all directions, he realized there was no chance of recovering the power reserves. Their world was doomed to barbarianism and the ensuing chaos of lost hope. The thought saddened him and he felt like he was dealt a mighty blow; it was hard to breathe but it had nothing to do with the atmosphere outside the bubble.

The dream of the Techs of trying to unite the planet under the banner of brotherhood by offering an alternative to the superstitions of the monks had turned into a nightmare. Soon the Dome would fail completely and the toxic environment of the Wastelands would cover the last refuge of his people, plunging most of them into an instantaneous, horrible death and a fight for survival among the unlucky few who did survived.

T'mar was also deep in thought, fighting with herself. She realized two things: First and foremost, it was highly unlikely that B'el was still even on the planet; and second, he had left and not taken her with him. She knew she had hurt him greatly, but he never let on, he never told her that he… cared. She had been disloyal to him and betrayed his trust, but what did he expect? He had taught her everything, well… almost everything. She knew he was working on a device that he said would change the face of the planet, but he never let on what it was or what it was supposed to do. Whenever she had asked about it, he always distracted her by showing her something else, teaching her something new. In that way she was able to learn what no other being had learned before or since.

She felt his hesitation at revealing his one secret and at times she knew he was wavering between telling her or not. In the end, he hadn't told her and her pre-occupation with his "project", this device, lessened and she soon forgot about it. After all, he never seemed to spend any time with it and since she had access to every room in the Castle she eventually decided he was just playing a loyalty game with her. The project was relegated to the back of her mind where she promptly stored it under useless information. Even when she first learned of the missing reserves, the thought didn't occur to her that B'el had taken it for his project. Her thinking was that he did take it but for another purpose entirely.

She knew he travelled back and forth between the worlds and at times she had followed him, finding willing participants on J'son's world to accommodate her. It was only when she encountered the purity of J'son's thoughts that she decided to focus on the permissible integration of her essence with those of J'son's people. Before, she had entered the minds of any entity willing or open enough to allow her entry, despite the danger or damage to the host. It was J'son that changed her mind, his decency and integrity, and she devoted herself to using her knowledge to help mankind. It was hard at first, but after she was able to communicate with J'son verbally, and later physically, did she finally make the necessary adjustment. B'el was right. To manifest on their world, the world of the dreamers, was to possess god-like power and the effect was intoxicating.

C'ton was having different issues and they focused mainly on his vanity. It angered him to realize that the greatest occult mind in the universe had left without divulging his secrets to a man. It infuriated him to know that a woman possessed superior knowledge to his and he didn't have access to it. If T'mar had been a man, he would have no problem accessing that knowledge. However, as it was, entering the mind of a female was an adventure in subtlety and deception. The chaotic currents of emotional interplay within the mind of a woman made it almost impossible for a man to navigate that terrain.

All learning was masculine based, very left brain, logical and domineering. It was the reason why women weren't allowed initiation into the higher ranks of the priesthood: there was too much uncertainty and the danger to the master was too great for most to accept the challenge. C'ton had almost lost his seat on the Council for taking in a female initiate and in the end had abandoned that seat to do so. He still maintained that position but hadn't returned to exercise his authority until just recently, which he didn't do after C'aad's death.

In the beginning, right after he met up with T'mar he had entered her mind as a form of love play, tickling her, so to speak, and caressing her erogenous zones directly. It never occurred to him then to rummage around looking into her hidden recesses. Thinking back now, he wondered if she would have let him, or maybe she had intentionally misdirected his mental wanderings, never allowing him to come too close. In all likelihood she was aware of his playful attitude and welcomed it, seeing he didn't have any ulterior motives. C'ton laughed out loud at this thought, startling the others by his outward show of absurdity. He thought about how he taught her how to block unwanted mental invasion, showing her how to ward off and cancel any intrusion. It was shortly after that he stopped going within her and the phenomenal sexual encounters ceased. He thought it was his teachings, but now he realized that she had played him and used his instructions as the excuse to keep him out. She must have known about B'el even then. What a silly old fool he was.

J'son was as confused as the others, but his confusion came as a conflict over what the Transcendentals had revealed to him. He was supposed to stop B'el, but stop him from doing what? If B'el had already left this planet and materialized on Earth where did he go and more importantly at what time did he chose to appear? How was he supposed to stop someone after they had already left, and again, stop him from doing what? The little he did remember of his time with the Transcendentals was starting to fade and the instructions he had been given didn't make sense.

He had been told there was going to be a power struggle and C'ton would be the instigator. J'son had assumed that C'ton would challenge B'el and the two of them would battle for supremacy, with C'ton, he hoped, being the victor. But as they moved closer to the Castle and C'ton's behavior became increasingly more erratic, J'son was starting to doubt that was what the Transcendentals had meant. The thought occurred to him then that maybe the confrontation would be between C'ton and T'mar, and that possible scenario scared him.

Their bubble fluctuated momentarily as J'son's dark thoughts gripped his mind. The others noticed it and dread seized them, realizing that their only hope of reaching the Castle lay in the mind of a human who could at any time leave them to die in the Wastelands. Why would he stay, what was holding him there, except his attachment to T'mar? If the Castle became too hairy for him, they all thought, he could just abandon them to their deaths. The fluctuating bubble crystallized that thought in their minds, bringing it to the fore.

Secretly, but residing within the minds of the three of them simultaneously, they decided to cultivate their friendship they had with J'son individually in hopes of using it to their advantage. It was a mistake for sure because it pit one against the other, but it was their only hope to keep from being left stranded out in the open. If they could make it to the Castle, J'son's services would no longer be needed. The three of them would survive as B'el had done, learning his secrets and putting them to use. That was the plan and the three of them, unbeknownst to the others, would tactfully convince J'son of their point of view.

The light of the Castle dominated the expanse before them. All of the stars had vanished behind the bright radiance and the sky was now brilliantly white, spreading outward in all directions. Behind them the sky was pitch black without any indication that the Dome was still operational. If the Dome was still in place, no sign of it could be seen. The glow of the beacon, or whatever it was, increased in magnitude the closer they approached, blending and then devouring the dark, consuming it until all that was left was the light. The sky in three directions was brighter than even the light of their sun, but it cast off no heat of any kind. The air was still cold, icy almost, crystal clear lacking clouds and extremely toxic.

"How is it that B'el could live out here?" J'son asked after a long period of silence. "I mean if the air is as toxic as it has been how does he breathe?"

"Well he—"

"With a spell—"

"It's generated," T'mar said, blocking off the others' explanation before they could give it. Each was eager to answer his question whether they had the right answer or not. "Within the Castle is a power generator, a transformer that he devised using the skills of the Techs. The generator takes the toxins out of the open space and converts them into breathable air. I'm not too familiar with the process, but it—"

"It's simple, really," T'mer said sounding self-important. "It converts the active energy floating around between the molecular toxins and binds them together on a sub-atomic level, rearranging them into the common oxygen and nitrogen mixture. The result is a breathable grid suitable for life. He may have developed the idea, but he needed us to assemble the parts based on his theorems."

"Yes, T'mer. We know how proud you are over the accomplishments of the Techs," T'mar snapped back. "There is also a shield generator that blocks out the harmful radiation from entering the Castle proper. Once inside, we will be protected from the harshness of this environment and won't need your bubble. It will also help our skin to heal. B'el should have some ointments and balms ready for just such a situation as ours. Rarely does one travel across the Wastelands and make it here without physical damage."

T'mar grew quiet remembering her first time crossing the Wastelands. She had managed to generate a bubble similar to J'son's, but it had failed before she could reach the entrance to the Castle. She had been covered in boils and tumors, practically crawling to the doorway, where she lost consciousness and fell into oblivion. When she awoke, lying comfortably on a soft, bed-like structure, B'el was staring down at her, smiling. She was only conscious for a few moments, but she remembered he had said to her: "I'm so glad you made it."

T'mar shivered at the memory and wrapped her arms around herself. The thought reminded her of how desperate she had been and how she would have done anything to keep from leaving that sanctuary. His physical representation at that time had been close to average in stark contrast to the rumors of a beautiful god dwelling in his personal heaven. He had blondish-brown hair, cut short and well kempt. He had facial hair around his mouth and he had off-white, slightly crooked teeth. But it was his smile that gave him the sense of being beautiful, full of charisma and trust at the same time.

He looked fairly normal outwardly but his penetrating blue-black eyes shone with an inner light of extreme intensity. They were hard to look at, powerful and full of knowledge, and so she would from that time forward continue to look at his pleasant, full lips and bright, promising smile. She remembered now what she had said to him in response to his greeting right before she passed out again. She had said, "I want to have your baby."

"That is so," C'ton had been saying, speaking to J'son, clarifying a particular point that T'mer had made. "At first, B'el had worked with all of us, Techs and monks equally. He showed no partiality and gave as freely as we required of him. This was before we realized he had access to the ancient knowledge. We didn't know at that time that he was feeding us what we wanted to hear in exchange for the Technology of the Techs and the wisdom of the monks. B'el was sort of a hybrid of the two schools of thoughts. In fact, it was he that pointed out the similarities between the two and was the first to suggest a common source.

"The Techs had broken away from the teachings of the monks in the distant past and developed their ways in isolation: measuring and testing, trial and error was their way. We emphasized the power of belief and use that part of our minds to inform the rational aspects. The Techs believe in nothing except what can be proved dimensionally. They actually think that you, J'son, and your world are just a mental aberration of our over-active imaginations. For them, you don't exist."

"That's not entirely true, J'son," T'mer countered. "It's not that we don't think you exist, but rather your existence might be based on fundamental laws that have yet to be discovered. We don't have an opinion on what the monks believe; we just don't see the evidence."

"But I'm standing here in front of you. Isn't that evidence enough? How do you explain my presence here?"

"Again, the most logical explanation is that you are a mental projection of either T'mar or C'ton. My bet is on T'mar. You two seem too close for you to be a manifestation of C'ton's. I would like, however, to have you tested away from T'mar's influence and see if you still possess a corporal body. You have yet to be separated from her even when you transferred back to your world. Remember, you supposedly did take her with you."

"Well, I think you all are just a figment of my imagination. How do I know this isn't some elaborate dream?"

"Exactly!"

They were quiet again, walking with their heads down, occasionally looking up at the massive, ever-increasing mountain that was B'el's Castle. Where in the distance it looked similar to the Temple, now closer up it was obvious that the two were polar opposites. Where the Temple was crafted, designed with skill and ability, the Castle was rough hewn and lacked rounded symmetry. It jutted out of the ground, rough and jagged, like the fangs of the mountain thrust up from the bowels of the planet. Two sharp, ragged shoulders, pointed up, flanking the central spire, which rose more than a thousand feet above them, giving J'son the impression of a raised middle finger, almost as if B'el were flipping off the Temple far behind them. The total height of the Castle was approximately three thousand feet above the sandy ground. There was nothing but desolation around the base with no signs of vegetation or animal life. The sand had objects embedded in it at various, random places that caused a reflection, making the ground shimmer, like in the desert.

The central spire did indeed have windows of sorts running up and around it, but unlike the Temple they were unevenly placed, as if someone had knocked holes from the inside out wherever an opening was needed. They were irregular-cut openings and appeared to have several different shapes, none of them square. It looked like they had been blown out and the resulting shape left as is. Light streamed out of these windows and cast web-like beams out across the Wastelands. Only in this respect did the Castle resemble that of the Temple. Also, one opening was cut, or blown out, near the ground level and situated in such a way that the light shined down, casting a bright, illuminated ray of light directly in the center and in front of the Castle. There a cave or tunnel could be seen set slightly back from the rest of the mountain. This was the entrance to the Castle of B'el.

As they approached the base of the mountain, walking along a packed path, a shadow was cast below the beam-like openings causing a dark area to form between the upper windows and the lower central window. The only light below the upper windows was the single beam directed at the entrance. They stood in that irregular circle of light feeling the heat of it warming their chilled bodies. They had finally made it across the Wastelands and the light and heat felt wonderful, lifting their spirits for the moment. They knew that their journey wasn't over and had only just begun. They weren't sure what they would find within this black mountain but didn't dwell on that thought just yet.

J'son gazed up at the opening directly overhead trying to peer into the interior but the light was too intense. Looking down, blinking madly, he shielded his eyes with his hand, opening them every few seconds to determine if his sight had returned. The light hurt his eyes, like staring at the sun for too long. The others seemed oblivious to his actions and he waited until he re-adjusted to the less intense area at his feet. The crystal-like objects that they had seen embedded into the sand were easily recognizable now up close. Reaching down, J'son picked up a smaller piece of glass and dropped it immediately, plunging his index finger deep into his mouth.

"Ouch, that hurts. I think I cut myself, but it burns."

"Those are as sharp as blades and probably as hot as molten lead," T'mar said, hiding a grin behind her hand. "You might want to be careful of anything you want to touch here in His Castle."

J'son pulled his blistering finger out of his mouth to find his print burned off and the tip smooth. There was no blood, but it was red and tender looking. The other three were smiling at him good naturedly, and seeing their humor made him smile, too. It had been a long trek and the promise of protection from the poisonous atmosphere was extremely welcomed.

J'son was about to ask C'ton when he thought it would be ok to drop the bubble when he noticed it was already gone. The intensity of the light had blinded him to the fact that his bubble had dissolved without him being aware. He still felt the power drain of the bubble, though, but couldn't see the shimmering outline of it. Stretching out his arms to the sides, he ran his fingers over and around what should have been the outer perimeter of the bubble. His fingers touched nothing but the light and he dropped them back down, slapping his thighs in the process.

Slowly, he started to walk to the edge of the light, keeping his hands before him, fumbling like a man caught in the brightness. He was almost to the edge when he heard T'mar call out to him.

"J'son! Stop, don't move. As soon as we entered this area all energy output was absorbed. You won't be able to replace your protection bubble until after you leave the boundary of the light, then it will be too late. You think your finger hurts now, wait until you are between the light and the dark." She approached him gently and calmly, laying her hands lightly on his shoulders. "That's the way we just came, sweetie. Here, let me show you the way inside."

Chapter Forty-One:

Rest and Healing

"It's a medical treatment center, similar to the one in the Temple. B'el had designed that one based on this one."

C'ton describing the function of the beds

The entrance was set back several feet into the mountain in a shallow scoop, not a tunnel or cave really, just a hollow blasted out of the rock face. Stepping into it they moved out of the light and back into the dark. At the back of this hollow was a large, wooden door, maybe ten feet high and half as wide. What struck J'son as strange was that the door was made of some type of wood, oak maybe, with deep veins and a visibly coarse texture. There wasn't a door knob or latch of any kind. There also didn't appear to be any hinges, just a large piece of wood resting between thick slabs of black rock like the very mountain had grown around the door.

"How do we get in?" J'son asked. "Knock?"

"In a way," T'mar said, smiling slyly. Placing her hand in the center of the door, palm inward and fingers pointing up, she extended it above her as high as she could reach, then in a rapid motion she lowered it, twisting her wrist mid way down so the fingers pointed down. Reaching almost to the bottom of the door keeping her knees straight, she raised her hand again, twisting it mid way and moving it to the right until she came to the edge.

Without touching the rock surrounding the door, she twisted her hand for the third time and glided it back across the door to the left, stopping before she touched the other side. Her lips had been moving during this procedure, and reaching the left side she removed her hand and let it drop to her side. Nothing happened for a few moments, and then a deep echo sounded on the other side of the door, a low, guttural hum. The volume rose until the entire entryway buzzed like a sustained Bass note. The percussion was almost unbearable, reaching a point of possible auditory damage, but then it subsided and all was quiet.

J'son stared at C'ton and T'mer wondering if they knew what was going on. It was T'mer who noticed J'son looking at him. "That's some doorbell, isn't it boy?"

A crack appeared down the center of the door from top to bottom, and without a sound the door swung open inward, revealing a long, dark passage whose end disappeared into the gloom. Stepping through quickly, the four of them entered the Castle one after the other before the door closed automatically behind them. T'mer was the last one to enter and his broad shoulders caught the edge of the thick door, turning him sideways and causing him to stumble through. Righting himself, he joined the others standing just inside. With the door closed, they found themselves in complete darkness again without the benefit of J'son's bubble.

"Follow me," T'mar said. She walked along the once familiar corridor without diverging to the left or right. After about fifty feet, they came to another door made of some type of metal. This door did have a handle and the large, metallic hinges were slightly bent, showing signs of a forcible entry. "T'mer, I'll need help with this, remember."

T'mer pushed through the others and stood before the ancient-looking door, sizing it up. "I thought I broke it down, but it stills looks to be in one piece. I remember prying the hinges off."

"So you did, but it appears B'el had it reinstalled. Hopefully he didn't bolt it from the other side."

T'mer tried the latch, hearing the mechanism click and pulled the door towards him. The door swung opened a crack and then stopped. Wrapping his large fingers between the door and the opening, he pulled on it with an audible grunt. The door opened a little bit more and then stopped again. Frustrated by his lack of success, he grabbed the opening and placed a foot against the rock framework for leverage. Pulling with all his strength, sweat pooling across his forehead, he jerked and yanked on the door, the cords in his muscular arms showing signs of strain. He was about to let go when the door, unexpectedly and of its own accord, glided open, sending him tumbling backwards to the floor. He lay there flat on his back staring up at the ceiling, panting. The light pouring out of the opening flooded the corridor with bizarre, lavender light.

C'ton chuckled to himself, and stepping over T'mer's prone body he entered the room beyond the door. Speaking over his shoulder, smiling brightly, he said, "I guess the old man still has a few tricks left up his sleeve."

J'son reached out a hand to help T'mer to his feet, which T'mer promptly smacked away.

"Don't be angry at J'son just because you have a bruised ego, T'mer." T'mar stepped around him and followed C'ton into the lighted room. J'son waited for T'mer to get up and then the two of them joined the others.

The room was circular in design but again looked like it had been blasted out with extreme heat. The rock was melted and smooth if irregular. The ceiling was maybe ten feet high and the total circumference was about fifty feet around; small compared to the actual mass of the mountain which contained it. The room was barren except for a glowing, amethyst-like crystal resting in the center of the room which sat on a raised lump of rock resembling a crude pedestal. Towards the back there was a reddish, dimly-lit, spiraling staircase. It was made out of rough-carved rock without handrails. Walking towards the stairs, passing the crystal on their left, the light source emitted a high-pitched, eerie squeal, almost as if it was screeching at them. The sound gave J'son the willies and he purposefully gave the glowing crystal a wide margin.

Approaching the first step, the four of them looked up through the winding stair as it rose into complete darkness, disappearing through an opening in the ceiling. C'ton was about to mount the stairs when T'mar caught him by the back of the neck and forcefully pulled him back, stopping him before he could put his foot on the first step. He spun around shocked that she had done that, but seeing the caution in her eyes he realized that he was about to make a serious mistake. Pointing to a handprint embedded into the central pillar on which the steps revolved, T'mar placed her left hand within it. Instantly, the stairs lit up, changing from the ruddy color of a moment before into a deep blue radiance that gave the staircase an inviting quality.

"I'm still keyed into the system it seems," T'mar said. "We'll all need to be careful in here. If we tried to mount the steps while it was still red, we wouldn't have made it to the second step. I'm sorry if I offended you, C'ton."

"Uh huh."

Slowly and with extreme caution, they mounted the stairs and ascended through the opening in the ceiling. T'mar was the first to emerge into the next room directly above the entry foyer. This room was much larger and expansive, widening out to fill the interior of the mountain. The room was lit by a central stone or crystal that looked like sapphire and gave off light resembling cobalt. It sat on its own pedestal like the room below but was proportionally larger. The walls were covered by different artifacts, some of metal, some of rock, some looking almost like a hologram made with light and still others seemingly organic in nature.

It was the organic pieces that caught J'son's eye and he walked over to the far wall on his left to study one up close. The animal, if one could call it that, had a head with multiple eyes and a flat, pancake-like face. There were no ears that he could see and it possessed four slits that he took to be its nose. It was naked, in that it didn't have any fur, and its small body was extremely wrinkled with a leathery texture. Judging by its expression, the creature looked scared and appeared to be cowering, like it was backed into a corner. It was resting in a hollow cut into the wall and was lit from above by a soft yellow light. The entire display had a sickening appearance and J'son backed away from it moments later.

"That was B'el's first attempt to bring an animal back from your world, J'son," T'mar said. "That's what all of these are: futile attempts to re-materialize here what he had discovered over here."

"But that doesn't look like anything that I am familiar with. In fact I don't recognize any of this stuff." Curiosity getting the best of him, J'son causally followed the curving wall pausing at each exhibition to study the object. The ones made out of metal appeared to be weapons of some sort, with sharp if not twisted protrusions resembling swords maybe. Others of the metal type could have been weaponry that shot projectiles. The objects made out of rock he took to be statuary, although resembling nothing he had ever seen before.

It was the holograms, though, that really caught his attention. Some were of the singular type while others had companions. They appeared to be alive, moving and undulating, but it was like they were caught between two worlds, in some type of inner dimension, existing here and there at the same time. These were the most recognizable and he could make out what he thought were mammals from earth, the most disturbing of which appeared to be humanoid. As he looked at them he could see an awareness coming from their distorted faces. One of them even reached out a mangled hand, looking directly at J'son and appeared to call out to him. Almost hypnotized by the image, J'son's mind filled with visions of horror and desperation and he thought he could hear it speaking to him. The thing kept saying the same thing: "Help me!"

"Turn away from that, J'son. There's nothing we can do for it, or any of those things." C'ton walked over to where he was standing and place a gentle but firm hand on his shoulder, pulling him away. "They are trapped in a nightmare from which they will never awake. B'el has captured their souls, their essence and now only the fading light of their spirit is all that's left of their pervious life. What he has done by using the black arts is truly shocking and disturbing. Come on. This room holds nothing of interest for us."

While C'ton's was talking with J'son, T'mar and T'mer were looking at each other with grim expressions. T'mer knew intimately what those lost souls were going through. When he had come to rescue T'mar so many cycles ago, he had been taken prisoner and his psyche locked away within one of those holograms. It was a computer program, really, and by simply deconstructing his molecular configuration and converting it into light waves he became a captive of B'el. It was only through T'mar's subversion that he was released. The experience still gave him chills and he shuddered at being in such close proximity to them.

"C'ton's right. We need to keep moving if we are to reach his control center without being detected."

"Don't you think by activating the system he already knows we're here?" C'ton asked, sounding snide and sarcastic. He didn't like how familiar T'mar was within the Castle and her management of the situation rubbed him the wrong way; her attitude sounded condescending. It was like she was calling the shots and he had to obey, having to trust that she wouldn't lead them astray. This was his first time within B'el's fortress and although he would recognize the various furnishings his curiosity kept him focused on reaching the upper floors. His plan was dependant on using B'el's power console. T'mar would have direct access to that panel and he needed her to activate it before he could carry out his idea. He knew he would have to use subtlety to keep her ignorant to the fact that it was he who wanted access.

"I mean," C'ton continued, sounding apologetic, "even if he has already departed the system he knows we are here and there is no telling what traps he has programmed. I'm sure he knew we were coming, especially you, T'mar. My suggestion is we, or I mean you, activate the system and disarm it. With J'son walking around looking at everything I afraid he might trigger the internal defenses and turn us all into a hologram. I believe we need to be ever vigilant and alert for any sign that we have been detected. It's strange, though, that we haven't had anyone come out to greet us, don't you think, T'mar?"

"I was just thinking that," T'mer said, visibly inspecting the walls for signs of surveillance.

"This is the hall where B'el met his visitors, but he didn't spy on them, T'mer. Their presence was known as soon as the wooden door was activated. It was there that he viewed his guests. Once they entered this chamber, however, he left them with privacy. He always liked the reaction this room caused and he waited to see their expression only after they left and entered the upper hall. That's where we will find the medical attention that we need. Well, all accept for J'son. I think B'el would have been surprised that he made it here unscathed."

⁓

They left that room feeling slightly ill, which was the intension, crossing the large hall and coming to a stop at an archway blasted out at the rear. Instead of a spiraling staircase, the archway led down a short corridor where it ended at the base of another staircase. The steps were wide and the rise fairly shallow, going up at a comfortable slant; but there were several of them and they wound around the far wall. T'mar was still in the lead, but J'son slid past her and took the steps two at a time, reaching the next level slightly out of breath. Bending over at the waist, he took in the air of the room and was pleasantly surprised by the sweetness of the fragrance.

"It smells pretty good up here. Why doesn't B'el have an elevator? Climbing all of these steps is wearing me out."

"A what?" T'mer asked reaching the top of the stairs, bringing up the rear.

"A transport tube, like at the Temple."

"All of this is planned," C'ton said, taking in the air in great gulps. "The idea is to keep his 'guests' off balanced so when he does show benevolence it makes him seem that much more humane."

The steps led out of a similar archway as below and into a rectangular room divided in half by a central hallway and partitioned off into different sized rooms to the left and right. The rooms, or more precisely cubicles, didn't have doors but were open facing the hallway with three walls separating the rooms from each other and no ceiling. Each room was lit by a different color giving the entire level a pleasing, rainbow-like glow. The ceiling was very high up and domed with a mural painted directly above and center. It showed a reclining figure resting on one bent elbow, his feet pointed towards the center, naked from the waist up, pointing a finger at the figures directly opposite. These figures were more or less naked young women with wings, presumably flying towards the reclining man, with stars over their heads and crystal-like stones in their opened hands.

The scene was very comforting, but staring up at it gave J'son a pain in his neck.

"How are you supposed to appreciate that way up there," he said.

"The idea, sweetie, is to lie on your back on those beds. It's very relaxing and some would say intoxicating." The tone of T'mar's voice was very seductive and when J'son looked at her to see the beds she was talking about, he caught her eye and he could almost read her thoughts. It was embarrassing and he quickly turned away to peer into the individual rooms.

Each room was distinct to itself, decorated with different furniture and areas to rest. Each chair or bed was designed to give the one occupying it an optimal view of the mural and the colorfully painted walls nicely accentuated the dominate color of each room, offering different and complimentary tones and shades. Some of the rooms were larger, some smaller, each having the appropriate amount of furnishings depending on its function. For larger groups, the room may contain several beds or only a single one filling the space. The smaller rooms, obviously designed for one, had a combination of a bed and a recliner.

There were cabinets lining the three walls about waist high with sliding glass doors and multiple shelves. The shelves were filled with several containers each with a label describing its contents. The labels were written in some form of pictogram, but the explicit graphics left no doubt what the containers held. Each room also contained skinny, curving lamps which stood on the floor and held florescence-like bulbs of opaque white in an umbrella-like canopy. The wispy necks of these devices ran to the floor and stood on four, delicate feet. The entire device was free moving and was capable of following the occupant wherever he went within the room.

"Pick a room, J'son, and try it out," T'mar said still expressing that sensual tone. "All of us are going to recuperate here for awhile. It's very… intoxicating."

"You're coming with me," T'mer ordered, taking T'mar roughly by the wrist and hauling her towards one of the larger rooms with only one bed. He tossed her down like a rag doll, face first and proceeded to rip her matted, furry clothes off, slapping her behind and opening wounds where her blisters were. Reaching out to the lamp-like device, he gripped it and bent it over the bed. "How do you turn this damn thing on?"

"Oh, T'mer," she said seductively." Let me help you with that."

C'ton was settling himself down into one of the smaller rooms, selecting the recliner over the bed. He motioned towards his lamp device and the thing scurried across the floor and bent over him, turning on its healing light, starting at the infra-red end of the spectrum and gradually increasing towards the ultra-violent. It also emitted a soothing, hypnotic hum which caused C'ton to close his eyes.

Almost immediately the red, bleeding sores which covered his face and body began to lighten in color and turn a healthy shade of pink. The hum was just loud enough to compensate for the external sounds coming from T'mar and T'mer's room opposite his, but it didn't go so far as becoming deafening. It was a sound cancellation device that produced the necessary frequencies required to balance out and cancel the other sounds, creating a zone of pleasing calm. C'ton was now embraced in a state of silence while being bathed in warm, therapeutic light.

J'son didn't know if he wanted to partake of the healing energies of the rooms and stood hesitant next to a small bed. A lamp moved over to him, twisting its face vertically, trying to cover as much of J'son's body with its light as it could. J'son avoided the light by moving over to one of the cabinets and began to study the labels. The illustrations spelled out graphically their purpose and he reached out to grab a bottle of pills that showed a head and face with a silly smile. The face looked drowsy and slightly stupid, the way people look after drinking all night. He put the bottle back and picked up a jar of cream that promised skin rejuvenation. He opened the jar and applied a small amount to a blemish on his arm. Instantly, the blemish evaporated and left a pleasant, tingling sensation that started to extend around his arm.

"The affect can become universal with a mild, light-frequency adjustment," a tinny voice intoned.

The voice startled him, considering that it sounded feminine and mechanical at the same time. He spun around to see the owner of that voice and saw the wimpy lamp staring at him, beginning to glow a carroty-red color.

"Who said that?"

A tiny grill that he hadn't seen before located just underneath the lamp canopy appeared to be the source and he studied it for a few moments in silence, waiting for it to say something else. The carroty glow increased in luminescence emitting a warm, soothing wash of light which soon covered his body from head to toe. Standing there, he felt very relaxed and he gazed at the bed laying a few feet away thinking how much he wanted to lie down.

Still bathed in the light, he bent over and reached out a hand to test the firmness of the bed, but stopped short, coming back to himself with a jerk. The light was still causing a deep feeling of relaxation and he fought the sensation, pulling himself away from the bed and the lamp. He stumbled backwards until he was out of the room and standing back in the hallway. Glancing to his left and right, he saw the other three in various states of stupor. Even T'mar and T'mer were lying still, naked, with dim-witted smiles plastered across their dense-looking faces. In their present state they were all very vulnerable and he decided then to avoid the rooms of healing.

Walking down the hall like a soldier on watch, he reached the far end and stood under the archway of yet another set of stairs. Looking up the stairwell, he could see a bright light coming through an opening at the top. He could also hear what he took to be the sounds of static electricity popping and snapping, like something out of a bad 1950's sci-fi movie. He smiled at the thought and started to climb the steps, pausing for a moment debating if his friends would be okay without him. Shrugging off any lingering concern, he continued up the long, spiraling steps to the next level above.

The stairs came to an end at the threshold of a large, brightly-lit room containing endless shelves stacked with miscellaneous leaves of paper, hard cover books bound with some type of leathery material, round plastic disks, cubes and other assorted storage devices. The shelves followed the curve of the room with rows in between and passageways running off in all directions. In front of these shelves were curved, semi-circular desks of a sort and flat monitors placed before comfortable metal chairs and partially submerged keyboards.

In the center of the room, to which the shelves circled, was a transparent, globe-like device that sat on a low base close to the floor. The interior of the globe radiated a misty-blue color, like white clouds hanging in a blue sky. A thin beam of light extended up from the top of the globe, casting a small circle of light on the ceiling overhead. The light flickered occasionally and a popping sound could be heard, like the zapping of a bug lamp. The occasion or frequency of the popping was irregular and J'son tried to determine exactly why it popped when it did.

He moved closer to the globe, winding his way around the shelving and could hear a slight hum that started from the base and increased in volume as it moved up the beam of light. Starting quietly at first, it climaxed once it reached the ceiling. ZzzzzzzzzAAP! Again, the rate of occurrence wasn't fixed and he couldn't determine why it popped when it did. He turned away from the globe and sat behind the closest monitor, fingering the keyboard, punching the keys, trying to get the monitor to light up.

To the left of the keyboard was a flat, green pad with slight impressions, like fingerprints. To the right of the keyboard was a square indentation, like an inverted cube cut into the surface of the desk. He stuck the tip of his finger into the one-inch square notch until it bottomed out and then pulled it out. He couldn't determine its purpose and then he focused his attention on the green pad to his left.

Aligning the tips of his fingers over the impressions, he slowly lowered his hand until he just barely touched the pad. Immediately, his hand was forced down flat, pressing into the gel-like surface until it was absorbed within the pad leaving just his wrist visible. The sound of the zapping speeded up, "Zap. Zap. Zap. Zap." And the glow of the globe intensified. The circle of light on the ceiling became larger and all the monitors lit up simultaneously. The room was buzzing and humming and zapping and J'son found himself falling into a type of trance.

He was still conscious and cognizant, but the reality of the room disappeared and he was thrown into a bright, luminous space where knowledge was readily available simply by reaching out and touching it. In this landscape, knowledge hung around him like fruit on a tree and he reached out to pluck the nearest one. It had the shape and appearance of an apple and he bit into it, at first tasting its sweet juices and then a rush exploded into his mind, filling his body with the learning of that particular fruit. The effect lasted only a moment, but left him with facts, information and data.

Coming back to himself but still in that other reality of the fruit grove, he reached out to another tree baring a different fruit and bit into that. Again, information and knowledge flooded his awareness and he was staggered by what he was learning in such a short period of time. He now had two completely different collections of information residing within him concurrently and the knowledge expanded his awareness of the world around him.

Contemplating this knowledge, he saw psychic tentacles branching out from the two bodies of knowledge connecting and joining with each other, producing a third information base. This third platform incorporated his latest knowledge with his recent memories, filling in the gaps and answering his many questions. The experience puffed him up and expanded his ego. He now believed there was nothing he couldn't understand and he "walked" through this forest observing the different fruits and taking those that were pleasing to him. He was aware that this process was momentary, but it seemed to him like he was gone for ages.

He was just about to leave the forest, the thought occurring to him to check on his friends, when he stumbled upon a tree unlike the others, possessing fruit hidden within the brambles of a thorny vine. He reached in, carefully twisting and bending his mind to avoid pricking himself, and plucked a blackish fruit the size of a cherry. Placing it in his mouth, he discovered it to be hard, marble-like and so decided to swallow it instead. The effect was instantaneous and he found himself staring at a book containing verses, poetry and prose with parts taking the form of a narrative.

It was written in an esoteric script which he understood and he read it from the title page to the back cover, pausing only to reflect on the wisdom of each passage. The title of the book was called "The Book of B'el," and it was filled with wisdom and wonder and power, revealing secrets of this world and all worlds. The book was unsettling in parts and laugh-out-loud funny in others. It appeared B'el had a sense of humor and the knowledge imparted in this manner resonated more deeply with J'son than the disturbing parts.

It spoke of the Transcendentals and hinted at who and what they were. The text wasn't dogmatic on this and left J'son wondering why they were so mysterious. It also spoke of B'el's master plan and how he did, indeed, expect T'mar and the others of find their way here. He had been playing them all along and how the culmination of his plan was about to begin. Its focal point was a portal he had opened on the top floor of his Castle and how he had needed J'son's special abilities to close it again, placing a warning that his, J'son's, failure to do this would jeopardize his world. It also explained that C'ton would try to prevent this and set himself up as the new master of the Castle.

The text implied that T'mer was expendable and with moving verse it mourned B'el's loss of T'mar as his mate. That part of the text touched J'son profoundly and he sensed a type of humanity within the tortured soul of B'el. J'son realized that B'el was just misunderstood and his heart ached at the loneliness B'el expressed. It was with tears in his eyes that J'son finally closed the book and left the forest, finding himself seated behind the monitor once again.

Chapter Forty-Two:

The Final Battle

"You fools! Know that the time for decision is upon you and your fate rests with the proper choice."

C'ton demanding obeisance

"What are you doing? You fool! Get away from there. You don't know what you are doing."

Sometime during J'son's mental browsing C'ton had come into the library and was now making his way to the center of the room, knocking over chairs and violently shoving desks out of the way. Reaching J'son, he pulled him away from the monitor and threw him to the floor. Standing over him, scowling down at him, the "X" very pronounced, C'ton was a seething cauldron of emotion. He stood clenching his teeth and working his hands into fists. An eerie glow came to his eyes, terrible and accusing. He pointed a long, stick-like finger down at J'son and was just about to make a big mistake when he stopped and turned to look at the entrance.

He heard T'mer and T'mar coming up the steps and quickly reached down, yanking J'son to his feet. He shoved him aside without saying anything and righted the chair J'son had been sitting in. He fumbled within the folds of his tunic and produced his info cube, rapidly inserting it into the space provided for it next to the keyboard. He sat down and fell into a trance similar to the one J'son had just experienced. After a few moments, he blinked his eyes and emerged from the trance smiling a wicked smile. He turned to look up at a disheveled J'son standing next to him and snorted a laugh.

"I won't need this anymore," he said, removing the info cube from the console. Turning in the chair, he tossed the info cube into the swirling inner light of the globe. The cube hit the globe and was absorbed into it with a loud zapping noise. The monitor, which had remained on while C'ton was at the desk, switched off and stared blankly like it had never been on. He stood up, smiling, showing J'son an uncomfortable friendliness by placing his cold, boney hand on his shoulder. He leaned in close and whispered into J'son's ear:

"We'll just keep this to ourselves for the time being."

T'mar and T'mer entered the library together, smiling and happy; their arms were wrapped around each other and they were laughing to themselves. T'mer was playfully biting her neck and she was lifting up her chin to give him better access. They stopped playing as soon as they saw J'son and C'ton standing next to the Globe. Something about the way J'son looked gave T'mar a strange feeling and she looked at T'mer to see if he had seen it, too. He returned her concern and the two of them continued to stare at the other two. Something had just happened and she didn't like the way J'son was responding to it.

"What's going on here, C'ton?" she asked. "You didn't plug into the library records, did you?"

"No, no. Our little friend was about to do just that when I advised him against it. Didn't I, J'son? Yes. I was about to explain to him the inherent dangers of such mischief when the two of you came in. There is nothing in these records that should concern us. What we need is access to the system grid to discover what B'el has been doing most recently. You can tap into that, T'mar. But I believe we have to go up two more levels to the control room. It's right above the living area, isn't that right, T'mar?"

"Yes that's true," she said slowly, not trusting the tone of his voice. She didn't know how long she and T'mer were under the influence of the healing baths, but she knew it was longer than C'ton. It bothered her that he didn't want to engage the library records, if simply out of curiosity. He was right that accessing them was dangerous, and habit forming, but the urge to discover B'el's secrets would override all caution. Why didn't he want to at least look?

"We can bypass B'el's main residence and enter the control level by taking a backdoor passage there to the left. It is a long, winding stair that will take us past several windows giving us a view of the outside. Of course, there won't be much to look at except sand and glass. We won't even be able to see the stars with this place lit up like a candle. At this height, though, we might be able to make out the rim of the Dome, if it is still in operation. If the Dome has collapsed, we may be the only sane people left on the planet." She said that last part eyeballing C'ton to see if those words had any effect on him.

J'son's head was buzzing and his thoughts were manic, wanting to say several things at the same time. He opened his mouth to speak but stuttered an incoherent string of syllables instead. "Iuuuuhbulyla."

"What was that, J'son?" T'mer said, making his way over to him and stopping before C'ton. He didn't like the way C'ton looked, either.

"Oh, nothing. Nothing," C'ton offered, squeezing J'son's shoulder roughly. "He's still feeling the effects of the healing baths, aren't you J'son?"

"J'son?" T'mar asked. "Are you okay? You don't look too good. You look different."

"Yeah. C'ton and I were just… well, let's get to the control room," he said changing the subject. Brushing C'ton's hand away he added, "B'el's energy creature is here somewhere; I can feel it. It's probably guarding the portal."

"The portal?"

"Shhhh. J'son didn't mean to say that. Portal! We don't know anything yet. All we have are hunches that B'el took the power reserves but to what purpose we still don't know."

"I know."

The four of them left the area surrounding the globe and skirted several rows of shelving, making their way to the outer wall. A rough hewn niche cut into the wall was hidden behind a large wall hanging of a battle scene reminiscent of medieval Earth. T'mer pulled the drape aside at T'mar's instruction, revealing a wooden door similar in construction to the main door they had entered far below.

T'mar placed her hand, palm side down, on the left side of the door and put the index finger of her right hand into a small hole located waist high in the door. The door clicked and she removed her finger, pushing the door gently with her left hand. The door opened into a dimly lit hallway that curved away and rounded the inside of the exterior wall of the Castle. They followed this passageway as it rose upward at a comfortable incline.

The passageway brightened considerably as they neared a thick opening large enough for the four of them to gaze out. There was no breeze and the light filtering outward came from a circular hole directly behind them that was covered by a crystal-like lens of some sort. The white light was soft and gentle and warm. Standing in front of the window the light from behind seemed to wrap itself around them in a soothing embrace.

It was hard to see beyond the window, but J'son thought he could see the curving shape of the Dome in the distance, a reddish hue against the black of night. This particular window was pointing due west, as directions go, and the light it emitted cast a finger of hope on the dim reflection of the Dome. The light of this window was giving power to the Dome, keeping it visible, if only weakly.

"Look! See what the light is doing?" asked J'son. "That is the beacon that will draw everyone here. They mustn't find the portal opened. That would be devastating to my planet. Come on, we have to find a way to close it." J'son raced away from the others, following the curving passageway as it wound its way around the inside of the exterior wall of the Castle, disappearing from sight.

"J'son! Wait. You don't know what's up ahead." T'mar sounded frantic.

"We can't let him near the portal," C'ton said. "T'mer, you have to stop him. Quickly, go after him. Take him out if you have to."

The passage ended abruptly at an arched doorway without a door. Cautiously stepping through, he entered a large, open room devoid of seating of any type except in the center. The place seemed alive with electricity and J'son had the uneasy feeling that he was being watched, or possibly hunted. He had the distinct impression that there was something else in the room besides him and he stayed at the doorway scanning the walls, floor and ceiling looking for any signs of danger.

To his left was a cage-like area. The bars of this cage let out a static-y sound and gave him the impression that the entire structure was electrified. The cage door was busted open from the inside out and he paid particular attention to what was still left inside. Located up in a corner was a rectangular metal box about the size of a shoe box. There was one blinking light and a small projection screen that looked similar to the lens of a 35mm camera. A dim, solid red light could be seen within the lens and it looked at J'son like an eyeball. It gave him a creepy feeling and he shuddered, turning away from it.

In the center of the room a Dais similar to the one in the Temple stood on a tripod over a circular, ringed opening in the floor. Out of the opening came an intense beam of white light that flowed upward, bathing the Dais in a wash of pure energy. Steps leading up to the Dais were hard to make out in the glowing light and hid a black smudge showing their location. Above the Dais was a concave, semi-spherical globe containing angled mirrors that reminded J'son of a disco ball. The light rising from the Dais hit this structure, changing it from white to multihued, where it was concentrated and collected.

The curving walls of this room were smooth and concaved, lined with transparent, floor to ceiling, glass-like panels that contained dials, gauges, switches and tiny monitors. Large, thick, black cables ran out from the bottom of these control panels and slithered across the floor in a haphazard manner ending and connecting to the raised ring opening underneath the Dais. Towards the back of the room, opposite the doorway was a rectangular platform painted white and surrounded on three sides by a railing that separated it from the rest of the room and contrasted with the jet-black floor. The railing contained a waist-high gate that swung on large hinges. The gate was closed and a blinking red light suggested it was locked.

A laser-looking device hung from the ceiling directly above the white area and was pointed straight down. The laser had an umbrella-shaped, parabolic protrusion with an antenna mounted in its center. A metallic ball with small, circular, encompassing lights rode on the back of the laser. The thing seemed to be turned on and a cone-shaped beam of energy cast a circular light on the floor. Within the cone of light was a distorted field of wavy lines and images. J'son couldn't make anything of the images, but he had the strange feeling that he was seeing into another dimension.

The air immediately surrounding the white area buzzed with electrical intensity and he could feel waves of movement flowing into it. A sound resembling the sucking in of air could be heard and just by walking into the room he felt like he was being pulled towards that area. He stopped a few feet inside the room, feeling the pull of the area opposite him and he leaned back against the drag, clutching the door opening for support.

T'mer was the first one to make it to the control room and he stopped just outside. Seeing J'son holding the opening, he grabbed his arm and pulled him back into the passageway. The two of them stood staring into the room without saying anything. Sounds of high-voltage current filled the passageway, a "zummmmmmming" hum that sounded dangerous and foreboding. Then, out of the corner of T'mer's eye he thought he saw movement, a quick flash that darted across the room and settled within the small cage to his left. He leaned into the room and cocked his head to look. The cage was seemingly empty, but he could see a milky-white patch on the floor, bleaching out the black rock. He studied the patch for a moment longer, waiting for it to move or change shape. The spot was motionless and looked like just a stain.

"What's the matter? Did you see something?"

"No, just that white spot inside the cage."

"What white spot?" J'son leaned his head in to look at the cage and quickly pulled it back in. "That wasn't there before. And now I can feel a presence, like something is in there."

"I feel it, too. That must be your energy creature you were worried about."

C'ton came up on them suddenly and without notice. He broke through their ranks and entered the room before either of them could say anything. C'ton was now in the center of the room staring up at the Dais, oblivious to any pull or covert observation. He seemed pleased with himself and proceeded to walk between the legs of the tripod, merging with the light. He mounted the stairs, clanking heavily on the metal steps as he ascended. He was about half way up, his body mostly obscured in the light, when T'mar called out to him.

"C'ton, don't go up there."

Stopping, he twisted his body to look over his shoulder. They couldn't see him clearly, but it was obvious to them that he was smiling. When he spoke, his voice came out sounding pompous and arrogant but also faint, as if from a great distance. "Why? Do you wish to sit here in my stead? Do you really believe you are worthy to take the seat of power?"

"C'ton, don't!" T'mar rushed into the room followed by T'mer and J'son, stopping just before the legs of the tripod. The ringed circle beneath the Dais erupted violently, raising a curtain of red fire, sealing off the landing leading up to the throne above.

C'ton started to laugh and continued his climb to the top. Once reaching the top, he turned and sat down without preamble. Immediately the red curtain dropped and the white light fell to a quiet mist gathering on the floor. The steps, Dais and throne were revealed in their entirety showing a simple structure. The chair had two armrests where C'ton placed his hands. There were a series of buttons on each support and he busied himself typing away at them. The room began to dim slightly and the black floor took on an odd illumination. The white, cordoned-off area directly behind him increased its illumination and the distortion field stabilized, decreasing the inward pull.

Within the field they all observed what looked to be a forest that J'son immediately recognized as trees from his world. It was a dense forest with bright sunlight streaming down through the leaves, streaking the ground with patches of light and dark. A dirt path lay before the opening and stretched out into the distance following the natural terrain of the forest floor. The trees reminded J'son of Northwestern America, but having never been there he couldn't be sure. The scale of the trees was hard to determine and he wasn't that familiar with the different types, but it didn't take a specialist to know that those trees were completely unlike the trees he had encountered here on this world.

"C'ton, what are you doing? C'ton, please."

T'mar stepped forward and reached out her hand to take the railing leading up the steps. Just as she was about to grasp the bar, a low, growling, hissing sound erupted behind her coming from the direction of the cage. Hearing the noise, the three of them turned around and looked at the cage. The white stain had moved and now instead of one large patch of white there were seven smaller stains; six were circular and paired together resembling paw prints while the seventh trailed behind them in a flat smudge. The circular patches were moving closer to the three of them in a lazy manner while the seventh part swayed back and forth, sweeping the black floor like a tail. They couldn't see a physical body, but it was obvious that whatever this thing was it was predatory.

"Ah! B'el's pet. You have seen it before, haven't you J'son. Or rather felt its presence. Here, let me help you see it more clearly."

C'ton punched another set of keys on his armrest and the room dimmed even more, revealing an electrified hulking beast that gave off the resemblance of a tiger with a massive head and thick, short legs. Its body was long and muscular with a tail as thick as a good sized tree that tapered off to a skinny point, capped by a flat, triangular shovel-like appendage. When it opened its large mouth, jagged, spike-like teeth hung in multiple rows. The entire creature shimmered but cast no shadow. It radiated energy but absorbed it, too.

T'mar stepped back away from the stairs and rejoined J'son and T'mer. T'mer put himself in front of the beast and kept the other two behind him. The creature skirted them and worked its way over to the Dais, lying down at the foot of one of the legs. His head was erect and he emitted that same dark, low, hissing growl, almost like it was purring. Just the sound of it sent shivers over their bodies and T'mer slowly backed away from the Dais and closer to the door, forcing J'son and T'mar backwards.

"Let's get out of here," he whispered over his shoulder. To his surprise, both J'son and T'mar refused, stepping to either side of him and stood in a straight line facing the creature and the Dais.

"I don't think so, T'mer."

"We're not going anywhere. Don't you know what has happened? We have to close that portal."

"You're not going to close anything, you fool. That portal, that doorway is our salvation. I alone control it and I will determine who will pass through its gate." C'ton stood up, waving his hand around the room, indicating the portal and the three of them. "This is the answer to our shared dilemma, T'mar. The whole world will come to us seeking deliverance. They will come to us and beg before this throne for our help and wisdom. I am the sole possessor of the truth and the gatekeeper. We will have our revenge on them and prove the inferiority of their beliefs. It is what you have wanted all along. If you join me, I will make you a Queen worthy of their subjection and worship."

J'son and T'mer were shocked into silence at C'ton's audacity, unable to comprehend the change that had occurred. T'mar, though, understood exactly what had happened and recognized the fervor to which C'ton spoke. It was the seat of power, the all-consuming draw of ultimate knowledge. C'ton had become like B'el in his quest for power, taking the mantle of kingship for himself. She wasn't too sure when the change occurred, at what point his mind became overthrown, but that didn't matter now. Looking up at him, seeing the fire in his eyes, the spirit of B'el possessing him, she knew there was only one thing she could do.

Unlike J'son, she didn't want to close the portal. Her overwhelming, irresistible desire of transporting between worlds without having to rely on a mortal was too great. Here was C'ton, now the true heir of B'el's wisdom, offering her what she hadn't been able to accept from B'el. She looked at J'son and T'mer, seeing their confusion, and weakness, and made the decision to join with C'ton. Together they would hold all worlds as Gods, dispensing judgment, and mercy, as she saw fit. T'mer would become a willing slave to her; he would be easy to convince. J'son, who only selfishly cared for his own, backward, enslaved world, would be harder to handle.

He was dangerous of course, but closing the portal was out of the question. J'son and his abilities were nothing compared to the power that was now within her reach. She didn't know if the power reserves from the

Temple would hold out through the long night, but all she needed was safe passage to the outer worlds. Once there, she could live out her life as a Goddess. Then, when the sun of her world came back around she would have the choice of returning or staying. Either way, she was one oath away from obtaining all her desires.

"C'ton, don't you know who you sound like?" J'son asked desperately. "Only B'el would presume complete domination of my world. T'mar, you should know that he had a storage device of some sort, a cube that he placed in a receptacle in the library. It was after that that his thoughts changed. He desired a portal of his own, but a part of him, the good that is in you, C'ton, resisted taking it by force. You could have used me at any point; I see that now. The power you possessed then was far greater than even T'mar knew. Why did you resist when you could have taken it at any time?"

"That is where you are mistaken, J'son," T'mar said, moving away from him, taking T'mer by the hand and leading him towards the Dais. "I have always known C'ton was the true ruler of our world. B'el was weakening; his time of lordship was coming to close. He knew it and that was why he needed me. His hope was that I would strengthen his rule and so prolong it. That portal represents a new beginning for our people. We will use that portal to infiltrate your world and teach you the true meaning of worship. Instead of possessing your dreams, we will become fully realized beings."

"Well spoken, my queen. Bow before my throne and take the oath of office."

T'mer stood beside T'mar like in a trance. He was docile and willing to do whatever T'mar requested of him. Through her witching ways she had implanted a scenario within him that became active once she had accepted C'ton's rule. All that remain to lock in his loyalty was the utterance of the oath. He wouldn't be the same, but his stubborn ways wouldn't be missed. He would become her play thing and warrior when the need arose.

"I can't let this happen," J'son said. Raising his hand before him and closing his eyes, he imagined his hometown and his beloved pet. Seizing the image within him, he projected his desire outward, pulling energy from the room in massive quantities. The floor moaned as energy was ripped away from it, shaking the foundations of the mountain itself.

"Stop what you are doing!" C'ton commanded. "You fool. You will bring the mountain down on top of us."

The portal grew wider as the energy rushed into the room without form, feeding the opening. The field destabilized and the somewhat stable pull of before became a raging current. T'mar and T'mer slipped from their positions and slid towards the gapping opening. Because of the unregulated influx of power, the portal no longer remained fixed on Earth and opened onto the neighboring galaxy, showing stars and constellations instead of trees and paths.

T'mer, acting by instinct, reached out and grabbed the far leg of the tripod, locking his hand around T'mar's wrist at the same time. T'mar's legs had slid across the threshold of the portal and were dangling within the perimeter of the field. The temperature was bitingly frigid and she screamed out in pain.

"Ahhhhhhhhhhhh!"

C'ton was frantically punching buttons trying to diminish the size of the portal to no avail. His energy creature, highly visible at this point, was slipping backward. Its thick claws had dug into the rock and were leaving deep, scraping grooves. Its tail was just within reach of T'mer and it flicked back and forth, striking him severely across the arm holding onto the tripod.

Each strike sent high-voltage electricity ripping through T'mer's body, loosening his grip on T'mar. He was just about to let go when the pull from the portal eased and the opening decreased in size. The field returned to a forest and T'mar was left lying on the floor with just her feet sticking in the dirt.

The abrupt change was occasioned by another presence in the room. J'son had managed to materialize his energy creature and now the two beasts were staring at each other, sizing the other one up. They both growled differently: a low hissing sound coming from C'ton's creature and a wolfing howl coming from J'son's. C'ton's creature took the initiative and pounced on the other one, landing claws first on the back of J'son's creature. A renewed howled issued out of it as it retreated and rolled away, regaining its footing and charging. J'son's creature lunged at the other, sending it sprawling backwards. The impact of the beast struck the tripod, causing it to tilt and C'ton fell out of his chair, hitting the floor with a thud.

T'mar and T'mer had recovered and stood up. T'mer was dazed but no longer in a trance. He appeared to be disoriented and unsure of what was happening. He looked at T'mar with confusion in his eyes, hoping she could explain what had happened. She returned his gaze and pointed at J'son who was standing back towards the door, making like he was about to leave. "Stop him," was all she could say.

The two energy creatures were pounding each other, showering the room with sparks and electrical fireflies. Each impact rocked the room, dislodging the globe and diverting the energy collected there. The wall panels twisted and warped, cracking the dials and gauges, throwing the controlled, power output into disarray. The rainbow colors reflected by the tilting globe showered the room, burning holes into the rock, opening up fissures that stretched across the floor. The creatures, more stable than the bipeds, straddled the cracks as they fought.

T'mer, in his rush to prevent J'son from leaving the room, fell into one of the crevices, clutching the edge.

"T'mer!"

C'ton struggled to his feet as each attack of the creatures rocked the room, bringing him back down. T'mar was limping on frostbitten feet but managed to grab hold of the railing surrounding the portal. Looking at the melee erupting all around her and seeing the portal still opened to the pleasant-looking forest, she threw herself into it as the room rocked again. She emerged on the other side looking back toward the control room.

T'mer was pulling himself up out of the crevice and turned to look at her. His face said it all and she felt a tinge of regret, seeing the pain and utter disappointment there. She stood there looking back into the room a moment longer then turned away from the opening, fully removing herself from the Planet of the Elohim.

The tripod came crashing down and the ringed circle exploded in a flame of fire. The globe fell and crashed on the floor beside C'ton, splintering into a thousand pieces. The portal closed and all that was left was a smoldering, white area and a bent, twisted rail. C'ton, staring in disbelief at the destruction, headed towards the door, feeling his way along the walls and jumping over the large cracks splintering the floor. The room broke into jagged sections and a massive gash kept C'ton from reaching the door.

"J'son, I'm sorry. Help me. Take me with you."

T'mer had made it out of the crevice and was standing close to J'son. He seemed defeated and small. His head hung down and he looked heartbroken. "How could she have left me?"

"It's okay T'mer. Here, take my hand. I can take you with me."

"Don't leave me, J'son. Don't leave me. I am your friend. I was fooled by blind ambition. Remember who I am. Take me with you."

J'son was just about to tell T'mer to go and get C'ton when the room rocked again and a section of the ceiling fell, placing a massive boulder between them and C'ton. He didn't know if the boulder landed on C'ton or not, but his cries for help stopped. It pained J'son to think that he would have to leave C'ton behind, dead or alive, but the choice had been made for him. The room was collapsing and the doorway they were standing under buckled, straining under the weight of the mountain. Time was running out and he tried to calm his mind enough to open that portal within himself and carry them through.

He had never imagined T'mer before and that would take concentration. As the room rocked and fell all around him, J'son closed his eyes and dreamed of his hometown. He saw his friend there and he reached out to him. His friend was smiling and he started to speak but J'son couldn't make out the sound. He watched his lips moving and tried to mimic the movements, forming the words for himself. The impression he got was a question. His friend was asking, "Who is that guy?"

With that inquiry, J'son knew he had managed to bring T'mer through with him. He opened his eyes and the room was gone, replaced by a quiet, wooded area he recognized as his hometown. He smiled at his friend and then turned to the hulking figure to his right. T'mer's face was clear and his eyes were bright. J'son smiled bigger showing teeth. He laughed to himself and then said, "Welcome to Earth."

Glossary

': The apostrophe represents a dialect, an accent, a form of enunciation and an inflection based on the one pronouncing it. It is similar to the difference between a southern accent and one from Australia. Depending on the title of the word it is attached, it can have various meanings and denotes the lineage and root of the original word to follow. Its sound is unpronounceable in the English language.

'cfr: The chief mediator for those living next to the Dome and those living in the Temple.

'che: Student.

'cud, gift of: A high-level ability to map distances without the need of physical markers.

'deh, cavern of: The cavern of 'deh was discovered by C'ber using the stick of the 'jun tree.

'dpr: Dome preservers are low-level monks who chant producing the vibrational wave forms necessary for Dome support.

'dsh: Derogatory.

'fbu: Small flower with blooms the size of an opened hand.

'gly: The great library found within the Temple.

'int: A flying, wasp-like insect with six wings and hard bodies resembling plastic.

'lav: Derogatory.

'lug: Derogatory.

'loh, cave of: The cave of lost hope. In the past it was a way to exit the Dome and cross the Wastelands. Now, however, in is a place of mediation. Why the cave was given its name is lost in time.

'mgl: Another derogatory term used by T'mer; A mongrel.

'mrn: Derogatory.

'ncr: A red crystal found in the cavern of 'deh. The radiance of the crystal allows one to mentally project outside the Dome.

'plc: Power leeches are large, snake-like, psychic creature with a huge head and a long, stick-like body resembling a cherry with its stem. It is magenta, almost black in color and feeds on the pineal gland.

'psi root: A medicinal plant with 6 to 8 spiny, orange, fleshy tentacles the thickness of a finger. The tentacles fold up like a cupped hand. Tiny ¼ inch long sprouts cover the tentacles and are red in color. The root is six inches long with a one-inch diameter.

'sec: Derogatory.

'slu: A derogatory term used by T'mer referring to J'son. It is a worm-like creature without a back bone.

'tok: The name of J'son's energy creature that resembles his beloved dog from earth but much larger. It is a thought form generated from his memories.

'tpo: A familiar that bonds with the Adepts.

'tyr: An apprentice.

'uog: Derogatory.

'vjc: Vent juice. Throughout the planet there exist cracks that allow sub-surface energy to rise up from deep within the planet. The gasses are a florescent blue and provide an energy reservoir for those in need.

vrn: Derogatory; vermin.

'vsn, lake of: The lake of vision is a smooth body of water at the foot of the mountains.

'vsn, platform of: The platform of vision is a natural rock structure resting between two hills above the lake. Sitting on this platform and staring at the mirror-like lake produces visions.

'wat: A poisonous, rat-like creature with pointed, needle-like legs. Walking across bare skin leaves tiny puncture wounds. The venom is used in certain monastic rituals for its psychedelic properties. J'son was accidentally infected by this creature.

'wrt: A heretic who has left the council of monks. D'nan called G'mra a 'wrt and believes C'ton to be one.

'yog: Heart-shaped, palm-sized orange fruit.

A: The capital letter before each proper name is a designation and a title in the religious hierarchy of the planet. It follows an alphabetic progression with "A" being the highest and denoting the abilities and training of the name it is attached. There is only one "A" designation belonging to the supreme god of the universe. B'el, because of his title, is the highest ranking monk on the planet and his sole ambition is to retain the title "AB'el for himself.

<u>**Adept**</u>: A high-level Tech that has shunned religion and has reached a sophisticated understanding of the universe.

<u>**C'aad**</u>: The High Priest and the supreme reigning member of the council. He is the highest religious authority of the Temple and the sole interpreter of all scripture. His primary completion is B'el; however because of a disagreement he sees C'ton as his chief rival.

<u>**C'art**</u>: The first High Priest who has since passed on into the grid.

<u>**C'ber**</u>: Council member and friend of C'ton's before he "crossed over".

<u>**C'ton**</u>: An ancient, high-ranking monk who has renounced his position on the council to pursuing the life of a wandering, ascetic monk. He normally wears a full-length robe with a long, braided beard. At one time he took T'mar to be his student only to be abandoned by her.

<u>**C'zag**</u>: Young council member promoted from the lower ranks.

<u>**D'nan/G'nan**</u>: The secretary to the High Priest. He is lower in rank to C'ton but assumes a higher position believing C'ton has lost his claim to a seat on the council by renouncing all affiliation to the Temple. He is the first one to remember T'mar from her younger incarnation.

<u>**F'bol**</u>: A 'dod, Dome dweller.

<u>**J'son**</u>: A young human male of average height and weight with shoulder-length blonde hair, blue eyes and modest muscular definition.

<u>**K'tum**</u>: Low level monk whose brain turned to mush trying the psychedelic 'psi root.

S'tan/T'tan: Tech from the City who helped T'mer design and build the mirrors to recharge the Dome. He was promoted to the designation of "S" while in the service of the Temple.

T'mar/G'mra: A beautiful, over-sexed woman with auburn hair, emerald eyes and a gorgeous body who at one point was J'son's dream girl. Her designation is misleading and although the "T" represents her ranking as a Tech way down in the hierarchy, she is nonetheless a high-ranking monk who has studied under B'el.

T'mer: A hot-tempered, muscle-bound Tech having the respect of those in the City who has a husband/wife relationship with T'mar.

Dome: Semi-spherical energy field that encompasses the Temple, City and all habitable areas; barrier that separates the habitable world from the Wastelands.

Transcendentals: Mysterious tall, blue, ethereal beings with long legs and arms who have transcended the boundaries of known reality.

Wastelands: A burned-out, contaminated area suffering the effects of nuclear fallout from a war that devastated the planet in the distant past. It is a region devoid of life. B'el's Castle resides in this area and is completely cut off from those living under the Dome. A limited few have braved the toxic environment in order to seek him out, but most have died before completing the trek. T'mar and T'mer are the only two to cross the Wastelands and make it back intact.